THE GRAPHIC NOVEL

WINDHAVEN

By George R. R. Martin

A SONG OF ICE AND FIRE
Book One: A Game of Thrones
Book Two: A Clash of Kings
Book Three: A Storm of Swords
Book Four: A Feast for Crows
Book Five: A Dance with Dragons
The World of Ice & Fire: The Untold History of Westeros and the Game of Thrones

Dying of the Light
Windhaven (with Lisa Tuttle)
Fevre Dream
The Armageddon Rag
Dead Man's Hand (with John J. Miller)

SHORT STORY COLLECTIONS
Dreamsongs: Volume I
Dreamsongs: Volume II
A Song for Lya and Other Stories
Songs of Stars and Shadows
Sandkings
Songs the Dead Men Sing
Nightflyers
Tuf Voyaging
Portraits of His Children
Quartet

Also by Lisa Tuttle

The Silver Bough
The Mysteries
The Pillow Friend
Windhaven (with George R. R. Martin)
Lost Futures
Gabriel
Familiar Spirit

SHORT STORY COLLECTIONS
A Spaceship Built of Stone
A Nest of Nightmares
Memories of the Body

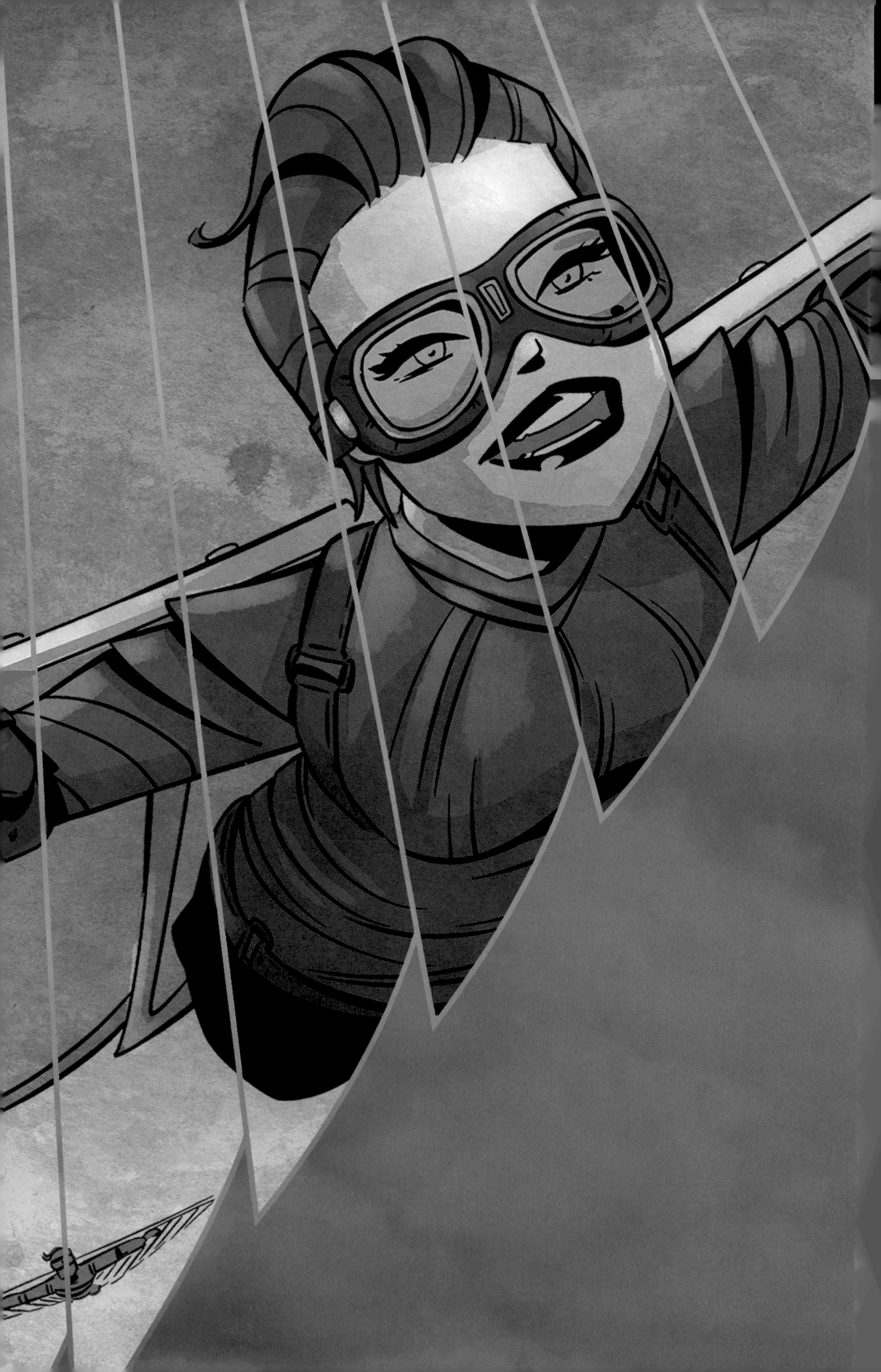

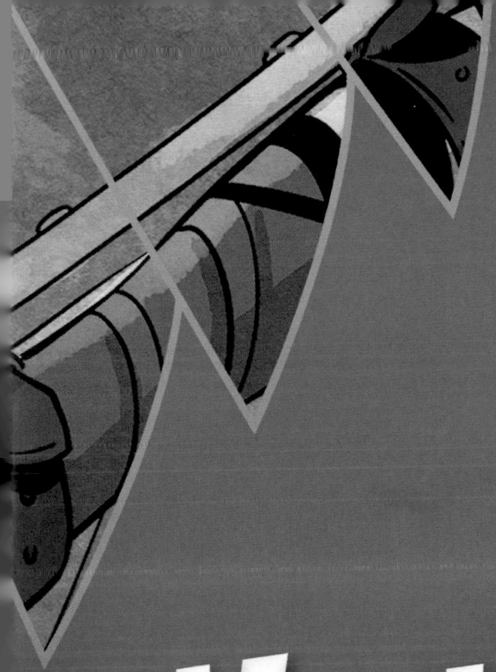

THE GRAPHIC NOVEL

WINDHAVEN

written by
George R. R. Martin & Lisa Tuttle

adapted by
Lisa Tuttle

art by
Elsa Charretier

colors by
Lauren Affe

lettering by
Bill Tortolini

Bantam Books • New York

Copyright © 2018 by George R. R. Martin and Lisa Tuttle

All rights reserved.

Published in the United States by Bantam Books,
an imprint of Random House, a division of
Penguin Random House LLC, New York.

Bantam BOOKS and the HOUSE colophon are registered
trademarks of Penguin Random House LLC.

Adapted from the novel *Windhaven* by George R. R. Martin and Lisa Tuttle
originally published in hardcover and in the United States by Simon & Schuster in
1981, copyright © 1981 by George R. R. Martin and Lisa Tuttle.

ISBN 978-0-553-39366-8
eBook ISBN 978-0-553-39367-5

Printed in China on acid-free paper by
RR Donnelley Asia Printing Solutions

2 4 6 8 9 7 5 3 1

First Edition

Graphic novel interior design by Bill Tortolini

Author's Note

I was twenty, and George R. R. Martin was twenty-four years old when we met for the first time—a couple of newbie writers (we said "neo-pros" in those days), each with a handful of stories in print, determined to make our names. A few months later, he suggested we write a story together.

Collaborating on "The Storms of Windhaven" in 1974 was so much fun (maybe not quite as exhilarating as flying, but words were our wings) and the response from readers was so positive that we had to write more. It took a few years, and many life changes, but eventually that story became a novel. (His second, my first.) *Windhaven* was published in hardcover in 1981, and since then there have been many more editions and translations.

This particular translation, into a graphic novel, was a very different trip— but likewise more fun than simply writing alone. I've been reminded often of those first, heady days of collaboration back in the 1970s, and feel privileged this time to have been able to work with the talented artists Elsa Charretier and Lauren Affe, our editor Anne Groell, and the rest of the team who have brought the world and characters George and I created to life in a new—and, if I may say it, absolutely brilliant—way. A big thank-you to them. To our audience: I hope you enjoy the journey as much as I did. Fly high!

Lisa Tuttle

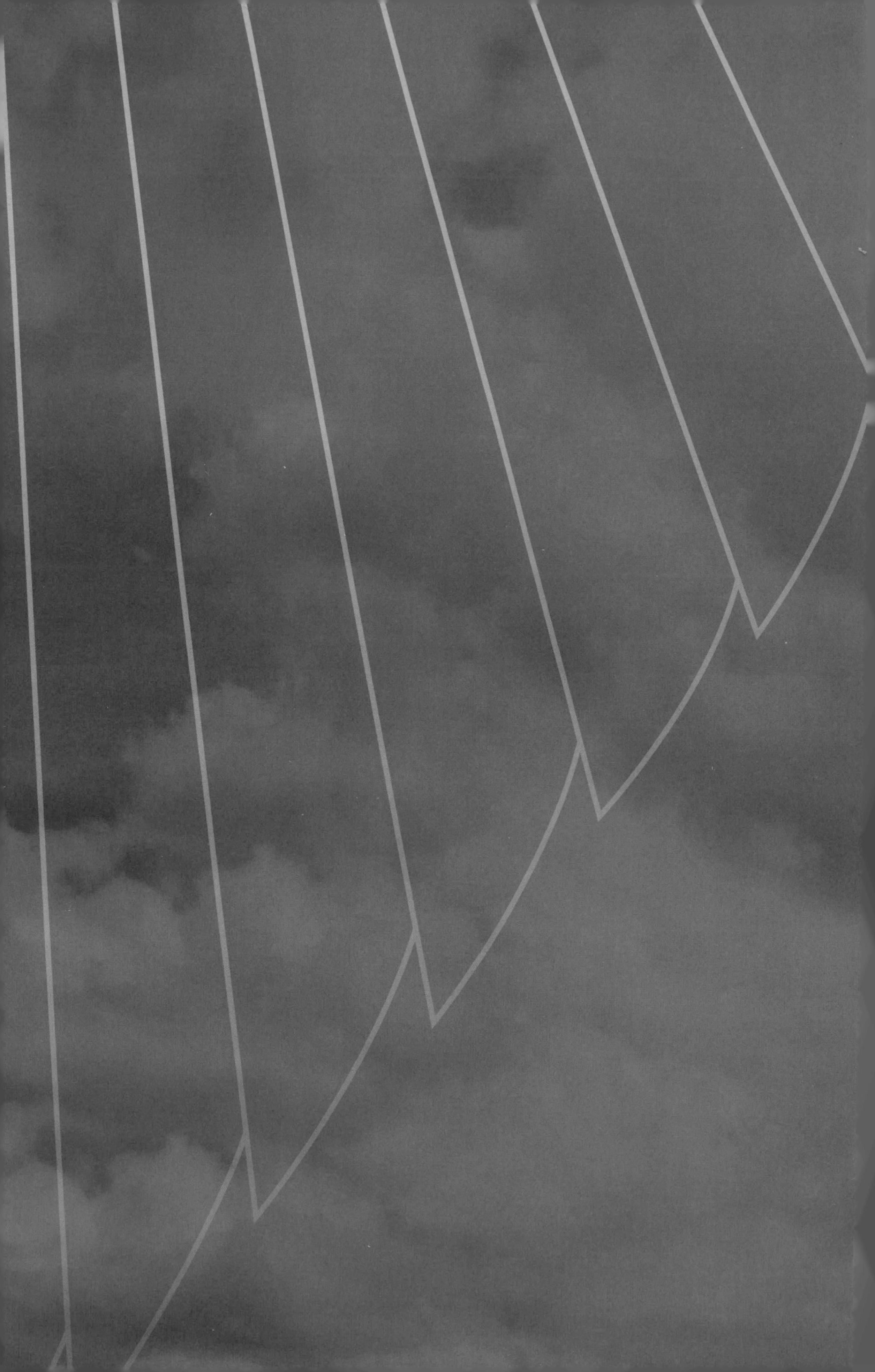

THE GRAPHIC NOVEL

WINDHAVEN

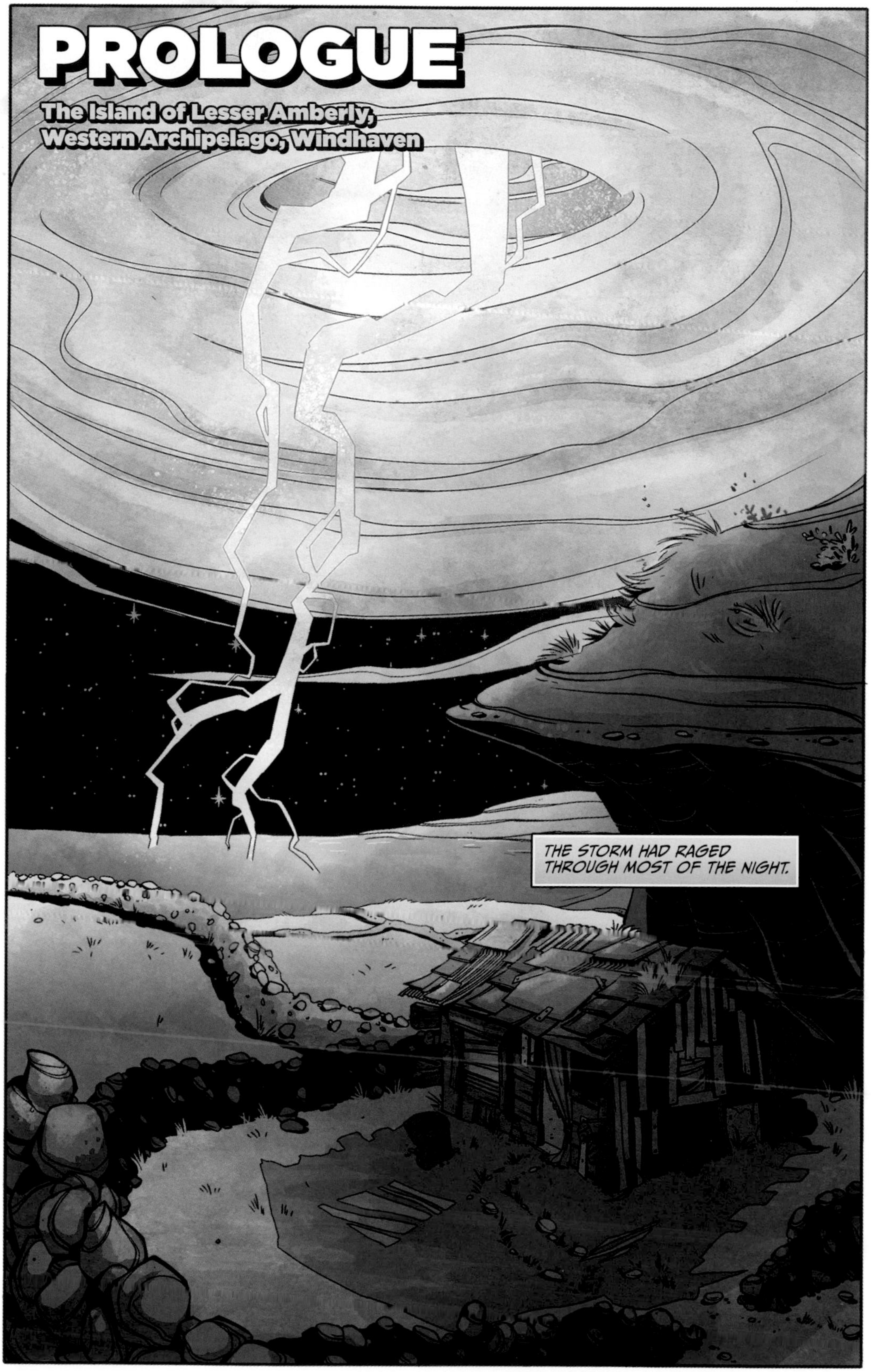
PROLOGUE
The Island of Lesser Amberly,
Western Archipelago, Windhaven
THE STORM HAD RAGED
THROUGH MOST OF THE NIGHT.

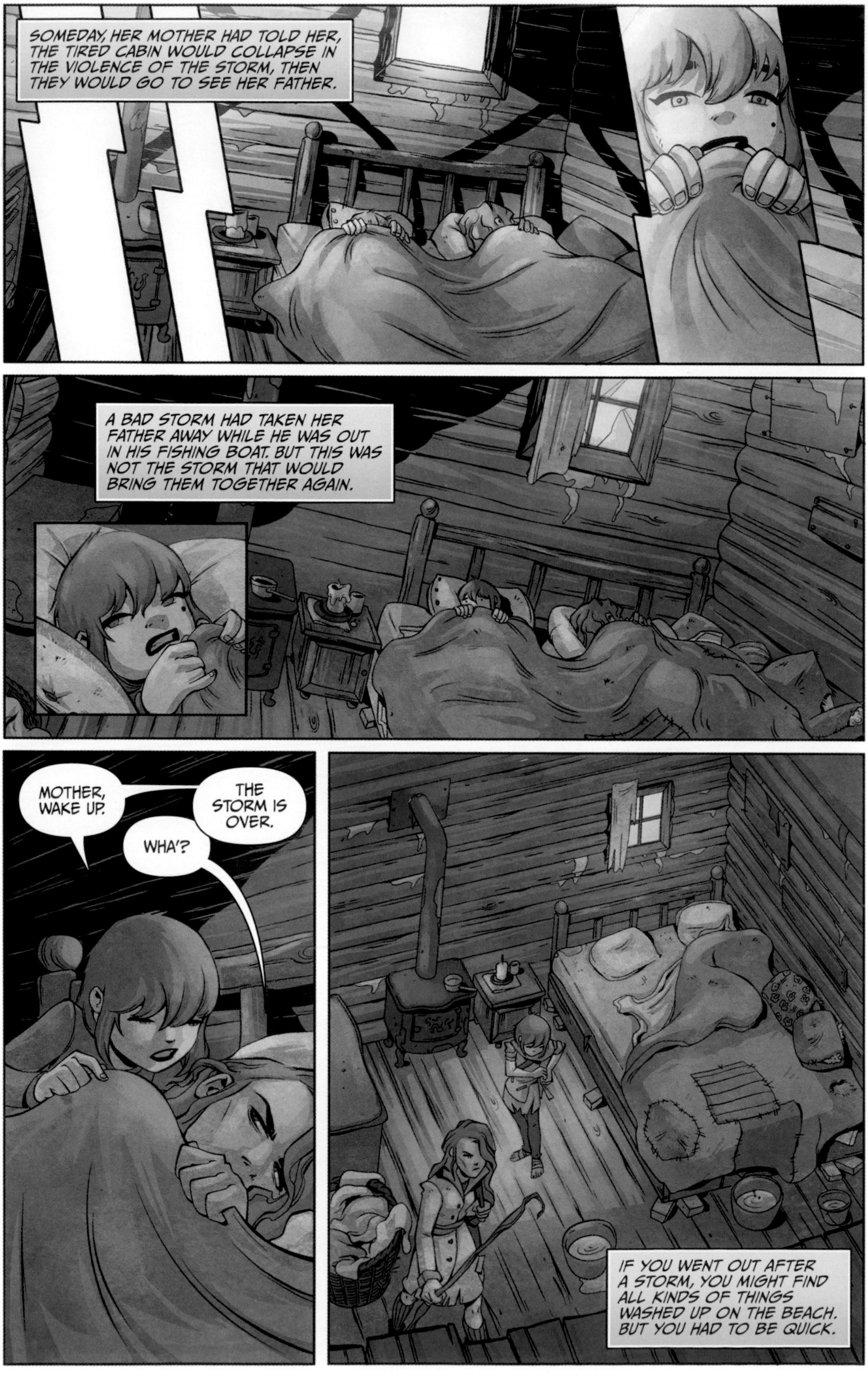
SOMEDAY, HER MOTHER HAD TOLD HER, THE TIRED CABIN WOULD COLLAPSE IN THE VIOLENCE OF THE STORM, THEN THEY WOULD GO TO SEE HER FATHER.
A BAD STORM HAD TAKEN HER FATHER AWAY WHILE HE WAS OUT IN HIS FISHING BOAT. BUT THIS WAS NOT THE STORM THAT WOULD BRING THEM TOGETHER AGAIN.
MOTHER, WAKE UP.
THE STORM IS OVER.
WHA'?
IF YOU WENT OUT AFTER A STORM, YOU MIGHT FIND ALL KINDS OF THINGS WASHED UP ON THE BEACH. BUT YOU HAD TO BE QUICK.

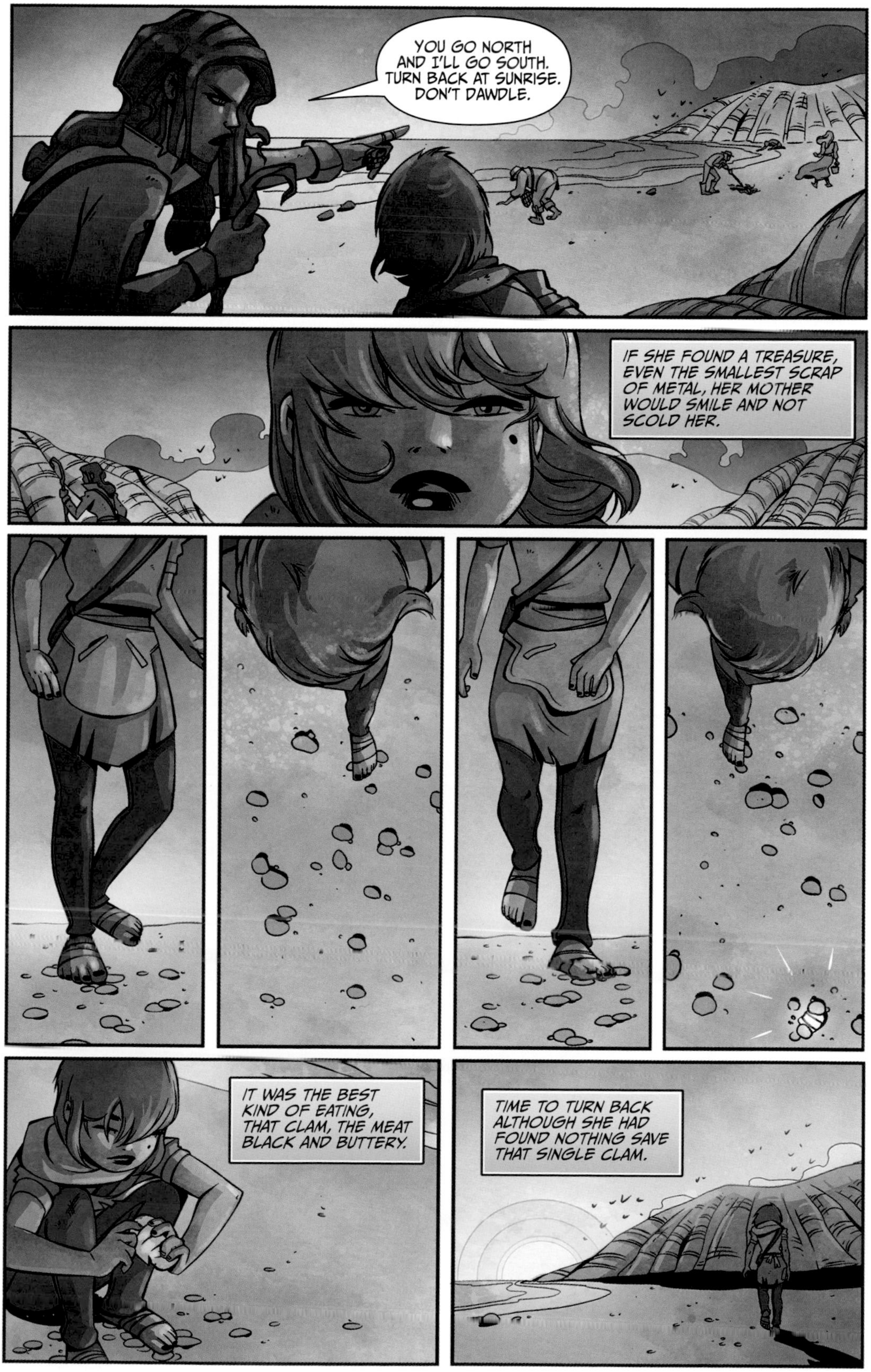
YOU GO NORTH AND I'LL GO SOUTH. TURN BACK AT SUNRISE. DON'T DAWDLE.
IF SHE FOUND A TREASURE, EVEN THE SMALLEST SCRAP OF METAL, HER MOTHER WOULD SMILE AND NOT SCOLD HER.
IT WAS THE BEST KIND OF EATING, THAT CLAM, THE MEAT BLACK AND BUTTERY.
TIME TO TURN BACK ALTHOUGH SHE HAD FOUND NOTHING SAVE THAT SINGLE CLAM.

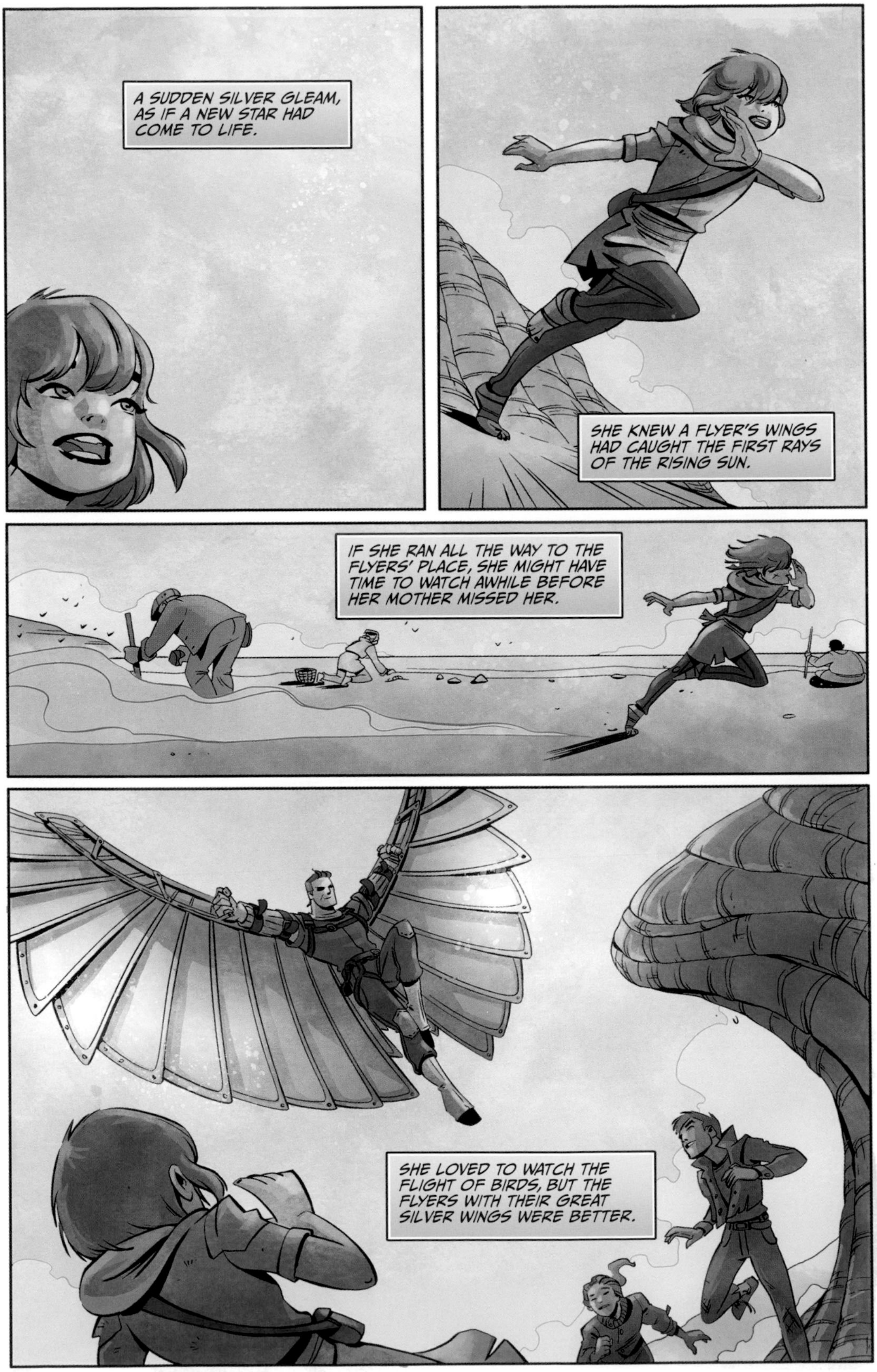
A SUDDEN SILVER GLEAM, AS IF A NEW STAR HAD COME TO LIFE.
SHE KNEW A FLYER'S WINGS HAD CAUGHT THE FIRST RAYS OF THE RISING SUN.
IF SHE RAN ALL THE WAY TO THE FLYERS' PLACE, SHE MIGHT HAVE TIME TO WATCH AWHILE BEFORE HER MOTHER MISSED HER.
SHE LOVED TO WATCH THE FLIGHT OF BIRDS, BUT THE FLYERS WITH THEIR GREAT SILVER WINGS WERE BETTER.

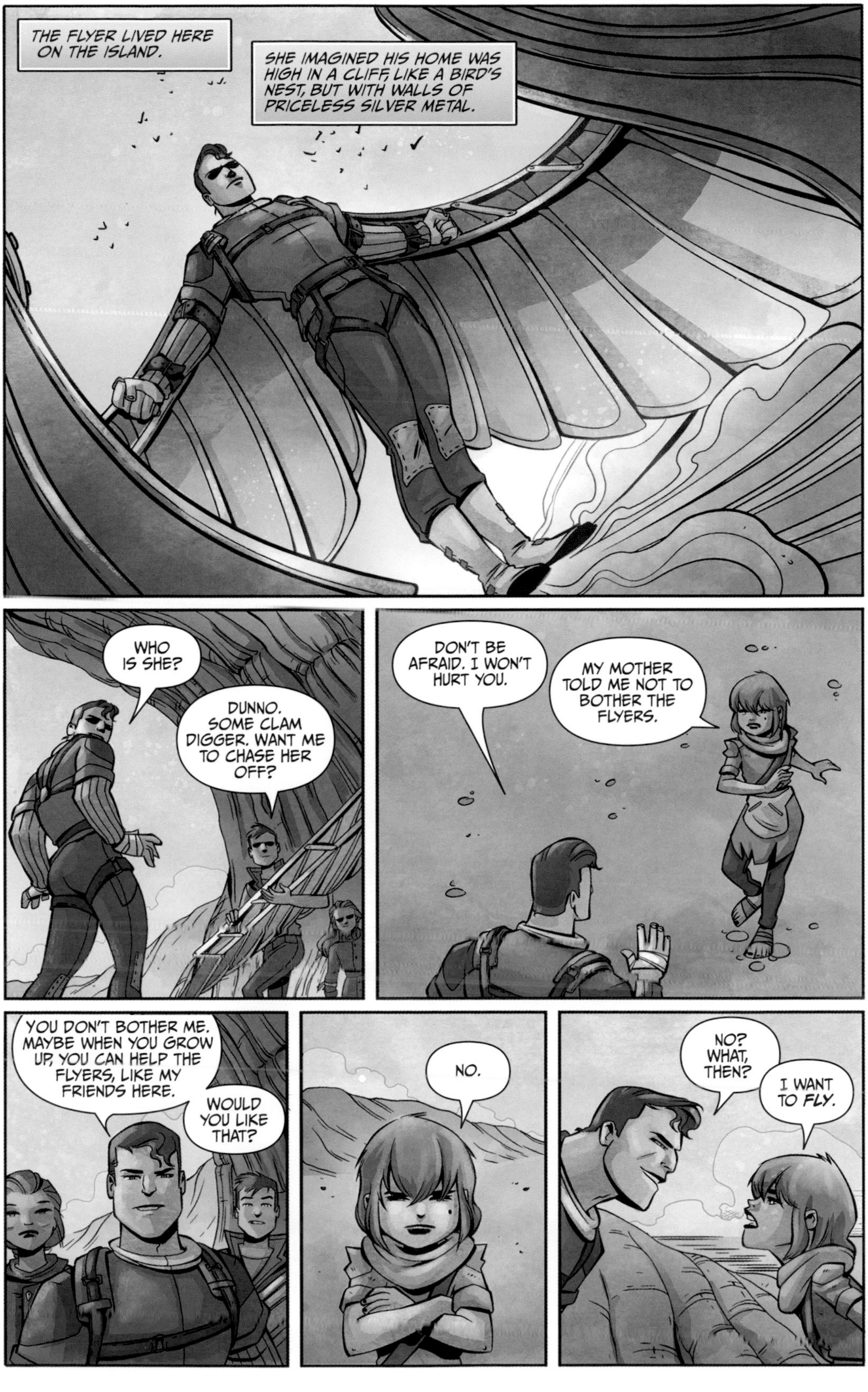
THE FLYER LIVED HERE ON THE ISLAND.
SHE IMAGINED HIS HOME WAS HIGH IN A CLIFF, LIKE A BIRD'S NEST, BUT WITH WALLS OF PRICELESS SILVER METAL.
WHO IS SHE?
DUNNO. SOME CLAM DIGGER. WANT ME TO CHASE HER OFF?
DON'T BE AFRAID. I WON'T HURT YOU.
MY MOTHER TOLD ME NOT TO BOTHER THE FLYERS.
YOU DON'T BOTHER ME. MAYBE WHEN YOU GROW UP, YOU CAN HELP THE FLYERS, LIKE MY FRIENDS HERE.
WOULD YOU LIKE THAT?
NO.
NO? WHAT, THEN?
I WANT TO *FLY*.

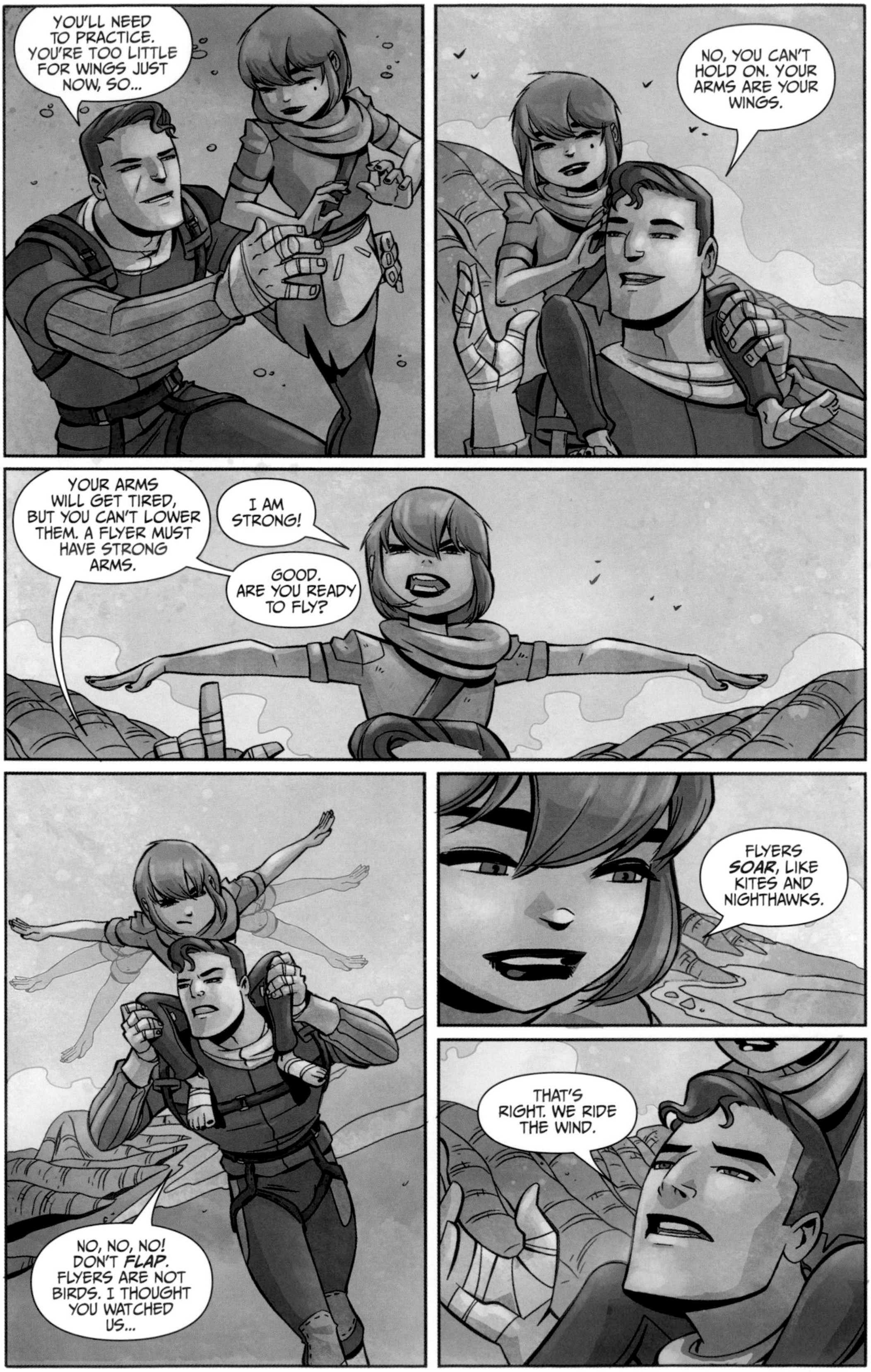

YOU'LL NEED TO PRACTICE. YOU'RE TOO LITTLE FOR WINGS JUST NOW, SO...
NO, YOU CAN'T HOLD ON. YOUR ARMS ARE YOUR WINGS.
YOUR ARMS WILL GET TIRED, BUT YOU CAN'T LOWER THEM. A FLYER MUST HAVE STRONG ARMS.
I AM STRONG!
GOOD. ARE YOU READY TO FLY?
NO, NO, NO! DON'T *FLAP*. FLYERS ARE NOT BIRDS. I THOUGHT YOU WATCHED US...
FLYERS *SOAR*, LIKE KITES AND NIGHTHAWKS.
THAT'S RIGHT. WE RIDE THE WIND.

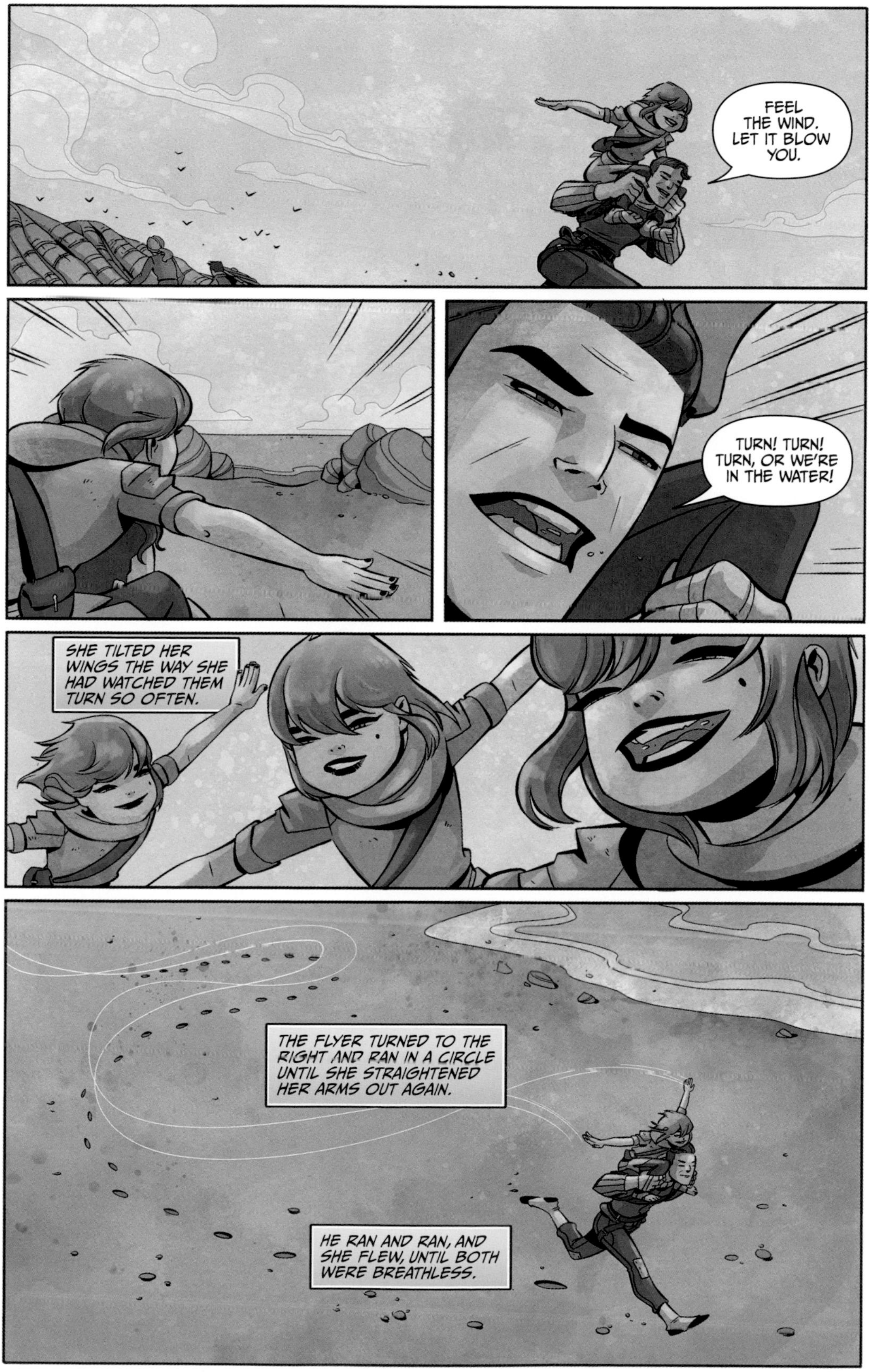
FEEL THE WIND. LET IT BLOW YOU.
TURN! TURN! TURN, OR WE'RE IN THE WATER!
SHE TILTED HER WINGS THE WAY SHE HAD WATCHED THEM TURN SO OFTEN.
THE FLYER TURNED TO THE RIGHT AND RAN IN A CIRCLE UNTIL SHE STRAIGHTENED HER ARMS OUT AGAIN.
HE RAN AND RAN, AND SHE FLEW, UNTIL BOTH WERE BREATHLESS.

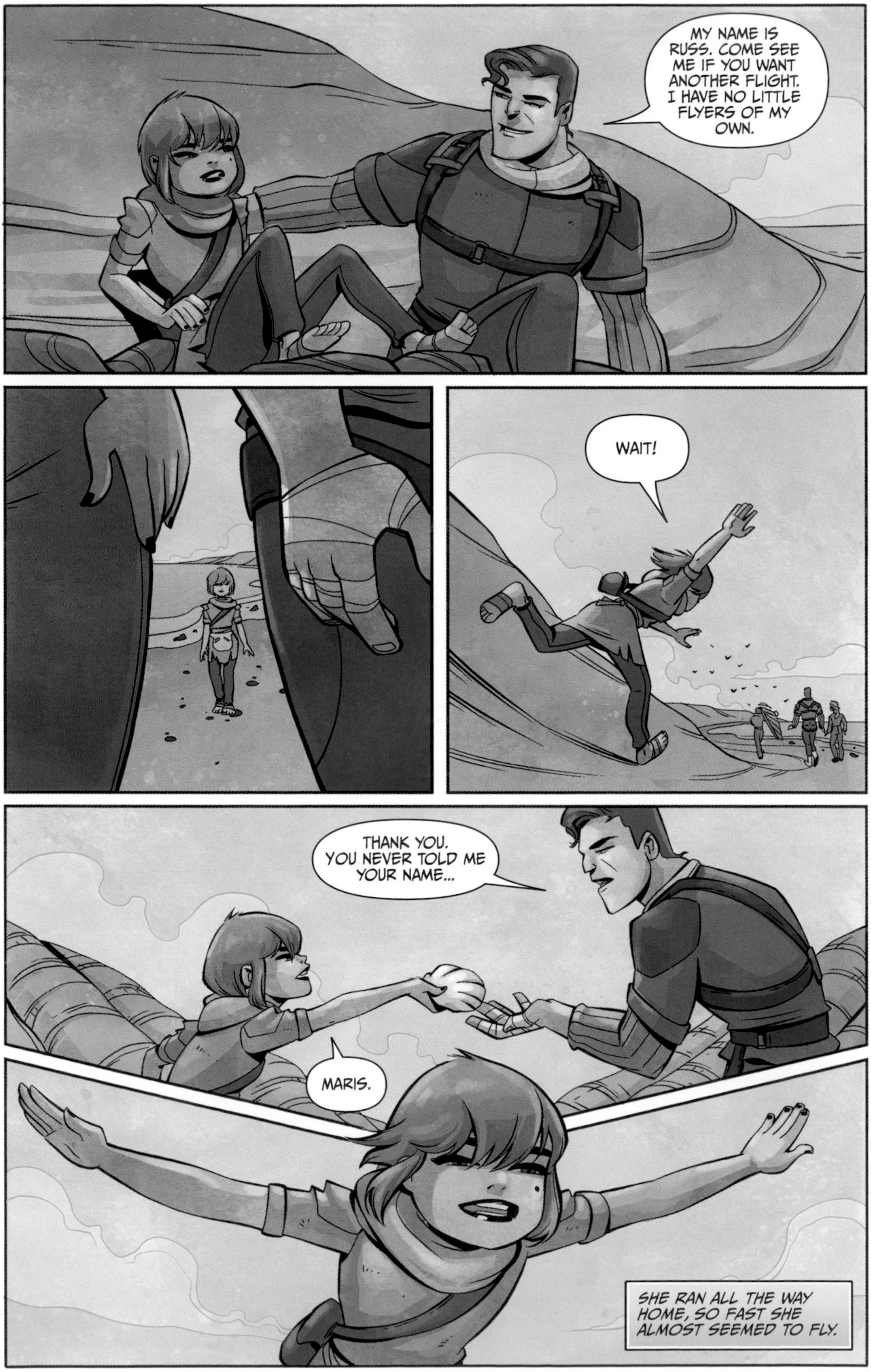
MY NAME IS RUSS. COME SEE ME IF YOU WANT ANOTHER FLIGHT. I HAVE NO LITTLE FLYERS OF MY OWN.
WAIT!
THANK YOU. YOU NEVER TOLD ME YOUR NAME...
MARIS.
SHE RAN ALL THE WAY HOME, SO FAST SHE ALMOST SEEMED TO FLY.

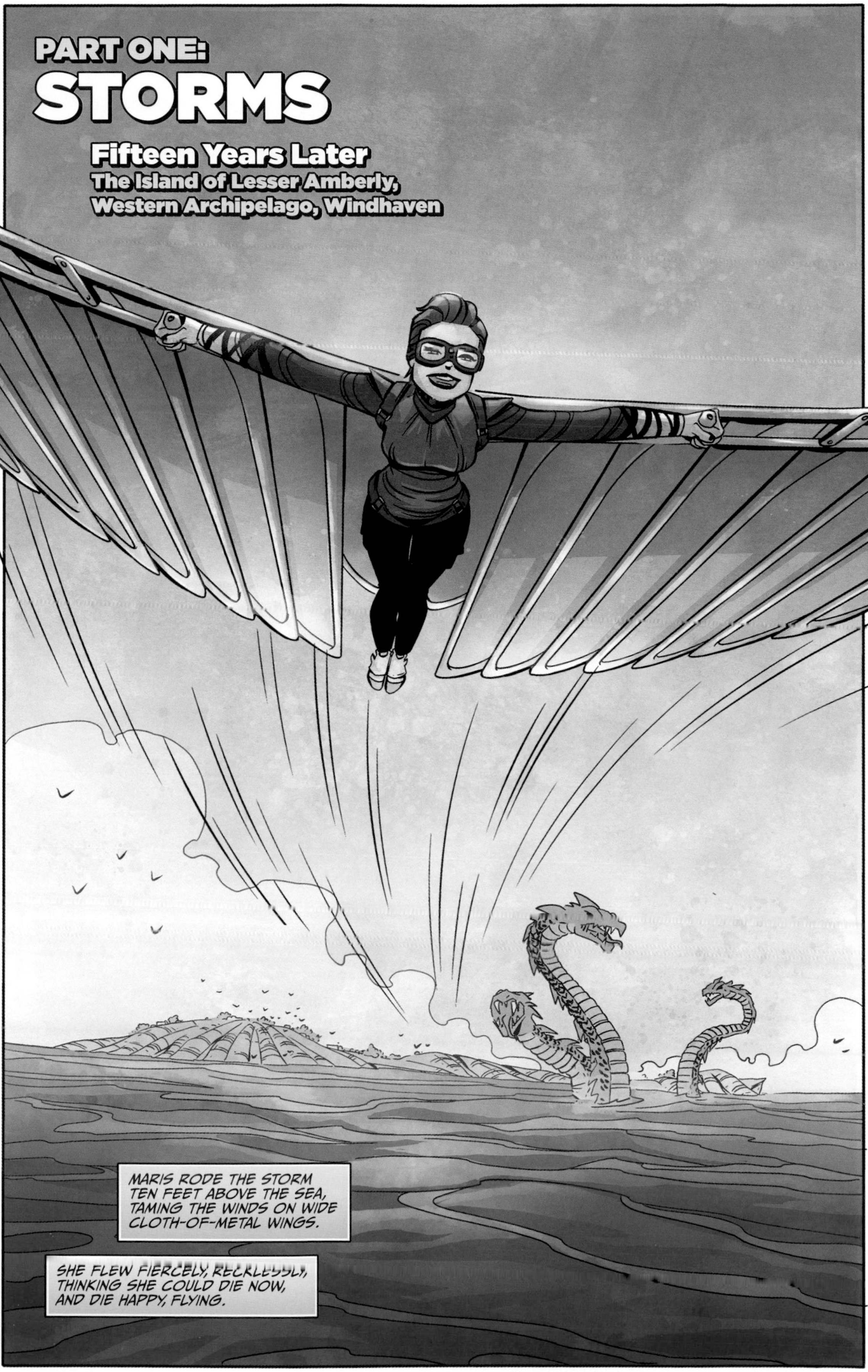
PART ONE:
STORMS
Fifteen Years Later
The Island of Lesser Amberly,
Western Archipelago, Windhaven
MARIS RODE THE STORM TEN FEET ABOVE THE SEA, TAMING THE WINDS ON WIDE CLOTH-OF-METAL WINGS.
SHE FLEW FIERCELY, RECKLESSLY, THINKING SHE COULD DIE NOW, AND DIE HAPPY, FLYING.

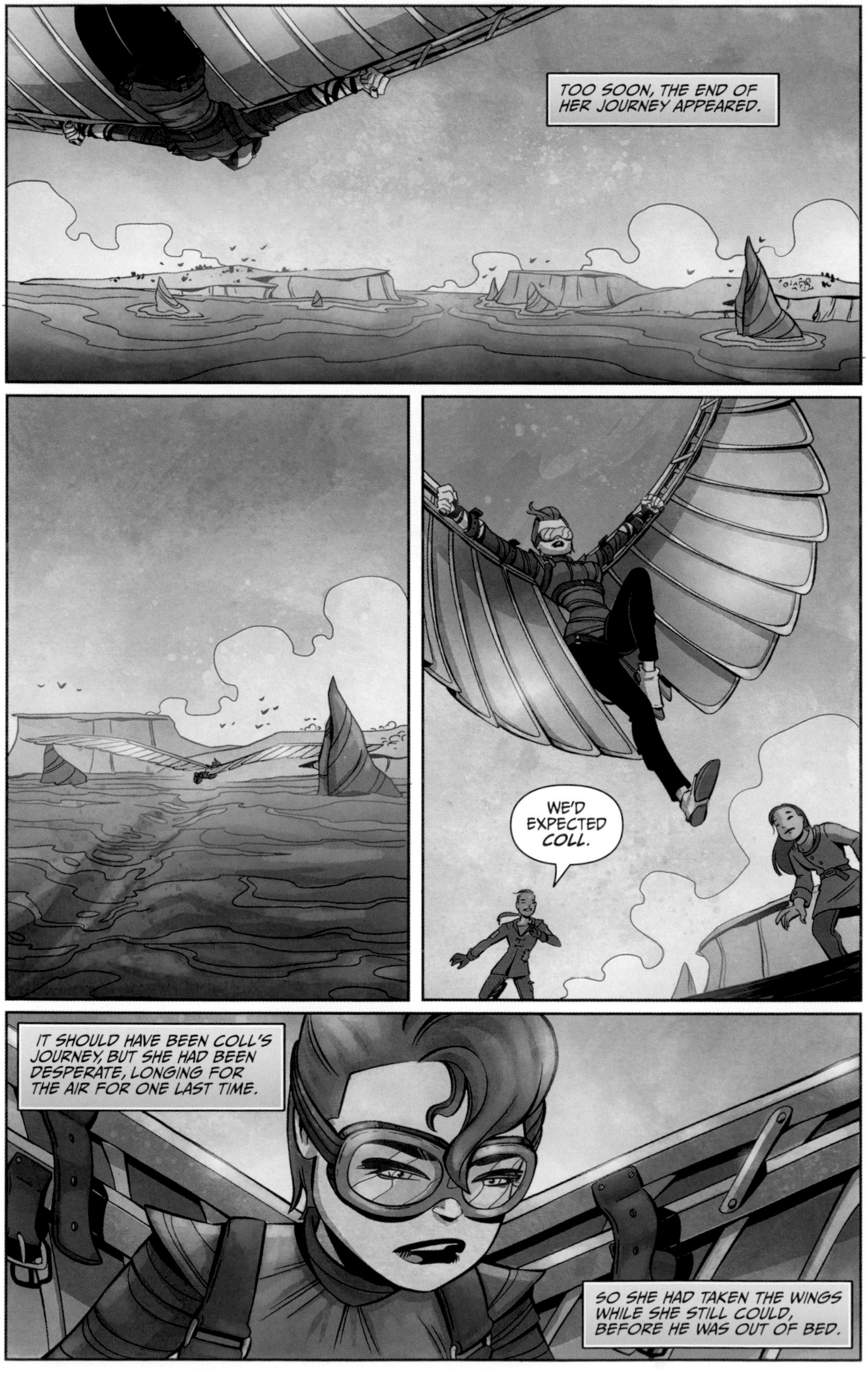
TOO SOON, THE END OF HER JOURNEY APPEARED.
WE'D EXPECTED COLL.
IT SHOULD HAVE BEEN COLL'S JOURNEY, BUT SHE HAD BEEN DESPERATE, LONGING FOR THE AIR FOR ONE LAST TIME.
SO SHE HAD TAKEN THE WINGS WHILE SHE STILL COULD, BEFORE HE WAS OUT OF BED.

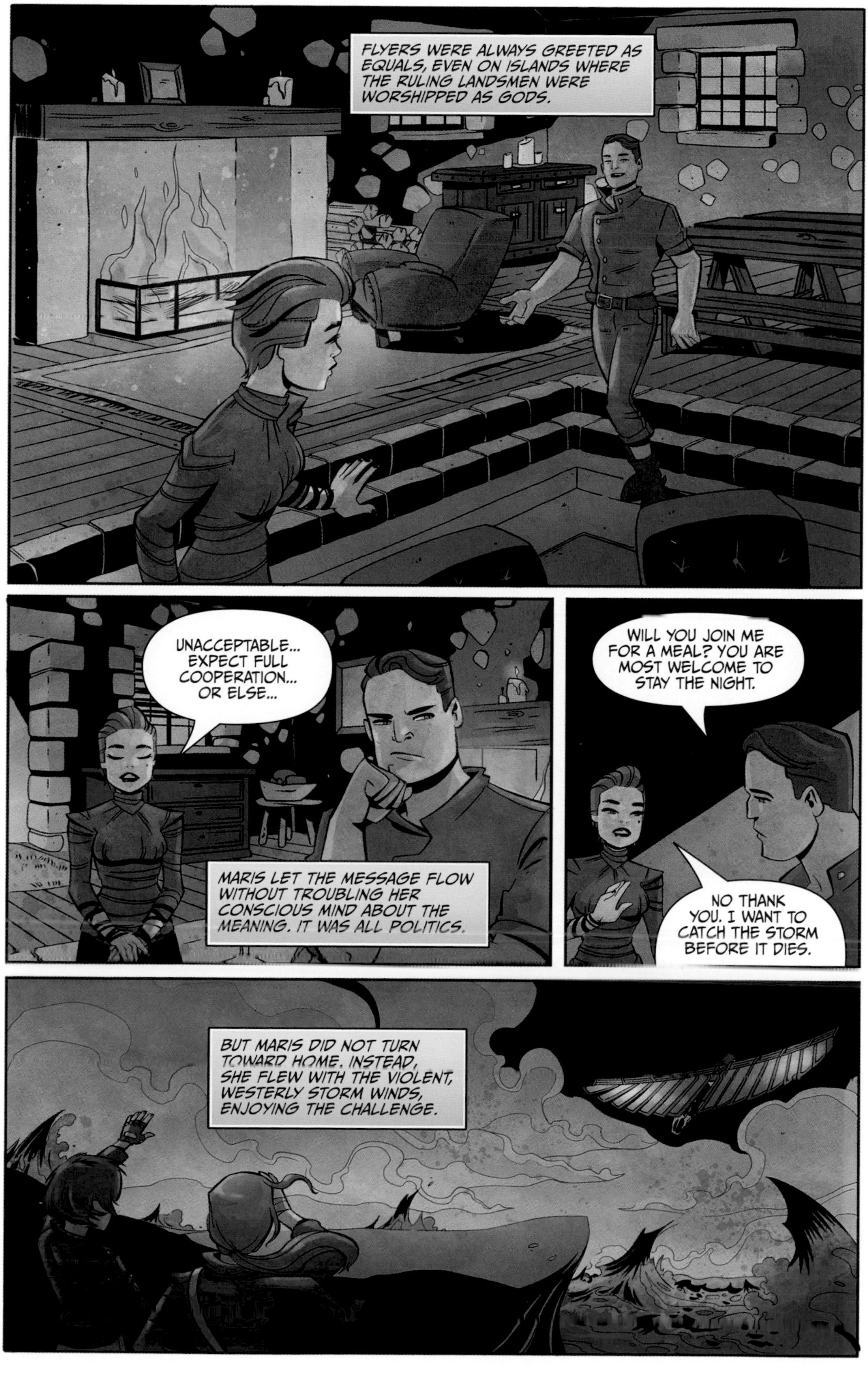
FLYERS WERE ALWAYS GREETED AS EQUALS, EVEN ON ISLANDS WHERE THE RULING LANDSMEN WERE WORSHIPPED AS GODS.
UNACCEPTABLE... EXPECT FULL COOPERATION... OR ELSE...
MARIS LET THE MESSAGE FLOW WITHOUT TROUBLING HER CONSCIOUS MIND ABOUT THE MEANING. IT WAS ALL POLITICS.
WILL YOU JOIN ME FOR A MEAL? YOU ARE MOST WELCOME TO STAY THE NIGHT.
NO THANK YOU. I WANT TO CATCH THE STORM BEFORE IT DIES.
BUT MARIS DID NOT TURN TOWARD HOME. INSTEAD, SHE FLEW WITH THE VIOLENT, WESTERLY STORM WINDS, ENJOYING THE CHALLENGE.

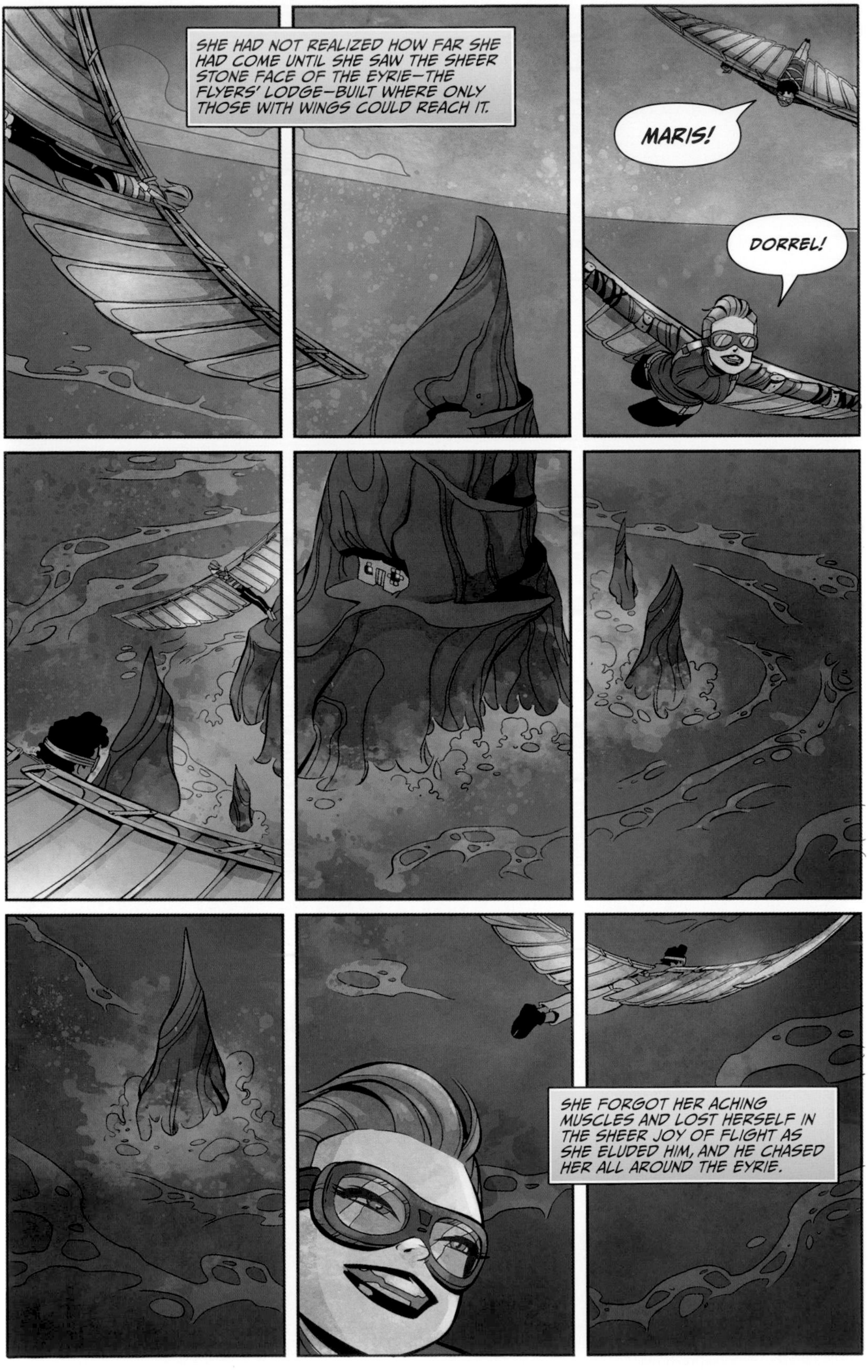
SHE HAD NOT REALIZED HOW FAR SHE HAD COME UNTIL SHE SAW THE SHEER STONE FACE OF THE EYRIE—THE FLYERS' LODGE—BUILT WHERE ONLY THOSE WITH WINGS COULD REACH IT.
MARIS!
DORREL!
SHE FORGOT HER ACHING MUSCLES AND LOST HERSELF IN THE SHEER JOY OF FLIGHT AS SHE ELUDED HIM, AND HE CHASED HER ALL AROUND THE EYRIE.

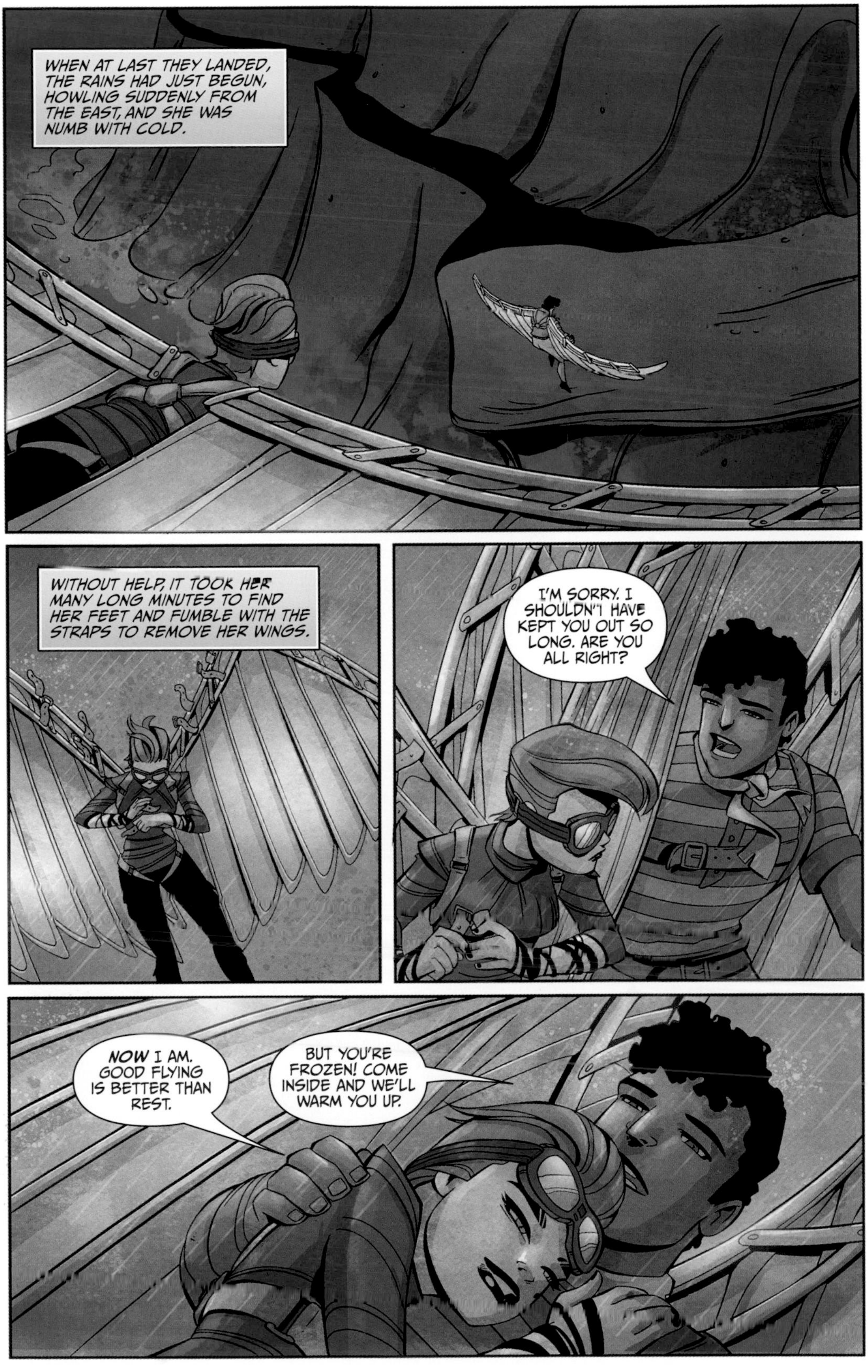
WHEN AT LAST THEY LANDED, THE RAINS HAD JUST BEGUN, HOWLING SUDDENLY FROM THE EAST, AND SHE WAS NUMB WITH COLD.
WITHOUT HELP, IT TOOK HER MANY LONG MINUTES TO FIND HER FEET AND FUMBLE WITH THE STRAPS TO REMOVE HER WINGS.
I'M SORRY. I SHOULDN'T HAVE KEPT YOU OUT SO LONG. ARE YOU ALL RIGHT?
NOW I AM. GOOD FLYING IS BETTER THAN REST.
BUT YOU'RE FROZEN! COME INSIDE AND WE'LL WARM YOU UP.

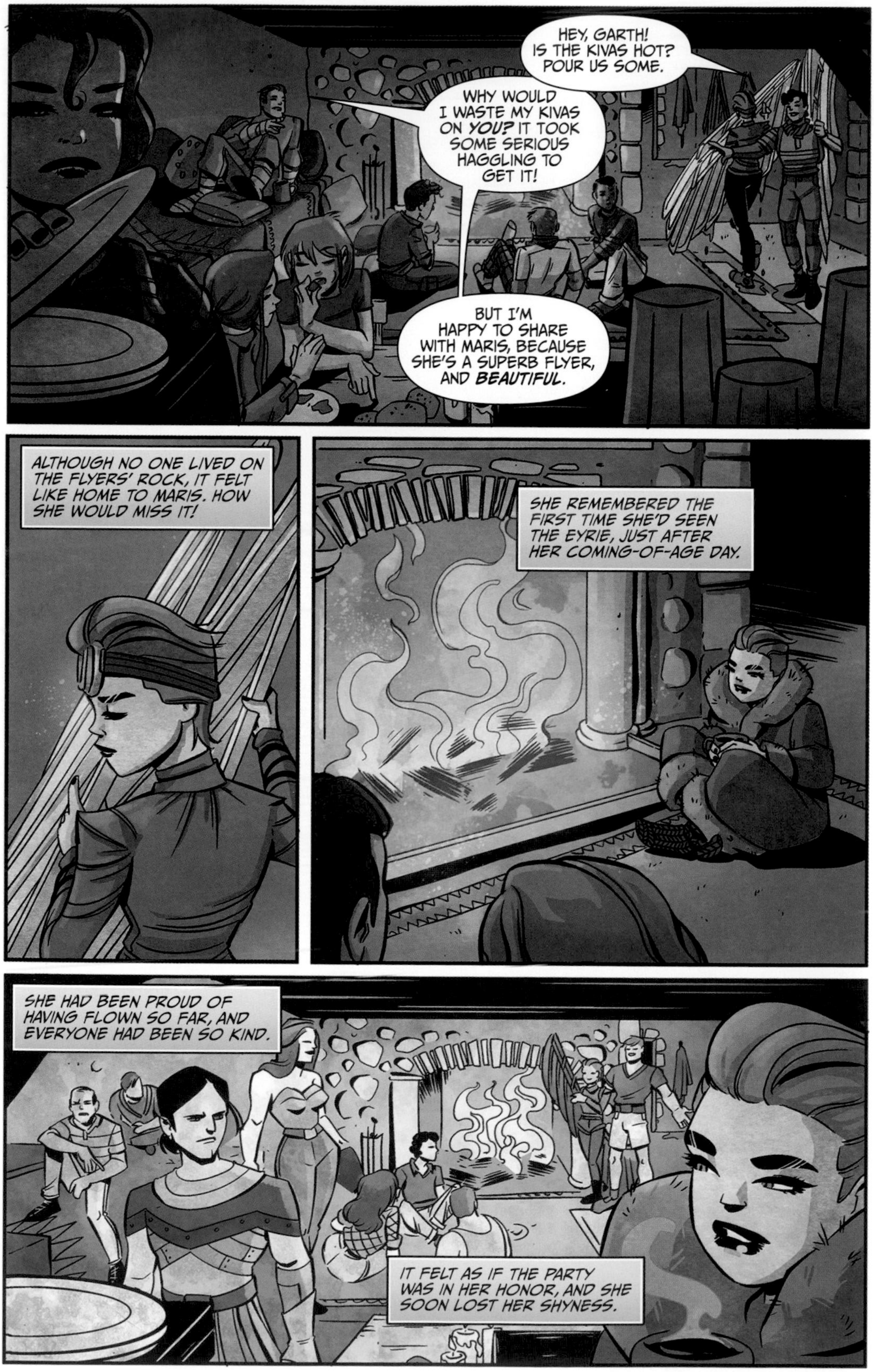
HEY, GARTH! IS THE KIVAS HOT? POUR US SOME.
WHY WOULD I WASTE MY KIVAS ON *YOU?* IT TOOK SOME SERIOUS HAGGLING TO GET IT!
BUT I'M HAPPY TO SHARE WITH MARIS, BECAUSE SHE'S A SUPERB FLYER, AND ***BEAUTIFUL***.
ALTHOUGH NO ONE LIVED ON THE FLYERS' ROCK, IT FELT LIKE HOME TO MARIS. HOW SHE WOULD MISS IT!
SHE REMEMBERED THE FIRST TIME SHE'D SEEN THE EYRIE, JUST AFTER HER COMING-OF-AGE DAY.
SHE HAD BEEN PROUD OF HAVING FLOWN SO FAR, AND EVERYONE HAD BEEN SO KIND.
IT FELT AS IF THE PARTY WAS IN HER HONOR, AND SHE SOON LOST HER SHYNESS.

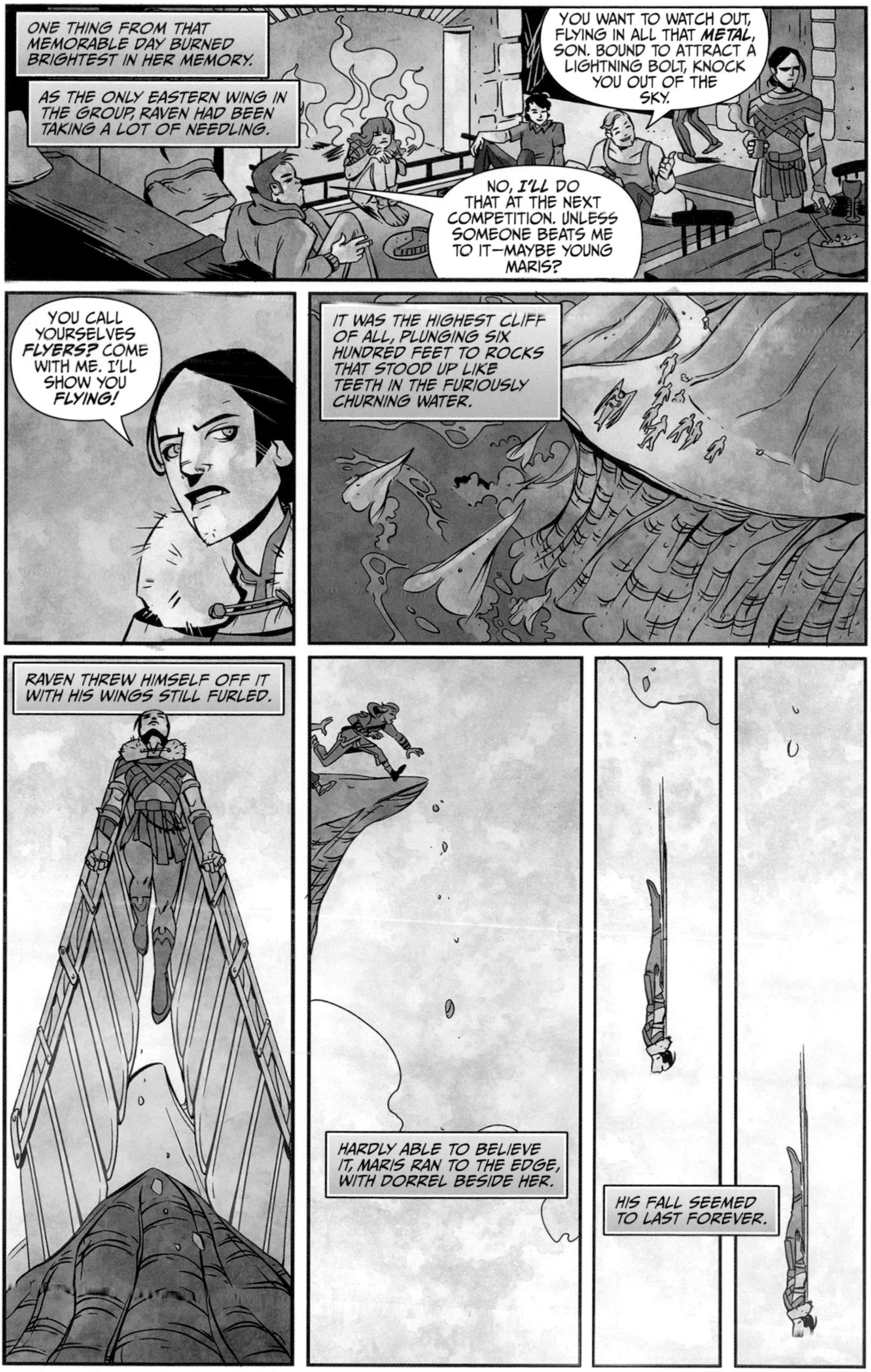
ONE THING FROM THAT MEMORABLE DAY BURNED BRIGHTEST IN HER MEMORY.
AS THE ONLY EASTERN WING IN THE GROUP, RAVEN HAD BEEN TAKING A LOT OF NEEDLING.
YOU WANT TO WATCH OUT, FLYING IN ALL THAT METAL, SON. BOUND TO ATTRACT A LIGHTNING BOLT, KNOCK YOU OUT OF THE SKY.
NO, I'LL DO THAT AT THE NEXT COMPETITION. UNLESS SOMEONE BEATS ME TO IT—MAYBE YOUNG MARIS?
YOU CALL YOURSELVES FLYERS? COME WITH ME. I'LL SHOW YOU FLYING!
IT WAS THE HIGHEST CLIFF OF ALL, PLUNGING SIX HUNDRED FEET TO ROCKS THAT STOOD UP LIKE TEETH IN THE FURIOUSLY CHURNING WATER.
RAVEN THREW HIMSELF OFF IT WITH HIS WINGS STILL FURLED.
HARDLY ABLE TO BELIEVE IT, MARIS RAN TO THE EDGE, WITH DORREL BESIDE HER.
HIS FALL SEEMED TO LAST FOREVER.

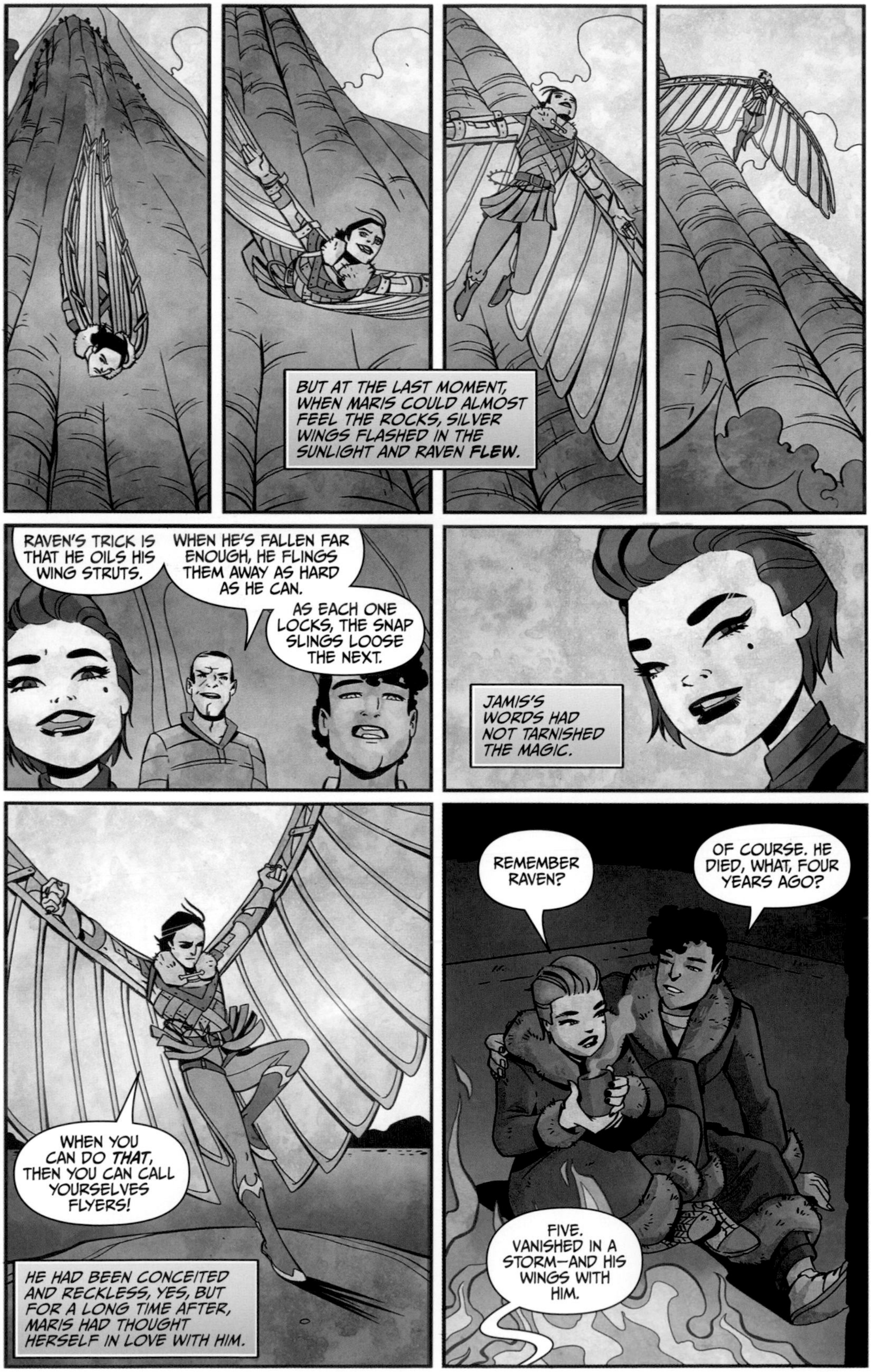
BUT AT THE LAST MOMENT, WHEN MARIS COULD ALMOST FEEL THE ROCKS, SILVER WINGS FLASHED IN THE SUNLIGHT AND RAVEN *FLEW*.
RAVEN'S TRICK IS THAT HE OILS HIS WING STRUTS.
WHEN HE'S FALLEN FAR ENOUGH, HE FLINGS THEM AWAY AS HARD AS HE CAN.
AS EACH ONE LOCKS, THE SNAP SLINGS LOOSE THE NEXT.
JAMIS'S WORDS HAD NOT TARNISHED THE MAGIC.
WHEN YOU CAN DO *THAT*, THEN YOU CAN CALL YOURSELVES FLYERS!
HE HAD BEEN CONCEITED AND RECKLESS, YES, BUT FOR A LONG TIME AFTER, MARIS HAD THOUGHT HERSELF IN LOVE WITH HIM.
REMEMBER RAVEN?
OF COURSE. HE DIED, WHAT, FOUR YEARS AGO?
FIVE. VANISHED IN A STORM—AND HIS WINGS WITH HIM.

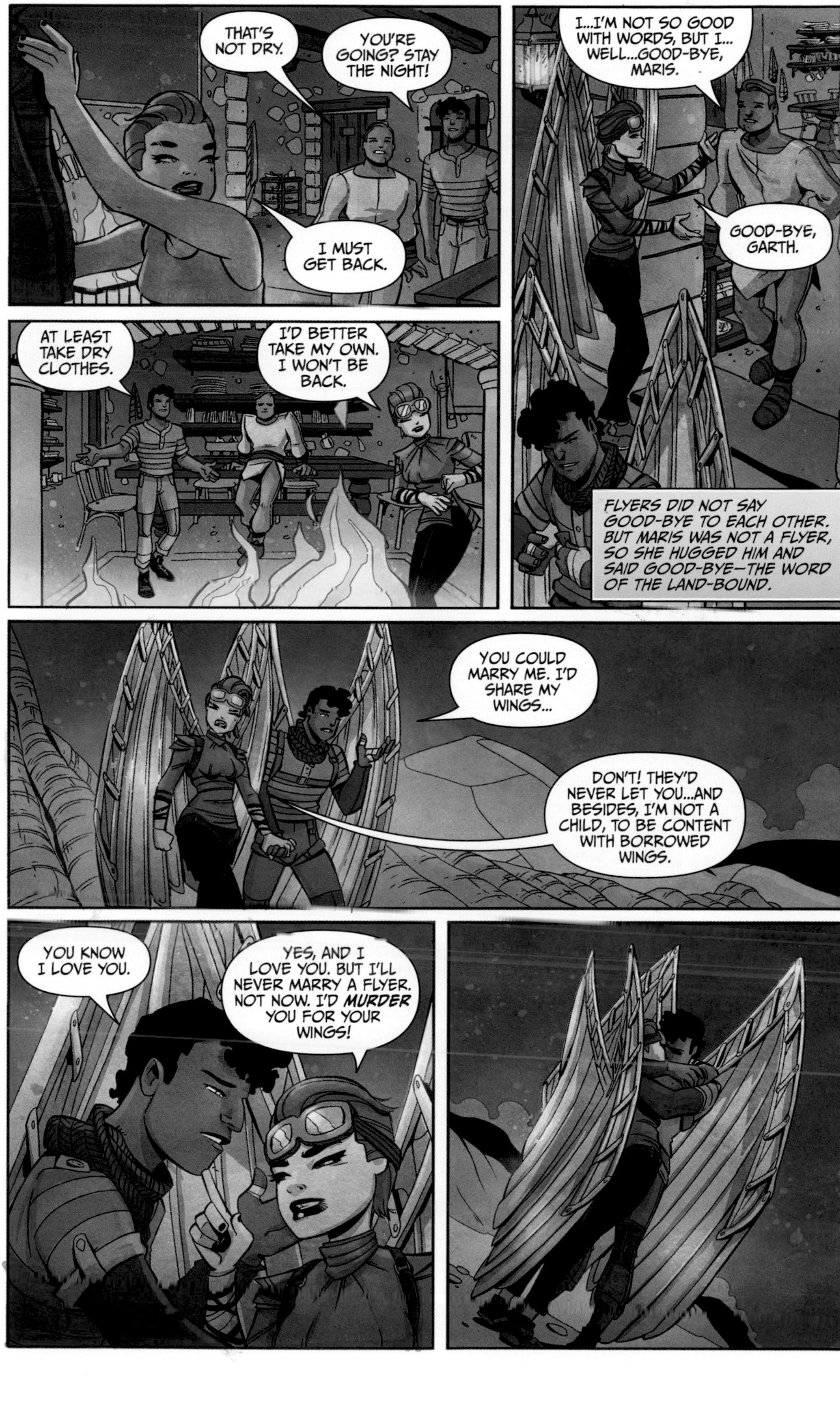
THAT'S NOT DRY.
YOU'RE GOING? STAY THE NIGHT!
I MUST GET BACK.
I...I'M NOT SO GOOD WITH WORDS, BUT I... WELL...GOOD-BYE, MARIS.
GOOD-BYE, GARTH.
AT LEAST TAKE DRY CLOTHES.
I'D BETTER TAKE MY OWN. I WON'T BE BACK.
FLYERS DID NOT SAY GOOD-BYE TO EACH OTHER. BUT MARIS WAS NOT A FLYER, SO SHE HUGGED HIM AND SAID GOOD-BYE—THE WORD OF THE LAND-BOUND.
YOU COULD MARRY ME. I'D SHARE MY WINGS...
DON'T! THEY'D NEVER LET YOU...AND BESIDES, I'M NOT A CHILD, TO BE CONTENT WITH BORROWED WINGS.
YOU KNOW I LOVE YOU.
YES, AND I LOVE YOU. BUT I'LL NEVER MARRY A FLYER. NOT NOW. I'D MURDER YOU FOR YOUR WINGS!

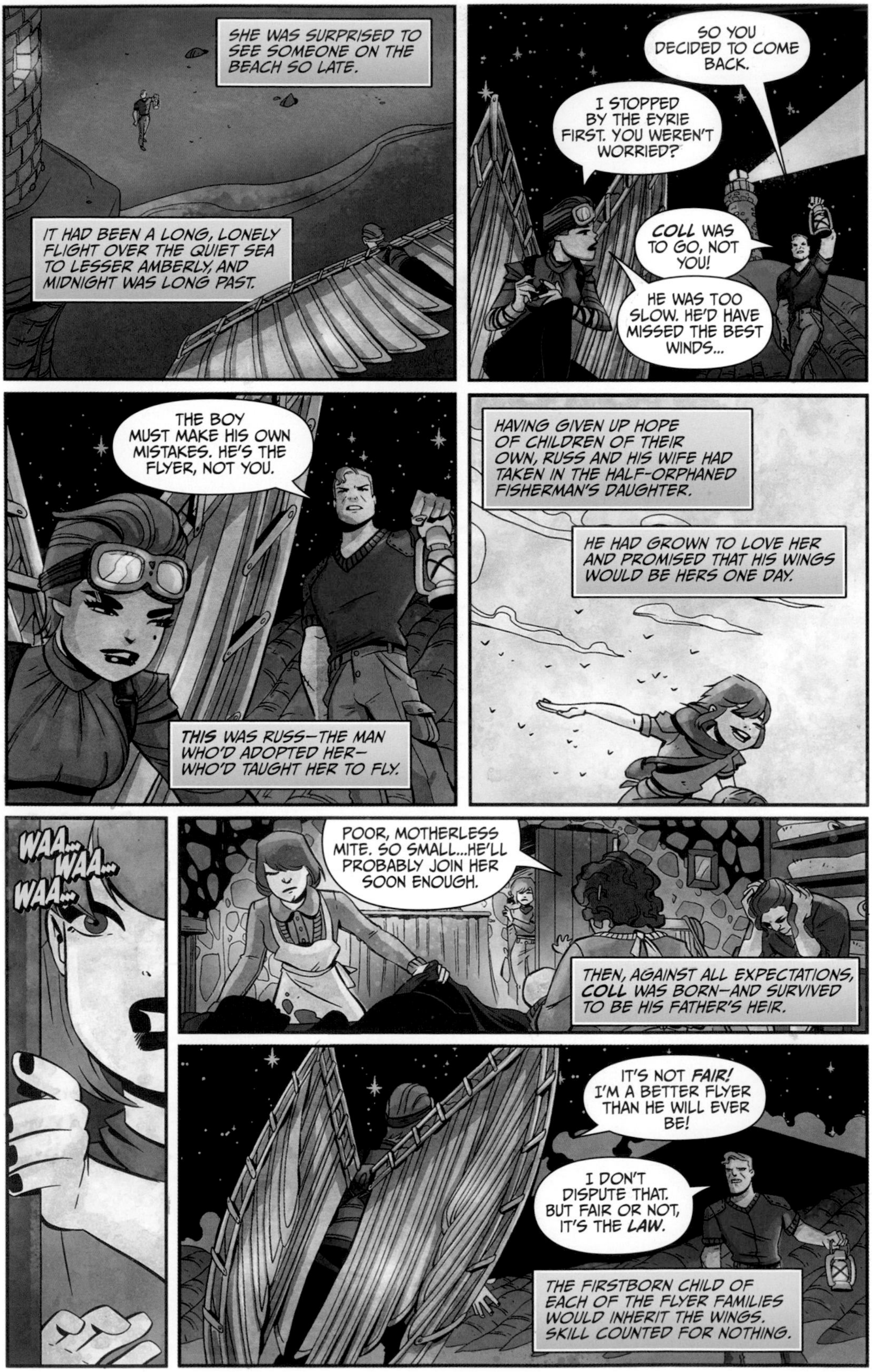
SHE WAS SURPRISED TO SEE SOMEONE ON THE BEACH SO LATE.
IT HAD BEEN A LONG, LONELY FLIGHT OVER THE QUIET SEA TO LESSER AMBERLY, AND MIDNIGHT WAS LONG PAST.
SO YOU DECIDED TO COME BACK.
I STOPPED BY THE EYRIE FIRST. YOU WEREN'T WORRIED?
COLL WAS TO GO, NOT YOU!
HE WAS TOO SLOW. HE'D HAVE MISSED THE BEST WINDS...
THE BOY MUST MAKE HIS OWN MISTAKES. HE'S THE FLYER, NOT YOU.
THIS WAS RUSS—THE MAN WHO'D ADOPTED HER—WHO'D TAUGHT HER TO FLY.
HAVING GIVEN UP HOPE OF CHILDREN OF THEIR OWN, RUSS AND HIS WIFE HAD TAKEN IN THE HALF-ORPHANED FISHERMAN'S DAUGHTER.
HE HAD GROWN TO LOVE HER AND PROMISED THAT HIS WINGS WOULD BE HERS ONE DAY.
WAA... WAA... WAA...
POOR, MOTHERLESS MITE. SO SMALL...HE'LL PROBABLY JOIN HER SOON ENOUGH.
THEN, AGAINST ALL EXPECTATIONS, COLL WAS BORN—AND SURVIVED TO BE HIS FATHER'S HEIR.
IT'S NOT FAIR! I'M A BETTER FLYER THAN HE WILL EVER BE!
I DON'T DISPUTE THAT. BUT FAIR OR NOT, IT'S THE LAW.
THE FIRSTBORN CHILD OF EACH OF THE FLYER FAMILIES WOULD INHERIT THE WINGS. SKILL COUNTED FOR NOTHING.

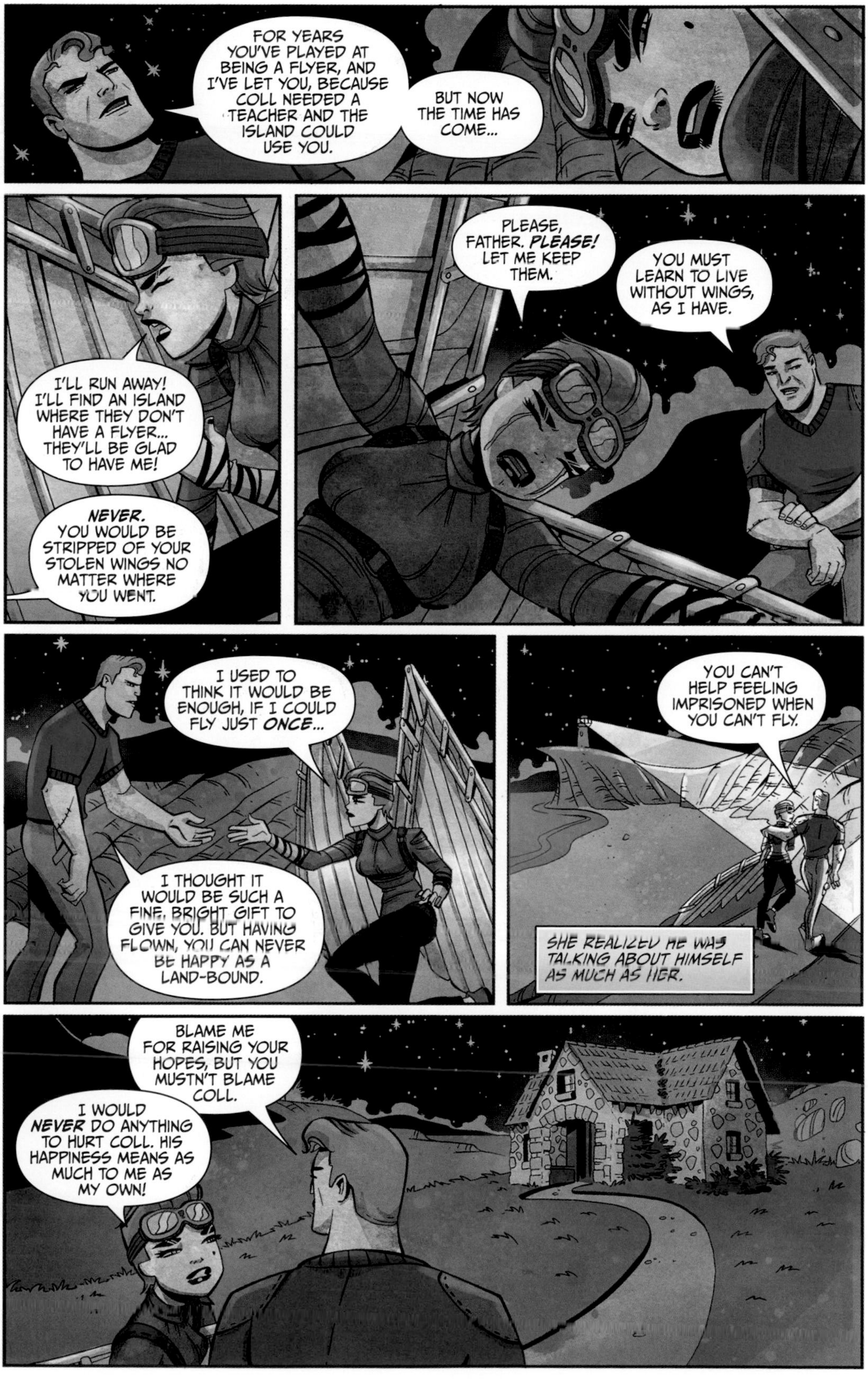
FOR YEARS YOU'VE PLAYED AT BEING A FLYER, AND I'VE LET YOU, BECAUSE COLL NEEDED A TEACHER AND THE ISLAND COULD USE YOU.
BUT NOW THE TIME HAS COME...
I'LL RUN AWAY! I'LL FIND AN ISLAND WHERE THEY DON'T HAVE A FLYER... THEY'LL BE GLAD TO HAVE ME!
NEVER. YOU WOULD BE STRIPPED OF YOUR STOLEN WINGS NO MATTER WHERE YOU WENT.
PLEASE, FATHER. PLEASE! LET ME KEEP THEM.
YOU MUST LEARN TO LIVE WITHOUT WINGS, AS I HAVE.
I USED TO THINK IT WOULD BE ENOUGH, IF I COULD FLY JUST ONCE...
I THOUGHT IT WOULD BE SUCH A FINE, BRIGHT GIFT TO GIVE YOU. BUT HAVING FLOWN, YOU CAN NEVER BE HAPPY AS A LAND-BOUND.
YOU CAN'T HELP FEELING IMPRISONED WHEN YOU CAN'T FLY.
SHE REALIZED HE WAS TALKING ABOUT HIMSELF AS MUCH AS HER.
BLAME ME FOR RAISING YOUR HOPES, BUT YOU MUSTN'T BLAME COLL.
I WOULD NEVER DO ANYTHING TO HURT COLL. HIS HAPPINESS MEANS AS MUCH TO ME AS MY OWN!

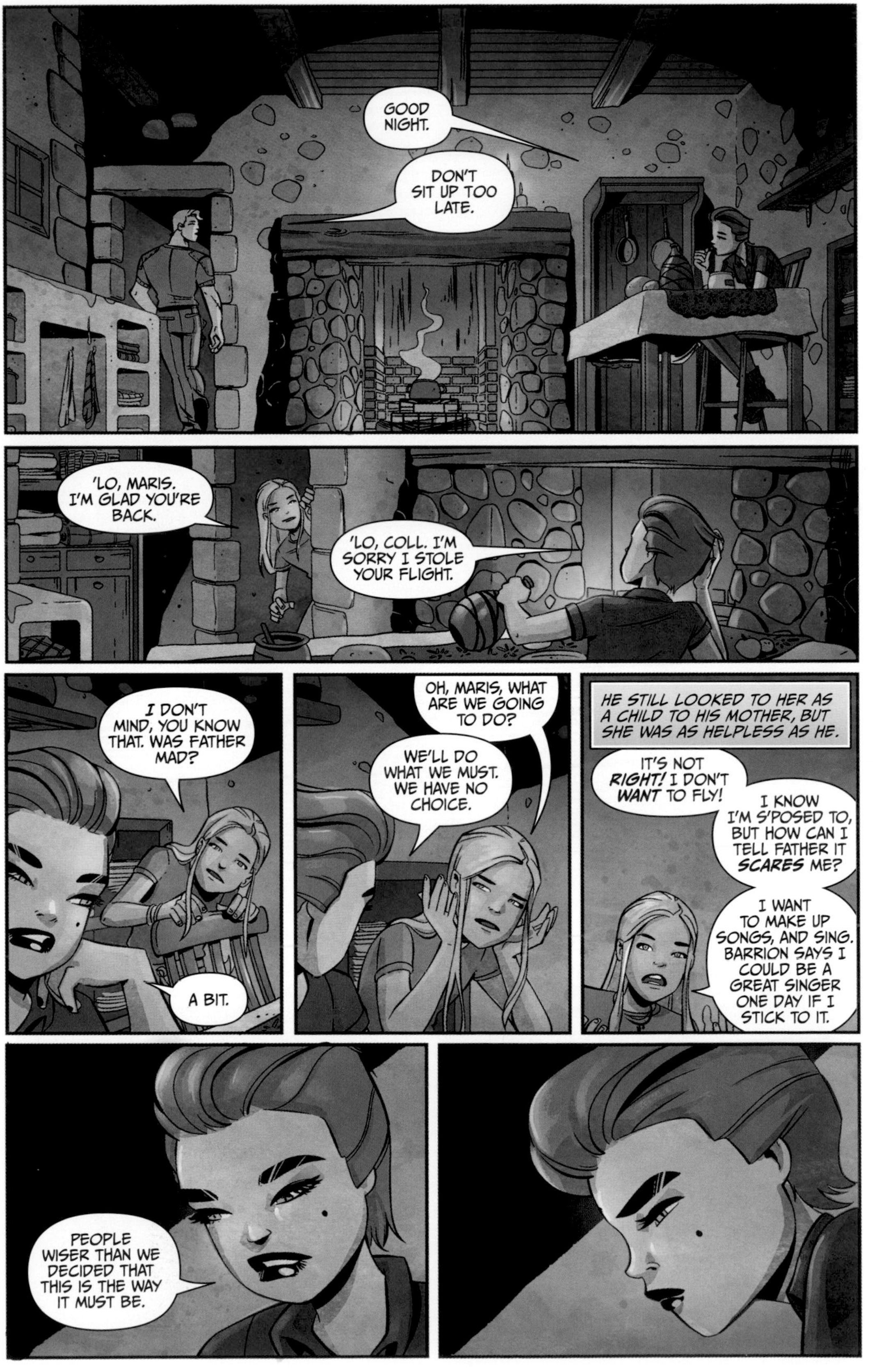
GOOD NIGHT.
DON'T SIT UP TOO LATE.
'LO, MARIS. I'M GLAD YOU'RE BACK.
'LO, COLL. I'M SORRY I STOLE YOUR FLIGHT.
I DON'T MIND, YOU KNOW THAT. WAS FATHER MAD?
A BIT.
OH, MARIS, WHAT ARE WE GOING TO DO?
WE'LL DO WHAT WE MUST. WE HAVE NO CHOICE.
HE STILL LOOKED TO HER AS A CHILD TO HIS MOTHER, BUT SHE WAS AS HELPLESS AS HE.
IT'S NOT RIGHT! I DON'T WANT TO FLY!
I KNOW I'M S'POSED TO, BUT HOW CAN I TELL FATHER IT SCARES ME?
I WANT TO MAKE UP SONGS, AND SING. BARRION SAYS I COULD BE A GREAT SINGER ONE DAY IF I STICK TO IT.
PEOPLE WISER THAN WE DECIDED THAT THIS IS THE WAY IT MUST BE.

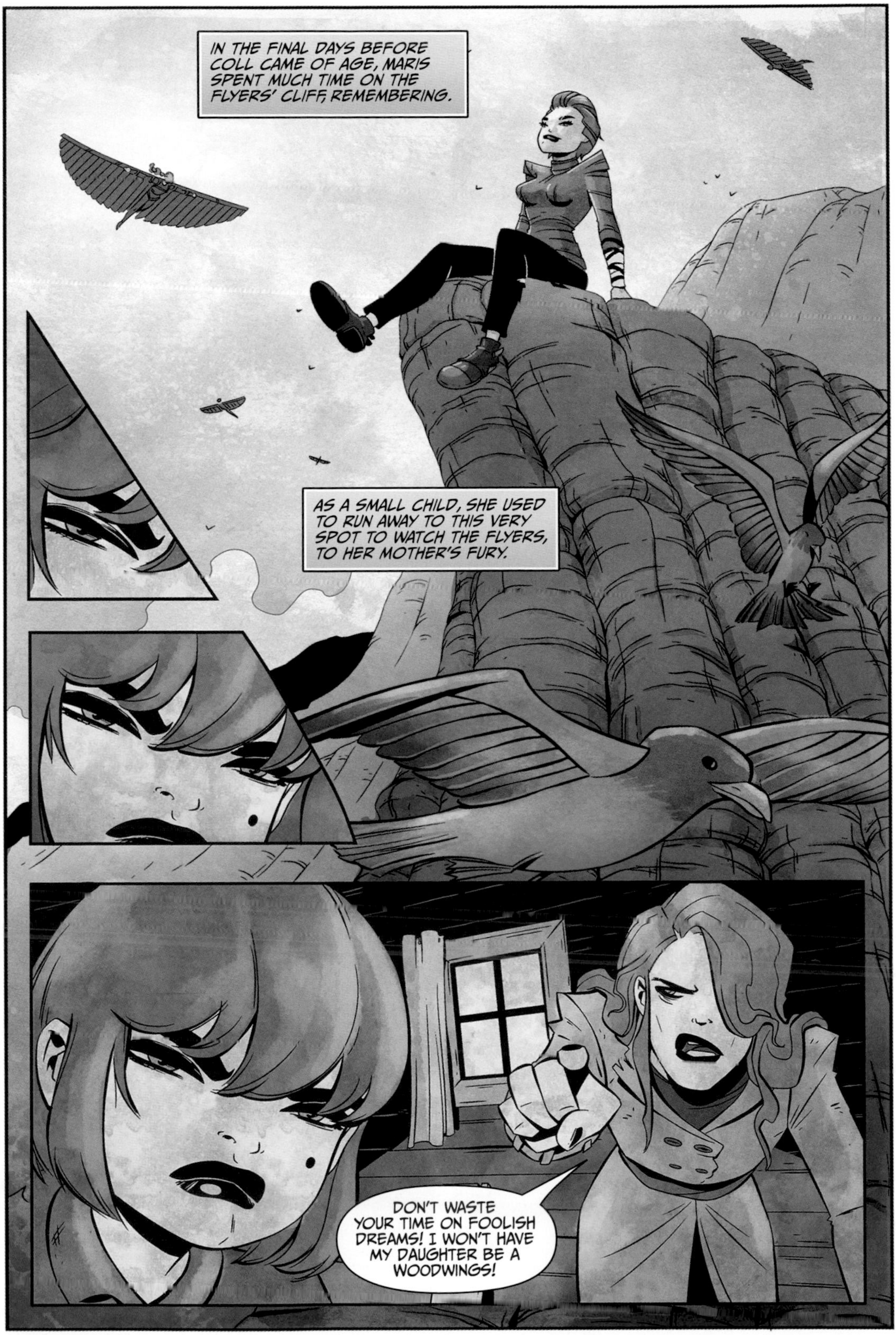
IN THE FINAL DAYS BEFORE COLL CAME OF AGE, MARIS SPENT MUCH TIME ON THE FLYERS' CLIFF, REMEMBERING.
AS A SMALL CHILD, SHE USED TO RUN AWAY TO THIS VERY SPOT TO WATCH THE FLYERS, TO HER MOTHER'S FURY.
DON'T WASTE YOUR TIME ON FOOLISH DREAMS! I WON'T HAVE MY DAUGHTER BE A WOODWINGS!

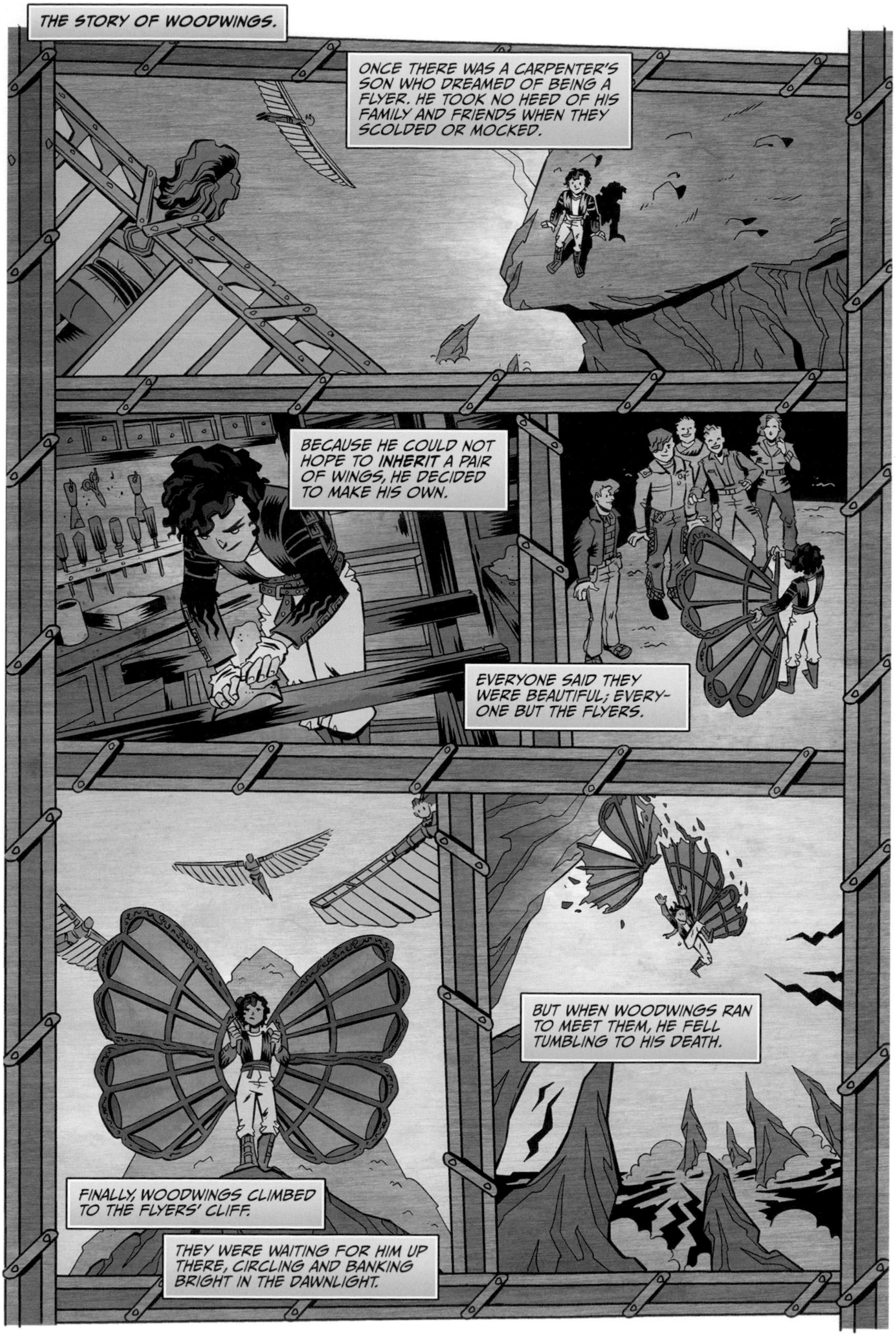
THE STORY OF WOODWINGS.
ONCE THERE WAS A CARPENTER'S SON WHO DREAMED OF BEING A FLYER. HE TOOK NO HEED OF HIS FAMILY AND FRIENDS WHEN THEY SCOLDED OR MOCKED.
BECAUSE HE COULD NOT HOPE TO INHERIT A PAIR OF WINGS, HE DECIDED TO MAKE HIS OWN.
EVERYONE SAID THEY WERE BEAUTIFUL; EVERY-ONE BUT THE FLYERS.
FINALLY, WOODWINGS CLIMBED TO THE FLYERS' CLIFF.
THEY WERE WAITING FOR HIM UP THERE, CIRCLING AND BANKING BRIGHT IN THE DAWNLIGHT.
BUT WHEN WOODWINGS RAN TO MEET THEM, HE FELL TUMBLING TO HIS DEATH.

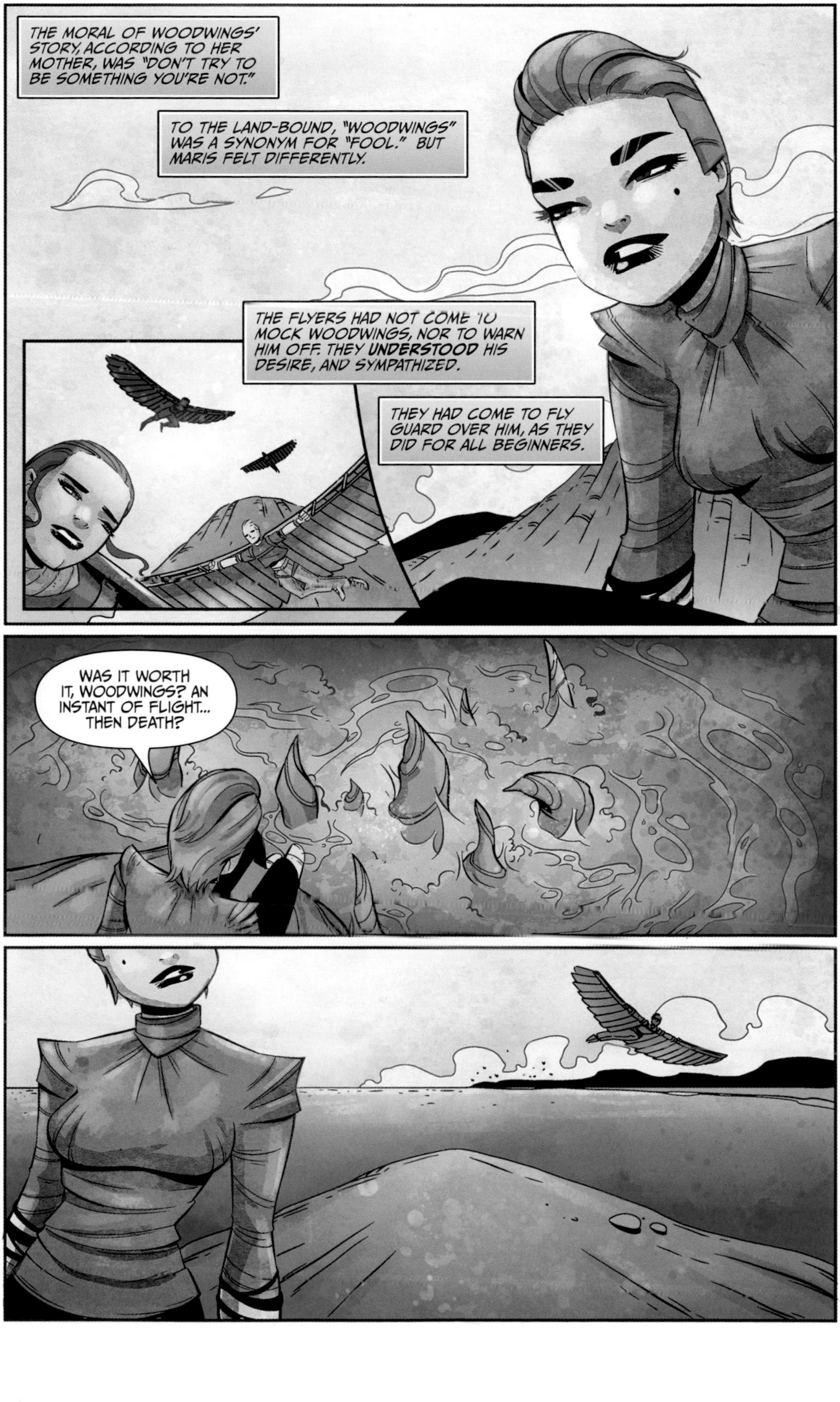
THE MORAL OF WOODWINGS' STORY, ACCORDING TO HER MOTHER, WAS "DON'T TRY TO BE SOMETHING YOU'RE NOT."
TO THE LAND-BOUND, "WOODWINGS" WAS A SYNONYM FOR "FOOL." BUT MARIS FELT DIFFERENTLY.
THE FLYERS HAD NOT COME TO MOCK WOODWINGS, NOR TO WARN HIM OFF. THEY UNDERSTOOD HIS DESIRE, AND SYMPATHIZED.
THEY HAD COME TO FLY GUARD OVER HIM, AS THEY DID FOR ALL BEGINNERS.
WAS IT WORTH IT, WOODWINGS? AN INSTANT OF FLIGHT... THEN DEATH?

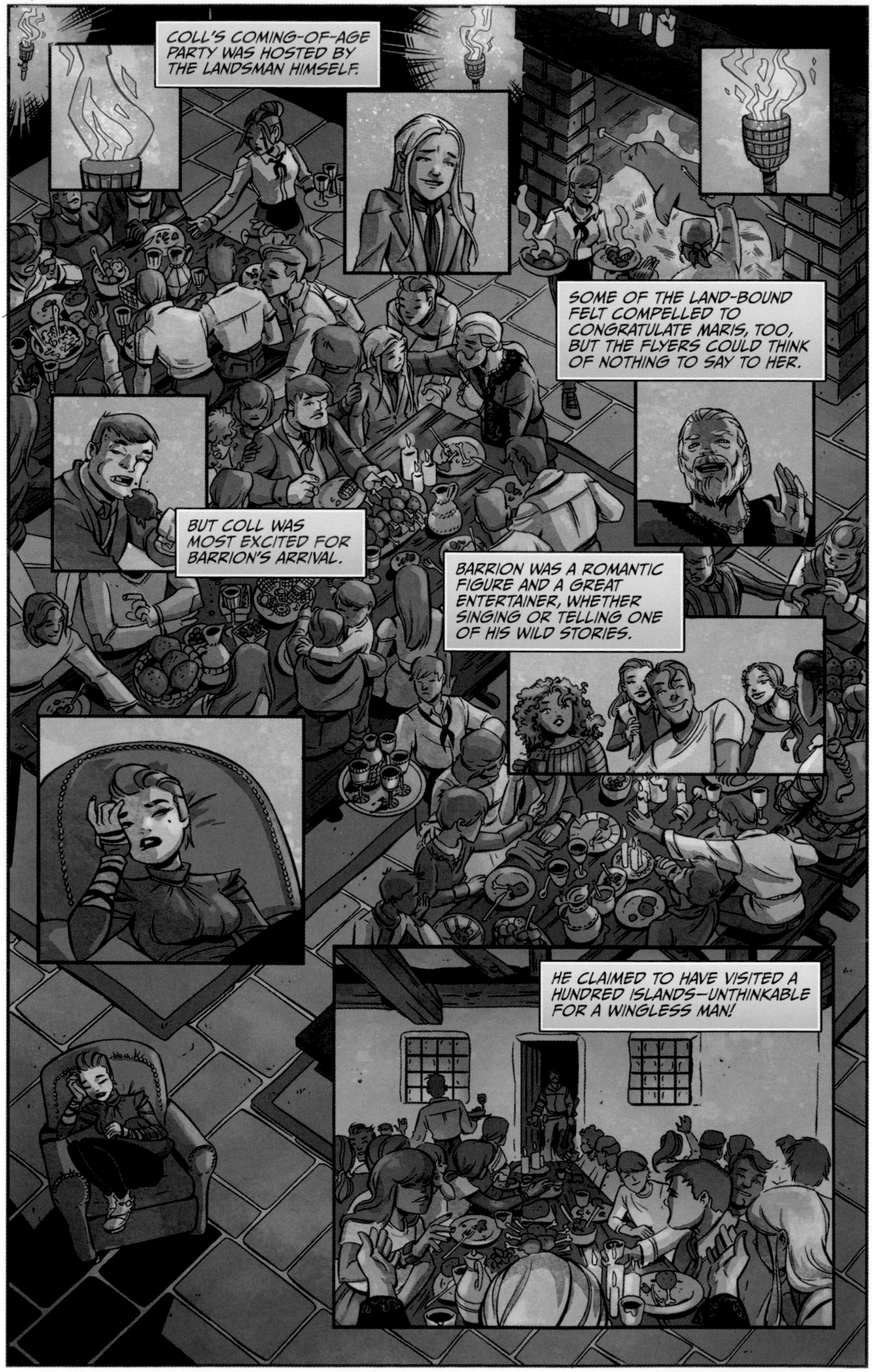
COLL'S COMING-OF-AGE PARTY WAS HOSTED BY THE LANDSMAN HIMSELF.
SOME OF THE LAND-BOUND FELT COMPELLED TO CONGRATULATE MARIS, TOO, BUT THE FLYERS COULD THINK OF NOTHING TO SAY TO HER.
BUT COLL WAS MOST EXCITED FOR BARRION'S ARRIVAL.
BARRION WAS A ROMANTIC FIGURE AND A GREAT ENTERTAINER, WHETHER SINGING OR TELLING ONE OF HIS WILD STORIES.
HE CLAIMED TO HAVE VISITED A HUNDRED ISLANDS—UNTHINKABLE FOR A WINGLESS MAN!

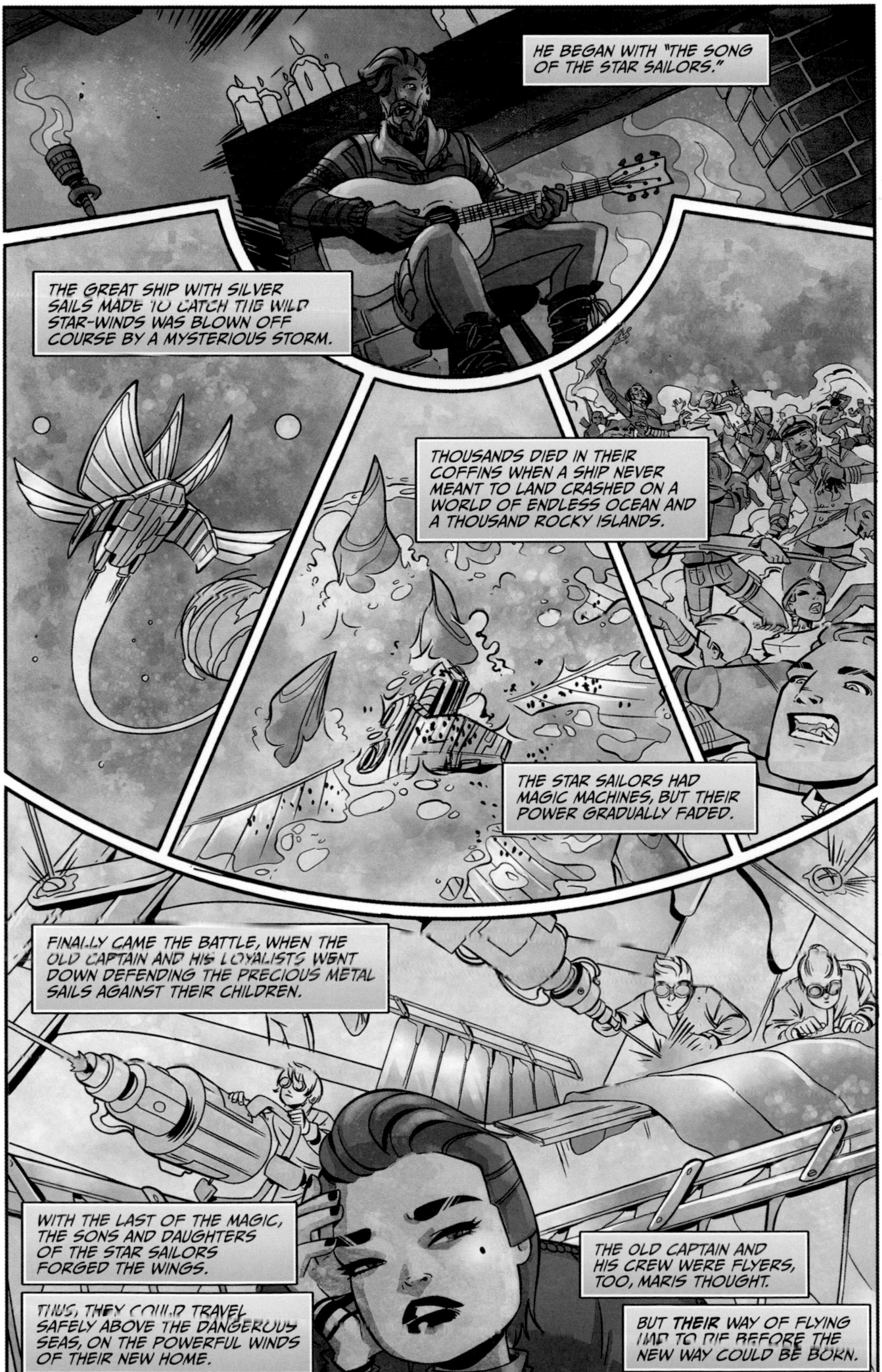
HE BEGAN WITH "THE SONG OF THE STAR SAILORS."
THE GREAT SHIP WITH SILVER SAILS MADE TO CATCH THE WILD STAR-WINDS WAS BLOWN OFF COURSE BY A MYSTERIOUS STORM.
THOUSANDS DIED IN THEIR COFFINS WHEN A SHIP NEVER MEANT TO LAND CRASHED ON A WORLD OF ENDLESS OCEAN AND A THOUSAND ROCKY ISLANDS.
THE STAR SAILORS HAD MAGIC MACHINES, BUT THEIR POWER GRADUALLY FADED.
FINALLY CAME THE BATTLE, WHEN THE OLD CAPTAIN AND HIS LOYALISTS WENT DOWN DEFENDING THE PRECIOUS METAL SAILS AGAINST THEIR CHILDREN.
WITH THE LAST OF THE MAGIC, THE SONS AND DAUGHTERS OF THE STAR SAILORS FORGED THE WINGS.
THUS, THEY COULD TRAVEL SAFELY ABOVE THE DANGEROUS SEAS, ON THE POWERFUL WINDS OF THEIR NEW HOME.
THE OLD CAPTAIN AND HIS CREW WERE FLYERS, TOO, MARIS THOUGHT.
BUT **THEIR** WAY OF FLYING HAD TO DIE BEFORE THE NEW WAY COULD BE BORN.

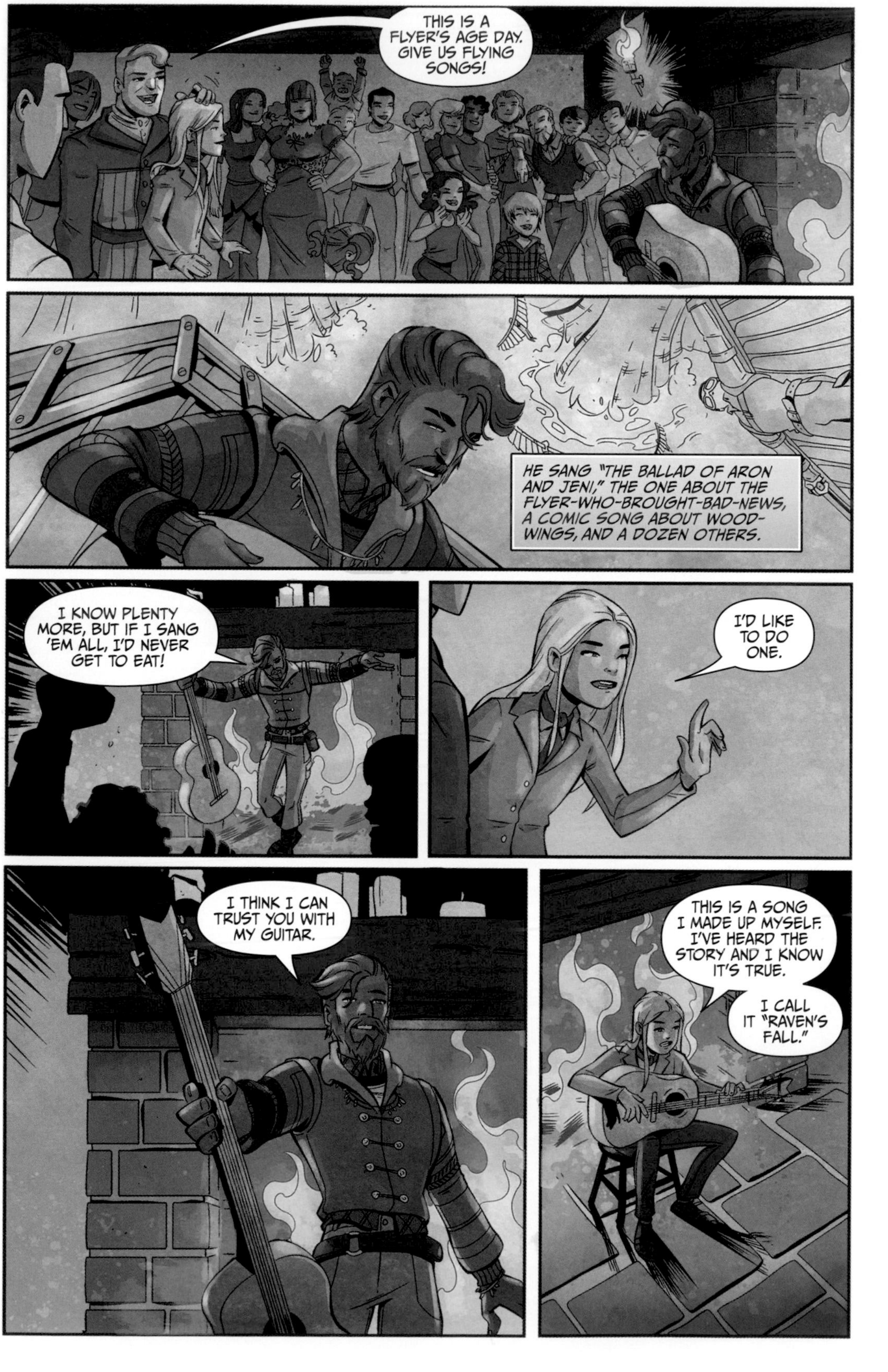

THIS IS A FLYER'S AGE DAY. GIVE US FLYING SONGS!
HE SANG "THE BALLAD OF ARON AND JENI," THE ONE ABOUT THE FLYER-WHO-BROUGHT-BAD-NEWS, A COMIC SONG ABOUT WOOD-WINGS, AND A DOZEN OTHERS.
I KNOW PLENTY MORE, BUT IF I SANG 'EM ALL, I'D NEVER GET TO EAT!
I'D LIKE TO DO ONE.
I THINK I CAN TRUST YOU WITH MY GUITAR.
THIS IS A SONG I MADE UP MYSELF. I'VE HEARD THE STORY AND I KNOW IT'S TRUE.
I CALL IT "RAVEN'S FALL."

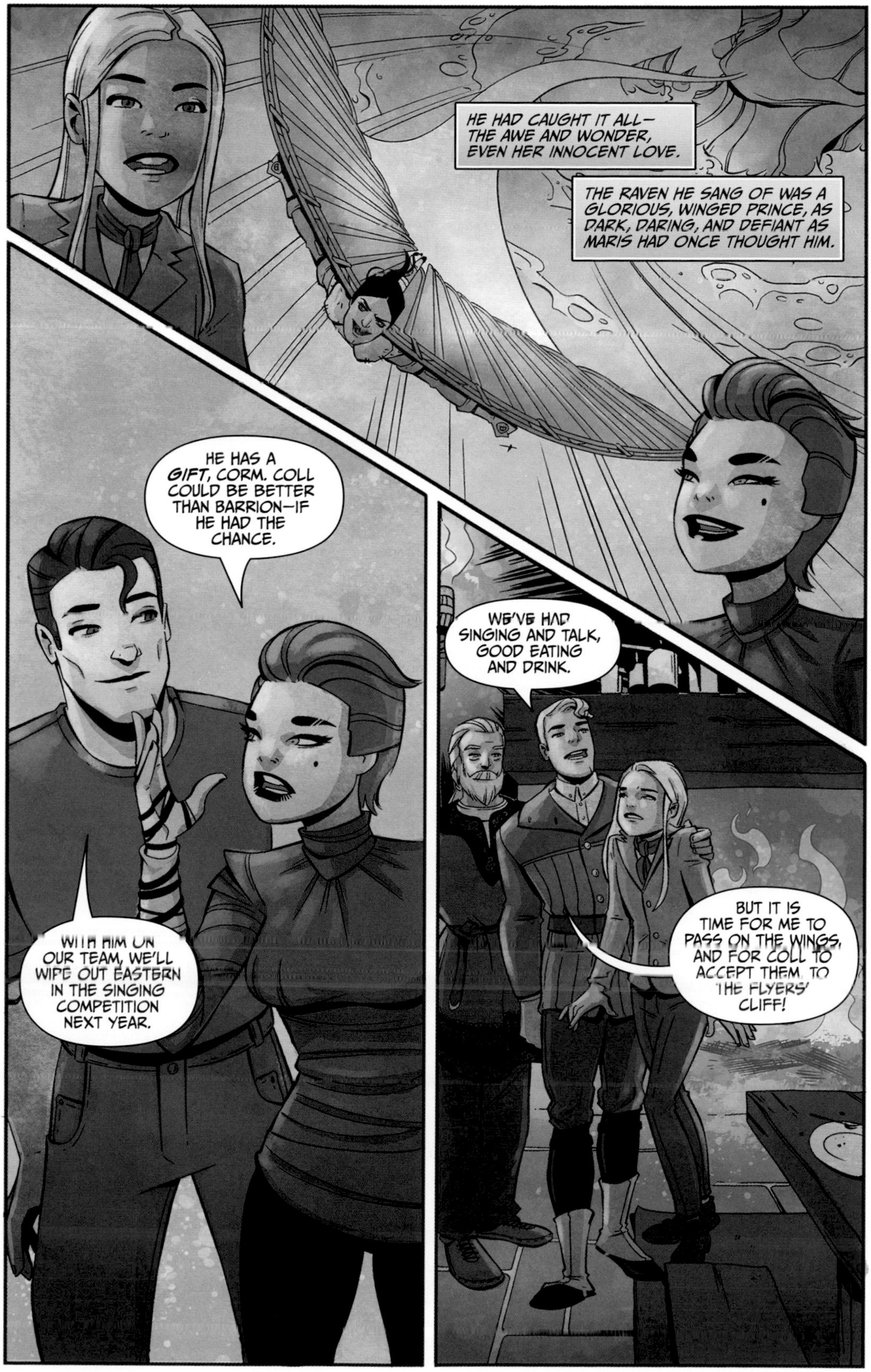
HE HAD CAUGHT IT ALL—THE AWE AND WONDER, EVEN HER INNOCENT LOVE.
THE RAVEN HE SANG OF WAS A GLORIOUS, WINGED PRINCE, AS DARK, DARING, AND DEFIANT AS MARIS HAD ONCE THOUGHT HIM.
HE HAS A GIFT, CORM. COLL COULD BE BETTER THAN BARRION—IF HE HAD THE CHANCE.
WITH HIM ON OUR TEAM, WE'LL WIPE OUT EASTERN IN THE SINGING COMPETITION NEXT YEAR.
WE'VE HAD SINGING AND TALK, GOOD EATING AND DRINK.
BUT IT IS TIME FOR ME TO PASS ON THE WINGS, AND FOR COLL TO ACCEPT THEM. TO THE FLYERS' CLIFF!

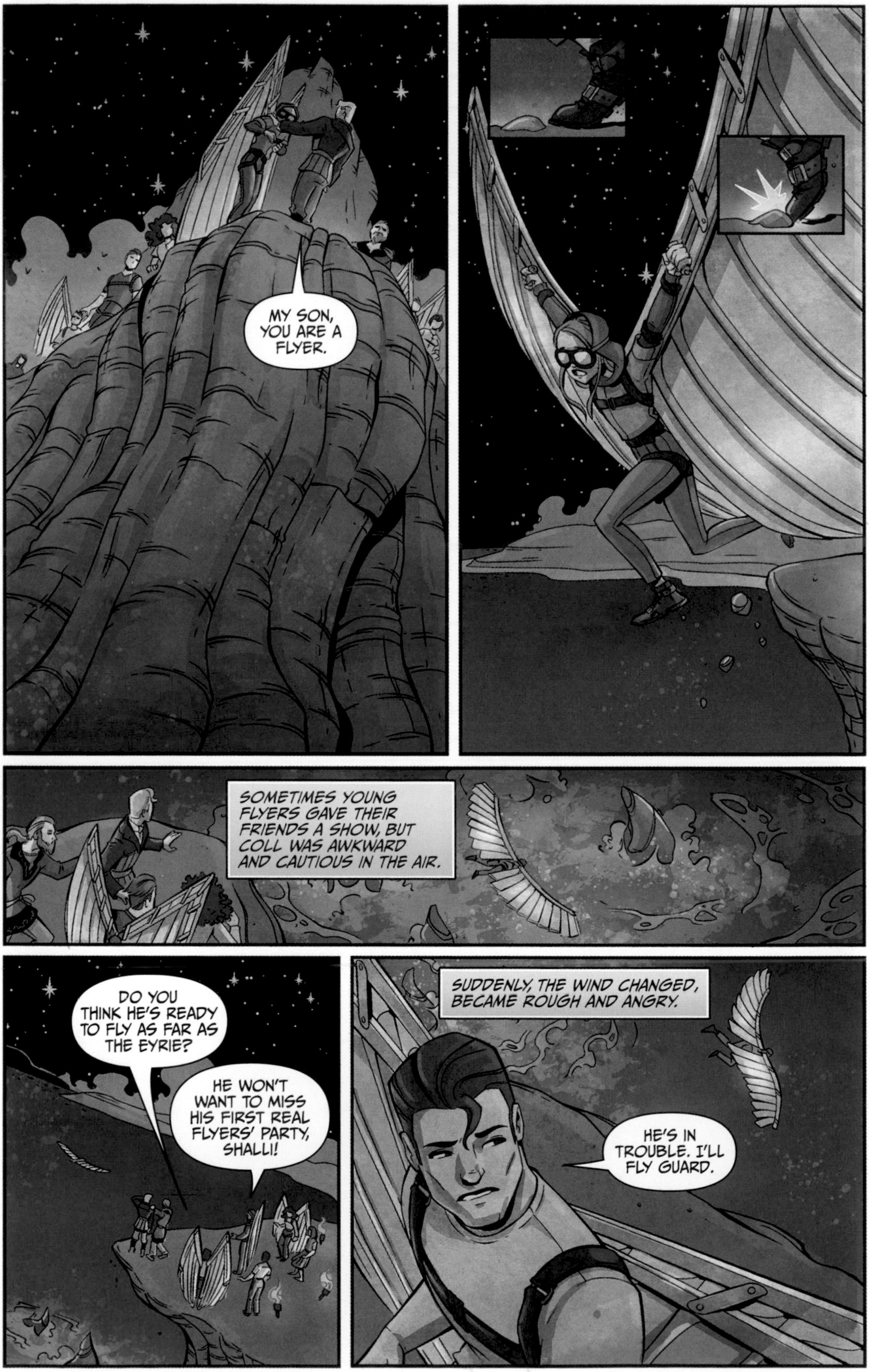
MY SON, YOU ARE A FLYER.
SOMETIMES YOUNG FLYERS GAVE THEIR FRIENDS A SHOW, BUT COLL WAS AWKWARD AND CAUTIOUS IN THE AIR.
DO YOU THINK HE'S READY TO FLY AS FAR AS THE EYRIE?
HE WON'T WANT TO MISS HIS FIRST REAL FLYERS' PARTY, SHALLI!
SUDDENLY, THE WIND CHANGED, BECAME ROUGH AND ANGRY.
HE'S IN TROUBLE. I'LL FLY GUARD.

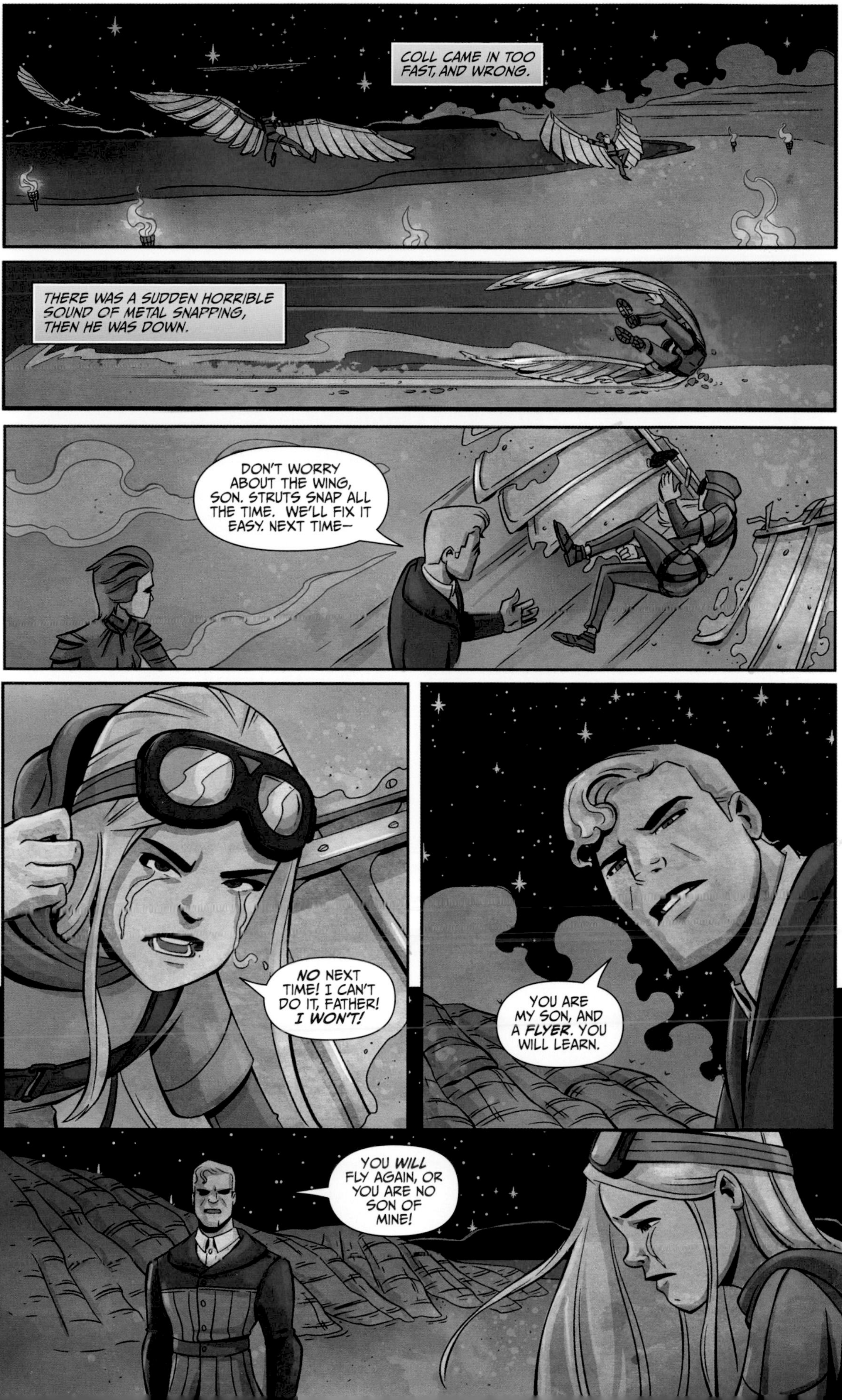
COLL CAME IN TOO FAST, AND WRONG.
THERE WAS A SUDDEN HORRIBLE SOUND OF METAL SNAPPING, THEN HE WAS DOWN.
DON'T WORRY ABOUT THE WING, SON. STRUTS SNAP ALL THE TIME. WE'LL FIX IT EASY. NEXT TIME—
NO NEXT TIME! I CAN'T DO IT, FATHER! I WON'T!
YOU ARE MY SON, AND A FLYER. YOU WILL LEARN.
YOU WILL FLY AGAIN, OR YOU ARE NO SON OF MINE!

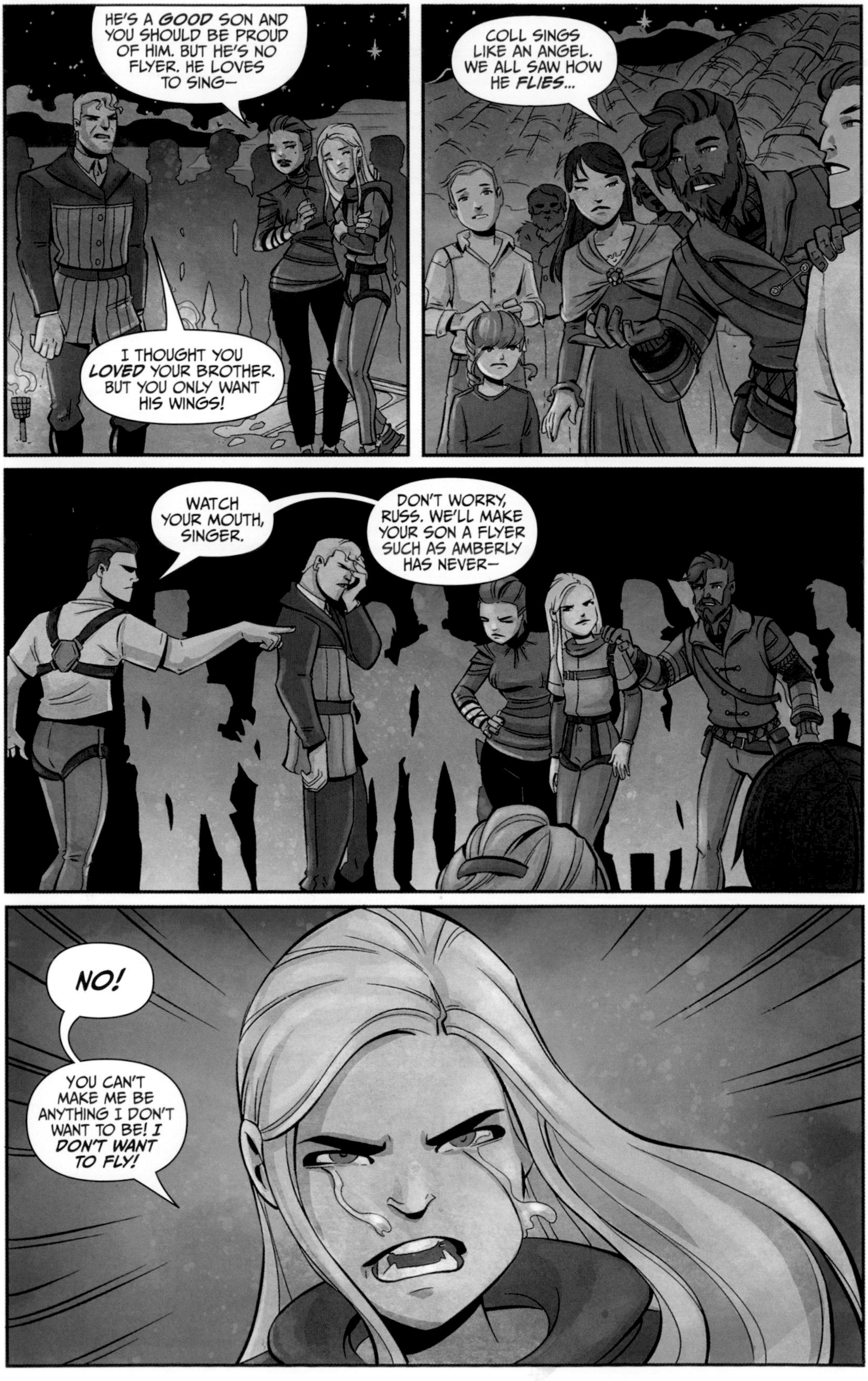
HE'S A GOOD SON AND YOU SHOULD BE PROUD OF HIM. BUT HE'S NO FLYER. HE LOVES TO SING—
I THOUGHT YOU LOVED YOUR BROTHER. BUT YOU ONLY WANT HIS WINGS!
COLL SINGS LIKE AN ANGEL. WE ALL SAW HOW HE FLIES...
WATCH YOUR MOUTH, SINGER.
DON'T WORRY, RUSS. WE'LL MAKE YOUR SON A FLYER SUCH AS AMBERLY HAS NEVER—
NO!
YOU CAN'T MAKE ME BE ANYTHING I DON'T WANT TO BE! I DON'T WANT TO FLY!

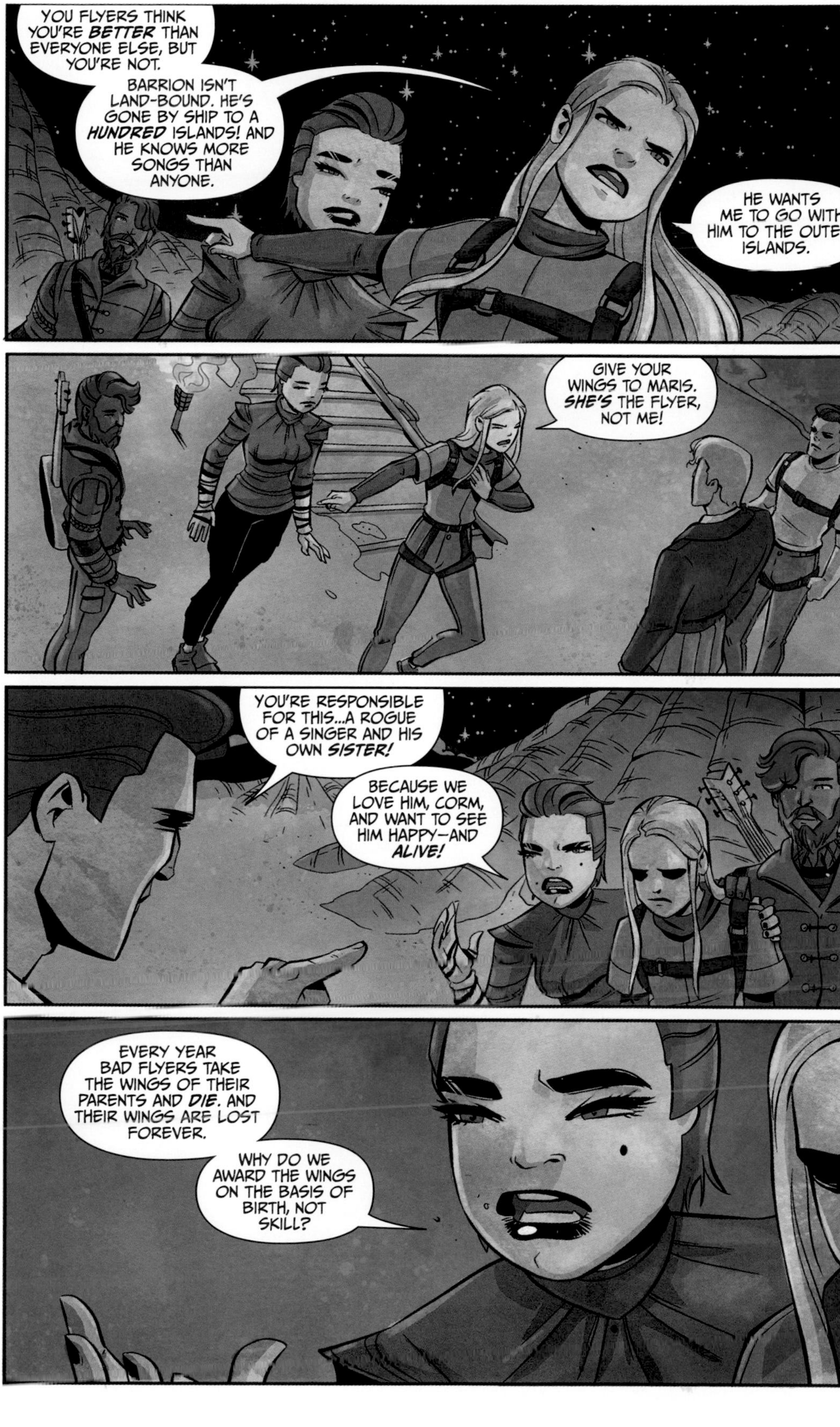
YOU FLYERS THINK YOU'RE BETTER THAN EVERYONE ELSE, BUT YOU'RE NOT.
BARRION ISN'T LAND-BOUND. HE'S GONE BY SHIP TO A HUNDRED ISLANDS! AND HE KNOWS MORE SONGS THAN ANYONE.
HE WANTS ME TO GO WITH HIM TO THE OUTER ISLANDS.
GIVE YOUR WINGS TO MARIS. SHE'S THE FLYER, NOT ME!
YOU'RE RESPONSIBLE FOR THIS...A ROGUE OF A SINGER AND HIS OWN SISTER!
BECAUSE WE LOVE HIM, CORM, AND WANT TO SEE HIM HAPPY—AND ALIVE!
EVERY YEAR BAD FLYERS TAKE THE WINGS OF THEIR PARENTS AND DIE. AND THEIR WINGS ARE LOST FOREVER.
WHY DO WE AWARD THE WINGS ON THE BASIS OF BIRTH, NOT SKILL?

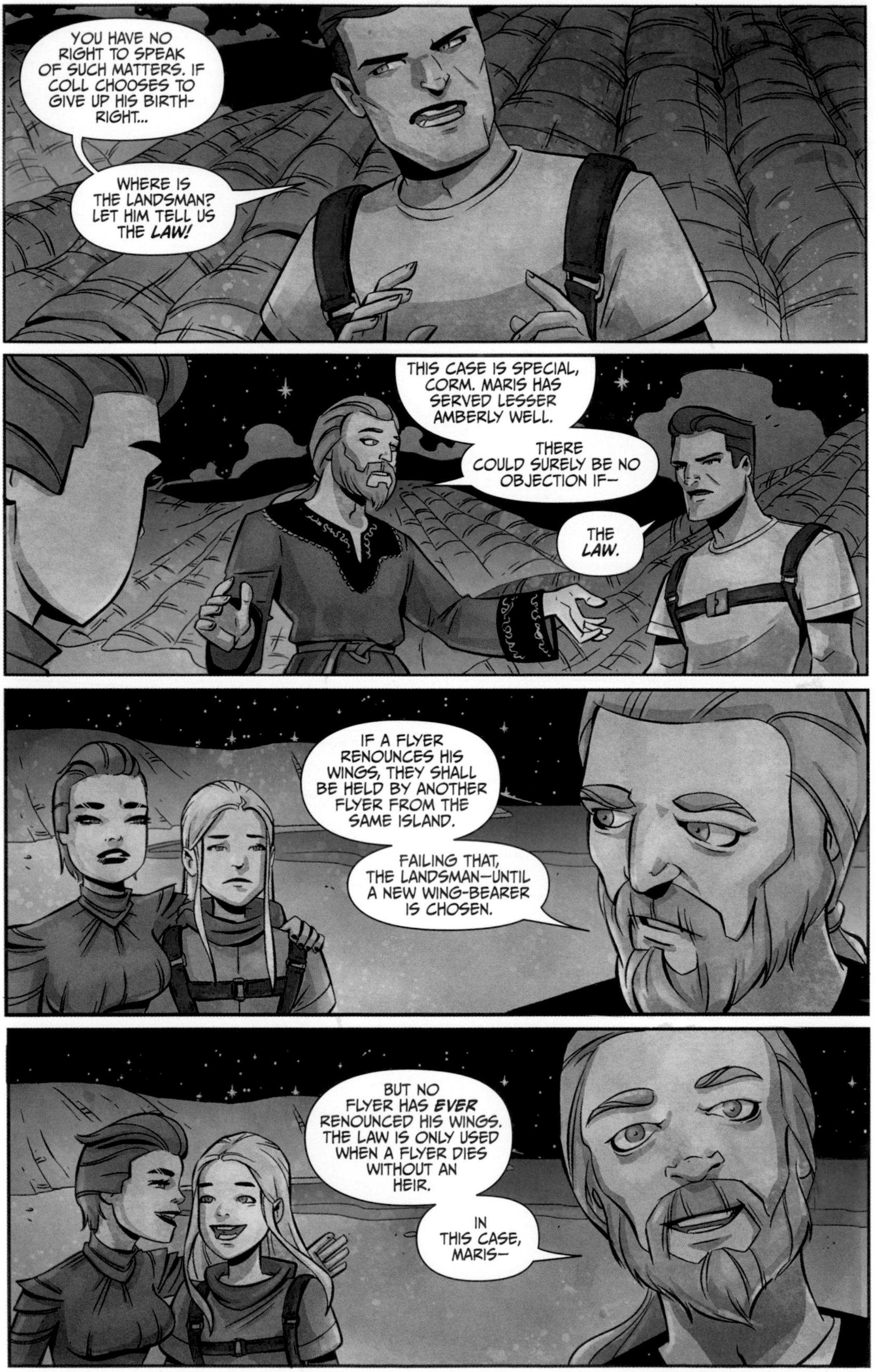
YOU HAVE NO RIGHT TO SPEAK OF SUCH MATTERS. IF COLL CHOOSES TO GIVE UP HIS BIRTH-RIGHT...
WHERE IS THE LANDSMAN? LET HIM TELL US THE *LAW!*
THIS CASE IS SPECIAL, CORM. MARIS HAS SERVED LESSER AMBERLY WELL.
THERE COULD SURELY BE NO OBJECTION IF—
THE *LAW.*
IF A FLYER RENOUNCES HIS WINGS, THEY SHALL BE HELD BY ANOTHER FLYER FROM THE SAME ISLAND.
FAILING THAT, THE LANDSMAN—UNTIL A NEW WING-BEARER IS CHOSEN.
BUT NO FLYER HAS *EVER* RENOUNCED HIS WINGS. THE LAW IS ONLY USED WHEN A FLYER DIES WITHOUT AN HEIR.
IN THIS CASE, MARIS—

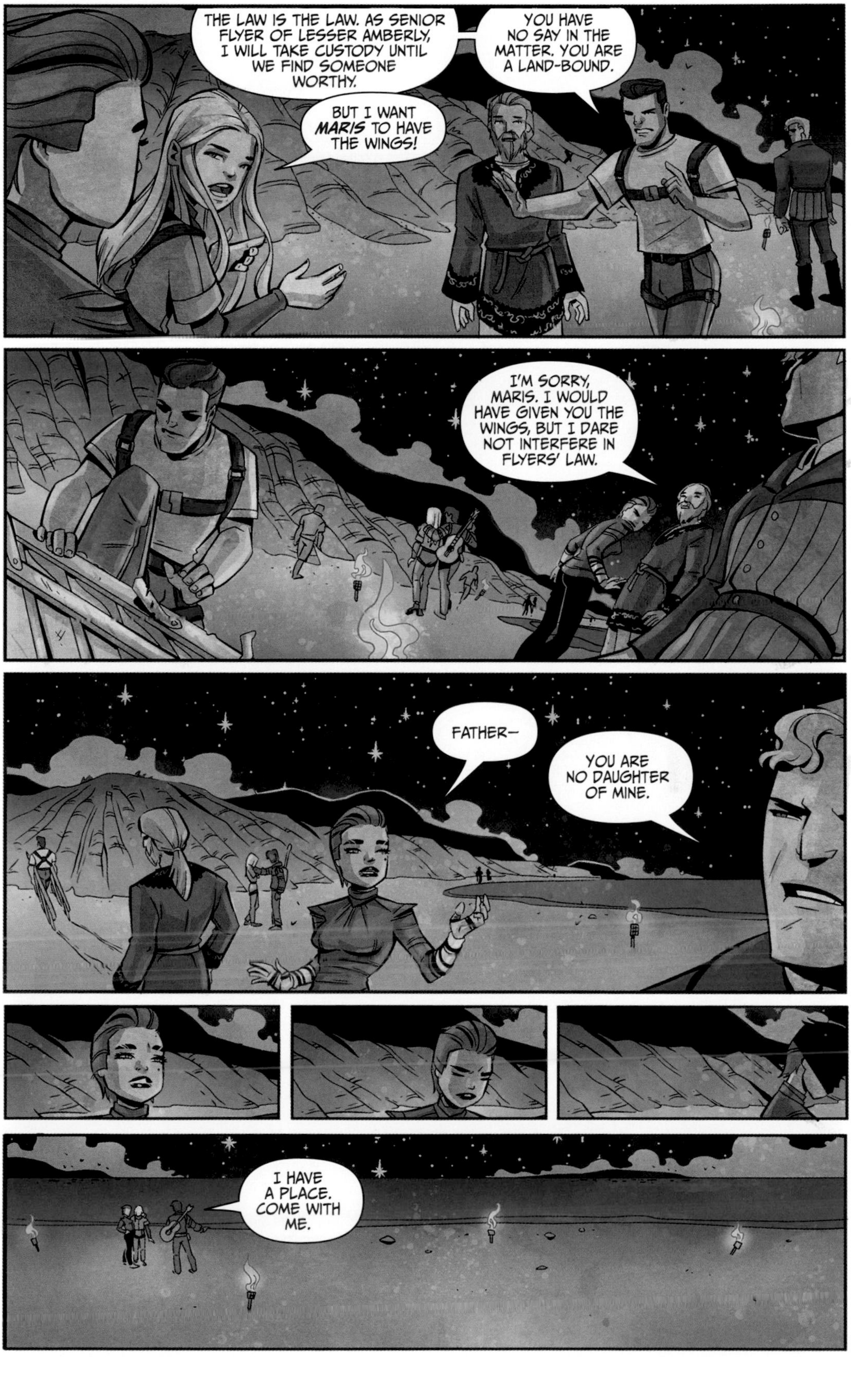

THE LAW IS THE LAW. AS SENIOR FLYER OF LESSER AMBERLY, I WILL TAKE CUSTODY UNTIL WE FIND SOMEONE WORTHY.
YOU HAVE NO SAY IN THE MATTER. YOU ARE A LAND-BOUND.
BUT I WANT **MARIS** TO HAVE THE WINGS!
I'M SORRY, MARIS. I WOULD HAVE GIVEN YOU THE WINGS, BUT I DARE NOT INTERFERE IN FLYERS' LAW.
FATHER—
YOU ARE NO DAUGHTER OF MINE.
I HAVE A PLACE. COME WITH ME.

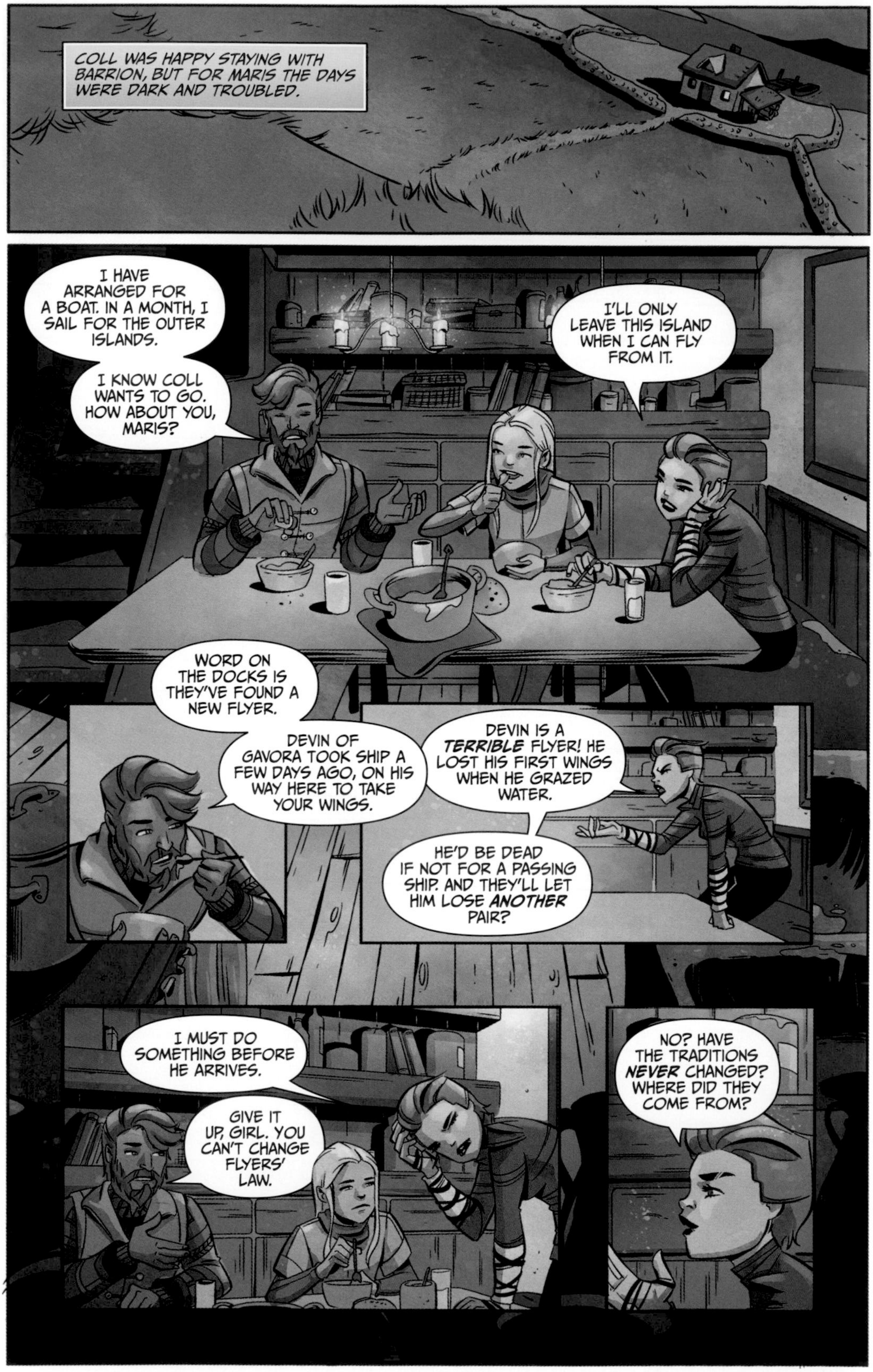
COLL WAS HAPPY STAYING WITH BARRION, BUT FOR MARIS THE DAYS WERE DARK AND TROUBLED.
I HAVE ARRANGED FOR A BOAT. IN A MONTH, I SAIL FOR THE OUTER ISLANDS.
I KNOW COLL WANTS TO GO. HOW ABOUT YOU, MARIS?
I'LL ONLY LEAVE THIS ISLAND WHEN I CAN FLY FROM IT.
WORD ON THE DOCKS IS THEY'VE FOUND A NEW FLYER.
DEVIN OF GAVORA TOOK SHIP A FEW DAYS AGO, ON HIS WAY HERE TO TAKE YOUR WINGS.
DEVIN IS A ***TERRIBLE*** FLYER! HE LOST HIS FIRST WINGS WHEN HE GRAZED WATER.
HE'D BE DEAD IF NOT FOR A PASSING SHIP. AND THEY'LL LET HIM LOSE ***ANOTHER*** PAIR?
I MUST DO SOMETHING BEFORE HE ARRIVES.
GIVE IT UP, GIRL. YOU CAN'T CHANGE FLYERS' LAW.
NO? HAVE THE TRADITIONS ***NEVER*** CHANGED? WHERE DID THEY COME FROM?

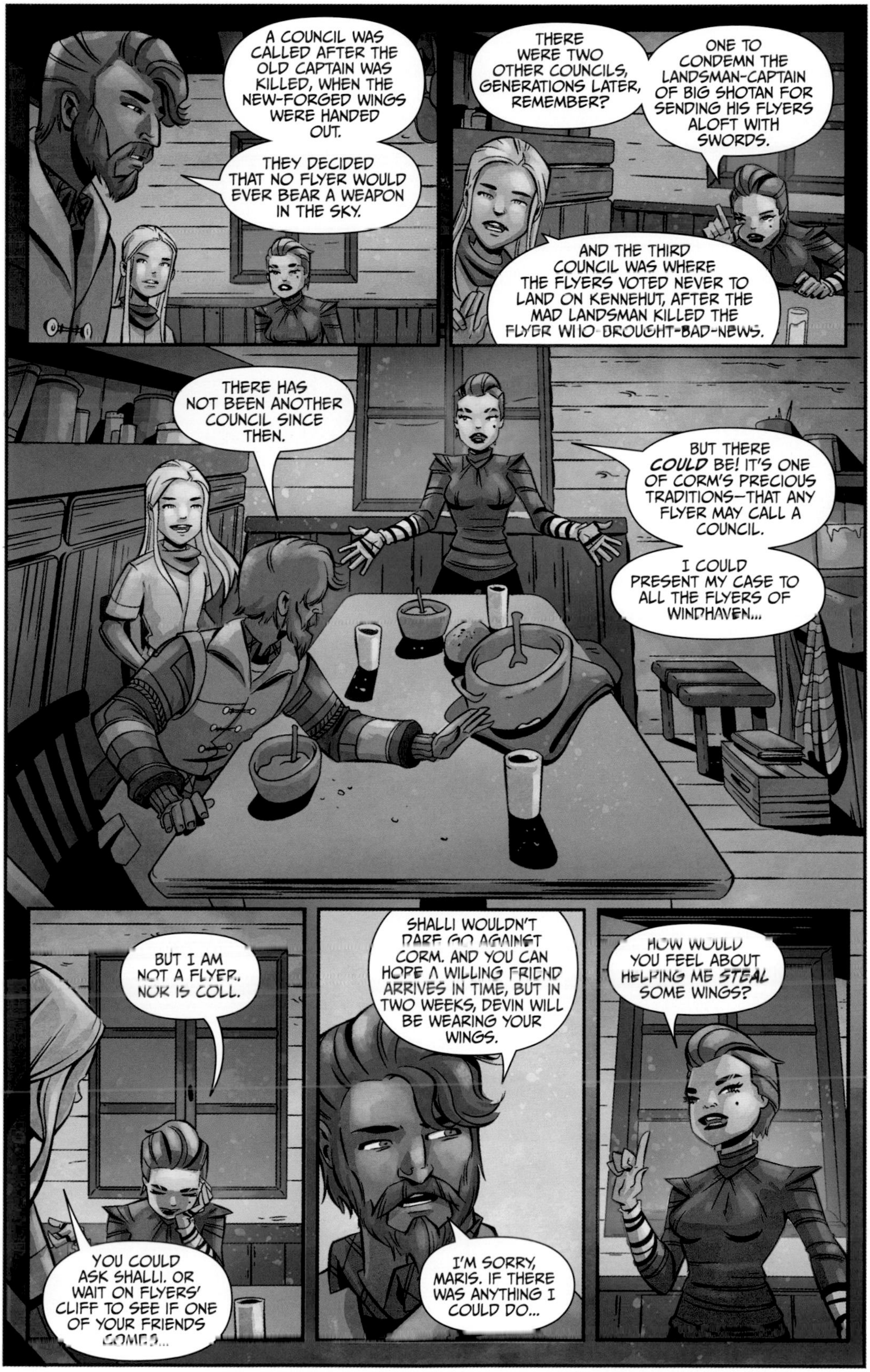
A COUNCIL WAS CALLED AFTER THE OLD CAPTAIN WAS KILLED, WHEN THE NEW-FORGED WINGS WERE HANDED OUT.
THEY DECIDED THAT NO FLYER WOULD EVER BEAR A WEAPON IN THE SKY.
THERE WERE TWO OTHER COUNCILS, GENERATIONS LATER, REMEMBER?
ONE TO CONDEMN THE LANDSMAN-CAPTAIN OF BIG SHOTAN FOR SENDING HIS FLYERS ALOFT WITH SWORDS.
AND THE THIRD COUNCIL WAS WHERE THE FLYERS VOTED NEVER TO LAND ON KENNEHUT, AFTER THE MAD LANDSMAN KILLED THE FLYER WHO BROUGHT BAD NEWS.
THERE HAS NOT BEEN ANOTHER COUNCIL SINCE THEN.
BUT THERE COULD BE! IT'S ONE OF CORM'S PRECIOUS TRADITIONS—THAT ANY FLYER MAY CALL A COUNCIL.
I COULD PRESENT MY CASE TO ALL THE FLYERS OF WINDHAVEN...
BUT I AM NOT A FLYER. NOR IS COLL.
YOU COULD ASK SHALLI. OR WAIT ON FLYERS' CLIFF TO SEE IF ONE OF YOUR FRIENDS COMES...
SHALLI WOULDN'T DARE GO AGAINST CORM. AND YOU CAN HOPE A WILLING FRIEND ARRIVES IN TIME, BUT IN TWO WEEKS, DEVIN WILL BE WEARING YOUR WINGS.
I'M SORRY, MARIS. IF THERE WAS ANYTHING I COULD DO...
HOW WOULD YOU FEEL ABOUT HELPING ME STEAL SOME WINGS?

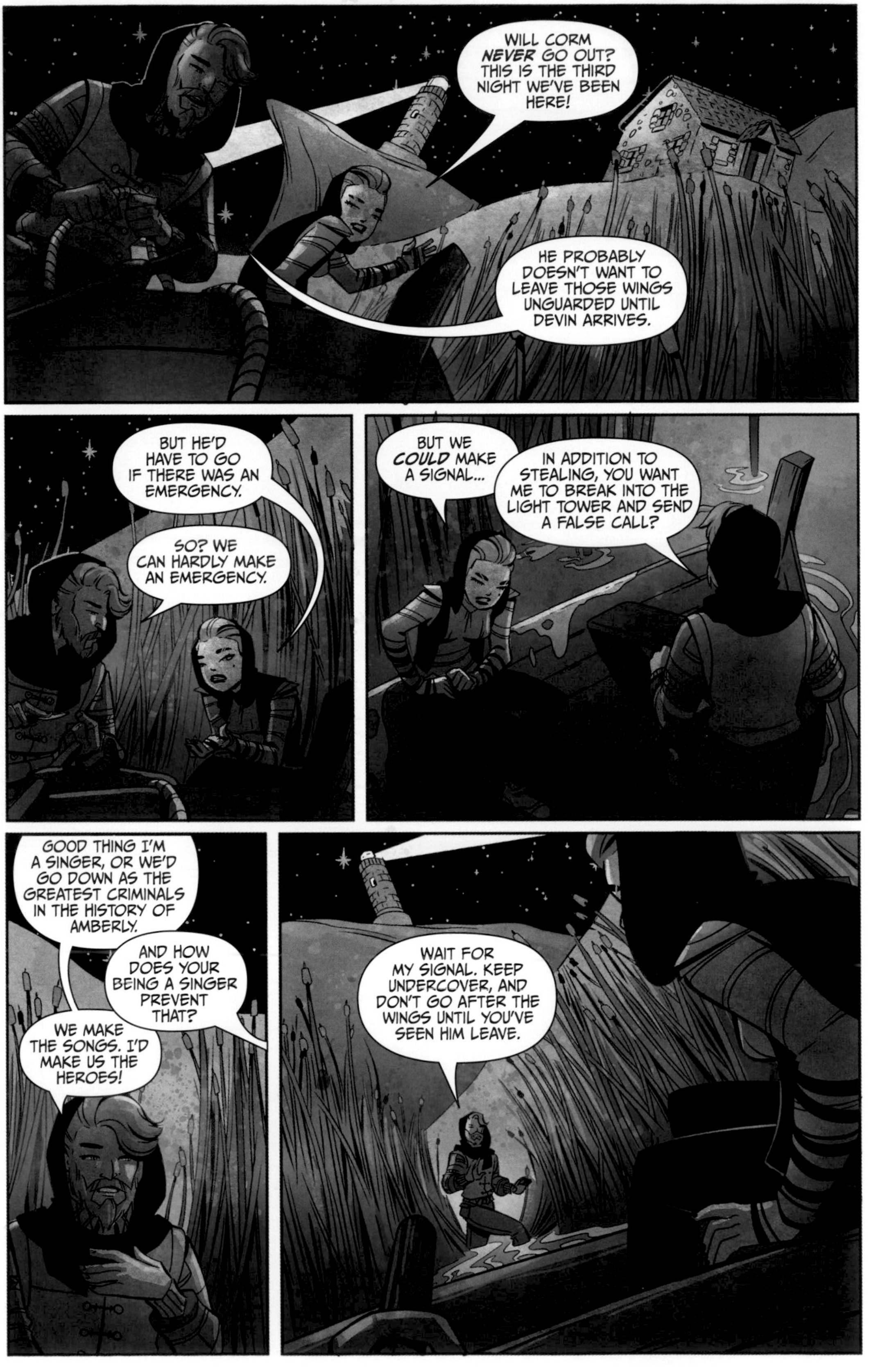
WILL CORM NEVER GO OUT? THIS IS THE THIRD NIGHT WE'VE BEEN HERE!
HE PROBABLY DOESN'T WANT TO LEAVE THOSE WINGS UNGUARDED UNTIL DEVIN ARRIVES.
BUT HE'D HAVE TO GO IF THERE WAS AN EMERGENCY.
SO? WE CAN HARDLY MAKE AN EMERGENCY.
BUT WE COULD MAKE A SIGNAL...
IN ADDITION TO STEALING, YOU WANT ME TO BREAK INTO THE LIGHT TOWER AND SEND A FALSE CALL?
GOOD THING I'M A SINGER, OR WE'D GO DOWN AS THE GREATEST CRIMINALS IN THE HISTORY OF AMBERLY.
AND HOW DOES YOUR BEING A SINGER PREVENT THAT?
WE MAKE THE SONGS. I'D MAKE US THE HEROES!
WAIT FOR MY SIGNAL. KEEP UNDERCOVER, AND DON'T GO AFTER THE WINGS UNTIL YOU'VE SEEN HIM LEAVE.

SHE TESTED EACH STRUT WITH HER FINGERS TO MAKE SURE THEY'D BEEN PROPERLY REPAIRED.

THEY'LL NEVER TAKE THEM FROM ME AGAIN.

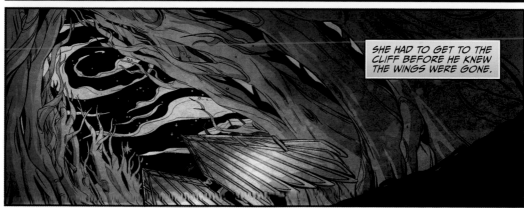

SHE HAD TO GET TO THE CLIFF BEFORE HE KNEW THE WINGS WERE GONE.

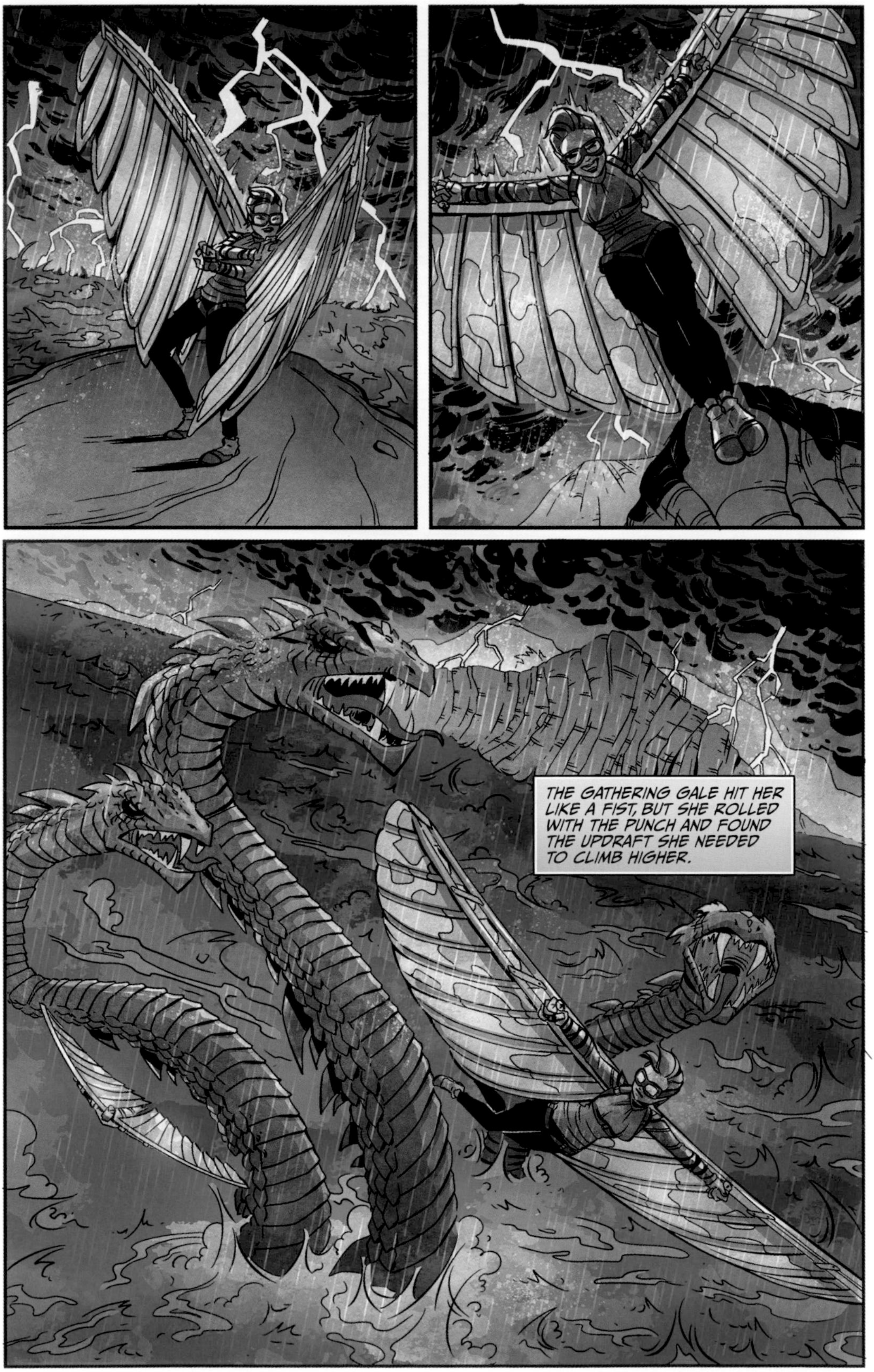
THE GATHERING GALE HIT HER LIKE A FIST, BUT SHE ROLLED WITH THE PUNCH AND FOUND THE UPDRAFT SHE NEEDED TO CLIMB HIGHER.

TURN! TURN BACK OR I'LL FORCE YOU DOWN!

CATCH ME IF YOU CAN!

A THOUSAND TIMES SHE'D PLAYED TAG IN THE SKY, BUT THIS CHASE WAS IN DEADLY EARNEST.

SHE FOUND THE CURRENTS THAT WOULD TAKE HER HIGHER, KNOWING THAT IF CORM GOT ABOVE HER AGAIN, HE WAS ANGRY ENOUGH TO FORCE HER DOWN INTO THE OCEAN.

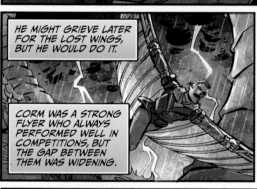

HE MIGHT GRIEVE LATER FOR THE LOST WINGS, BUT HE WOULD DO IT.

CORM WAS A STRONG FLYER WHO ALWAYS PERFORMED WELL IN COMPETITIONS, BUT THE GAP BETWEEN THEM WAS WIDENING.

EVEN BETTER: THE STORM WAS MORE DISTANT.

GIVE UP OUTCAST! NO ONE WILL LET YOU LAND...

YET SHE KNEW HE WOULDN'T BE ABLE TO CATCH HER. THE WINDS WERE HERS NOW.

MARIS WAITED UNTIL SHE COULD NO LONGER SEE HIS WINGS BEFORE CHANGING COURSE, KNOWING CORM WOULD CONTINUE BLINDLY AHEAD ON THE SILVER WIND'S UNTIL HE GAVE UP.

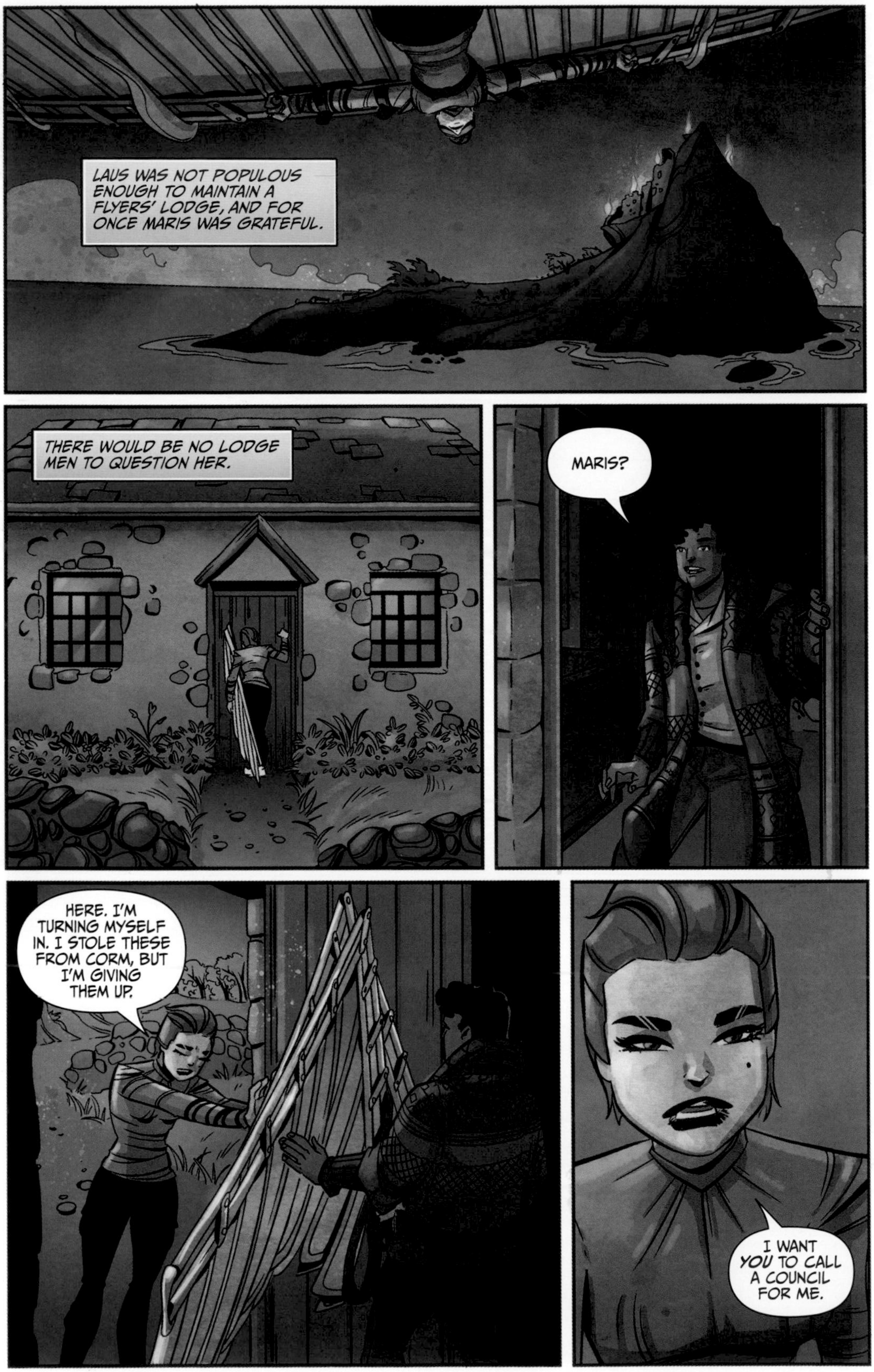
LAUS WAS NOT POPULOUS ENOUGH TO MAINTAIN A FLYERS' LODGE, AND FOR ONCE MARIS WAS GRATEFUL.
THERE WOULD BE NO LODGE MEN TO QUESTION HER.
MARIS?
HERE. I'M TURNING MYSELF IN. I STOLE THESE FROM CORM, BUT I'M GIVING THEM UP.
I WANT *YOU* TO CALL A COUNCIL FOR ME.

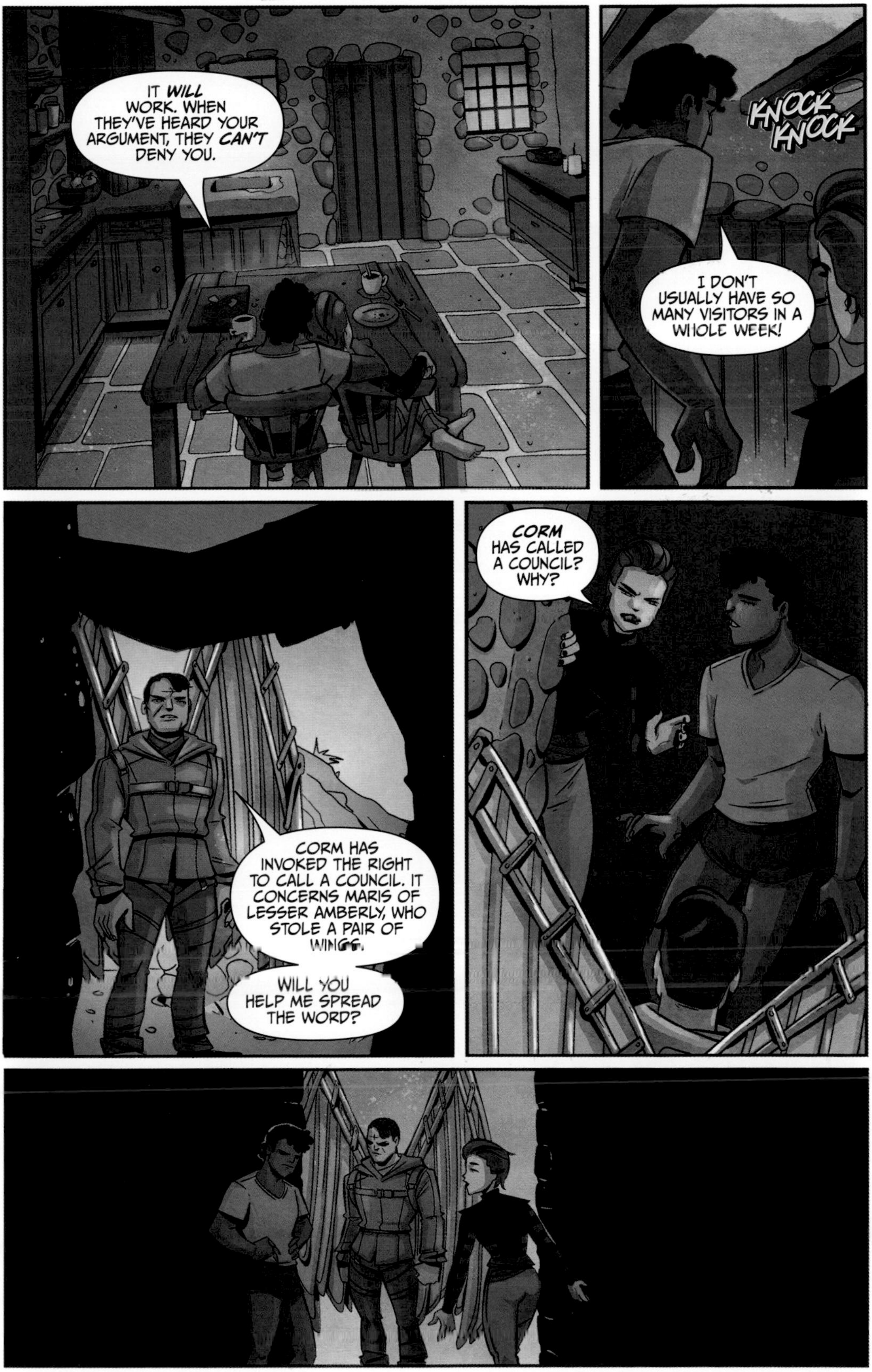

IT WILL WORK. WHEN THEY'VE HEARD YOUR ARGUMENT, THEY CAN'T DENY YOU.
KNOCK KNOCK
I DON'T USUALLY HAVE SO MANY VISITORS IN A WHOLE WEEK!
CORM HAS INVOKED THE RIGHT TO CALL A COUNCIL. IT CONCERNS MARIS OF LESSER AMBERLY, WHO STOLE A PAIR OF WINGS.
WILL YOU HELP ME SPREAD THE WORD?
CORM HAS CALLED A COUNCIL? WHY?

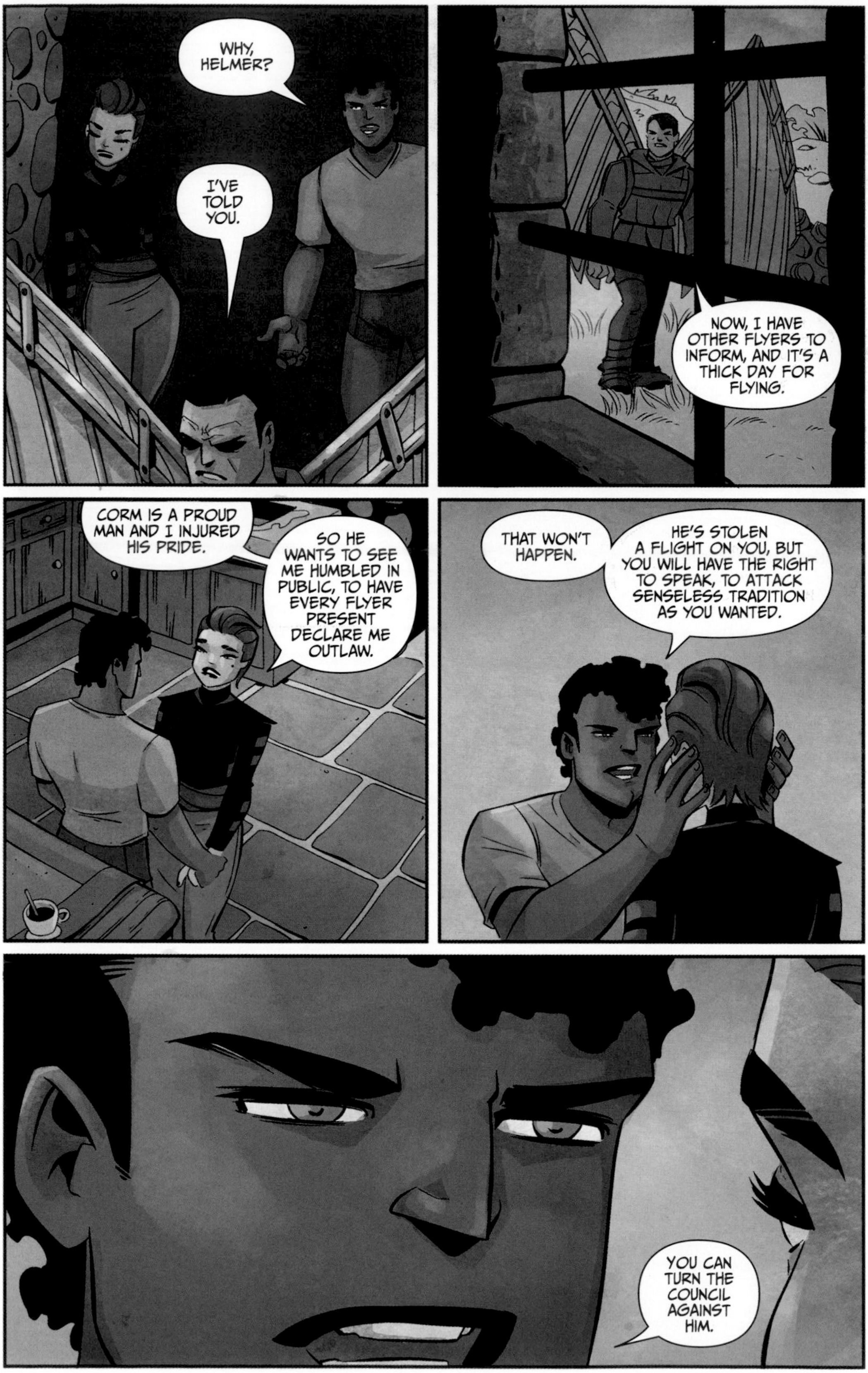
WHY, HELMER?
I'VE TOLD YOU.
NOW, I HAVE OTHER FLYERS TO INFORM, AND IT'S A THICK DAY FOR FLYING.
CORM IS A PROUD MAN AND I INJURED HIS PRIDE.
SO HE WANTS TO SEE ME HUMBLED IN PUBLIC, TO HAVE EVERY FLYER PRESENT DECLARE ME OUTLAW.
THAT WON'T HAPPEN.
HE'S STOLEN A FLIGHT ON YOU, BUT YOU WILL HAVE THE RIGHT TO SPEAK, TO ATTACK SENSELESS TRADITION AS YOU WANTED.
YOU CAN TURN THE COUNCIL AGAINST HIM.

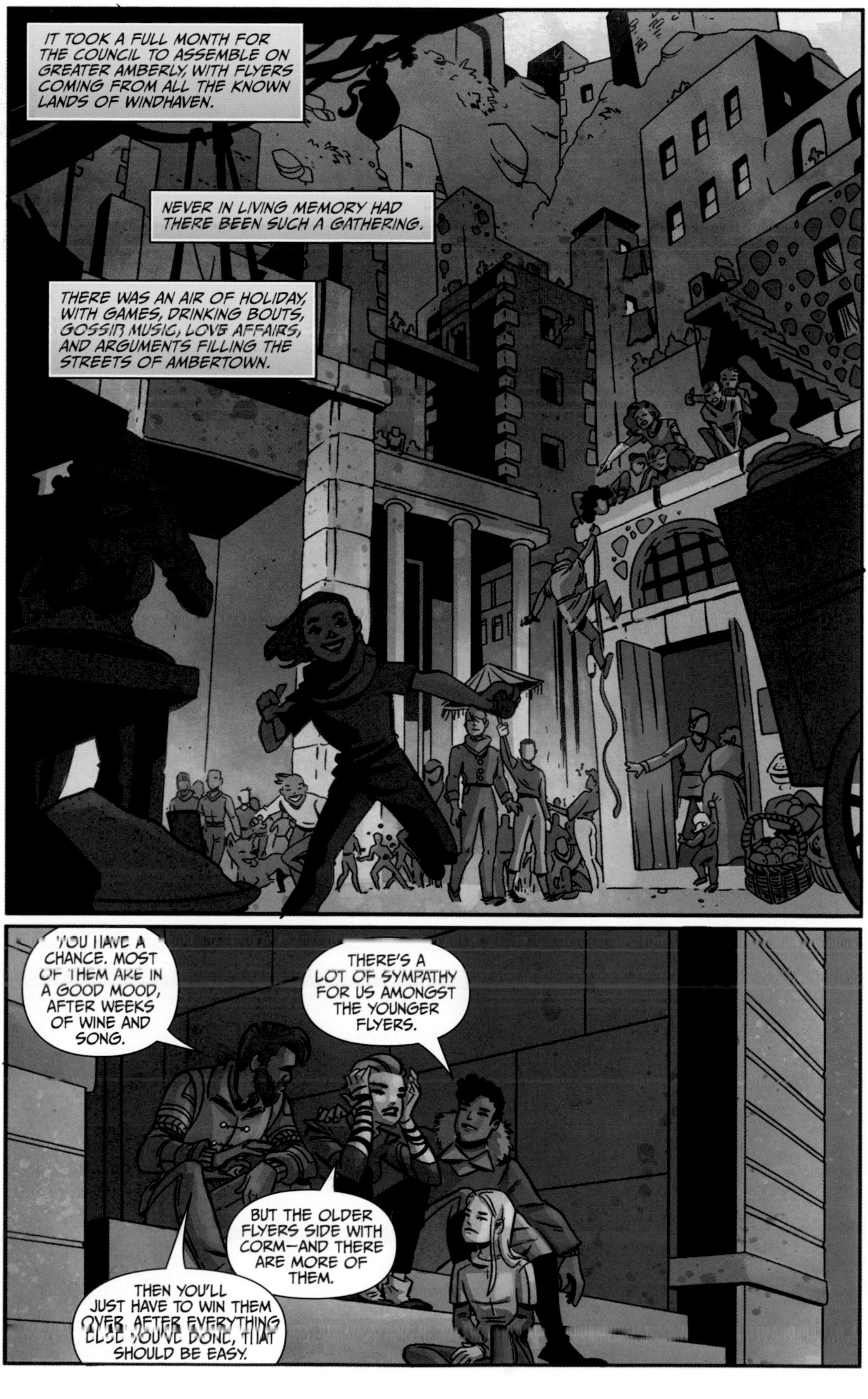
IT TOOK A FULL MONTH FOR THE COUNCIL TO ASSEMBLE ON GREATER AMBERLY, WITH FLYERS COMING FROM ALL THE KNOWN LANDS OF WINDHAVEN.
NEVER IN LIVING MEMORY HAD THERE BEEN SUCH A GATHERING.
THERE WAS AN AIR OF HOLIDAY, WITH GAMES, DRINKING BOUTS, GOSSIP, MUSIC, LOVE AFFAIRS, AND ARGUMENTS FILLING THE STREETS OF AMBERTOWN.
YOU HAVE A CHANCE. MOST OF THEM ARE IN A GOOD MOOD, AFTER WEEKS OF WINE AND SONG.
THERE'S A LOT OF SYMPATHY FOR US AMONGST THE YOUNGER FLYERS.
BUT THE OLDER FLYERS SIDE WITH CORM—AND THERE ARE MORE OF THEM.
THEN YOU'LL JUST HAVE TO WIN THEM OVER. AFTER EVERYTHING ELSE YOU'VE DONE, THAT SHOULD BE EASY.

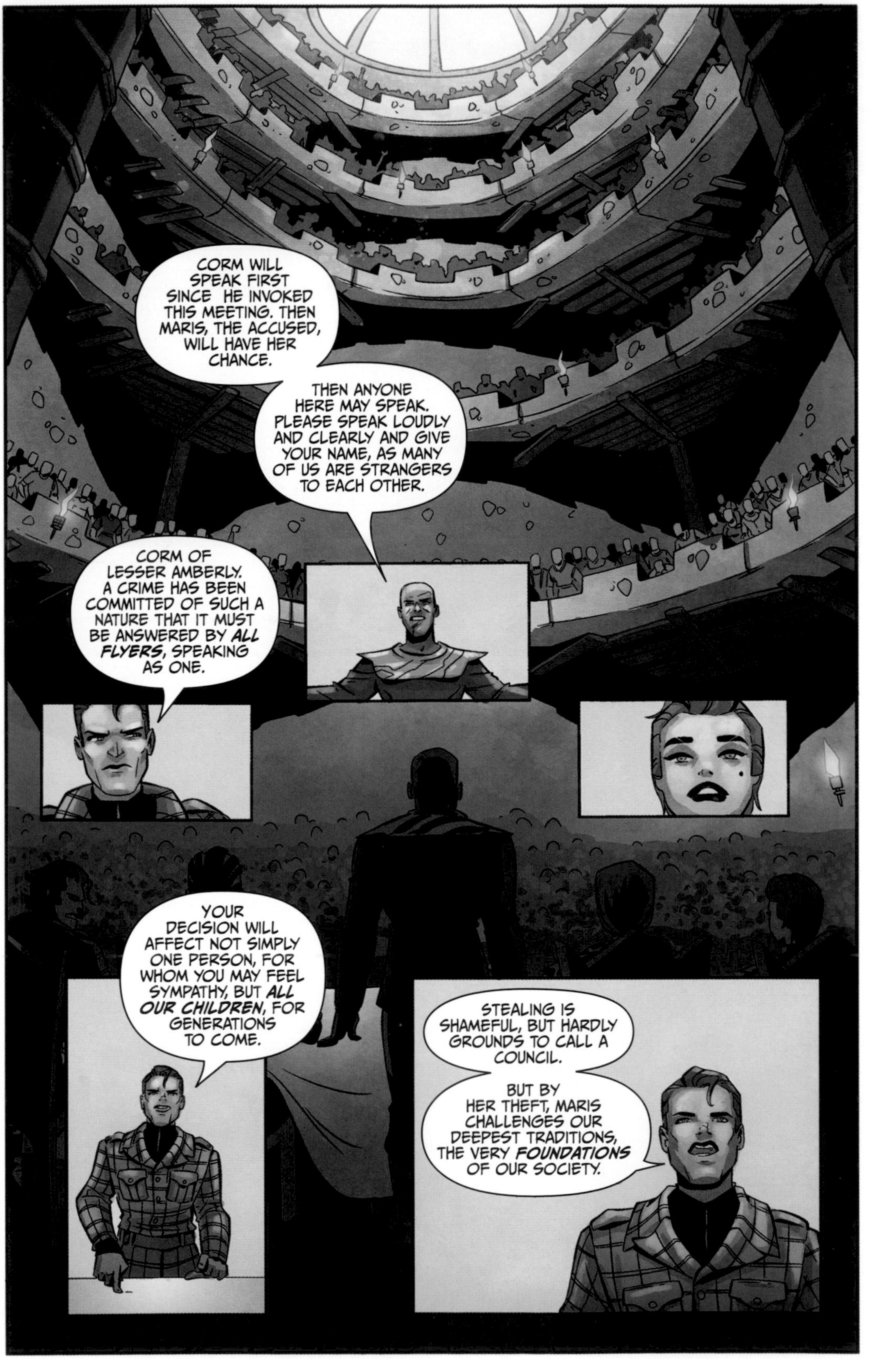
CORM WILL SPEAK FIRST SINCE HE INVOKED THIS MEETING. THEN MARIS, THE ACCUSED, WILL HAVE HER CHANCE.
THEN ANYONE HERE MAY SPEAK. PLEASE SPEAK LOUDLY AND CLEARLY AND GIVE YOUR NAME, AS MANY OF US ARE STRANGERS TO EACH OTHER.
CORM OF LESSER AMBERLY. A CRIME HAS BEEN COMMITTED OF SUCH A NATURE THAT IT MUST BE ANSWERED BY ALL FLYERS, SPEAKING AS ONE.
YOUR DECISION WILL AFFECT NOT SIMPLY ONE PERSON, FOR WHOM YOU MAY FEEL SYMPATHY, BUT ALL OUR CHILDREN, FOR GENERATIONS TO COME.
STEALING IS SHAMEFUL, BUT HARDLY GROUNDS TO CALL A COUNCIL.
BUT BY HER THEFT, MARIS CHALLENGES OUR DEEPEST TRADITIONS, THE VERY FOUNDATIONS OF OUR SOCIETY.

I CALL UPON THE FLYERS OF WINDHAVEN TO NAME MARIS, FORMERLY OF LESSER AMBERLY, *THIEF* AND *OUTLAW*.

AND TO PLEDGE THAT NONE WILL LAND ON ANY ISLAND SHE CALLS HOME.

IN THE AWFUL SILENCE THAT FOLLOWED, MARIS KNEW HOW MUCH DANGER SHE WAS IN AND HOW DEEPLY SHE HAD OFFENDED CORM.

HE WOULD TAKE *EVERYTHING* FROM HER.

MARIS, WILL YOU REPLY?

I CANNOT DENY THE THEFT. I STOLE THE WINGS OUT OF DESPERATION, AS MY ONLY CHANCE TO REACH A FLYER WHO COULD CALL COUNCIL.

BUT I SURRENDERED THE WINGS TO HIM AT ONCE.

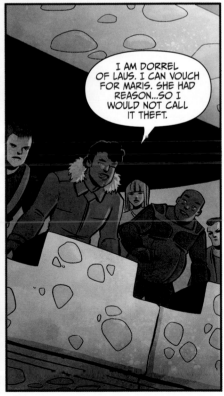

I AM DORREL OF LAUS. I CAN VOUCH FOR MARIS. SHE HAD REASON...SO I WOULD NOT CALL IT THEFT.

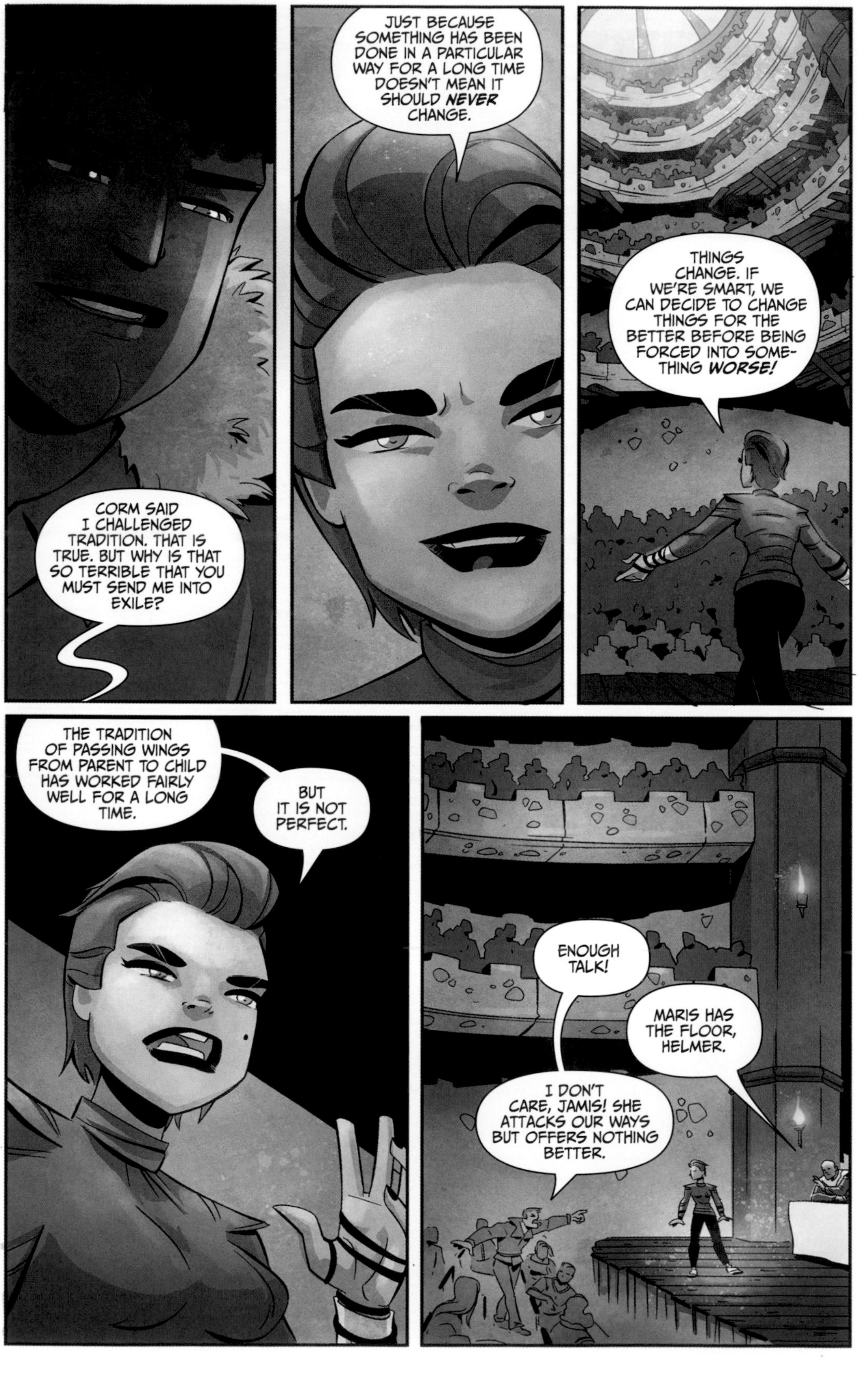
CORM SAID I CHALLENGED TRADITION. THAT IS TRUE. BUT WHY IS THAT SO TERRIBLE THAT YOU MUST SEND ME INTO EXILE?
JUST BECAUSE SOMETHING HAS BEEN DONE IN A PARTICULAR WAY FOR A LONG TIME DOESN'T MEAN IT SHOULD NEVER CHANGE.
THINGS CHANGE. IF WE'RE SMART, WE CAN DECIDE TO CHANGE THINGS FOR THE BETTER BEFORE BEING FORCED INTO SOMETHING WORSE!
THE TRADITION OF PASSING WINGS FROM PARENT TO CHILD HAS WORKED FAIRLY WELL FOR A LONG TIME.
BUT IT IS NOT PERFECT.
ENOUGH TALK!
MARIS HAS THE FLOOR, HELMER.
I DON'T CARE, JAMIS! SHE ATTACKS OUR WAYS BUT OFFERS NOTHING BETTER.

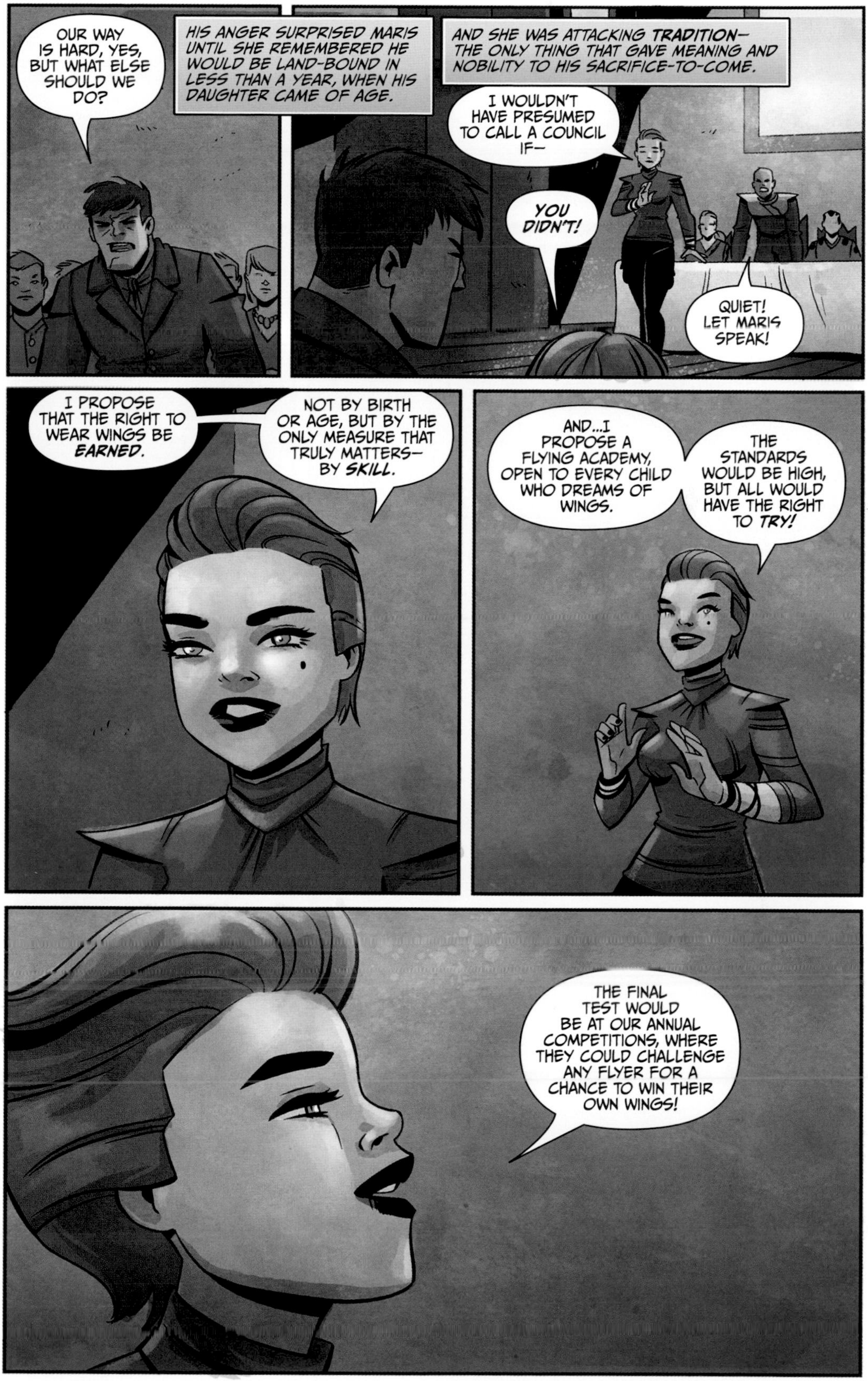
OUR WAY IS HARD, YES, BUT WHAT ELSE SHOULD WE DO?
HIS ANGER SURPRISED MARIS UNTIL SHE REMEMBERED HE WOULD BE LAND-BOUND IN LESS THAN A YEAR, WHEN HIS DAUGHTER CAME OF AGE.
AND SHE WAS ATTACKING TRADITION— THE ONLY THING THAT GAVE MEANING AND NOBILITY TO HIS SACRIFICE-TO-COME.
I WOULDN'T HAVE PRESUMED TO CALL A COUNCIL IF—
YOU DIDN'T!
QUIET! LET MARIS SPEAK!
I PROPOSE THAT THE RIGHT TO WEAR WINGS BE EARNED.
NOT BY BIRTH OR AGE, BUT BY THE ONLY MEASURE THAT TRULY MATTERS— BY SKILL.
AND...I PROPOSE A FLYING ACADEMY, OPEN TO EVERY CHILD WHO DREAMS OF WINGS.
THE STANDARDS WOULD BE HIGH, BUT ALL WOULD HAVE THE RIGHT TO TRY!
THE FINAL TEST WOULD BE AT OUR ANNUAL COMPETITIONS, WHERE THEY COULD CHALLENGE ANY FLYER FOR A CHANCE TO WIN THEIR OWN WINGS!

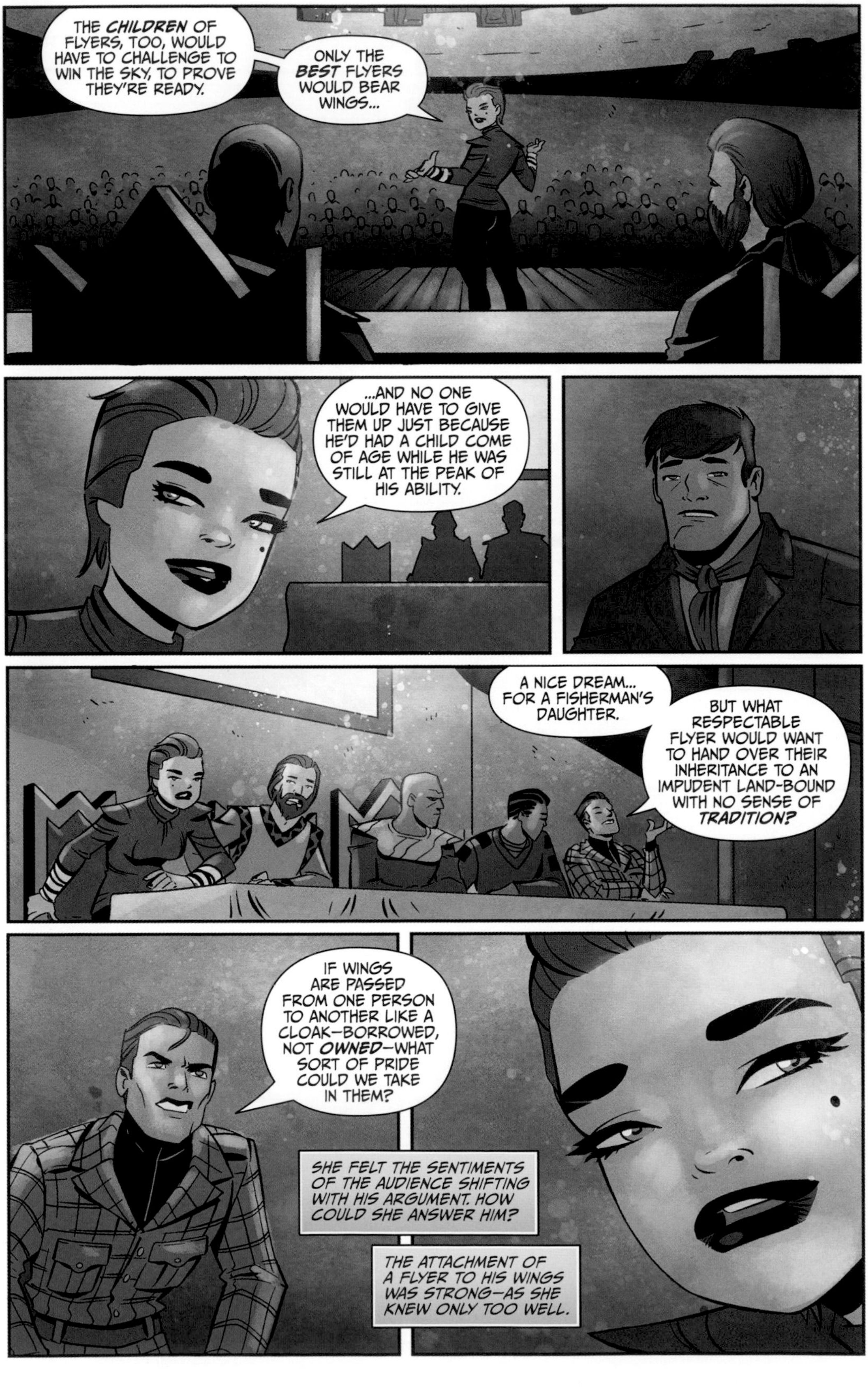
THE *CHILDREN* OF FLYERS, TOO, WOULD HAVE TO CHALLENGE TO WIN THE SKY, TO PROVE THEY'RE READY.
ONLY THE *BEST* FLYERS WOULD BEAR WINGS...
...AND NO ONE WOULD HAVE TO GIVE THEM UP JUST BECAUSE HE'D HAD A CHILD COME OF AGE WHILE HE WAS STILL AT THE PEAK OF HIS ABILITY.
A NICE DREAM... FOR A FISHERMAN'S DAUGHTER.
BUT WHAT RESPECTABLE FLYER WOULD WANT TO HAND OVER THEIR INHERITANCE TO AN IMPUDENT LAND-BOUND WITH NO SENSE OF *TRADITION?*
IF WINGS ARE PASSED FROM ONE PERSON TO ANOTHER LIKE A CLOAK—BORROWED, NOT *OWNED*—WHAT SORT OF PRIDE COULD WE TAKE IN THEM?
SHE FELT THE SENTIMENTS OF THE AUDIENCE SHIFTING WITH HIS ARGUMENT. HOW COULD SHE ANSWER HIM?
THE ATTACHMENT OF A FLYER TO HIS WINGS WAS STRONG—AS SHE KNEW ONLY TOO WELL.

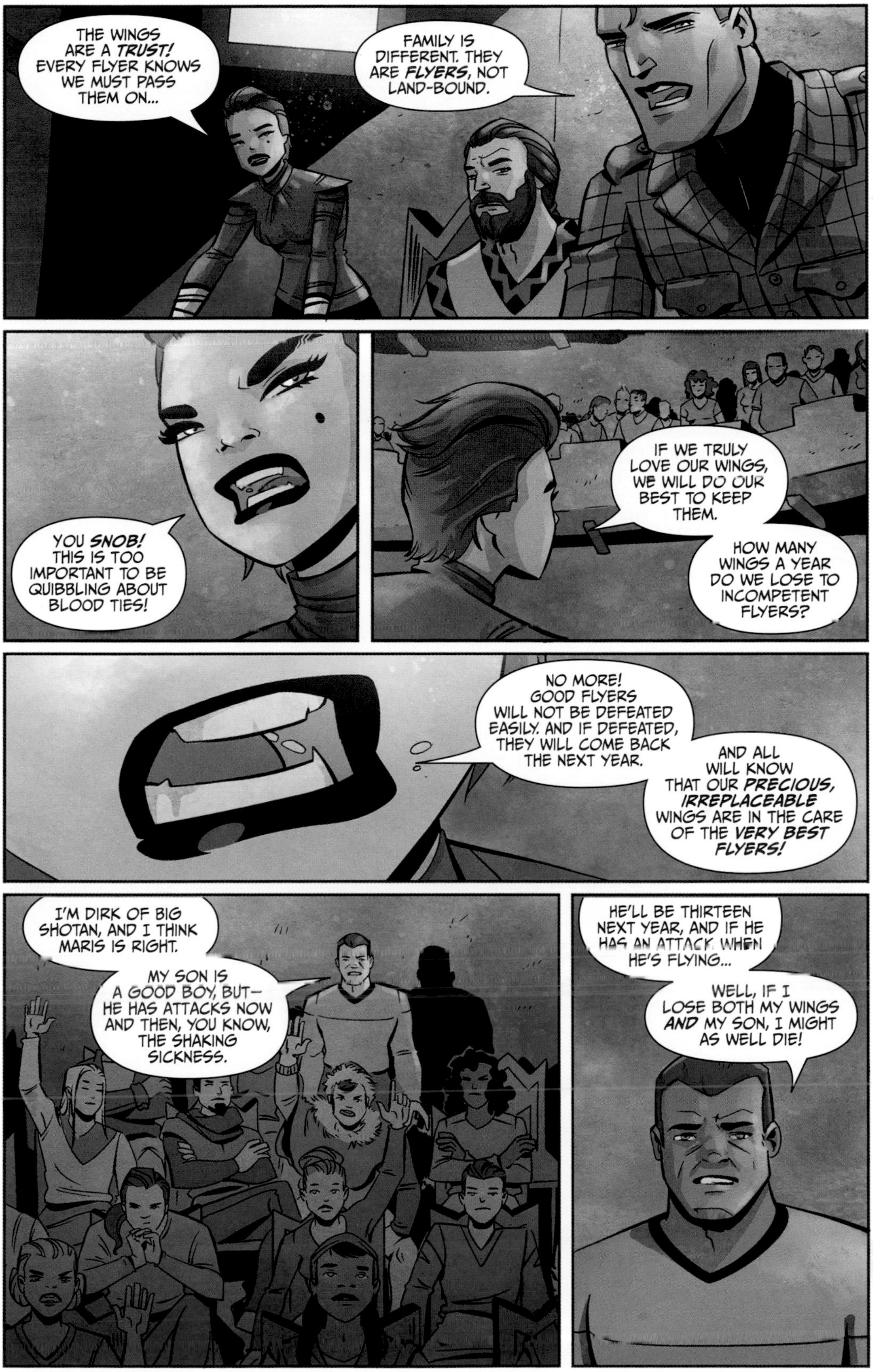
THE WINGS ARE A *TRUST!* EVERY FLYER KNOWS WE MUST PASS THEM ON...
FAMILY IS DIFFERENT. THEY ARE *FLYERS*, NOT LAND-BOUND.
YOU *SNOB!* THIS IS TOO IMPORTANT TO BE QUIBBLING ABOUT BLOOD TIES!
IF WE TRULY LOVE OUR WINGS, WE WILL DO OUR BEST TO KEEP THEM.
HOW MANY WINGS A YEAR DO WE LOSE TO INCOMPETENT FLYERS?
NO MORE! GOOD FLYERS WILL NOT BE DEFEATED EASILY. AND IF DEFEATED, THEY WILL COME BACK THE NEXT YEAR.
AND ALL WILL KNOW THAT OUR *PRECIOUS, IRREPLACEABLE* WINGS ARE IN THE CARE OF THE *VERY BEST FLYERS!*
I'M DIRK OF BIG SHOTAN, AND I THINK MARIS IS RIGHT.
MY SON IS A GOOD BOY, BUT— HE HAS ATTACKS NOW AND THEN, YOU KNOW, THE SHAKING SICKNESS.
HE'LL BE THIRTEEN NEXT YEAR, AND IF HE HAS AN ATTACK WHEN HE'S FLYING...
WELL, IF I LOSE BOTH MY WINGS *AND* MY SON, I MIGHT AS WELL DIE!

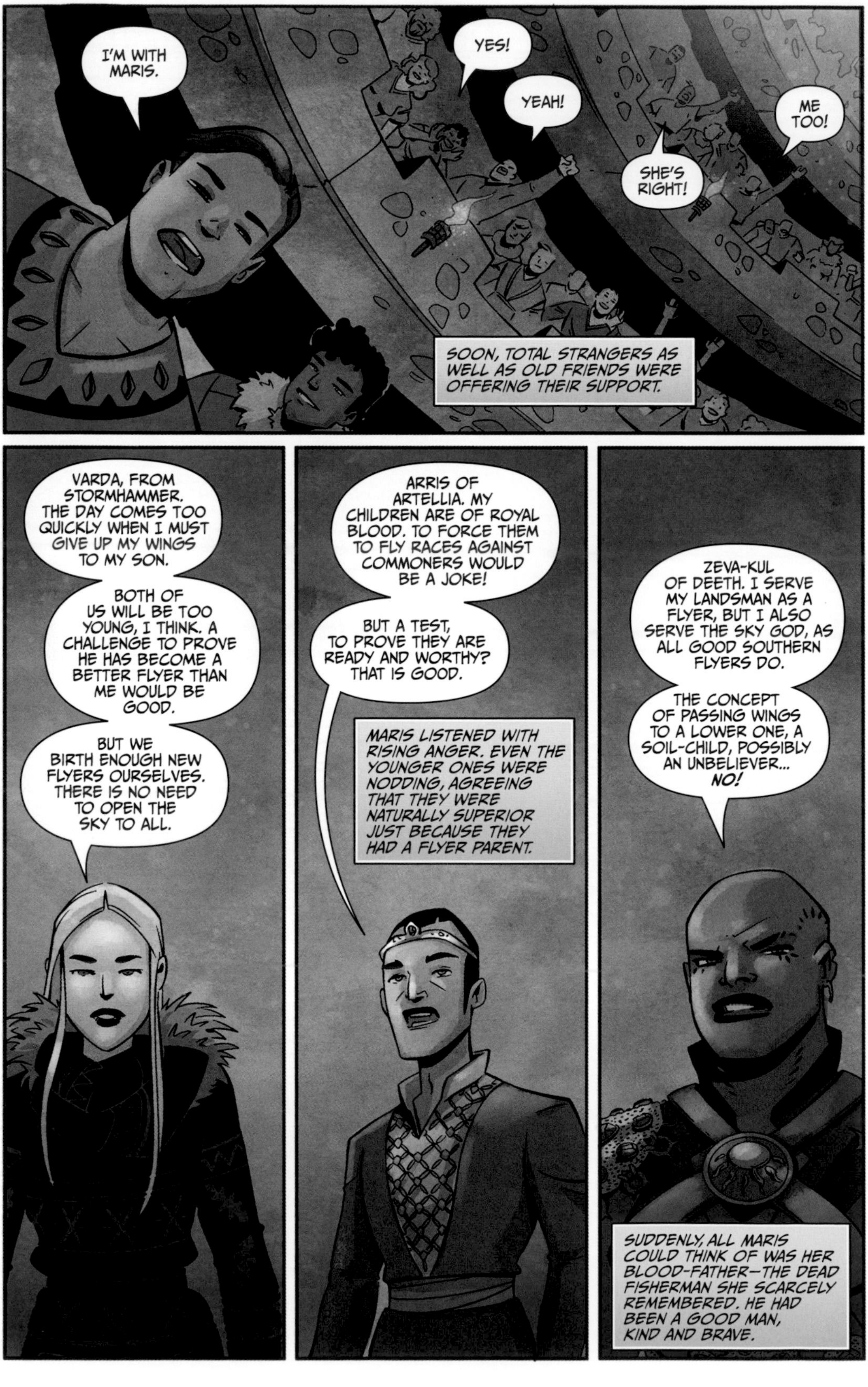
I'M WITH MARIS.
YES!
YEAH!
SHE'S RIGHT!
ME TOO!
SOON, TOTAL STRANGERS AS WELL AS OLD FRIENDS WERE OFFERING THEIR SUPPORT.
VARDA, FROM STORMHAMMER. THE DAY COMES TOO QUICKLY WHEN I MUST GIVE UP MY WINGS TO MY SON.
BOTH OF US WILL BE TOO YOUNG, I THINK. A CHALLENGE TO PROVE HE HAS BECOME A BETTER FLYER THAN ME WOULD BE GOOD.
BUT WE BIRTH ENOUGH NEW FLYERS OURSELVES. THERE IS NO NEED TO OPEN THE SKY TO ALL.
ARRIS OF ARTELLIA. MY CHILDREN ARE OF ROYAL BLOOD. TO FORCE THEM TO FLY RACES AGAINST COMMONERS WOULD BE A JOKE!
BUT A TEST, TO PROVE THEY ARE READY AND WORTHY? THAT IS GOOD.
MARIS LISTENED WITH RISING ANGER. EVEN THE YOUNGER ONES WERE NODDING, AGREEING THAT THEY WERE NATURALLY SUPERIOR JUST BECAUSE THEY HAD A FLYER PARENT.
ZEVA-KUL OF DEETH. I SERVE MY LANDSMAN AS A FLYER, BUT I ALSO SERVE THE SKY GOD, AS ALL GOOD SOUTHERN FLYERS DO.
THE CONCEPT OF PASSING WINGS TO A LOWER ONE, A SOIL-CHILD, POSSIBLY AN UNBELIEVER... NO!
SUDDENLY, ALL MARIS COULD THINK OF WAS HER BLOOD-FATHER—THE DEAD FISHERMAN SHE SCARCELY REMEMBERED. HE HAD BEEN A GOOD MAN, KIND AND BRAVE.

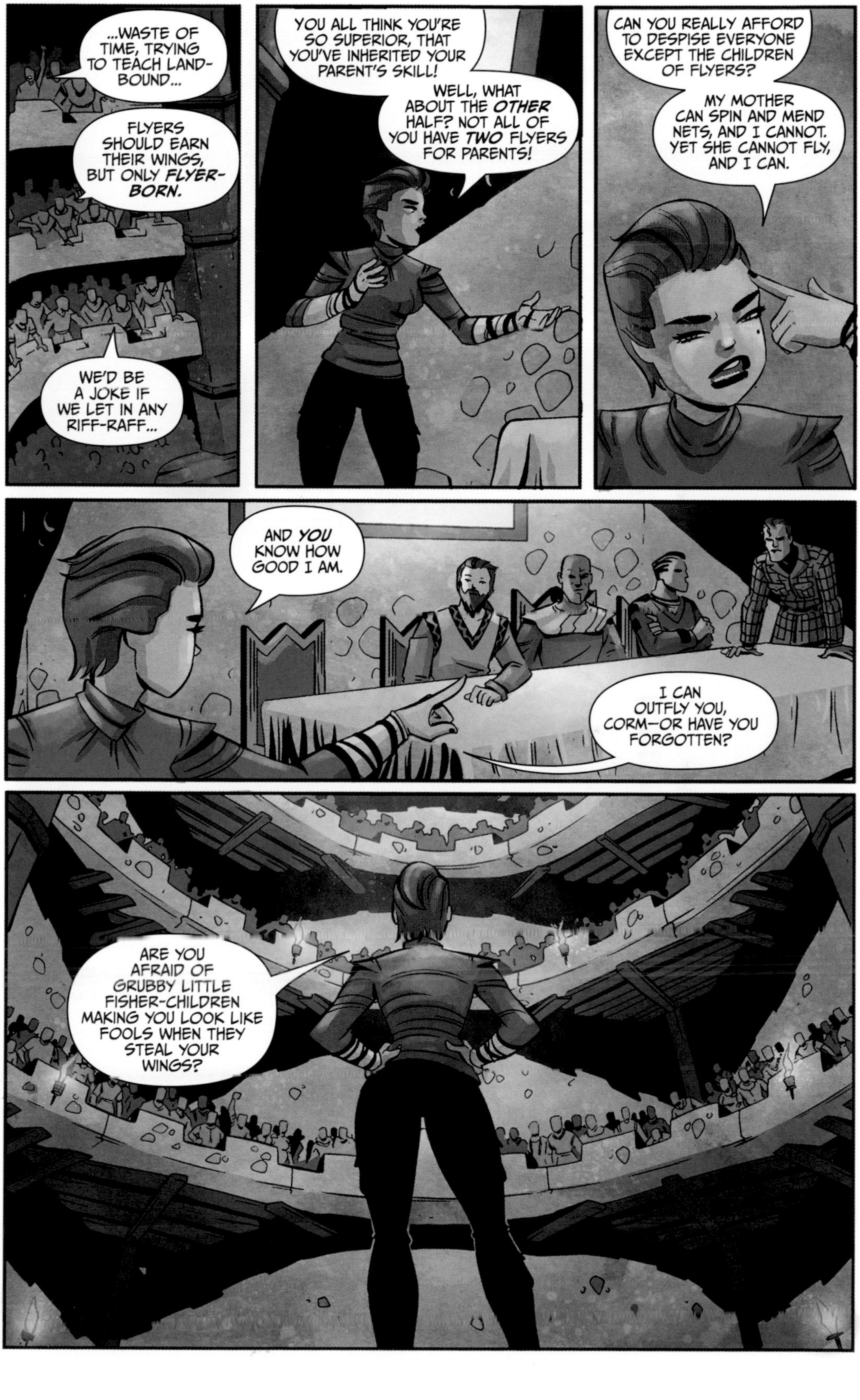
...WASTE OF TIME, TRYING TO TEACH LAND-BOUND...
FLYERS SHOULD EARN THEIR WINGS, BUT ONLY FLYER-BORN.
WE'D BE A JOKE IF WE LET IN ANY RIFF-RAFF...
YOU ALL THINK YOU'RE SO SUPERIOR, THAT YOU'VE INHERITED YOUR PARENT'S SKILL!
WELL, WHAT ABOUT THE OTHER HALF? NOT ALL OF YOU HAVE TWO FLYERS FOR PARENTS!
CAN YOU REALLY AFFORD TO DESPISE EVERYONE EXCEPT THE CHILDREN OF FLYERS?
MY MOTHER CAN SPIN AND MEND NETS, AND I CANNOT. YET SHE CANNOT FLY, AND I CAN.
AND YOU KNOW HOW GOOD I AM.
I CAN OUTFLY YOU, CORM—OR HAVE YOU FORGOTTEN?
ARE YOU AFRAID OF GRUBBY LITTLE FISHER-CHILDREN MAKING YOU LOOK LIKE FOOLS WHEN THEY STEAL YOUR WINGS?

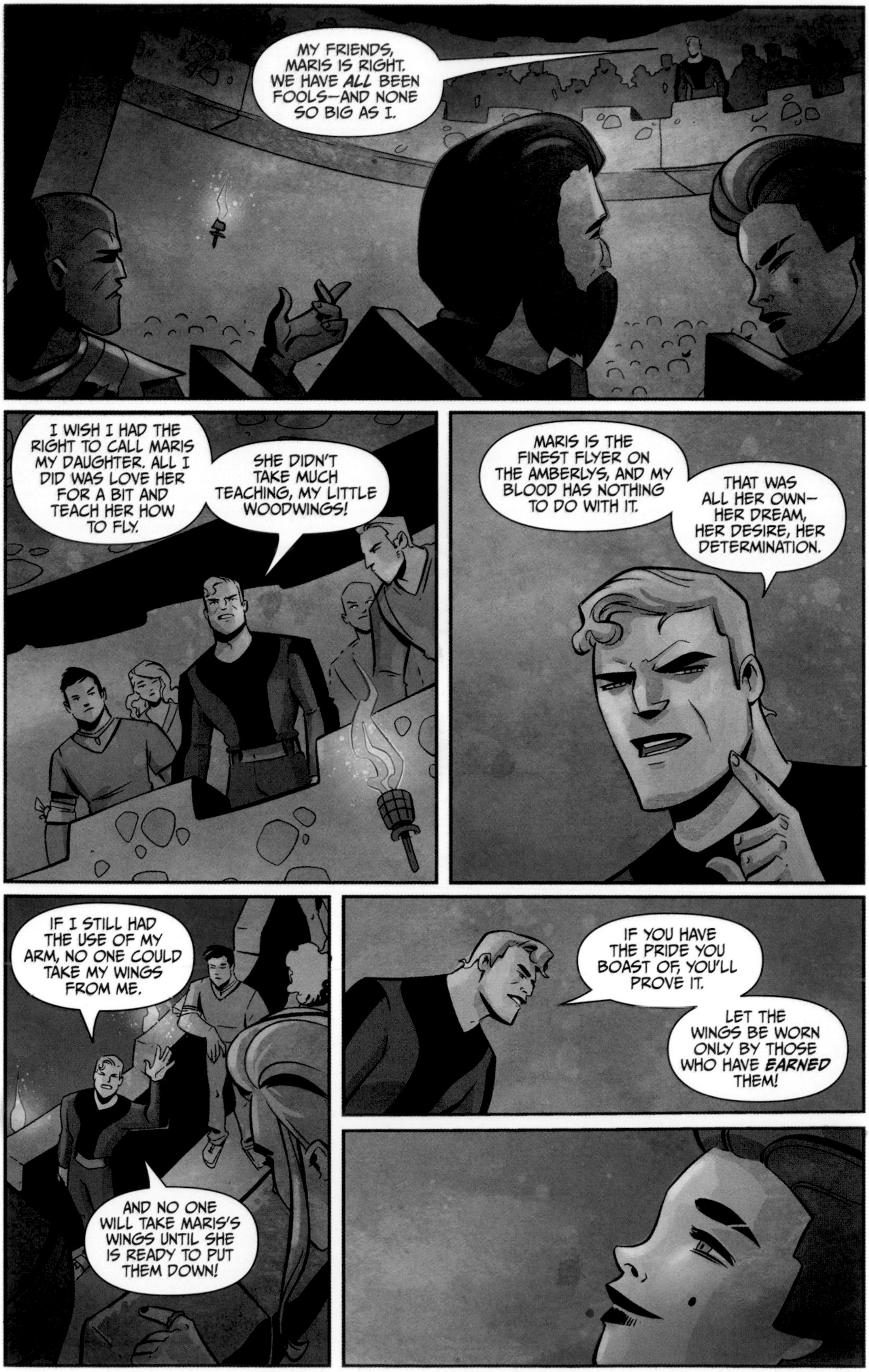
MY FRIENDS, MARIS IS RIGHT. WE HAVE ALL BEEN FOOLS—AND NONE SO BIG AS I.
I WISH I HAD THE RIGHT TO CALL MARIS MY DAUGHTER. ALL I DID WAS LOVE HER FOR A BIT AND TEACH HER HOW TO FLY.
SHE DIDN'T TAKE MUCH TEACHING, MY LITTLE WOODWINGS!
MARIS IS THE FINEST FLYER ON THE AMBERLYS, AND MY BLOOD HAS NOTHING TO DO WITH IT.
THAT WAS ALL HER OWN—HER DREAM, HER DESIRE, HER DETERMINATION.
IF I STILL HAD THE USE OF MY ARM, NO ONE COULD TAKE MY WINGS FROM ME.
AND NO ONE WILL TAKE MARIS'S WINGS UNTIL SHE IS READY TO PUT THEM DOWN!
IF YOU HAVE THE PRIDE YOU BOAST OF, YOU'LL PROVE IT.
LET THE WINGS BE WORN ONLY BY THOSE WHO HAVE EARNED THEM!

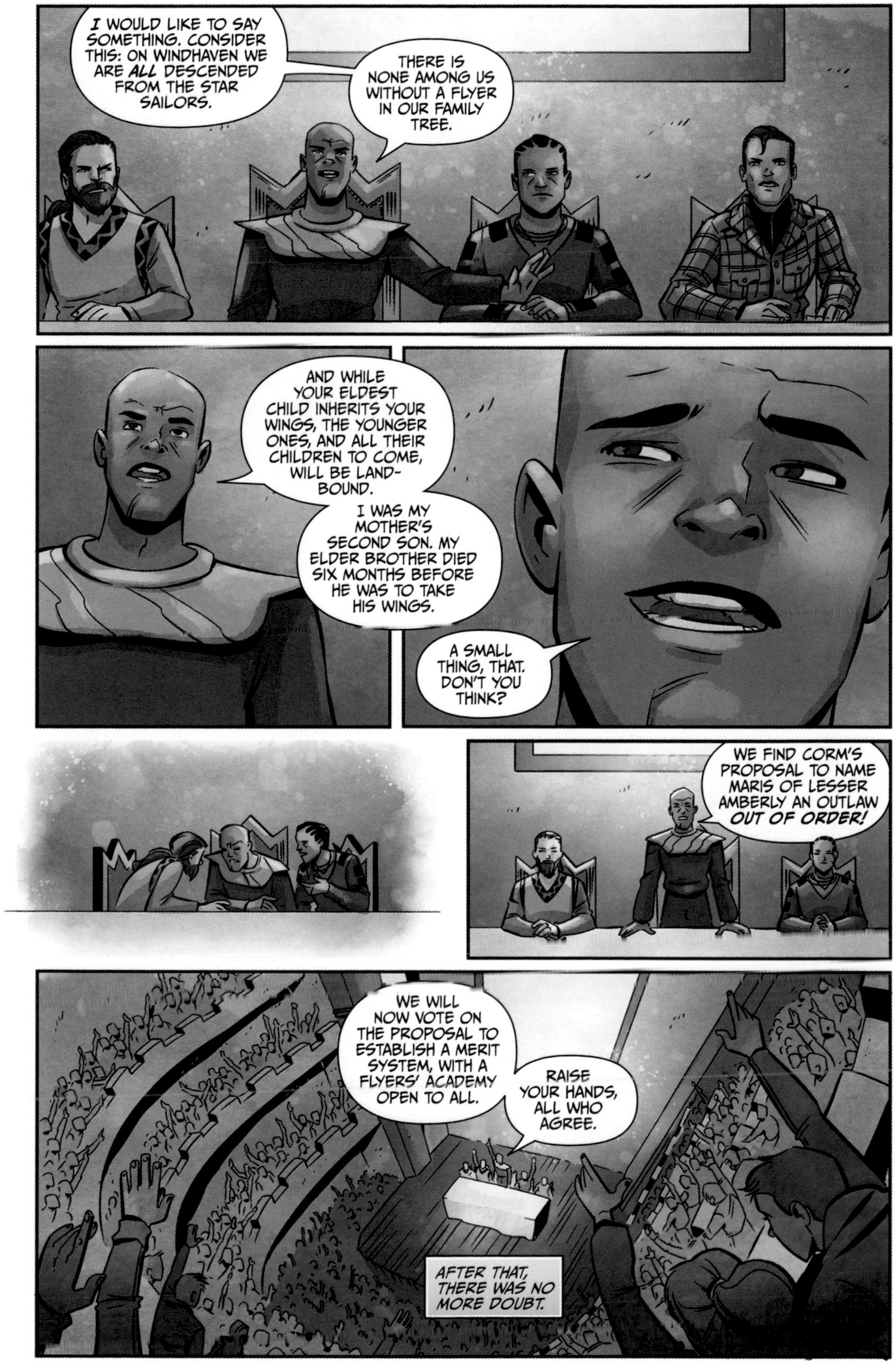

I WOULD LIKE TO SAY SOMETHING. CONSIDER THIS: ON WINDHAVEN WE ARE *ALL* DESCENDED FROM THE STAR SAILORS.
THERE IS NONE AMONG US WITHOUT A FLYER IN OUR FAMILY TREE.
AND WHILE YOUR ELDEST CHILD INHERITS YOUR WINGS, THE YOUNGER ONES, AND ALL THEIR CHILDREN TO COME, WILL BE LAND-BOUND.
I WAS MY MOTHER'S SECOND SON. MY ELDER BROTHER DIED SIX MONTHS BEFORE HE WAS TO TAKE HIS WINGS.
A SMALL THING, THAT. DON'T YOU THINK?
WE FIND CORM'S PROPOSAL TO NAME MARIS OF LESSER AMBERLY AN OUTLAW *OUT OF ORDER!*
WE WILL NOW VOTE ON THE PROPOSAL TO ESTABLISH A MERIT SYSTEM, WITH A FLYERS' ACADEMY OPEN TO ALL.
RAISE YOUR HANDS, ALL WHO AGREE.
AFTER THAT, THERE WAS NO MORE DOUBT.

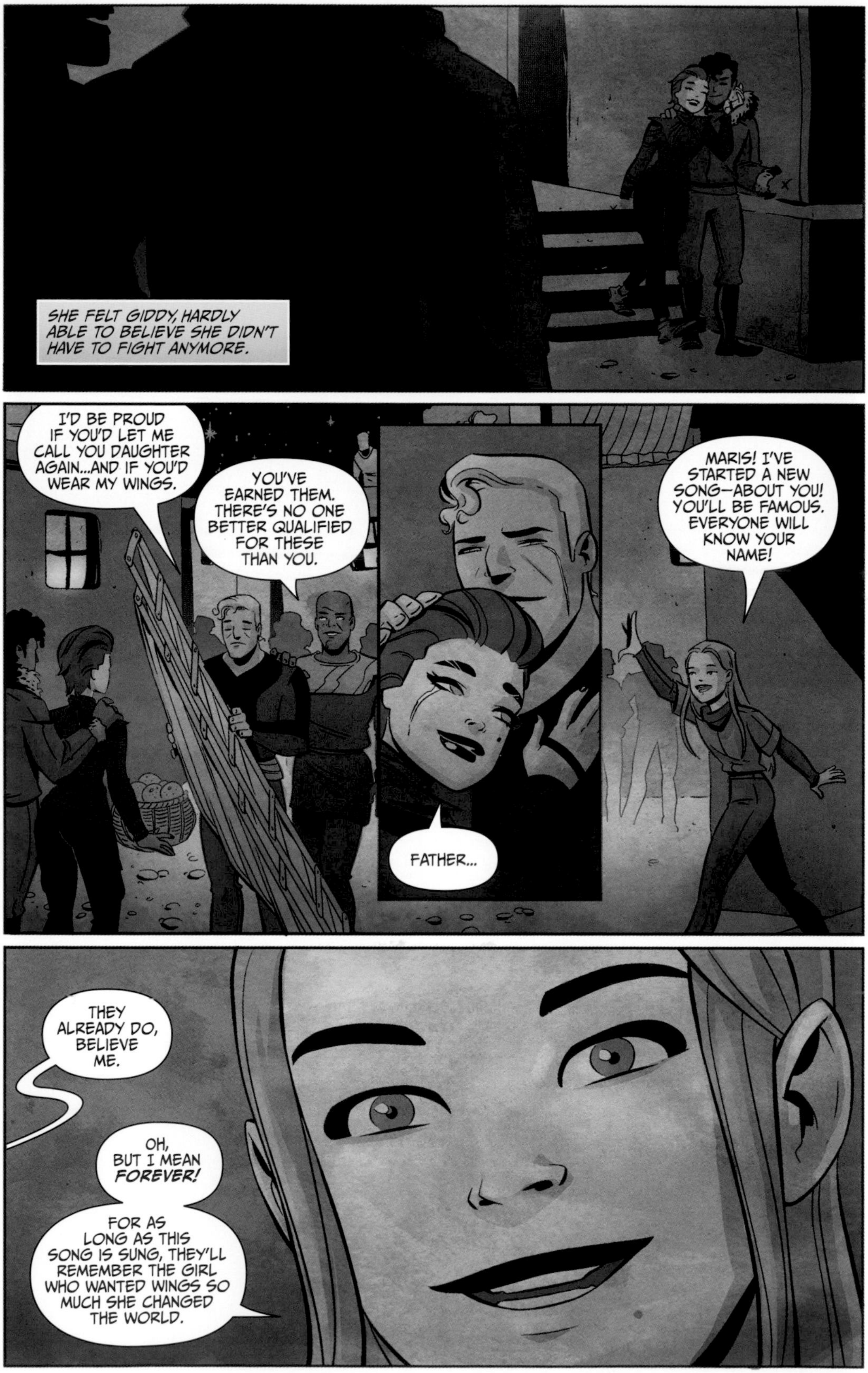
SHE FELT GIDDY, HARDLY ABLE TO BELIEVE SHE DIDN'T HAVE TO FIGHT ANYMORE.
I'D BE PROUD IF YOU'D LET ME CALL YOU DAUGHTER AGAIN...AND IF YOU'D WEAR MY WINGS.
YOU'VE EARNED THEM. THERE'S NO ONE BETTER QUALIFIED FOR THESE THAN YOU.
FATHER...
MARIS! I'VE STARTED A NEW SONG—ABOUT YOU! YOU'LL BE FAMOUS. EVERYONE WILL KNOW YOUR NAME!
THEY ALREADY DO, BELIEVE ME.
OH, BUT I MEAN *FOREVER!*
FOR AS LONG AS THIS SONG IS SUNG, THEY'LL REMEMBER THE GIRL WHO WANTED WINGS SO MUCH SHE CHANGED THE WORLD.

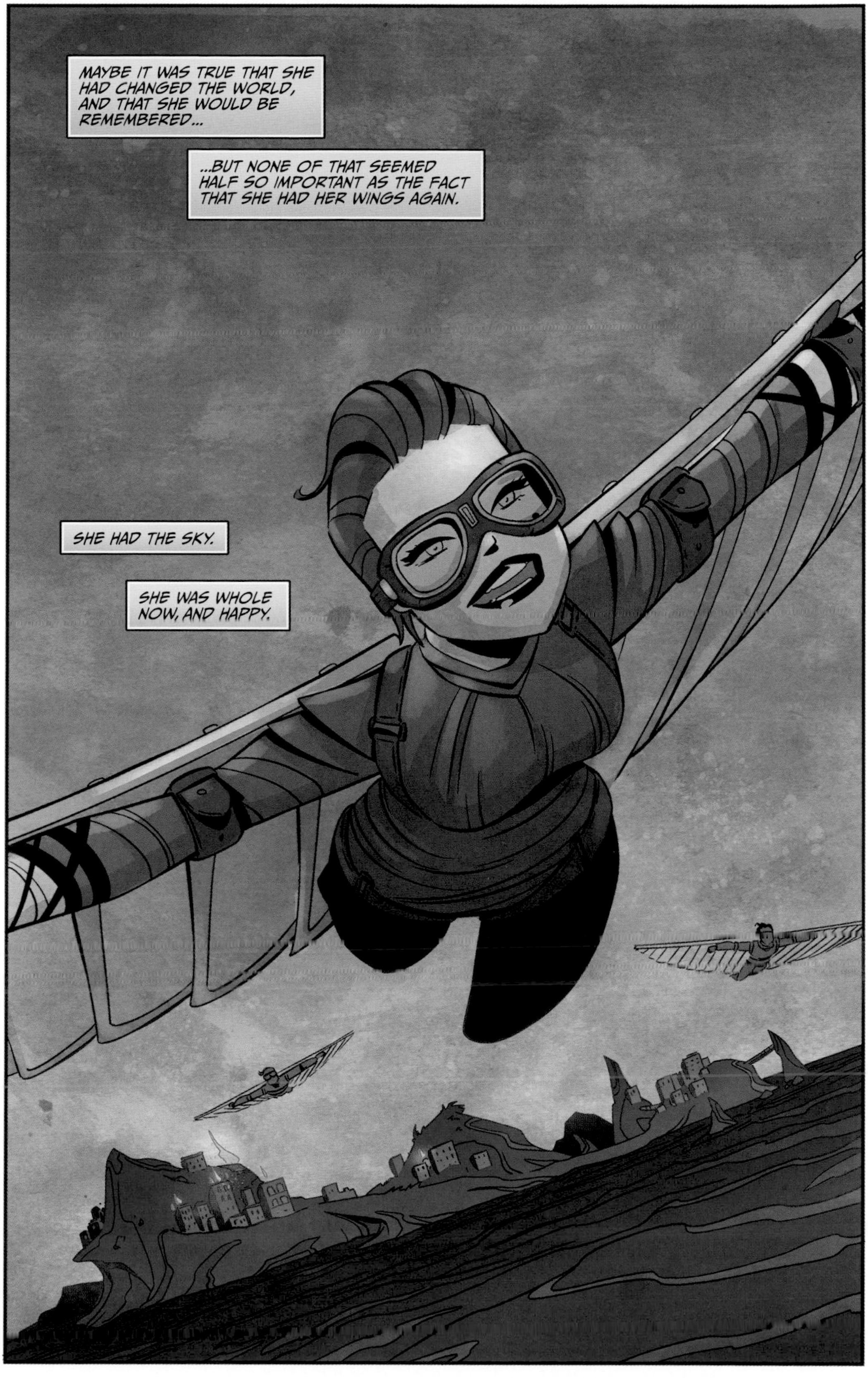
MAYBE IT WAS TRUE THAT SHE HAD CHANGED THE WORLD, AND THAT SHE WOULD BE REMEMBERED...
...BUT NONE OF THAT SEEMED HALF SO IMPORTANT AS THE FACT THAT SHE HAD HER WINGS AGAIN.
SHE HAD THE SKY.
SHE WAS WHOLE NOW, AND HAPPY.

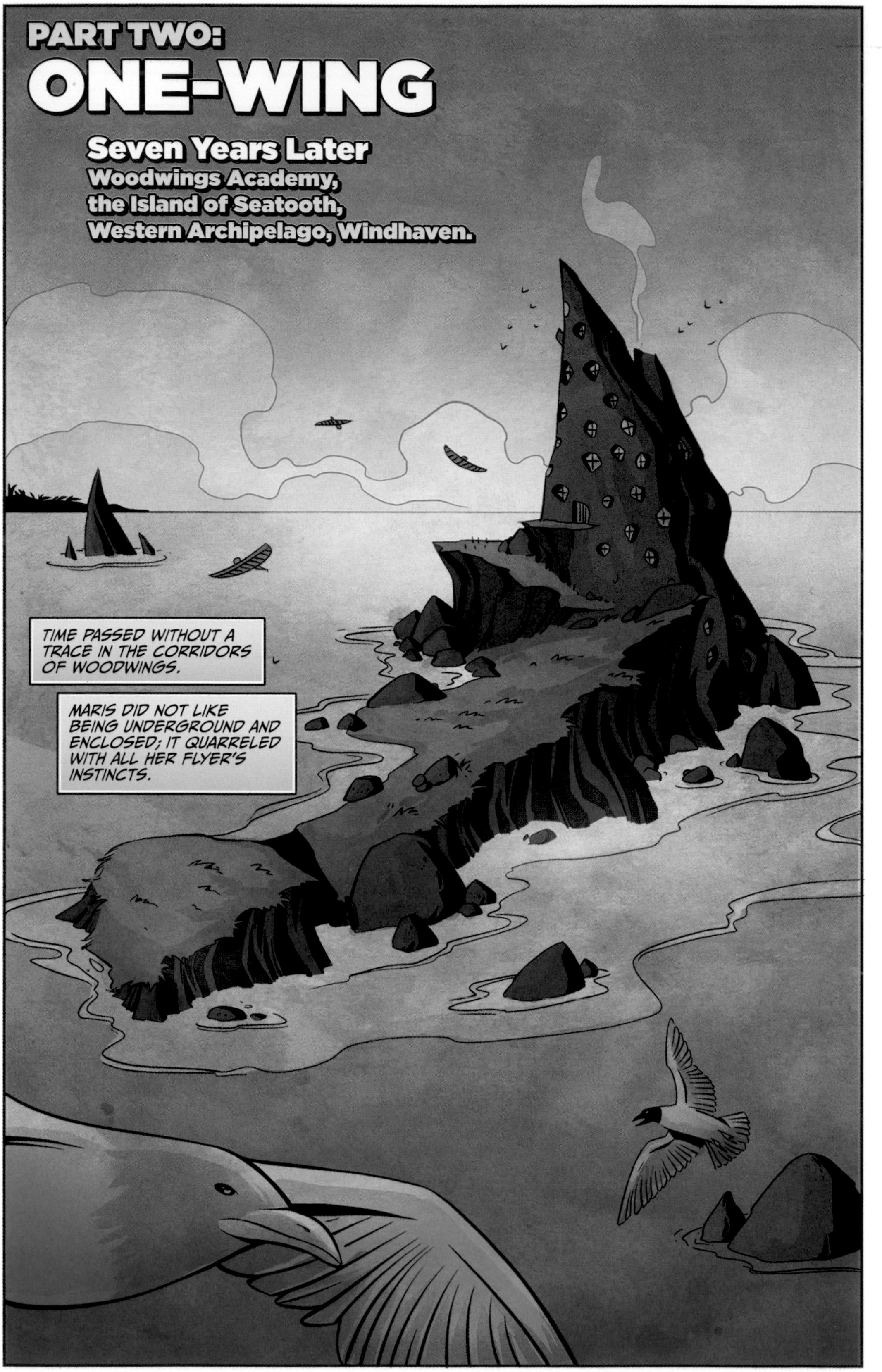
PART TWO:
ONE-WING
Seven Years Later
Woodwings Academy,
the Island of Seatooth,
Western Archipelago, Windhaven.
TIME PASSED WITHOUT A TRACE IN THE CORRIDORS OF WOODWINGS.
MARIS DID NOT LIKE BEING UNDERGROUND AND ENCLOSED; IT QUARRELED WITH ALL HER FLYER'S INSTINCTS.

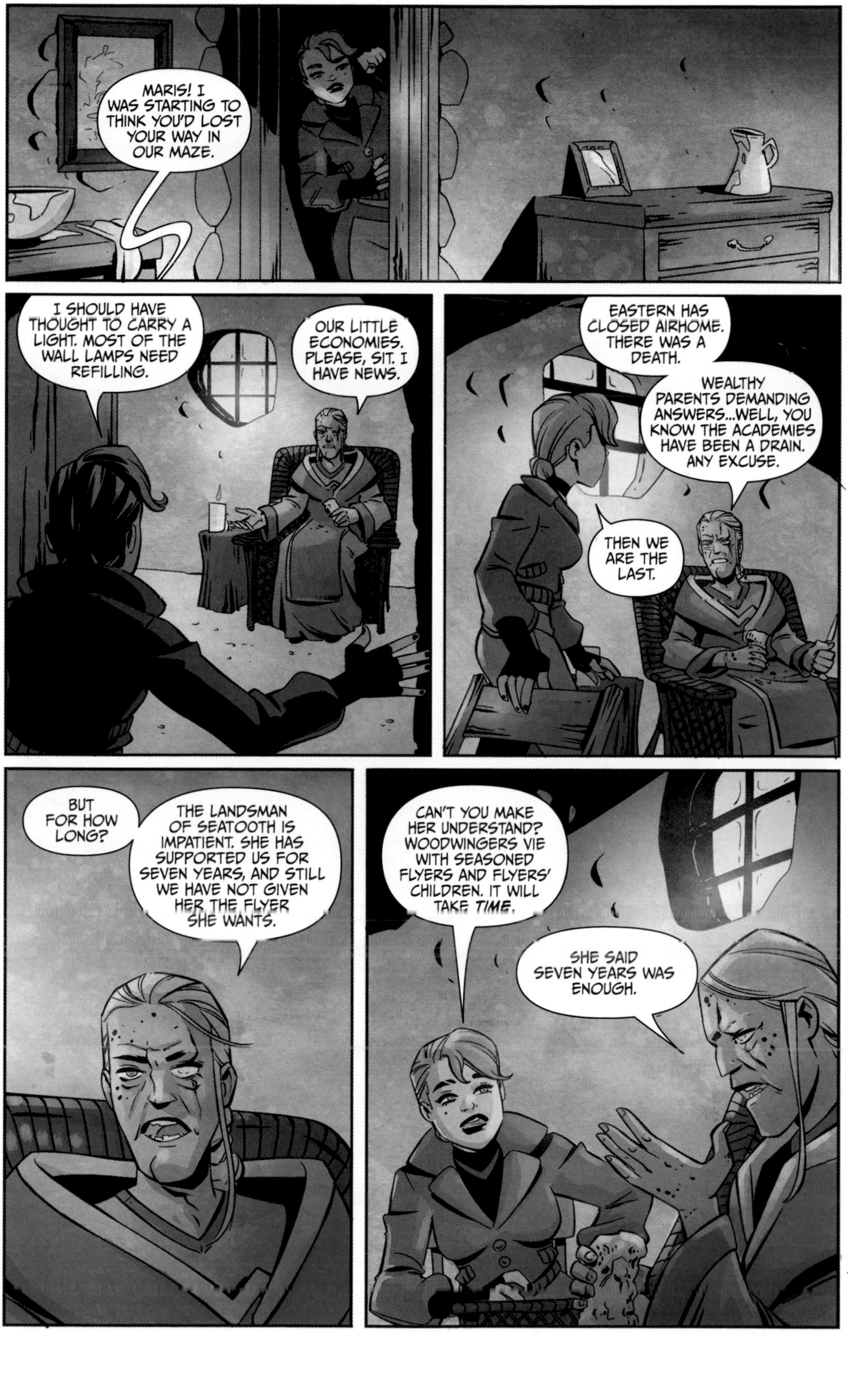
MARIS! I WAS STARTING TO THINK YOU'D LOST YOUR WAY IN OUR MAZE.
I SHOULD HAVE THOUGHT TO CARRY A LIGHT. MOST OF THE WALL LAMPS NEED REFILLING.
OUR LITTLE ECONOMIES. PLEASE, SIT. I HAVE NEWS.
EASTERN HAS CLOSED AIRHOME. THERE WAS A DEATH.
WEALTHY PARENTS DEMANDING ANSWERS...WELL, YOU KNOW THE ACADEMIES HAVE BEEN A DRAIN. ANY EXCUSE.
THEN WE ARE THE LAST.
BUT FOR HOW LONG?
THE LANDSMAN OF SEATOOTH IS IMPATIENT. SHE HAS SUPPORTED US FOR SEVEN YEARS, AND STILL WE HAVE NOT GIVEN HER THE FLYER SHE WANTS.
CAN'T YOU MAKE HER UNDERSTAND? WOODWINGERS VIE WITH SEASONED FLYERS AND FLYERS' CHILDREN. IT WILL TAKE *TIME*.
SHE SAID SEVEN YEARS WAS ENOUGH.

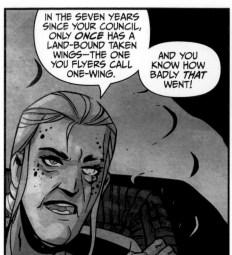

IN THE SEVEN YEARS SINCE YOUR COUNCIL, ONLY *ONCE* HAS A LAND-BOUND TAKEN WINGS—THE ONE YOU FLYERS CALL ONE-WING.

AND YOU KNOW HOW BADLY *THAT* WENT!

BUT I DIDN'T CALL YOU HERE TO COMFORT ME.

ONE OF THE STUDENTS FROM EASTERN IS COMING HERE, HOPING I WILL SPONSOR HIM IN THE NEXT COMPETITION.

HERE? FROM *EASTERN?* WITHOUT WINGS?

THE VOYAGE IS LONG AND HAZARDOUS. I WILL NOT BEGRUDGE HIM ADMISSION.

HE WILL BENEFIT FROM YOUR ADVICE.

I HOPE I HAVEN'T BEEN WORKING YOU TOO HARD, BUT IT'S SO GOOD FOR THE CHILDREN, TO HAVE A REAL FLYER TO SHOW THEM HOW IT'S DONE.

I'M AFRAID I MUST RETURN TO LESSER AMBERLY. I'VE BEEN AWAY TOO LONG.

HMPH. YOUR ISLAND HAS TWO OTHER FLYERS, AND SEATOOTH HAS *NONE.*

WITHOUT YOUR HELP TO PREPARE THE STUDENTS FOR THEIR CHALLENGES...

I'LL BE BACK AS SOON AS I CAN.

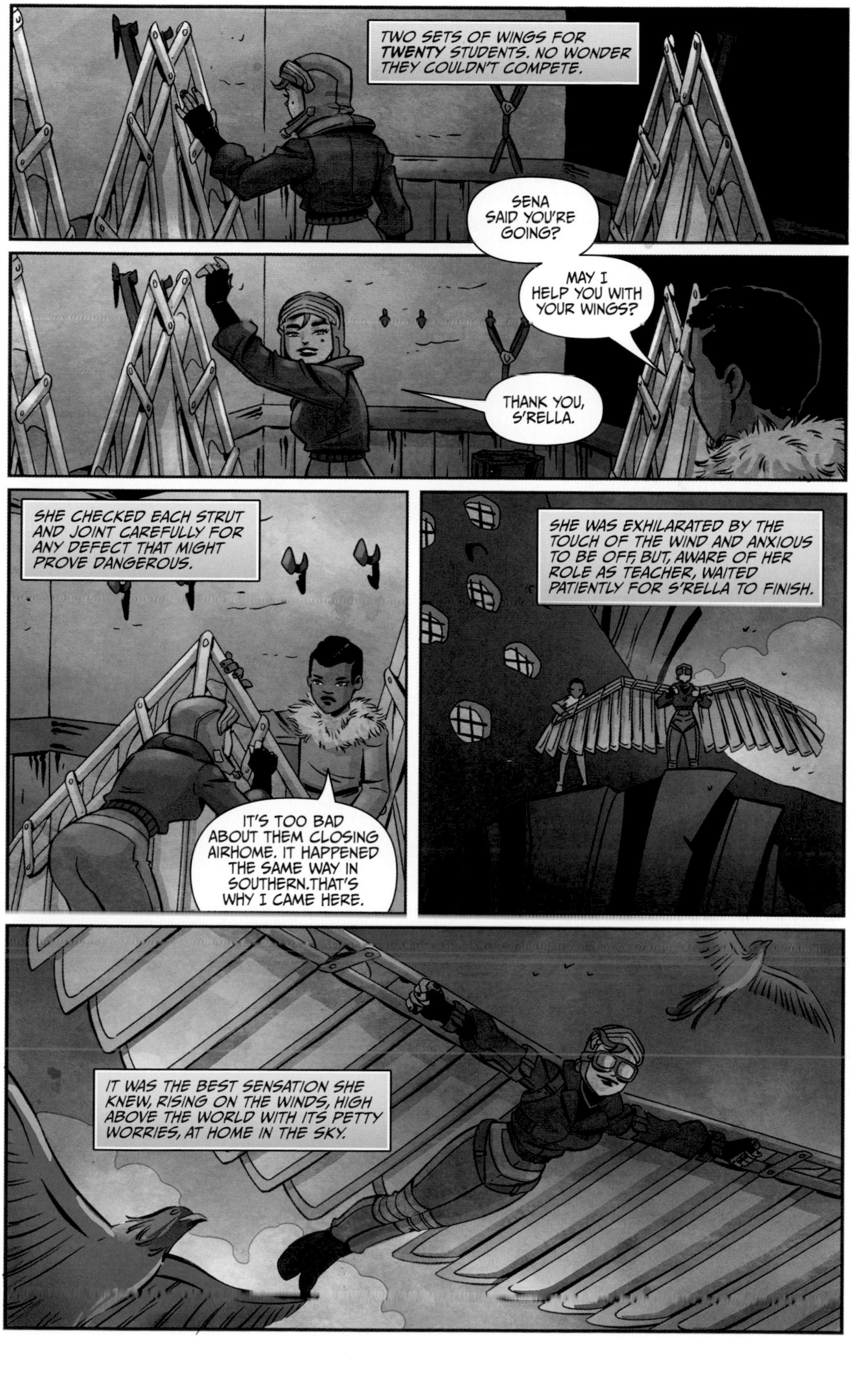
TWO SETS OF WINGS FOR TWENTY STUDENTS. NO WONDER THEY COULDN'T COMPETE.
SENA SAID YOU'RE GOING?
MAY I HELP YOU WITH YOUR WINGS?
THANK YOU, S'RELLA.
SHE CHECKED EACH STRUT AND JOINT CAREFULLY FOR ANY DEFECT THAT MIGHT PROVE DANGEROUS.
IT'S TOO BAD ABOUT THEM CLOSING AIRHOME. IT HAPPENED THE SAME WAY IN SOUTHERN.THAT'S WHY I CAME HERE.
SHE WAS EXHILARATED BY THE TOUCH OF THE WIND AND ANXIOUS TO BE OFF, BUT, AWARE OF HER ROLE AS TEACHER, WAITED PATIENTLY FOR S'RELLA TO FINISH.
IT WAS THE BEST SENSATION SHE KNEW, RISING ON THE WINDS, HIGH ABOVE THE WORLD WITH ITS PETTY WORRIES, AT HOME IN THE SKY.

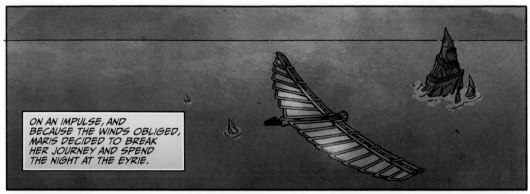

ON AN IMPULSE, AND BECAUSE THE WINDS OBLIGED, MARIS DECIDED TO BREAK HER JOURNEY AND SPEND THE NIGHT AT THE EYRIE.

DORREL!

I'VE BEEN ON SEATOOTH NEARLY TWO WEEKS...

YOU SPEND TOO MUCH TIME THERE. SENA GETS *PAID* TO TEACH THEM. YOU DON'T.

BUT I'M HAPPY TO HELP. YOU SHOULD COME, SPEND A WEEK WITH ME THERE.

WE'D SHARE A ROOM...

I'D LOVE TO SPEND A WEEK WITH YOU—ANYWHERE BUT WOODWINGS!

I WON'T TRAIN A BUNCH OF LAND-BOUNDS TO TAKE THE WINGS FROM MY FRIENDS.

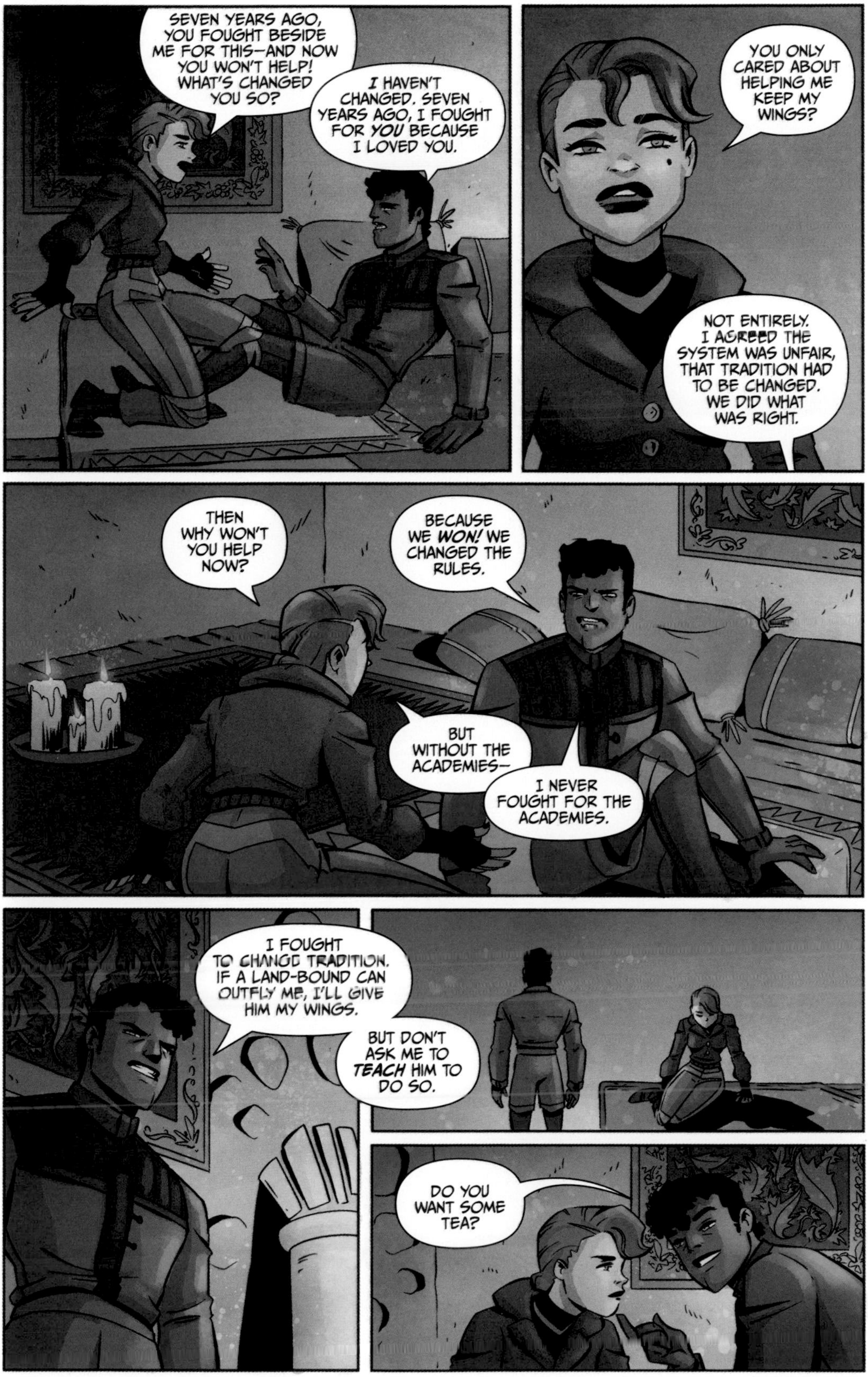
SEVEN YEARS AGO, YOU FOUGHT BESIDE ME FOR THIS—AND NOW YOU WON'T HELP! WHAT'S CHANGED YOU SO?
I HAVEN'T CHANGED. SEVEN YEARS AGO, I FOUGHT FOR YOU BECAUSE I LOVED YOU.
YOU ONLY CARED ABOUT HELPING ME KEEP MY WINGS?
NOT ENTIRELY. I AGREED THE SYSTEM WAS UNFAIR, THAT TRADITION HAD TO BE CHANGED. WE DID WHAT WAS RIGHT.
THEN WHY WON'T YOU HELP NOW?
BECAUSE WE WON! WE CHANGED THE RULES.
BUT WITHOUT THE ACADEMIES—
I NEVER FOUGHT FOR THE ACADEMIES.
I FOUGHT TO CHANGE TRADITION. IF A LAND-BOUND CAN OUTFLY ME, I'LL GIVE HIM MY WINGS.
BUT DON'T ASK ME TO TEACH HIM TO DO SO.
DO YOU WANT SOME TEA?

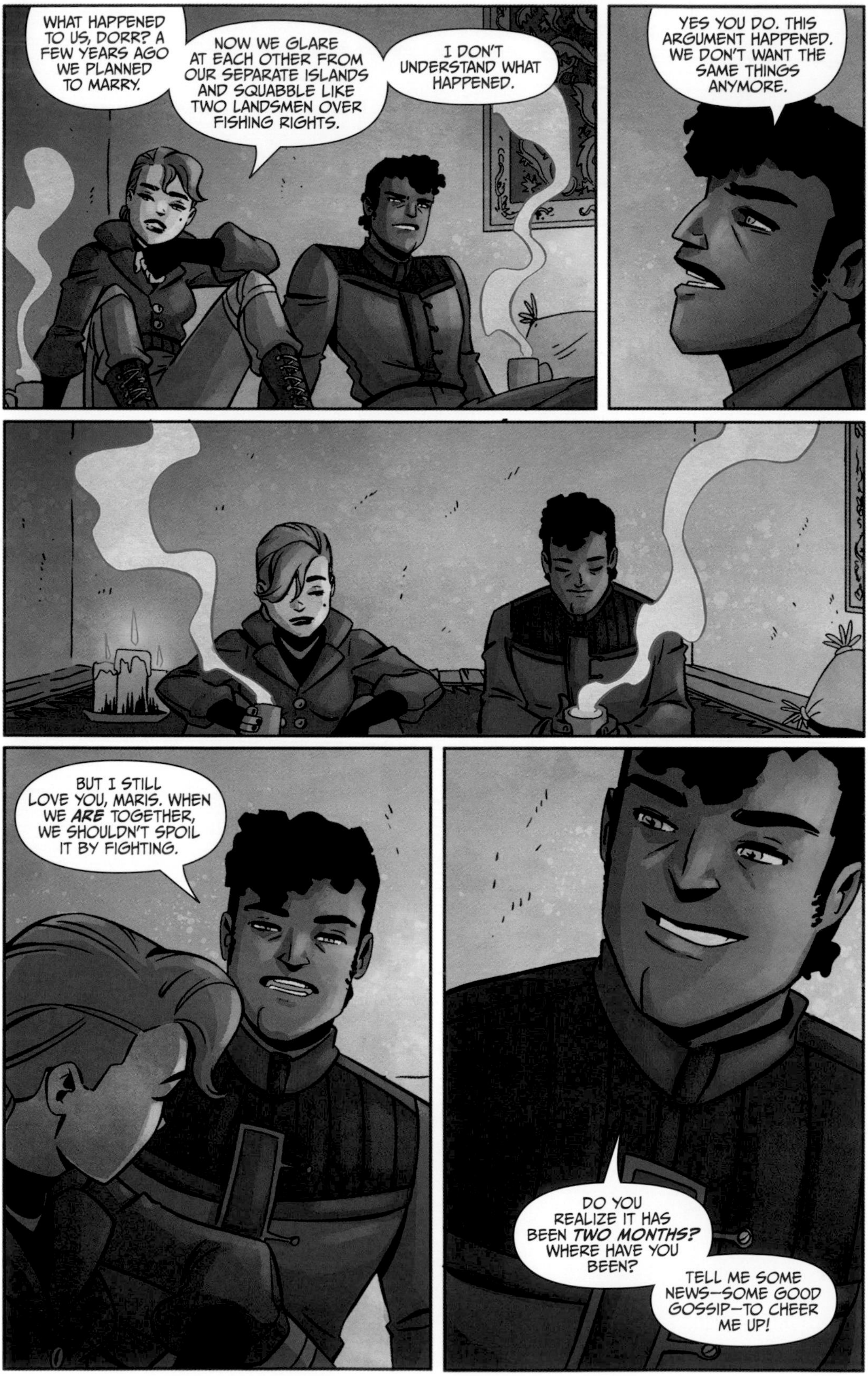
WHAT HAPPENED TO US, DORR? A FEW YEARS AGO WE PLANNED TO MARRY.
NOW WE GLARE AT EACH OTHER FROM OUR SEPARATE ISLANDS AND SQUABBLE LIKE TWO LANDSMEN OVER FISHING RIGHTS.
I DON'T UNDERSTAND WHAT HAPPENED.
YES YOU DO. THIS ARGUMENT HAPPENED. WE DON'T WANT THE SAME THINGS ANYMORE.
BUT I STILL LOVE YOU, MARIS. WHEN WE *ARE* TOGETHER, WE SHOULDN'T SPOIL IT BY FIGHTING.
DO YOU REALIZE IT HAS BEEN *TWO MONTHS?* WHERE HAVE YOU BEEN?
TELL ME SOME NEWS—SOME GOOD GOSSIP—TO CHEER ME UP!

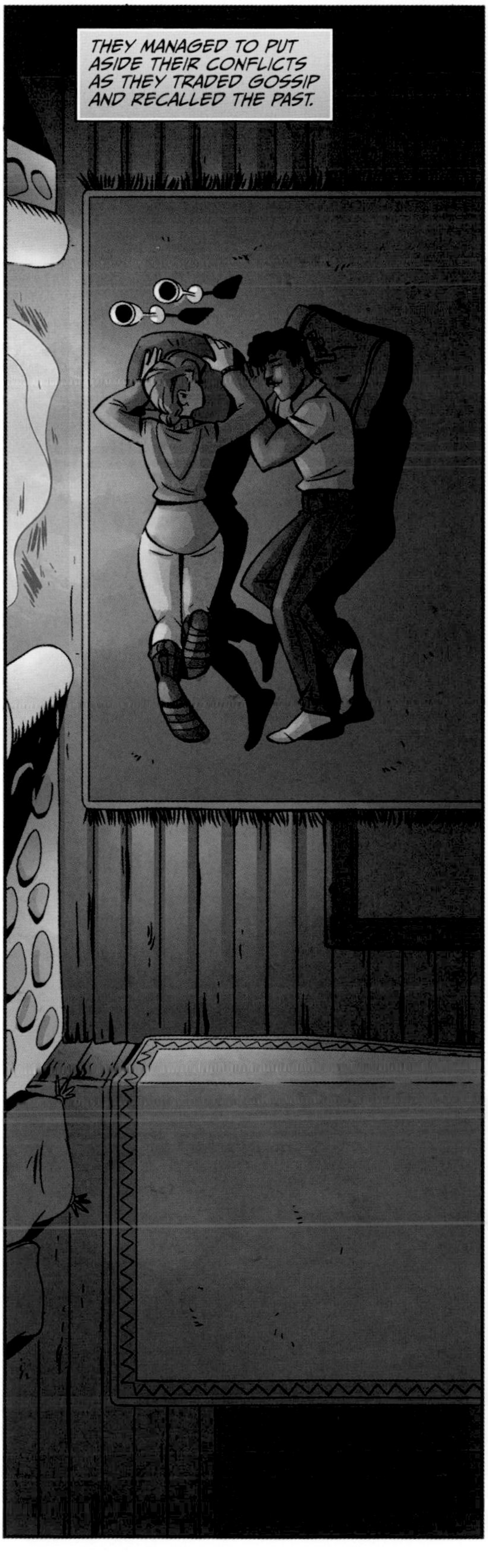
THEY MANAGED TO PUT ASIDE THEIR CONFLICTS AS THEY TRADED GOSSIP AND RECALLED THE PAST.

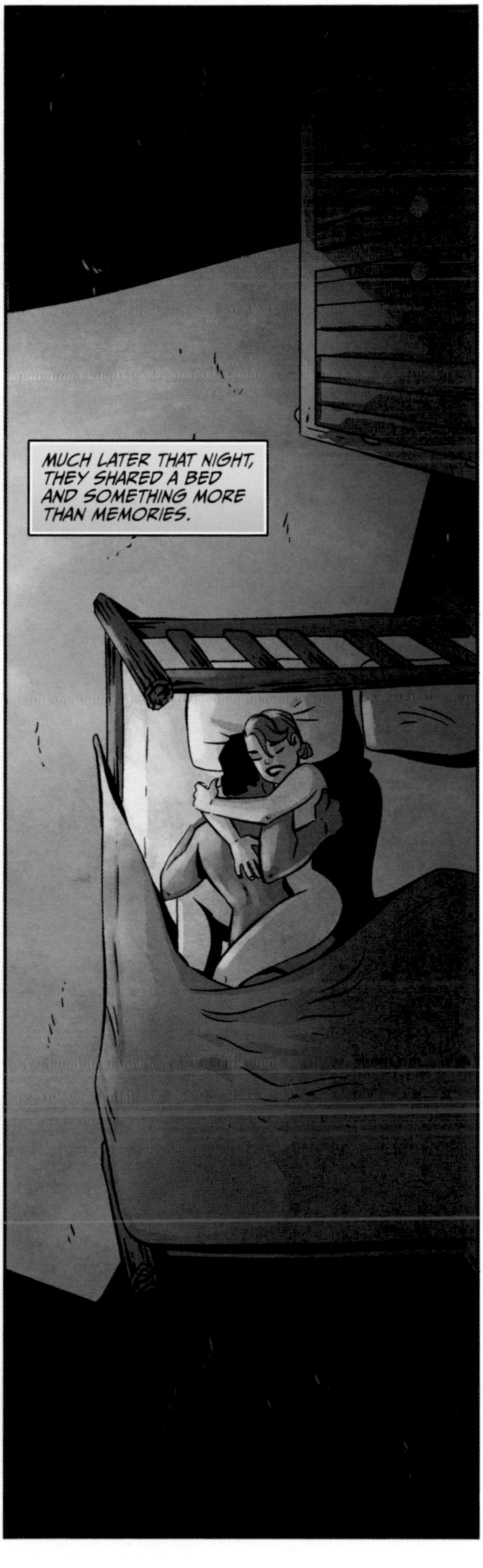
MUCH LATER THAT NIGHT, THEY SHARED A BED AND SOMETHING MORE THAN MEMORIES.

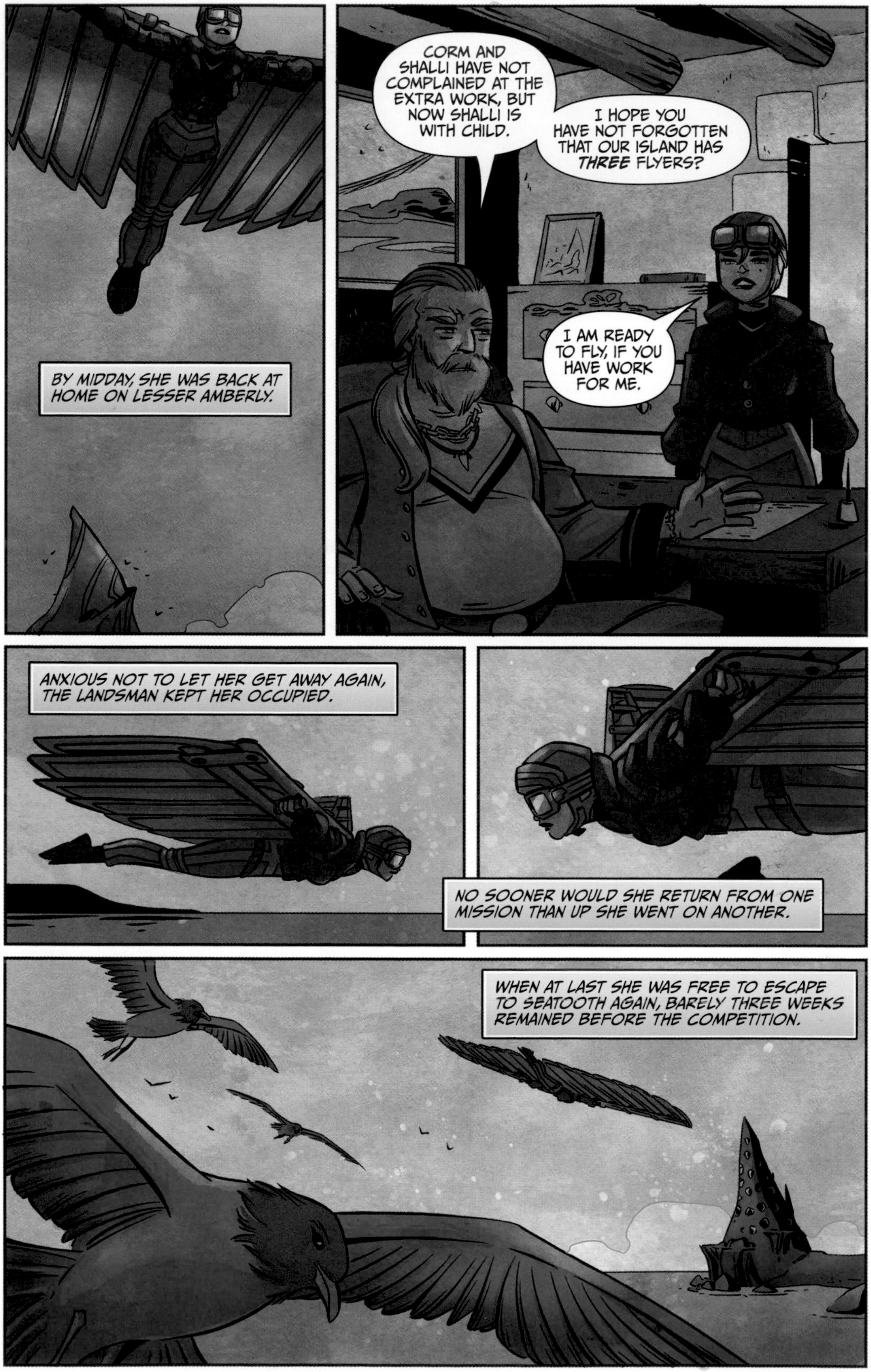
BY MIDDAY, SHE WAS BACK AT HOME ON LESSER AMBERLY.
CORM AND SHALLI HAVE NOT COMPLAINED AT THE EXTRA WORK, BUT NOW SHALLI IS WITH CHILD.
I HOPE YOU HAVE NOT FORGOTTEN THAT OUR ISLAND HAS THREE FLYERS?
I AM READY TO FLY, IF YOU HAVE WORK FOR ME.
ANXIOUS NOT TO LET HER GET AWAY AGAIN, THE LANDSMAN KEPT HER OCCUPIED.
NO SOONER WOULD SHE RETURN FROM ONE MISSION THAN UP SHE WENT ON ANOTHER.
WHEN AT LAST SHE WAS FREE TO ESCAPE TO SEATOOTH AGAIN, BARELY THREE WEEKS REMAINED BEFORE THE COMPETITION.

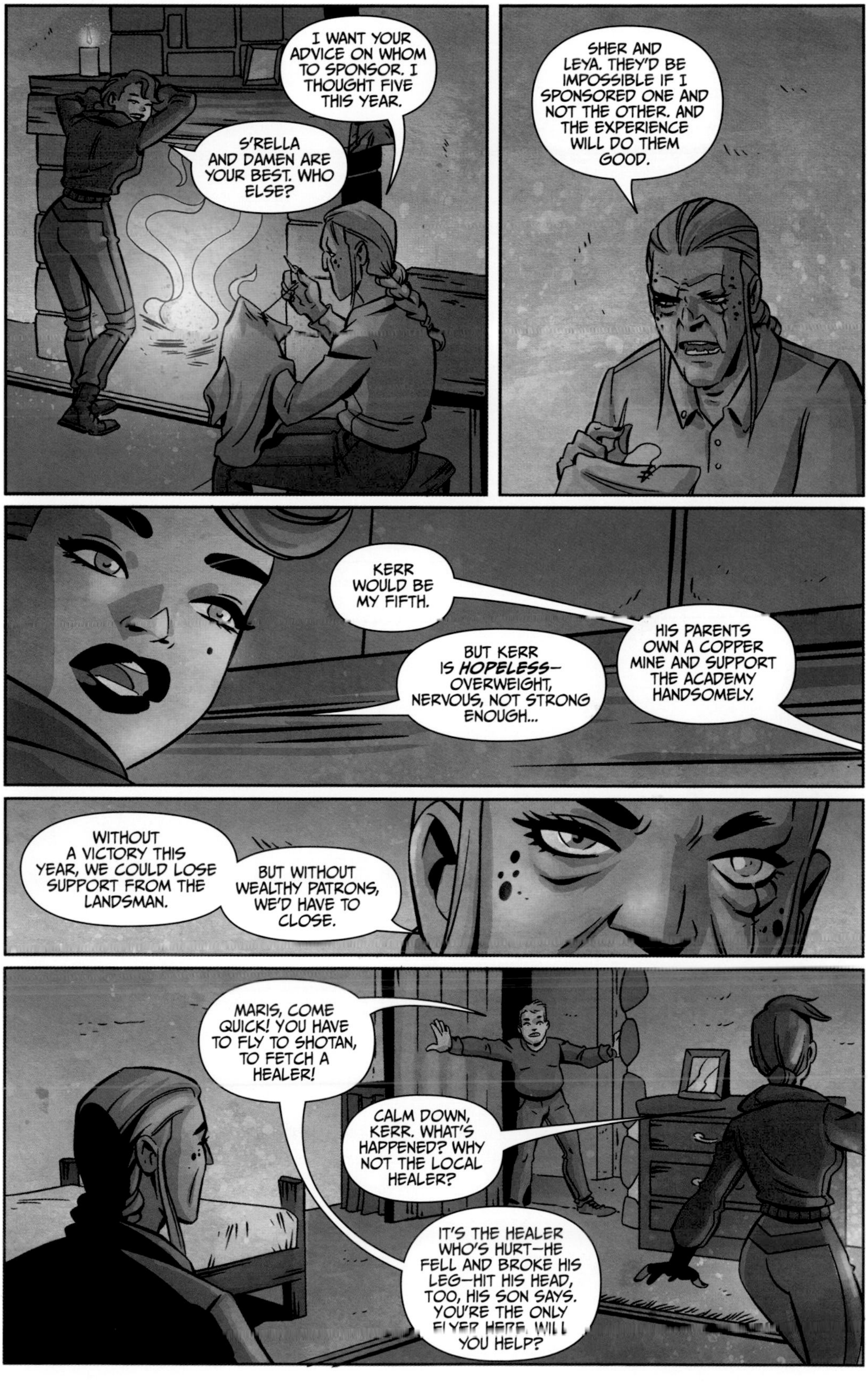
I WANT YOUR ADVICE ON WHOM TO SPONSOR. I THOUGHT FIVE THIS YEAR.
S'RELLA AND DAMEN ARE YOUR BEST. WHO ELSE?
SHER AND LEYA. THEY'D BE IMPOSSIBLE IF I SPONSORED ONE AND NOT THE OTHER. AND THE EXPERIENCE WILL DO THEM GOOD.
KERR WOULD BE MY FIFTH.
BUT KERR IS ***HOPELESS***— OVERWEIGHT, NERVOUS, NOT STRONG ENOUGH...
HIS PARENTS OWN A COPPER MINE AND SUPPORT THE ACADEMY HANDSOMELY.
WITHOUT A VICTORY THIS YEAR, WE COULD LOSE SUPPORT FROM THE LANDSMAN.
BUT WITHOUT WEALTHY PATRONS, WE'D HAVE TO CLOSE.
MARIS, COME QUICK! YOU HAVE TO FLY TO SHOTAN, TO FETCH A HEALER!
CALM DOWN, KERR. WHAT'S HAPPENED? WHY NOT THE LOCAL HEALER?
IT'S THE HEALER WHO'S HURT—HE FELL AND BROKE HIS LEG—HIT HIS HEAD, TOO, HIS SON SAYS. YOU'RE THE ONLY FLYER HERE. WILL YOU HELP?

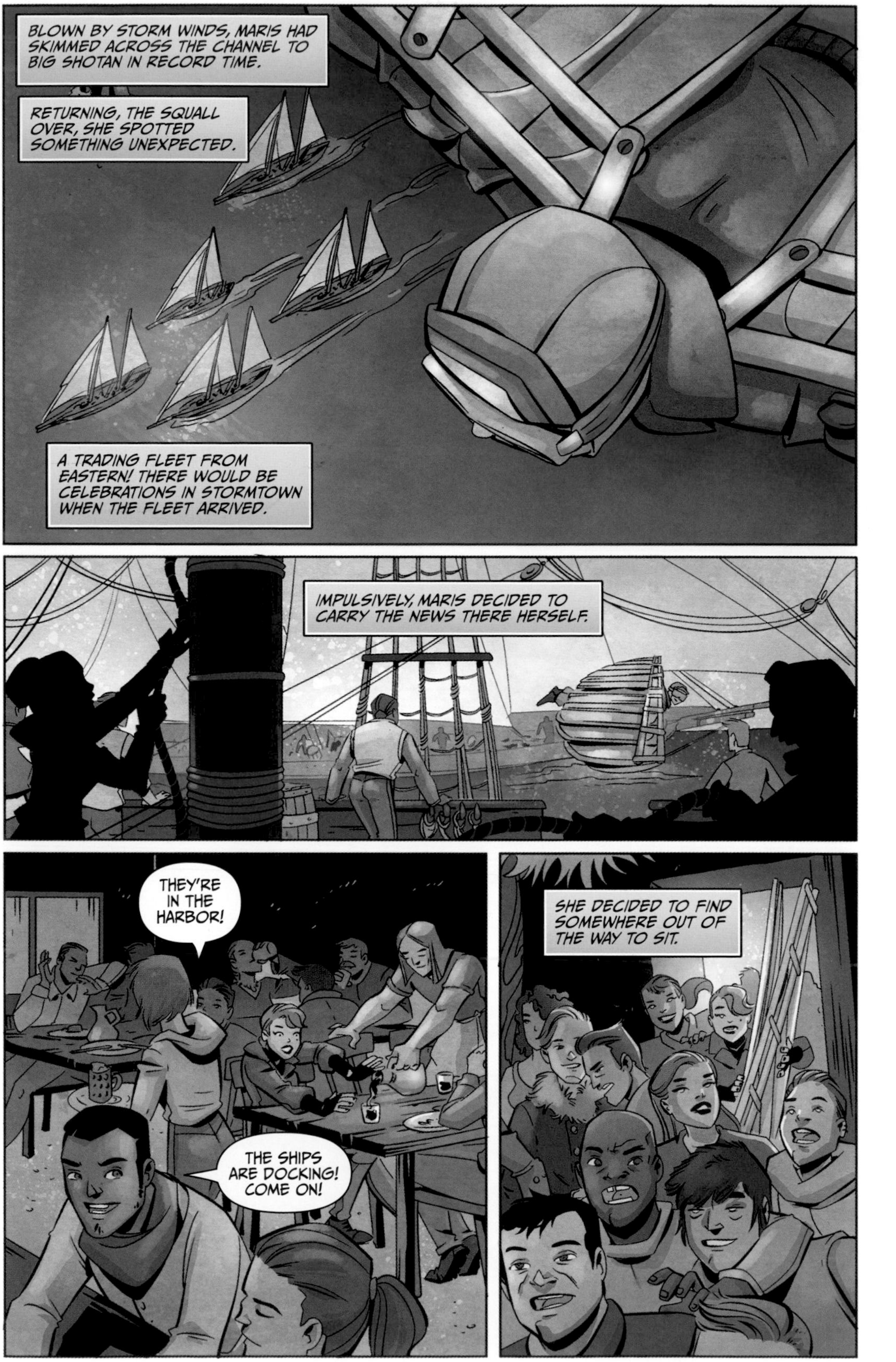
BLOWN BY STORM WINDS, MARIS HAD SKIMMED ACROSS THE CHANNEL TO BIG SHOTAN IN RECORD TIME.
RETURNING, THE SQUALL OVER, SHE SPOTTED SOMETHING UNEXPECTED.
A TRADING FLEET FROM EASTERN! THERE WOULD BE CELEBRATIONS IN STORMTOWN WHEN THE FLEET ARRIVED.
IMPULSIVELY, MARIS DECIDED TO CARRY THE NEWS THERE HERSELF.
THEY'RE IN THE HARBOR!
THE SHIPS ARE DOCKING! COME ON!
SHE DECIDED TO FIND SOMEWHERE OUT OF THE WAY TO SIT.

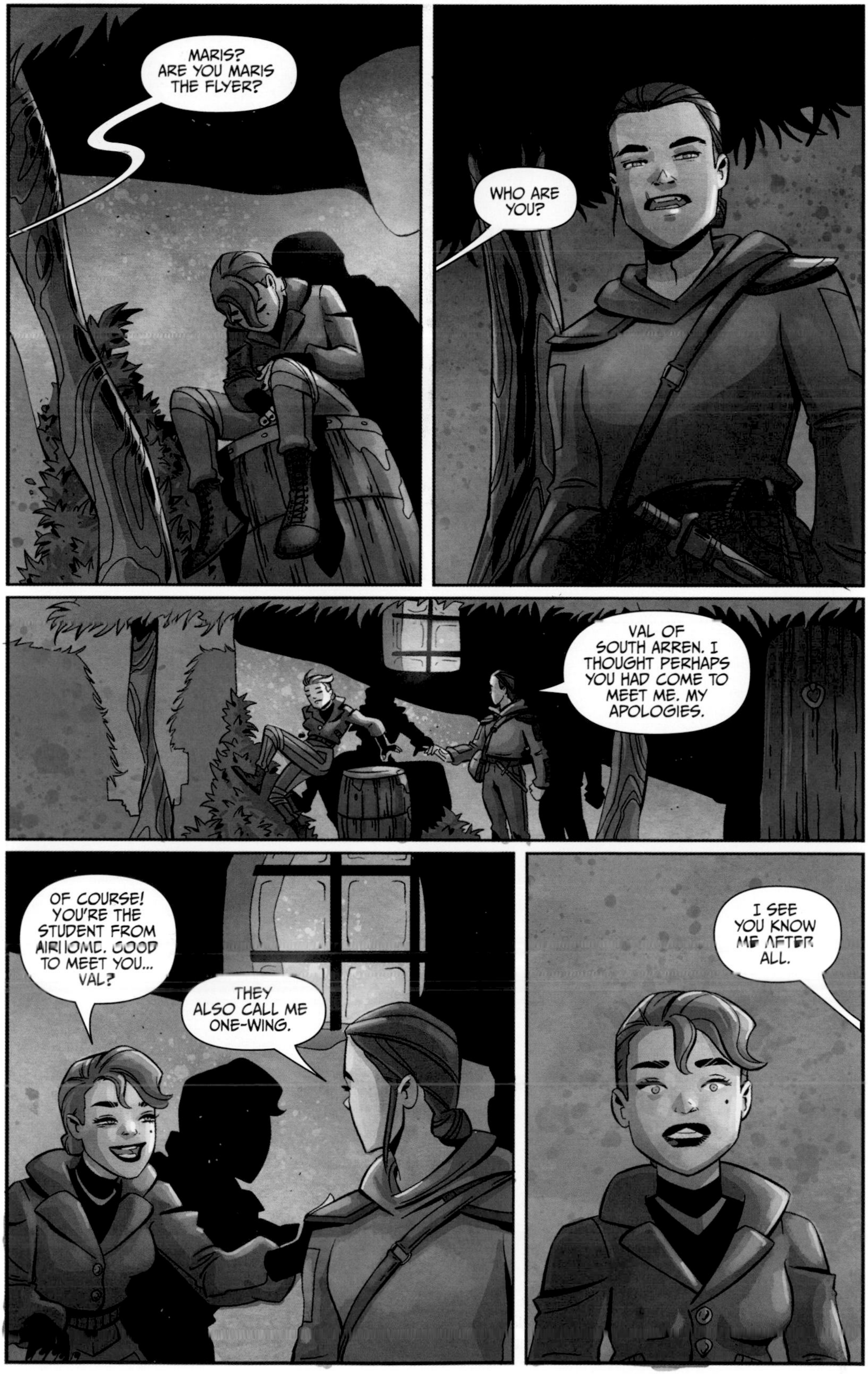
MARIS? ARE YOU MARIS THE FLYER?
WHO ARE YOU?
VAL OF SOUTH ARREN. I THOUGHT PERHAPS YOU HAD COME TO MEET ME. MY APOLOGIES.
OF COURSE! YOU'RE THE STUDENT FROM AIRHOME. GOOD TO MEET YOU... VAL?
THEY ALSO CALL ME ONE-WING.
I SEE YOU KNOW ME AFTER ALL.

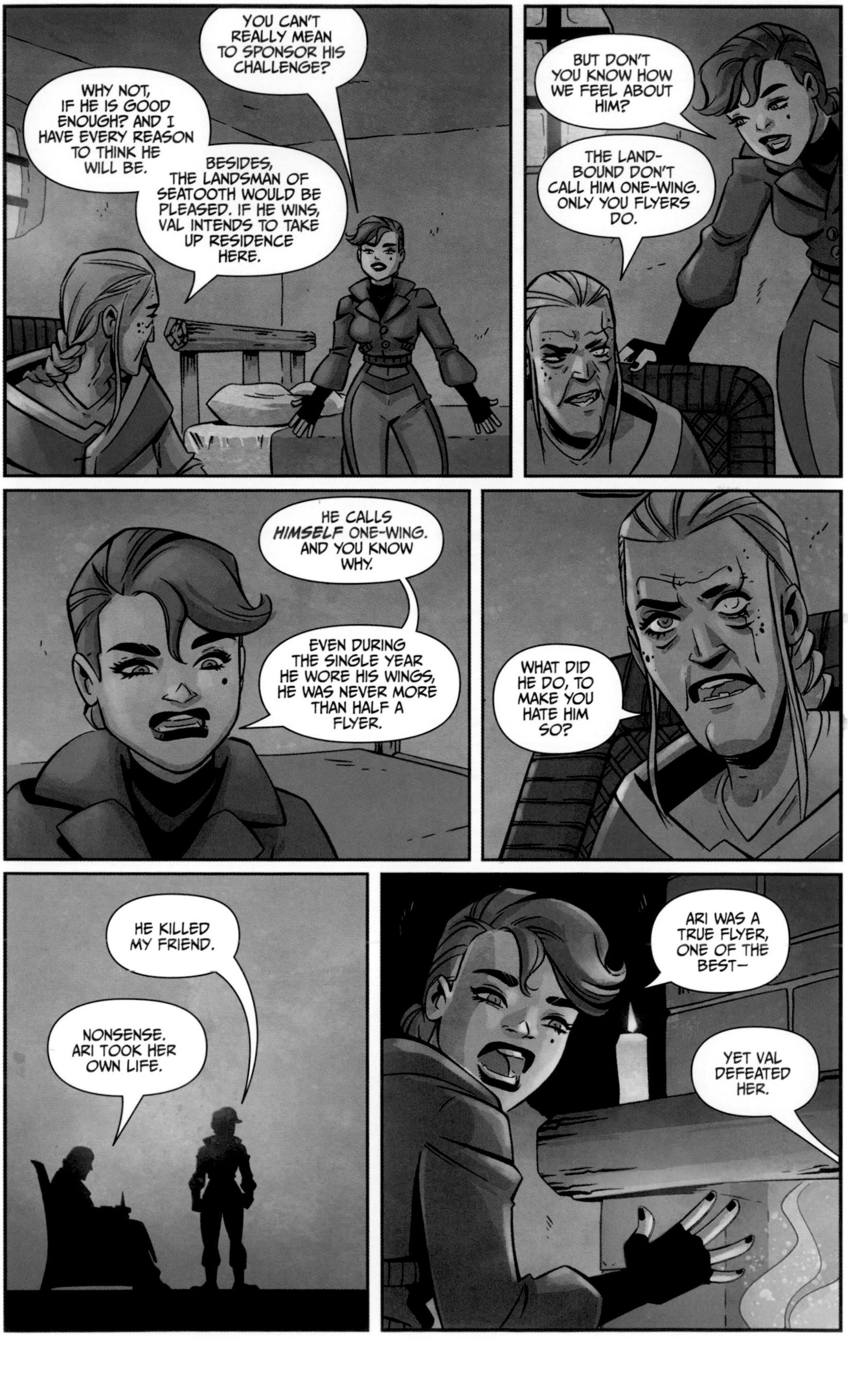
YOU CAN'T REALLY MEAN TO SPONSOR HIS CHALLENGE?
WHY NOT, IF HE IS GOOD ENOUGH? AND I HAVE EVERY REASON TO THINK HE WILL BE.
BESIDES, THE LANDSMAN OF SEATOOTH WOULD BE PLEASED. IF HE WINS, VAL INTENDS TO TAKE UP RESIDENCE HERE.
BUT DON'T YOU KNOW HOW WE FEEL ABOUT HIM?
THE LAND-BOUND DON'T CALL HIM ONE-WING. ONLY YOU FLYERS DO.
HE CALLS *HIMSELF* ONE-WING. AND YOU KNOW WHY.
EVEN DURING THE SINGLE YEAR HE WORE HIS WINGS, HE WAS NEVER MORE THAN HALF A FLYER.
WHAT DID HE DO, TO MAKE YOU HATE HIM SO?
HE KILLED MY FRIEND.
NONSENSE. ARI TOOK HER OWN LIFE.
ARI WAS A TRUE FLYER, ONE OF THE BEST—
YET VAL DEFEATED HER.

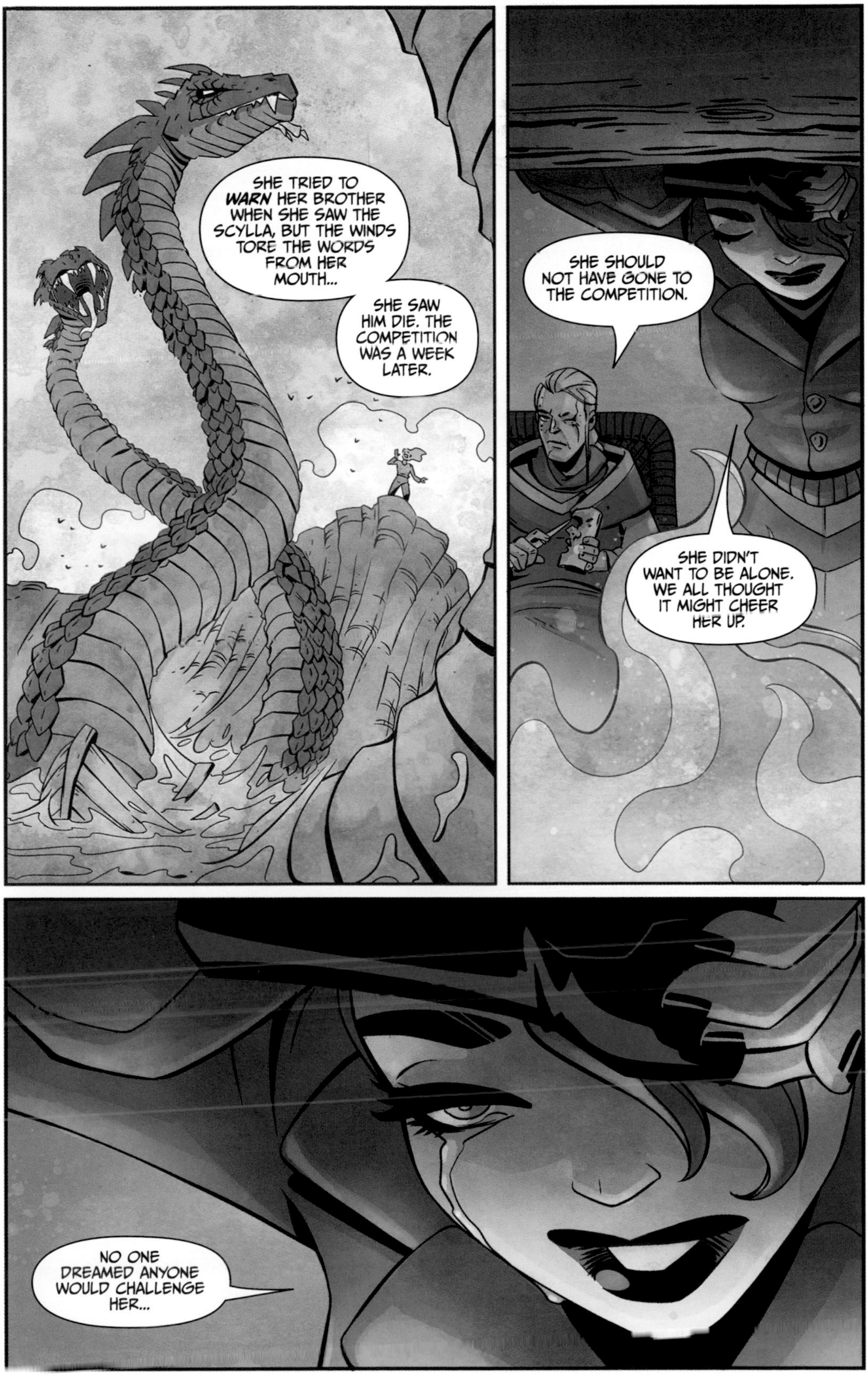
SHE TRIED TO *WARN* HER BROTHER WHEN SHE SAW THE SCYLLA, BUT THE WINDS TORE THE WORDS FROM HER MOUTH...
SHE SAW HIM DIE. THE COMPETITION WAS A WEEK LATER.
SHE SHOULD NOT HAVE GONE TO THE COMPETITION.
SHE DIDN'T WANT TO BE ALONE. WE ALL THOUGHT IT MIGHT CHEER HER UP.
NO ONE DREAMED ANYONE WOULD CHALLENGE HER...

SHE KNEW THE RULES SET BY THE COUNCIL. *YOUR* COUNCIL, MARIS!

RULES? WHAT ABOUT *FAIRNESS?* WHEN THAT BOY CHALLENGED HER—

YES, *BOY.* HE WAS FIFTEEN!

HE KNEW WHAT HE WAS DOING. THE JUDGES TRIED TO EXPLAIN THINGS TO HIM, BUT HE WOULD NOT WITHDRAW HIS CHALLENGE.

HE FLEW WELL AND ARI FLEW BADLY, AND THAT WAS IT. HE HAD HER WINGS.

A MONTH LATER, SHE KILLED HERSELF.

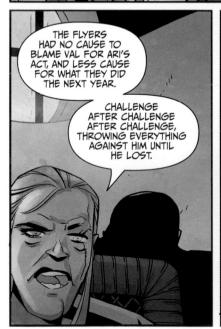

THE FLYERS HAD NO CAUSE TO BLAME VAL FOR ARI'S ACT, AND LESS CAUSE FOR WHAT THEY DID THE NEXT YEAR.

CHALLENGE AFTER CHALLENGE AFTER CHALLENGE, THROWING EVERYTHING AGAINST HIM UNTIL HE LOST.

THERE WAS NO RULE AGAINST MULTIPLE CHALLENGES THEN!

YET THERE IS NOW. BECAUSE IT WASN'T FAIR.

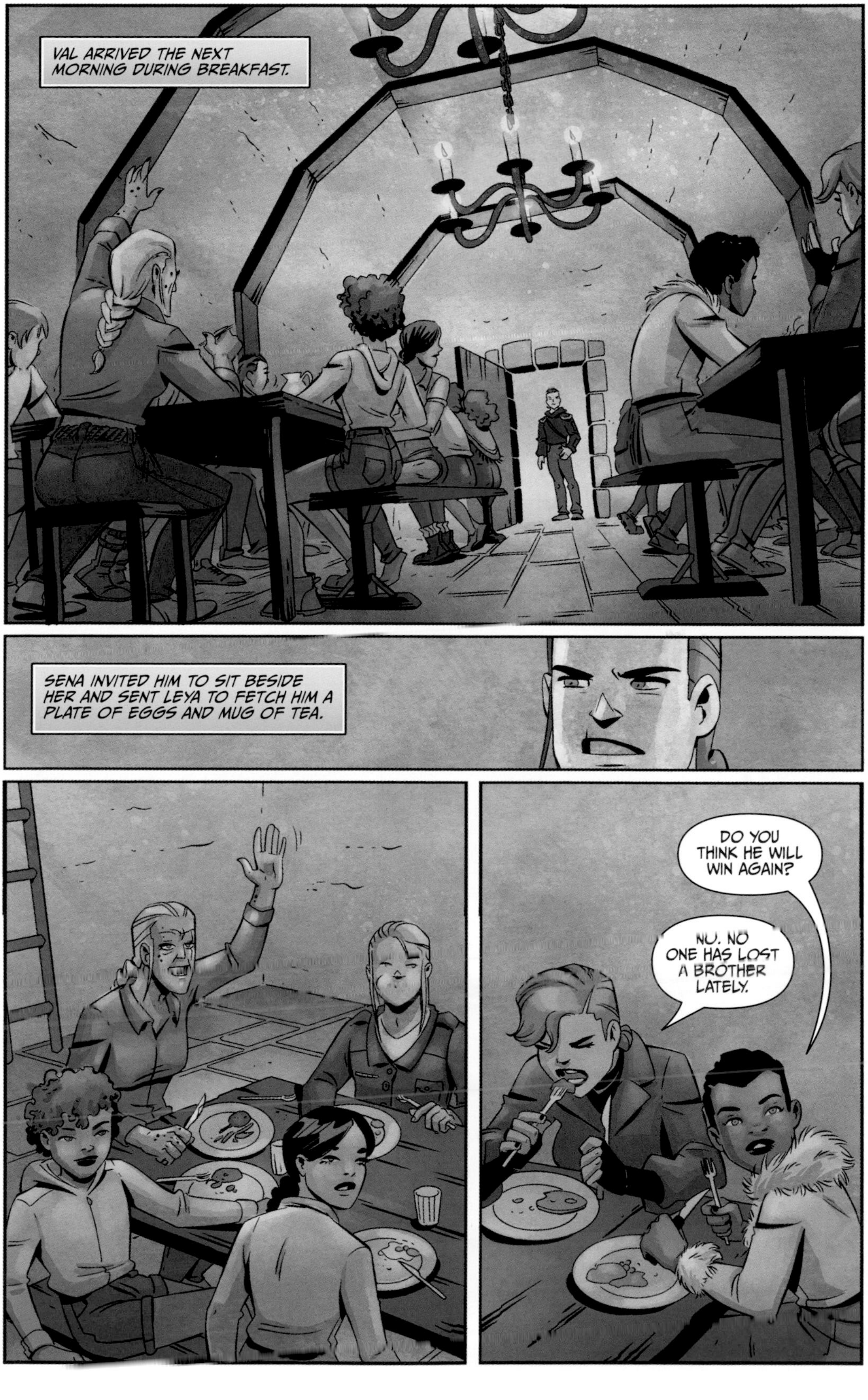
VAL ARRIVED THE NEXT MORNING DURING BREAKFAST.
SENA INVITED HIM TO SIT BESIDE HER AND SENT LEYA TO FETCH HIM A PLATE OF EGGS AND MUG OF TEA.
DO YOU THINK HE WILL WIN AGAIN?
NO. NO ONE HAS LOST A BROTHER LATELY.

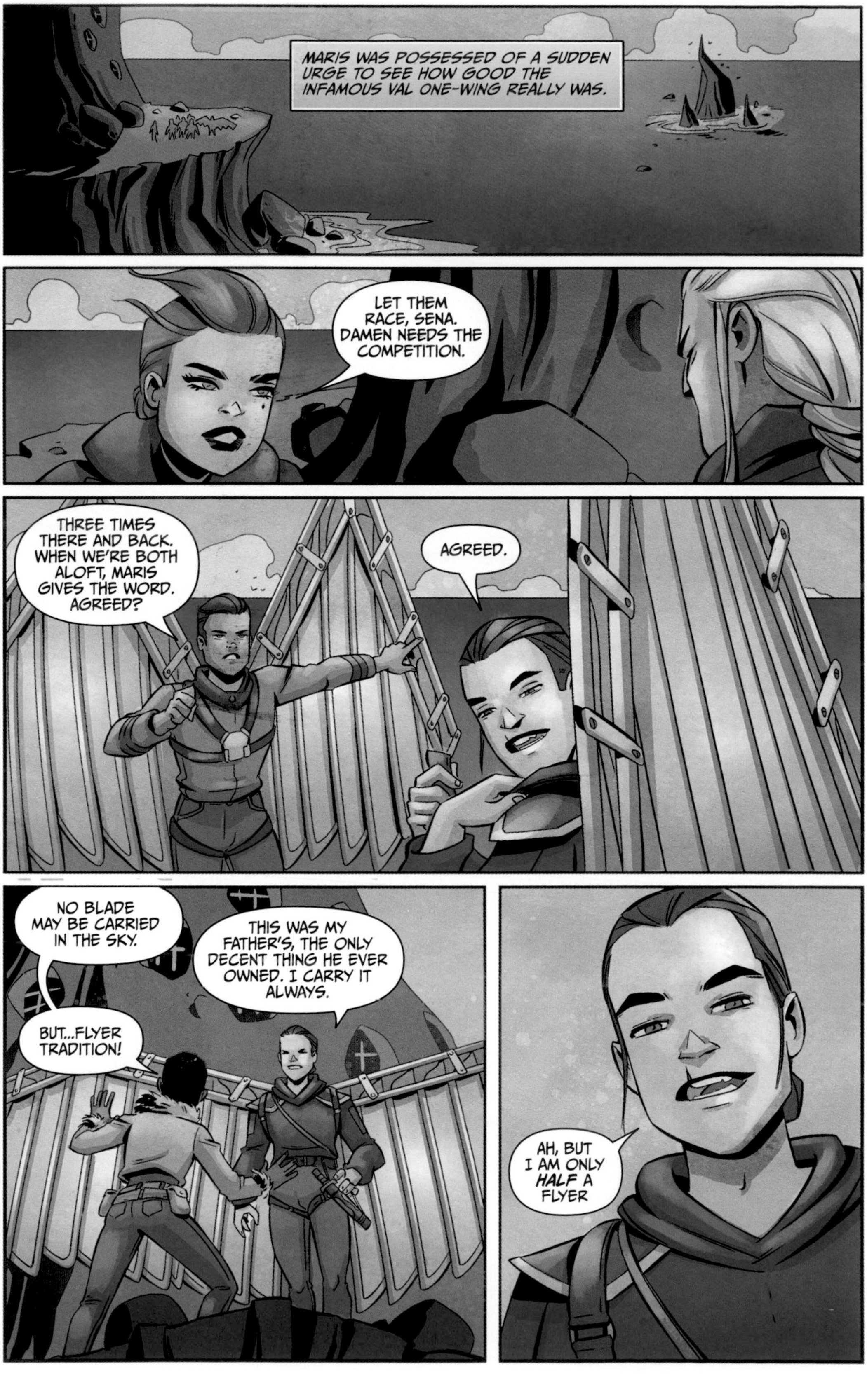
MARIS WAS POSSESSED OF A SUDDEN URGE TO SEE HOW GOOD THE INFAMOUS VAL ONE-WING REALLY WAS.
LET THEM RACE, SENA. DAMEN NEEDS THE COMPETITION.
THREE TIMES THERE AND BACK. WHEN WE'RE BOTH ALOFT, MARIS GIVES THE WORD. AGREED?
AGREED.
NO BLADE MAY BE CARRIED IN THE SKY.
BUT...FLYER TRADITION!
THIS WAS MY FATHER'S, THE ONLY DECENT THING HE EVER OWNED. I CARRY IT ALWAYS.
AH, BUT I AM ONLY *HALF* A FLYER

DAMEN REACHED THE ROCKS WELL AHEAD OF VAL. BUT FALTERED AS HE CAME AROUND AND SEEMED LESS STEADY COMING BACK.

DAMEN'S BEATING HIM!

VAL HAS WON IT.

WHAT? NO, LOOK, MARIS, DAMEN IS WELL AHEAD!

DAMEN IS JUST RIDING THE WINDS. VAL IS USING THEM.

HE WAS SEARCHING FOR THE RIGHT WIND, AND NOW HE'S FOUND IT. WATCH.

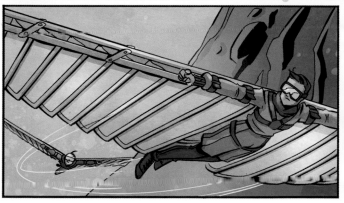

I WON'T STAY TO CONGRATULATE HIM.

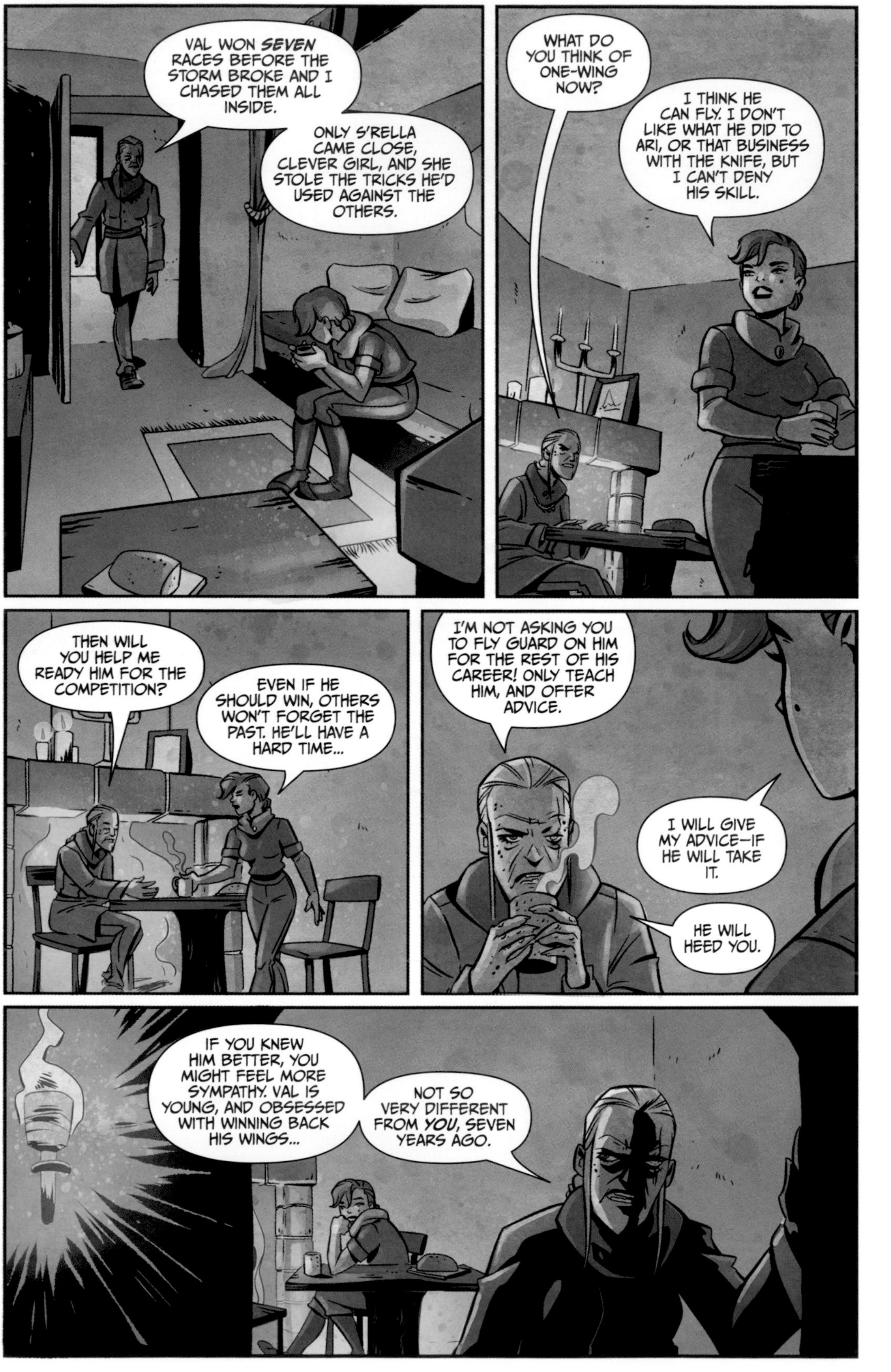
VAL WON *SEVEN* RACES BEFORE THE STORM BROKE AND I CHASED THEM ALL INSIDE.
ONLY S'RELLA CAME CLOSE, CLEVER GIRL, AND SHE STOLE THE TRICKS HE'D USED AGAINST THE OTHERS.
WHAT DO YOU THINK OF ONE-WING NOW?
I THINK HE CAN FLY. I DON'T LIKE WHAT HE DID TO ARI, OR THAT BUSINESS WITH THE KNIFE, BUT I CAN'T DENY HIS SKILL.
THEN WILL YOU HELP ME READY HIM FOR THE COMPETITION?
EVEN IF HE SHOULD WIN, OTHERS WON'T FORGET THE PAST. HE'LL HAVE A HARD TIME...
I'M NOT ASKING YOU TO FLY GUARD ON HIM FOR THE REST OF HIS CAREER! ONLY TEACH HIM, AND OFFER ADVICE.
I WILL GIVE MY ADVICE—IF HE WILL TAKE IT.
HE WILL HEED YOU.
IF YOU KNEW HIM BETTER, YOU MIGHT FEEL MORE SYMPATHY. VAL IS YOUNG, AND OBSESSED WITH WINNING BACK HIS WINGS...
NOT SO VERY DIFFERENT FROM *YOU*, SEVEN YEARS AGO.

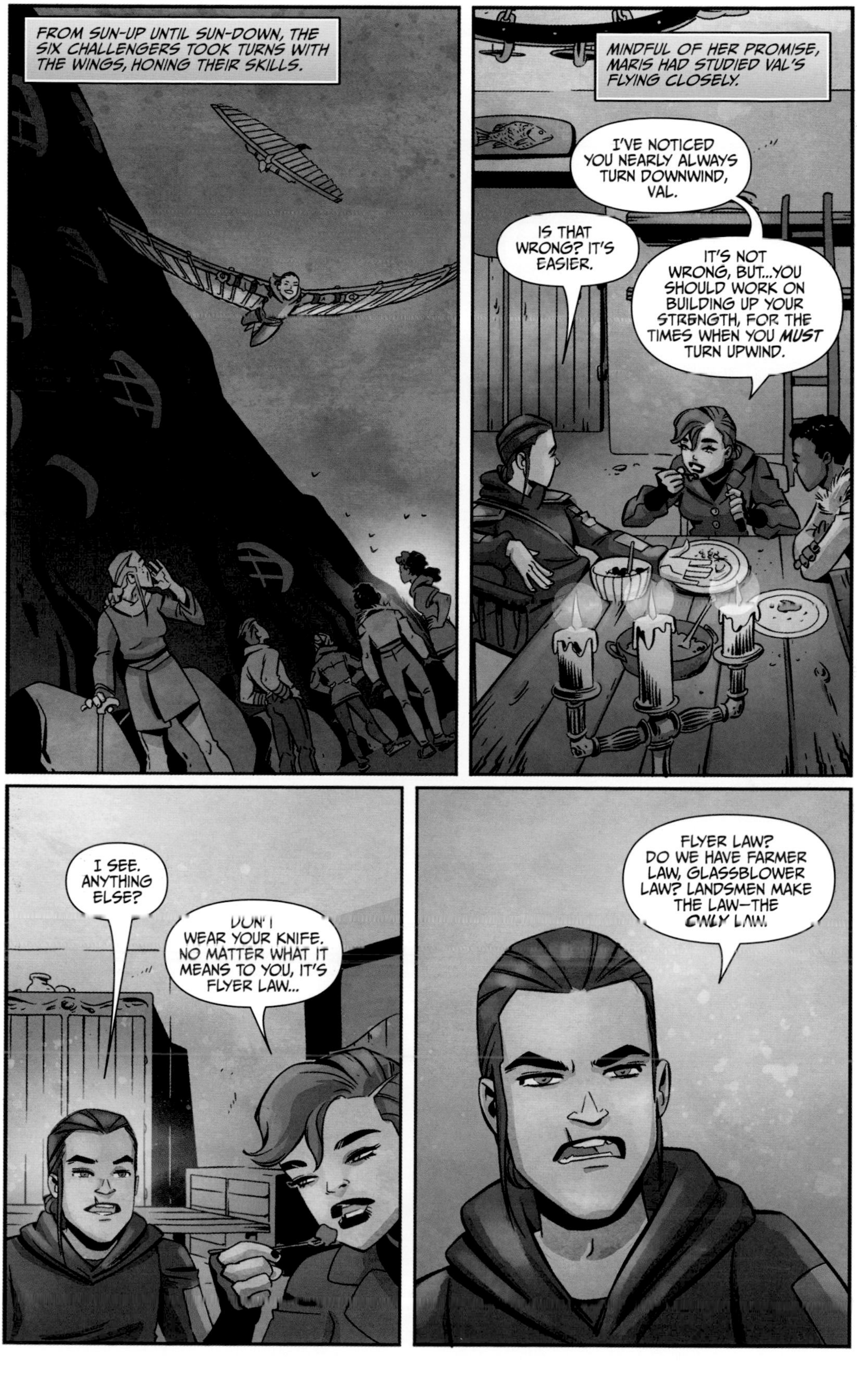
FROM SUN-UP UNTIL SUN-DOWN, THE SIX CHALLENGERS TOOK TURNS WITH THE WINGS, HONING THEIR SKILLS.
MINDFUL OF HER PROMISE, MARIS HAD STUDIED VAL'S FLYING CLOSELY.
I'VE NOTICED YOU NEARLY ALWAYS TURN DOWNWIND, VAL.
IS THAT WRONG? IT'S EASIER.
IT'S NOT WRONG, BUT...YOU SHOULD WORK ON BUILDING UP YOUR STRENGTH, FOR THE TIMES WHEN YOU **MUST** TURN UPWIND.
I SEE. ANYTHING ELSE?
DON'T WEAR YOUR KNIFE. NO MATTER WHAT IT MEANS TO YOU, IT'S FLYER LAW...
FLYER LAW? DO WE HAVE FARMER LAW, GLASSBLOWER LAW? LANDSMEN MAKE THE LAW—THE **ONLY** LAW.

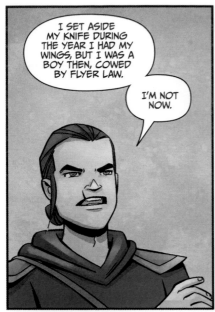

I SET ASIDE MY KNIFE DURING THE YEAR I HAD MY WINGS, BUT I WAS A BOY THEN, COWED BY FLYER LAW.

I'M NOT NOW.

BUT, VAL, IF YOU'RE GOING TO BE A FLYER—

I NEVER SAID I WAS GOING TO BE A FLYER. ONLY THAT I INTEND TO WIN WINGS AND FLY.

AND DON'T FORGET YOUR BIRTH, S'RELLA. EVEN IF YOU WIN, YOU ARE NOT GOING TO BE A FLYER EITHER.

YOU'LL ALWAYS BE CONSIDERED HALF A FLYER, LIKE ME.

A ONE-WING.

THAT'S NOT TRUE! I WAS NOT BORN OF FLYERS, BUT THEY'VE ACCEPTED ME!

HAVE THEY?

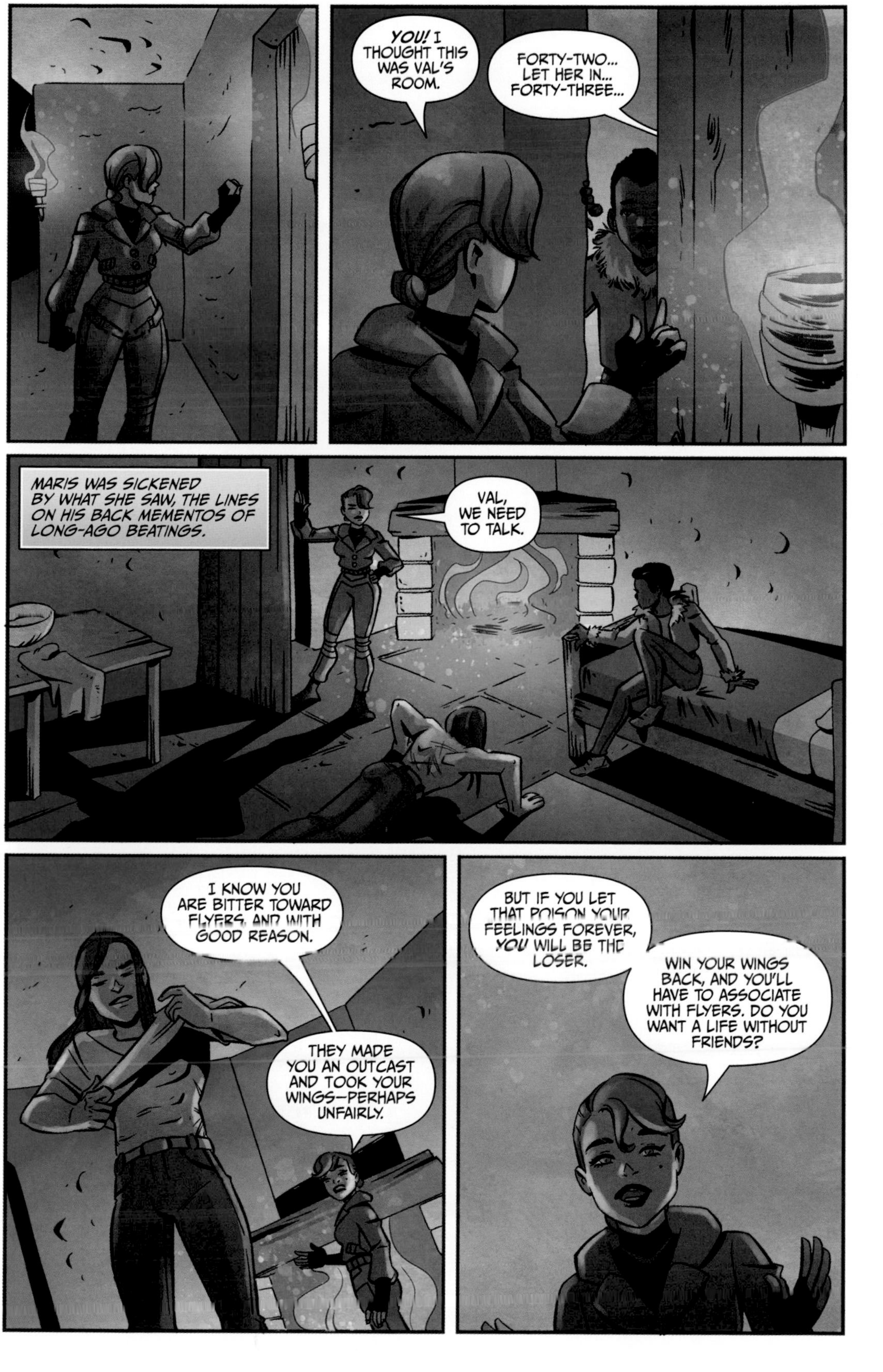
YOU! I THOUGHT THIS WAS VAL'S ROOM.
FORTY-TWO... LET HER IN... FORTY-THREE...
MARIS WAS SICKENED BY WHAT SHE SAW, THE LINES ON HIS BACK MEMENTOS OF LONG-AGO BEATINGS.
VAL, WE NEED TO TALK.
I KNOW YOU ARE BITTER TOWARD FLYERS, AND WITH GOOD REASON.
THEY MADE YOU AN OUTCAST AND TOOK YOUR WINGS—PERHAPS UNFAIRLY.
BUT IF YOU LET THAT POISON YOUR FEELINGS FOREVER, YOU WILL BE THE LOSER.
WIN YOUR WINGS BACK, AND YOU'LL HAVE TO ASSOCIATE WITH FLYERS. DO YOU WANT A LIFE WITHOUT FRIENDS?

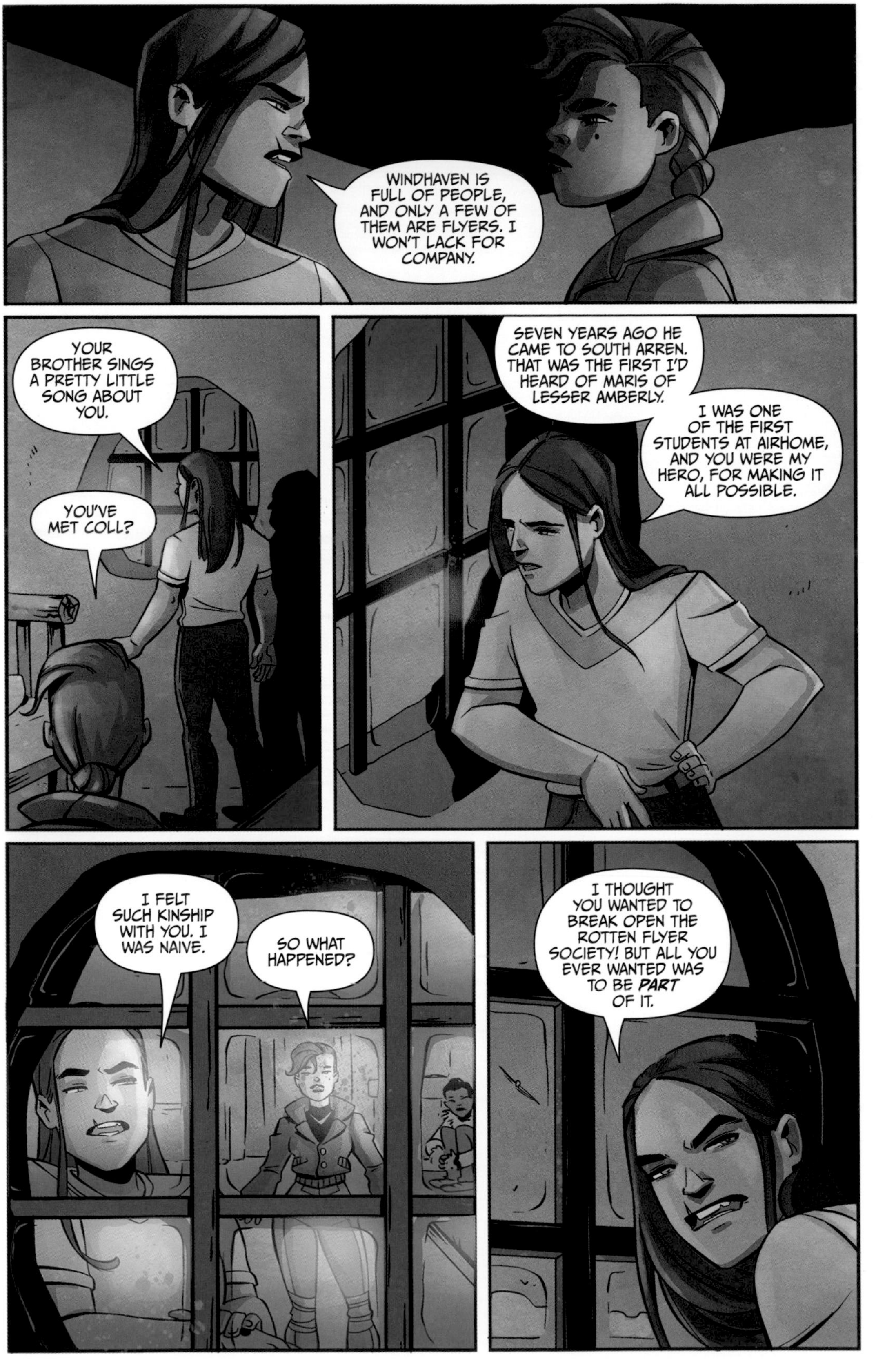
WINDHAVEN IS FULL OF PEOPLE, AND ONLY A FEW OF THEM ARE FLYERS. I WON'T LACK FOR COMPANY.
YOUR BROTHER SINGS A PRETTY LITTLE SONG ABOUT YOU.
YOU'VE MET COLL?
SEVEN YEARS AGO HE CAME TO SOUTH ARREN. THAT WAS THE FIRST I'D HEARD OF MARIS OF LESSER AMBERLY.
I WAS ONE OF THE FIRST STUDENTS AT AIRHOME, AND YOU WERE MY HERO, FOR MAKING IT ALL POSSIBLE.
I FELT SUCH KINSHIP WITH YOU. I WAS NAIVE.
SO WHAT HAPPENED?
I THOUGHT YOU WANTED TO BREAK OPEN THE ROTTEN FLYER SOCIETY! BUT ALL YOU EVER WANTED WAS TO BE *PART* OF IT.

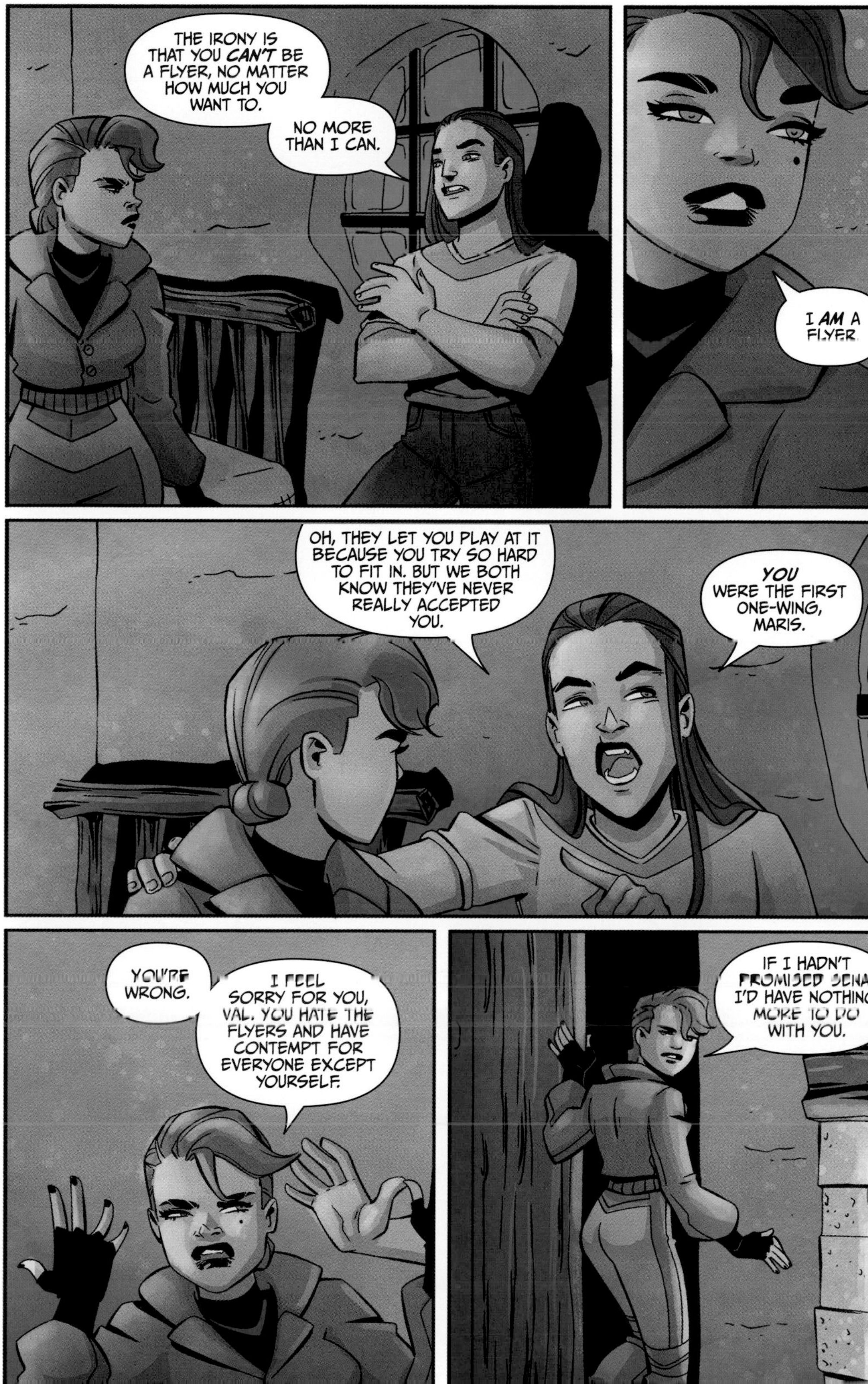
THE IRONY IS THAT YOU CAN'T BE A FLYER, NO MATTER HOW MUCH YOU WANT TO.
NO MORE THAN I CAN.
I AM A FLYER.
OH, THEY LET YOU PLAY AT IT BECAUSE YOU TRY SO HARD TO FIT IN. BUT WE BOTH KNOW THEY'VE NEVER REALLY ACCEPTED YOU.
YOU WERE THE FIRST ONE-WING, MARIS.
YOU'RE WRONG.
I FEEL SORRY FOR YOU, VAL. YOU HATE THE FLYERS AND HAVE CONTEMPT FOR EVERYONE EXCEPT YOURSELF.
IF I HADN'T PROMISED SENA, I'D HAVE NOTHING MORE TO DO WITH YOU.

AT THE END OF EVERY DAY OF TRAINING, MARIS RACED EACH STUDENT INDIVIDUALLY.

ONE DAY THE WEATHER CHANGED, WITH ICY WINDS FROM THE NORTH.

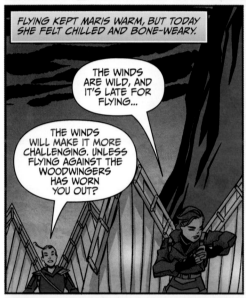

FLYING KEPT MARIS WARM, BUT TODAY SHE FELT CHILLED AND BONE-WEARY.

THE WINDS ARE WILD, AND IT'S LATE FOR FLYING...

THE WINDS WILL MAKE IT MORE CHALLENGING. UNLESS FLYING AGAINST THE WOODWINGERS HAS WORN YOU OUT?

I ONCE FLEW THIRTY HOURS WITHOUT A REST. AN AFTERNOON OF PLAY DOESN'T WEAR ME OUT.

WHEN SHE SAW HIS MOCKING SMILE, SHE KNEW SHE HAD FALLEN INTO HIS TRAP.

THE USUAL? THREE TIMES OUT AND BACK?

WHO WILL JUDGE US?

WE'LL KNOW. THAT'S ALL THAT MATTERS.

A SHOCK COURSED THROUGH HER AS VAL IMMEDIATELY SURGED AHEAD. FLYING AGAINST THE WOODWINGERS HAD MADE HER SOFT.

DETERMINED TO OVERTAKE HIM, SHE FLEW DANGEROUSLY CLOSE ON HER SECOND PASS, AND HER WINGTIP GRAZED THE SPIRE.

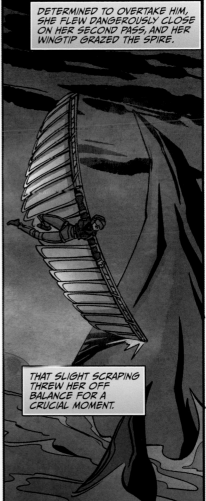

THAT SLIGHT SCRAPING THREW HER OFF BALANCE FOR A CRUCIAL MOMENT.

THE WINDS STALLED HER WITH UNPREDICTABLE GUSTS, SEEMING TO FAVOR VAL.

SEEING HIM GLIDING SO HIGH ABOVE, SHE KNEW SHE HAD LOST THE RACE.

I WON'T TELL ANYONE.

I DON'T CARE WHAT YOU SAY—

YOU HAD BEEN FLYING ALL DAY. WE BOTH KNOW I COULD NEVER HAVE BEATEN YOU IF WE WERE BOTH FRESH.

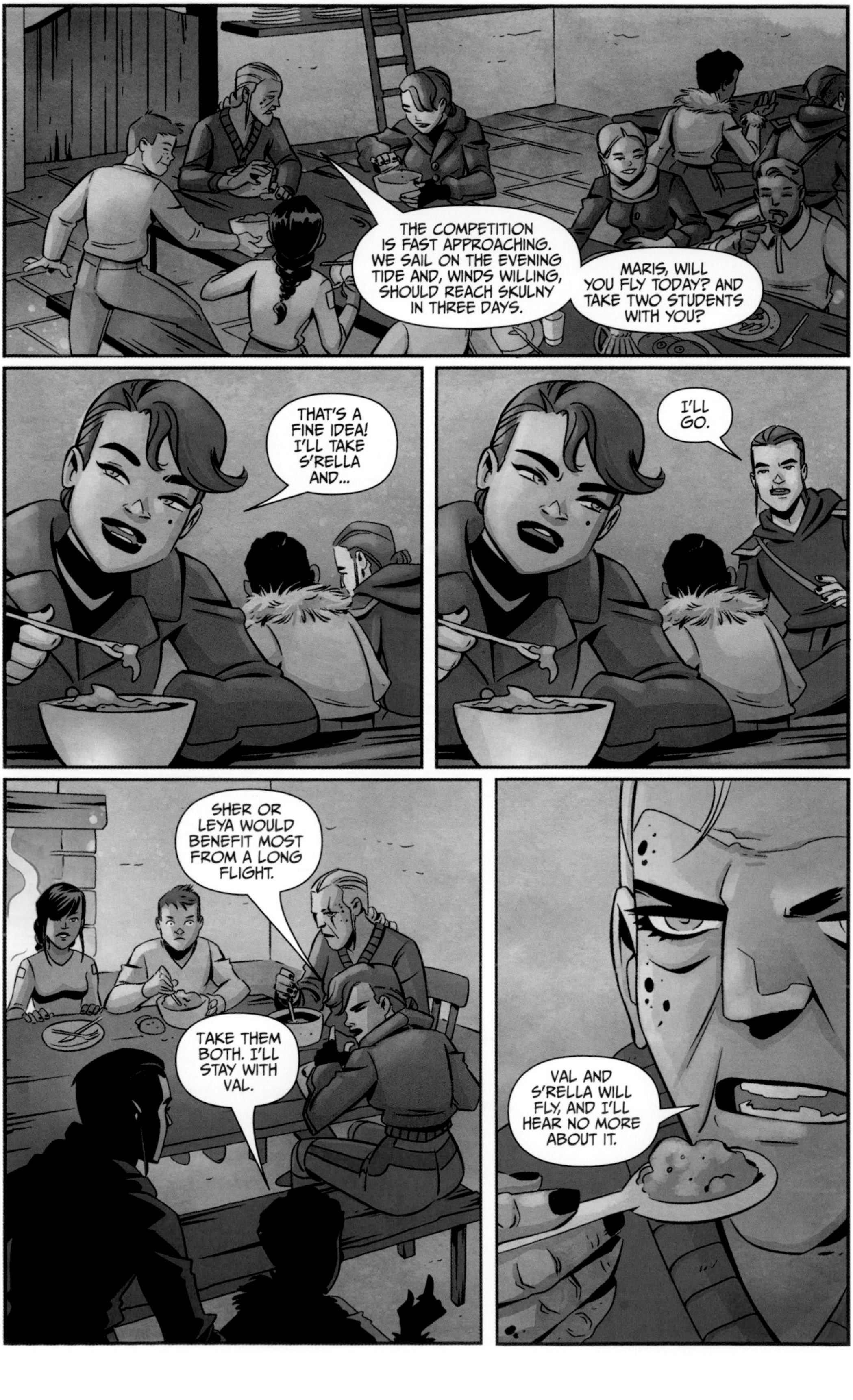
THE COMPETITION IS FAST APPROACHING. WE SAIL ON THE EVENING TIDE AND, WINDS WILLING, SHOULD REACH SKULNY IN THREE DAYS.
MARIS, WILL YOU FLY TODAY? AND TAKE TWO STUDENTS WITH YOU?
THAT'S A FINE IDEA! I'LL TAKE S'RELLA AND...
I'LL GO.
SHER OR LEYA WOULD BENEFIT MOST FROM A LONG FLIGHT.
TAKE THEM BOTH. I'LL STAY WITH VAL.
VAL AND S'RELLA WILL FLY, AND I'LL HEAR NO MORE ABOUT IT.

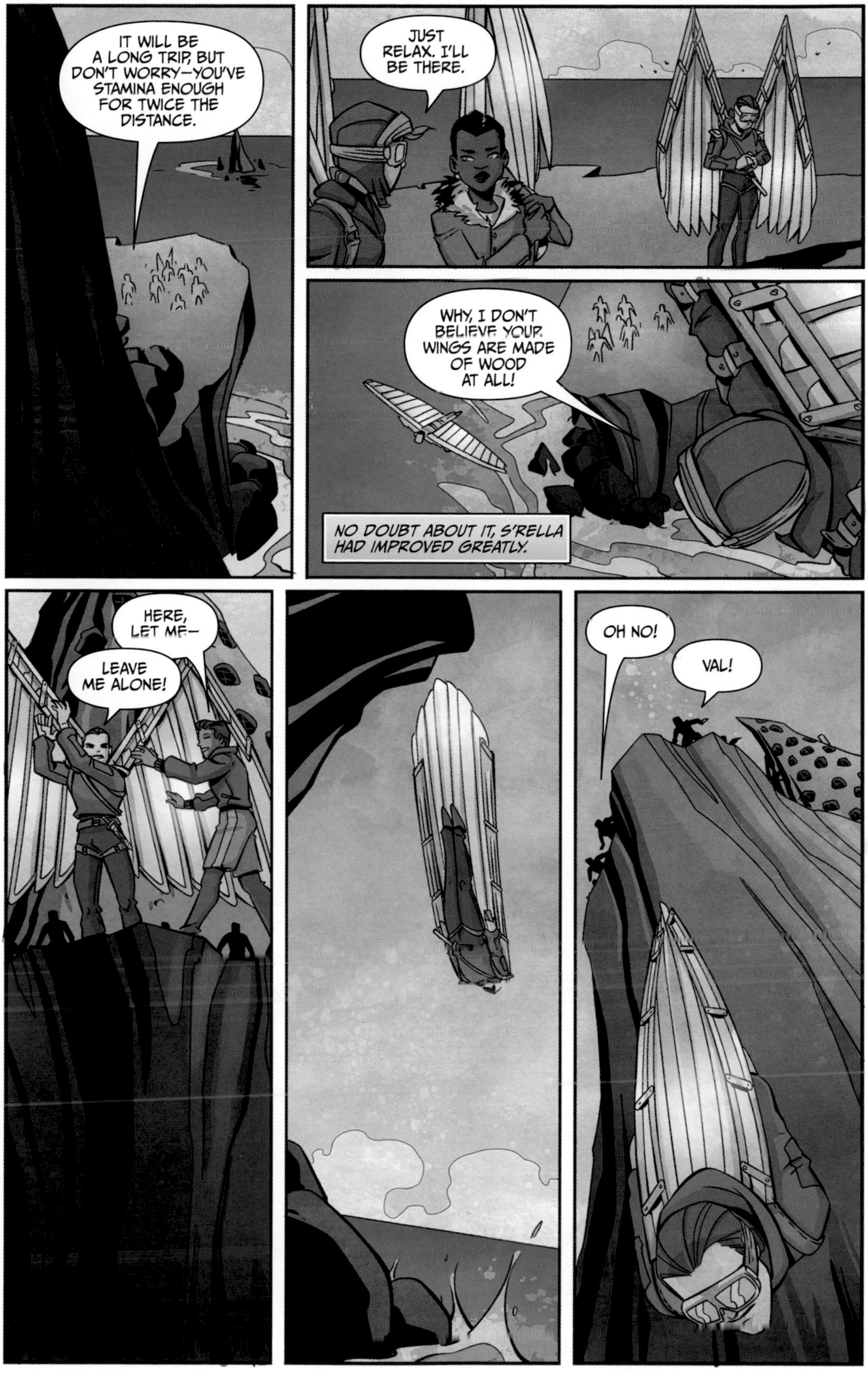
IT WILL BE A LONG TRIP, BUT DON'T WORRY—YOU'VE STAMINA ENOUGH FOR TWICE THE DISTANCE.
JUST RELAX. I'LL BE THERE.
WHY, I DON'T BELIEVE YOUR WINGS ARE MADE OF WOOD AT ALL!
NO DOUBT ABOUT IT, S'RELLA HAD IMPROVED GREATLY.
HERE, LET ME—
LEAVE ME ALONE!
OH NO!
VAL!

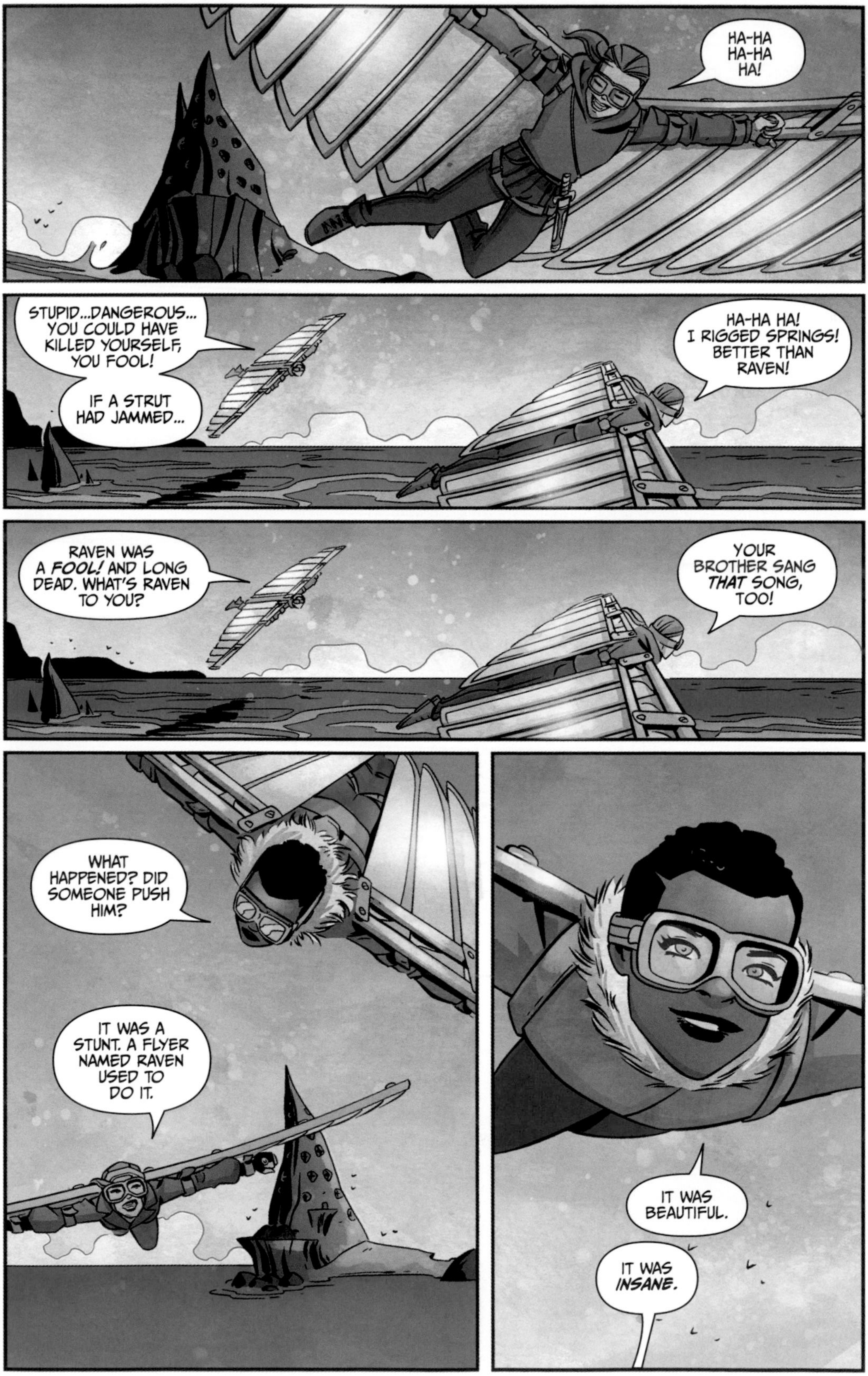
HA-HA HA-HA HA!
STUPID...DANGEROUS... YOU COULD HAVE KILLED YOURSELF, YOU FOOL!
IF A STRUT HAD JAMMED...
HA-HA HA! I RIGGED SPRINGS! BETTER THAN RAVEN!
RAVEN WAS A FOOL! AND LONG DEAD. WHAT'S RAVEN TO YOU?
YOUR BROTHER SANG THAT SONG, TOO!
WHAT HAPPENED? DID SOMEONE PUSH HIM?
IT WAS A STUNT. A FLYER NAMED RAVEN USED TO DO IT.
IT WAS BEAUTIFUL.
IT WAS INSANE.

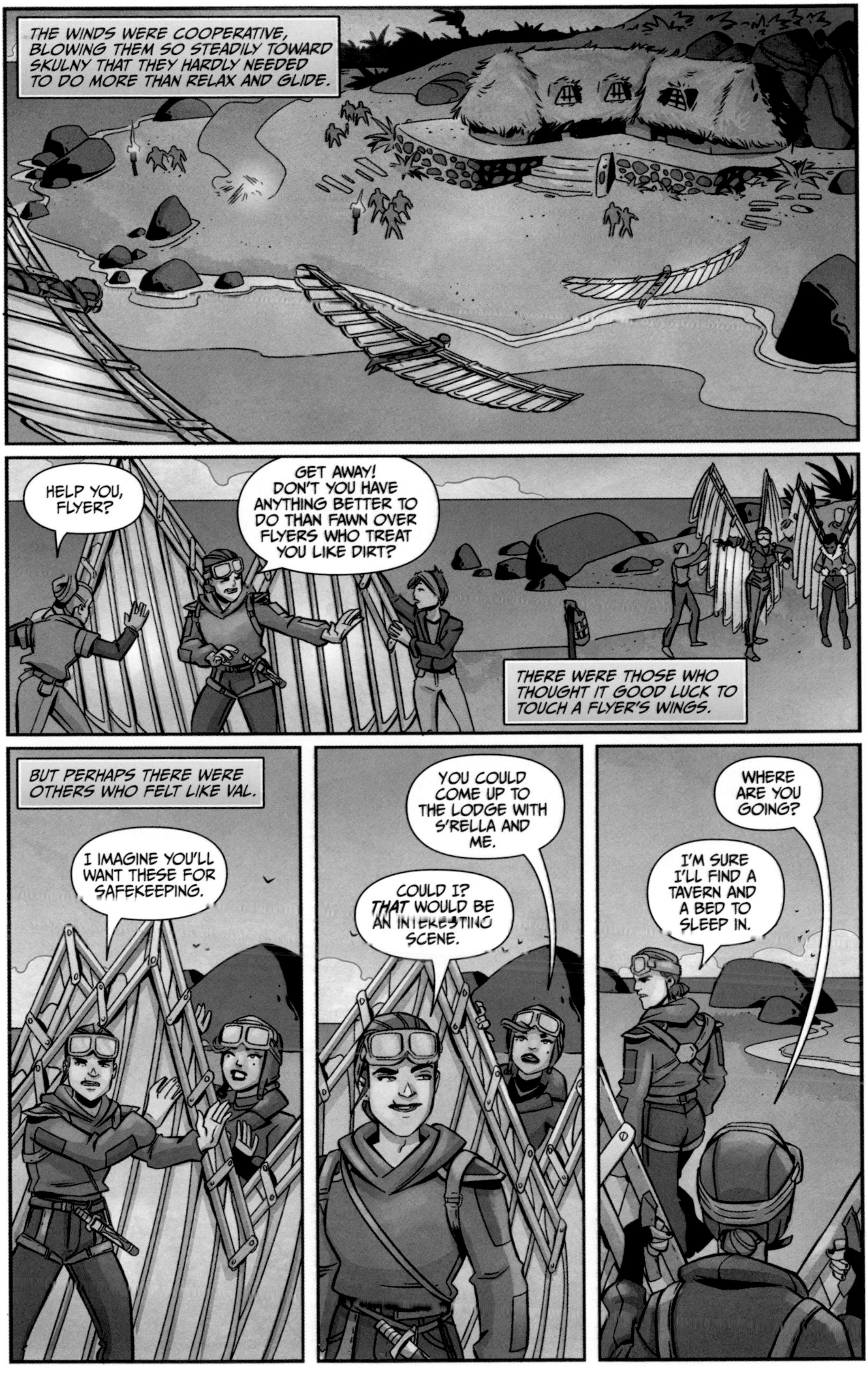

THE WINDS WERE COOPERATIVE, BLOWING THEM SO STEADILY TOWARD SKULNY THAT THEY HARDLY NEEDED TO DO MORE THAN RELAX AND GLIDE.
HELP YOU, FLYER?
GET AWAY! DON'T YOU HAVE ANYTHING BETTER TO DO THAN FAWN OVER FLYERS WHO TREAT YOU LIKE DIRT?
THERE WERE THOSE WHO THOUGHT IT GOOD LUCK TO TOUCH A FLYER'S WINGS.
BUT PERHAPS THERE WERE OTHERS WHO FELT LIKE VAL.
I IMAGINE YOU'LL WANT THESE FOR SAFEKEEPING.
YOU COULD COME UP TO THE LODGE WITH S'RELLA AND ME.
COULD I? *THAT* WOULD BE AN INTERESTING SCENE.
WHERE ARE YOU GOING?
I'M SURE I'LL FIND A TAVERN AND A BED TO SLEEP IN.

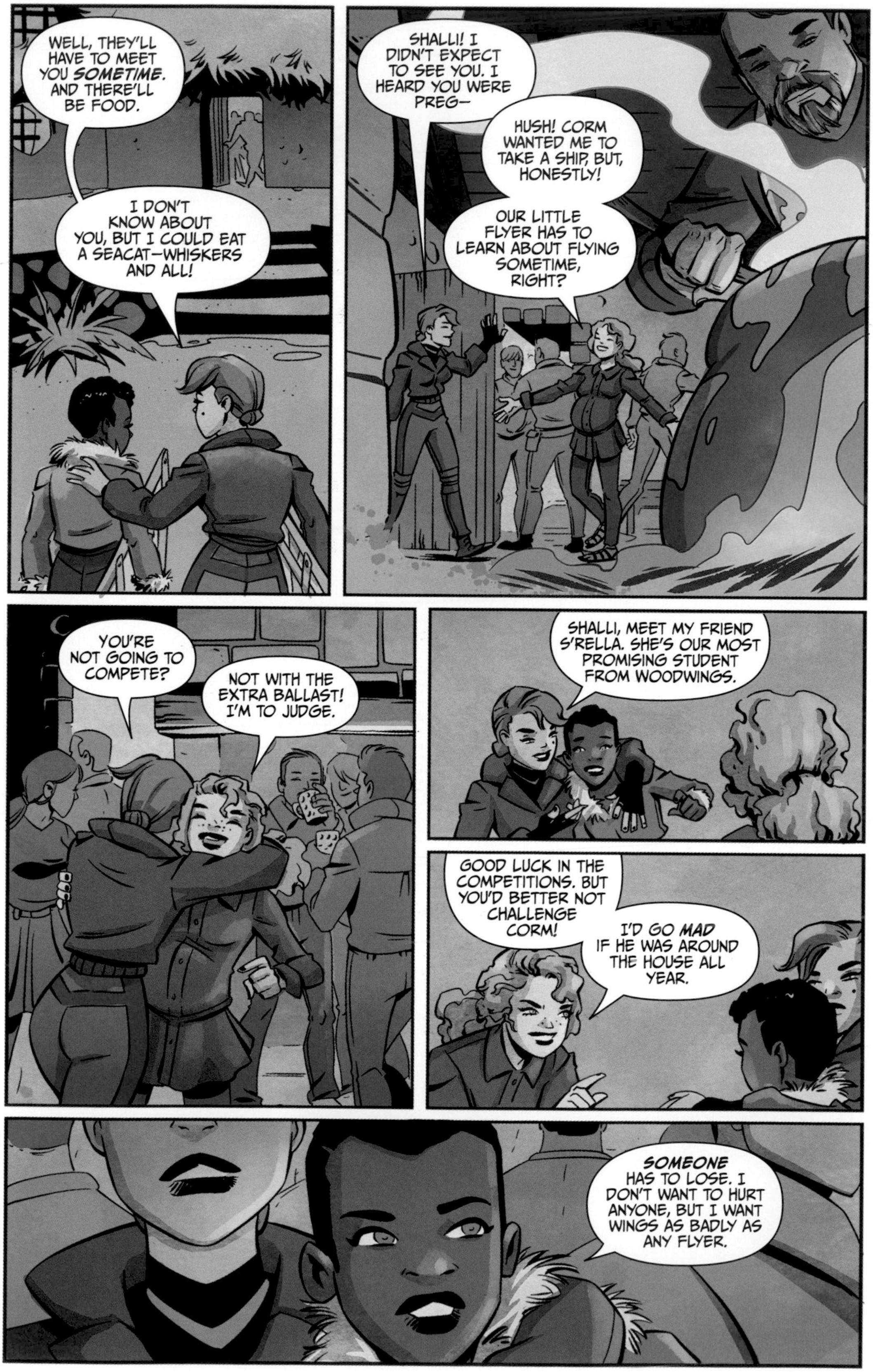
WELL, THEY'LL HAVE TO MEET YOU *SOMETIME*. AND THERE'LL BE FOOD.
I DON'T KNOW ABOUT YOU, BUT I COULD EAT A SEACAT—WHISKERS AND ALL!
SHALLI! I DIDN'T EXPECT TO SEE YOU. I HEARD YOU WERE PREG—
HUSH! CORM WANTED ME TO TAKE A SHIP, BUT, HONESTLY!
OUR LITTLE FLYER HAS TO LEARN ABOUT FLYING SOMETIME, RIGHT?
YOU'RE NOT GOING TO COMPETE?
NOT WITH THE EXTRA BALLAST! I'M TO JUDGE.
SHALLI, MEET MY FRIEND S'RELLA. SHE'S OUR MOST PROMISING STUDENT FROM WOODWINGS.
GOOD LUCK IN THE COMPETITIONS. BUT YOU'D BETTER NOT CHALLENGE CORM!
I'D GO *MAD* IF HE WAS AROUND THE HOUSE ALL YEAR.
SOMEONE HAS TO LOSE. I DON'T WANT TO HURT ANYONE, BUT I WANT WINGS AS BADLY AS ANY FLYER.

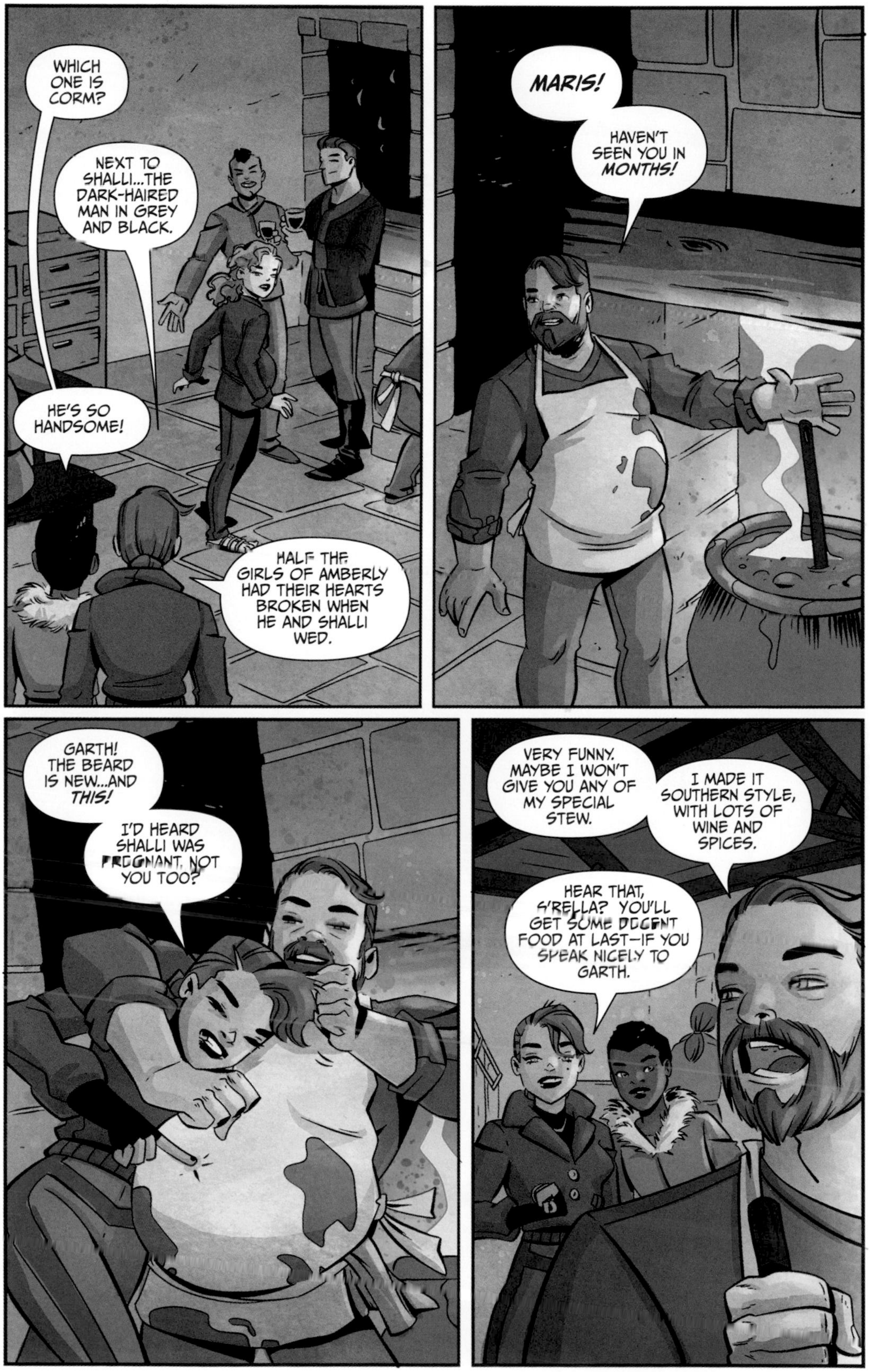
WHICH ONE IS CORM?
NEXT TO SHALLI...THE DARK-HAIRED MAN IN GREY AND BLACK.
HE'S SO HANDSOME!
HALF THE GIRLS OF AMBERLY HAD THEIR HEARTS BROKEN WHEN HE AND SHALLI WED.
MARIS!
HAVEN'T SEEN YOU IN *MONTHS!*
GARTH! THE BEARD IS NEW...AND *THIS!*
I'D HEARD SHALLI WAS PREGNANT, NOT YOU TOO?
VERY FUNNY. MAYBE I WON'T GIVE YOU ANY OF MY SPECIAL STEW.
I MADE IT SOUTHERN STYLE, WITH LOTS OF WINE AND SPICES.
HEAR THAT, S'RELLA? YOU'LL GET SOME DECENT FOOD AT LAST—IF YOU SPEAK NICELY TO GARTH.

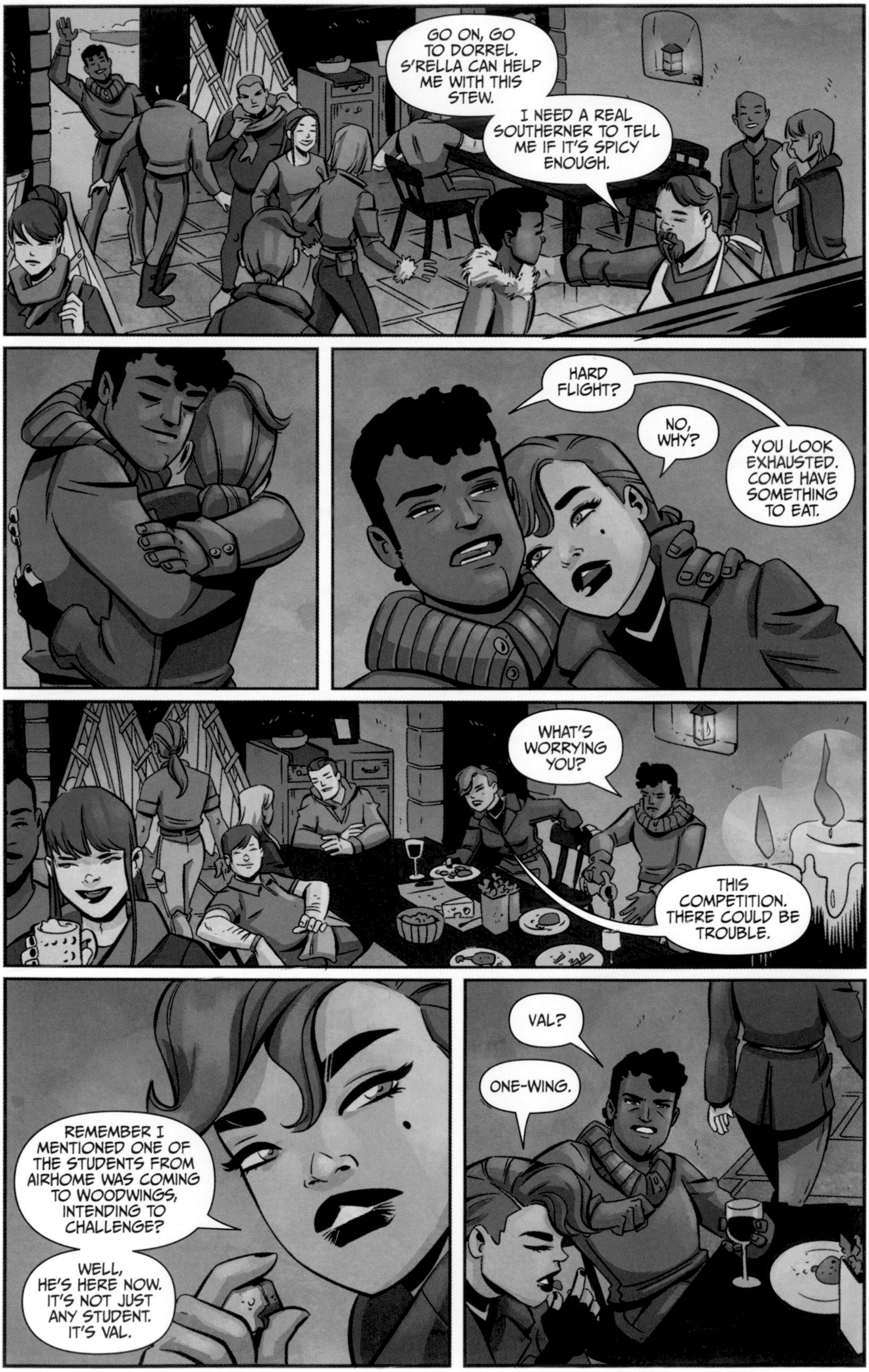
GO ON, GO TO DORREL. S'RELLA CAN HELP ME WITH THIS STEW.
I NEED A REAL SOUTHERNER TO TELL ME IF IT'S SPICY ENOUGH.
HARD FLIGHT?
NO, WHY?
YOU LOOK EXHAUSTED. COME HAVE SOMETHING TO EAT.
WHAT'S WORRYING YOU?
THIS COMPETITION. THERE COULD BE TROUBLE.
REMEMBER I MENTIONED ONE OF THE STUDENTS FROM AIRHOME WAS COMING TO WOODWINGS, INTENDING TO CHALLENGE?
WELL, HE'S HERE NOW. IT'S NOT JUST ANY STUDENT. IT'S VAL.
VAL?
ONE-WING.

ONE-WING? I NEVER EXPECTED HIM TO TRY AGAIN. DOES HE EXPECT TO BE WELCOMED?

HE KNOWS BETTER. AND HIS OPINION OF FLYERS IS JUST AS LOW...

WELL, I DON'T IMAGINE HE'LL WIN. NO ONE HAS LOST A RELATIVE LATELY.

ALTHOUGH THE GIBE WAS NO DIFFERENT FROM WHAT SHE HAD SAID THE DAY VAL ARRIVED AT THE ACADEMY, IT NOW STRUCK MARIS AS CRUEL.

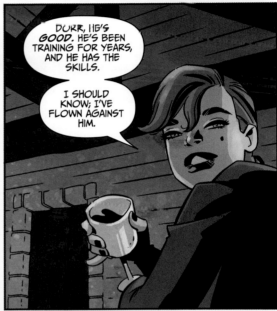

DORR, HE'S *GOOD.* HE'S BEEN TRAINING FOR YEARS, AND HE HAS THE SKILLS.

I SHOULD KNOW; I'VE FLOWN AGAINST HIM.

FLOWN AGAINST...

PLEASE DON'T TELL ME YOU'VE BEEN *HELPING* HIM?

HE WAS A STUDENT. SENA ASKED ME TO WORK WITH HIM.

COME OUTSIDE. WE CAN'T TALK ABOUT THIS WHERE ANYONE MIGHT OVERHEAR.

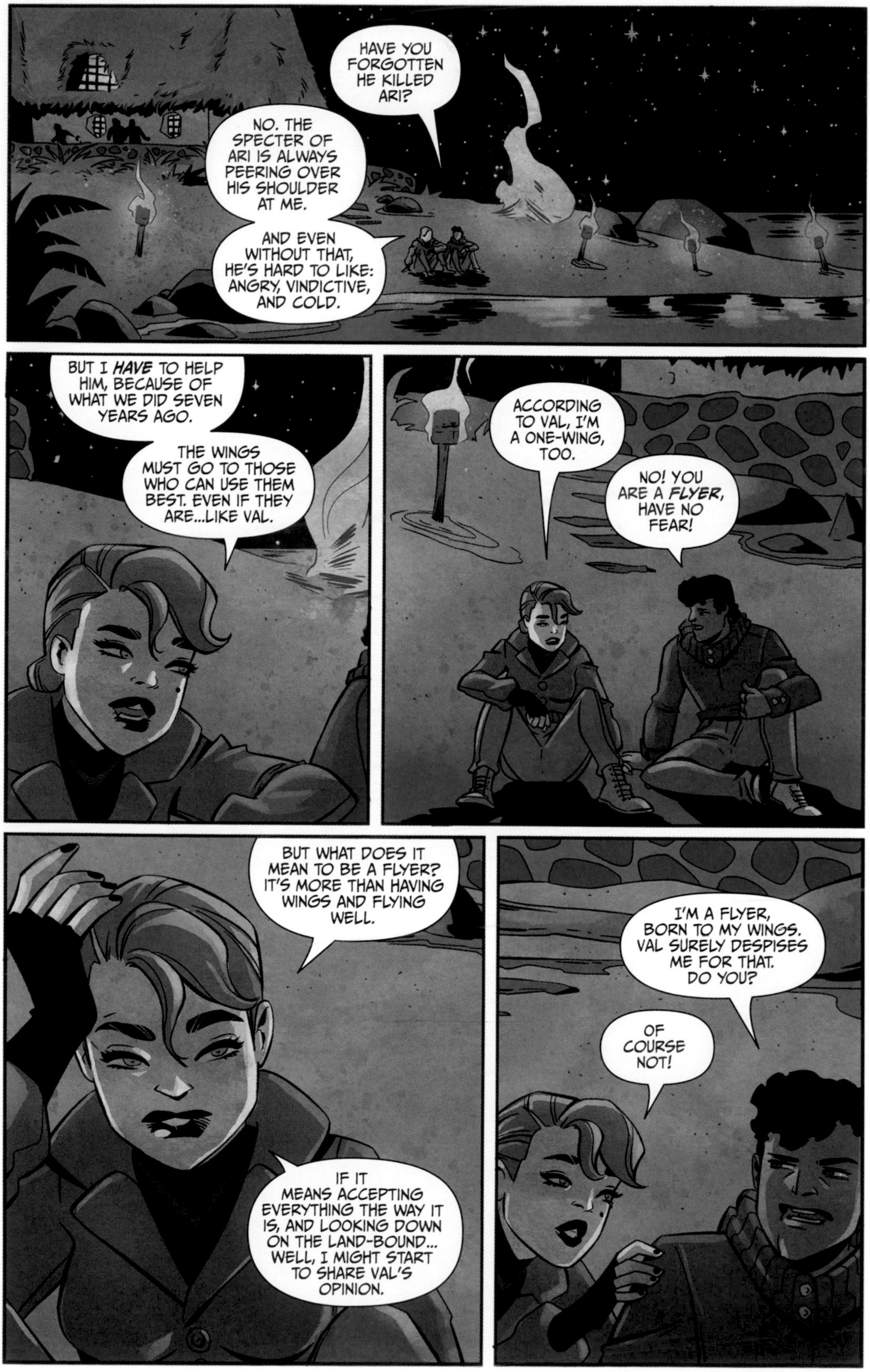
HAVE YOU FORGOTTEN HE KILLED ARI?
NO. THE SPECTER OF ARI IS ALWAYS PEERING OVER HIS SHOULDER AT ME.
AND EVEN WITHOUT THAT, HE'S HARD TO LIKE: ANGRY, VINDICTIVE, AND COLD.
BUT I *HAVE* TO HELP HIM, BECAUSE OF WHAT WE DID SEVEN YEARS AGO.
THE WINGS MUST GO TO THOSE WHO CAN USE THEM BEST. EVEN IF THEY ARE...LIKE VAL.
ACCORDING TO VAL, I'M A ONE-WING, TOO.
NO! YOU ARE A *FLYER*, HAVE NO FEAR!
BUT WHAT DOES IT MEAN TO BE A FLYER? IT'S MORE THAN HAVING WINGS AND FLYING WELL.
IF IT MEANS ACCEPTING EVERYTHING THE WAY IT IS, AND LOOKING DOWN ON THE LAND-BOUND... WELL, I MIGHT START TO SHARE VAL'S OPINION.
I'M A FLYER, BORN TO MY WINGS. VAL SURELY DESPISES ME FOR THAT. DO YOU?
OF COURSE NOT!

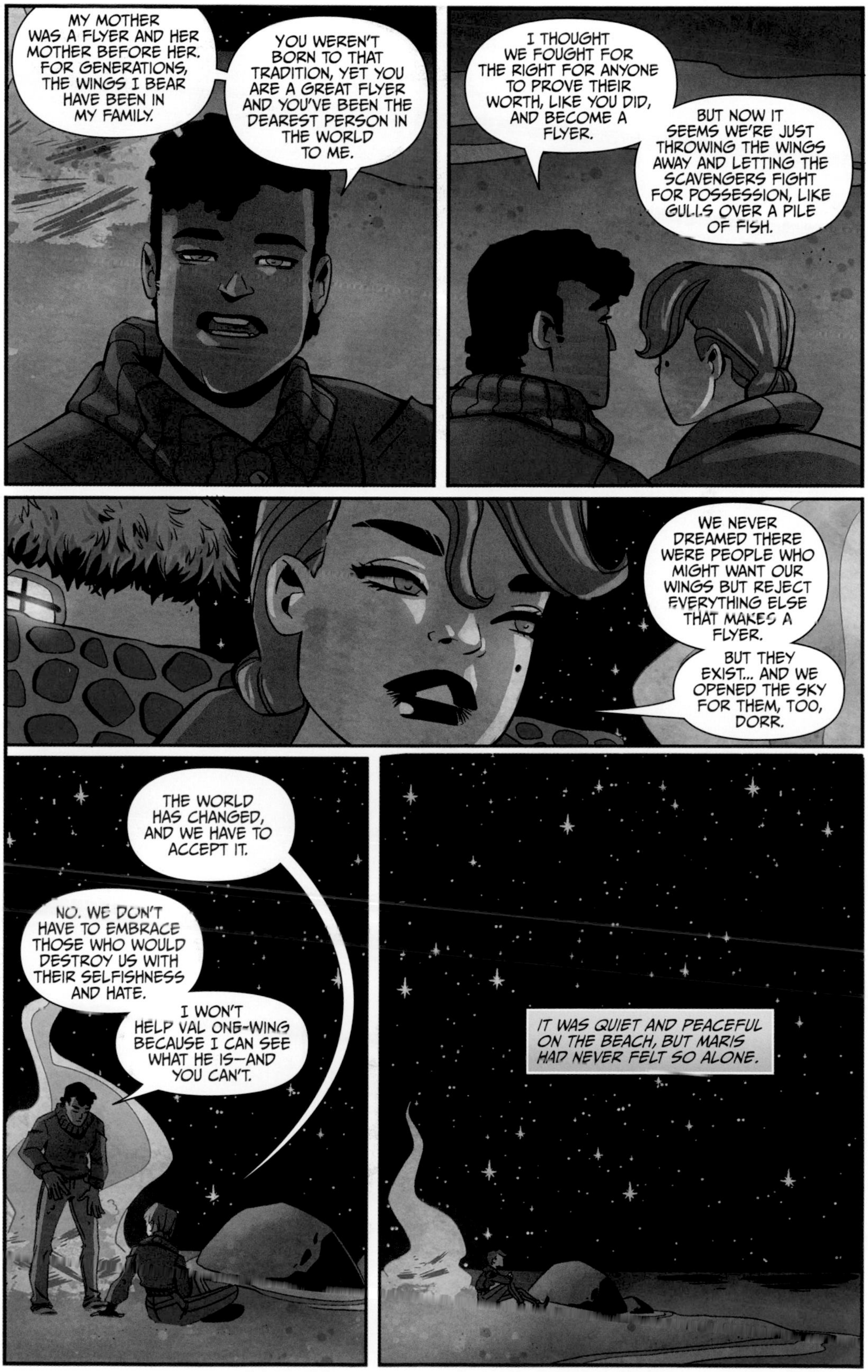
MY MOTHER WAS A FLYER AND HER MOTHER BEFORE HER. FOR GENERATIONS, THE WINGS I BEAR HAVE BEEN IN MY FAMILY.
YOU WEREN'T BORN TO THAT TRADITION, YET YOU ARE A GREAT FLYER AND YOU'VE BEEN THE DEAREST PERSON IN THE WORLD TO ME.
I THOUGHT WE FOUGHT FOR THE RIGHT FOR ANYONE TO PROVE THEIR WORTH, LIKE YOU DID, AND BECOME A FLYER.
BUT NOW IT SEEMS WE'RE JUST THROWING THE WINGS AWAY AND LETTING THE SCAVENGERS FIGHT FOR POSSESSION, LIKE GULLS OVER A PILE OF FISH.
WE NEVER DREAMED THERE WERE PEOPLE WHO MIGHT WANT OUR WINGS BUT REJECT EVERYTHING ELSE THAT MAKES A FLYER.
BUT THEY EXIST... AND WE OPENED THE SKY FOR THEM, TOO, DORR.
THE WORLD HAS CHANGED, AND WE HAVE TO ACCEPT IT.
NO. WE DON'T HAVE TO EMBRACE THOSE WHO WOULD DESTROY US WITH THEIR SELFISHNESS AND HATE.
I WON'T HELP VAL ONE-WING BECAUSE I CAN SEE WHAT HE IS—AND YOU CAN'T.
IT WAS QUIET AND PEACEFUL ON THE BEACH, BUT MARIS HAD NEVER FELT SO ALONE.

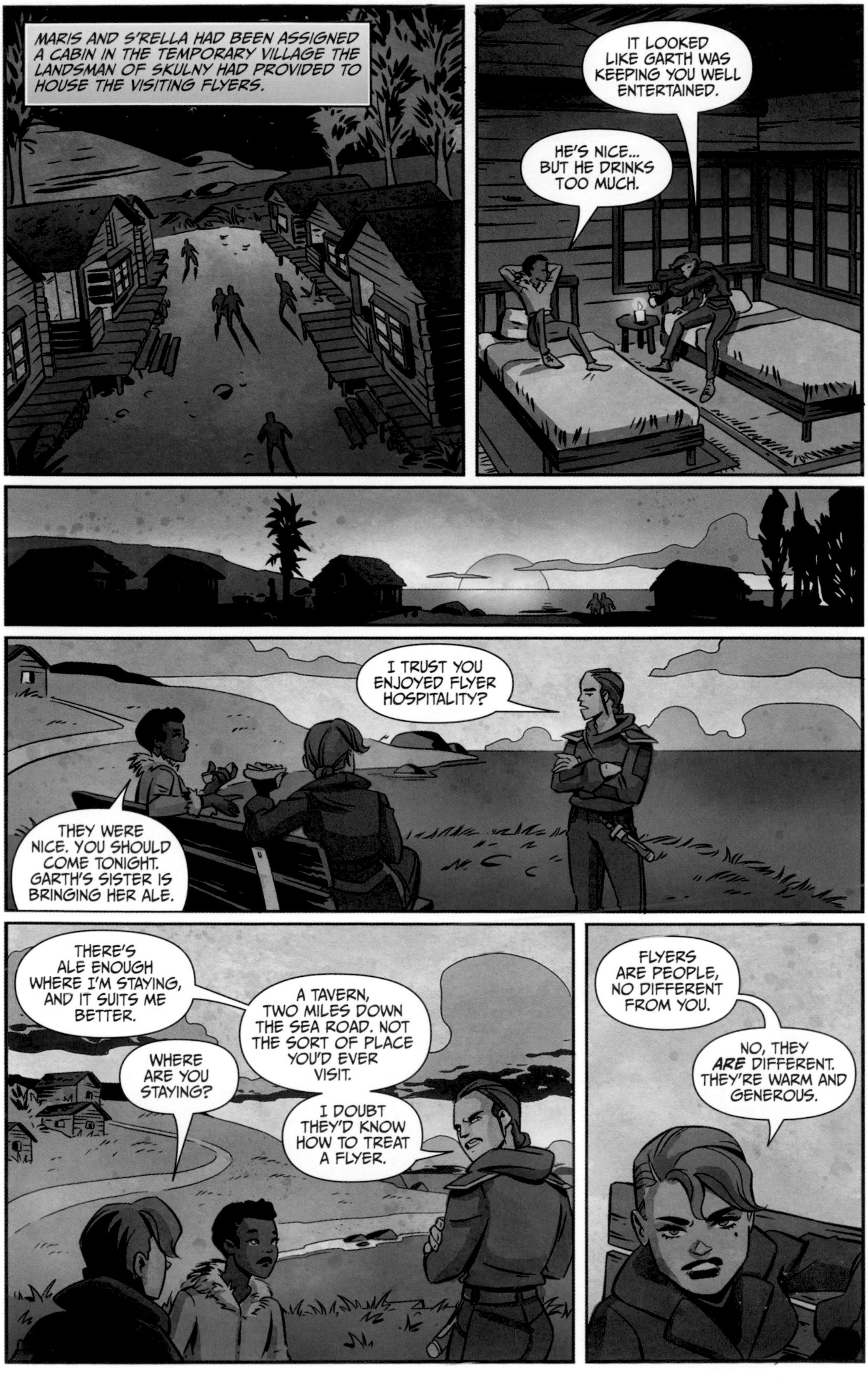
MARIS AND S'RELLA HAD BEEN ASSIGNED A CABIN IN THE TEMPORARY VILLAGE THE LANDSMAN OF SKULNY HAD PROVIDED TO HOUSE THE VISITING FLYERS.
IT LOOKED LIKE GARTH WAS KEEPING YOU WELL ENTERTAINED.
HE'S NICE... BUT HE DRINKS TOO MUCH.
I TRUST YOU ENJOYED FLYER HOSPITALITY?
THEY WERE NICE. YOU SHOULD COME TONIGHT. GARTH'S SISTER IS BRINGING HER ALE.
THERE'S ALE ENOUGH WHERE I'M STAYING, AND IT SUITS ME BETTER.
WHERE ARE YOU STAYING?
A TAVERN, TWO MILES DOWN THE SEA ROAD. NOT THE SORT OF PLACE YOU'D EVER VISIT.
I DOUBT THEY'D KNOW HOW TO TREAT A FLYER.
FLYERS ARE PEOPLE, NO DIFFERENT FROM YOU.
NO, THEY *ARE* DIFFERENT. THEY'RE WARM AND GENEROUS.

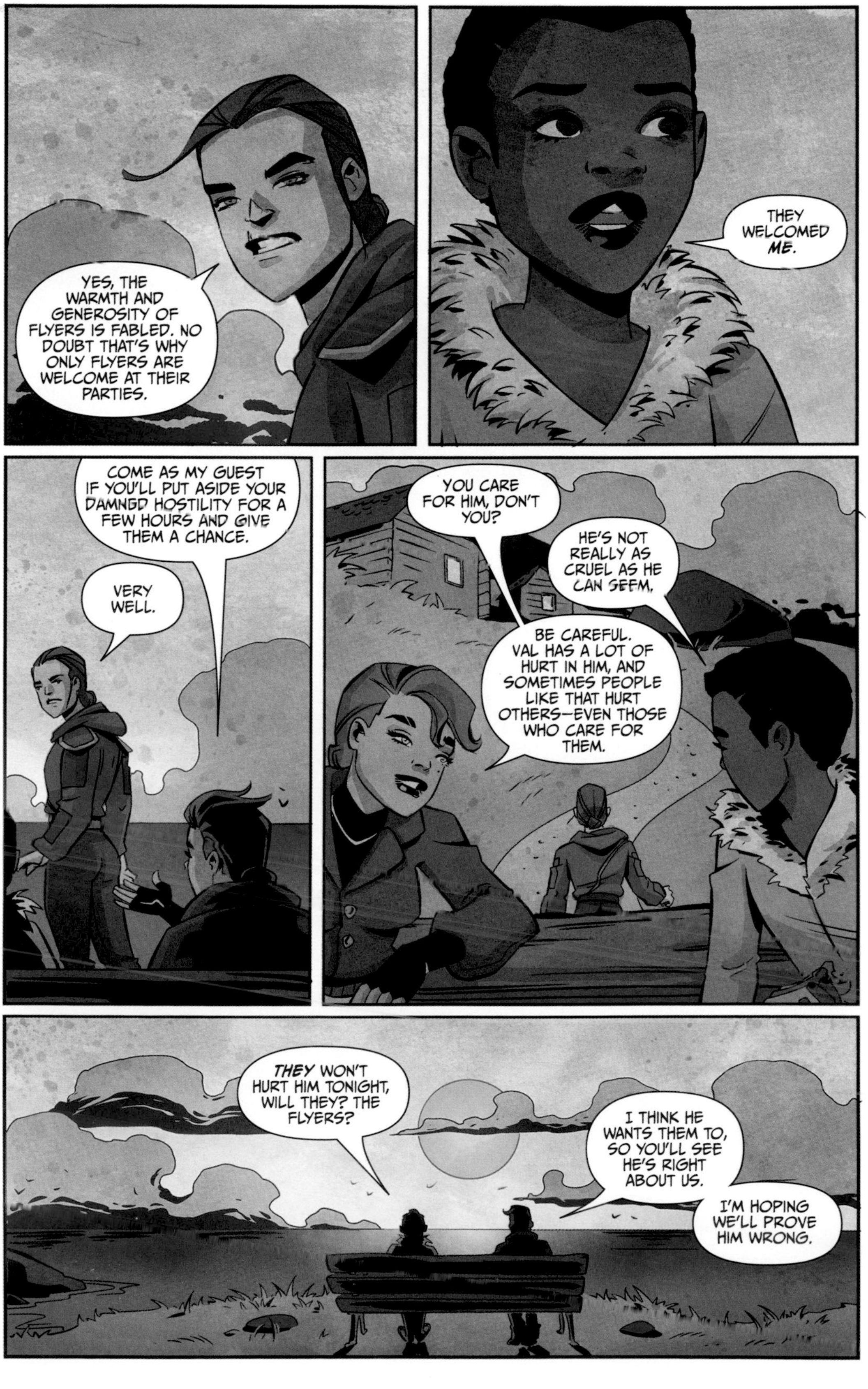
YES, THE WARMTH AND GENEROSITY OF FLYERS IS FABLED. NO DOUBT THAT'S WHY ONLY FLYERS ARE WELCOME AT THEIR PARTIES.
THEY WELCOMED *ME*.
COME AS MY GUEST IF YOU'LL PUT ASIDE YOUR DAMNED HOSTILITY FOR A FEW HOURS AND GIVE THEM A CHANCE.
VERY WELL.
YOU CARE FOR HIM, DON'T YOU?
HE'S NOT REALLY AS CRUEL AS HE CAN SEEM.
BE CAREFUL. VAL HAS A LOT OF HURT IN HIM, AND SOMETIMES PEOPLE LIKE THAT HURT OTHERS—EVEN THOSE WHO CARE FOR THEM.
THEY WON'T HURT HIM TONIGHT, WILL THEY? THE FLYERS?
I THINK HE WANTS THEM TO, SO YOU'LL SEE HE'S RIGHT ABOUT US.
I'M HOPING WE'LL PROVE HIM WRONG.

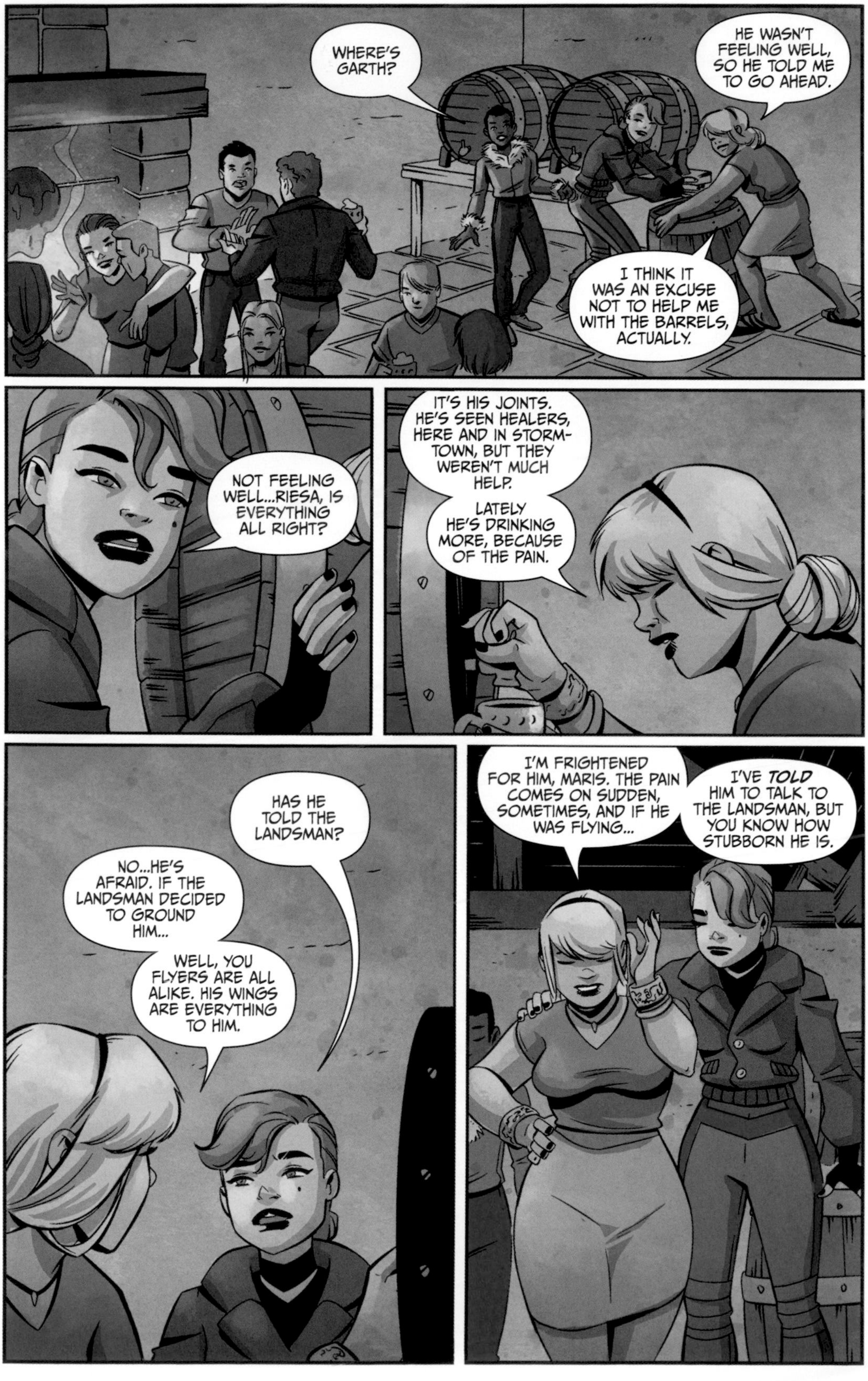
WHERE'S GARTH?
HE WASN'T FEELING WELL, SO HE TOLD ME TO GO AHEAD.
I THINK IT WAS AN EXCUSE NOT TO HELP ME WITH THE BARRELS, ACTUALLY.
NOT FEELING WELL...RIESA, IS EVERYTHING ALL RIGHT?
IT'S HIS JOINTS. HE'S SEEN HEALERS, HERE AND IN STORM-TOWN, BUT THEY WEREN'T MUCH HELP.
LATELY HE'S DRINKING MORE, BECAUSE OF THE PAIN.
HAS HE TOLD THE LANDSMAN?
NO...HE'S AFRAID. IF THE LANDSMAN DECIDED TO GROUND HIM...
WELL, YOU FLYERS ARE ALL ALIKE. HIS WINGS ARE EVERYTHING TO HIM.
I'M FRIGHTENED FOR HIM, MARIS. THE PAIN COMES ON SUDDEN, SOMETIMES, AND IF HE WAS FLYING...
I'VE *TOLD* HIM TO TALK TO THE LANDSMAN, BUT YOU KNOW HOW STUBBORN HE IS.

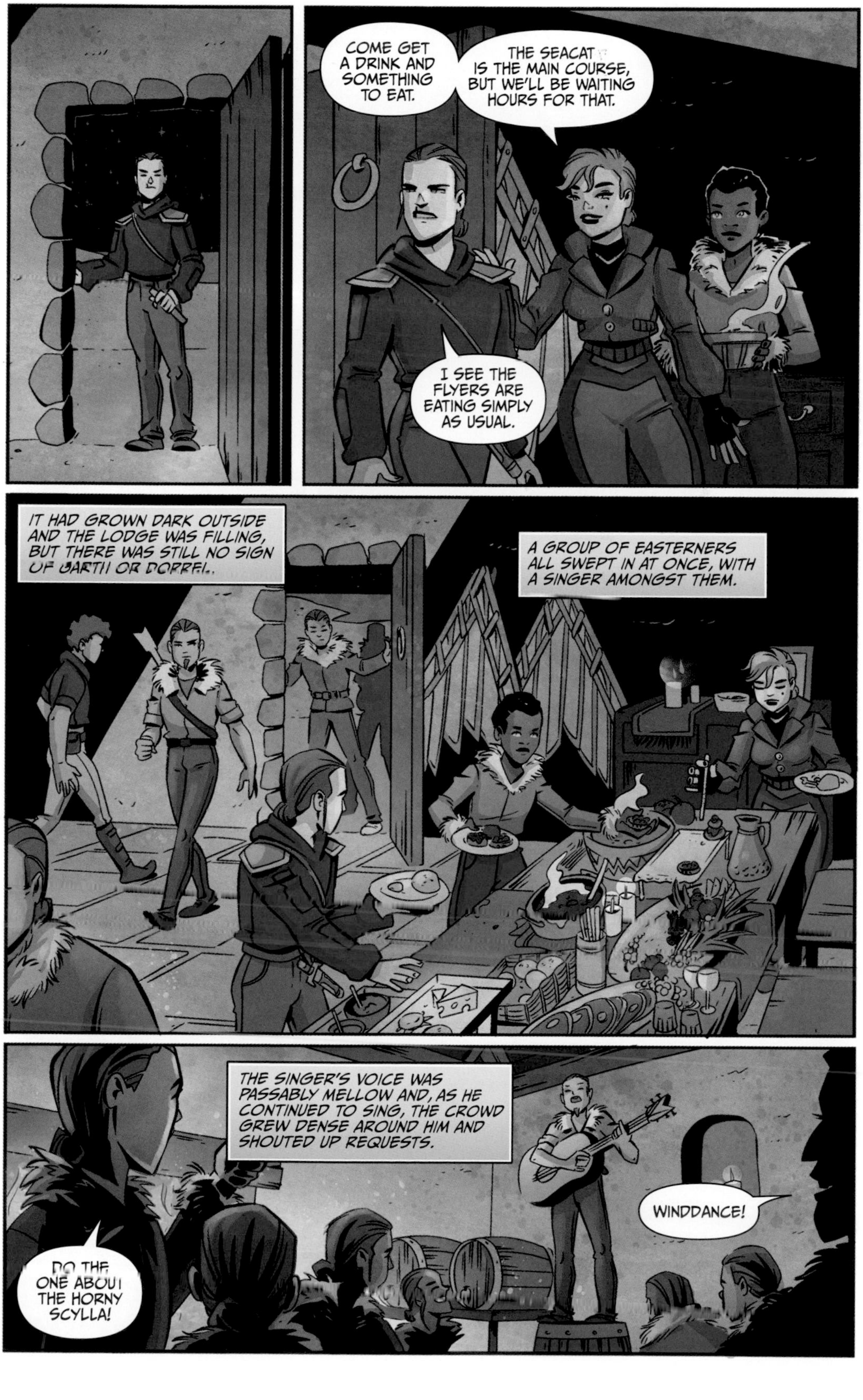
COME GET A DRINK AND SOMETHING TO EAT.
THE SEACAT IS THE MAIN COURSE, BUT WE'LL BE WAITING HOURS FOR THAT.
I SEE THE FLYERS ARE EATING SIMPLY AS USUAL.
IT HAD GROWN DARK OUTSIDE AND THE LODGE WAS FILLING, BUT THERE WAS STILL NO SIGN OF GARTH OR DORREL.
A GROUP OF EASTERNERS ALL SWEPT IN AT ONCE, WITH A SINGER AMONGST THEM.
THE SINGER'S VOICE WAS PASSABLY MELLOW AND, AS HE CONTINUED TO SING, THE CROWD GREW DENSE AROUND HIM AND SHOUTED UP REQUESTS.
WINDDANCE!
DO THE ONE ABOUT THE HORNY SCYLLA!

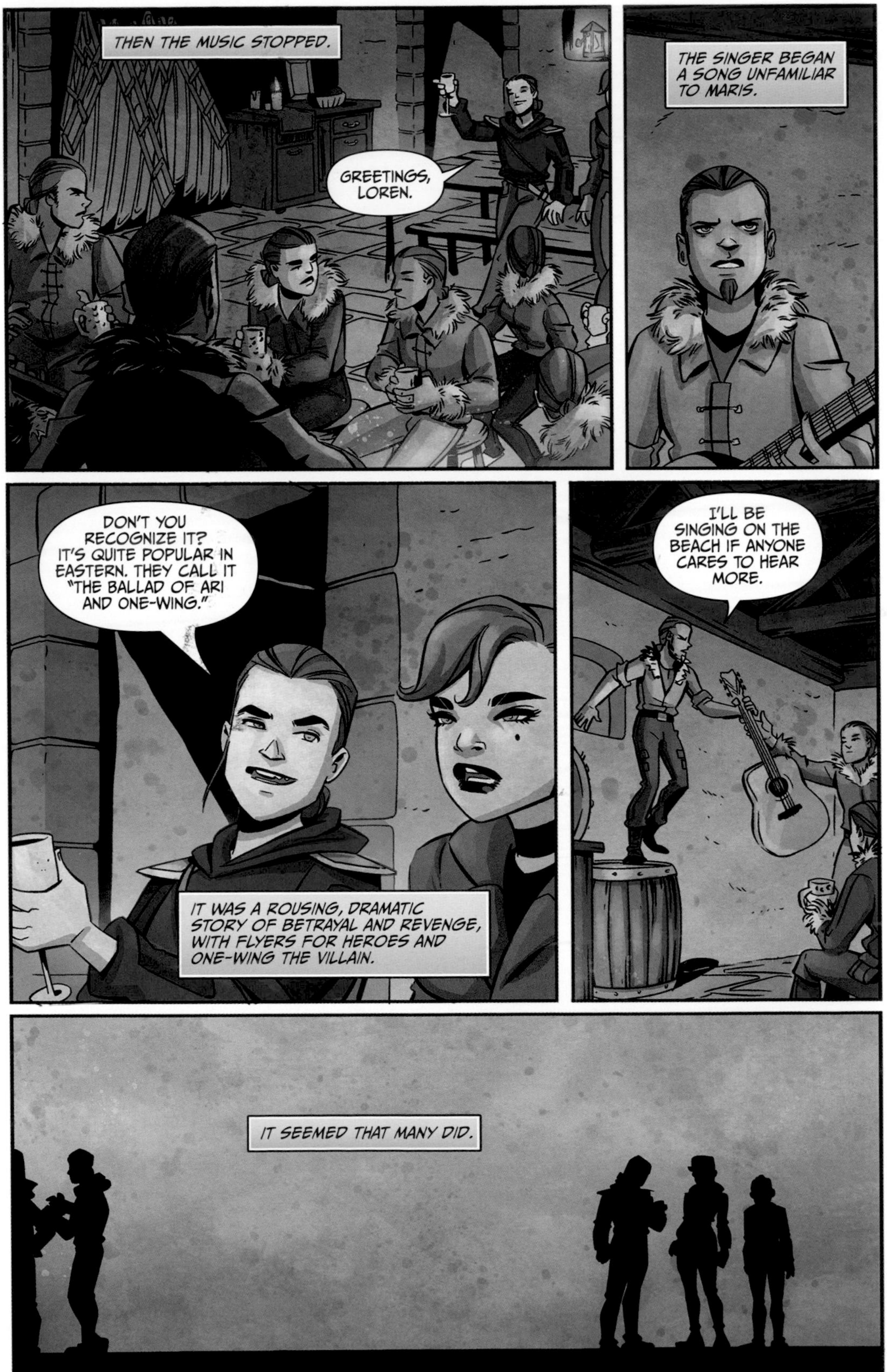
THEN THE MUSIC STOPPED.
GREETINGS, LOREN.
THE SINGER BEGAN A SONG UNFAMILIAR TO MARIS.
DON'T YOU RECOGNIZE IT? IT'S QUITE POPULAR IN EASTERN. THEY CALL IT "THE BALLAD OF ARI AND ONE-WING."
IT WAS A ROUSING, DRAMATIC STORY OF BETRAYAL AND REVENGE, WITH FLYERS FOR HEROES AND ONE-WING THE VILLAIN.
I'LL BE SINGING ON THE BEACH IF ANYONE CARES TO HEAR MORE.
IT SEEMED THAT MANY DID.

YOU HAVEN'T INTRODUCED ME TO YOUR FLYER FRIENDS YET.

I'M VAL OF SOUTH ARREN, AND THIS IS S'RELLA.

I ADMIRE YOUR COURAGE, ONE-WING, BUT NOTHING ELSE.

THIS IS A *FLYERS'* LODGE. WHAT IS YOUR BUSINESS HERE?

THEY ARE MY GUESTS. DO YOU QUESTION MY RIGHT TO BE HERE?

NO, ONLY YOUR TASTE IN COMPANIONS.

WHAT HAPPENED TO MY PARTY? IF THERE WAS A FIGHT, I'LL WRING THE NECK OF THE FOOL WHO STARTED IT!

FLYERS HAVE NO BUSINESS FIGHTING LIKE LAND-BOUND ROWDIES.

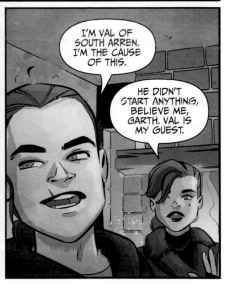

I'M VAL OF SOUTH ARREN. I'M THE CAUSE OF THIS.

HE DIDN'T START ANYTHING, BELIEVE ME, GARTH. VAL IS MY GUEST.

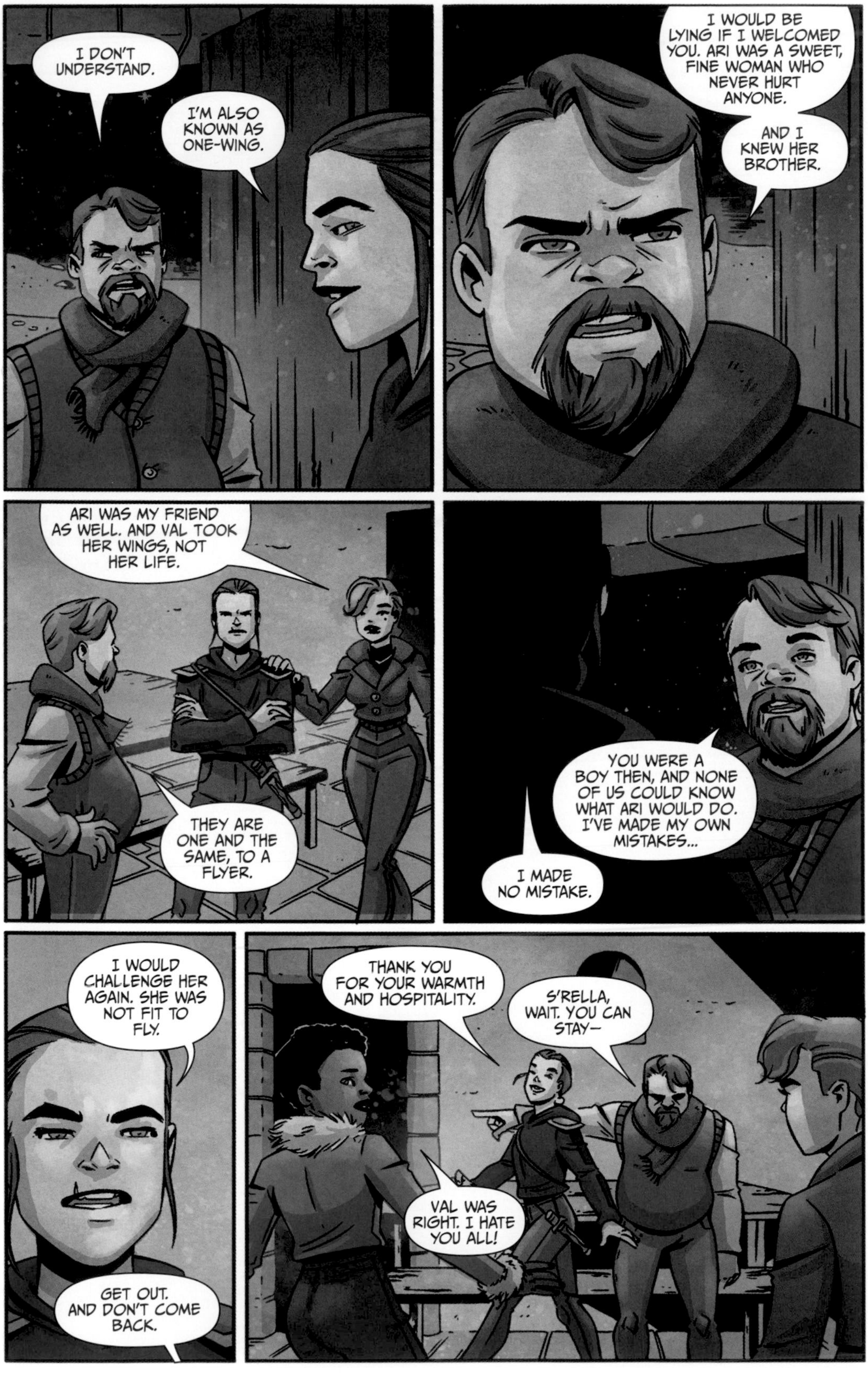
I DON'T UNDERSTAND.
I'M ALSO KNOWN AS ONE-WING.
I WOULD BE LYING IF I WELCOMED YOU. ARI WAS A SWEET, FINE WOMAN WHO NEVER HURT ANYONE.
AND I KNEW HER BROTHER.
ARI WAS MY FRIEND AS WELL. AND VAL TOOK HER WINGS, NOT HER LIFE.
THEY ARE ONE AND THE SAME, TO A FLYER.
YOU WERE A BOY THEN, AND NONE OF US COULD KNOW WHAT ARI WOULD DO. I'VE MADE MY OWN MISTAKES...
I MADE NO MISTAKE.
I WOULD CHALLENGE HER AGAIN. SHE WAS NOT FIT TO FLY.
GET OUT. AND DON'T COME BACK.
THANK YOU FOR YOUR WARMTH AND HOSPITALITY.
S'RELLA, WAIT. YOU CAN STAY—
VAL WAS RIGHT. I HATE YOU ALL!

S'RELLA HAD NOT SPENT THE NIGHT IN THEIR CABIN BUT TURNED UP THE NEXT MORNING WITH VAL, BOTH EAGER TO PRACTICE.

LATER, MARIS WAS RESTING WHEN SHE WAS STARTLED BY A POUNDING AT THE DOOR.

WHAM WHAM WHAM

I AM ARAK. I HAVE FLOWN FOR SOUTH ARREN THESE THIRTY YEARS. I WOULD SPEAK TO YOU ABOUT VAL ONE-WING.

DO YOU KNOW THE STOCK HE SPRINGS FROM? HIS PARENTS WERE FROM LOMARRON.

MINERS?

LANDSGUARD. PROFESSIONAL KILLERS, A BIT TOO FOND OF THEIR WORK.

HIS FATHER KILLED A MAN, BREAKING A TRUCE, SO THE FAMILY HAD TO FLEE. THEY CAME TO SOUTH ARREN IN A STOLEN BOAT.

ONE NIGHT THE FATHER GOT DRUNK AND TALKED TOO MUCH. WORD REACHED THE LANDSMAN, THEN LOMARRON. HE WAS HANGED AS A THIEF AND A MURDERER.

I TOOK PITY ON THE POOR WIDOW, TOOK HER IN AS MY HOUSEKEEPER, AND RAISED VAL WITH MY OWN SON.

I SET HIM A GOOD EXAMPLE, GAVE HIM EVERY CHANCE, AND WHAT DOES HE DO BUT STEAL FROM ME! BAD BLOOD.

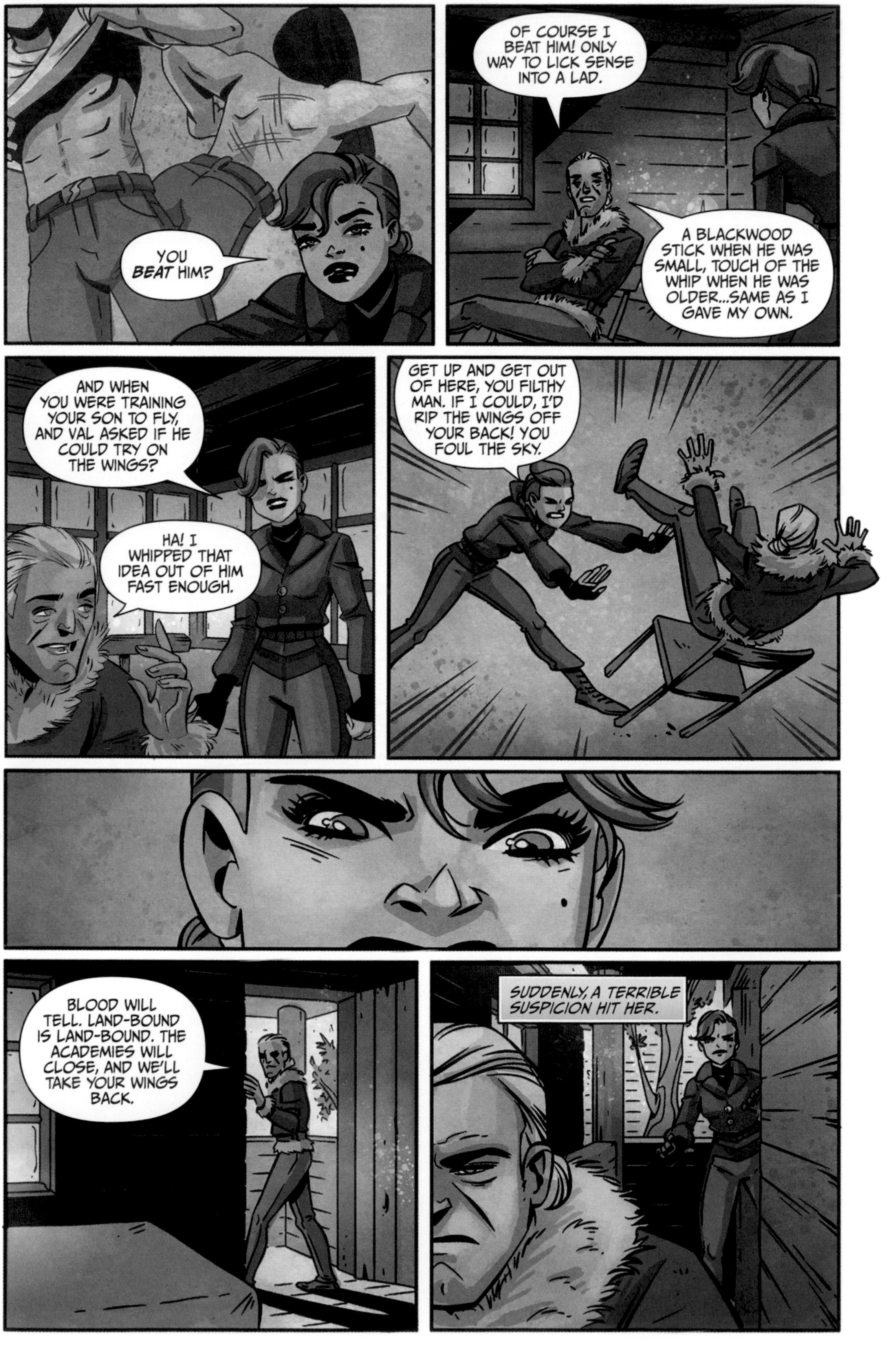
YOU BEAT HIM?
OF COURSE I BEAT HIM! ONLY WAY TO LICK SENSE INTO A LAD.
A BLACKWOOD STICK WHEN HE WAS SMALL, TOUCH OF THE WHIP WHEN HE WAS OLDER...SAME AS I GAVE MY OWN.
AND WHEN YOU WERE TRAINING YOUR SON TO FLY, AND VAL ASKED IF HE COULD TRY ON THE WINGS?
HA! I WHIPPED THAT IDEA OUT OF HIM FAST ENOUGH.
GET UP AND GET OUT OF HERE, YOU FILTHY MAN. IF I COULD, I'D RIP THE WINGS OFF YOUR BACK! YOU FOUL THE SKY.
BLOOD WILL TELL. LAND-BOUND IS LAND-BOUND. THE ACADEMIES WILL CLOSE, AND WE'LL TAKE YOUR WINGS BACK.
SUDDENLY, A TERRIBLE SUSPICION HIT HER.

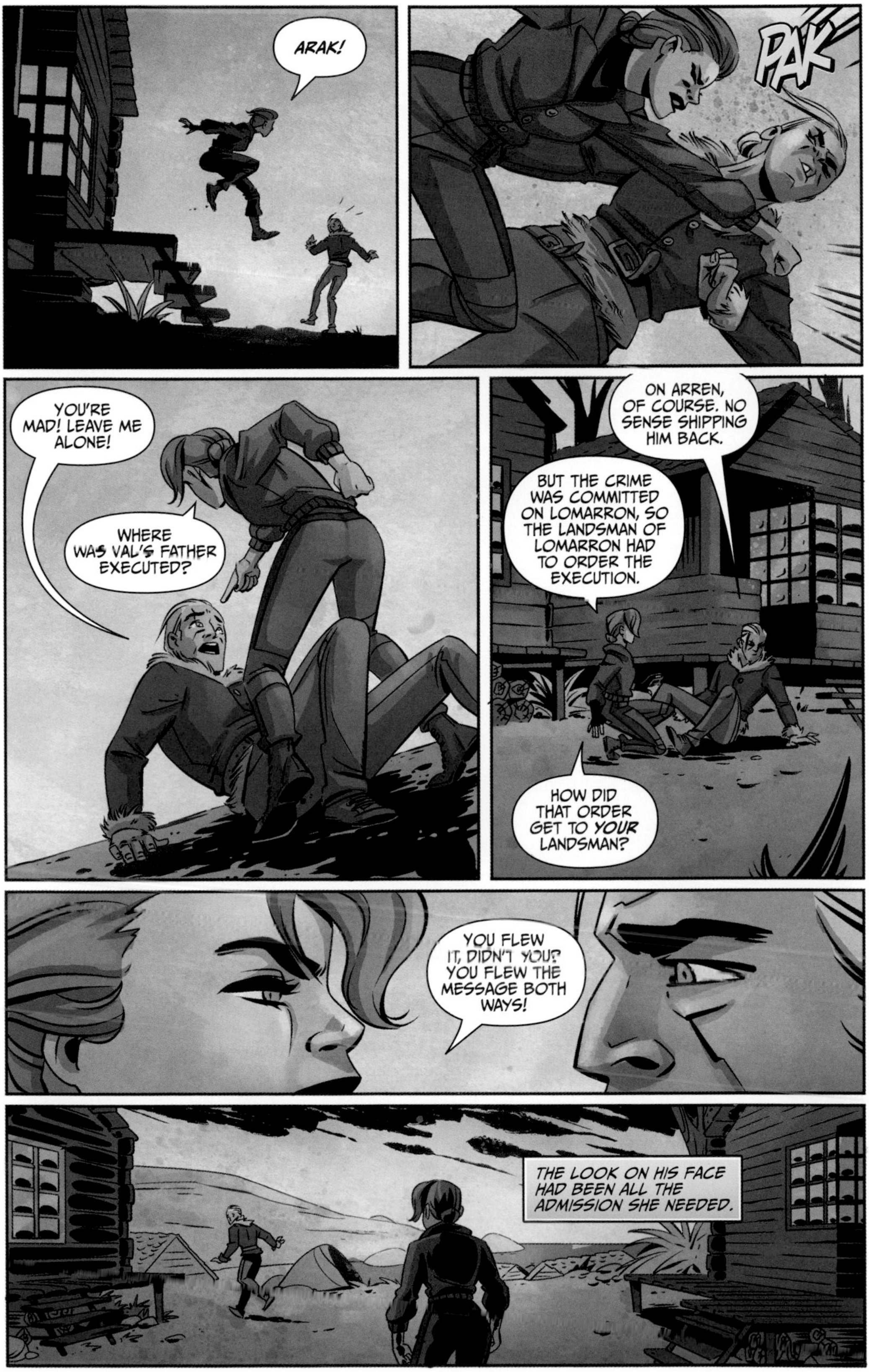
ARAK!
PAK
YOU'RE MAD! LEAVE ME ALONE!
WHERE WAS VAL'S FATHER EXECUTED?
ON ARREN, OF COURSE. NO SENSE SHIPPING HIM BACK.
BUT THE CRIME WAS COMMITTED ON LOMARRON, SO THE LANDSMAN OF LOMARRON HAD TO ORDER THE EXECUTION.
HOW DID THAT ORDER GET TO *YOUR* LANDSMAN?
YOU FLEW IT, DIDN'T YOU? YOU FLEW THE MESSAGE BOTH WAYS!
THE LOOK ON HIS FACE HAD BEEN ALL THE ADMISSION SHE NEEDED.

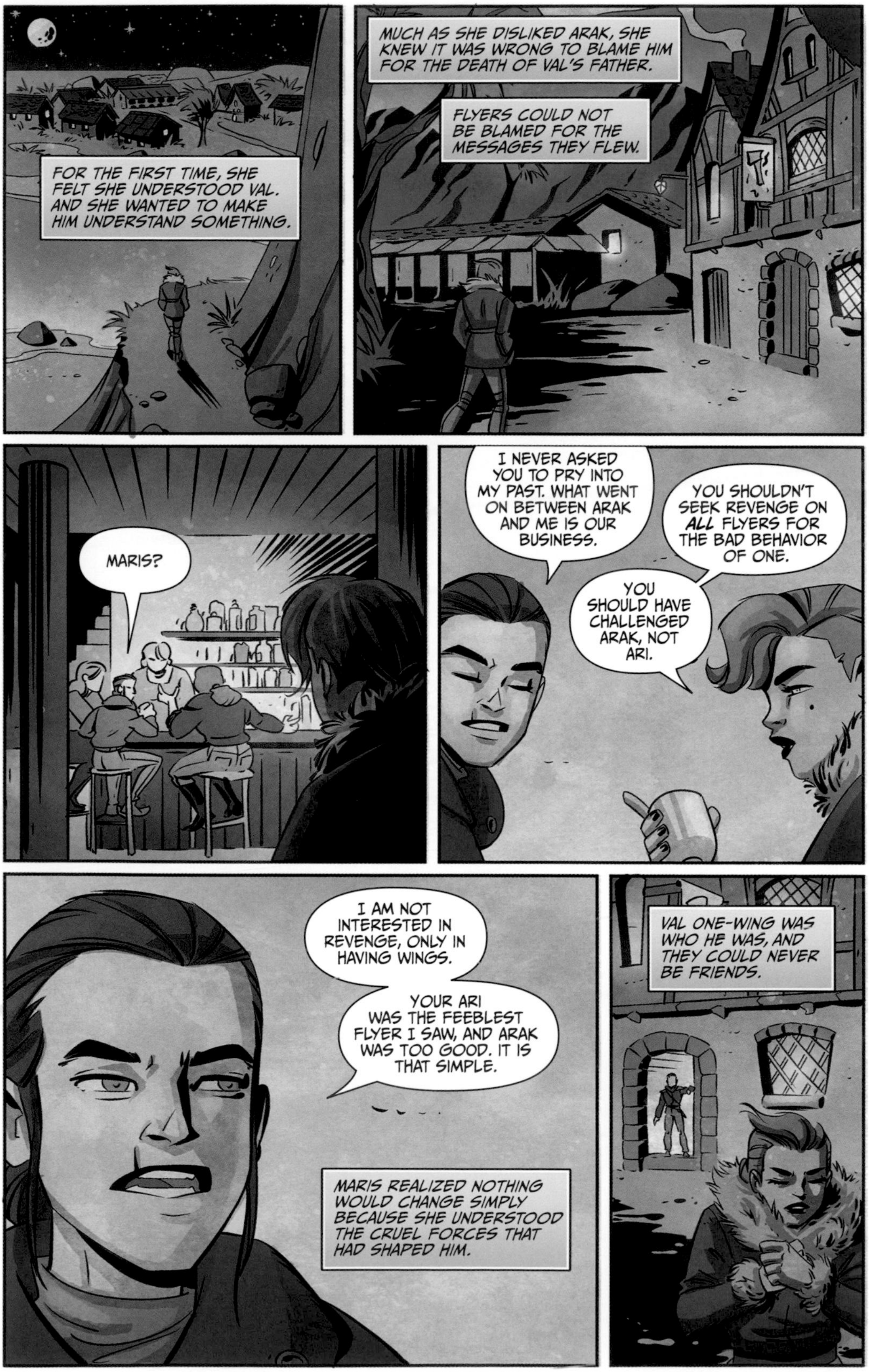

FOR THE FIRST TIME, SHE FELT SHE UNDERSTOOD VAL. AND SHE WANTED TO MAKE HIM UNDERSTAND SOMETHING.
MUCH AS SHE DISLIKED ARAK, SHE KNEW IT WAS WRONG TO BLAME HIM FOR THE DEATH OF VAL'S FATHER.
FLYERS COULD NOT BE BLAMED FOR THE MESSAGES THEY FLEW.
MARIS?
I NEVER ASKED YOU TO PRY INTO MY PAST. WHAT WENT ON BETWEEN ARAK AND ME IS OUR BUSINESS.
YOU SHOULDN'T SEEK REVENGE ON ALL FLYERS FOR THE BAD BEHAVIOR OF ONE.
YOU SHOULD HAVE CHALLENGED ARAK, NOT ARI.
I AM NOT INTERESTED IN REVENGE, ONLY IN HAVING WINGS.
YOUR ARI WAS THE FEEBLEST FLYER I SAW, AND ARAK WAS TOO GOOD. IT IS THAT SIMPLE.
MARIS REALIZED NOTHING WOULD CHANGE SIMPLY BECAUSE SHE UNDERSTOOD THE CRUEL FORCES THAT HAD SHAPED HIM.
VAL ONE-WING WAS WHO HE WAS, AND THEY COULD NEVER BE FRIENDS.

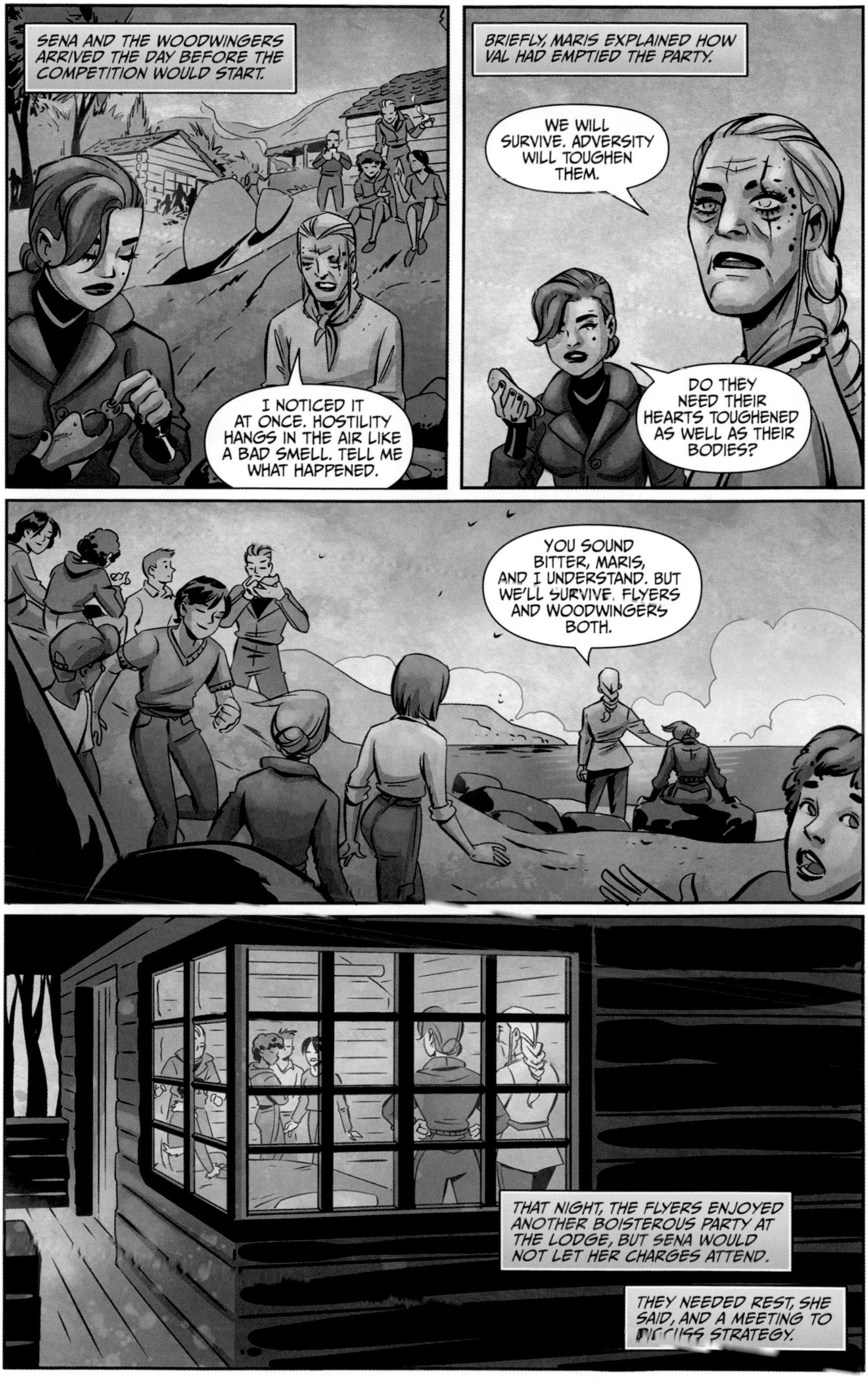
SENA AND THE WOODWINGERS ARRIVED THE DAY BEFORE THE COMPETITION WOULD START.
I NOTICED IT AT ONCE. HOSTILITY HANGS IN THE AIR LIKE A BAD SMELL. TELL ME WHAT HAPPENED.
BRIEFLY, MARIS EXPLAINED HOW VAL HAD EMPTIED THE PARTY.
WE WILL SURVIVE. ADVERSITY WILL TOUGHEN THEM.
DO THEY NEED THEIR HEARTS TOUGHENED AS WELL AS THEIR BODIES?
YOU SOUND BITTER, MARIS, AND I UNDERSTAND. BUT WE'LL SURVIVE. FLYERS AND WOODWINGERS BOTH.
THAT NIGHT, THE FLYERS ENJOYED ANOTHER BOISTEROUS PARTY AT THE LODGE, BUT SENA WOULD NOT LET HER CHARGES ATTEND.
THEY NEEDED REST, SHE SAID, AND A MEETING TO DISCUSS STRATEGY.

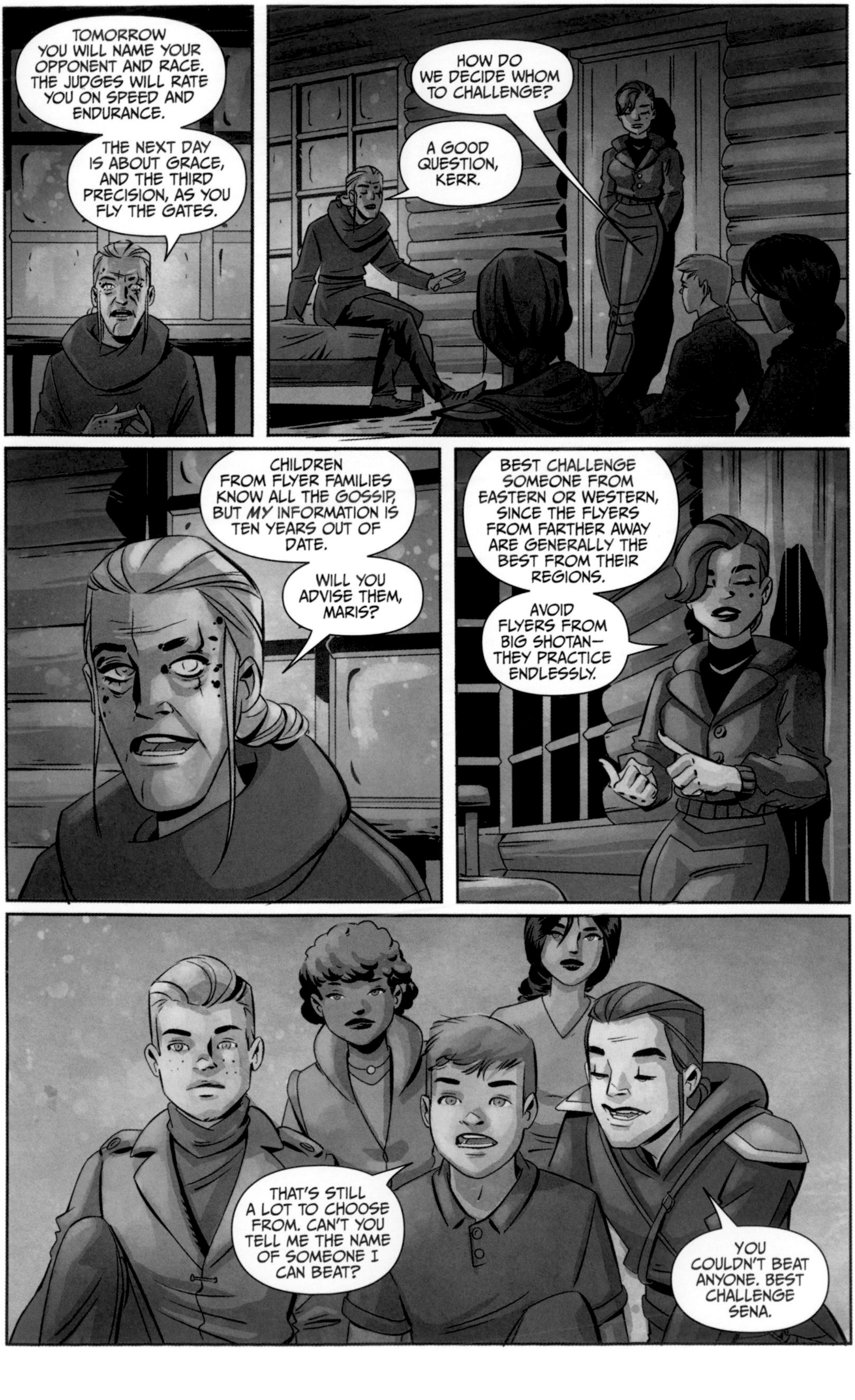
TOMORROW YOU WILL NAME YOUR OPPONENT AND RACE. THE JUDGES WILL RATE YOU ON SPEED AND ENDURANCE.
THE NEXT DAY IS ABOUT GRACE, AND THE THIRD PRECISION, AS YOU FLY THE GATES.
HOW DO WE DECIDE WHOM TO CHALLENGE?
A GOOD QUESTION, KERR.
CHILDREN FROM FLYER FAMILIES KNOW ALL THE GOSSIP, BUT *MY* INFORMATION IS TEN YEARS OUT OF DATE.
WILL YOU ADVISE THEM, MARIS?
BEST CHALLENGE SOMEONE FROM EASTERN OR WESTERN, SINCE THE FLYERS FROM FARTHER AWAY ARE GENERALLY THE BEST FROM THEIR REGIONS.
AVOID FLYERS FROM BIG SHOTAN— THEY PRACTICE ENDLESSLY.
THAT'S STILL A LOT TO CHOOSE FROM. CAN'T YOU TELL ME THE NAME OF SOMEONE I CAN BEAT?
YOU COULDN'T BEAT ANYONE. BEST CHALLENGE SENA.

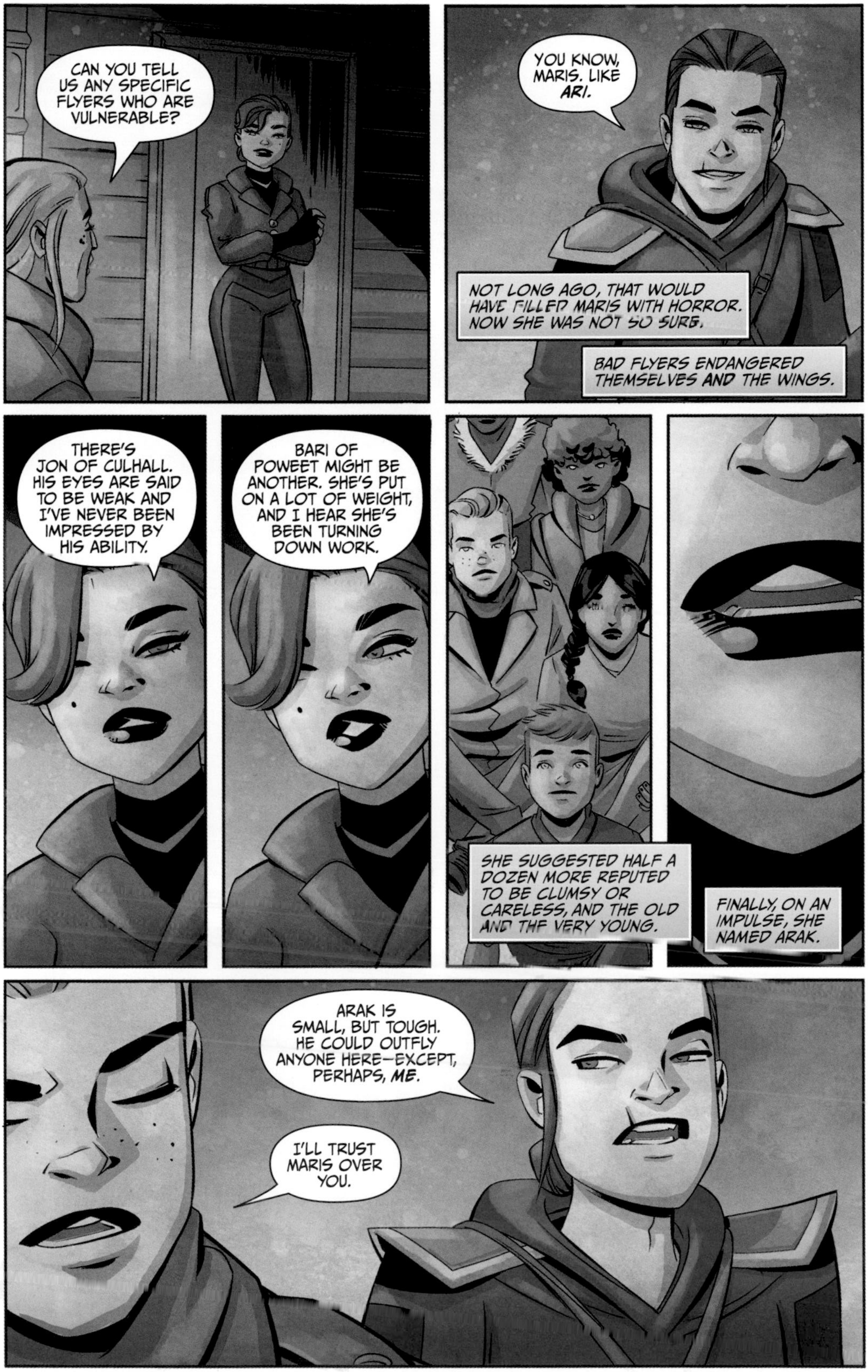
CAN YOU TELL US ANY SPECIFIC FLYERS WHO ARE VULNERABLE?
YOU KNOW, MARIS. LIKE ARI.
NOT LONG AGO, THAT WOULD HAVE FILLED MARIS WITH HORROR. NOW SHE WAS NOT SO SURE.
BAD FLYERS ENDANGERED THEMSELVES AND THE WINGS.
THERE'S JON OF CULHALL. HIS EYES ARE SAID TO BE WEAK AND I'VE NEVER BEEN IMPRESSED BY HIS ABILITY.
BARI OF POWEET MIGHT BE ANOTHER. SHE'S PUT ON A LOT OF WEIGHT, AND I HEAR SHE'S BEEN TURNING DOWN WORK.
SHE SUGGESTED HALF A DOZEN MORE REPUTED TO BE CLUMSY OR CARELESS, AND THE OLD AND THE VERY YOUNG.
FINALLY, ON AN IMPULSE, SHE NAMED ARAK.
ARAK IS SMALL, BUT TOUGH. HE COULD OUTFLY ANYONE HERE—EXCEPT, PERHAPS, ME.
I'LL TRUST MARIS OVER YOU.

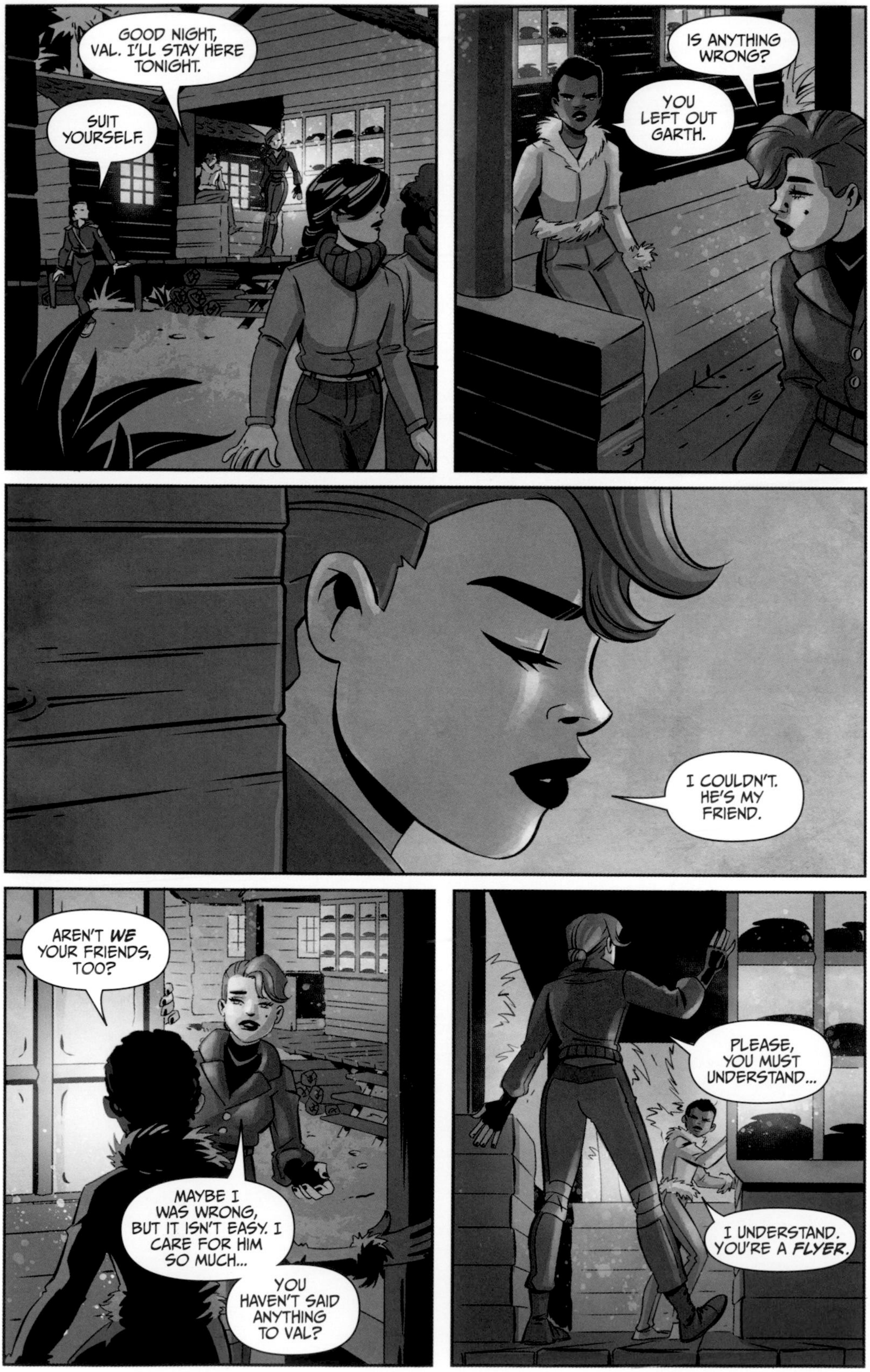
GOOD NIGHT, VAL. I'LL STAY HERE TONIGHT.
SUIT YOURSELF.
IS ANYTHING WRONG?
YOU LEFT OUT GARTH.
I COULDN'T. HE'S MY FRIEND.
AREN'T *WE* YOUR FRIENDS, TOO?
MAYBE I WAS WRONG, BUT IT ISN'T EASY. I CARE FOR HIM SO MUCH...
YOU HAVEN'T SAID ANYTHING TO VAL?
PLEASE, YOU MUST UNDERSTAND...
I UNDERSTAND. YOU'RE A *FLYER*.

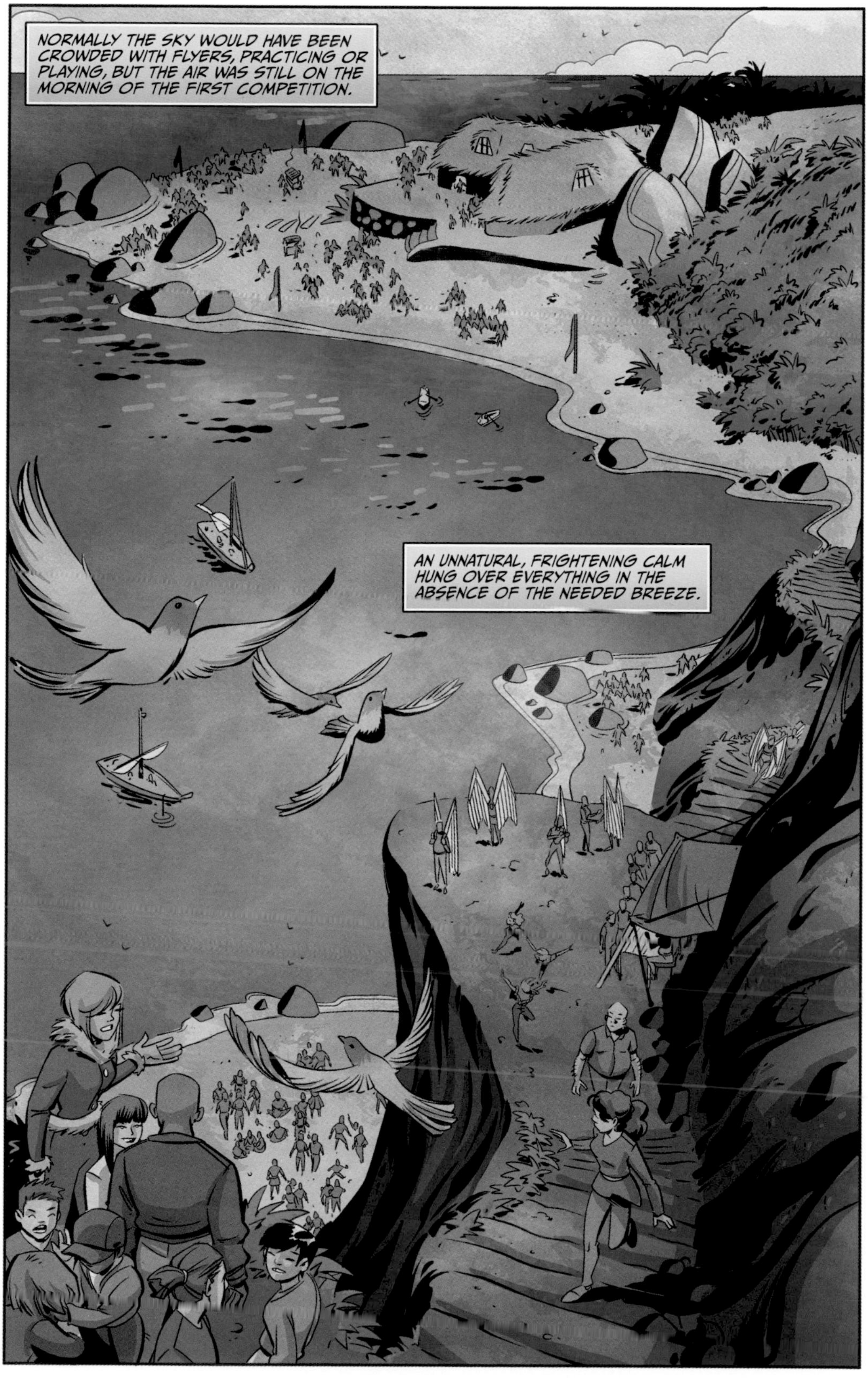
NORMALLY THE SKY WOULD HAVE BEEN CROWDED WITH FLYERS, PRACTICING OR PLAYING, BUT THE AIR WAS STILL ON THE MORNING OF THE FIRST COMPETITION.
AN UNNATURAL, FRIGHTENING CALM HUNG OVER EVERYTHING IN THE ABSENCE OF THE NEEDED BREEZE.

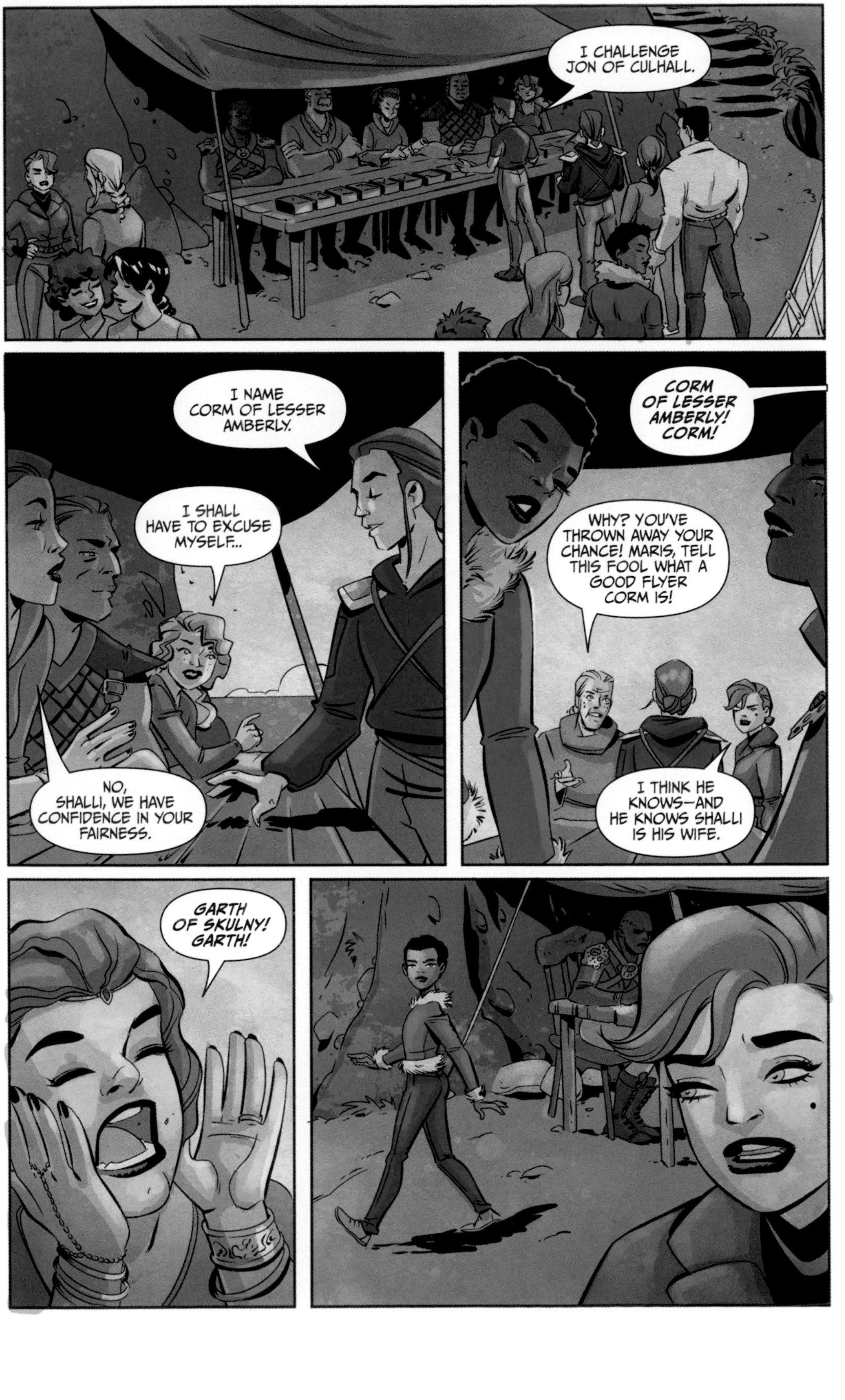
I CHALLENGE JON OF CULHALL.
I NAME CORM OF LESSER AMBERLY.
I SHALL HAVE TO EXCUSE MYSELF...
NO, SHALLI, WE HAVE CONFIDENCE IN YOUR FAIRNESS.
CORM OF LESSER AMBERLY! CORM!
WHY? YOU'VE THROWN AWAY YOUR CHANCE! MARIS, TELL THIS FOOL WHAT A GOOD FLYER CORM IS!
I THINK HE KNOWS—AND HE KNOWS SHALLI IS HIS WIFE.
GARTH OF SKULNY! GARTH!

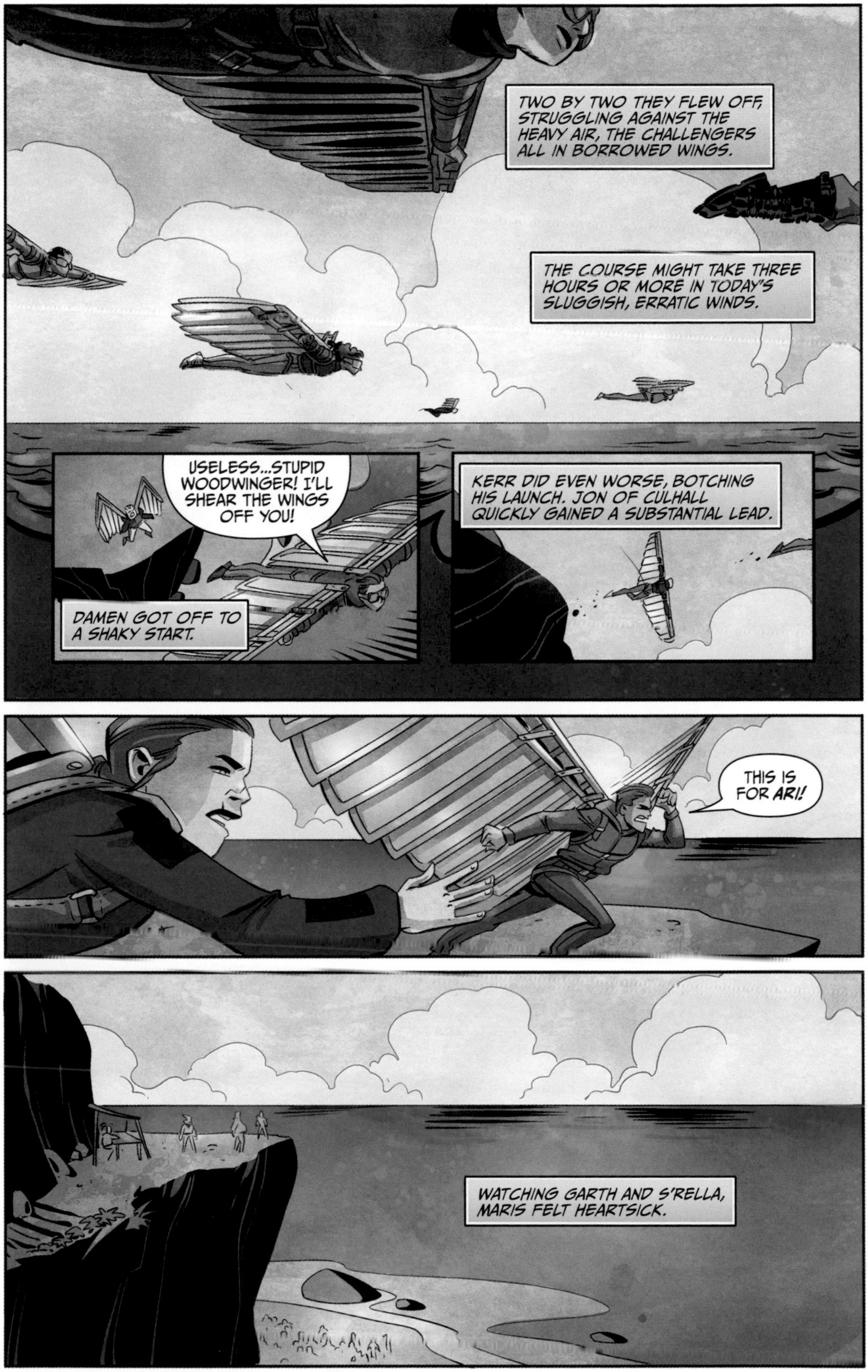
TWO BY TWO THEY FLEW OFF, STRUGGLING AGAINST THE HEAVY AIR, THE CHALLENGERS ALL IN BORROWED WINGS.
THE COURSE MIGHT TAKE THREE HOURS OR MORE IN TODAY'S SLUGGISH, ERRATIC WINDS.
USELESS...STUPID WOODWINGER! I'LL SHEAR THE WINGS OFF YOU!
DAMEN GOT OFF TO A SHAKY START.
KERR DID EVEN WORSE, BOTCHING HIS LAUNCH. JON OF CULHALL QUICKLY GAINED A SUBSTANTIAL LEAD.
THIS IS FOR ARI!
WATCHING GARTH AND S'RELLA, MARIS FELT HEARTSICK.

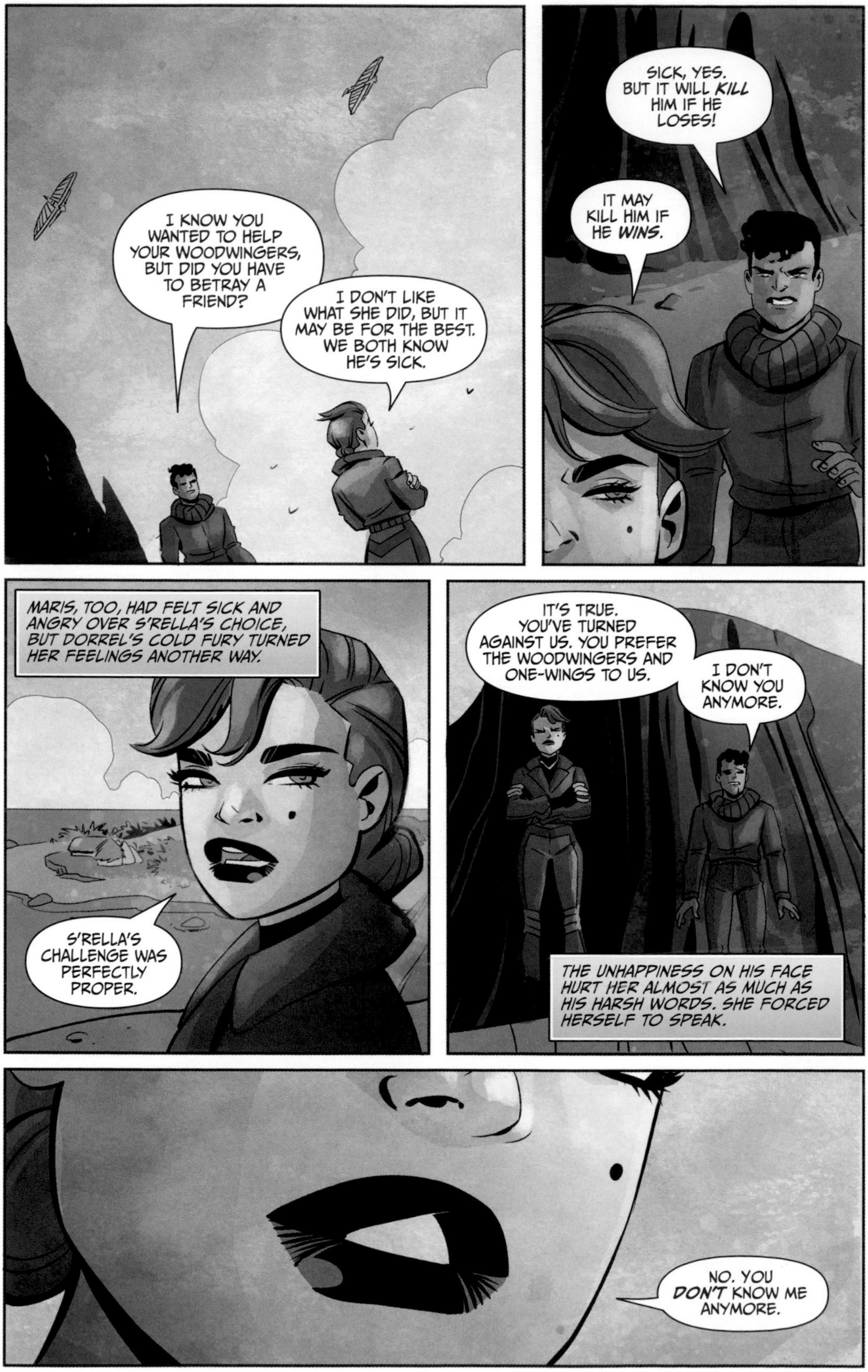
I KNOW YOU WANTED TO HELP YOUR WOODWINGERS, BUT DID YOU HAVE TO BETRAY A FRIEND?
I DON'T LIKE WHAT SHE DID, BUT IT MAY BE FOR THE BEST. WE BOTH KNOW HE'S SICK.
SICK, YES. BUT IT WILL *KILL* HIM IF HE LOSES!
IT MAY KILL HIM IF HE *WINS*.
MARIS, TOO, HAD FELT SICK AND ANGRY OVER S'RELLA'S CHOICE, BUT DORREL'S COLD FURY TURNED HER FEELINGS ANOTHER WAY.
S'RELLA'S CHALLENGE WAS PERFECTLY PROPER.
IT'S TRUE. YOU'VE TURNED AGAINST US. YOU PREFER THE WOODWINGERS AND ONE-WINGS TO US.
I DON'T KNOW YOU ANYMORE.
THE UNHAPPINESS ON HIS FACE HURT HER ALMOST AS MUCH AS HIS HARSH WORDS. SHE FORCED HERSELF TO SPEAK.
NO. YOU *DON'T* KNOW ME ANYMORE.

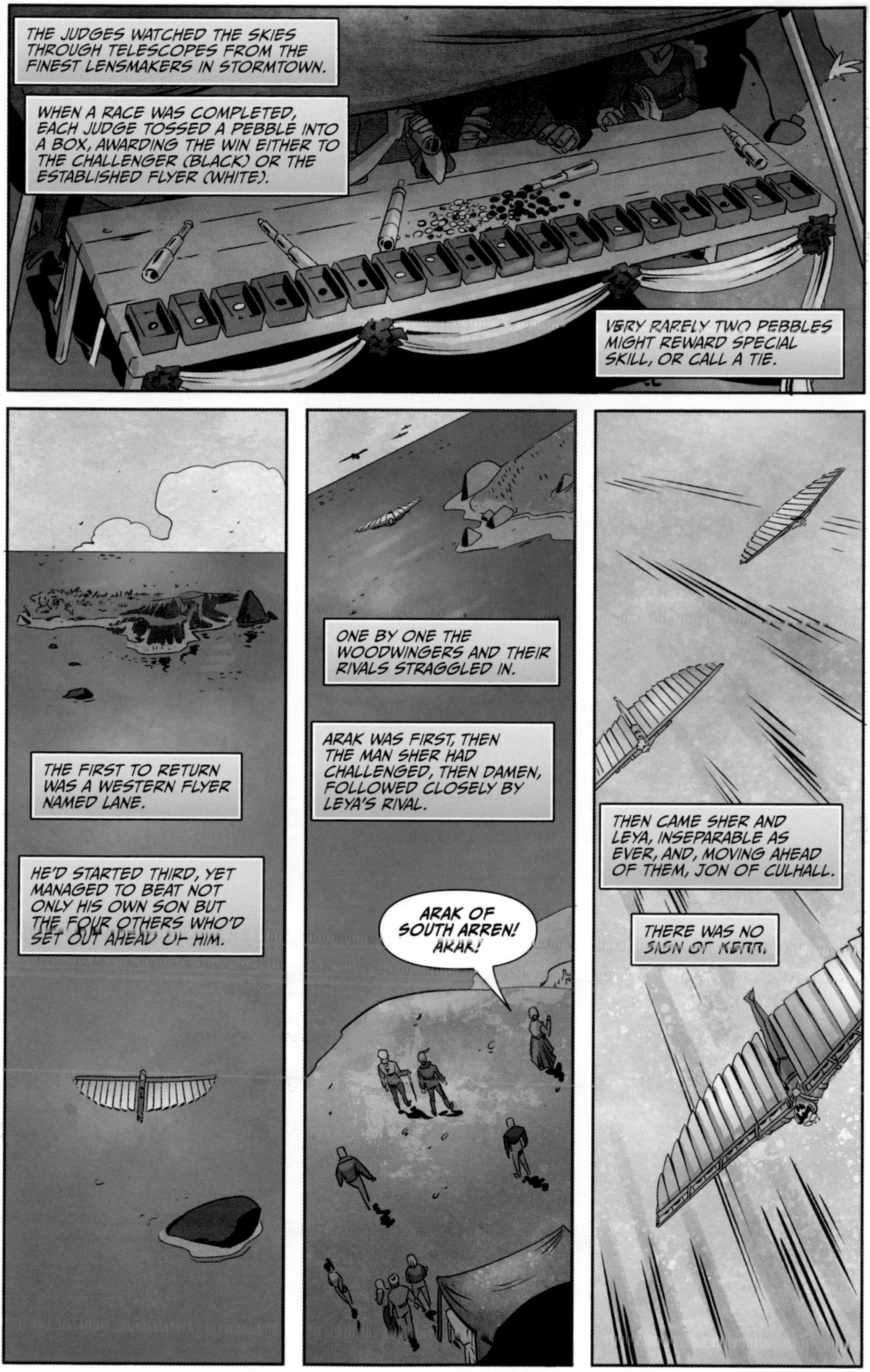

THE JUDGES WATCHED THE SKIES THROUGH TELESCOPES FROM THE FINEST LENSMAKERS IN STORMTOWN.
WHEN A RACE WAS COMPLETED, EACH JUDGE TOSSED A PEBBLE INTO A BOX, AWARDING THE WIN EITHER TO THE CHALLENGER (BLACK) OR THE ESTABLISHED FLYER (WHITE).
VERY RARELY TWO PEBBLES MIGHT REWARD SPECIAL SKILL, OR CALL A TIE.
THE FIRST TO RETURN WAS A WESTERN FLYER NAMED LANE.
HE'D STARTED THIRD, YET MANAGED TO BEAT NOT ONLY HIS OWN SON BUT THE FOUR OTHERS WHO'D SET OUT AHEAD OF HIM.
ONE BY ONE THE WOODWINGERS AND THEIR RIVALS STRAGGLED IN.
ARAK WAS FIRST, THEN THE MAN SHER HAD CHALLENGED, THEN DAMEN, FOLLOWED CLOSELY BY LEYA'S RIVAL.
ARAK OF SOUTH ARREN! ARAK!
THEN CAME SHER AND LEYA, INSEPARABLE AS EVER, AND, MOVING AHEAD OF THEM, JON OF CULHALL.
THERE WAS NO SIGN OF KERR.

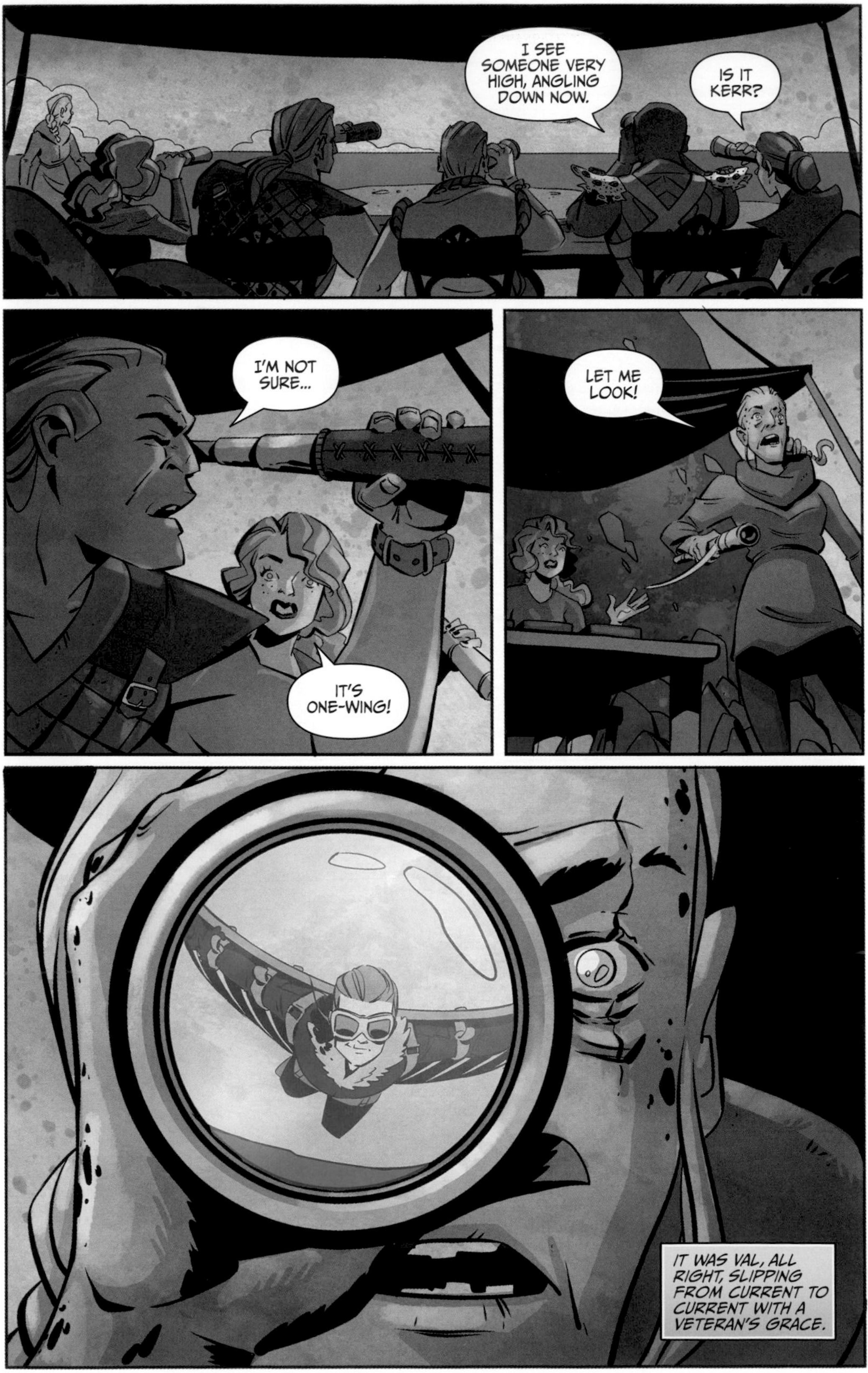
I SEE SOMEONE VERY HIGH, ANGLING DOWN NOW.
IS IT KERR?
I'M NOT SURE...
IT'S ONE-WING!
LET ME LOOK!
IT WAS VAL, ALL RIGHT, SLIPPING FROM CURRENT TO CURRENT WITH A VETERAN'S GRACE.

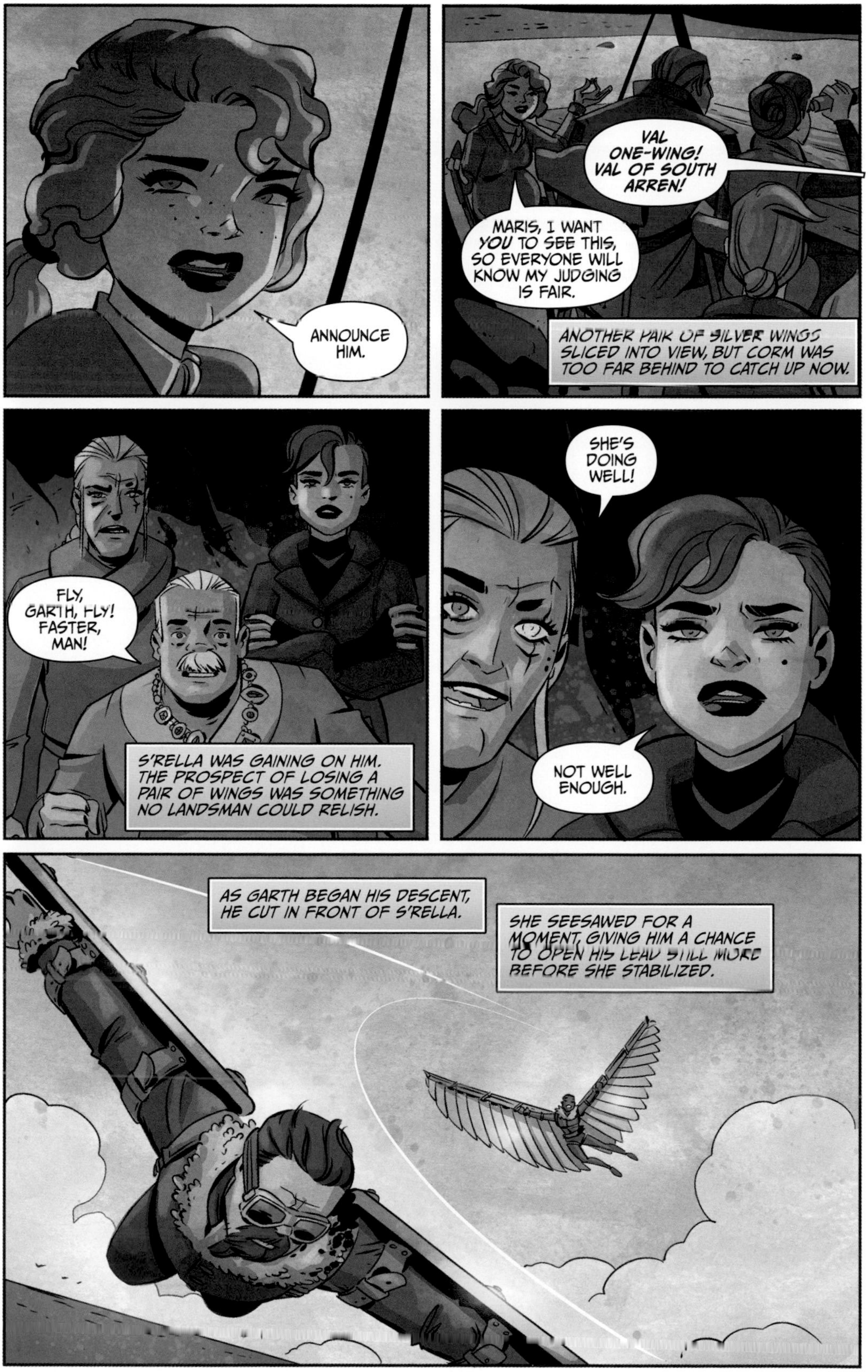
ANNOUNCE HIM.
VAL ONE-WING! VAL OF SOUTH ARREN!
MARIS, I WANT YOU TO SEE THIS, SO EVERYONE WILL KNOW MY JUDGING IS FAIR.
ANOTHER PAIR OF SILVER WINGS SLICED INTO VIEW, BUT CORM WAS TOO FAR BEHIND TO CATCH UP NOW.
FLY, GARTH, FLY! FASTER, MAN!
S'RELLA WAS GAINING ON HIM. THE PROSPECT OF LOSING A PAIR OF WINGS WAS SOMETHING NO LANDSMAN COULD RELISH.
SHE'S DOING WELL!
NOT WELL ENOUGH.
AS GARTH BEGAN HIS DESCENT, HE CUT IN FRONT OF S'RELLA.
SHE SEESAWED FOR A MOMENT, GIVING HIM A CHANCE TO OPEN HIS LEAD STILL MORE BEFORE SHE STABILIZED.

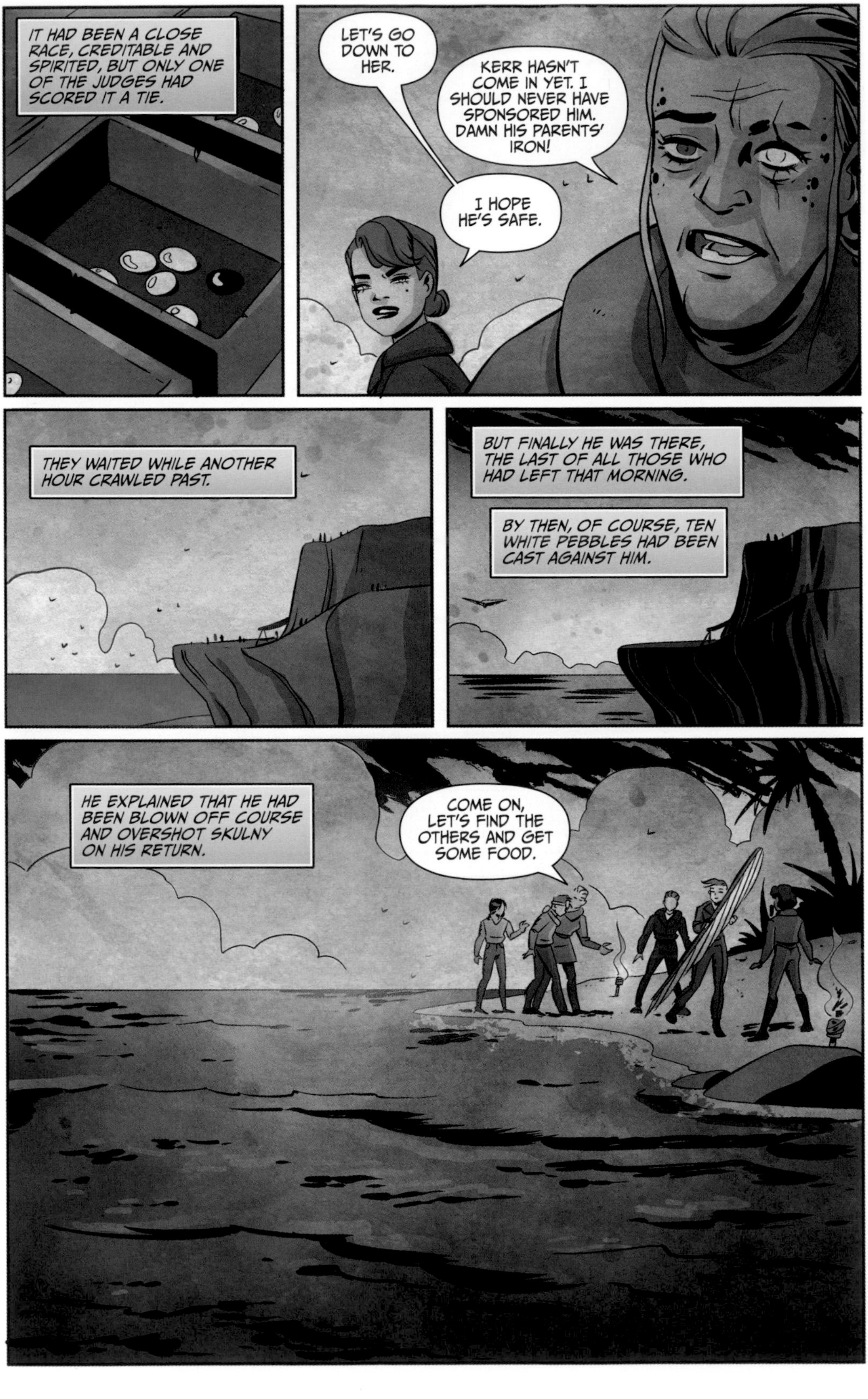
IT HAD BEEN A CLOSE RACE, CREDITABLE AND SPIRITED, BUT ONLY ONE OF THE JUDGES HAD SCORED IT A TIE.
LET'S GO DOWN TO HER.
KERR HASN'T COME IN YET. I SHOULD NEVER HAVE SPONSORED HIM. DAMN HIS PARENTS' IRON!
I HOPE HE'S SAFE.
THEY WAITED WHILE ANOTHER HOUR CRAWLED PAST.
BUT FINALLY HE WAS THERE, THE LAST OF ALL THOSE WHO HAD LEFT THAT MORNING.
BY THEN, OF COURSE, TEN WHITE PEBBLES HAD BEEN CAST AGAINST HIM.
HE EXPLAINED THAT HE HAD BEEN BLOWN OFF COURSE AND OVERSHOT SKULNY ON HIS RETURN.
COME ON, LET'S FIND THE OTHERS AND GET SOME FOOD.

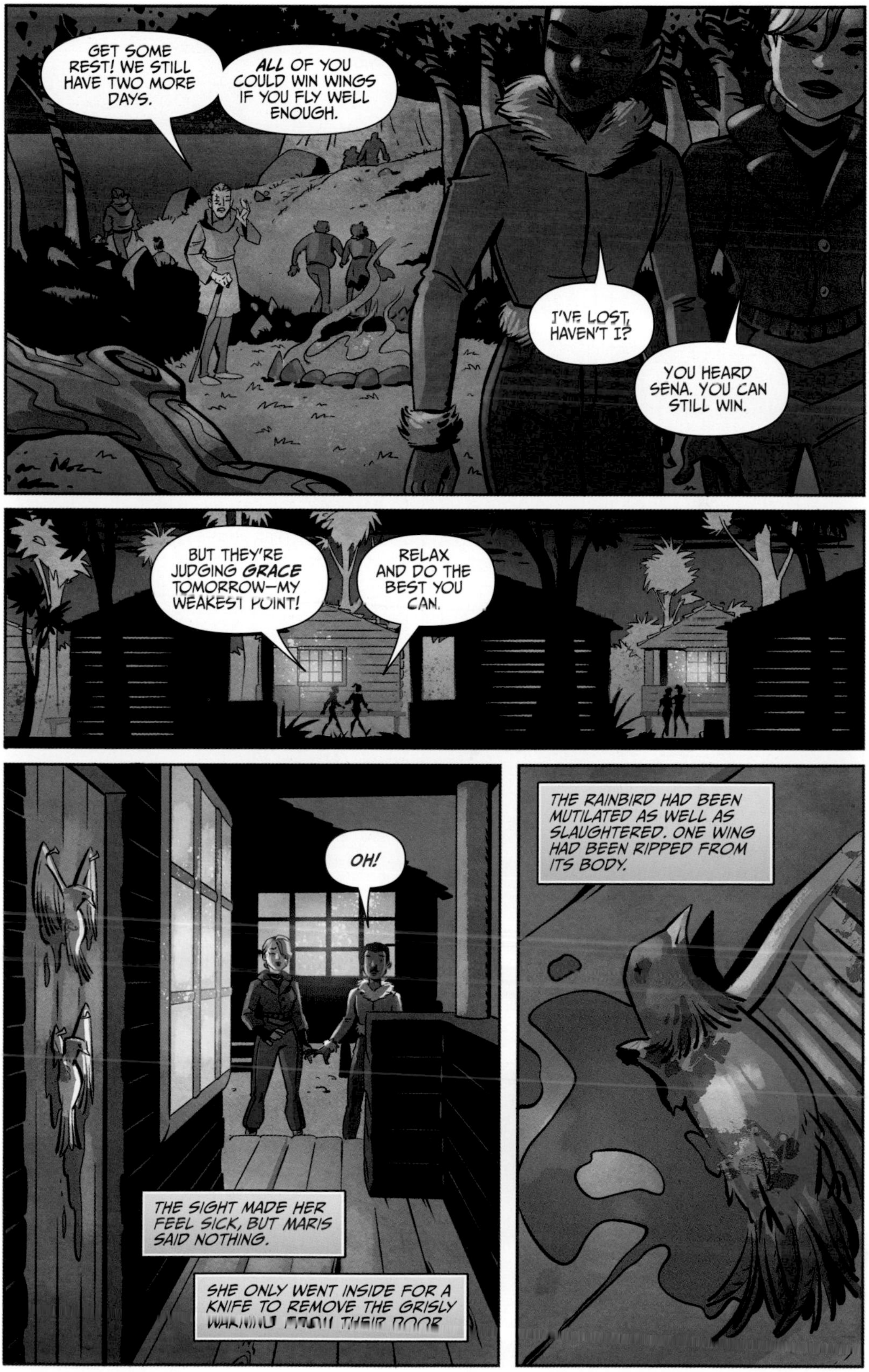
GET SOME REST! WE STILL HAVE TWO MORE DAYS.
ALL OF YOU COULD WIN WINGS IF YOU FLY WELL ENOUGH.
I'VE LOST, HAVEN'T I?
YOU HEARD SENA. YOU CAN STILL WIN.
BUT THEY'RE JUDGING GRACE TOMORROW—MY WEAKEST POINT!
RELAX AND DO THE BEST YOU CAN.
OH!
THE SIGHT MADE HER FEEL SICK, BUT MARIS SAID NOTHING.
SHE ONLY WENT INSIDE FOR A KNIFE TO REMOVE THE GRISLY WARNING FROM THEIR DOOR
THE RAINBIRD HAD BEEN MUTILATED AS WELL AS SLAUGHTERED. ONE WING HAD BEEN RIPPED FROM ITS BODY.

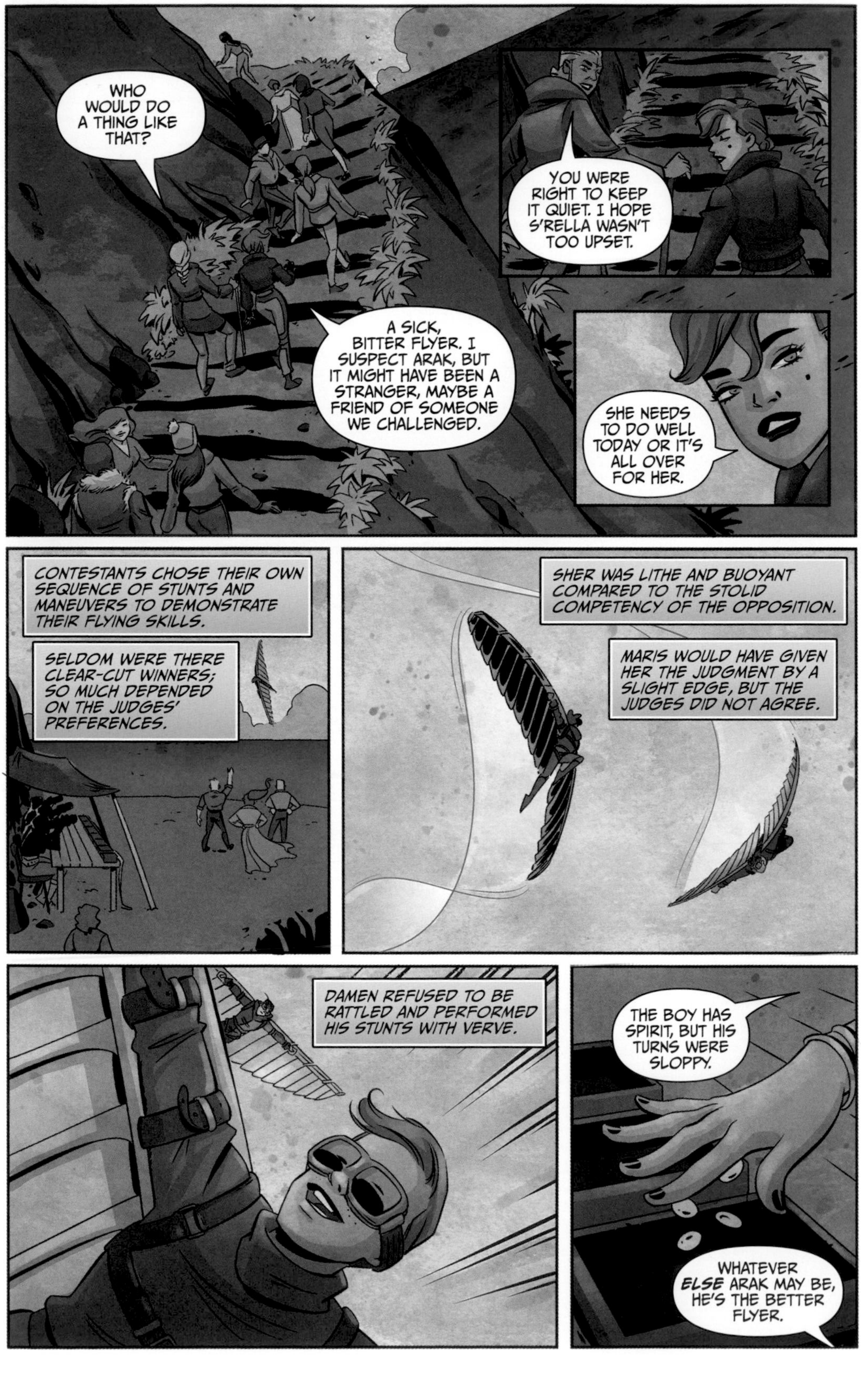

WHO WOULD DO A THING LIKE THAT?
A SICK, BITTER FLYER. I SUSPECT ARAK, BUT IT MIGHT HAVE BEEN A STRANGER, MAYBE A FRIEND OF SOMEONE WE CHALLENGED.
YOU WERE RIGHT TO KEEP IT QUIET. I HOPE S'RELLA WASN'T TOO UPSET.
SHE NEEDS TO DO WELL TODAY OR IT'S ALL OVER FOR HER.
CONTESTANTS CHOSE THEIR OWN SEQUENCE OF STUNTS AND MANEUVERS TO DEMONSTRATE THEIR FLYING SKILLS.
SELDOM WERE THERE CLEAR-CUT WINNERS; SO MUCH DEPENDED ON THE JUDGES' PREFERENCES.
SHER WAS LITHE AND BUOYANT COMPARED TO THE STOLID COMPETENCY OF THE OPPOSITION.
MARIS WOULD HAVE GIVEN HER THE JUDGMENT BY A SLIGHT EDGE, BUT THE JUDGES DID NOT AGREE.
DAMEN REFUSED TO BE RATTLED AND PERFORMED HIS STUNTS WITH VERVE.
THE BOY HAS SPIRIT, BUT HIS TURNS WERE SLOPPY.
WHATEVER ELSE ARAK MAY BE, HE'S THE BETTER FLYER.

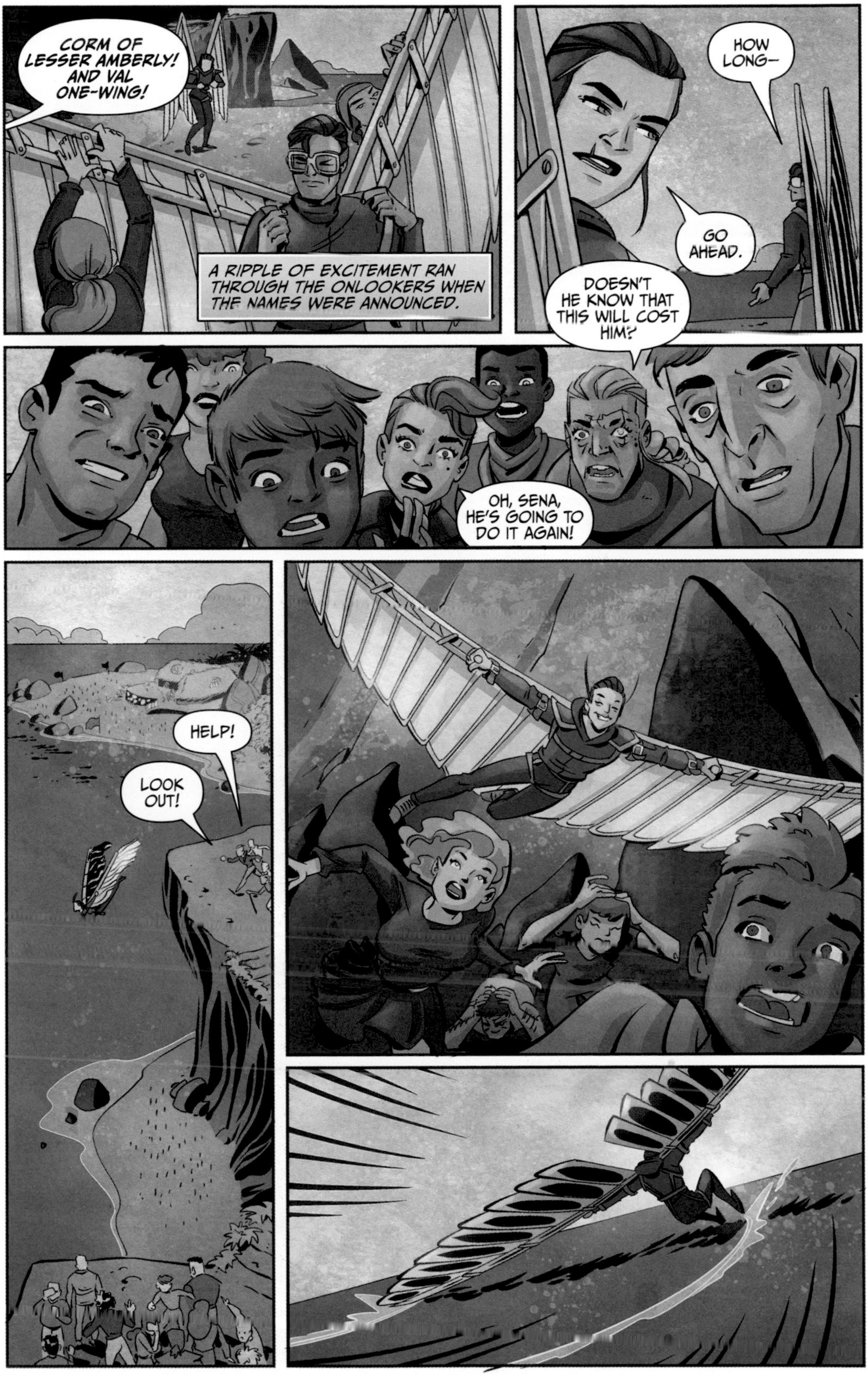
CORM OF LESSER AMBERLY! AND VAL ONE-WING!
A RIPPLE OF EXCITEMENT RAN THROUGH THE ONLOOKERS WHEN THE NAMES WERE ANNOUNCED.
HOW LONG—
GO AHEAD.
DOESN'T HE KNOW THAT THIS WILL COST HIM?
OH, SENA, HE'S GOING TO DO IT AGAIN!
HELP!
LOOK OUT!

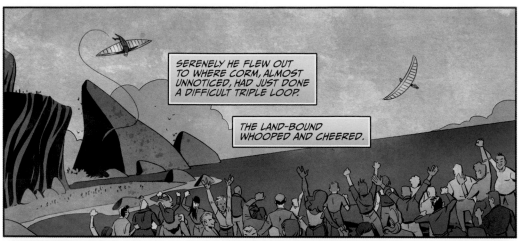

SERENELY HE FLEW OUT TO WHERE CORM, ALMOST UNNOTICED, HAD JUST DONE A DIFFICULT TRIPLE LOOP.

THE LAND-BOUND WHOOPED AND CHEERED.

DAMN! EVEN *RAVEN* NEVER DID IT BETTER!

A CHEAP TRICK. DANGEROUS, TOO.

I'VE NEVER SEEN ANYTHING LIKE IT! HOW DID HE *DO* IT?

VAL FLEW WELL, BUT CORM FLEW BETTER, WITH GRACE AND THE SKILL OF LONG PRACTICE.

BUT AFTER RAVEN'S FALL, NO AMOUNT OF FINESSE MATTERED.

ONE FOOLHARDY STUNT DOES NOT CHANGE THE FACT THAT CORM WAS SUPERIOR OVERALL.

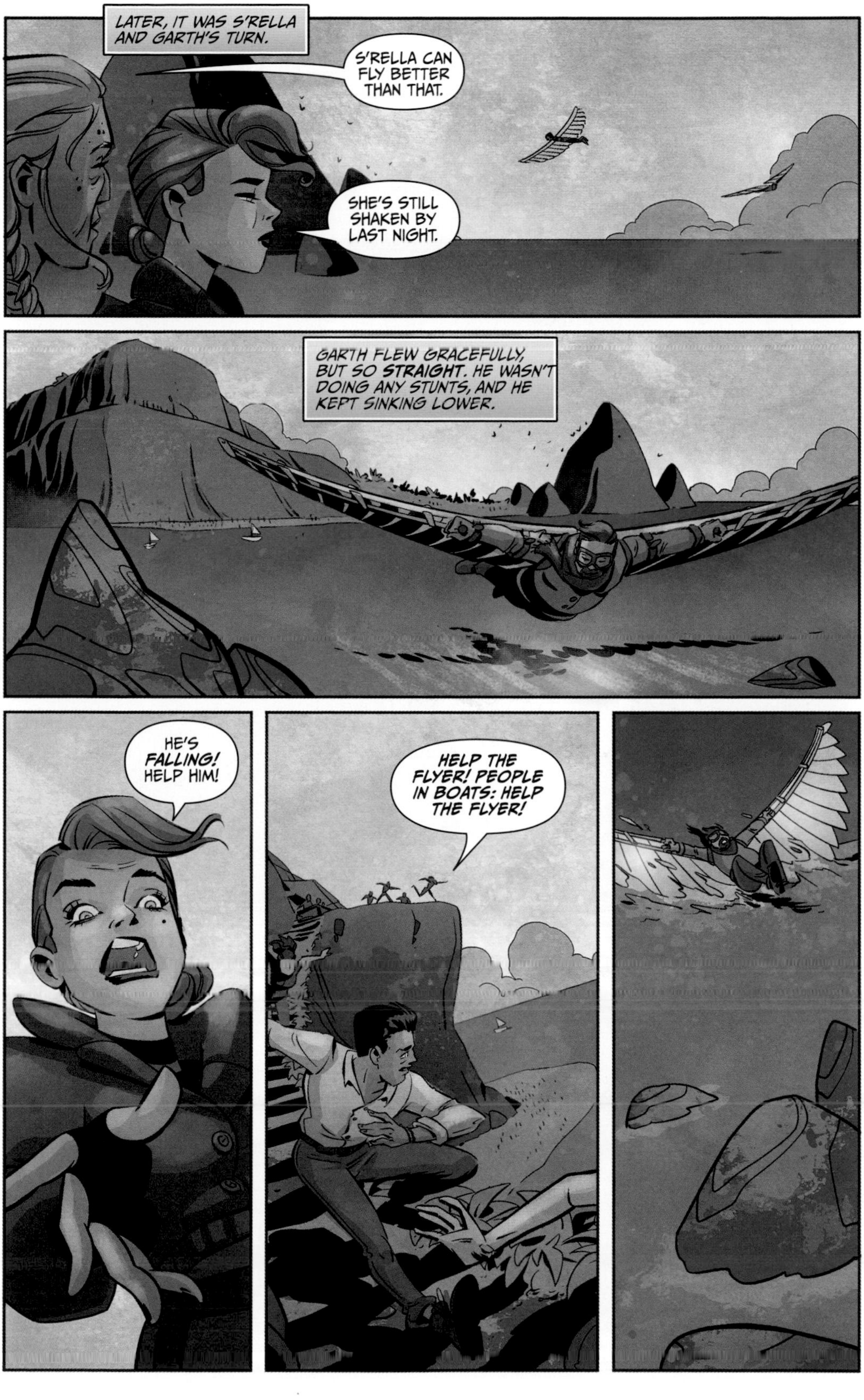
LATER, IT WAS S'RELLA AND GARTH'S TURN.
S'RELLA CAN FLY BETTER THAN THAT.
SHE'S STILL SHAKEN BY LAST NIGHT.
GARTH FLEW GRACEFULLY, BUT SO STRAIGHT. HE WASN'T DOING ANY STUNTS, AND HE KEPT SINKING LOWER.
HE'S FALLING! HELP HIM!
HELP THE FLYER! PEOPLE IN BOATS: HELP THE FLYER!

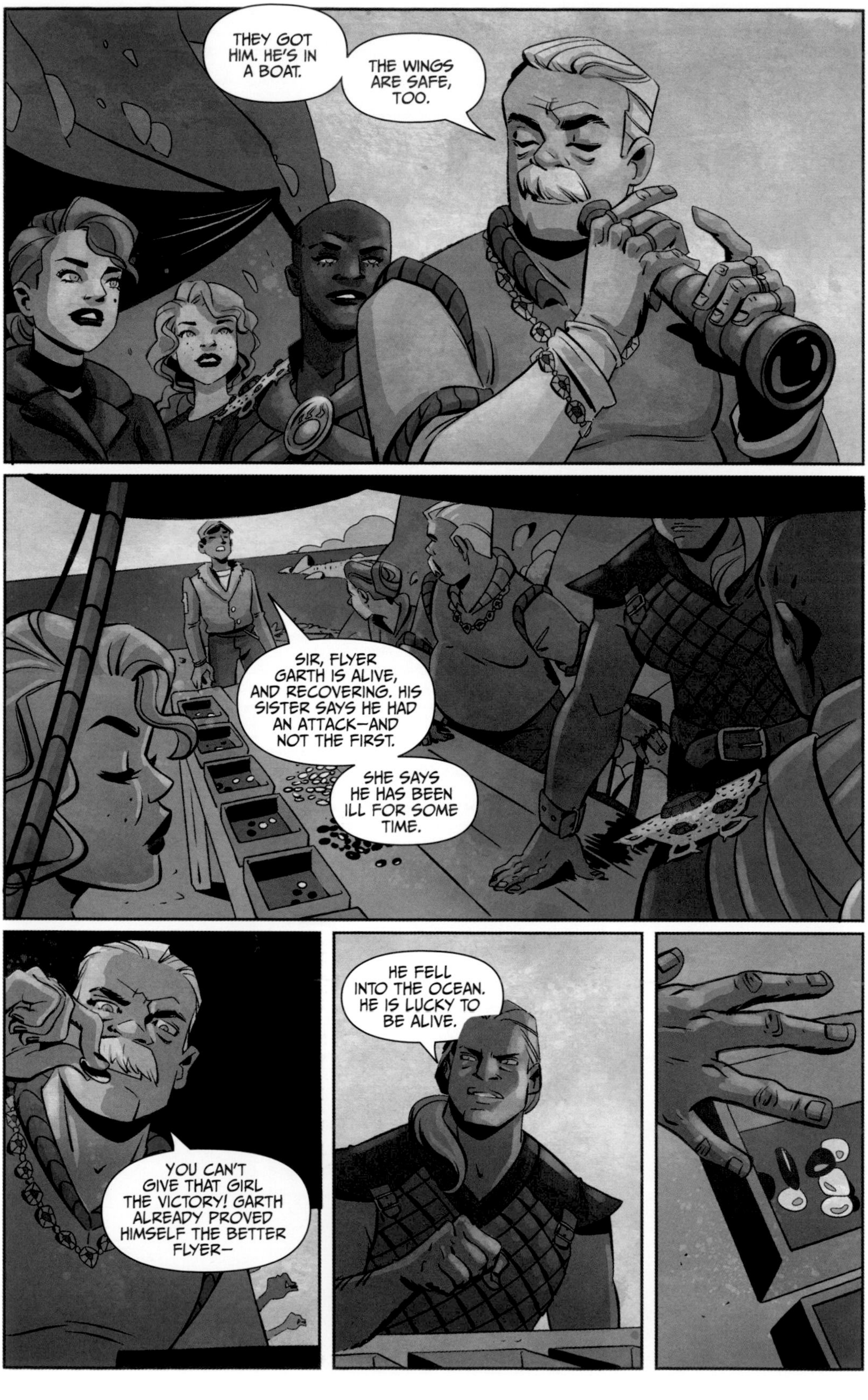
THEY GOT HIM. HE'S IN A BOAT.
THE WINGS ARE SAFE, TOO.
SIR, FLYER GARTH IS ALIVE, AND RECOVERING. HIS SISTER SAYS HE HAD AN ATTACK—AND NOT THE FIRST.
SHE SAYS HE HAS BEEN ILL FOR SOME TIME.
YOU CAN'T GIVE THAT GIRL THE VICTORY! GARTH ALREADY PROVED HIMSELF THE BETTER FLYER—
HE FELL INTO THE OCEAN. HE IS LUCKY TO BE ALIVE.

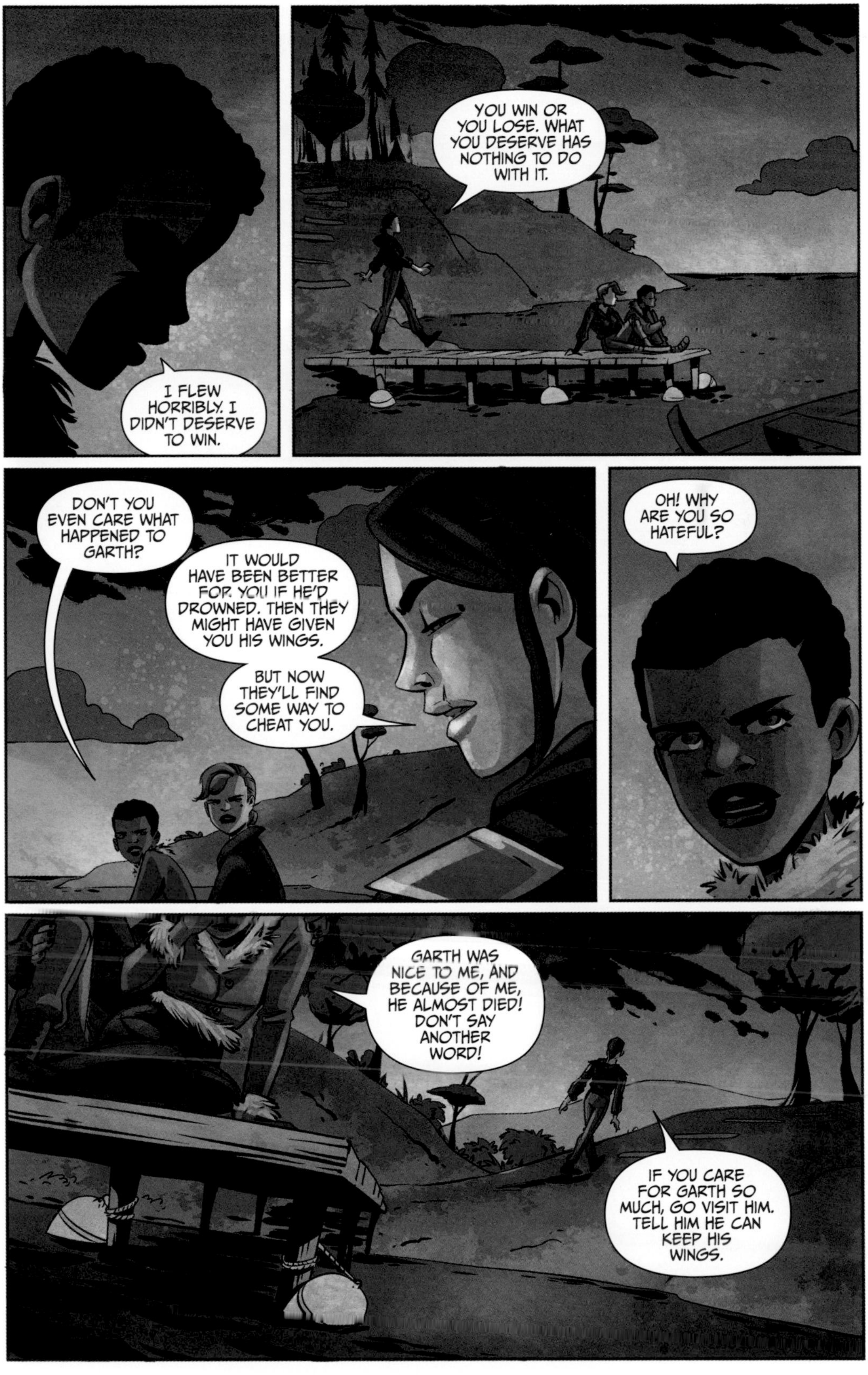
I FLEW HORRIBLY. I DIDN'T DESERVE TO WIN.
YOU WIN OR YOU LOSE. WHAT YOU DESERVE HAS NOTHING TO DO WITH IT.
DON'T YOU EVEN CARE WHAT HAPPENED TO GARTH?
IT WOULD HAVE BEEN BETTER FOR YOU IF HE'D DROWNED. THEN THEY MIGHT HAVE GIVEN YOU HIS WINGS.
BUT NOW THEY'LL FIND SOME WAY TO CHEAT YOU.
OH! WHY ARE YOU SO HATEFUL?
GARTH WAS NICE TO ME, AND BECAUSE OF ME, HE ALMOST DIED! DON'T SAY ANOTHER WORD!
IF YOU CARE FOR GARTH SO MUCH, GO VISIT HIM. TELL HIM HE CAN KEEP HIS WINGS.

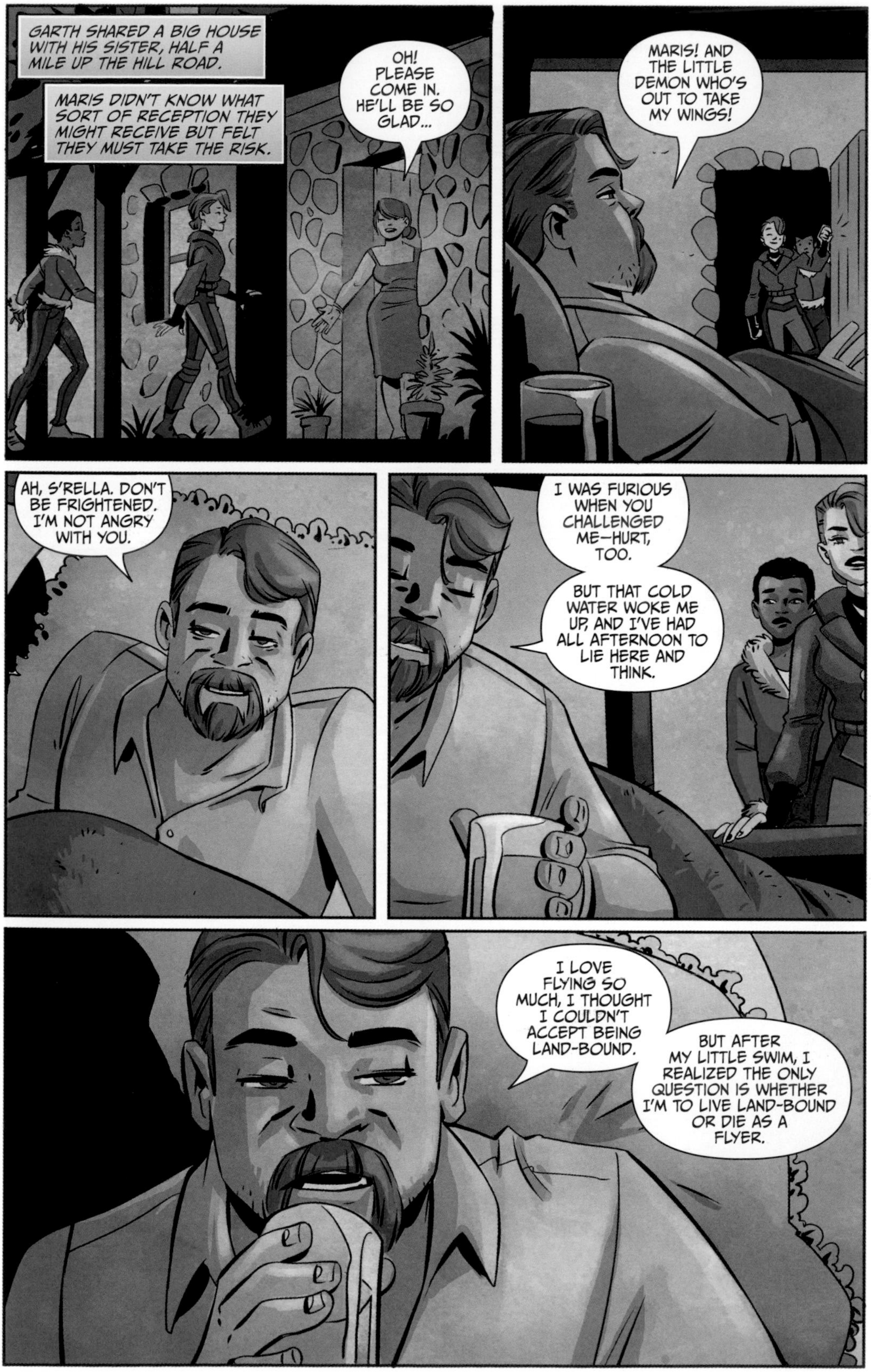
GARTH SHARED A BIG HOUSE WITH HIS SISTER, HALF A MILE UP THE HILL ROAD.
MARIS DIDN'T KNOW WHAT SORT OF RECEPTION THEY MIGHT RECEIVE BUT FELT THEY MUST TAKE THE RISK.
OH! PLEASE COME IN. HE'LL BE SO GLAD...
MARIS! AND THE LITTLE DEMON WHO'S OUT TO TAKE MY WINGS!
AH, S'RELLA. DON'T BE FRIGHTENED. I'M NOT ANGRY WITH YOU.
I WAS FURIOUS WHEN YOU CHALLENGED ME—HURT, TOO.
BUT THAT COLD WATER WOKE ME UP, AND I'VE HAD ALL AFTERNOON TO LIE HERE AND THINK.
I LOVE FLYING SO MUCH, I THOUGHT I COULDN'T ACCEPT BEING LAND-BOUND.
BUT AFTER MY LITTLE SWIM, I REALIZED THE ONLY QUESTION IS WHETHER I'M TO LIVE LAND-BOUND OR DIE AS A FLYER.

WHAT I MEAN TO SAY IS THAT I CAN'T COMPETE TOMORROW. I'M NOT EVEN GOING TO TRY.

THE SEA—WITH A LITTLE HELP FROM MY SISTER—BROUGHT ME TO MY SENSES. THE WINGS ARE YOURS.

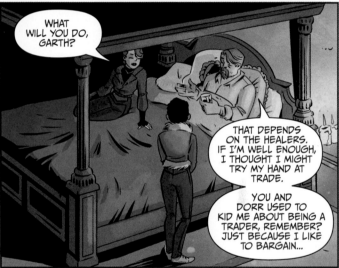

WHAT WILL YOU DO, GARTH?

THAT DEPENDS ON THE HEALERS. IF I'M WELL ENOUGH, I THOUGHT I MIGHT TRY MY HAND AT TRADE.

YOU AND DORR USED TO KID ME ABOUT BEING A TRADER, REMEMBER? JUST BECAUSE I LIKE TO BARGAIN...

SOME TRADER I TURNED OUT TO BE... GIVE MY WINGS TO S'RELLA, BUT WHAT DOES SHE GIVE *ME*?

IT'S SO DAMNED ROTTEN...

PROMISE YOU'LL COME AND SEE ME. BAD ENOUGH TO LOSE MY WINGS, THE WIND, AND FREEDOM, BUT IF I LOSE MY FRIENDS...

I PROMISE.

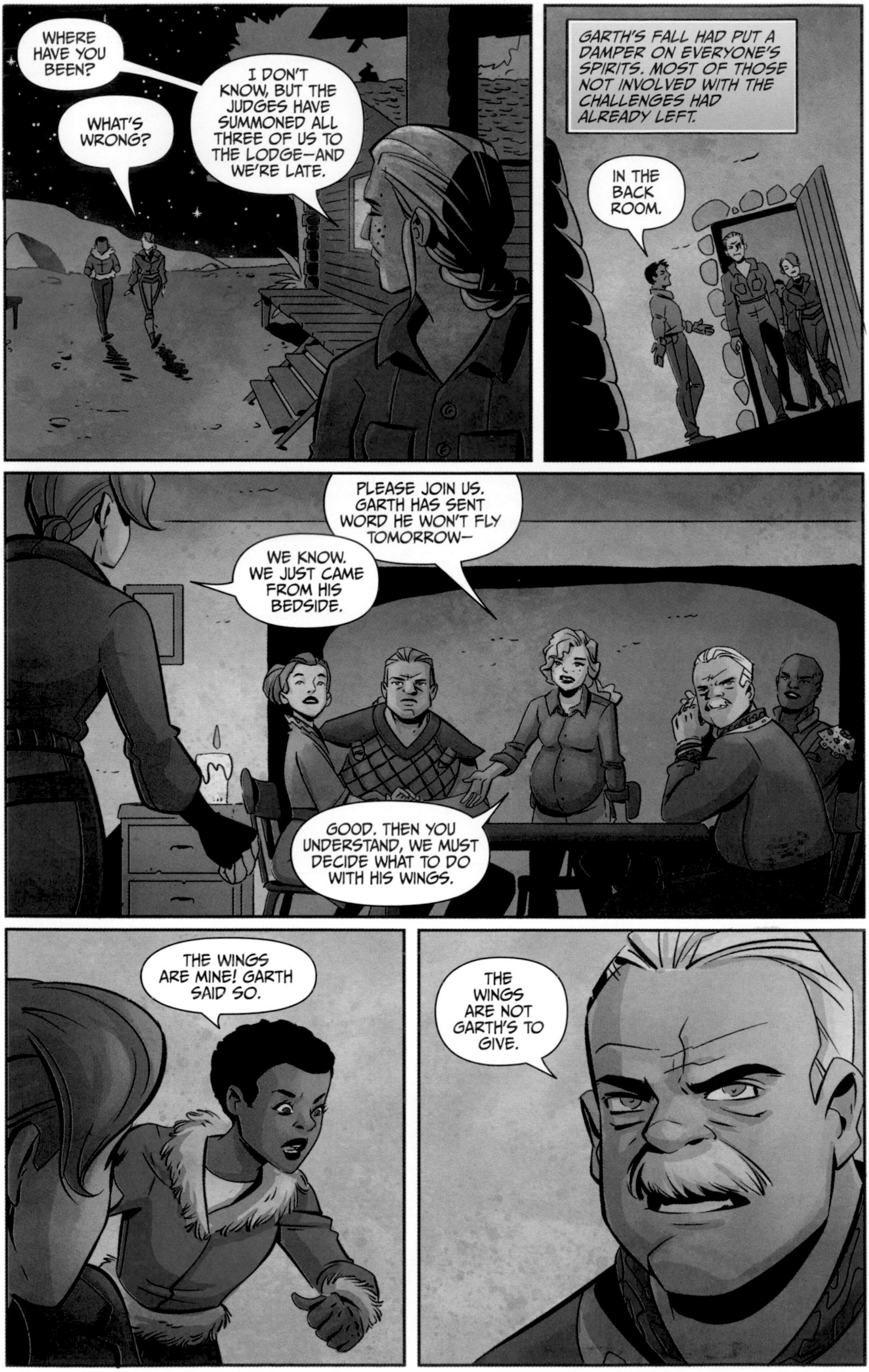

WHERE HAVE YOU BEEN?
WHAT'S WRONG?
I DON'T KNOW, BUT THE JUDGES HAVE SUMMONED ALL THREE OF US TO THE LODGE—AND WE'RE LATE.
GARTH'S FALL HAD PUT A DAMPER ON EVERYONE'S SPIRITS. MOST OF THOSE NOT INVOLVED WITH THE CHALLENGES HAD ALREADY LEFT.
IN THE BACK ROOM.
PLEASE JOIN US. GARTH HAS SENT WORD HE WON'T FLY TOMORROW—
WE KNOW. WE JUST CAME FROM HIS BEDSIDE.
GOOD. THEN YOU UNDERSTAND, WE MUST DECIDE WHAT TO DO WITH HIS WINGS.
THE WINGS ARE MINE! GARTH SAID SO.
THE WINGS ARE NOT GARTH'S TO GIVE.

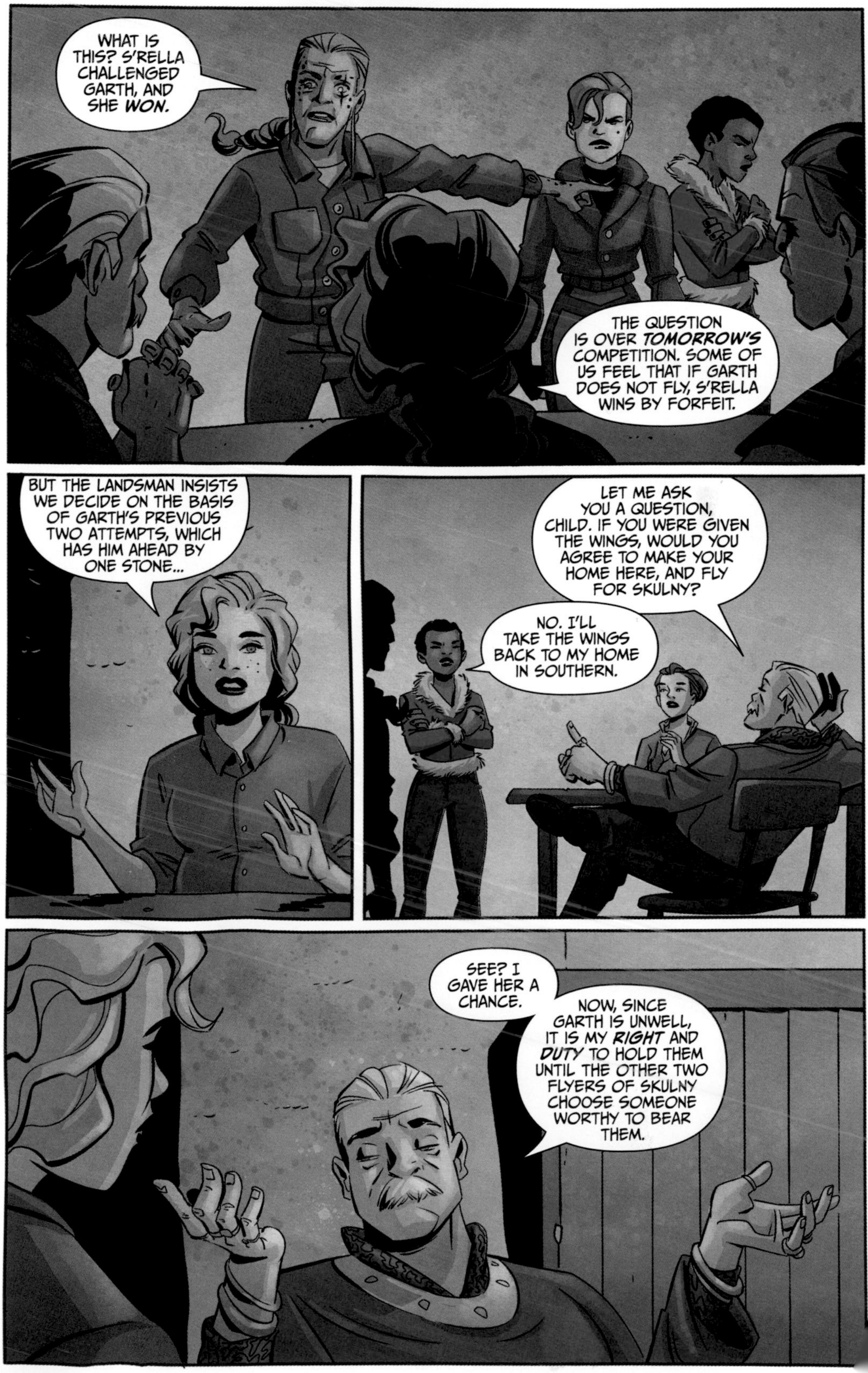
WHAT IS THIS? S'RELLA CHALLENGED GARTH, AND SHE WON.
THE QUESTION IS OVER TOMORROW'S COMPETITION. SOME OF US FEEL THAT IF GARTH DOES NOT FLY, S'RELLA WINS BY FORFEIT.
BUT THE LANDSMAN INSISTS WE DECIDE ON THE BASIS OF GARTH'S PREVIOUS TWO ATTEMPTS, WHICH HAS HIM AHEAD BY ONE STONE...
LET ME ASK YOU A QUESTION, CHILD. IF YOU WERE GIVEN THE WINGS, WOULD YOU AGREE TO MAKE YOUR HOME HERE, AND FLY FOR SKULNY?
NO. I'LL TAKE THE WINGS BACK TO MY HOME IN SOUTHERN.
SEE? I GAVE HER A CHANCE.
NOW, SINCE GARTH IS UNWELL, IT IS MY RIGHT AND DUTY TO HOLD THEM UNTIL THE OTHER TWO FLYERS OF SKULNY CHOOSE SOMEONE WORTHY TO BEAR THEM.

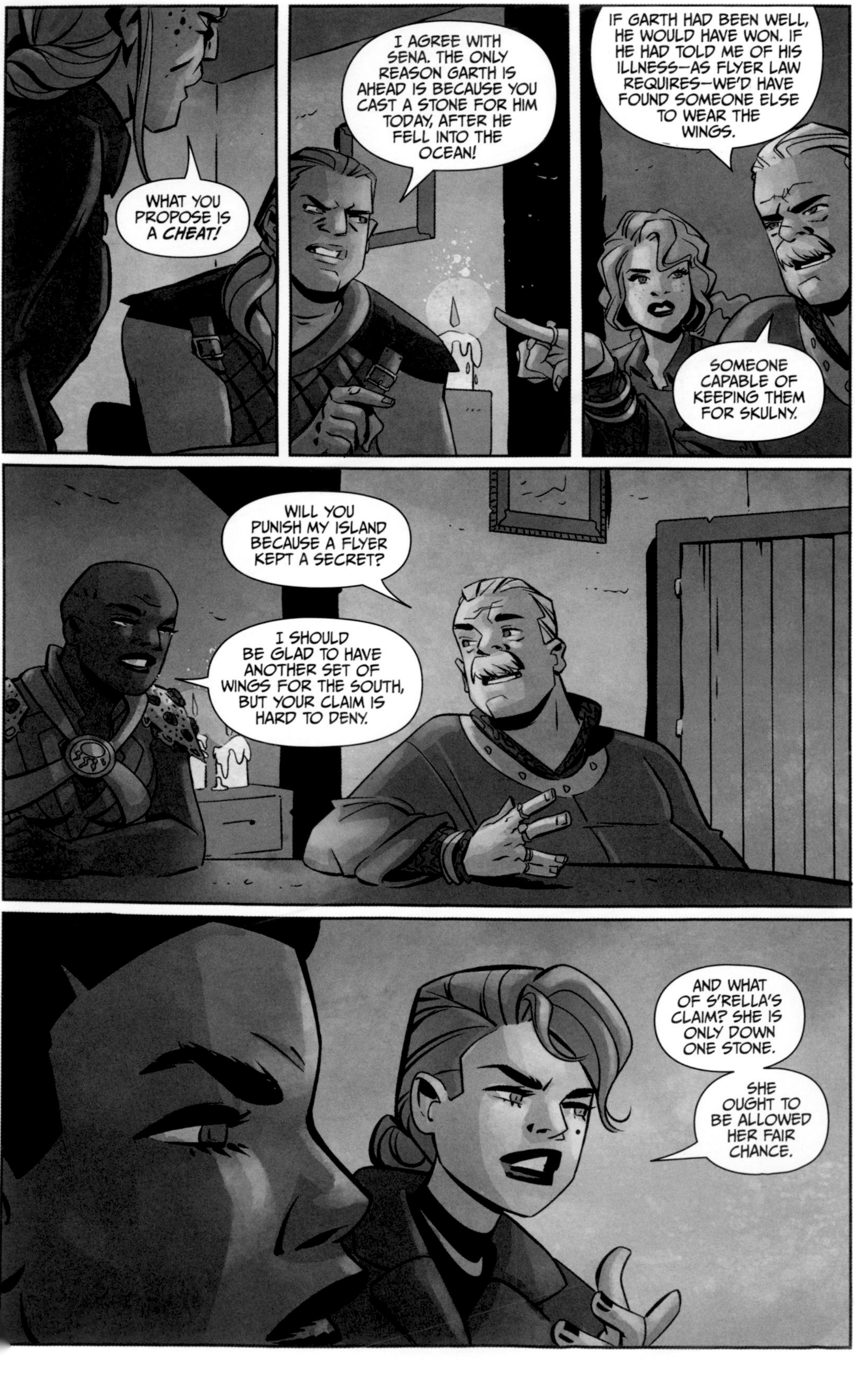
WHAT YOU PROPOSE IS A *CHEAT!*
I AGREE WITH SENA. THE ONLY REASON GARTH IS AHEAD IS BECAUSE YOU CAST A STONE FOR HIM TODAY, AFTER HE FELL INTO THE OCEAN!
IF GARTH HAD BEEN WELL, HE WOULD HAVE WON. IF HE HAD TOLD ME OF HIS ILLNESS—AS FLYER LAW REQUIRES—WE'D HAVE FOUND SOMEONE ELSE TO WEAR THE WINGS.
SOMEONE CAPABLE OF KEEPING THEM FOR SKULNY.
WILL YOU PUNISH MY ISLAND BECAUSE A FLYER KEPT A SECRET?
I SHOULD BE GLAD TO HAVE ANOTHER SET OF WINGS FOR THE SOUTH, BUT YOUR CLAIM IS HARD TO DENY.
AND WHAT OF S'RELLA'S CLAIM? SHE IS ONLY DOWN ONE STONE.
SHE OUGHT TO BE ALLOWED HER FAIR CHANCE.

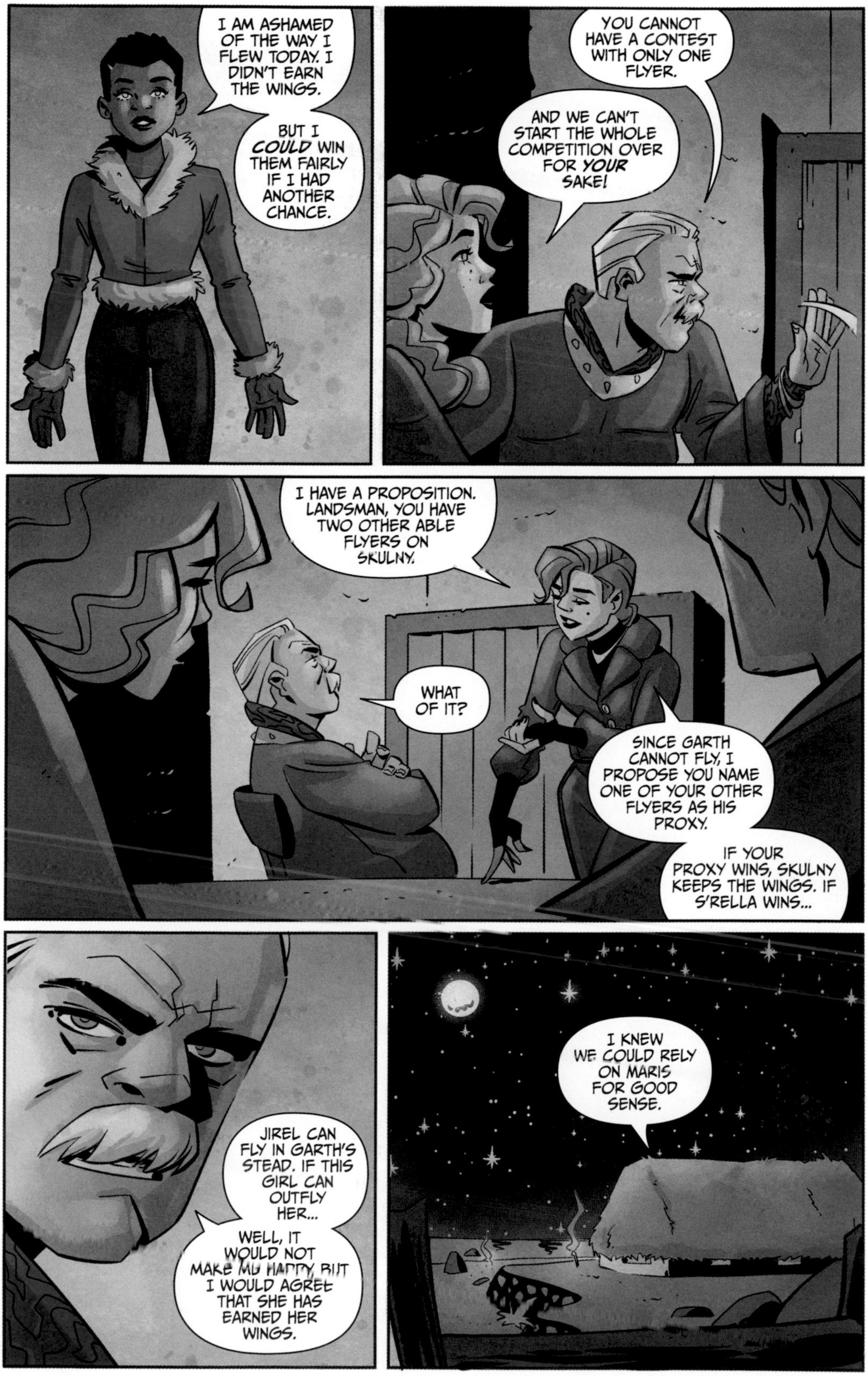
I AM ASHAMED OF THE WAY I FLEW TODAY. I DIDN'T EARN THE WINGS.
BUT I COULD WIN THEM FAIRLY IF I HAD ANOTHER CHANCE.
YOU CANNOT HAVE A CONTEST WITH ONLY ONE FLYER.
AND WE CAN'T START THE WHOLE COMPETITION OVER FOR YOUR SAKE!
I HAVE A PROPOSITION. LANDSMAN, YOU HAVE TWO OTHER ABLE FLYERS ON SKULNY.
WHAT OF IT?
SINCE GARTH CANNOT FLY, I PROPOSE YOU NAME ONE OF YOUR OTHER FLYERS AS HIS PROXY.
IF YOUR PROXY WINS, SKULNY KEEPS THE WINGS. IF S'RELLA WINS...
JIREL CAN FLY IN GARTH'S STEAD. IF THIS GIRL CAN OUTFLY HER...
WELL, IT WOULD NOT MAKE MY HAPPY, BUT I WOULD AGREE THAT SHE HAS EARNED HER WINGS.
I KNEW WE COULD RELY ON MARIS FOR GOOD SENSE.

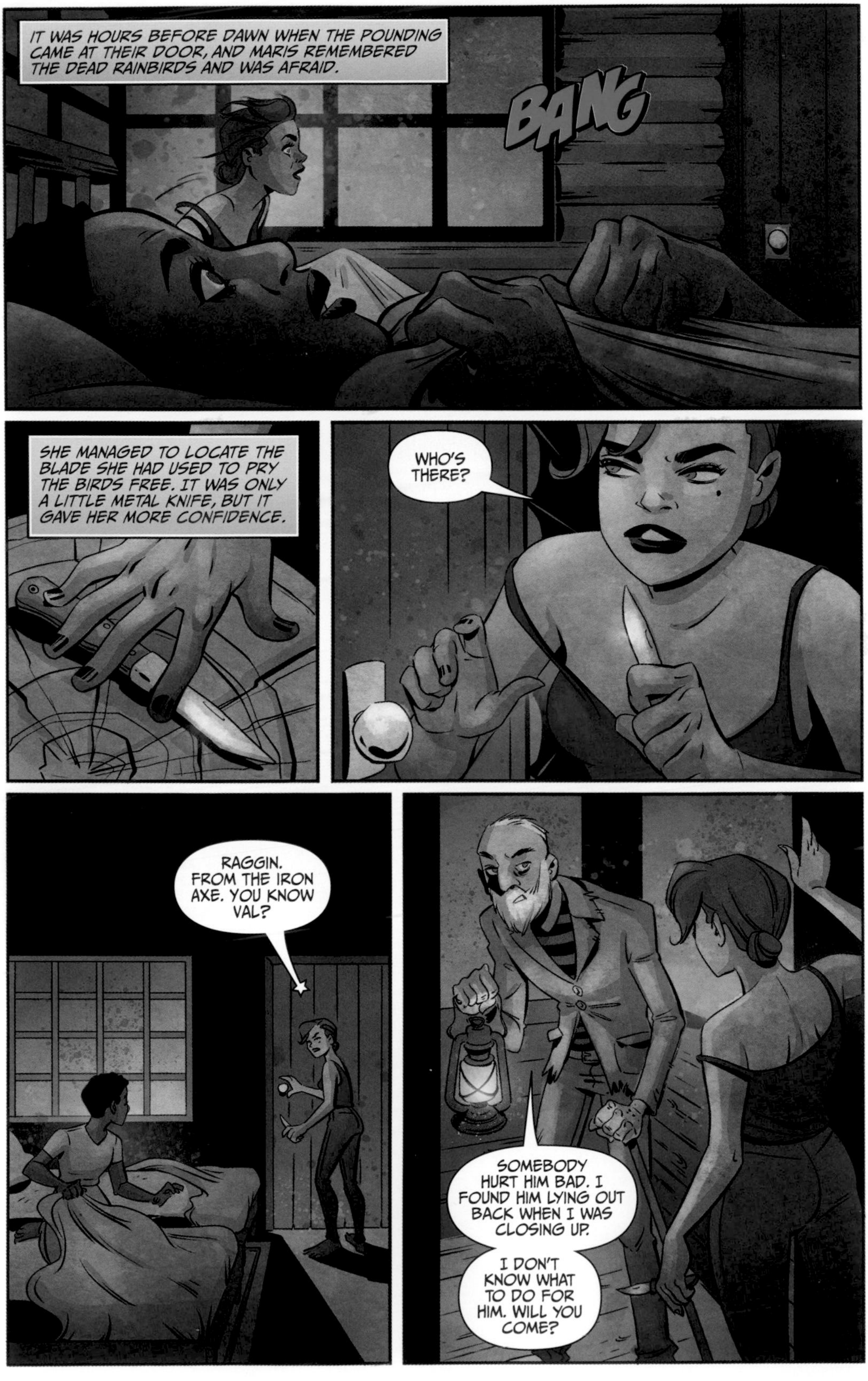
IT WAS HOURS BEFORE DAWN WHEN THE POUNDING CAME AT THEIR DOOR, AND MARIS REMEMBERED THE DEAD RAINBIRDS AND WAS AFRAID.
BANG
SHE MANAGED TO LOCATE THE BLADE SHE HAD USED TO PRY THE BIRDS FREE. IT WAS ONLY A LITTLE METAL KNIFE, BUT IT GAVE HER MORE CONFIDENCE.
WHO'S THERE?
RAGGIN. FROM THE IRON AXE. YOU KNOW VAL?
SOMEBODY HURT HIM BAD. I FOUND HIM LYING OUT BACK WHEN I WAS CLOSING UP.
I DON'T KNOW WHAT TO DO FOR HIM. WILL YOU COME?

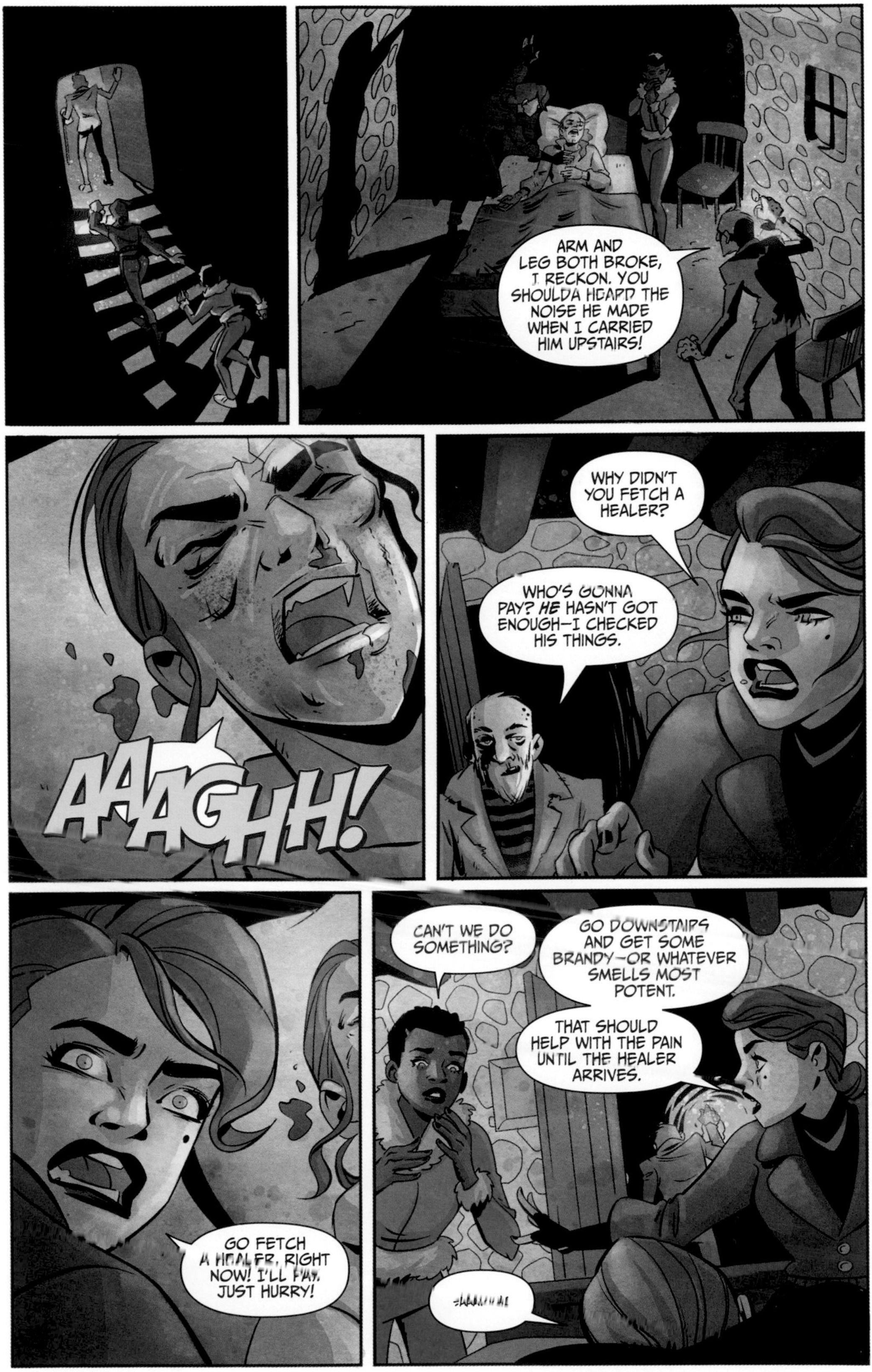
ARM AND LEG BOTH BROKE, I RECKON. YOU SHOULDA HEARD THE NOISE HE MADE WHEN I CARRIED HIM UPSTAIRS!
AAAGHH!
WHY DIDN'T YOU FETCH A HEALER?
WHO'S GONNA PAY? HE HASN'T GOT ENOUGH—I CHECKED HIS THINGS.
GO FETCH A HEALER, RIGHT NOW! I'LL PAY. JUST HURRY!
CAN'T WE DO SOMETHING?
GO DOWNSTAIRS AND GET SOME BRANDY—OR WHATEVER SMELLS MOST POTENT.
THAT SHOULD HELP WITH THE PAIN UNTIL THE HEALER ARRIVES.

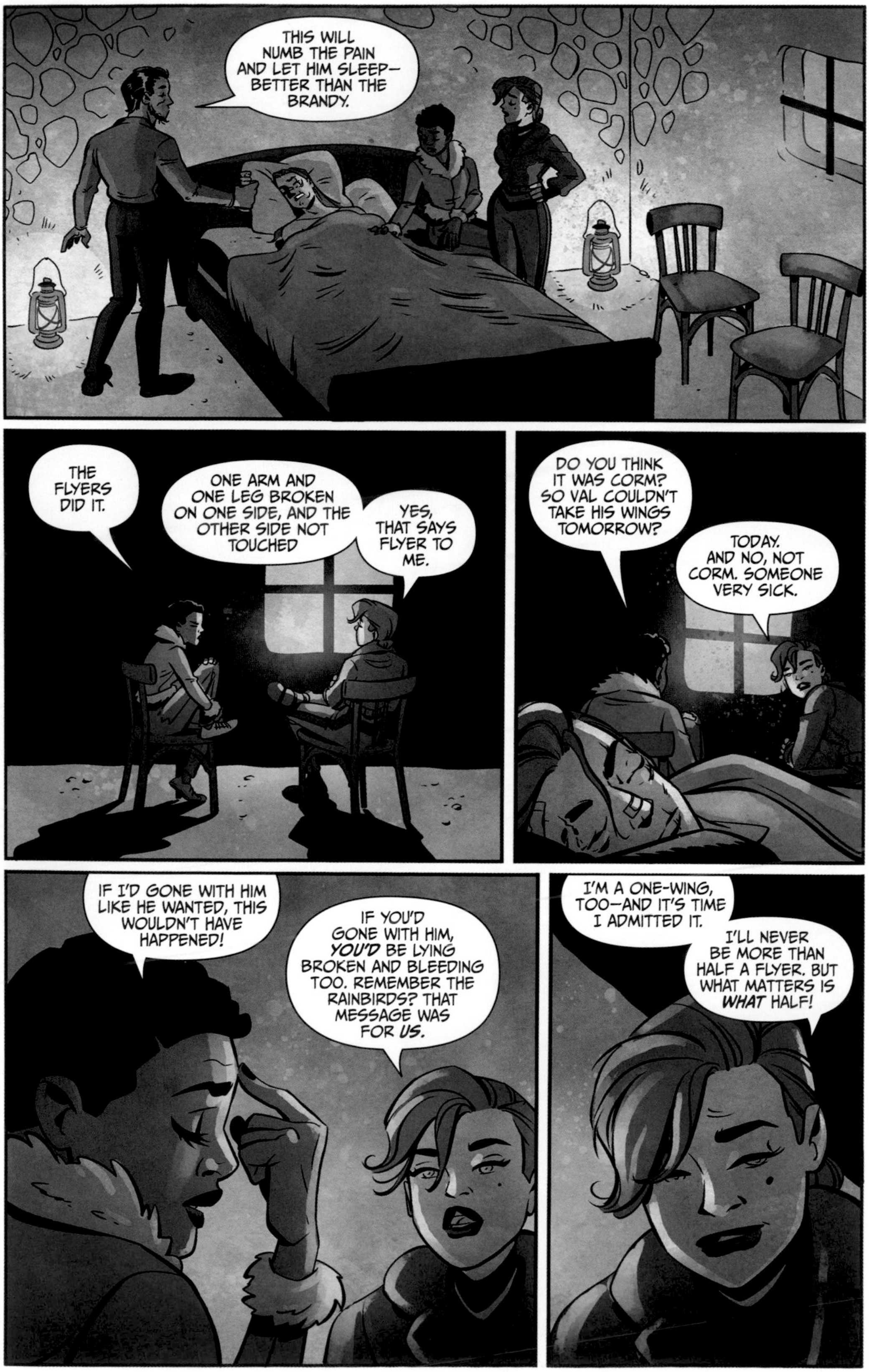
THIS WILL NUMB THE PAIN AND LET HIM SLEEP—BETTER THAN THE BRANDY.
THE FLYERS DID IT.
ONE ARM AND ONE LEG BROKEN ON ONE SIDE, AND THE OTHER SIDE NOT TOUCHED
YES, THAT SAYS FLYER TO ME.
DO YOU THINK IT WAS CORM? SO VAL COULDN'T TAKE HIS WINGS TOMORROW?
TODAY. AND NO, NOT CORM. SOMEONE VERY SICK.
IF I'D GONE WITH HIM LIKE HE WANTED, THIS WOULDN'T HAVE HAPPENED!
IF YOU'D GONE WITH HIM, *YOU'D* BE LYING BROKEN AND BLEEDING TOO. REMEMBER THE RAINBIRDS? THAT MESSAGE WAS FOR *US*.
I'M A ONE-WING, TOO—AND IT'S TIME I ADMITTED IT.
I'LL NEVER BE MORE THAN HALF A FLYER. BUT WHAT MATTERS IS *WHAT* HALF!

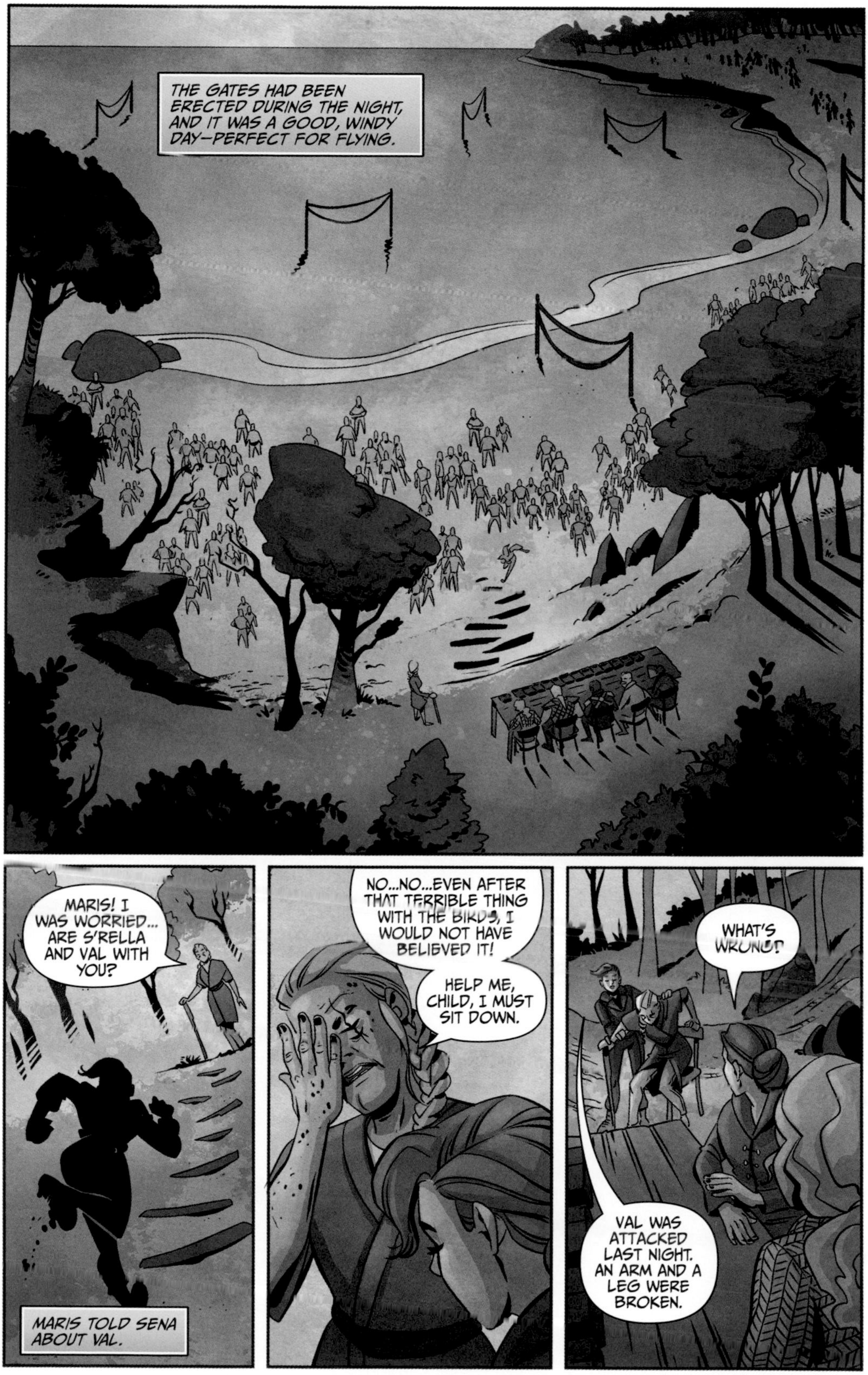
THE GATES HAD BEEN ERECTED DURING THE NIGHT, AND IT WAS A GOOD, WINDY DAY—PERFECT FOR FLYING.
MARIS! I WAS WORRIED... ARE S'RELLA AND VAL WITH YOU?
MARIS TOLD SENA ABOUT VAL.
NO...NO...EVEN AFTER THAT TERRIBLE THING WITH THE BIRDS, I WOULD NOT HAVE BELIEVED IT!
HELP ME, CHILD, I MUST SIT DOWN.
WHAT'S WRONG?
VAL WAS ATTACKED LAST NIGHT. AN ARM AND A LEG WERE BROKEN.

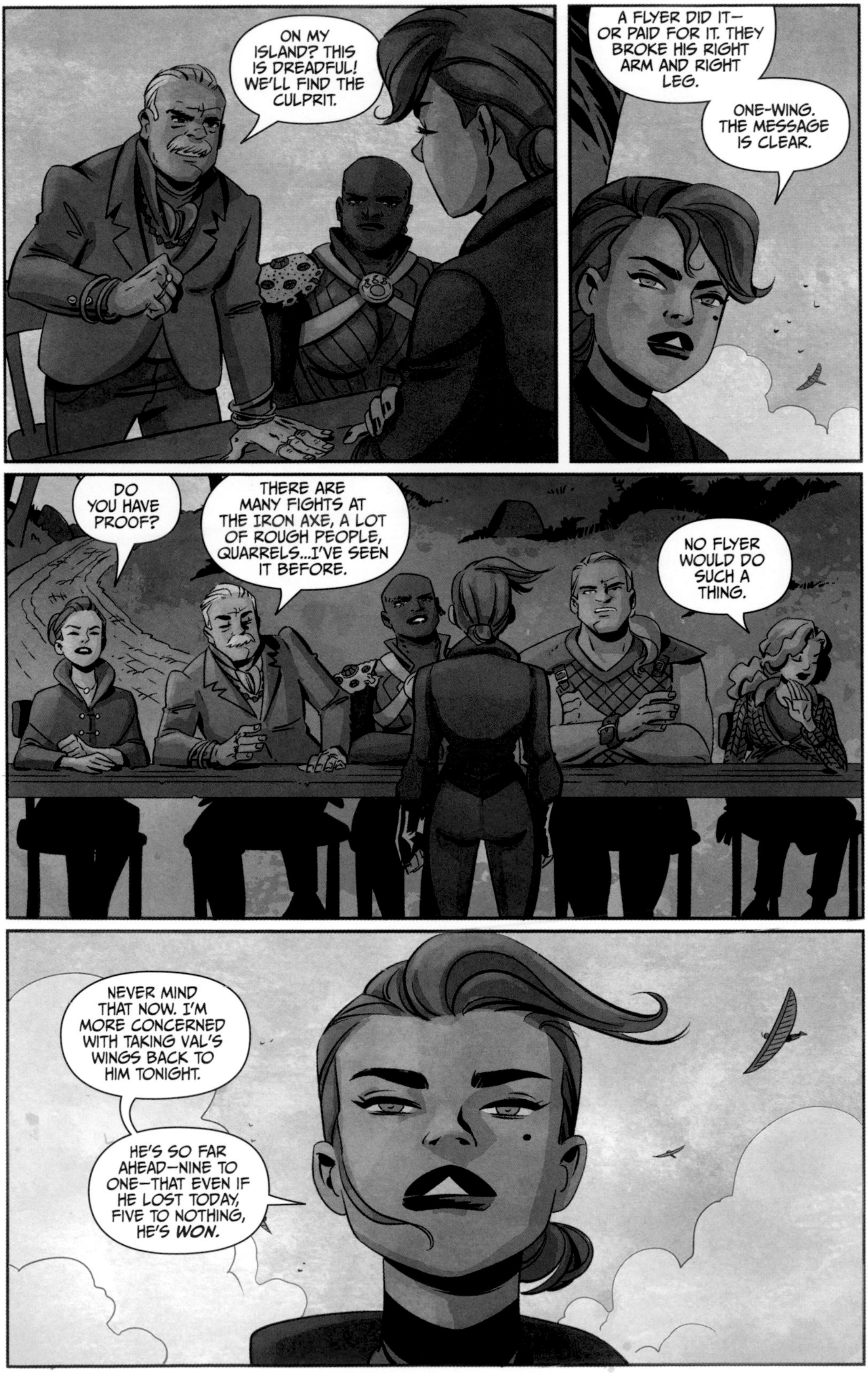
ON MY ISLAND? THIS IS DREADFUL! WE'LL FIND THE CULPRIT.
A FLYER DID IT—OR PAID FOR IT. THEY BROKE HIS RIGHT ARM AND RIGHT LEG.
ONE-WING. THE MESSAGE IS CLEAR.
DO YOU HAVE PROOF?
THERE ARE MANY FIGHTS AT THE IRON AXE, A LOT OF ROUGH PEOPLE, QUARRELS...I'VE SEEN IT BEFORE.
NO FLYER WOULD DO SUCH A THING.
NEVER MIND THAT NOW. I'M MORE CONCERNED WITH TAKING VAL'S WINGS BACK TO HIM TONIGHT.
HE'S SO FAR AHEAD—NINE TO ONE—THAT EVEN IF HE LOST TODAY, FIVE TO NOTHING, HE'S **WON.**

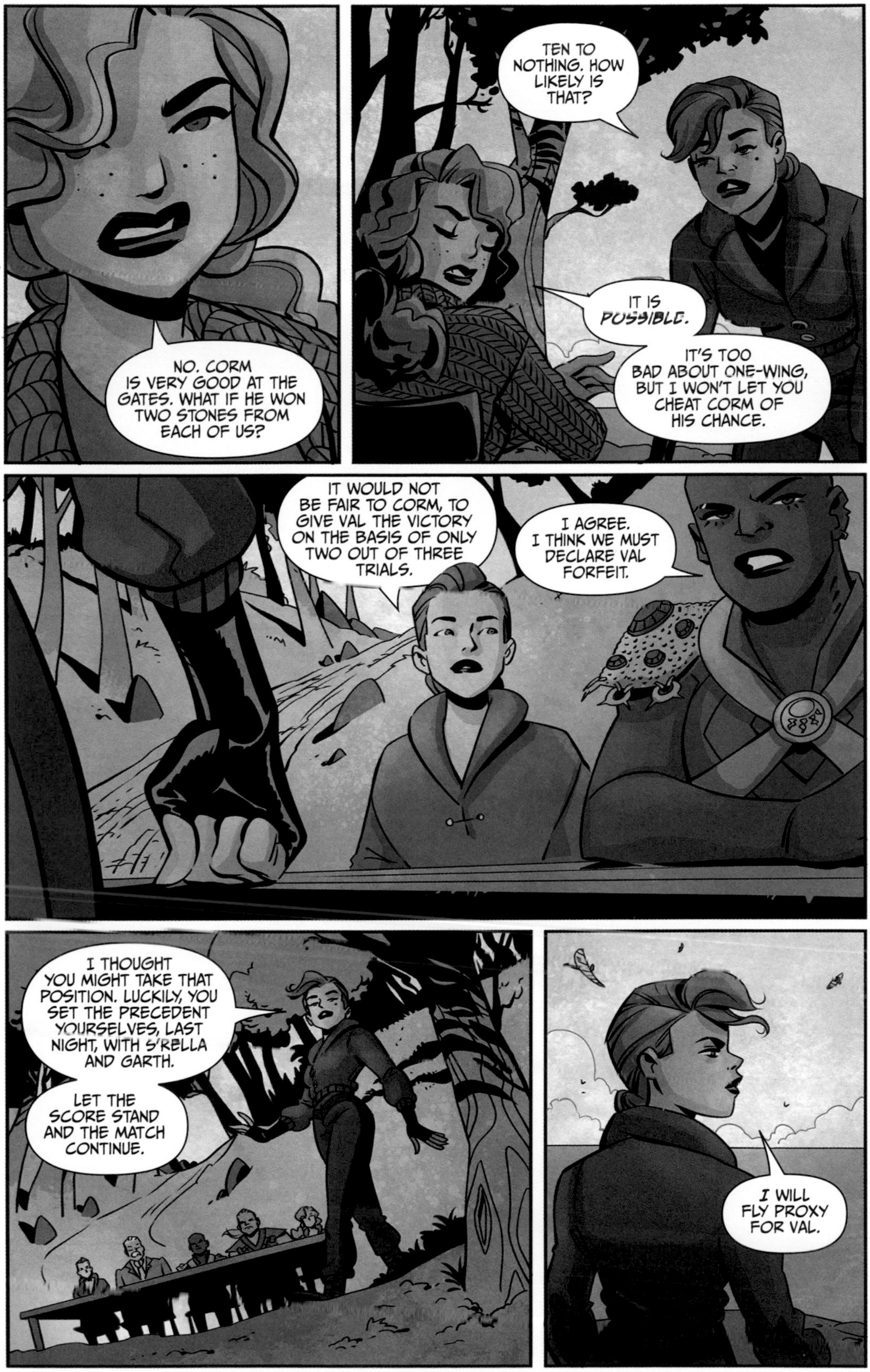
NO. CORM IS VERY GOOD AT THE GATES. WHAT IF HE WON TWO STONES FROM EACH OF US?
TEN TO NOTHING. HOW LIKELY IS THAT?
IT IS POSSIBLE.
IT'S TOO BAD ABOUT ONE-WING, BUT I WON'T LET YOU CHEAT CORM OF HIS CHANCE.
IT WOULD NOT BE FAIR TO CORM, TO GIVE VAL THE VICTORY ON THE BASIS OF ONLY TWO OUT OF THREE TRIALS.
I AGREE. I THINK WE MUST DECLARE VAL FORFEIT.
I THOUGHT YOU MIGHT TAKE THAT POSITION. LUCKILY, YOU SET THE PRECEDENT YOURSELVES, LAST NIGHT, WITH S'RELLA AND GARTH.
LET THE SCORE STAND AND THE MATCH CONTINUE.
I WILL FLY PROXY FOR VAL.

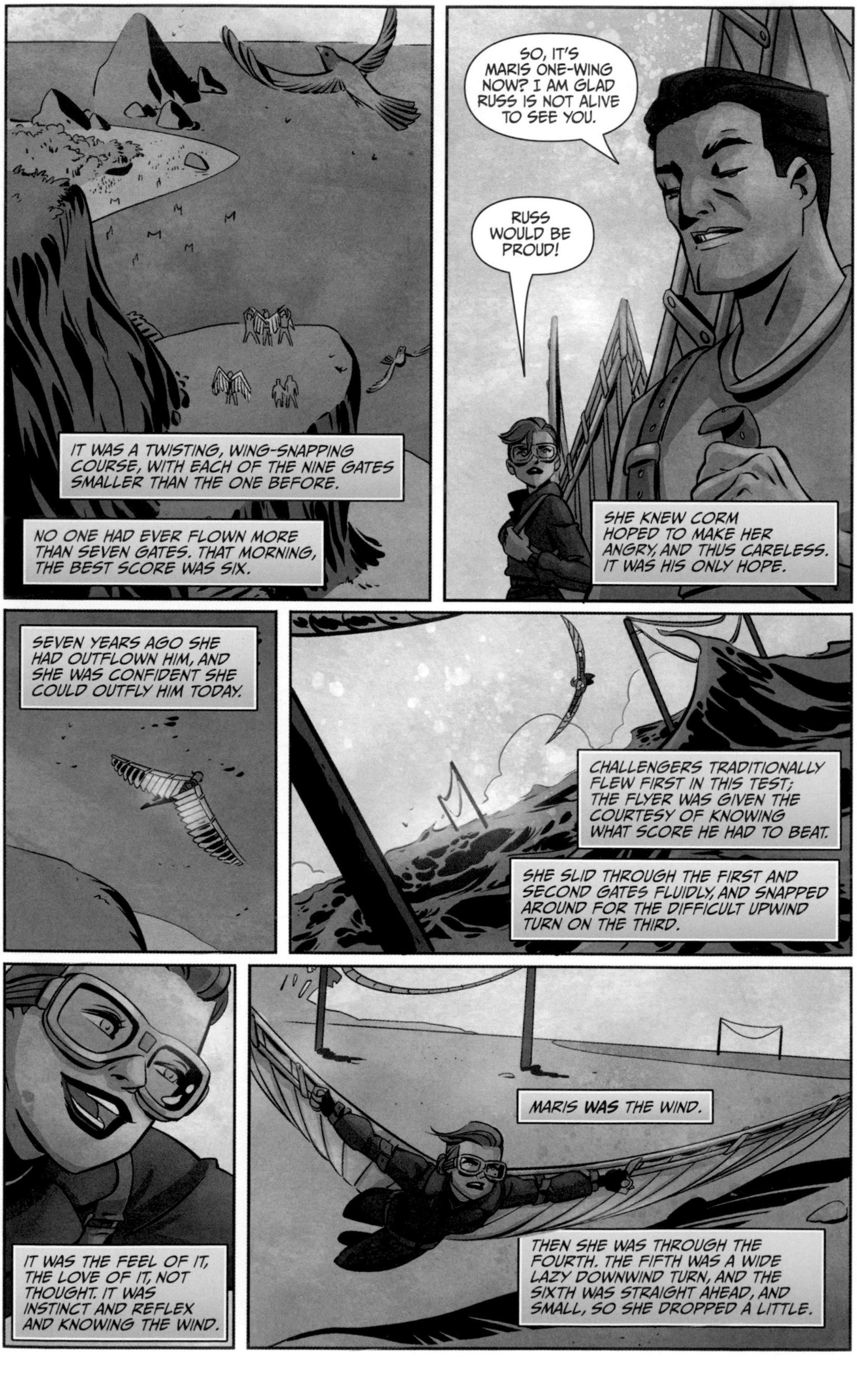
IT WAS A TWISTING, WING-SNAPPING COURSE, WITH EACH OF THE NINE GATES SMALLER THAN THE ONE BEFORE.
NO ONE HAD EVER FLOWN MORE THAN SEVEN GATES. THAT MORNING, THE BEST SCORE WAS SIX.
SO, IT'S MARIS ONE-WING NOW? I AM GLAD RUSS IS NOT ALIVE TO SEE YOU.
RUSS WOULD BE PROUD!
SHE KNEW CORM HOPED TO MAKE HER ANGRY, AND THUS CARELESS. IT WAS HIS ONLY HOPE.
SEVEN YEARS AGO SHE HAD OUTFLOWN HIM, AND SHE WAS CONFIDENT SHE COULD OUTFLY HIM TODAY.
CHALLENGERS TRADITIONALLY FLEW FIRST IN THIS TEST; THE FLYER WAS GIVEN THE COURTESY OF KNOWING WHAT SCORE HE HAD TO BEAT.
SHE SLID THROUGH THE FIRST AND SECOND GATES FLUIDLY, AND SNAPPED AROUND FOR THE DIFFICULT UPWIND TURN ON THE THIRD.
IT WAS THE FEEL OF IT, THE LOVE OF IT, NOT THOUGHT. IT WAS INSTINCT AND REFLEX AND KNOWING THE WIND.
MARIS WAS THE WIND.
THEN SHE WAS THROUGH THE FOURTH. THE FIFTH WAS A WIDE LAZY DOWNWIND TURN, AND THE SIXTH WAS STRAIGHT AHEAD, AND SMALL, SO SHE DROPPED A LITTLE.

IN A HEARTBEAT, IT WAS OVER. A SUDDEN COLD DOWNDRAFT CLUTCHED AT HER FOR AN INSTANT, BUT THAT WAS ENOUGH FOR HER WINGS TO BRUSH THE GROUND AND END IT.

FIVE. NOT THE BEST SCORE OF THE DAY, BUT A GOOD SCORE, AND ENOUGH.

CORM KNEW IT, TOO. HE WAS TOO FAR BEHIND TO WIN UNLESS HE BROKE ALL THE RECORDS AND COLLECTED TWO VOTES FROM EVERY JUDGE.

DISHEARTENED, HE FAILED AT THE FOURTH GATE.

S'RELLA THE WOODWINGER. JIREL OF SKULNY, PROXY FOR GARTH OF SKULNY.

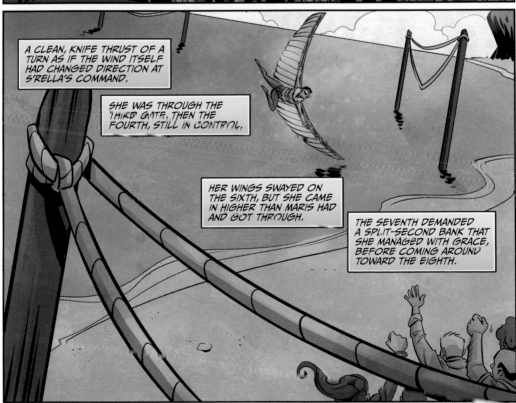

A CLEAN, KNIFE THRUST OF A TURN AS IF THE WIND ITSELF HAD CHANGED DIRECTION AT S'RELLA'S COMMAND.

SHE WAS THROUGH THE THIRD GATE, THEN THE FOURTH, STILL IN CONTROL.

HER WINGS SWAYED ON THE SIXTH, BUT SHE CAME IN HIGHER THAN MARIS HAD AND GOT THROUGH.

THE SEVENTH DEMANDED A SPLIT-SECOND BANK THAT SHE MANAGED WITH GRACE, BEFORE COMING AROUND TOWARD THE EIGHTH.

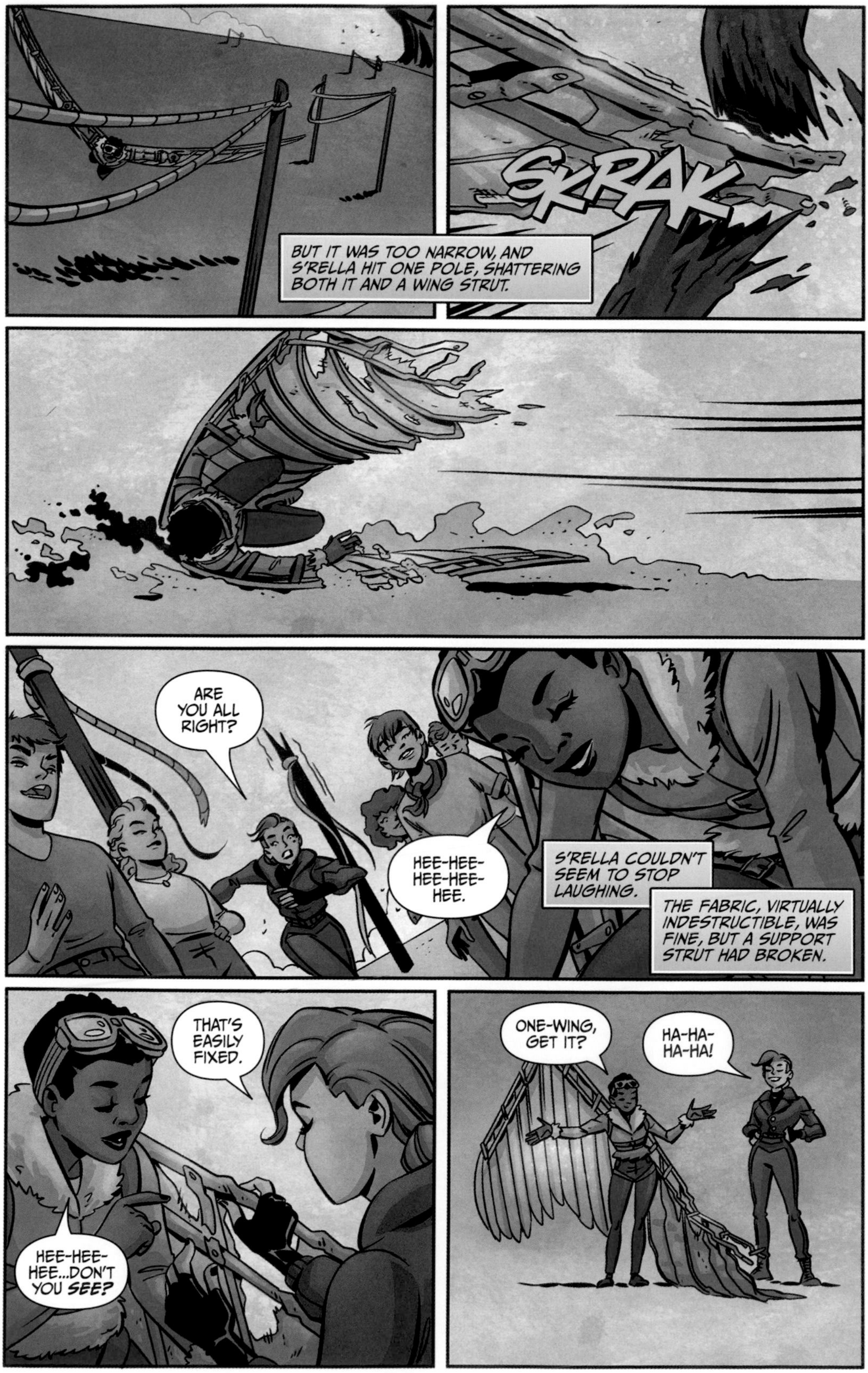
SKRAK
BUT IT WAS TOO NARROW, AND S'RELLA HIT ONE POLE, SHATTERING BOTH IT AND A WING STRUT.
ARE YOU ALL RIGHT?
HEE-HEE-HEE-HEE-HEE.
S'RELLA COULDN'T SEEM TO STOP LAUGHING.
THE FABRIC, VIRTUALLY INDESTRUCTIBLE, WAS FINE, BUT A SUPPORT STRUT HAD BROKEN.
THAT'S EASILY FIXED.
HEE-HEE-HEE...DON'T YOU ***SEE?***
ONE-WING, GET IT?
HA-HA-HA-HA!

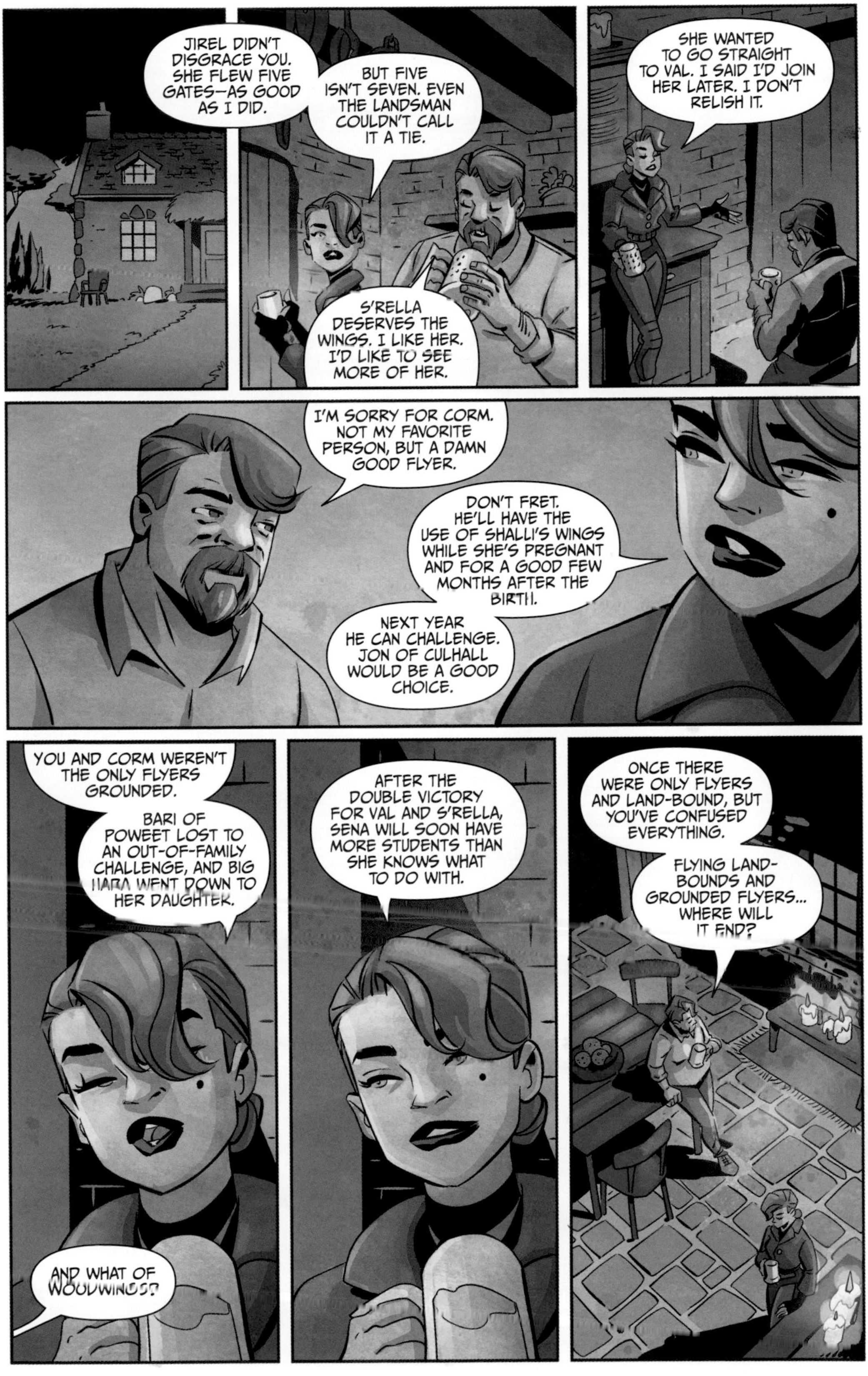
JIREL DIDN'T DISGRACE YOU. SHE FLEW FIVE GATES—AS GOOD AS I DID.
BUT FIVE ISN'T SEVEN. EVEN THE LANDSMAN COULDN'T CALL IT A TIE.
S'RELLA DESERVES THE WINGS. I LIKE HER. I'D LIKE TO SEE MORE OF HER.
SHE WANTED TO GO STRAIGHT TO VAL. I SAID I'D JOIN HER LATER. I DON'T RELISH IT.
I'M SORRY FOR CORM. NOT MY FAVORITE PERSON, BUT A DAMN GOOD FLYER.
DON'T FRET. HE'LL HAVE THE USE OF SHALLI'S WINGS WHILE SHE'S PREGNANT AND FOR A GOOD FEW MONTHS AFTER THE BIRTH.
NEXT YEAR HE CAN CHALLENGE. JON OF CULHALL WOULD BE A GOOD CHOICE.
YOU AND CORM WEREN'T THE ONLY FLYERS GROUNDED.
BARI OF POWEET LOST TO AN OUT-OF-FAMILY CHALLENGE, AND BIG HARA WENT DOWN TO HER DAUGHTER.
AND WHAT OF WOODWINGS?
AFTER THE DOUBLE VICTORY FOR VAL AND S'RELLA, SENA WILL SOON HAVE MORE STUDENTS THAN SHE KNOWS WHAT TO DO WITH.
ONCE THERE WERE ONLY FLYERS AND LAND-BOUND, BUT YOU'VE CONFUSED EVERYTHING.
FLYING LAND-BOUNDS AND GROUNDED FLYERS... WHERE WILL IT END?

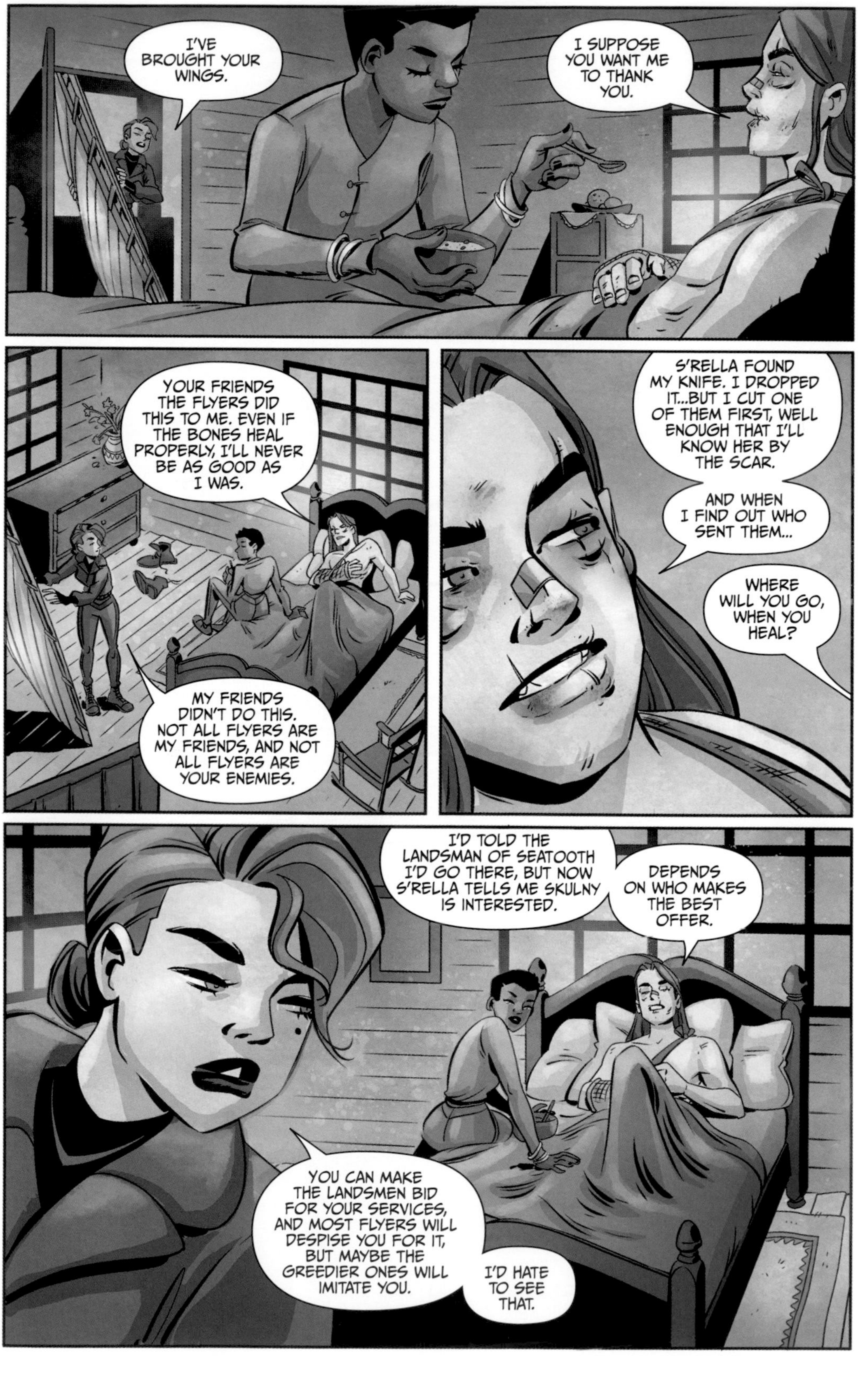
I'VE BROUGHT YOUR WINGS.
I SUPPOSE YOU WANT ME TO THANK YOU.
YOUR FRIENDS THE FLYERS DID THIS TO ME. EVEN IF THE BONES HEAL PROPERLY, I'LL NEVER BE AS GOOD AS I WAS.
MY FRIENDS DIDN'T DO THIS. NOT ALL FLYERS ARE MY FRIENDS, AND NOT ALL FLYERS ARE YOUR ENEMIES.
S'RELLA FOUND MY KNIFE. I DROPPED IT...BUT I CUT ONE OF THEM FIRST, WELL ENOUGH THAT I'LL KNOW HER BY THE SCAR.
AND WHEN I FIND OUT WHO SENT THEM...
WHERE WILL YOU GO, WHEN YOU HEAL?
I'D TOLD THE LANDSMAN OF SEATOOTH I'D GO THERE, BUT NOW S'RELLA TELLS ME SKULNY IS INTERESTED.
DEPENDS ON WHO MAKES THE BEST OFFER.
YOU CAN MAKE THE LANDSMEN BID FOR YOUR SERVICES, AND MOST FLYERS WILL DESPISE YOU FOR IT, BUT MAYBE THE GREEDIER ONES WILL IMITATE YOU.
I'D HATE TO SEE THAT.

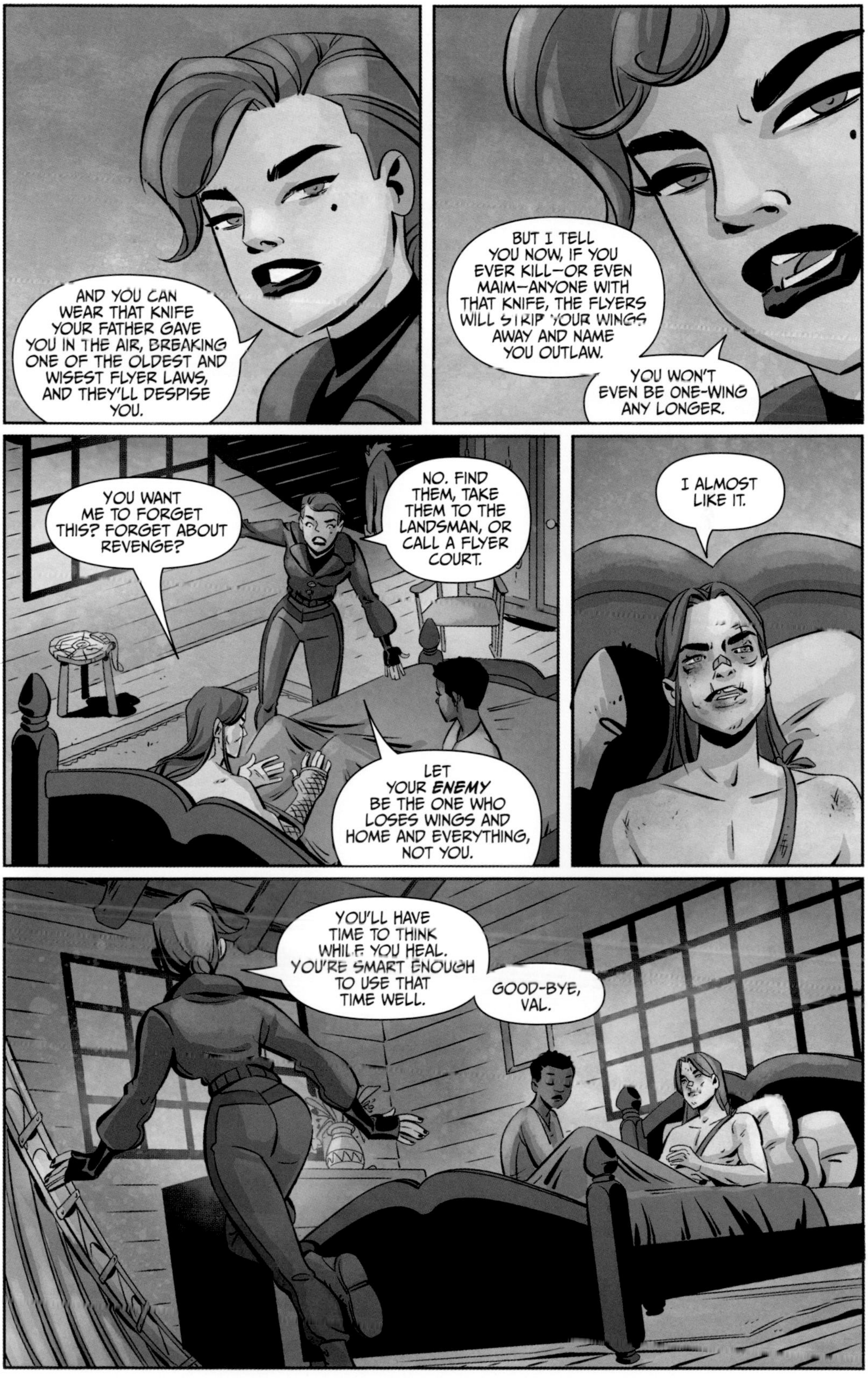

AND YOU CAN WEAR THAT KNIFE YOUR FATHER GAVE YOU IN THE AIR, BREAKING ONE OF THE OLDEST AND WISEST FLYER LAWS, AND THEY'LL DESPISE YOU.
BUT I TELL YOU NOW, IF YOU EVER KILL—OR EVEN MAIM—ANYONE WITH THAT KNIFE, THE FLYERS WILL STRIP YOUR WINGS AWAY AND NAME YOU OUTLAW.
YOU WON'T EVEN BE ONE-WING ANY LONGER.
YOU WANT ME TO FORGET THIS? FORGET ABOUT REVENGE?
NO. FIND THEM, TAKE THEM TO THE LANDSMAN, OR CALL A FLYER COURT.
LET YOUR ***ENEMY*** BE THE ONE WHO LOSES WINGS AND HOME AND EVERYTHING, NOT YOU.
I ALMOST LIKE IT.
YOU'LL HAVE TIME TO THINK WHILE YOU HEAL. YOU'RE SMART ENOUGH TO USE THAT TIME WELL.
GOOD-BYE, VAL.

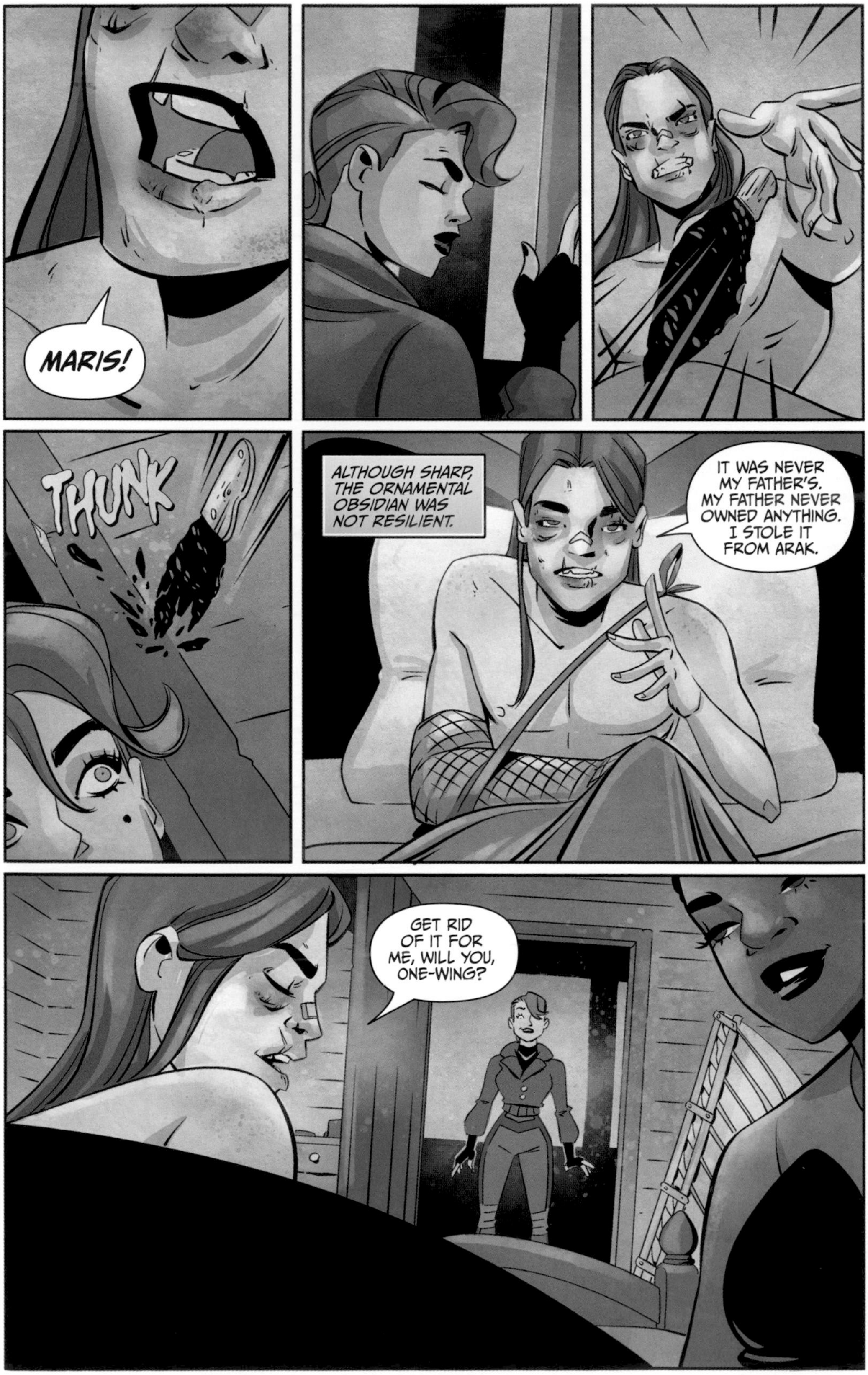
MARIS!
THUNK
ALTHOUGH SHARP, THE ORNAMENTAL OBSIDIAN WAS NOT RESILIENT.
IT WAS NEVER MY FATHER'S. MY FATHER NEVER OWNED ANYTHING. I STOLE IT FROM ARAK.
GET RID OF IT FOR ME, WILL YOU, ONE-WING?

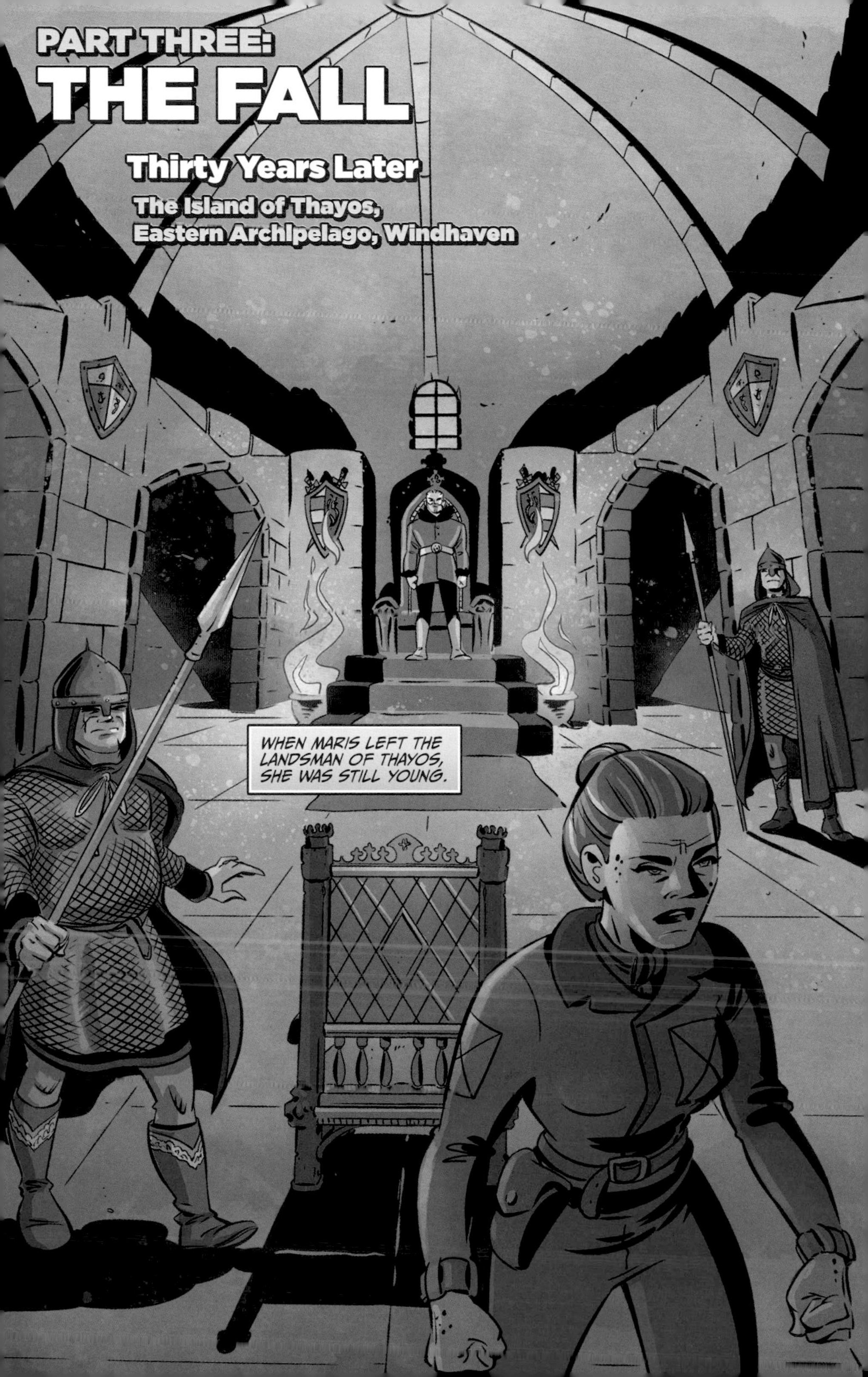
PART THREE:
THE FALL
Thirty Years Later
The Island of Thayos,
Eastern Archipelago, Windhaven
WHEN MARIS LEFT THE LANDSMAN OF THAYOS, SHE WAS STILL YOUNG.

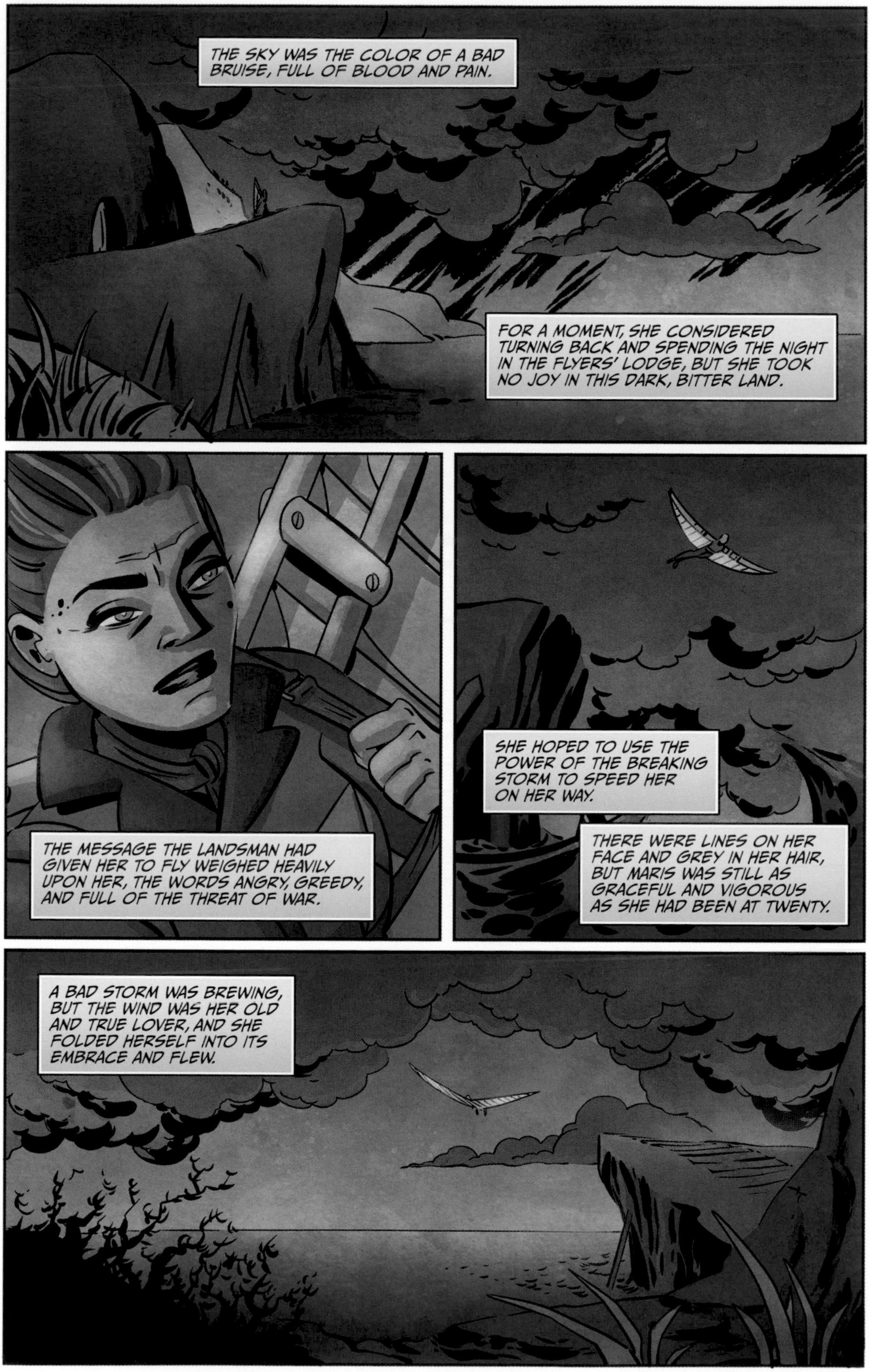
THE SKY WAS THE COLOR OF A BAD BRUISE, FULL OF BLOOD AND PAIN.
FOR A MOMENT, SHE CONSIDERED TURNING BACK AND SPENDING THE NIGHT IN THE FLYERS' LODGE, BUT SHE TOOK NO JOY IN THIS DARK, BITTER LAND.
THE MESSAGE THE LANDSMAN HAD GIVEN HER TO FLY WEIGHED HEAVILY UPON HER, THE WORDS ANGRY, GREEDY, AND FULL OF THE THREAT OF WAR.
SHE HOPED TO USE THE POWER OF THE BREAKING STORM TO SPEED HER ON HER WAY.
THERE WERE LINES ON HER FACE AND GREY IN HER HAIR, BUT MARIS WAS STILL AS GRACEFUL AND VIGOROUS AS SHE HAD BEEN AT TWENTY.
A BAD STORM WAS BREWING, BUT THE WIND WAS HER OLD AND TRUE LOVER, AND SHE FOLDED HERSELF INTO ITS EMBRACE AND FLEW.

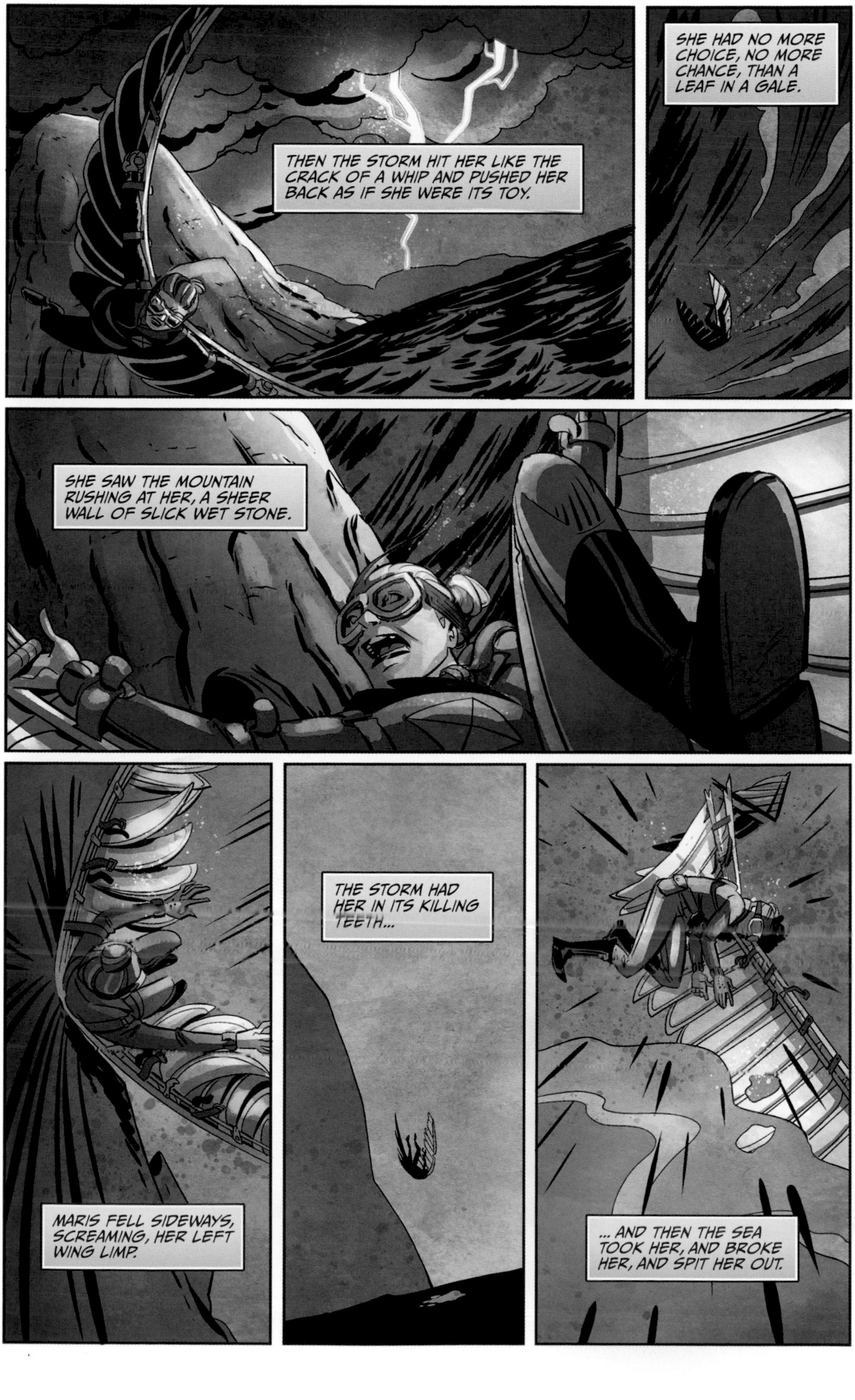
THEN THE STORM HIT HER LIKE THE CRACK OF A WHIP AND PUSHED HER BACK AS IF SHE WERE ITS TOY.
SHE HAD NO MORE CHOICE, NO MORE CHANCE, THAN A LEAF IN A GALE.
SHE SAW THE MOUNTAIN RUSHING AT HER, A SHEER WALL OF SLICK WET STONE.
MARIS FELL SIDEWAYS, SCREAMING, HER LEFT WING LIMP.
THE STORM HAD HER IN ITS KILLING TEETH...
... AND THEN THE SEA TOOK HER, AND BROKE HER, AND SPIT HER OUT.

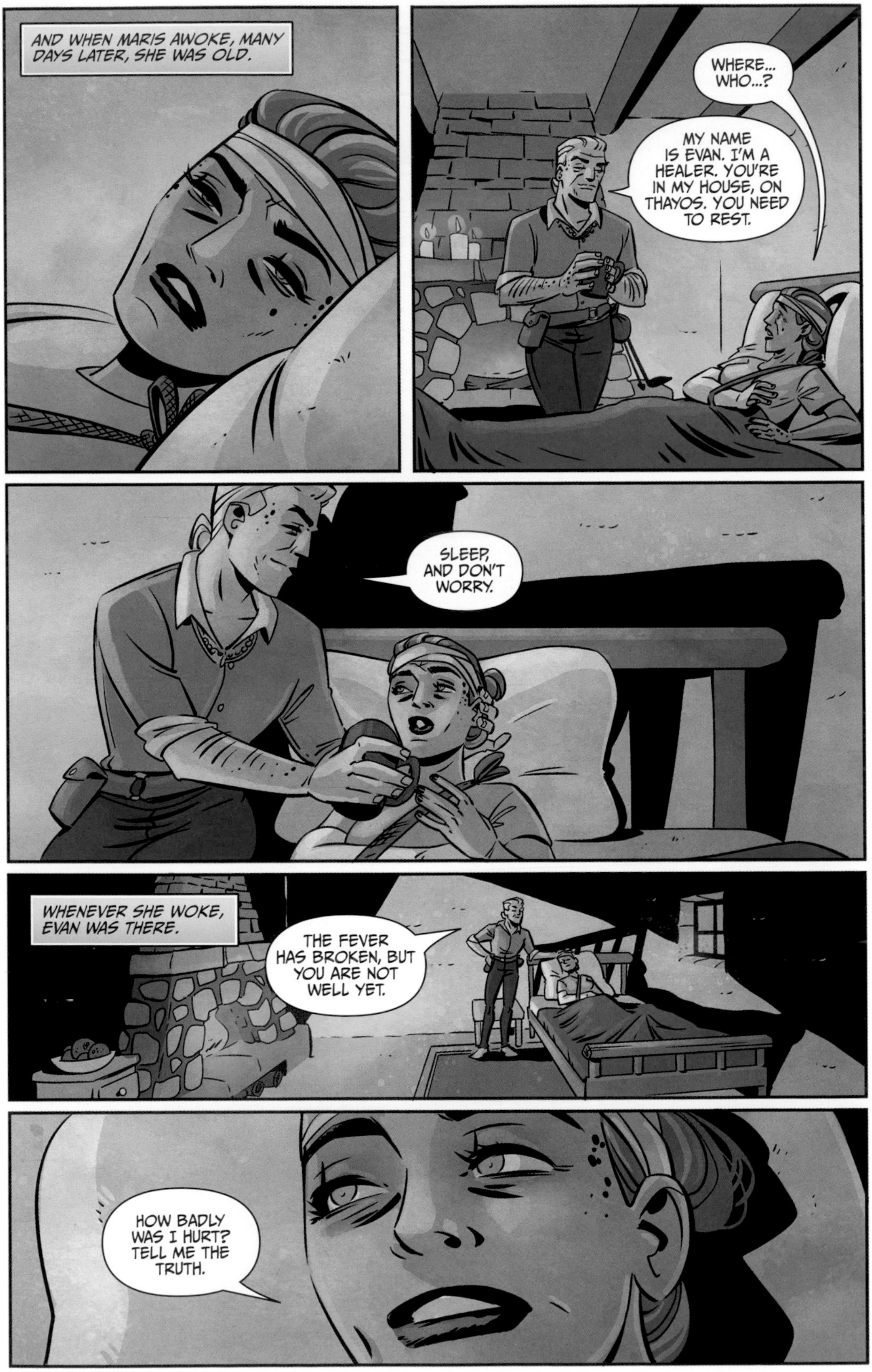
AND WHEN MARIS AWOKE, MANY DAYS LATER, SHE WAS OLD.
WHERE... WHO...?
MY NAME IS EVAN. I'M A HEALER. YOU'RE IN MY HOUSE, ON THAYOS. YOU NEED TO REST.
SLEEP, AND DON'T WORRY.
WHENEVER SHE WOKE, EVAN WAS THERE.
THE FEVER HAS BROKEN, BUT YOU ARE NOT WELL YET.
HOW BADLY WAS I HURT? TELL ME THE TRUTH.

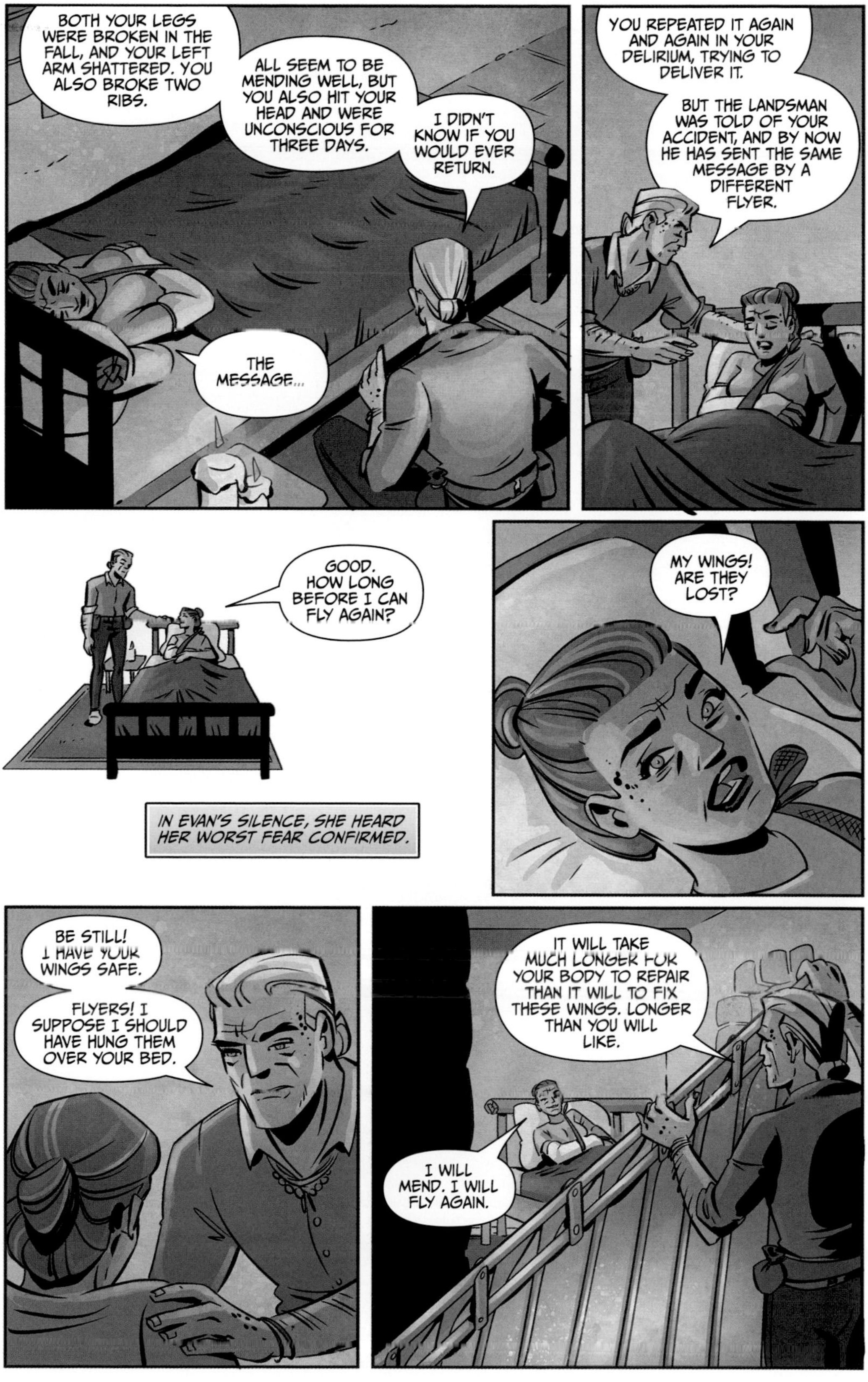
BOTH YOUR LEGS WERE BROKEN IN THE FALL, AND YOUR LEFT ARM SHATTERED. YOU ALSO BROKE TWO RIBS.
ALL SEEM TO BE MENDING WELL, BUT YOU ALSO HIT YOUR HEAD AND WERE UNCONSCIOUS FOR THREE DAYS.
I DIDN'T KNOW IF YOU WOULD EVER RETURN.
THE MESSAGE...
YOU REPEATED IT AGAIN AND AGAIN IN YOUR DELIRIUM, TRYING TO DELIVER IT.
BUT THE LANDSMAN WAS TOLD OF YOUR ACCIDENT, AND BY NOW HE HAS SENT THE SAME MESSAGE BY A DIFFERENT FLYER.
GOOD. HOW LONG BEFORE I CAN FLY AGAIN?
IN EVAN'S SILENCE, SHE HEARD HER WORST FEAR CONFIRMED.
MY WINGS! ARE THEY LOST?
BE STILL! I HAVE YOUR WINGS SAFE.
FLYERS! I SUPPOSE I SHOULD HAVE HUNG THEM OVER YOUR BED.
IT WILL TAKE MUCH LONGER FOR YOUR BODY TO REPAIR THAN IT WILL TO FIX THESE WINGS. LONGER THAN YOU WILL LIKE.
I WILL MEND. I WILL FLY AGAIN.

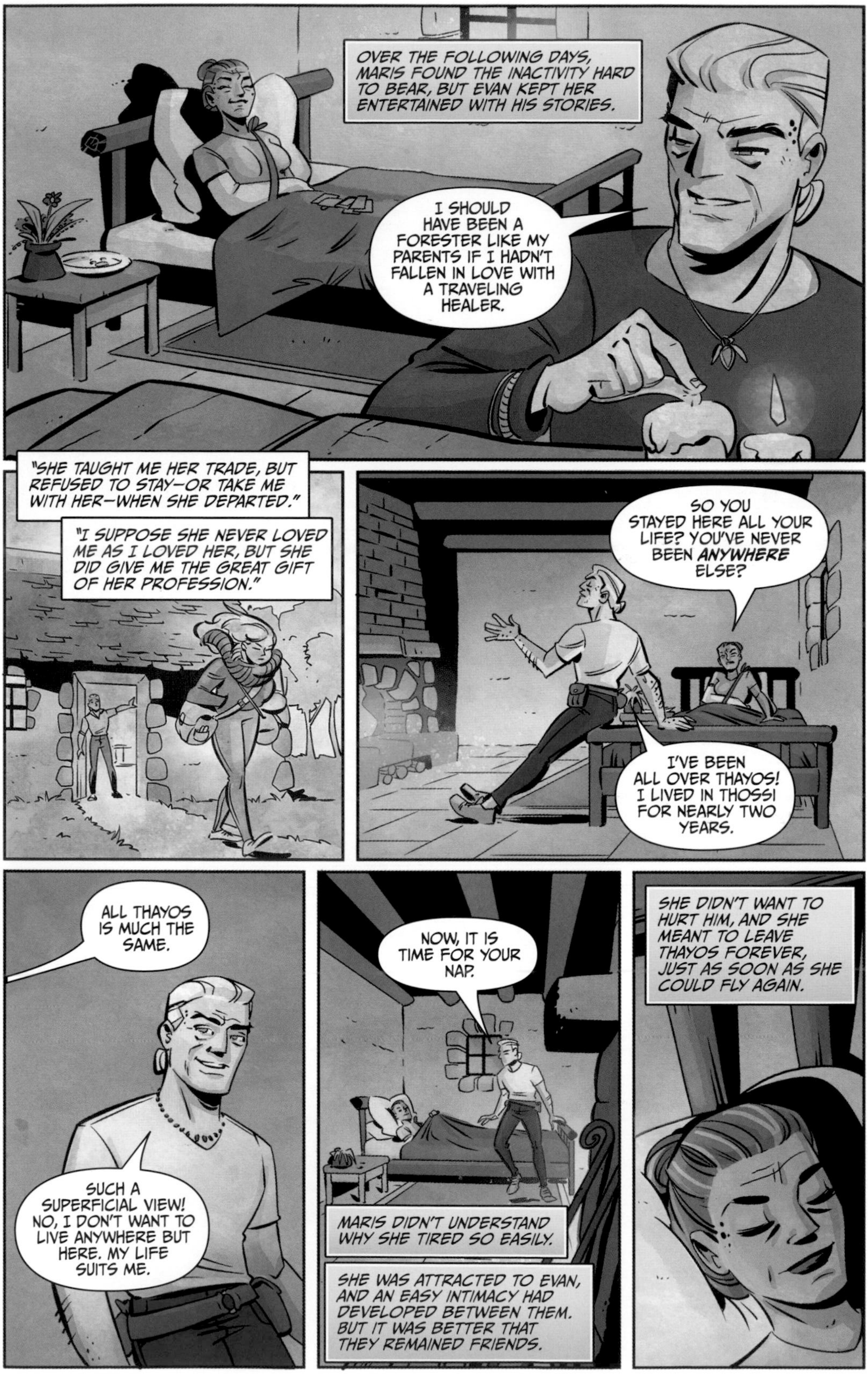
OVER THE FOLLOWING DAYS, MARIS FOUND THE INACTIVITY HARD TO BEAR, BUT EVAN KEPT HER ENTERTAINED WITH HIS STORIES.
I SHOULD HAVE BEEN A FORESTER LIKE MY PARENTS IF I HADN'T FALLEN IN LOVE WITH A TRAVELING HEALER.
"SHE TAUGHT ME HER TRADE, BUT REFUSED TO STAY—OR TAKE ME WITH HER—WHEN SHE DEPARTED."
"I SUPPOSE SHE NEVER LOVED ME AS I LOVED HER, BUT SHE DID GIVE ME THE GREAT GIFT OF HER PROFESSION."
SO YOU STAYED HERE ALL YOUR LIFE? YOU'VE NEVER BEEN ANYWHERE ELSE?
I'VE BEEN ALL OVER THAYOS! I LIVED IN THOSSI FOR NEARLY TWO YEARS.
ALL THAYOS IS MUCH THE SAME.
SUCH A SUPERFICIAL VIEW! NO, I DON'T WANT TO LIVE ANYWHERE BUT HERE. MY LIFE SUITS ME.
NOW, IT IS TIME FOR YOUR NAP.
MARIS DIDN'T UNDERSTAND WHY SHE TIRED SO EASILY.
SHE WAS ATTRACTED TO EVAN, AND AN EASY INTIMACY HAD DEVELOPED BETWEEN THEM. BUT IT WAS BETTER THAT THEY REMAINED FRIENDS.
SHE DIDN'T WANT TO HURT HIM, AND SHE MEANT TO LEAVE THAYOS FOREVER, JUST AS SOON AS SHE COULD FLY AGAIN.

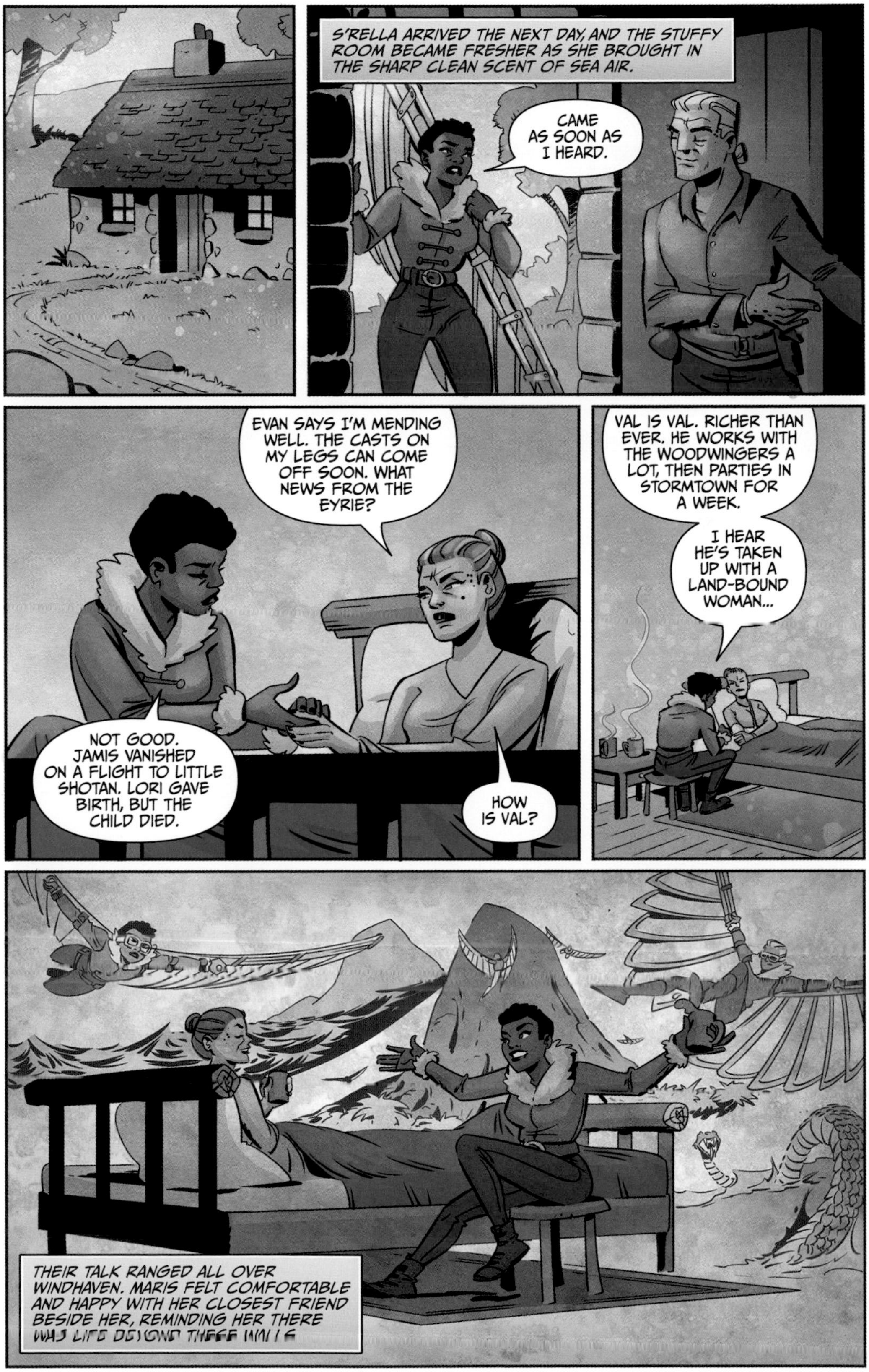
S'RELLA ARRIVED THE NEXT DAY, AND THE STUFFY ROOM BECAME FRESHER AS SHE BROUGHT IN THE SHARP CLEAN SCENT OF SEA AIR.
CAME AS SOON AS I HEARD.
EVAN SAYS I'M MENDING WELL. THE CASTS ON MY LEGS CAN COME OFF SOON. WHAT NEWS FROM THE EYRIE?
NOT GOOD. JAMIS VANISHED ON A FLIGHT TO LITTLE SHOTAN. LORI GAVE BIRTH, BUT THE CHILD DIED.
HOW IS VAL?
VAL IS VAL. RICHER THAN EVER. HE WORKS WITH THE WOODWINGERS A LOT, THEN PARTIES IN STORMTOWN FOR A WEEK.
I HEAR HE'S TAKEN UP WITH A LAND-BOUND WOMAN...
THEIR TALK RANGED ALL OVER WINDHAVEN. MARIS FELT COMFORTABLE AND HAPPY WITH HER CLOSEST FRIEND BESIDE HER, REMINDING HER THERE WAS LIFE BEYOND THESE WALLS.

THEY SAY THERE WILL BE WAR HERE SOON, BUT I DON'T KNOW WHY.

A ROCK, MIDWAY BETWEEN THAYOS AND THRANE. NO ONE CARED ABOUT IT UNTIL IRON WAS FOUND.

NOW THE TWO ISLANDS ARE ARGUING THEIR CLAIMS.

THE MESSAGE I WAS TO FLY TO THRANE WAS SO FULL OF THREATS, I'M SURPRISED WAR HASN'T ALREADY BROKEN OUT.

OUR FLYERS HAVEN'T HAD A DAY'S REST. TYA HAS CARRIED PROMISES TO DOZENS OF POTENTIAL ALLIES BUT KEEPS COMING BACK WITH REFUSALS.

AND WITHOUT ALLIES, THE LANDSMAN DARES NOT ATTACK.

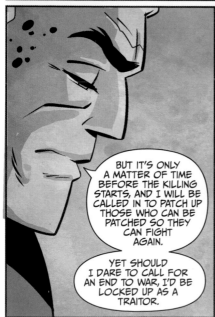

BUT IT'S ONLY A MATTER OF TIME BEFORE THE KILLING STARTS, AND I WILL BE CALLED IN TO PATCH UP THOSE WHO CAN BE PATCHED SO THEY CAN FIGHT AGAIN.

YET SHOULD I DARE TO CALL FOR AN END TO WAR, I'D BE LOCKED UP AS A TRAITOR.

I FEEL GUILTY SOMETIMES, ABOUT WHAT HAPPENS AS A RESULT OF SOME OF THE MESSAGES I FLY.

DON'T. YOU'RE NOT RESPONSIBLE.

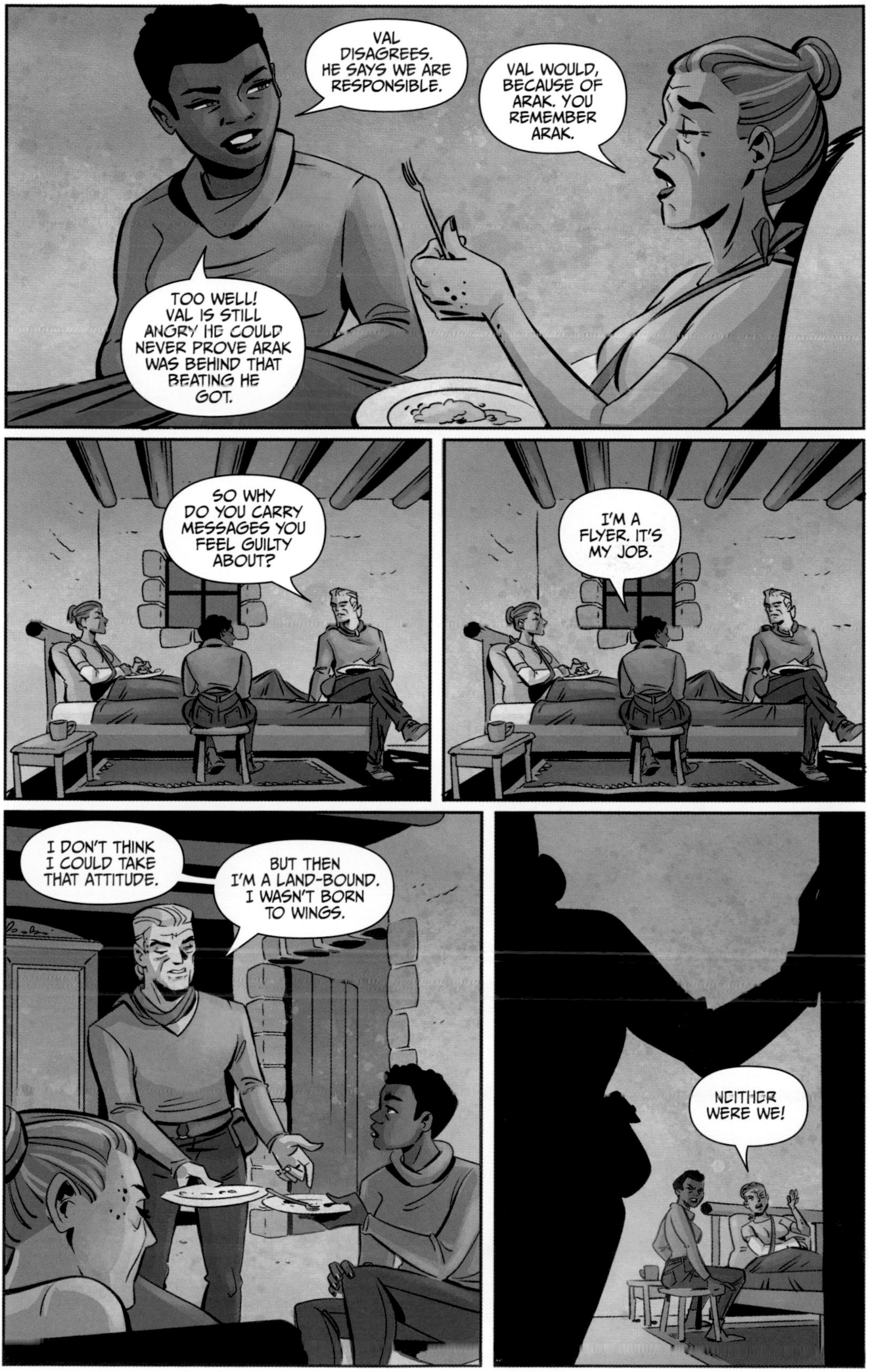
VAL DISAGREES. HE SAYS WE ARE RESPONSIBLE.
VAL WOULD, BECAUSE OF ARAK. YOU REMEMBER ARAK.
TOO WELL! VAL IS STILL ANGRY HE COULD NEVER PROVE ARAK WAS BEHIND THAT BEATING HE GOT.
SO WHY DO YOU CARRY MESSAGES YOU FEEL GUILTY ABOUT?
I'M A FLYER. IT'S MY JOB.
I DON'T THINK I COULD TAKE THAT ATTITUDE.
BUT THEN I'M A LAND-BOUND. I WASN'T BORN TO WINGS.
NEITHER WERE WE!

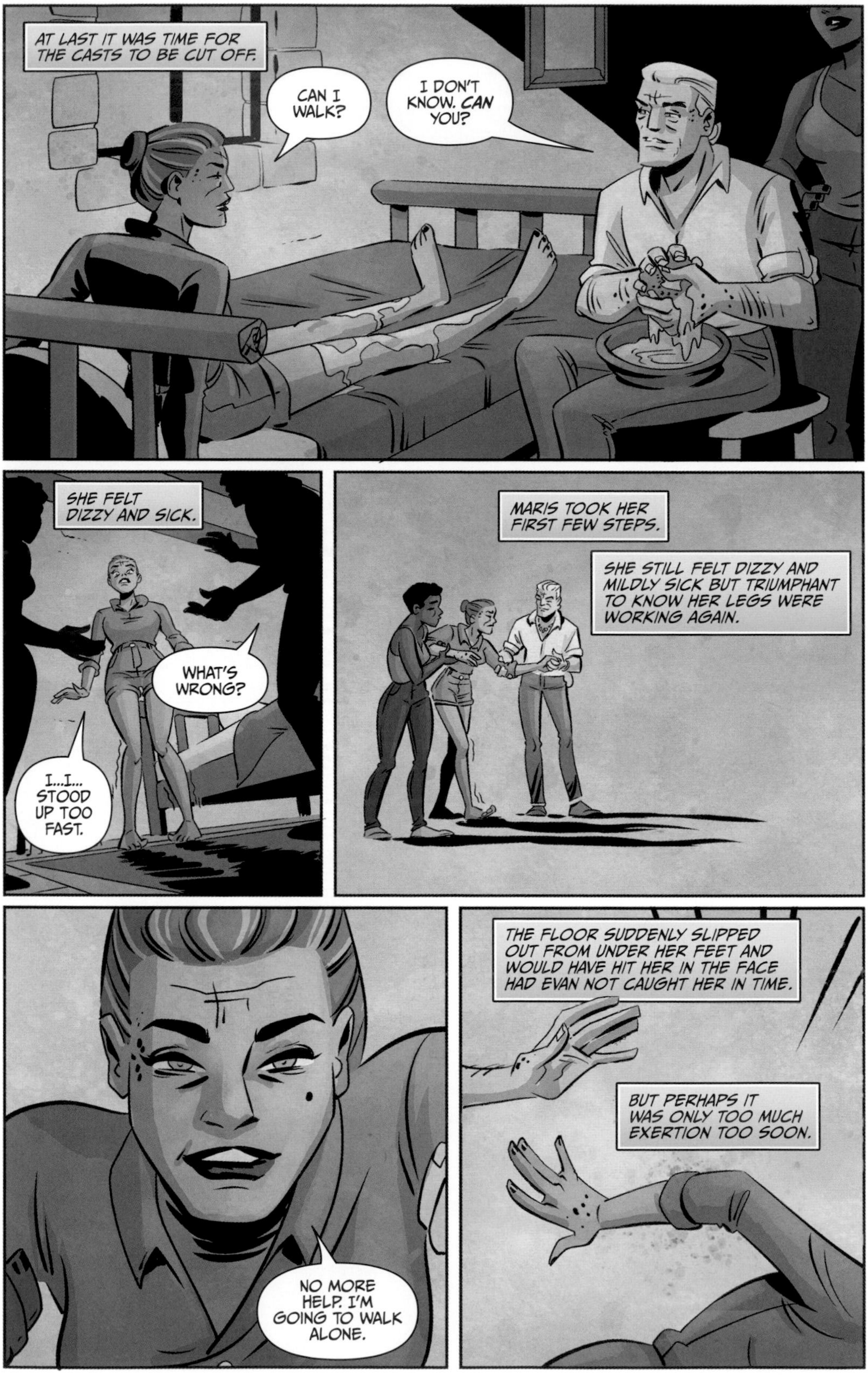
AT LAST IT WAS TIME FOR THE CASTS TO BE CUT OFF.
CAN I WALK?
I DON'T KNOW. CAN YOU?
SHE FELT DIZZY AND SICK.
WHAT'S WRONG?
I...I... STOOD UP TOO FAST.
MARIS TOOK HER FIRST FEW STEPS.
SHE STILL FELT DIZZY AND MILDLY SICK BUT TRIUMPHANT TO KNOW HER LEGS WERE WORKING AGAIN.
NO MORE HELP. I'M GOING TO WALK ALONE.
THE FLOOR SUDDENLY SLIPPED OUT FROM UNDER HER FEET AND WOULD HAVE HIT HER IN THE FACE HAD EVAN NOT CAUGHT HER IN TIME.
BUT PERHAPS IT WAS ONLY TOO MUCH EXERTION TOO SOON.

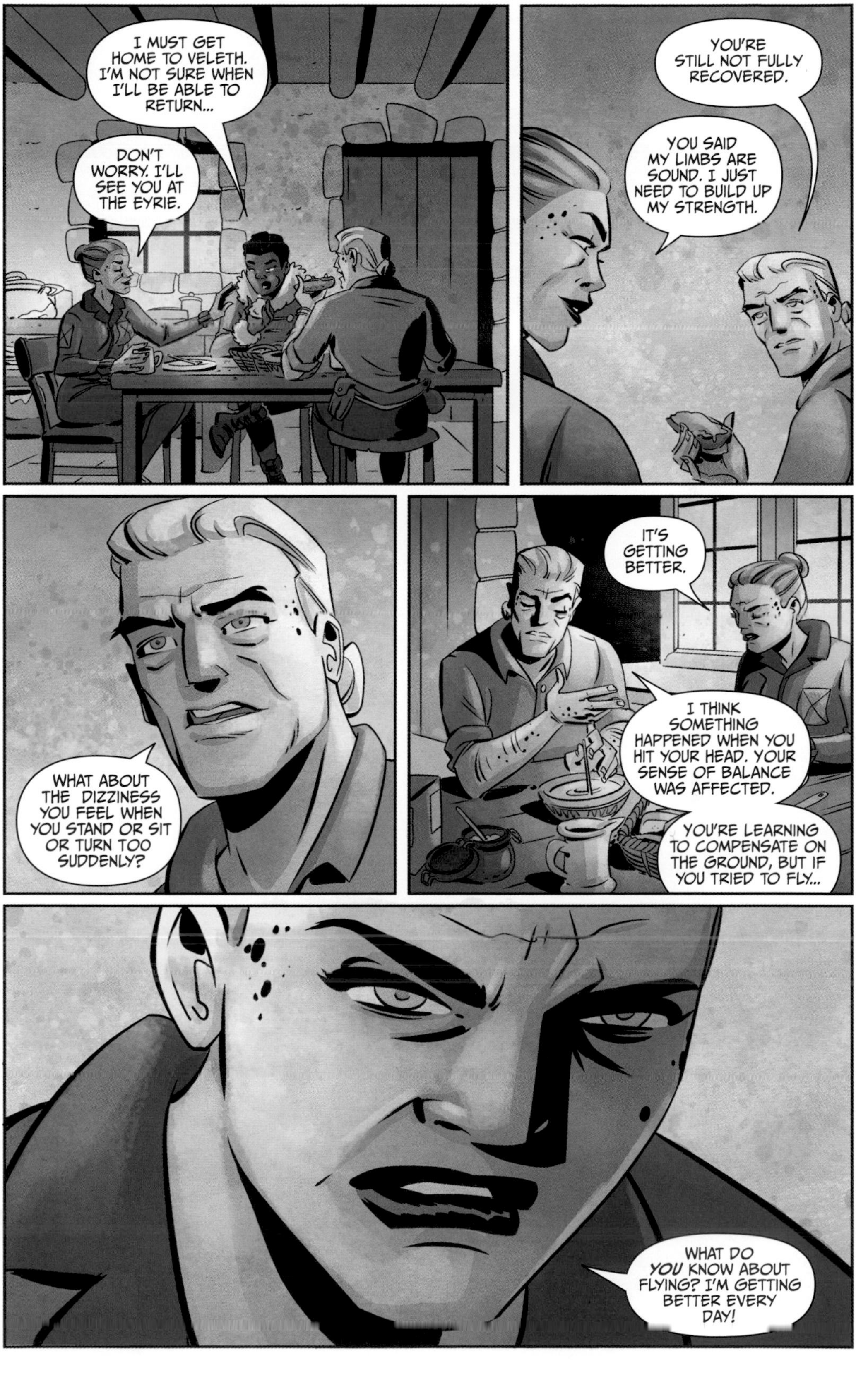
I MUST GET HOME TO VELETH. I'M NOT SURE WHEN I'LL BE ABLE TO RETURN...
DON'T WORRY. I'LL SEE YOU AT THE EYRIE.
YOU'RE STILL NOT FULLY RECOVERED.
YOU SAID MY LIMBS ARE SOUND. I JUST NEED TO BUILD UP MY STRENGTH.
WHAT ABOUT THE DIZZINESS YOU FEEL WHEN YOU STAND OR SIT OR TURN TOO SUDDENLY?
IT'S GETTING BETTER.
I THINK SOMETHING HAPPENED WHEN YOU HIT YOUR HEAD. YOUR SENSE OF BALANCE WAS AFFECTED.
YOU'RE LEARNING TO COMPENSATE ON THE GROUND, BUT IF YOU TRIED TO FLY...
WHAT DO *YOU* KNOW ABOUT FLYING? I'M GETTING BETTER EVERY DAY!

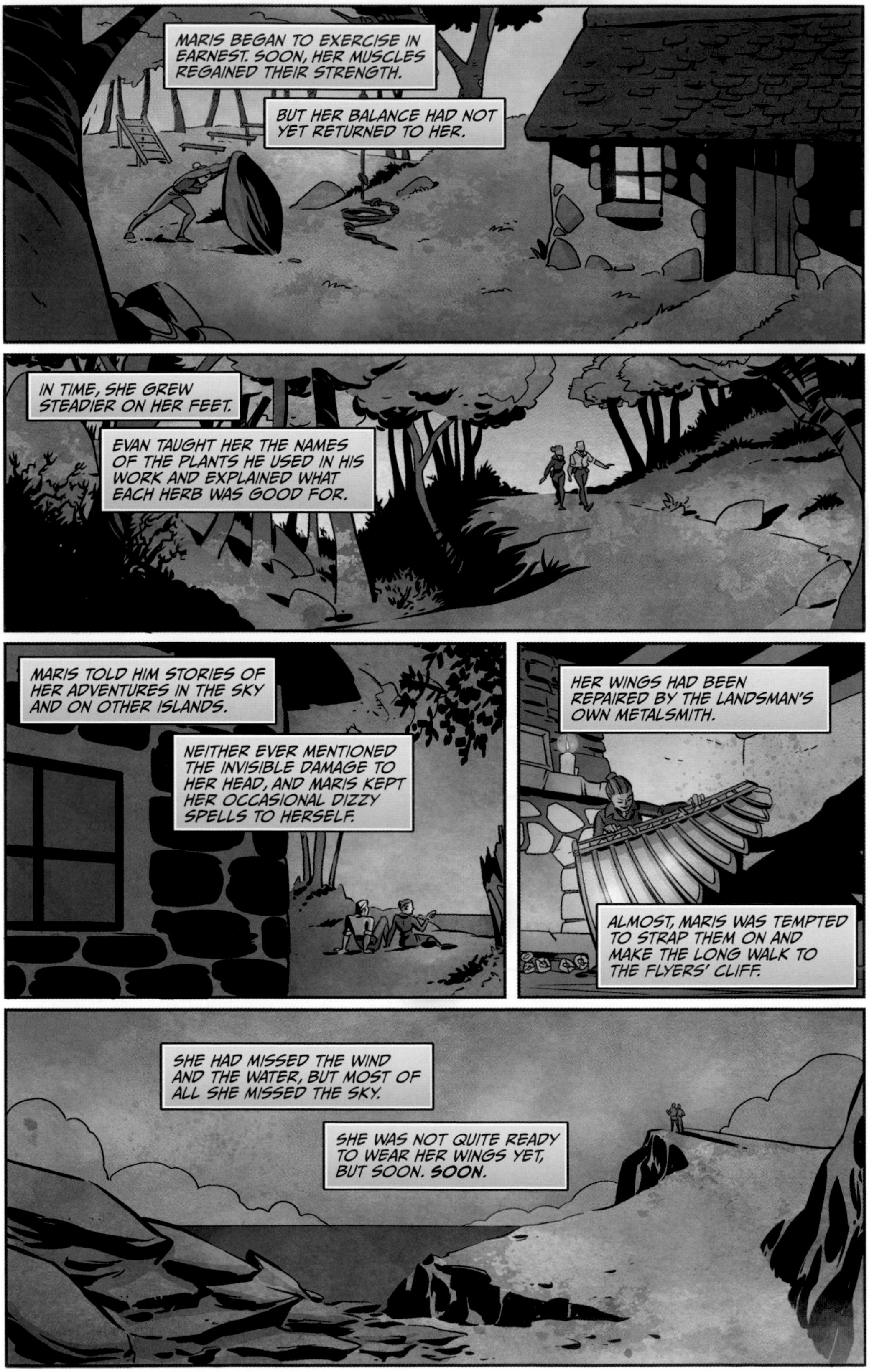
MARIS BEGAN TO EXERCISE IN EARNEST. SOON, HER MUSCLES REGAINED THEIR STRENGTH.
BUT HER BALANCE HAD NOT YET RETURNED TO HER.
IN TIME, SHE GREW STEADIER ON HER FEET.
EVAN TAUGHT HER THE NAMES OF THE PLANTS HE USED IN HIS WORK AND EXPLAINED WHAT EACH HERB WAS GOOD FOR.
MARIS TOLD HIM STORIES OF HER ADVENTURES IN THE SKY AND ON OTHER ISLANDS.
NEITHER EVER MENTIONED THE INVISIBLE DAMAGE TO HER HEAD, AND MARIS KEPT HER OCCASIONAL DIZZY SPELLS TO HERSELF.
HER WINGS HAD BEEN REPAIRED BY THE LANDSMAN'S OWN METALSMITH.
ALMOST, MARIS WAS TEMPTED TO STRAP THEM ON AND MAKE THE LONG WALK TO THE FLYERS' CLIFF.
SHE HAD MISSED THE WIND AND THE WATER, BUT MOST OF ALL SHE MISSED THE SKY.
SHE WAS NOT QUITE READY TO WEAR HER WINGS YET, BUT SOON. SOON.

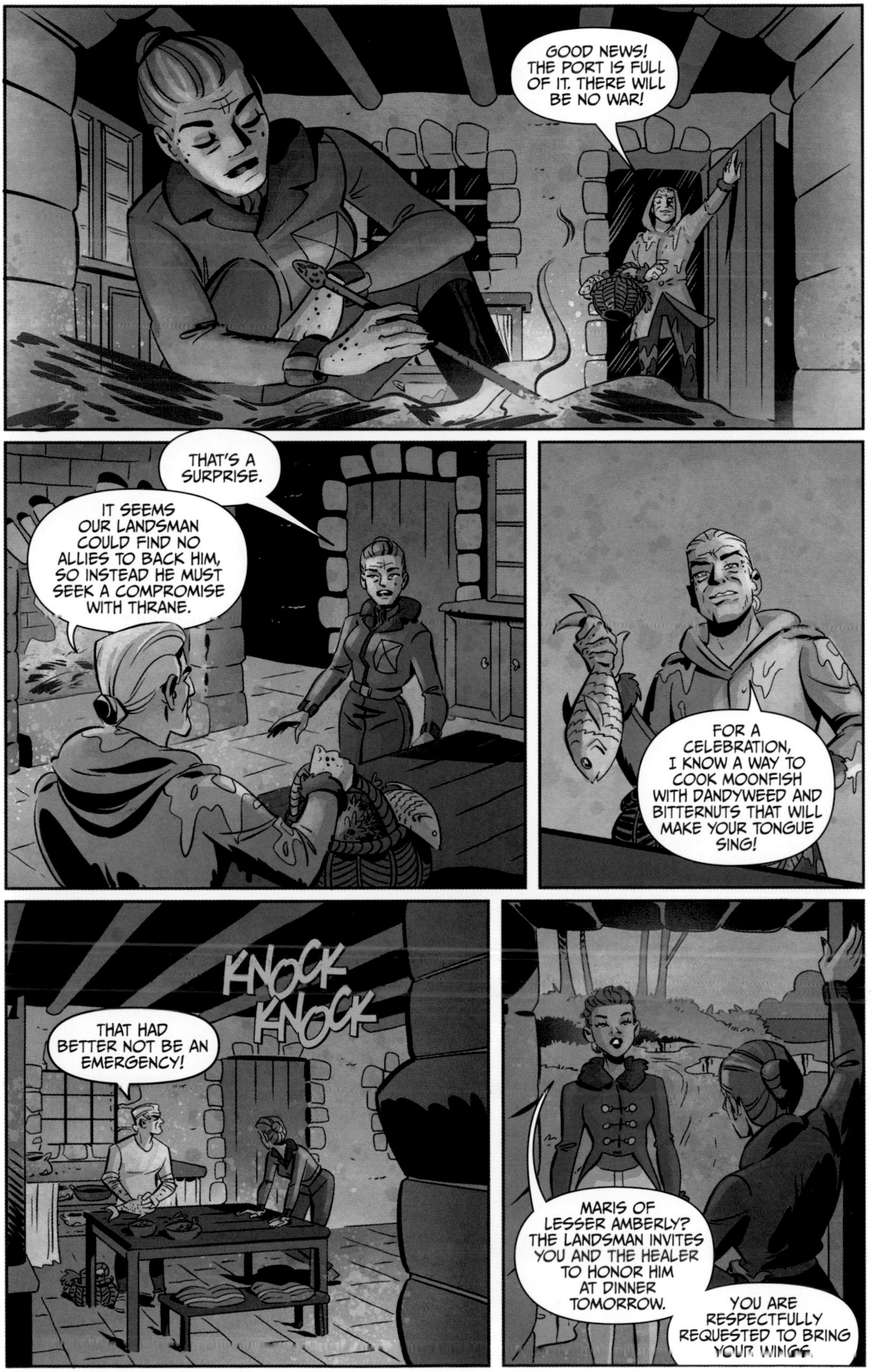
GOOD NEWS! THE PORT IS FULL OF IT. THERE WILL BE NO WAR!
THAT'S A SURPRISE.
IT SEEMS OUR LANDSMAN COULD FIND NO ALLIES TO BACK HIM, SO INSTEAD HE MUST SEEK A COMPROMISE WITH THRANE.
FOR A CELEBRATION, I KNOW A WAY TO COOK MOONFISH WITH DANDYWEED AND BITTERNUTS THAT WILL MAKE YOUR TONGUE SING!
KNOCK KNOCK
THAT HAD BETTER NOT BE AN EMERGENCY!
MARIS OF LESSER AMBERLY? THE LANDSMAN INVITES YOU AND THE HEALER TO HONOR HIM AT DINNER TOMORROW.
YOU ARE RESPECTFULLY REQUESTED TO BRING YOUR WINGS.

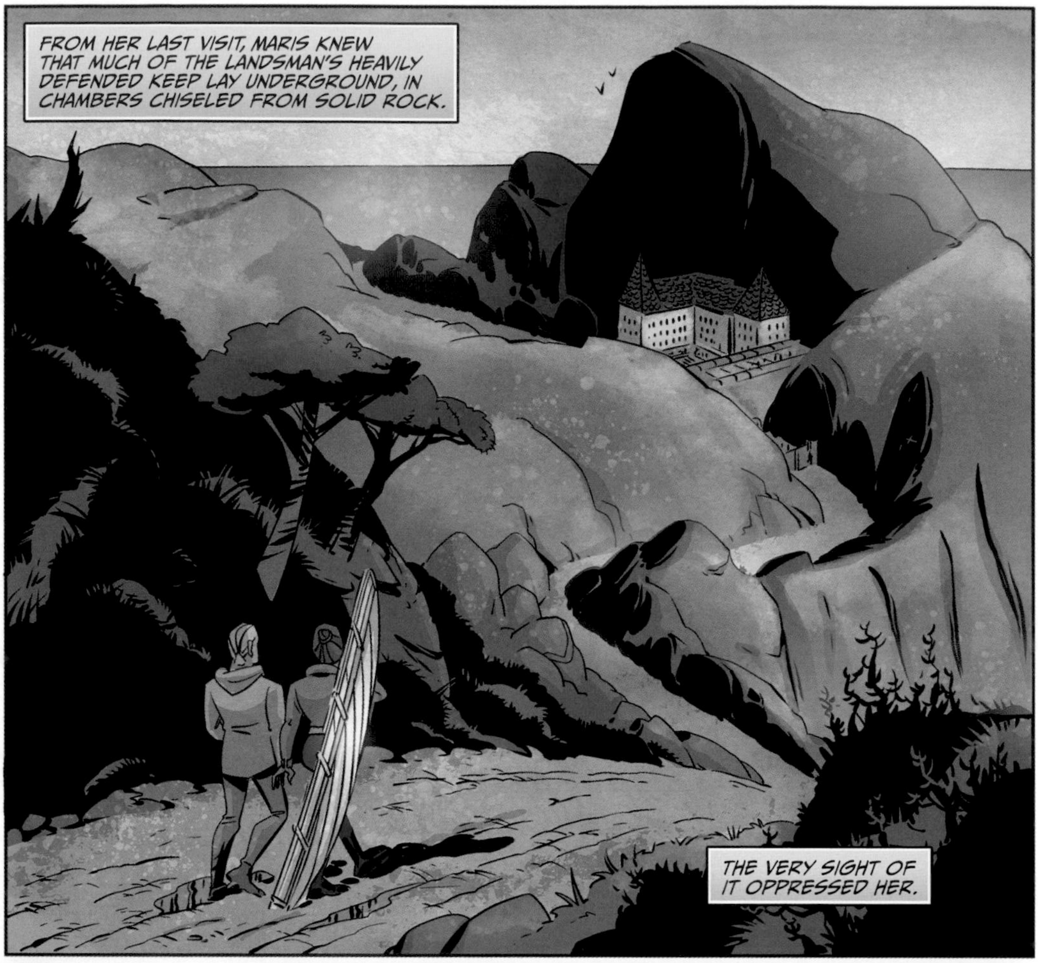
FROM HER LAST VISIT, MARIS KNEW THAT MUCH OF THE LANDSMAN'S HEAVILY DEFENDED KEEP LAY UNDERGROUND, IN CHAMBERS CHISELED FROM SOLID ROCK.
THE VERY SIGHT OF IT OPPRESSED HER.

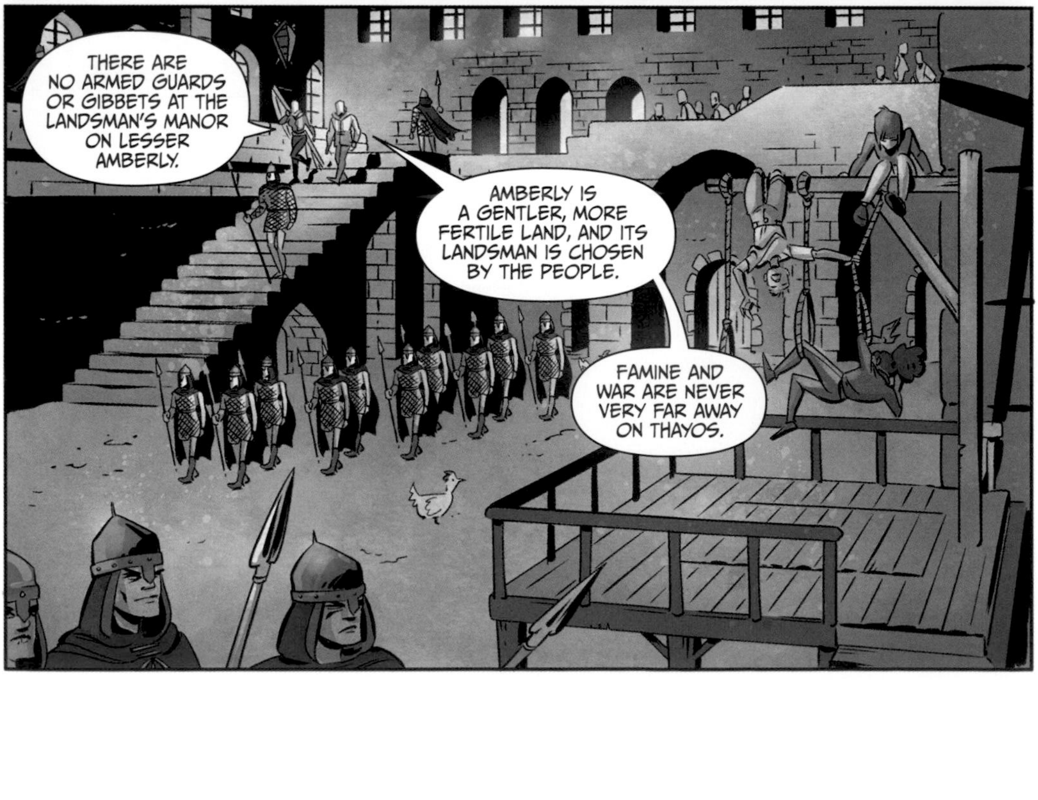
THERE ARE NO ARMED GUARDS OR GIBBETS AT THE LANDSMAN'S MANOR ON LESSER AMBERLY.
AMBERLY IS A GENTLER, MORE FERTILE LAND, AND ITS LANDSMAN IS CHOSEN BY THE PEOPLE.
FAMINE AND WAR ARE NEVER VERY FAR AWAY ON THAYOS.

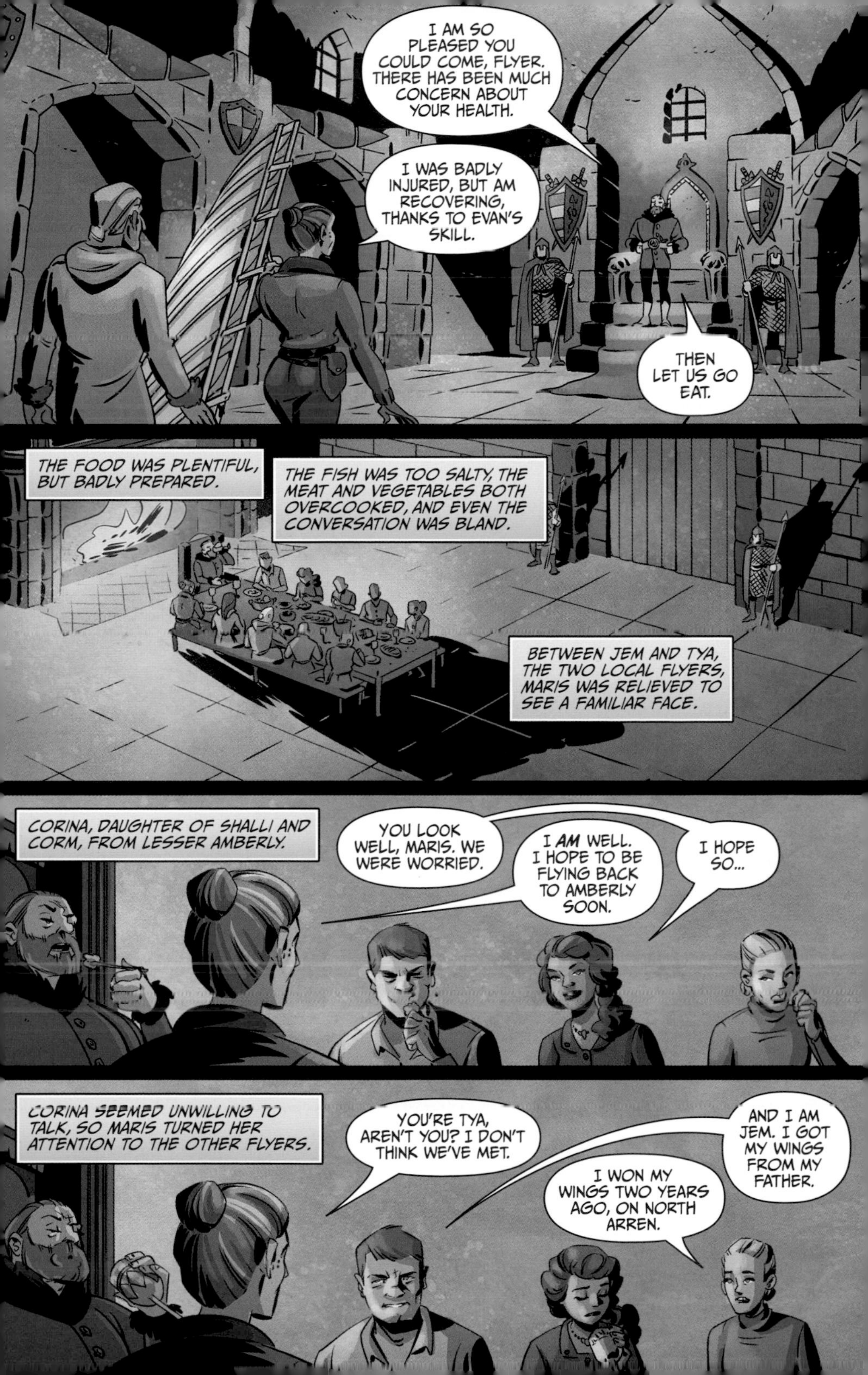
I AM SO PLEASED YOU COULD COME, FLYER. THERE HAS BEEN MUCH CONCERN ABOUT YOUR HEALTH.
I WAS BADLY INJURED, BUT AM RECOVERING, THANKS TO EVAN'S SKILL.
THEN LET US GO EAT.
THE FOOD WAS PLENTIFUL, BUT BADLY PREPARED.
THE FISH WAS TOO SALTY, THE MEAT AND VEGETABLES BOTH OVERCOOKED, AND EVEN THE CONVERSATION WAS BLAND.
BETWEEN JEM AND TYA, THE TWO LOCAL FLYERS, MARIS WAS RELIEVED TO SEE A FAMILIAR FACE.
CORINA, DAUGHTER OF SHALLI AND CORM, FROM LESSER AMBERLY.
YOU LOOK WELL, MARIS. WE WERE WORRIED.
I *AM* WELL. I HOPE TO BE FLYING BACK TO AMBERLY SOON.
I HOPE SO...
CORINA SEEMED UNWILLING TO TALK, SO MARIS TURNED HER ATTENTION TO THE OTHER FLYERS.
YOU'RE TYA, AREN'T YOU? I DON'T THINK WE'VE MET.
I WON MY WINGS TWO YEARS AGO, ON NORTH ARREN.
AND I AM JEM. I GOT MY WINGS FROM MY FATHER.

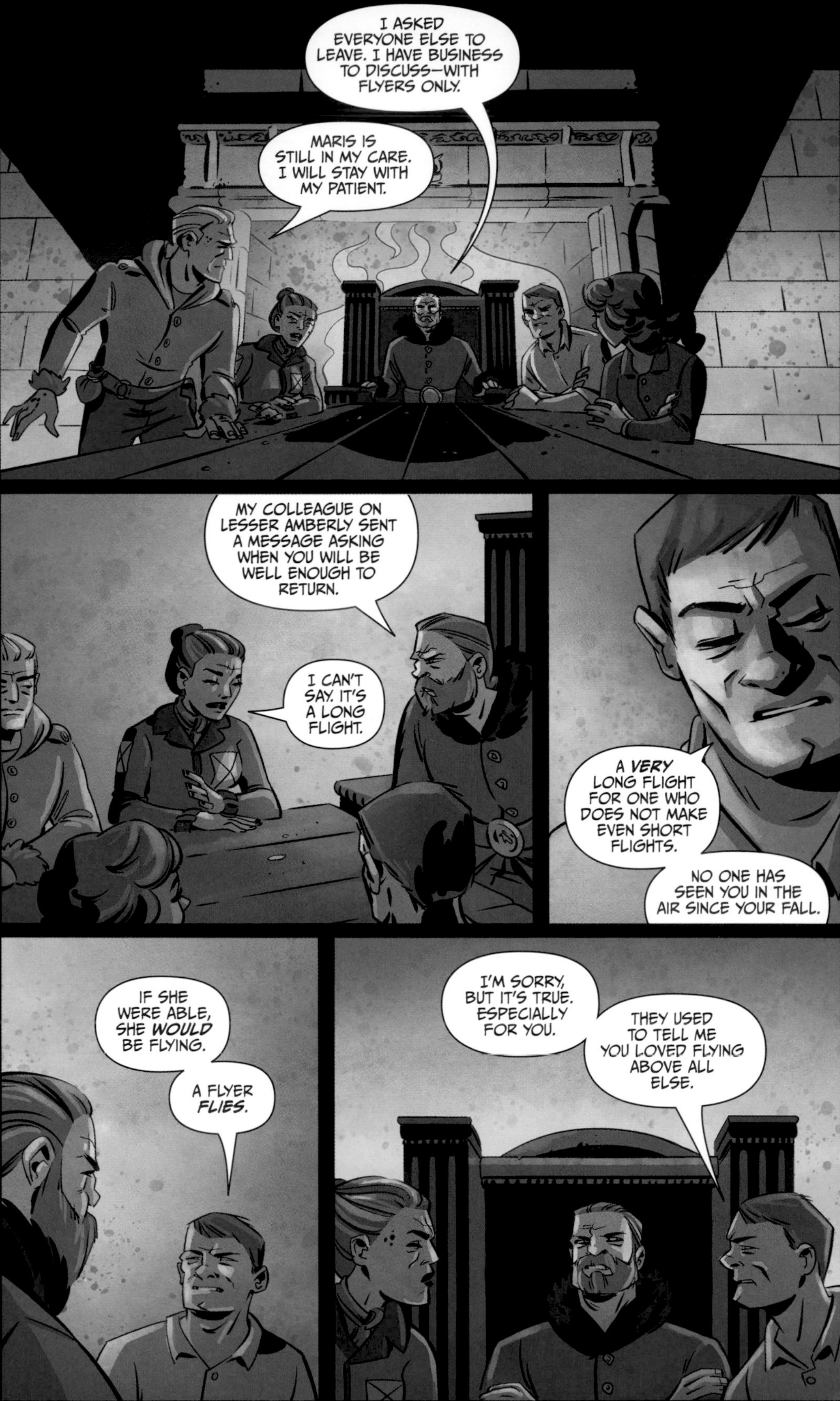
I ASKED EVERYONE ELSE TO LEAVE. I HAVE BUSINESS TO DISCUSS—WITH FLYERS ONLY.
MARIS IS STILL IN MY CARE. I WILL STAY WITH MY PATIENT.
MY COLLEAGUE ON LESSER AMBERLY SENT A MESSAGE ASKING WHEN YOU WILL BE WELL ENOUGH TO RETURN.
I CAN'T SAY. IT'S A LONG FLIGHT.
A *VERY* LONG FLIGHT FOR ONE WHO DOES NOT MAKE EVEN SHORT FLIGHTS.
NO ONE HAS SEEN YOU IN THE AIR SINCE YOUR FALL.
IF SHE WERE ABLE, SHE *WOULD* BE FLYING.
A FLYER *FLIES*.
I'M SORRY, BUT IT'S TRUE. ESPECIALLY FOR YOU.
THEY USED TO TELL ME YOU LOVED FLYING ABOVE ALL ELSE.

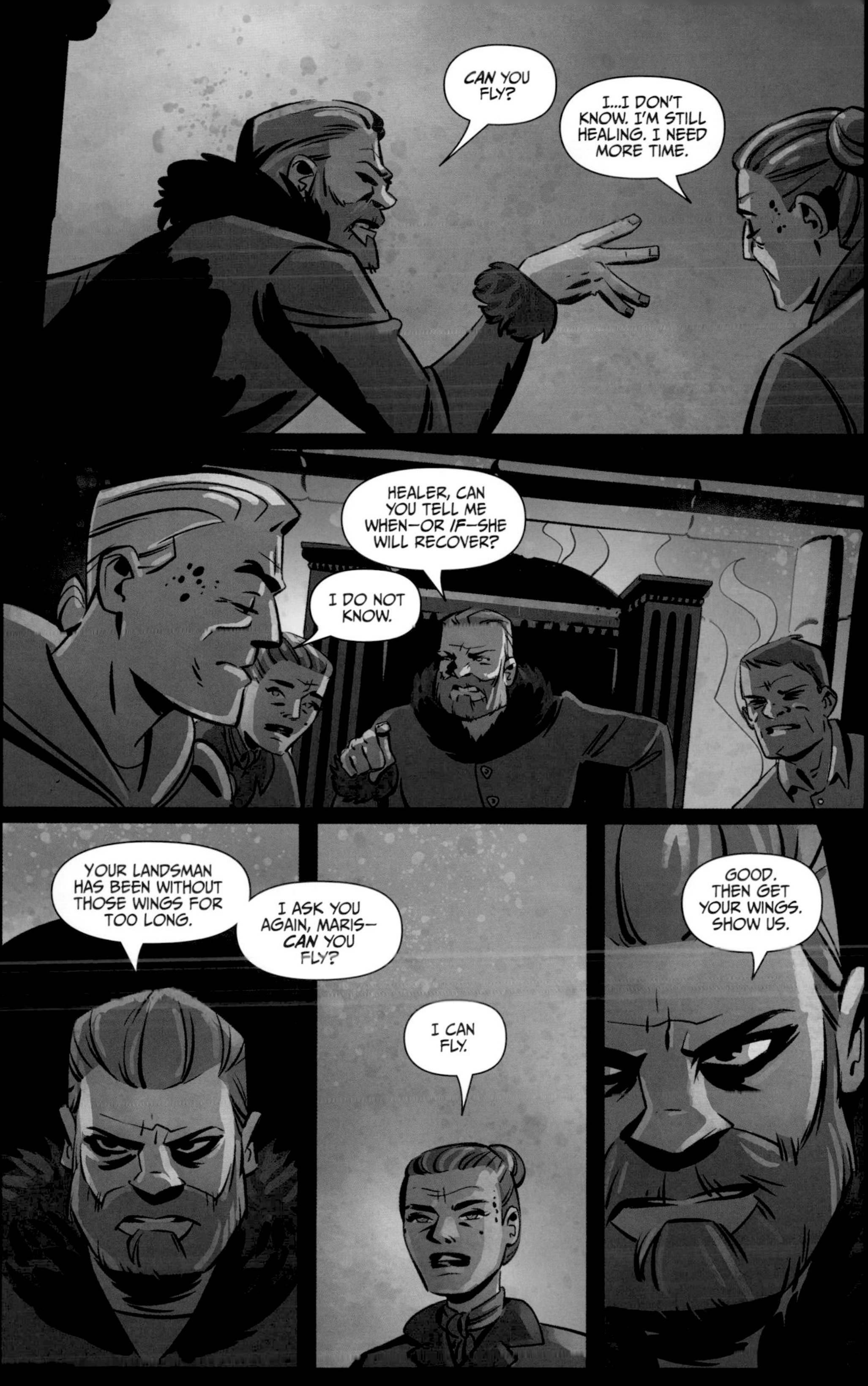

CAN YOU FLY?
I...I DON'T KNOW. I'M STILL HEALING. I NEED MORE TIME.
HEALER, CAN YOU TELL ME WHEN—OR *IF*—SHE WILL RECOVER?
I DO NOT KNOW.
YOUR LANDSMAN HAS BEEN WITHOUT THOSE WINGS FOR TOO LONG.
I ASK YOU AGAIN, MARIS—*CAN* YOU FLY?
I CAN FLY.
GOOD. THEN GET YOUR WINGS. SHOW US.

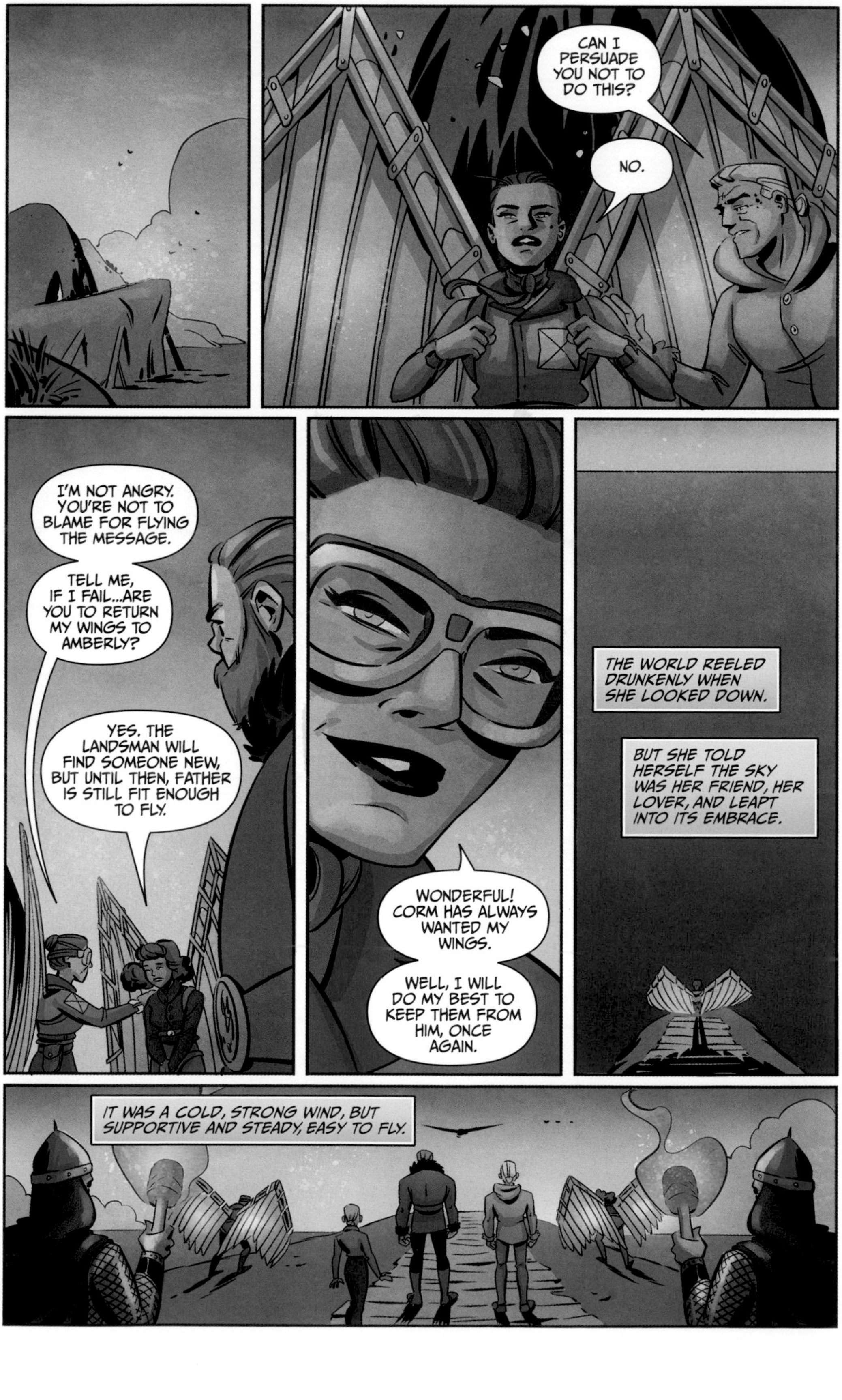
CAN I PERSUADE YOU NOT TO DO THIS?
NO.
I'M NOT ANGRY. YOU'RE NOT TO BLAME FOR FLYING THE MESSAGE.
TELL ME, IF I FAIL...ARE YOU TO RETURN MY WINGS TO AMBERLY?
YES. THE LANDSMAN WILL FIND SOMEONE NEW, BUT UNTIL THEN, FATHER IS STILL FIT ENOUGH TO FLY.
WONDERFUL! CORM HAS ALWAYS WANTED MY WINGS.
WELL, I WILL DO MY BEST TO KEEP THEM FROM HIM, ONCE AGAIN.
THE WORLD REELED DRUNKENLY WHEN SHE LOOKED DOWN.
BUT SHE TOLD HERSELF THE SKY WAS HER FRIEND, HER LOVER, AND LEAPT INTO ITS EMBRACE.
IT WAS A COLD, STRONG WIND, BUT SUPPORTIVE AND STEADY, EASY TO FLY.

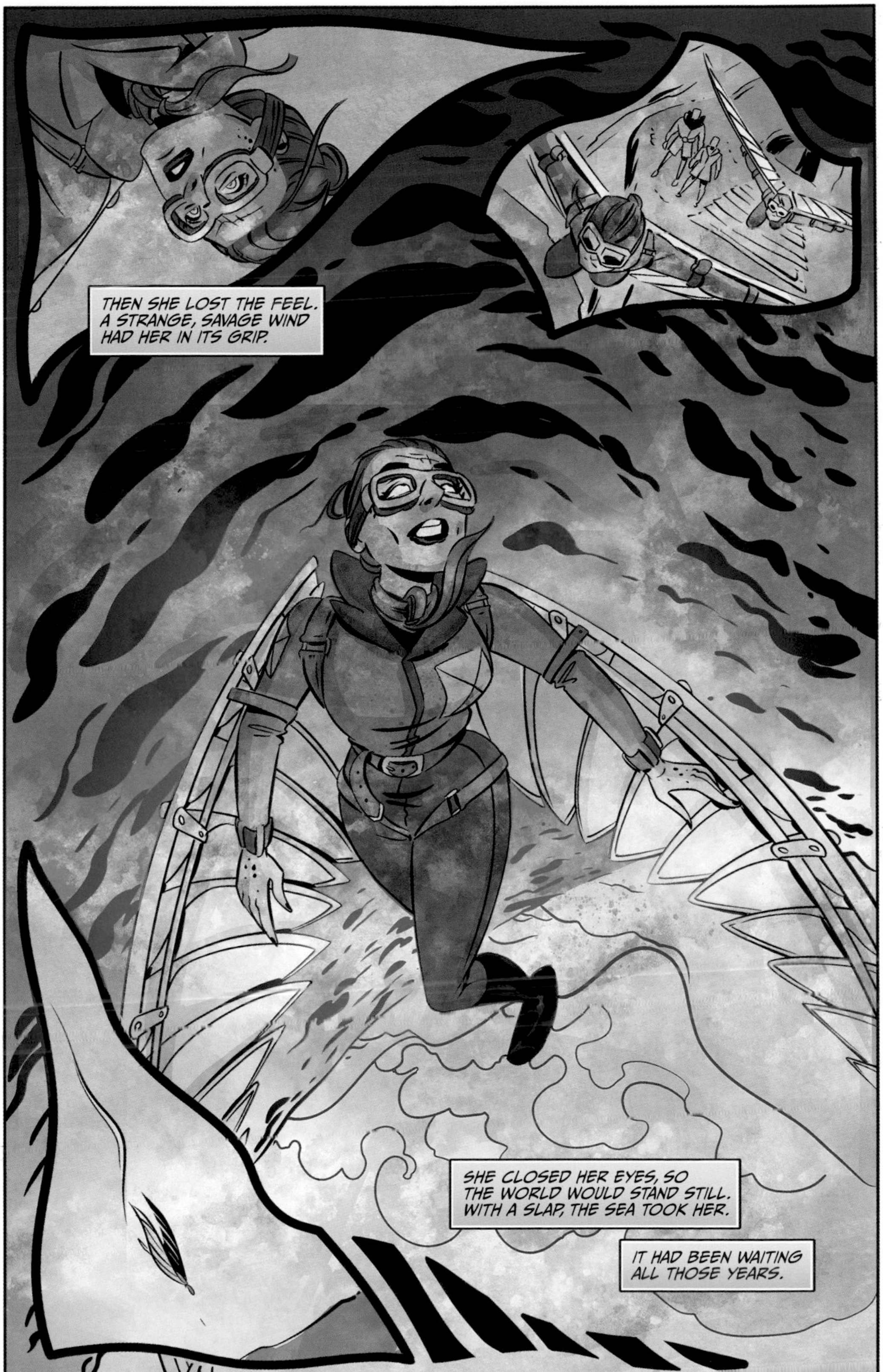
THEN SHE LOST THE FEEL. A STRANGE, SAVAGE WIND HAD HER IN ITS GRIP.
SHE CLOSED HER EYES, SO THE WORLD WOULD STAND STILL. WITH A SLAP, THE SEA TOOK HER.
IT HAD BEEN WAITING ALL THOSE YEARS.

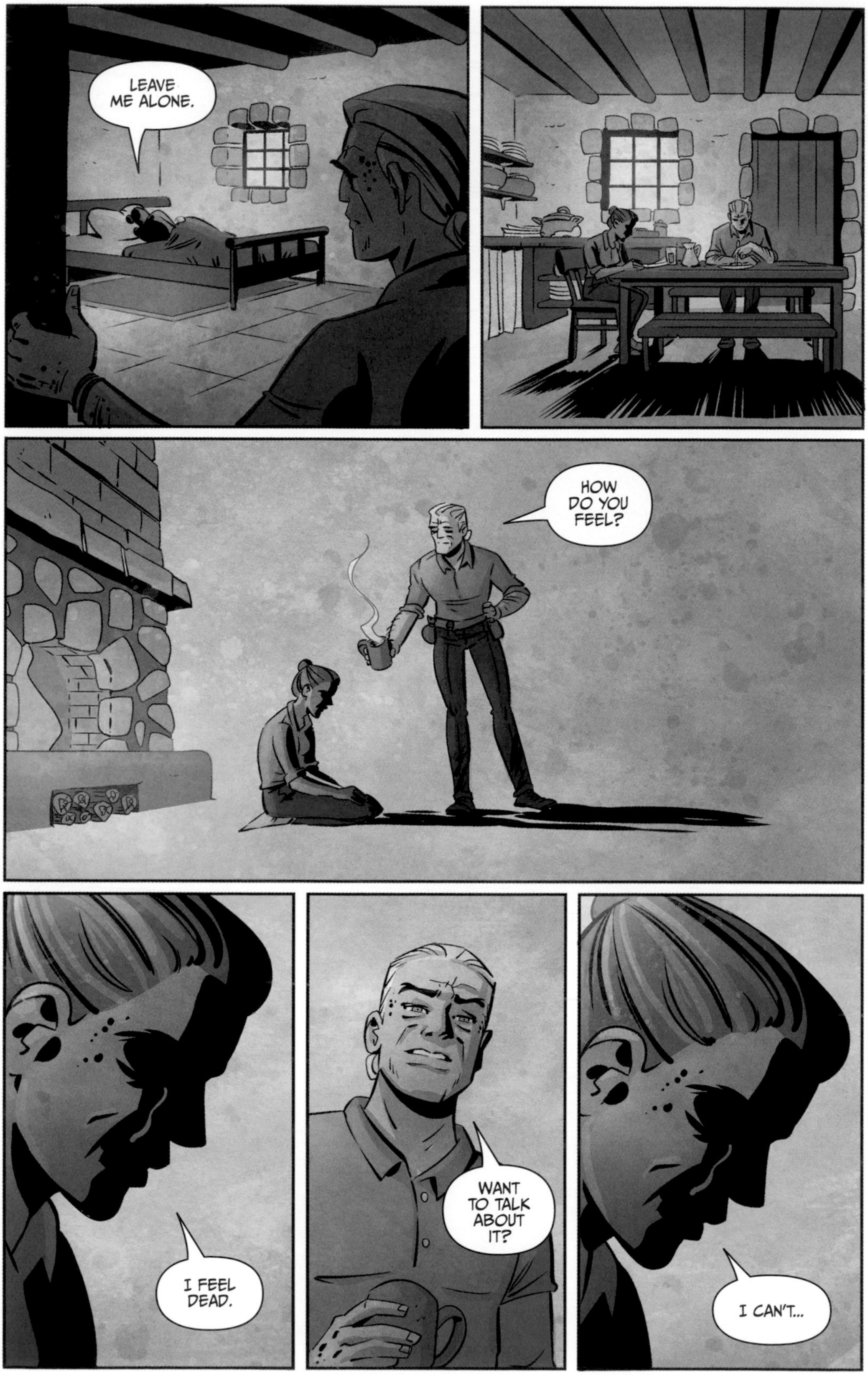
LEAVE ME ALONE.
HOW DO YOU FEEL?
I FEEL DEAD.
WANT TO TALK ABOUT IT?
I CAN'T...

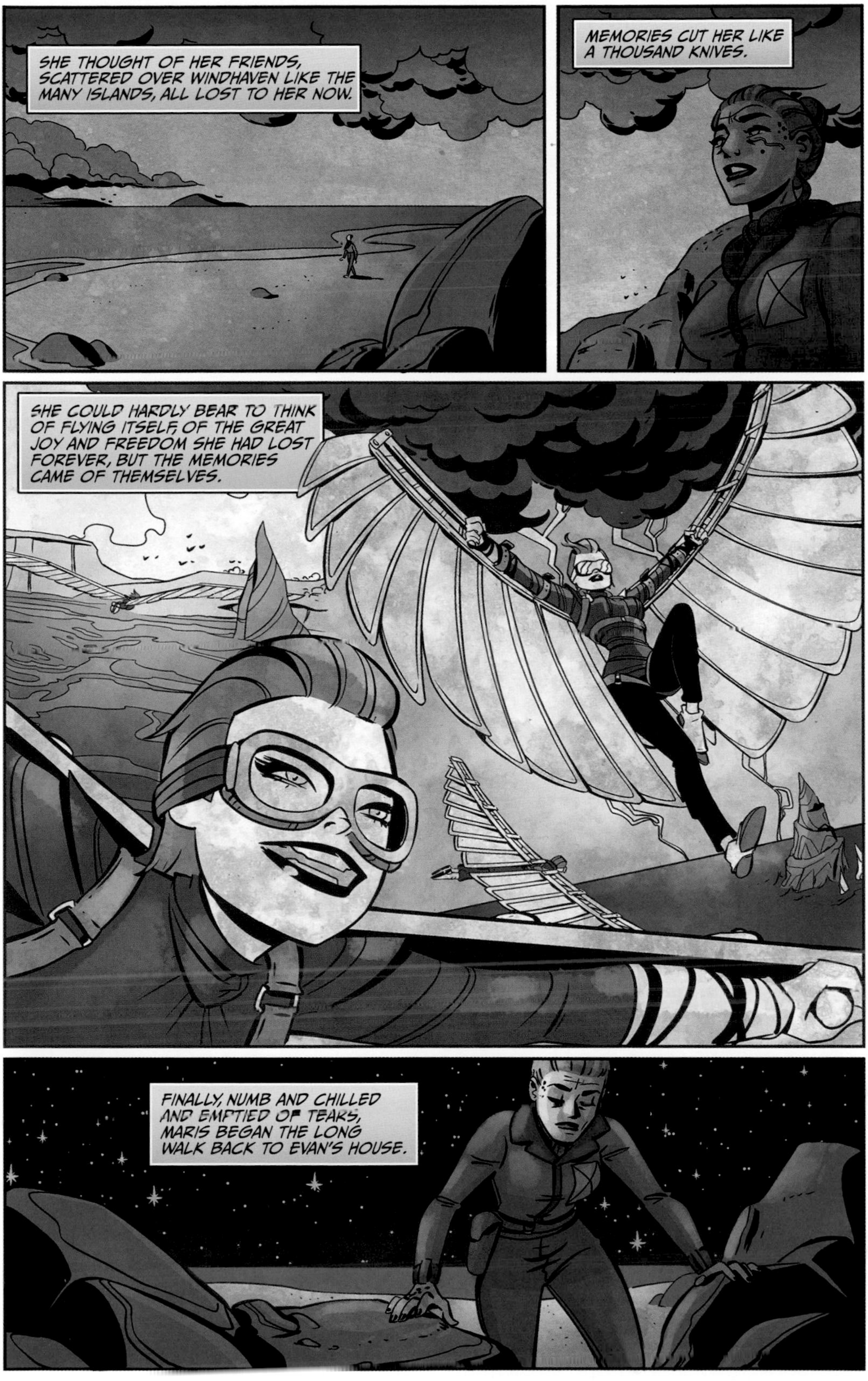
SHE THOUGHT OF HER FRIENDS, SCATTERED OVER WINDHAVEN LIKE THE MANY ISLANDS, ALL LOST TO HER NOW.
MEMORIES CUT HER LIKE A THOUSAND KNIVES.
SHE COULD HARDLY BEAR TO THINK OF FLYING ITSELF, OF THE GREAT JOY AND FREEDOM SHE HAD LOST FOREVER, BUT THE MEMORIES CAME OF THEMSELVES.
FINALLY, NUMB AND CHILLED AND EMPTIED OF TEARS, MARIS BEGAN THE LONG WALK BACK TO EVAN'S HOUSE.

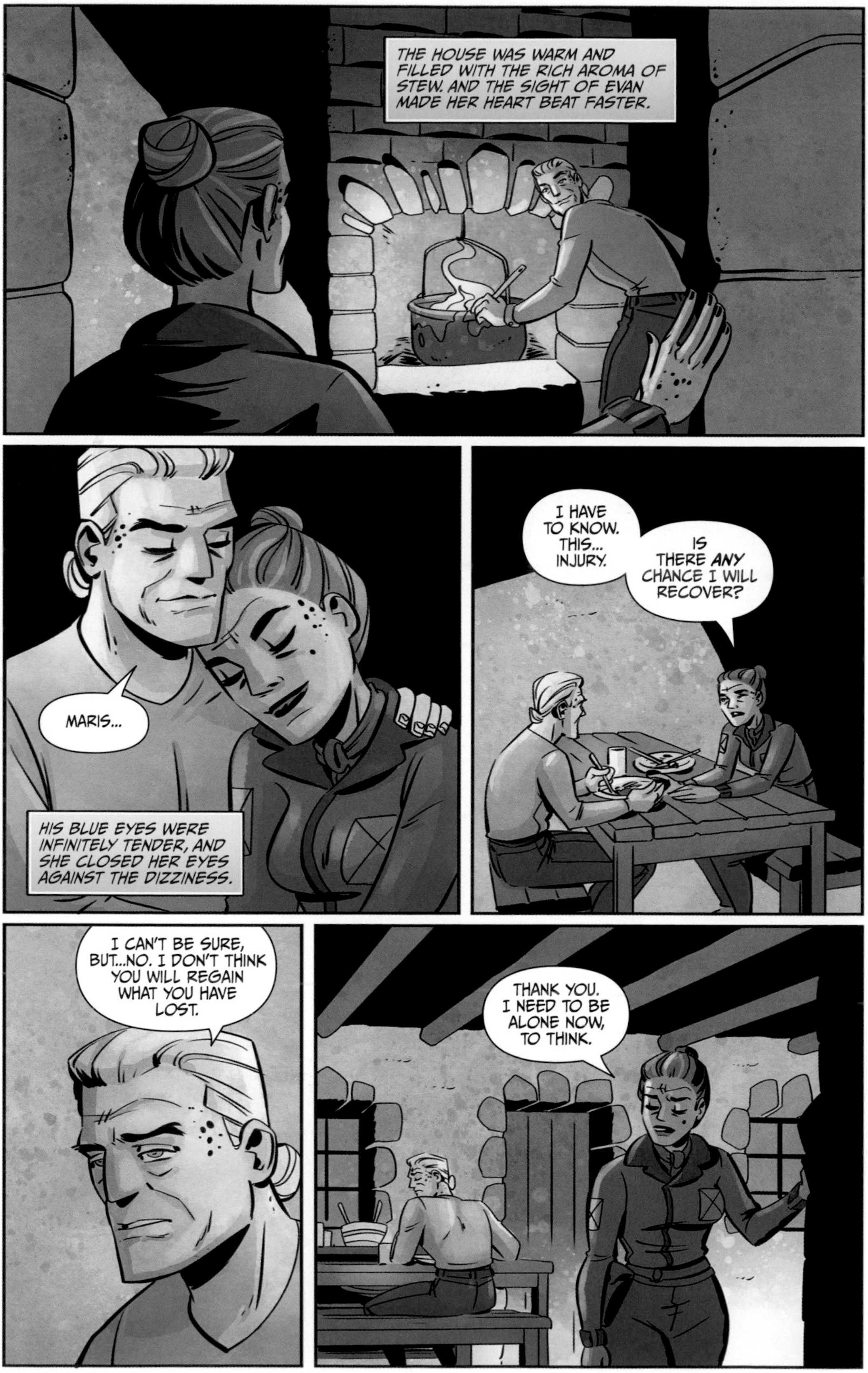
THE HOUSE WAS WARM AND FILLED WITH THE RICH AROMA OF STEW. AND THE SIGHT OF EVAN MADE HER HEART BEAT FASTER.
MARIS...
HIS BLUE EYES WERE INFINITELY TENDER, AND SHE CLOSED HER EYES AGAINST THE DIZZINESS.
I HAVE TO KNOW. THIS... INJURY.
IS THERE ANY CHANCE I WILL RECOVER?
I CAN'T BE SURE, BUT...NO. I DON'T THINK YOU WILL REGAIN WHAT YOU HAVE LOST.
THANK YOU. I NEED TO BE ALONE NOW, TO THINK.

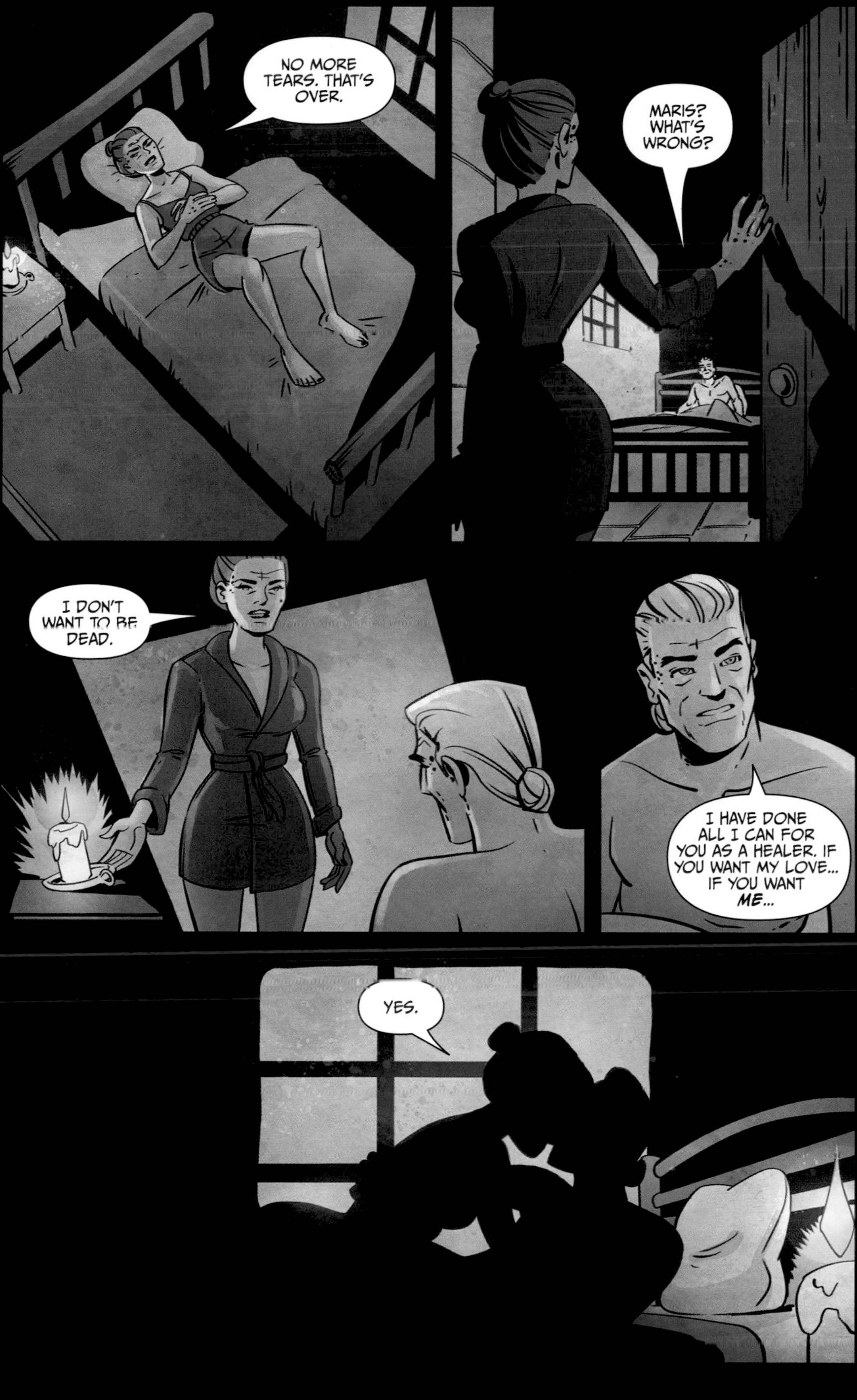
NO MORE TEARS. THAT'S OVER.
MARIS? WHAT'S WRONG?
I DON'T WANT TO BE DEAD.
I HAVE DONE ALL I CAN FOR YOU AS A HEALER. IF YOU WANT MY LOVE... IF YOU WANT *ME*...
YES.

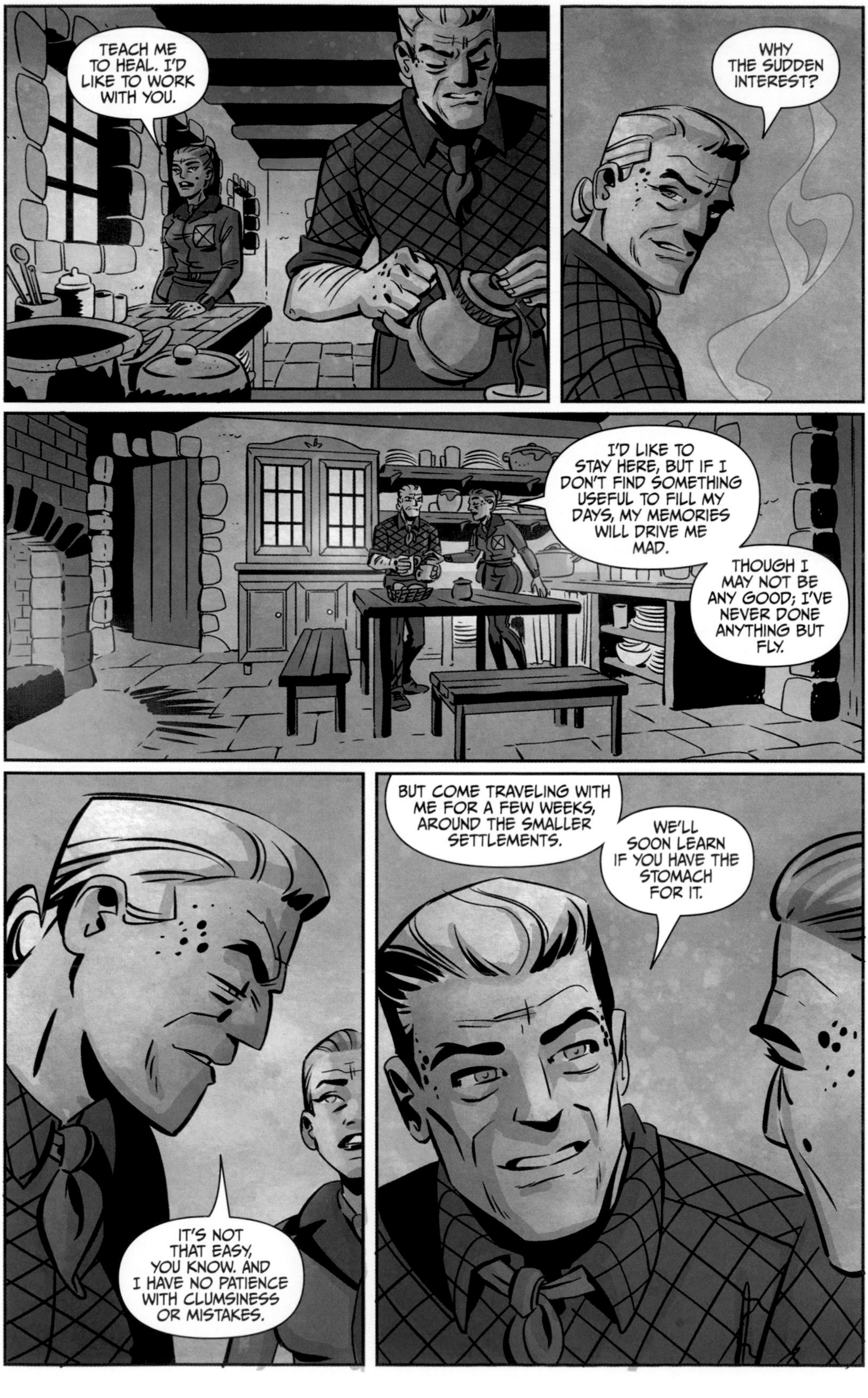
TEACH ME TO HEAL. I'D LIKE TO WORK WITH YOU.
WHY THE SUDDEN INTEREST?
I'D LIKE TO STAY HERE, BUT IF I DON'T FIND SOMETHING USEFUL TO FILL MY DAYS, MY MEMORIES WILL DRIVE ME MAD.
THOUGH I MAY NOT BE ANY GOOD; I'VE NEVER DONE ANYTHING BUT FLY.
IT'S NOT THAT EASY, YOU KNOW. AND I HAVE NO PATIENCE WITH CLUMSINESS OR MISTAKES.
BUT COME TRAVELING WITH ME FOR A FEW WEEKS, AROUND THE SMALLER SETTLEMENTS.
WE'LL SOON LEARN IF YOU HAVE THE STOMACH FOR IT.

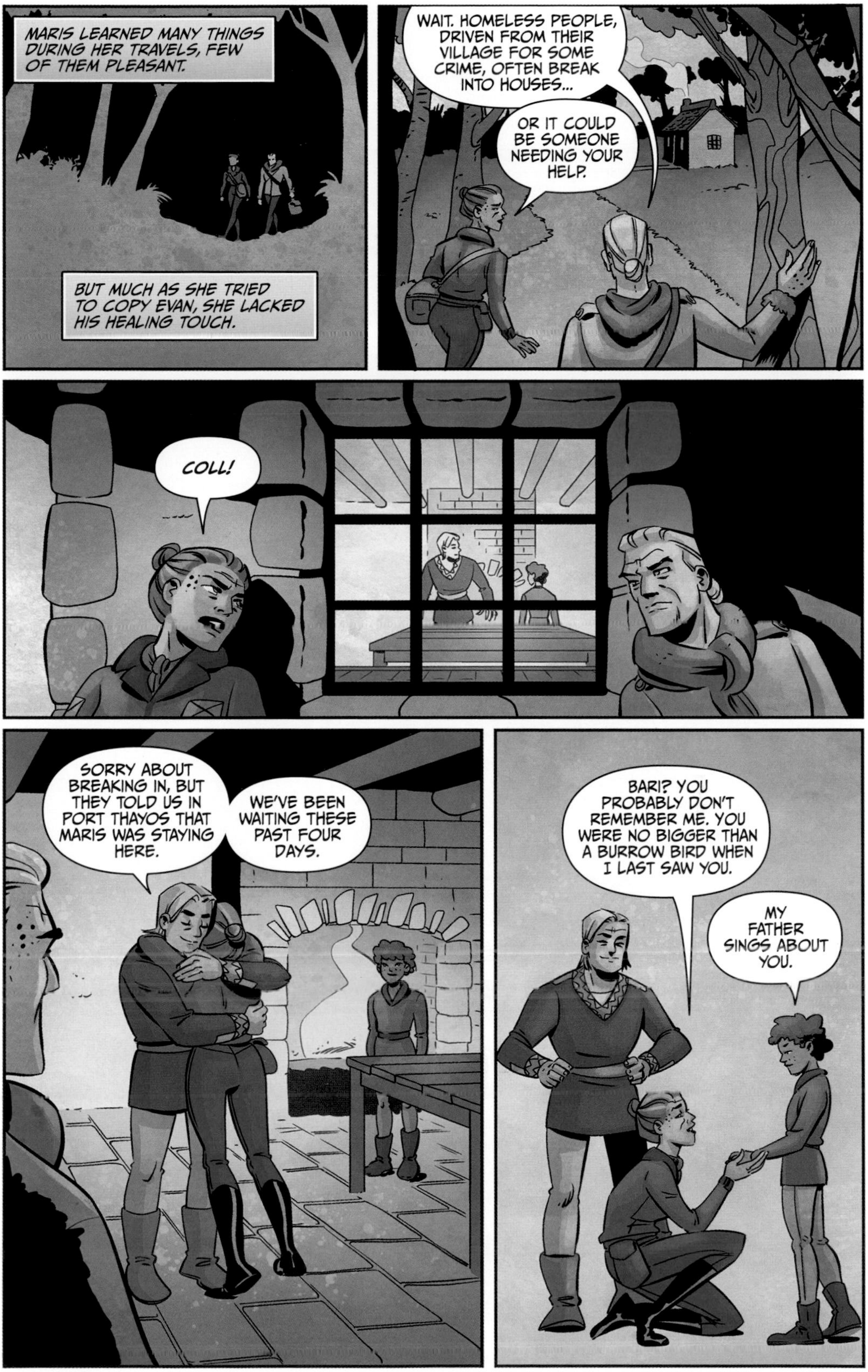
MARIS LEARNED MANY THINGS DURING HER TRAVELS, FEW OF THEM PLEASANT.
BUT MUCH AS SHE TRIED TO COPY EVAN, SHE LACKED HIS HEALING TOUCH.
WAIT. HOMELESS PEOPLE, DRIVEN FROM THEIR VILLAGE FOR SOME CRIME, OFTEN BREAK INTO HOUSES...
OR IT COULD BE SOMEONE NEEDING YOUR HELP.
COLL!
SORRY ABOUT BREAKING IN, BUT THEY TOLD US IN PORT THAYOS THAT MARIS WAS STAYING HERE.
WE'VE BEEN WAITING THESE PAST FOUR DAYS.
BARI? YOU PROBABLY DON'T REMEMBER ME. YOU WERE NO BIGGER THAN A BURROW BIRD WHEN I LAST SAW YOU.
MY FATHER SINGS ABOUT YOU.

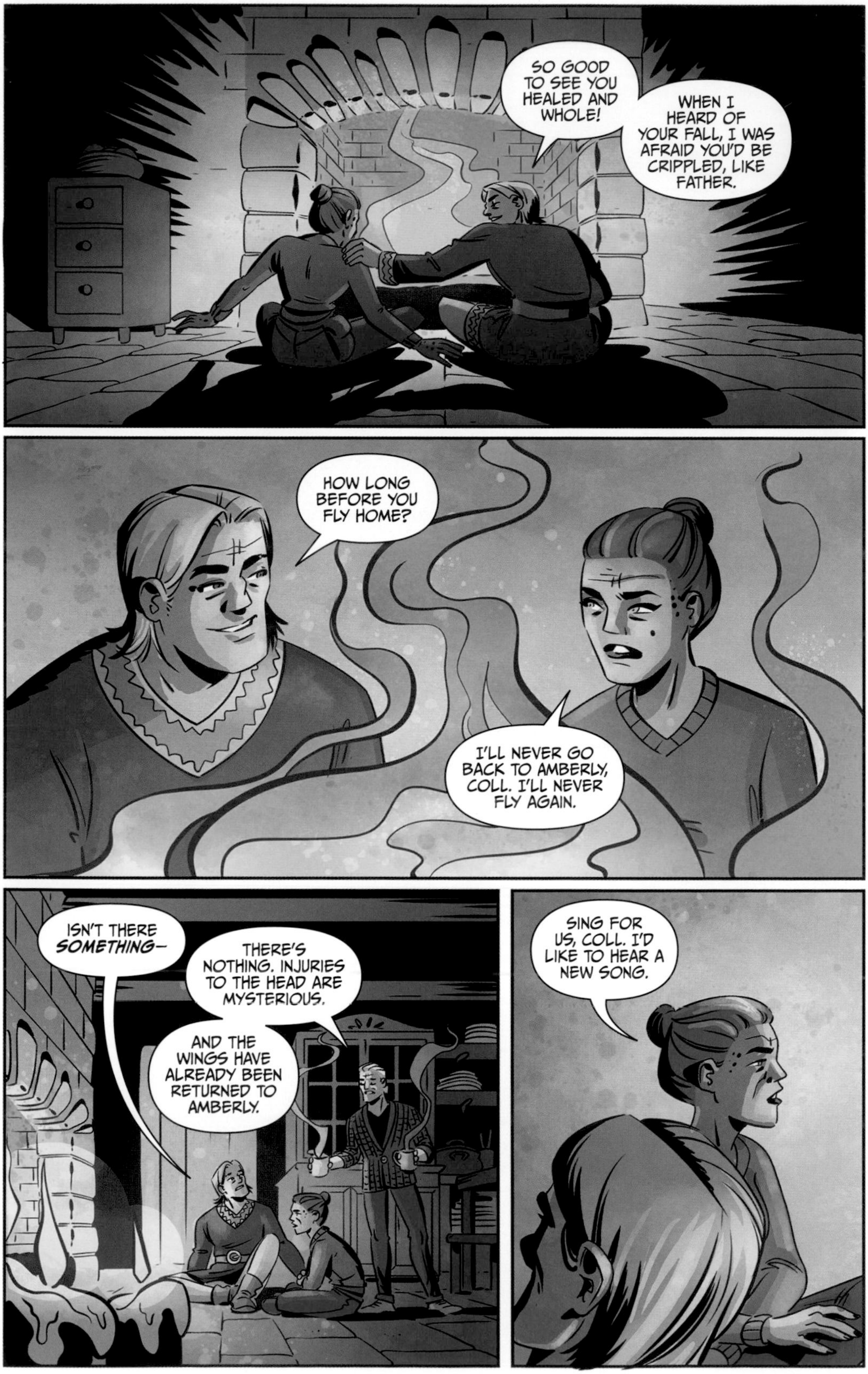
SO GOOD TO SEE YOU HEALED AND WHOLE!
WHEN I HEARD OF YOUR FALL, I WAS AFRAID YOU'D BE CRIPPLED, LIKE FATHER.
HOW LONG BEFORE YOU FLY HOME?
I'LL NEVER GO BACK TO AMBERLY, COLL. I'LL NEVER FLY AGAIN.
ISN'T THERE *SOMETHING*—
THERE'S NOTHING. INJURIES TO THE HEAD ARE MYSTERIOUS.
AND THE WINGS HAVE ALREADY BEEN RETURNED TO AMBERLY.
SING FOR US, COLL. I'D LIKE TO HEAR A NEW SONG.

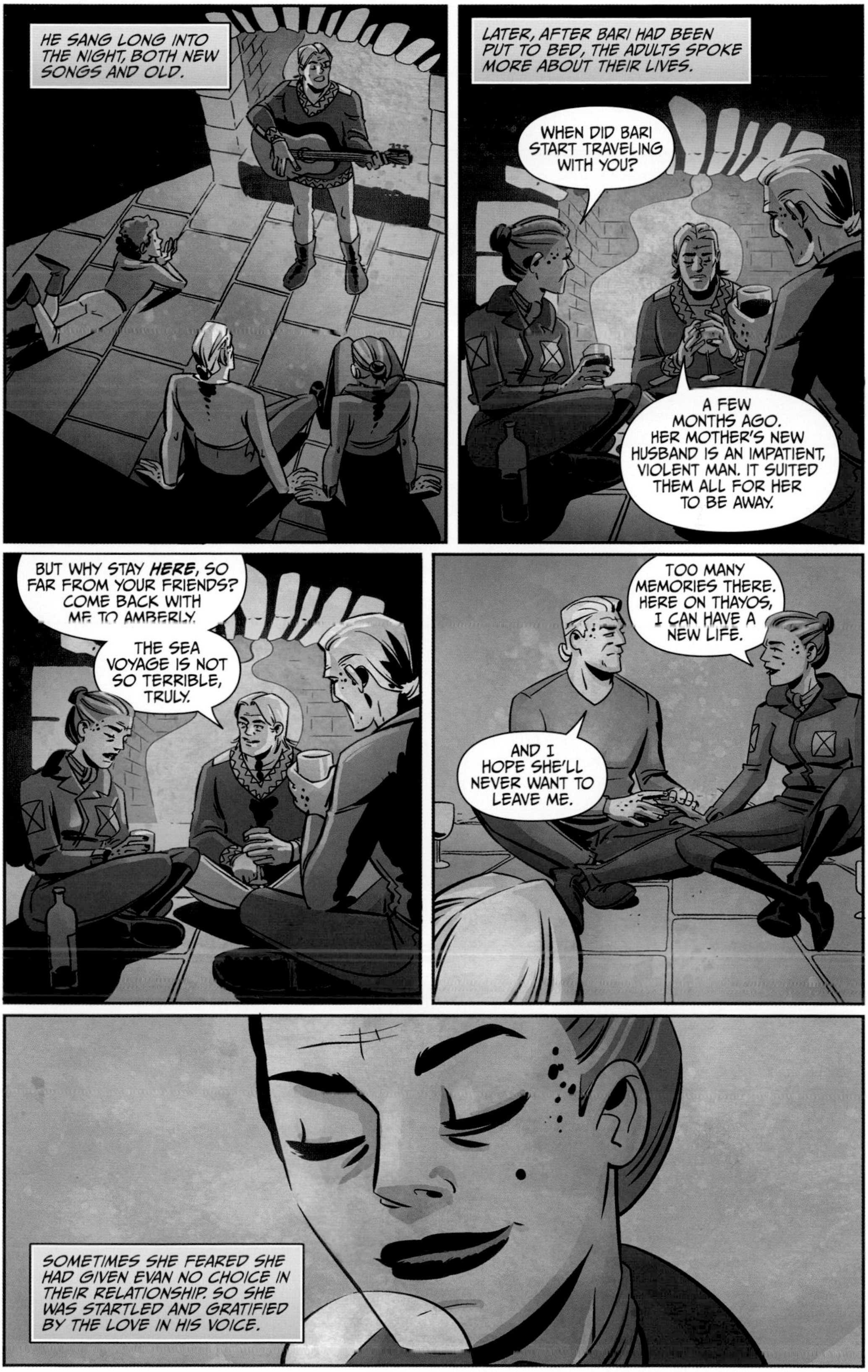
HE SANG LONG INTO THE NIGHT, BOTH NEW SONGS AND OLD.
LATER, AFTER BARI HAD BEEN PUT TO BED, THE ADULTS SPOKE MORE ABOUT THEIR LIVES.
WHEN DID BARI START TRAVELING WITH YOU?
A FEW MONTHS AGO. HER MOTHER'S NEW HUSBAND IS AN IMPATIENT, VIOLENT MAN. IT SUITED THEM ALL FOR HER TO BE AWAY.
BUT WHY STAY HERE, SO FAR FROM YOUR FRIENDS? COME BACK WITH ME TO AMBERLY.
THE SEA VOYAGE IS NOT SO TERRIBLE, TRULY.
TOO MANY MEMORIES THERE. HERE ON THAYOS, I CAN HAVE A NEW LIFE.
AND I HOPE SHE'LL NEVER WANT TO LEAVE ME.
SOMETIMES SHE FEARED SHE HAD GIVEN EVAN NO CHOICE IN THEIR RELATIONSHIP. SO SHE WAS STARTLED AND GRATIFIED BY THE LOVE IN HIS VOICE.

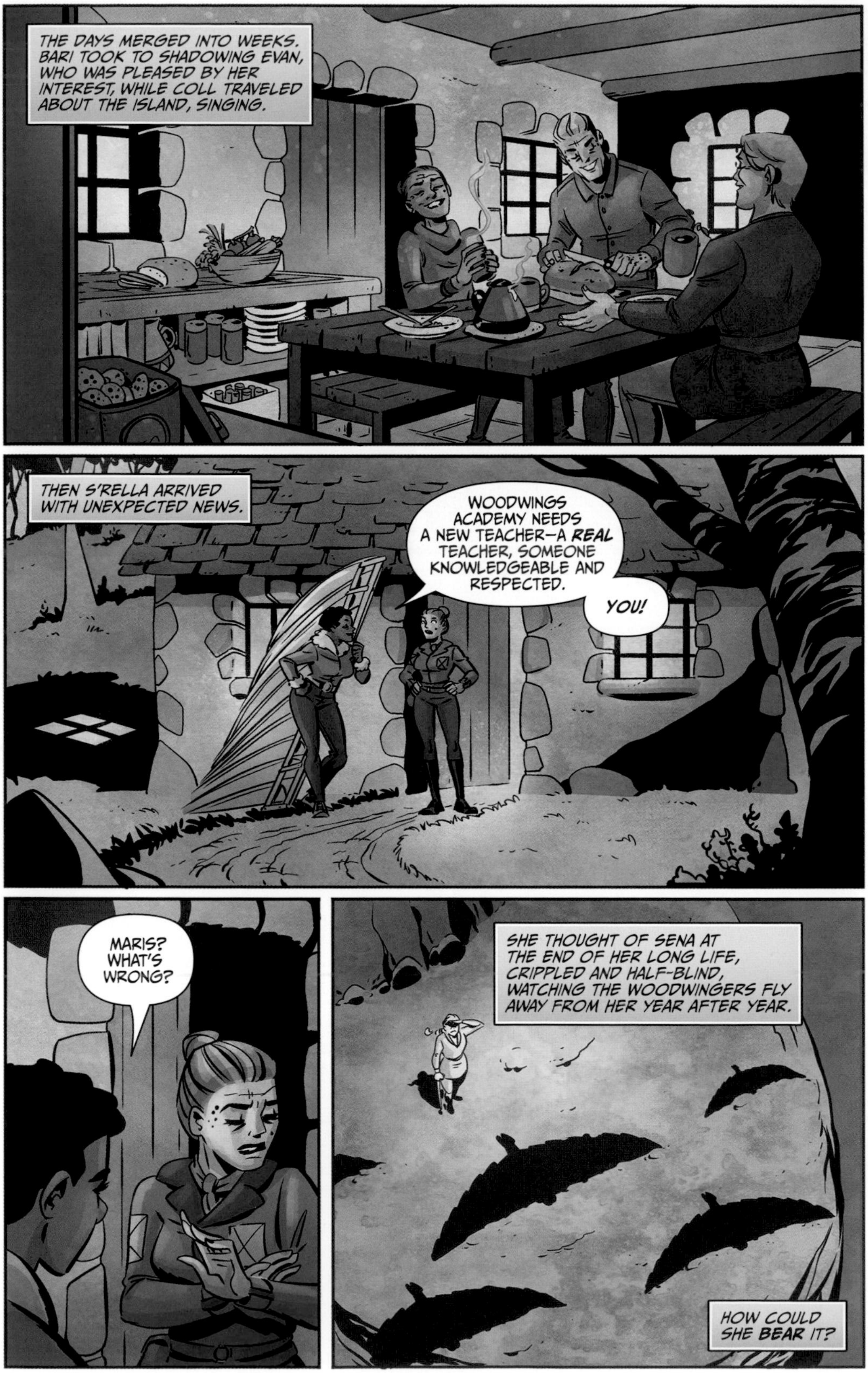
THE DAYS MERGED INTO WEEKS. BARI TOOK TO SHADOWING EVAN, WHO WAS PLEASED BY HER INTEREST, WHILE COLL TRAVELED ABOUT THE ISLAND, SINGING.
THEN S'RELLA ARRIVED WITH UNEXPECTED NEWS.
WOODWINGS ACADEMY NEEDS A NEW TEACHER—A **REAL** TEACHER, SOMEONE KNOWLEDGEABLE AND RESPECTED.
YOU!
MARIS? WHAT'S WRONG?
SHE THOUGHT OF SENA AT THE END OF HER LONG LIFE, CRIPPLED AND HALF-BLIND, WATCHING THE WOODWINGERS FLY AWAY FROM HER YEAR AFTER YEAR.
HOW COULD SHE **BEAR** IT?

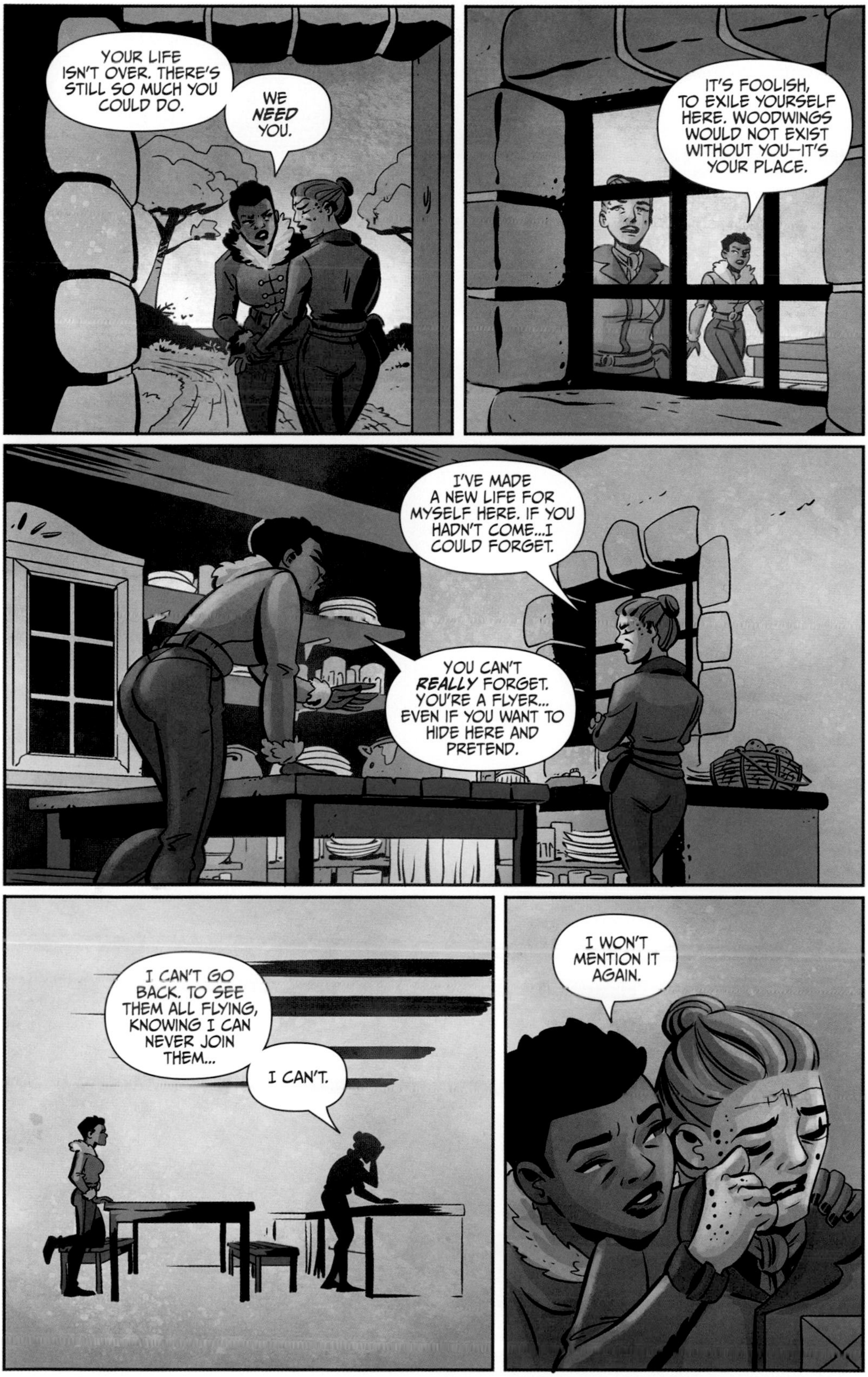
YOUR LIFE ISN'T OVER. THERE'S STILL SO MUCH YOU COULD DO.
WE *NEED* YOU.
IT'S FOOLISH, TO EXILE YOURSELF HERE. WOODWINGS WOULD NOT EXIST WITHOUT YOU—IT'S YOUR PLACE.
I'VE MADE A NEW LIFE FOR MYSELF HERE. IF YOU HADN'T COME...I COULD FORGET.
YOU CAN'T *REALLY* FORGET. YOU'RE A FLYER... EVEN IF YOU WANT TO HIDE HERE AND PRETEND.
I CAN'T GO BACK. TO SEE THEM ALL FLYING, KNOWING I CAN NEVER JOIN THEM...
I CAN'T.
I WON'T MENTION IT AGAIN.

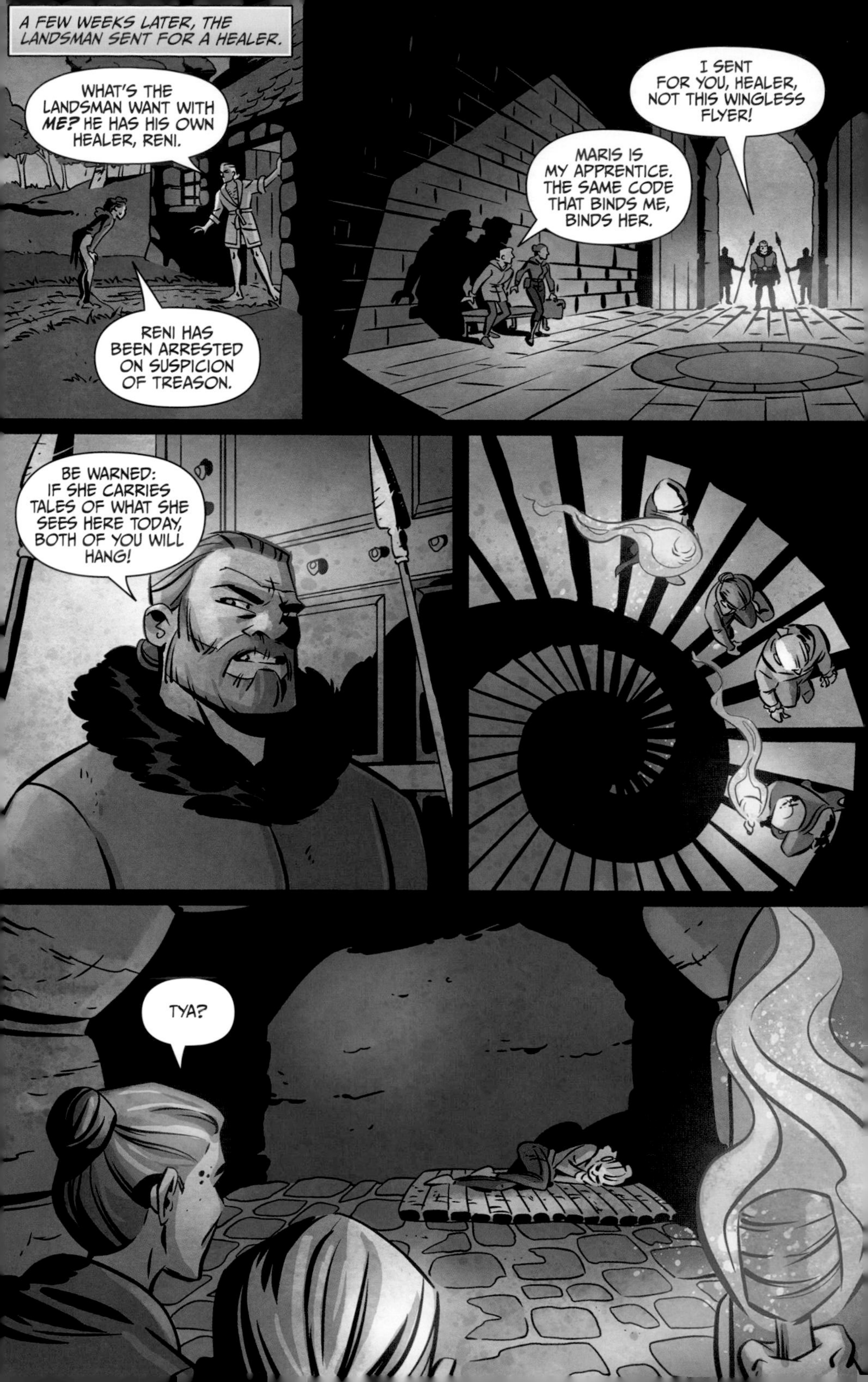
A FEW WEEKS LATER, THE LANDSMAN SENT FOR A HEALER.
WHAT'S THE LANDSMAN WANT WITH *ME?* HE HAS HIS OWN HEALER, RENI.
RENI HAS BEEN ARRESTED ON SUSPICION OF TREASON.
I SENT FOR YOU, HEALER, NOT THIS WINGLESS FLYER!
MARIS IS MY APPRENTICE. THE SAME CODE THAT BINDS ME, BINDS HER.
BE WARNED: IF SHE CARRIES TALES OF WHAT SHE SEES HERE TODAY, BOTH OF YOU WILL HANG!
TYA?

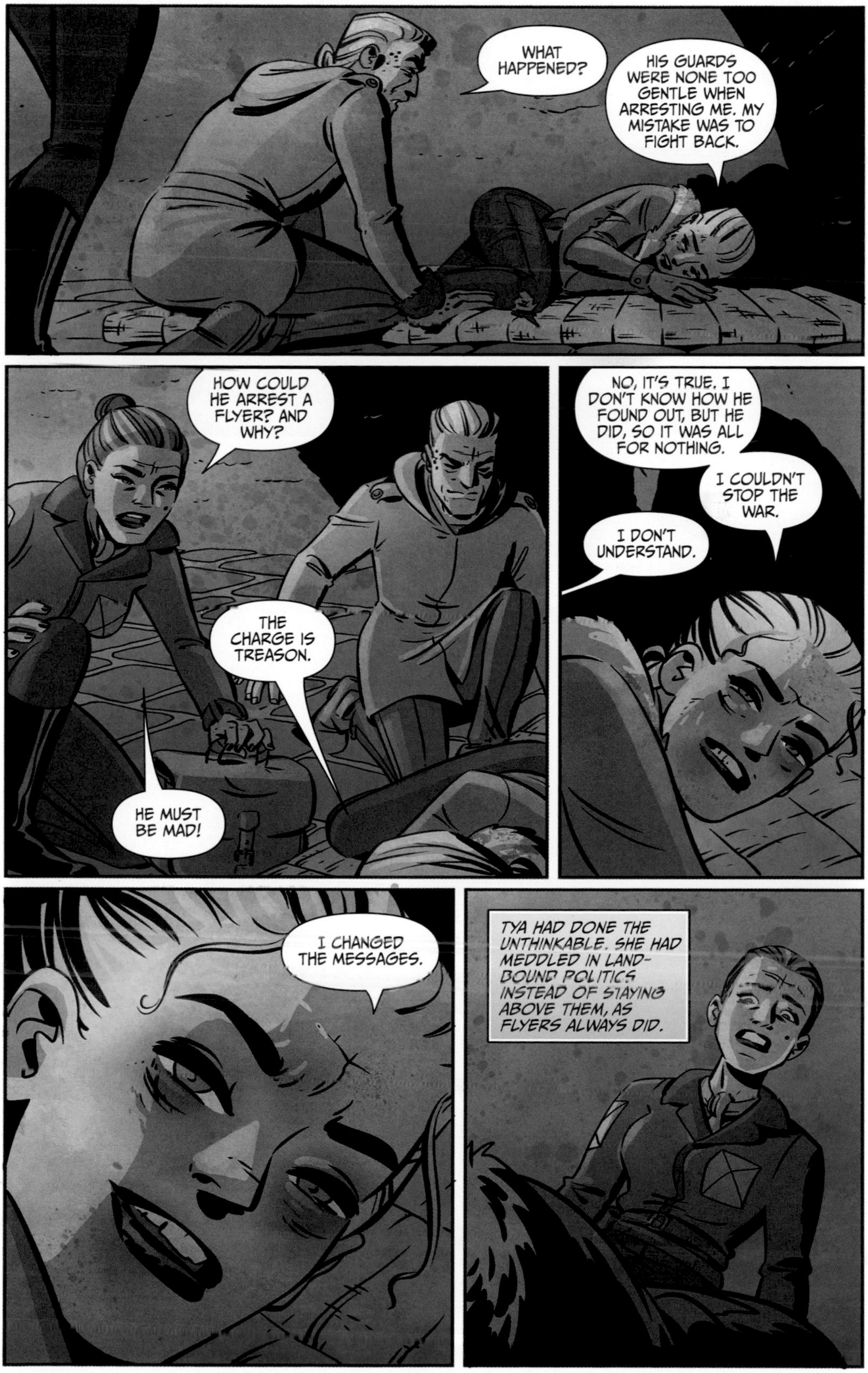
WHAT HAPPENED?
HIS GUARDS WERE NONE TOO GENTLE WHEN ARRESTING ME. MY MISTAKE WAS TO FIGHT BACK.
HOW COULD HE ARREST A FLYER? AND WHY?
THE CHARGE IS TREASON.
HE MUST BE MAD!
NO, IT'S TRUE. I DON'T KNOW HOW HE FOUND OUT, BUT HE DID, SO IT WAS ALL FOR NOTHING.
I COULDN'T STOP THE WAR.
I DON'T UNDERSTAND.
I CHANGED THE MESSAGES.
TYA HAD DONE THE UNTHINKABLE. SHE HAD MEDDLED IN LAND-BOUND POLITICS INSTEAD OF STAYING ABOVE THEM, AS FLYERS ALWAYS DID.

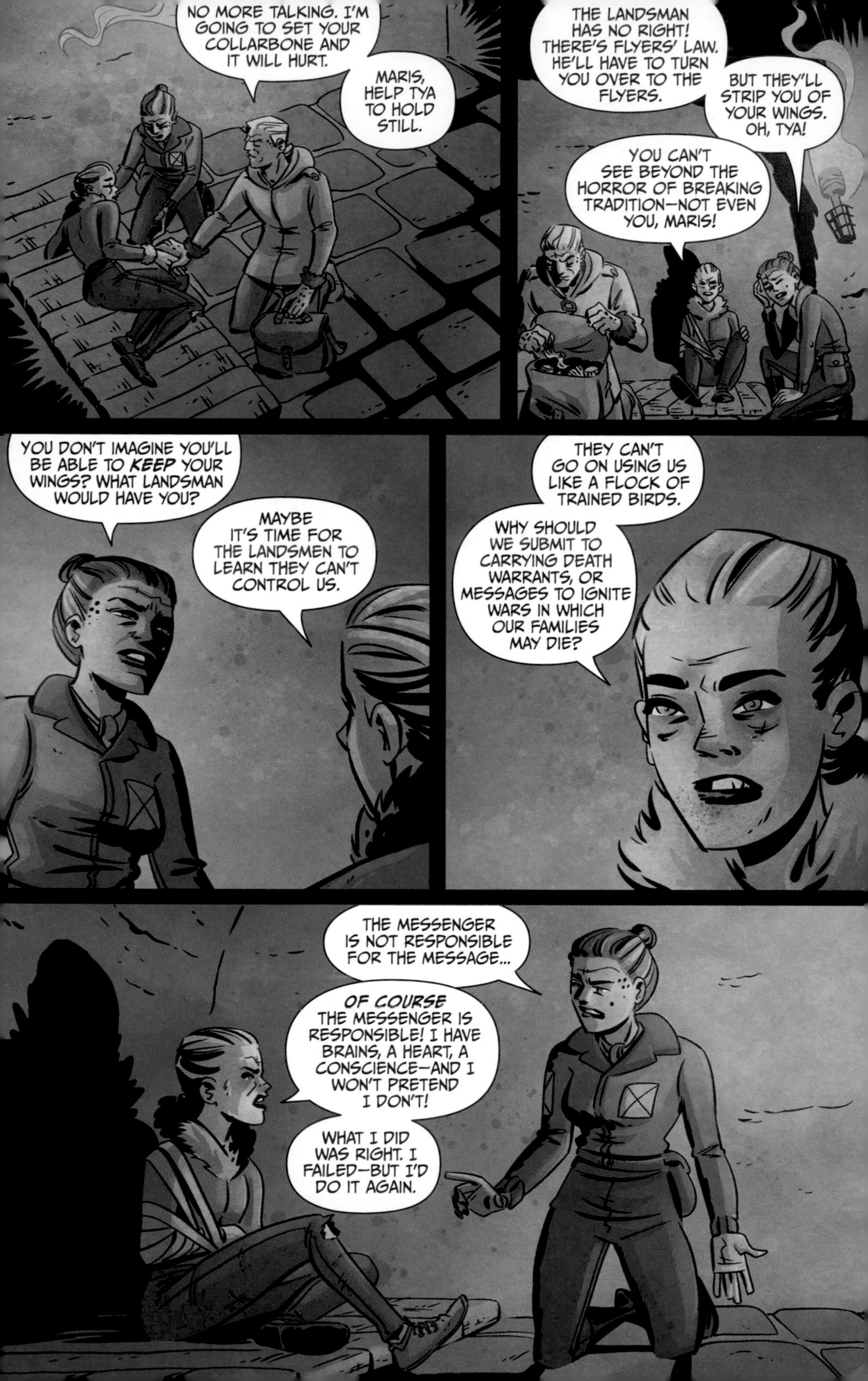
NO MORE TALKING. I'M GOING TO SET YOUR COLLARBONE AND IT WILL HURT.
MARIS, HELP TYA TO HOLD STILL.
THE LANDSMAN HAS NO RIGHT! THERE'S FLYERS' LAW. HE'LL HAVE TO TURN YOU OVER TO THE FLYERS.
BUT THEY'LL STRIP YOU OF YOUR WINGS. OH, TYA!
YOU CAN'T SEE BEYOND THE HORROR OF BREAKING TRADITION—NOT EVEN YOU, MARIS!
YOU DON'T IMAGINE YOU'LL BE ABLE TO *KEEP* YOUR WINGS? WHAT LANDSMAN WOULD HAVE YOU?
MAYBE IT'S TIME FOR THE LANDSMEN TO LEARN THEY CAN'T CONTROL US.
THEY CAN'T GO ON USING US LIKE A FLOCK OF TRAINED BIRDS.
WHY SHOULD WE SUBMIT TO CARRYING DEATH WARRANTS, OR MESSAGES TO IGNITE WARS IN WHICH OUR FAMILIES MAY DIE?
THE MESSENGER IS NOT RESPONSIBLE FOR THE MESSAGE...
OF COURSE THE MESSENGER IS RESPONSIBLE! I HAVE BRAINS, A HEART, A CONSCIENCE—AND I WON'T PRETEND I DON'T!
WHAT I DID WAS RIGHT. I FAILED—BUT I'D DO IT AGAIN.

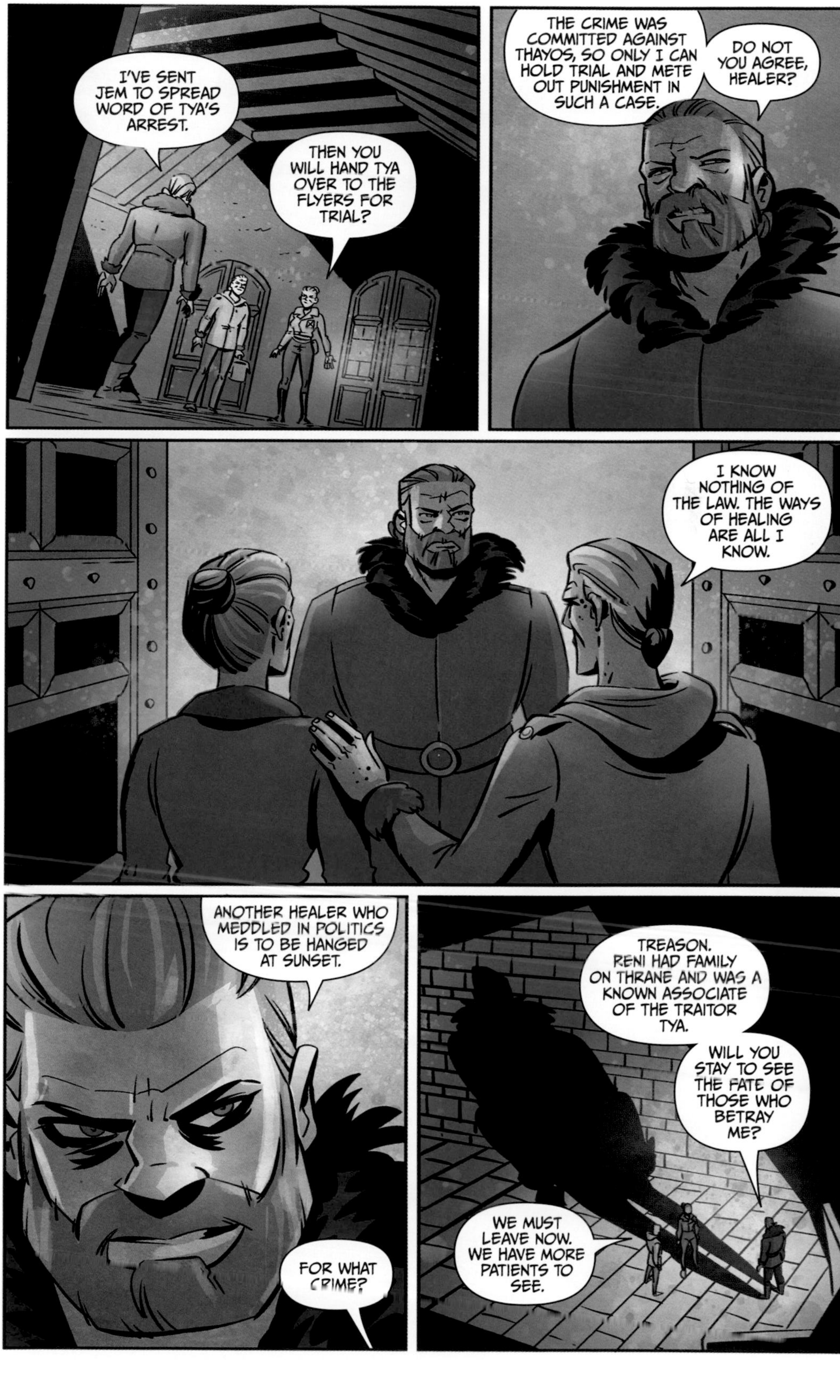
I'VE SENT JEM TO SPREAD WORD OF TYA'S ARREST.
THEN YOU WILL HAND TYA OVER TO THE FLYERS FOR TRIAL?
THE CRIME WAS COMMITTED AGAINST THAYOS, SO ONLY I CAN HOLD TRIAL AND METE OUT PUNISHMENT IN SUCH A CASE.
DO NOT YOU AGREE, HEALER?
I KNOW NOTHING OF THE LAW. THE WAYS OF HEALING ARE ALL I KNOW.
ANOTHER HEALER WHO MEDDLED IN POLITICS IS TO BE HANGED AT SUNSET.
FOR WHAT CRIME?
TREASON. RENI HAD FAMILY ON THRANE AND WAS A KNOWN ASSOCIATE OF THE TRAITOR TYA.
WILL YOU STAY TO SEE THE FATE OF THOSE WHO BETRAY ME?
WE MUST LEAVE NOW. WE HAVE MORE PATIENTS TO SEE.

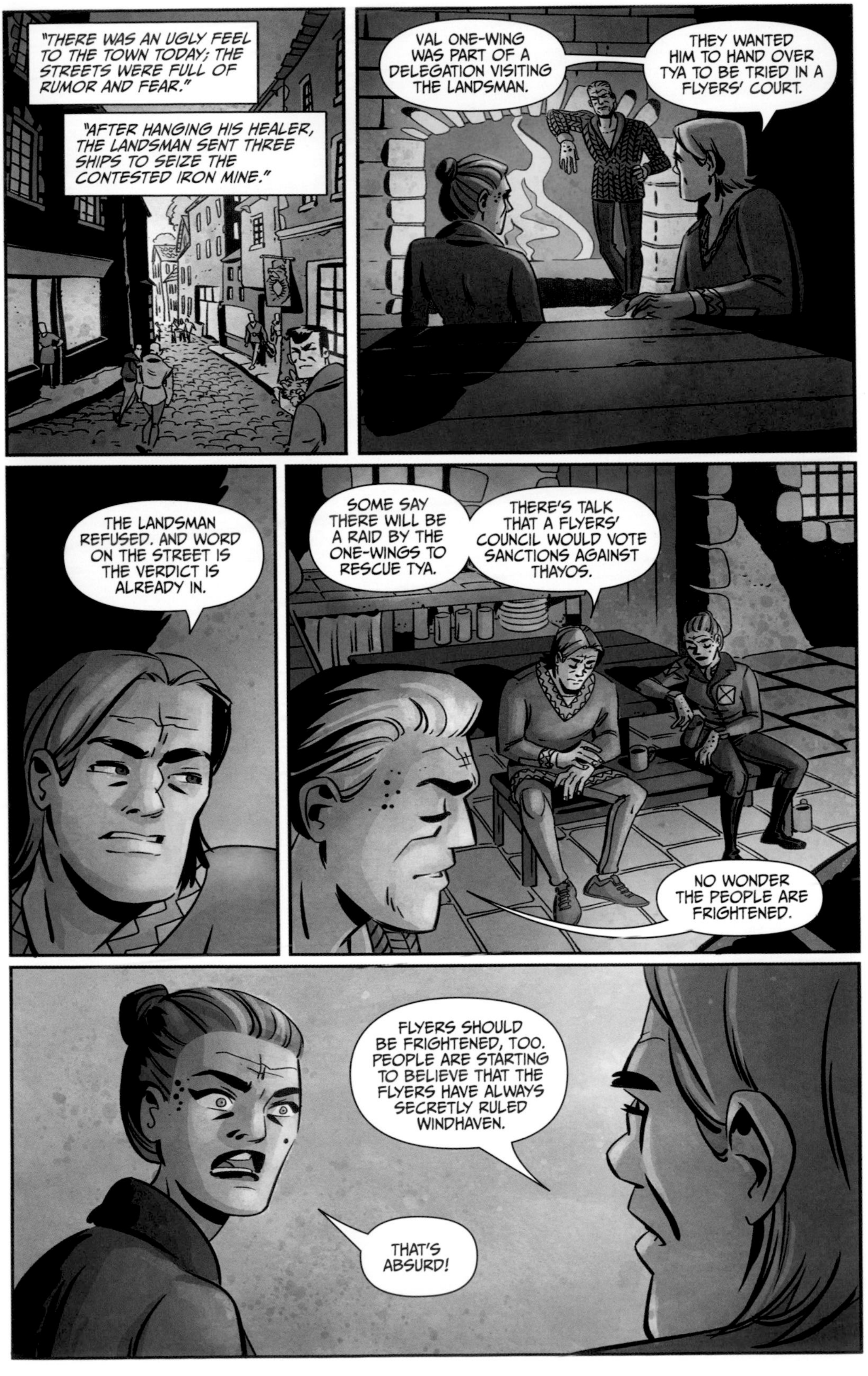
"THERE WAS AN UGLY FEEL TO THE TOWN TODAY; THE STREETS WERE FULL OF RUMOR AND FEAR."
"AFTER HANGING HIS HEALER, THE LANDSMAN SENT THREE SHIPS TO SEIZE THE CONTESTED IRON MINE."
VAL ONE-WING WAS PART OF A DELEGATION VISITING THE LANDSMAN.
THEY WANTED HIM TO HAND OVER TYA TO BE TRIED IN A FLYERS' COURT.
THE LANDSMAN REFUSED. AND WORD ON THE STREET IS THE VERDICT IS ALREADY IN.
SOME SAY THERE WILL BE A RAID BY THE ONE-WINGS TO RESCUE TYA.
THERE'S TALK THAT A FLYERS' COUNCIL WOULD VOTE SANCTIONS AGAINST THAYOS.
NO WONDER THE PEOPLE ARE FRIGHTENED.
FLYERS SHOULD BE FRIGHTENED, TOO. PEOPLE ARE STARTING TO BELIEVE THAT THE FLYERS HAVE ALWAYS SECRETLY RULED WINDHAVEN.
THAT'S ABSURD!

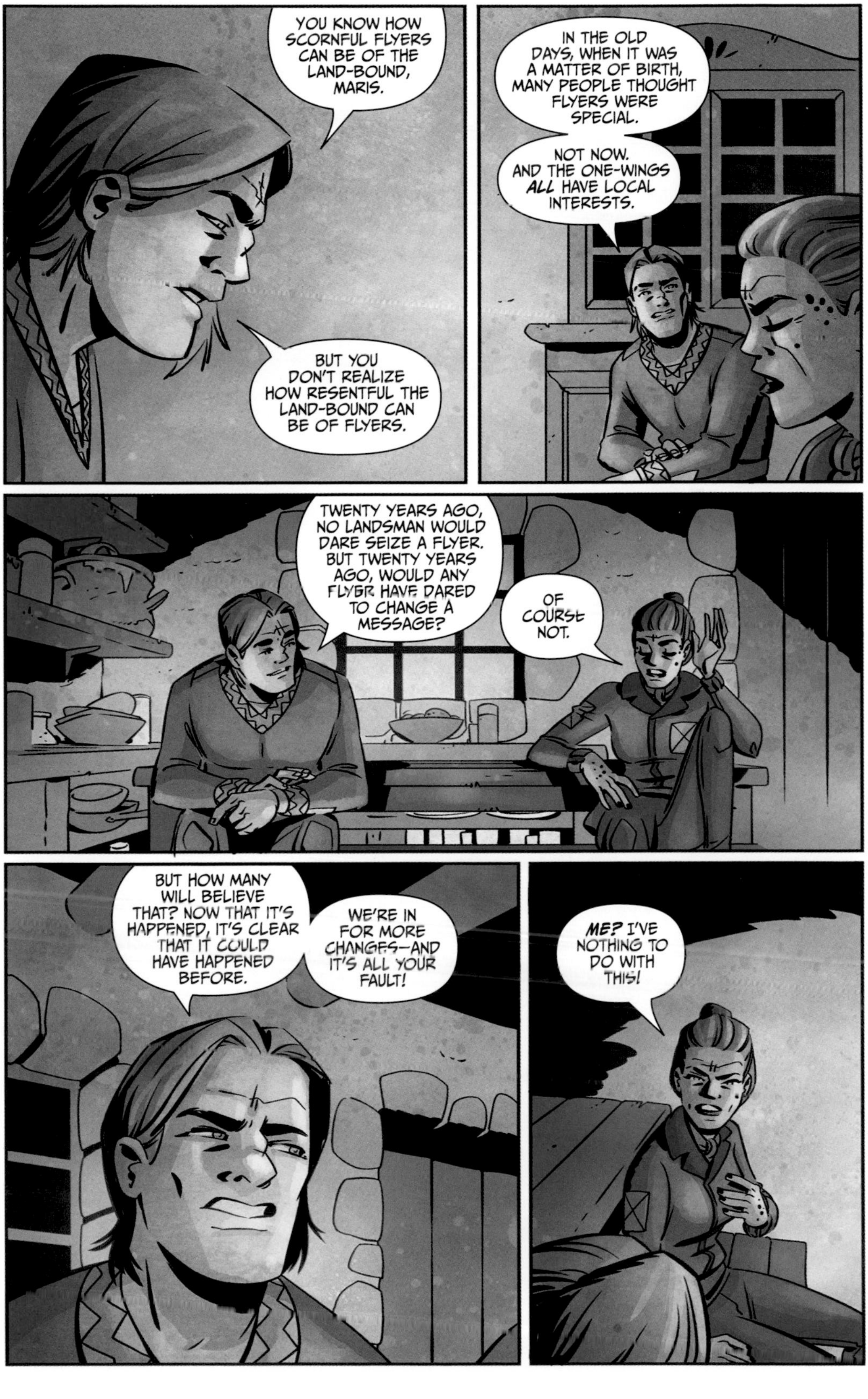
YOU KNOW HOW SCORNFUL FLYERS CAN BE OF THE LAND-BOUND, MARIS.
BUT YOU DON'T REALIZE HOW RESENTFUL THE LAND-BOUND CAN BE OF FLYERS.
IN THE OLD DAYS, WHEN IT WAS A MATTER OF BIRTH, MANY PEOPLE THOUGHT FLYERS WERE SPECIAL.
NOT NOW. AND THE ONE-WINGS ALL HAVE LOCAL INTERESTS.
TWENTY YEARS AGO, NO LANDSMAN WOULD DARE SEIZE A FLYER. BUT TWENTY YEARS AGO, WOULD ANY FLYER HAVE DARED TO CHANGE A MESSAGE?
OF COURSE NOT.
BUT HOW MANY WILL BELIEVE THAT? NOW THAT IT'S HAPPENED, IT'S CLEAR THAT IT COULD HAVE HAPPENED BEFORE.
WE'RE IN FOR MORE CHANGES—AND IT'S ALL YOUR FAULT!
ME? I'VE NOTHING TO DO WITH THIS!

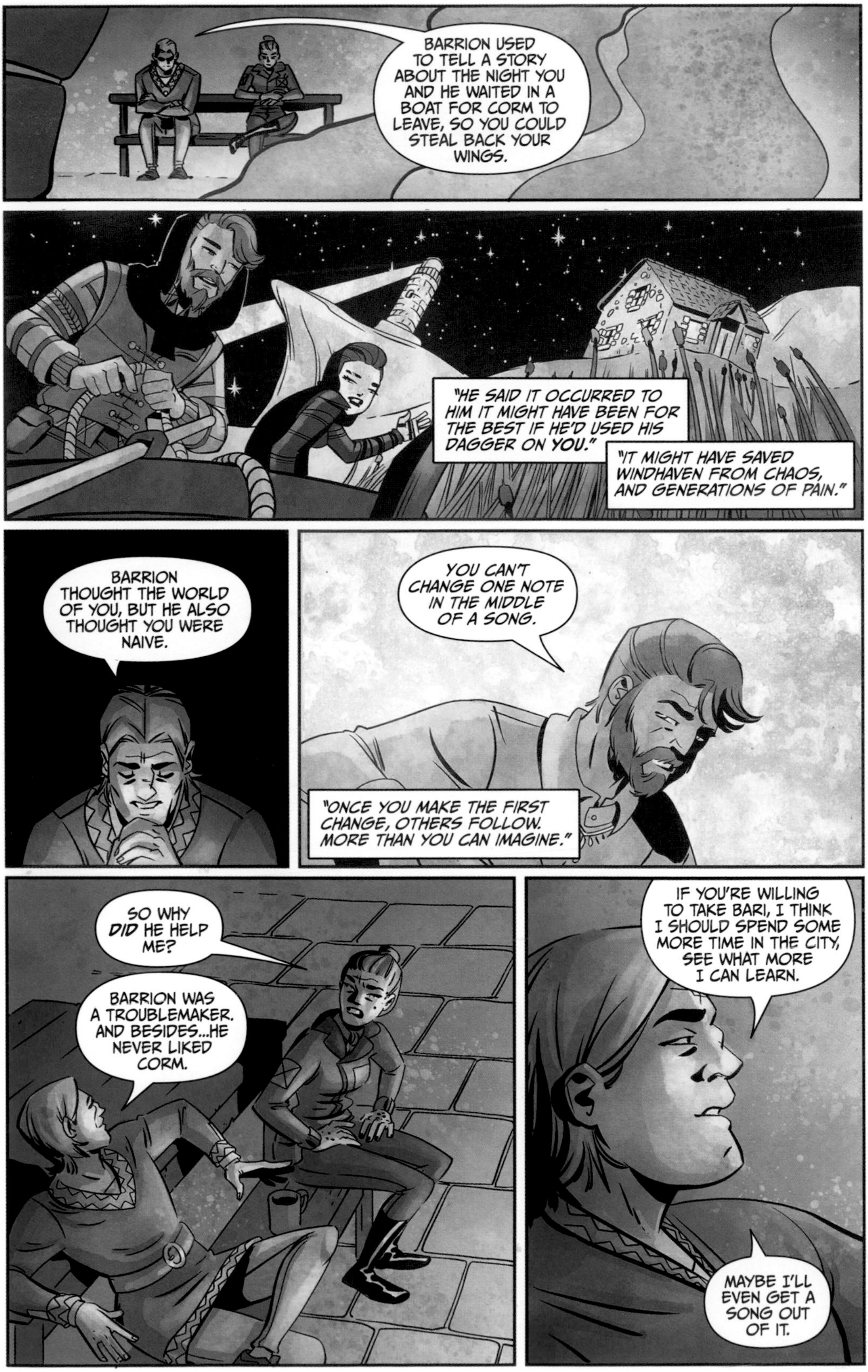
BARRION USED TO TELL A STORY ABOUT THE NIGHT YOU AND HE WAITED IN A BOAT FOR CORM TO LEAVE, SO YOU COULD STEAL BACK YOUR WINGS.
"HE SAID IT OCCURRED TO HIM IT MIGHT HAVE BEEN FOR THE BEST IF HE'D USED HIS DAGGER ON YOU."
"IT MIGHT HAVE SAVED WINDHAVEN FROM CHAOS, AND GENERATIONS OF PAIN."
BARRION THOUGHT THE WORLD OF YOU, BUT HE ALSO THOUGHT YOU WERE NAIVE.
YOU CAN'T CHANGE ONE NOTE IN THE MIDDLE OF A SONG.
"ONCE YOU MAKE THE FIRST CHANGE, OTHERS FOLLOW. MORE THAN YOU CAN IMAGINE."
SO WHY DID HE HELP ME?
BARRION WAS A TROUBLEMAKER. AND BESIDES...HE NEVER LIKED CORM.
IF YOU'RE WILLING TO TAKE BARI, I THINK I SHOULD SPEND SOME MORE TIME IN THE CITY, SEE WHAT MORE I CAN LEARN.
MAYBE I'LL EVEN GET A SONG OUT OF IT.

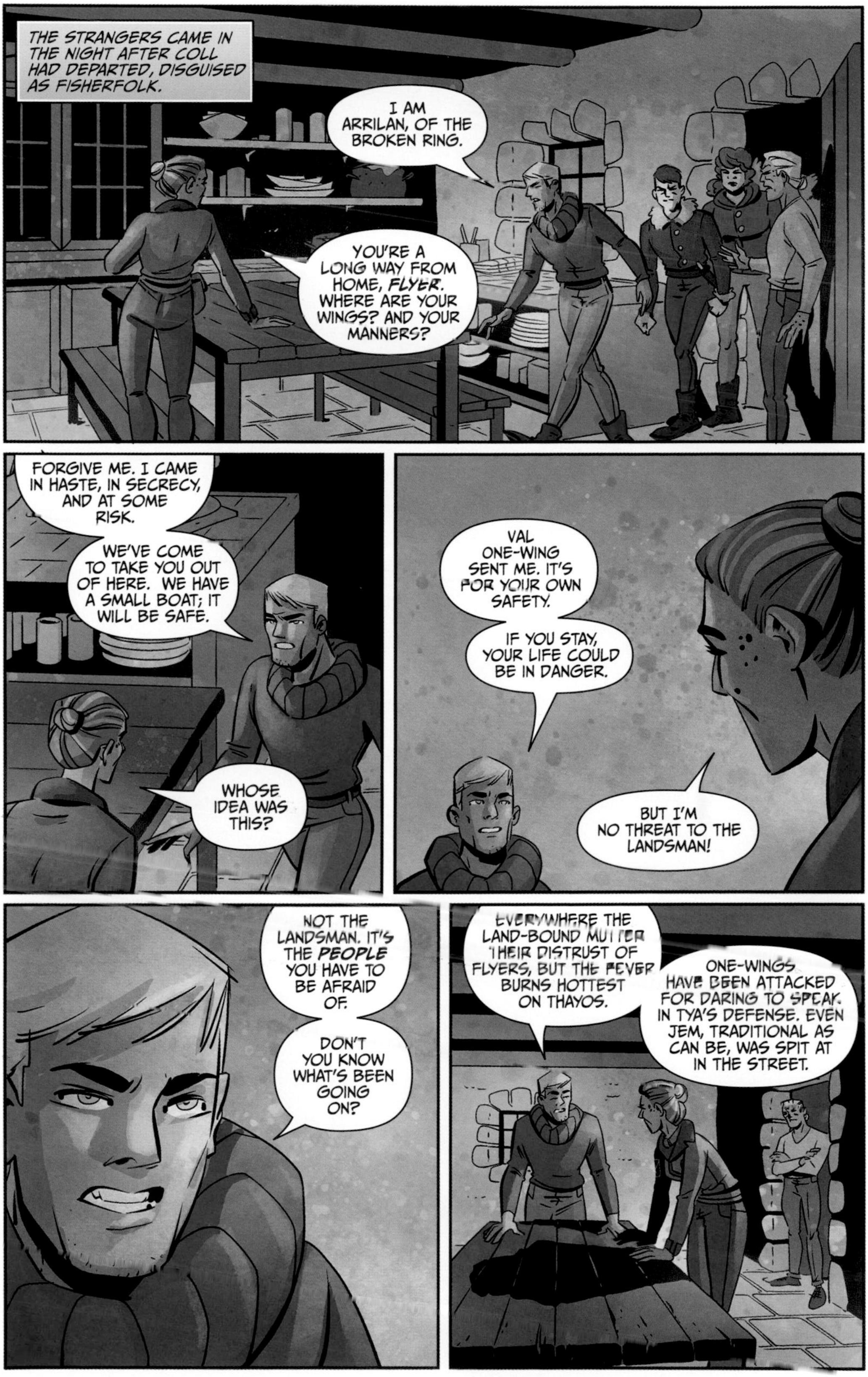
THE STRANGERS CAME IN THE NIGHT AFTER COLL HAD DEPARTED, DISGUISED AS FISHERFOLK.
I AM ARRILAN, OF THE BROKEN RING.
YOU'RE A LONG WAY FROM HOME, FLYER. WHERE ARE YOUR WINGS? AND YOUR MANNERS?
FORGIVE ME. I CAME IN HASTE, IN SECRECY, AND AT SOME RISK.
WE'VE COME TO TAKE YOU OUT OF HERE. WE HAVE A SMALL BOAT; IT WILL BE SAFE.
WHOSE IDEA WAS THIS?
VAL ONE-WING SENT ME. IT'S FOR YOUR OWN SAFETY.
IF YOU STAY, YOUR LIFE COULD BE IN DANGER.
BUT I'M NO THREAT TO THE LANDSMAN!
NOT THE LANDSMAN. IT'S THE PEOPLE YOU HAVE TO BE AFRAID OF.
DON'T YOU KNOW WHAT'S BEEN GOING ON?
EVERYWHERE THE LAND-BOUND MUTTER THEIR DISTRUST OF FLYERS, BUT THE FEVER BURNS HOTTEST ON THAYOS.
ONE-WINGS HAVE BEEN ATTACKED FOR DARING TO SPEAK IN TYA'S DEFENSE. EVEN JEM, TRADITIONAL AS CAN BE, WAS SPIT AT IN THE STREET.

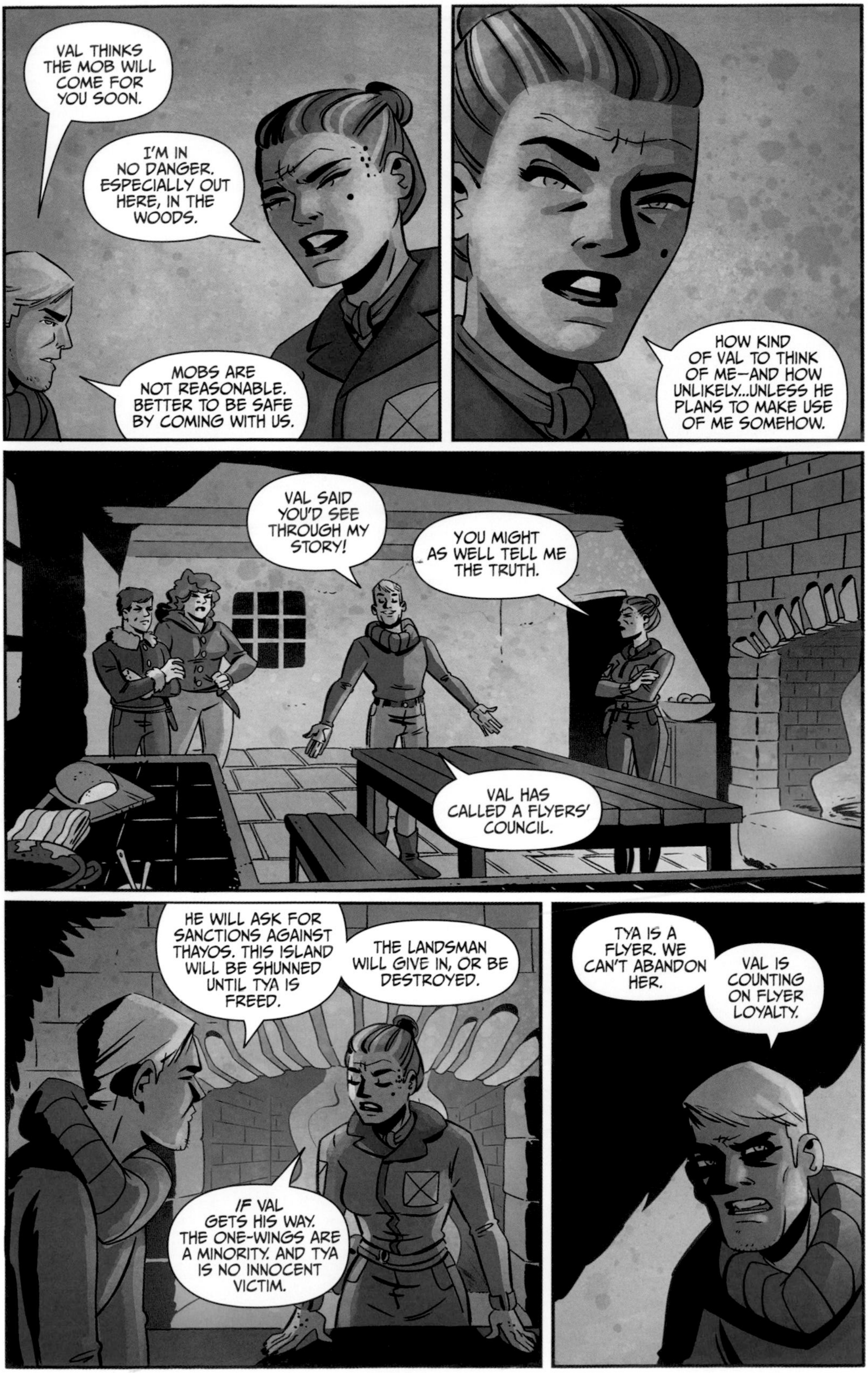
VAL THINKS THE MOB WILL COME FOR YOU SOON.
I'M IN NO DANGER. ESPECIALLY OUT HERE, IN THE WOODS.
MOBS ARE NOT REASONABLE. BETTER TO BE SAFE BY COMING WITH US.
HOW KIND OF VAL TO THINK OF ME—AND HOW UNLIKELY...UNLESS HE PLANS TO MAKE USE OF ME SOMEHOW.
VAL SAID YOU'D SEE THROUGH MY STORY!
YOU MIGHT AS WELL TELL ME THE TRUTH.
VAL HAS CALLED A FLYERS' COUNCIL.
HE WILL ASK FOR SANCTIONS AGAINST THAYOS. THIS ISLAND WILL BE SHUNNED UNTIL TYA IS FREED.
THE LANDSMAN WILL GIVE IN, OR BE DESTROYED.
IF VAL GETS HIS WAY. THE ONE-WINGS ARE A MINORITY. AND TYA IS NO INNOCENT VICTIM.
TYA IS A FLYER. WE CAN'T ABANDON HER.
VAL IS COUNTING ON FLYER LOYALTY.

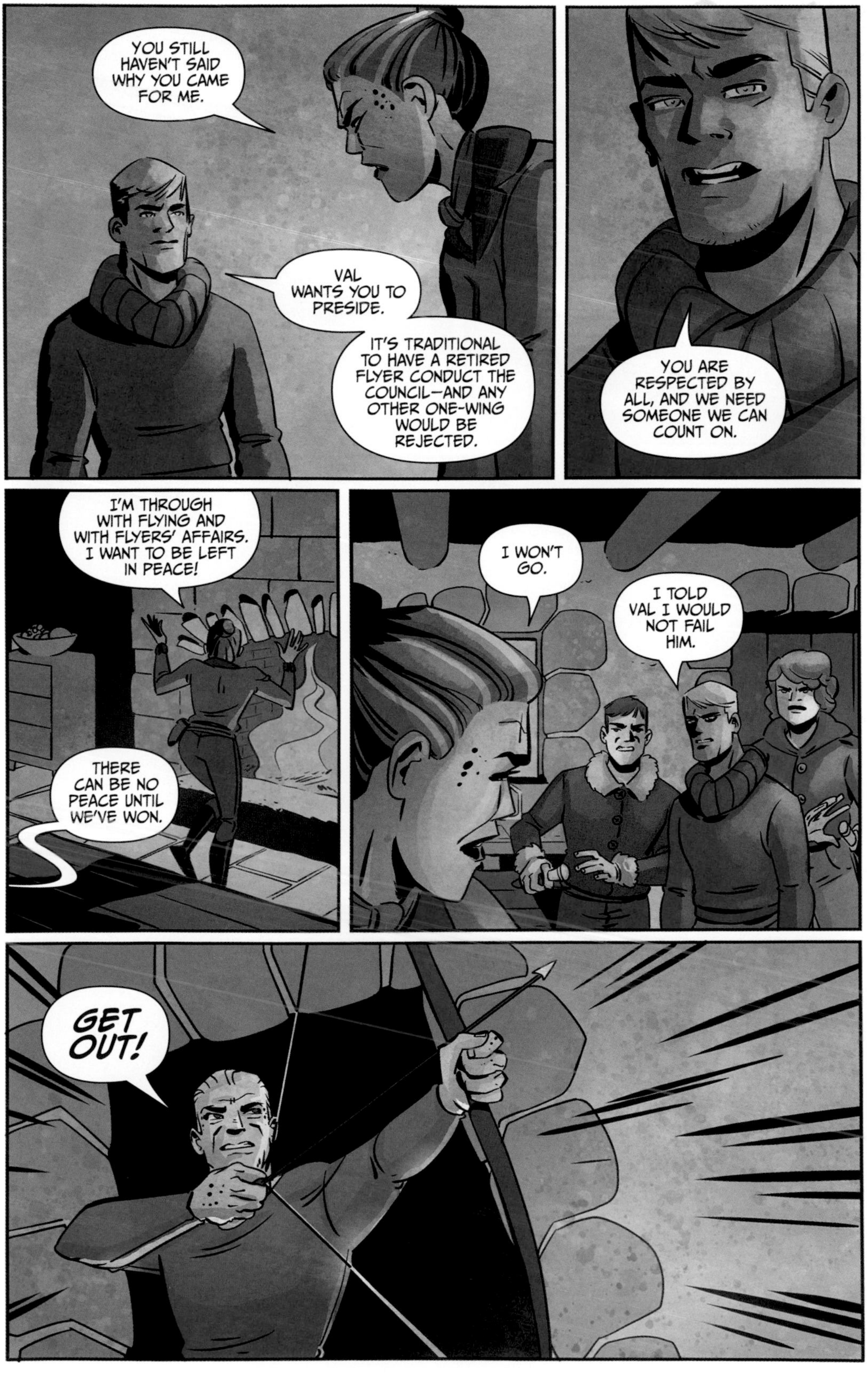
YOU STILL HAVEN'T SAID WHY YOU CAME FOR ME.
VAL WANTS YOU TO PRESIDE.
IT'S TRADITIONAL TO HAVE A RETIRED FLYER CONDUCT THE COUNCIL—AND ANY OTHER ONE-WING WOULD BE REJECTED.
YOU ARE RESPECTED BY ALL, AND WE NEED SOMEONE WE CAN COUNT ON.
I'M THROUGH WITH FLYING AND WITH FLYERS' AFFAIRS. I WANT TO BE LEFT IN PEACE!
THERE CAN BE NO PEACE UNTIL WE'VE WON.
I WON'T GO.
I TOLD VAL I WOULD NOT FAIL HIM.
GET OUT!

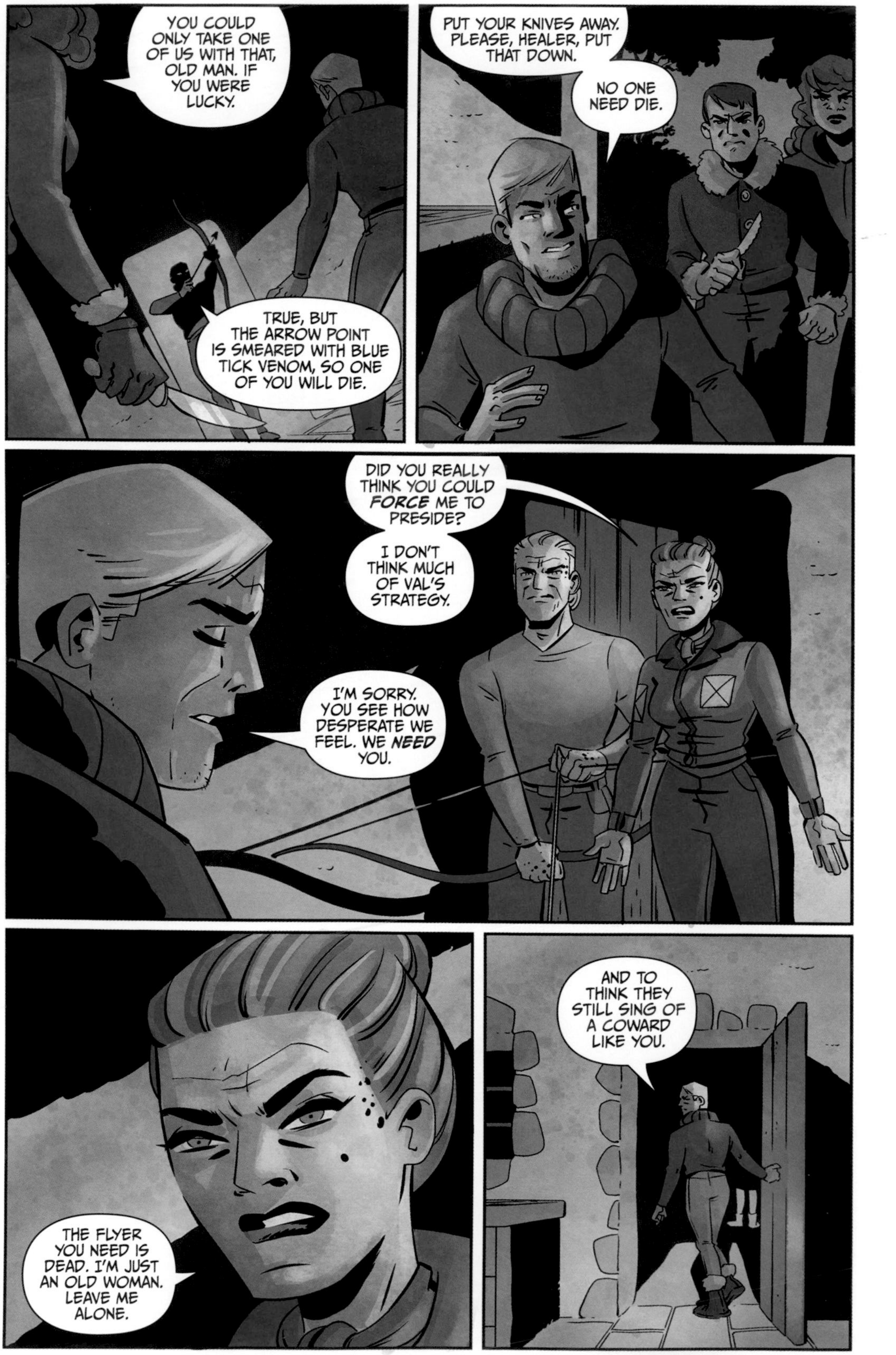
YOU COULD ONLY TAKE ONE OF US WITH THAT, OLD MAN. IF YOU WERE LUCKY.
TRUE, BUT THE ARROW POINT IS SMEARED WITH BLUE TICK VENOM, SO ONE OF YOU WILL DIE.
PUT YOUR KNIVES AWAY. PLEASE, HEALER, PUT THAT DOWN.
NO ONE NEED DIE.
DID YOU REALLY THINK YOU COULD *FORCE* ME TO PRESIDE?
I DON'T THINK MUCH OF VAL'S STRATEGY.
I'M SORRY. YOU SEE HOW DESPERATE WE FEEL. WE *NEED* YOU.
THE FLYER YOU NEED IS DEAD. I'M JUST AN OLD WOMAN. LEAVE ME ALONE.
AND TO THINK THEY STILL SING OF A COWARD LIKE YOU.

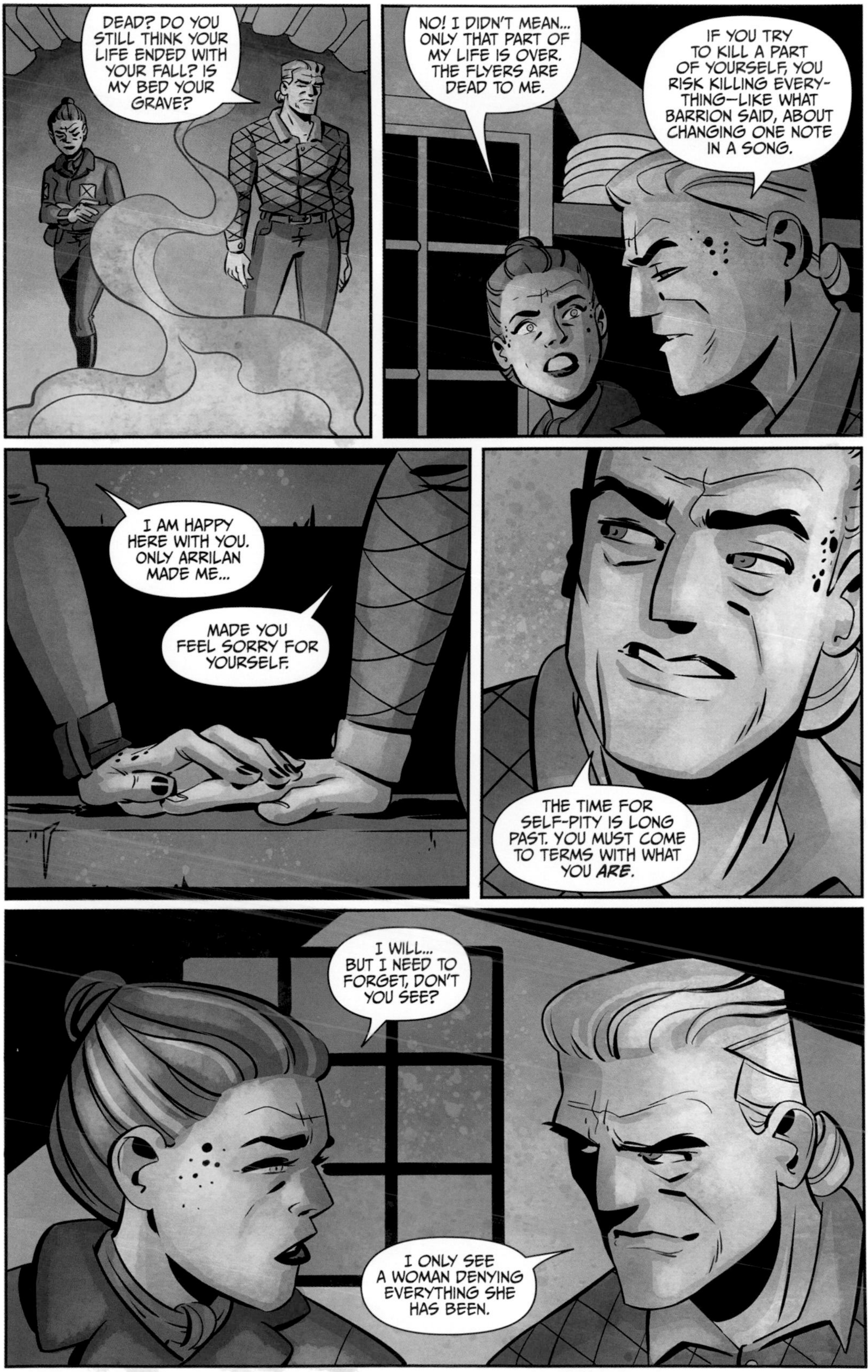
DEAD? DO YOU STILL THINK YOUR LIFE ENDED WITH YOUR FALL? IS MY BED YOUR GRAVE?
NO! I DIDN'T MEAN... ONLY THAT PART OF MY LIFE IS OVER. THE FLYERS ARE DEAD TO ME.
IF YOU TRY TO KILL A PART OF YOURSELF, YOU RISK KILLING EVERY-THING—LIKE WHAT BARRION SAID, ABOUT CHANGING ONE NOTE IN A SONG.
I AM HAPPY HERE WITH YOU. ONLY ARRILAN MADE ME...
MADE YOU FEEL SORRY FOR YOURSELF.
THE TIME FOR SELF-PITY IS LONG PAST. YOU MUST COME TO TERMS WITH WHAT YOU *ARE*.
I WILL... BUT I NEED TO FORGET, DON'T YOU SEE?
I ONLY SEE A WOMAN DENYING EVERYTHING SHE HAS BEEN.

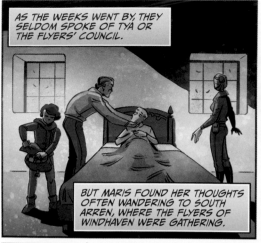

AS THE WEEKS WENT BY, THEY SELDOM SPOKE OF TYA OR THE FLYERS' COUNCIL.

BUT MARIS FOUND HER THOUGHTS OFTEN WANDERING TO SOUTH ARREN, WHERE THE FLYERS OF WINDHAVEN WERE GATHERING.

ALL HER FRIENDS WOULD BE THERE, AND THE SHEEN OF THEIR WINGS AND THE SOUND OF THEIR LAUGHTER WOULD FILL THE SKY.

SHE TRIED NOT TO THINK OF IT, BUT THE MEMORIES CAME UNBIDDEN, AND IN HER DREAMS SHE FLEW AGAIN.

LOOK, HERE IS THE SWEETSONG EVAN WANTED.

NO, THAT'S LIAR'S WEED. IT'S NO GOOD.

DADDY?

MORE THAN SIX WEEKS AFTER HE'D GONE TRAVELING, COLL RETURNED. AND HE WAS NOT ALONE.

THE LANDSMAN DECIDED TO DETAIN ME UNTIL THE COUNCIL HAD ENDED.

WHEN S'RELLA FLEW IN, JUST AFTERWARD, HE MADE HER STAY, TOO—ALONG WITH EVERY OTHER FLYER AND SINGER HE COULD FIND.

WE WERE HIS WITNESSES. HE WANTS US TO SPREAD THE WORD, SO EVERY-ONE WILL KNOW WHAT HE DID.

TYA OF THAYOS WAS HANGED YESTERDAY AT SUNSET.

SHE TRIED TO MAKE A SPEECH, BUT THE LANDSMAN WOULD NOT ALLOW IT.

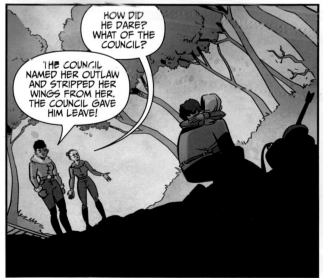

HOW DID HE DARE? WHAT OF THE COUNCIL?

THE COUNCIL NAMED HER OUTLAW AND STRIPPED HER WINGS FROM HER. THE COUNCIL GAVE HIM LEAVE!

THE LANDSMAN MADE HER WEAR HER WINGS FOR THE HANGING. HE JOKED ABOUT IT.

HE TOLD HER TO USE HER WINGS TO BREAK *THIS* FALL AND FLY AWAY.

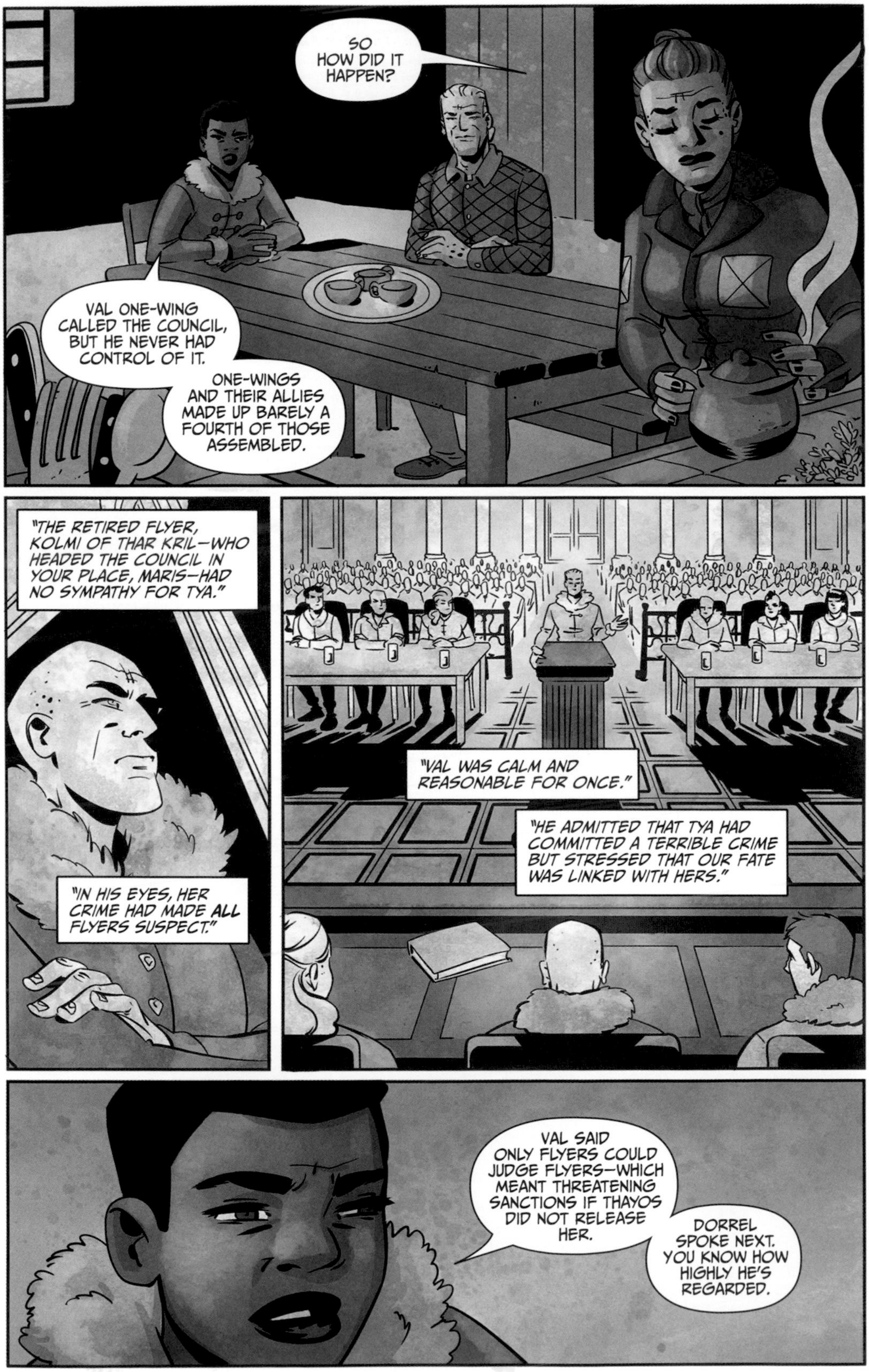
SO HOW DID IT HAPPEN?
VAL ONE-WING CALLED THE COUNCIL, BUT HE NEVER HAD CONTROL OF IT.
ONE-WINGS AND THEIR ALLIES MADE UP BARELY A FOURTH OF THOSE ASSEMBLED.
"THE RETIRED FLYER, KOLMI OF THAR KRIL—WHO HEADED THE COUNCIL IN YOUR PLACE, MARIS—HAD NO SYMPATHY FOR TYA."
"IN HIS EYES, HER CRIME HAD MADE **ALL** FLYERS SUSPECT."
"VAL WAS CALM AND REASONABLE FOR ONCE."
"HE ADMITTED THAT TYA HAD COMMITTED A TERRIBLE CRIME BUT STRESSED THAT OUR FATE WAS LINKED WITH HERS."
VAL SAID ONLY FLYERS COULD JUDGE FLYERS—WHICH MEANT THREATENING SANCTIONS IF THAYOS DID NOT RELEASE HER.
DORREL SPOKE NEXT. YOU KNOW HOW HIGHLY HE'S REGARDED.

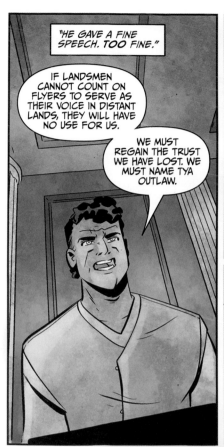

"HE GAVE A FINE SPEECH. *TOO FINE.*"

IF LANDSMEN CANNOT COUNT ON FLYERS TO SERVE AS THEIR VOICE IN DISTANT LANDS, THEY WILL HAVE NO USE FOR US.

WE MUST REGAIN THE TRUST WE HAVE LOST. WE MUST NAME TYA OUTLAW.

VAL'S PROPOSAL WAS VOTED DOWN IN A MINUTE, AND THE COUNCIL NAMED TYA OUTLAW.

OF COURSE, WE DIDN'T TELL THE LANDSMAN TO HANG HER. WE WENT SO FAR AS TO ASK HIM *NOT* TO.

OUR LANDSMAN SELDOM HEEDS REQUESTS.

THAT WAS THE END OF IT FOR ME. THAT WAS WHEN THE ONE-WINGS LEFT.

WE HELD OUR *OWN* COUNCIL, AND VOTED TO IMPOSE SANCTIONS ON THAYOS.

"KATINN AND I FLEW HERE TO TELL HIM NO ONE-WING WOULD EVER SERVE HIM UNLESS TYA WAS FREED."

YOUR KIND ARE UNFIT TO BE FLYERS. I WILL SHOW YOU WHAT I THINK OF ONE-WINGS!

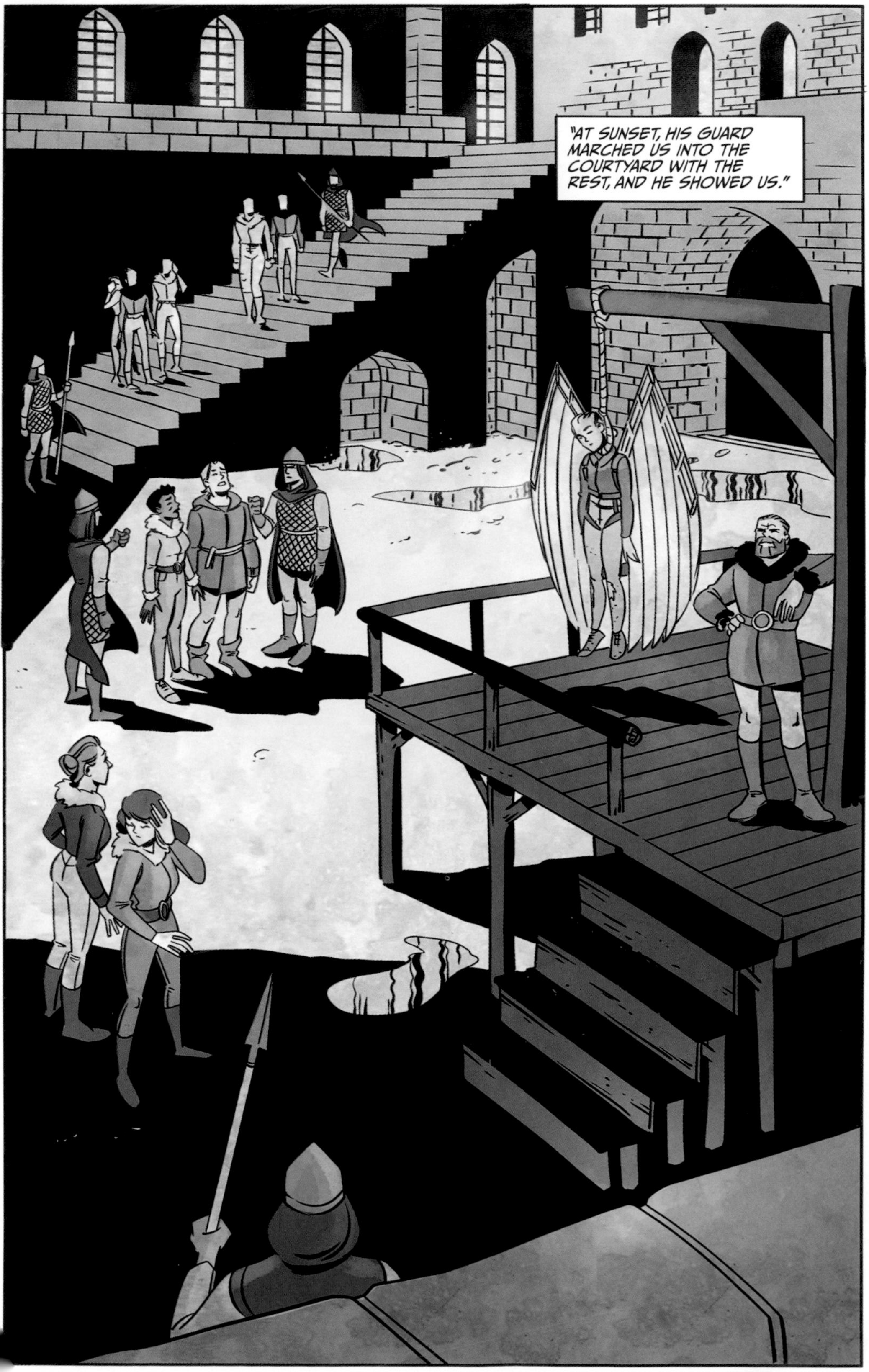
"AT SUNSET, HIS GUARD MARCHED US INTO THE COURTYARD WITH THE REST, AND HE SHOWED US."

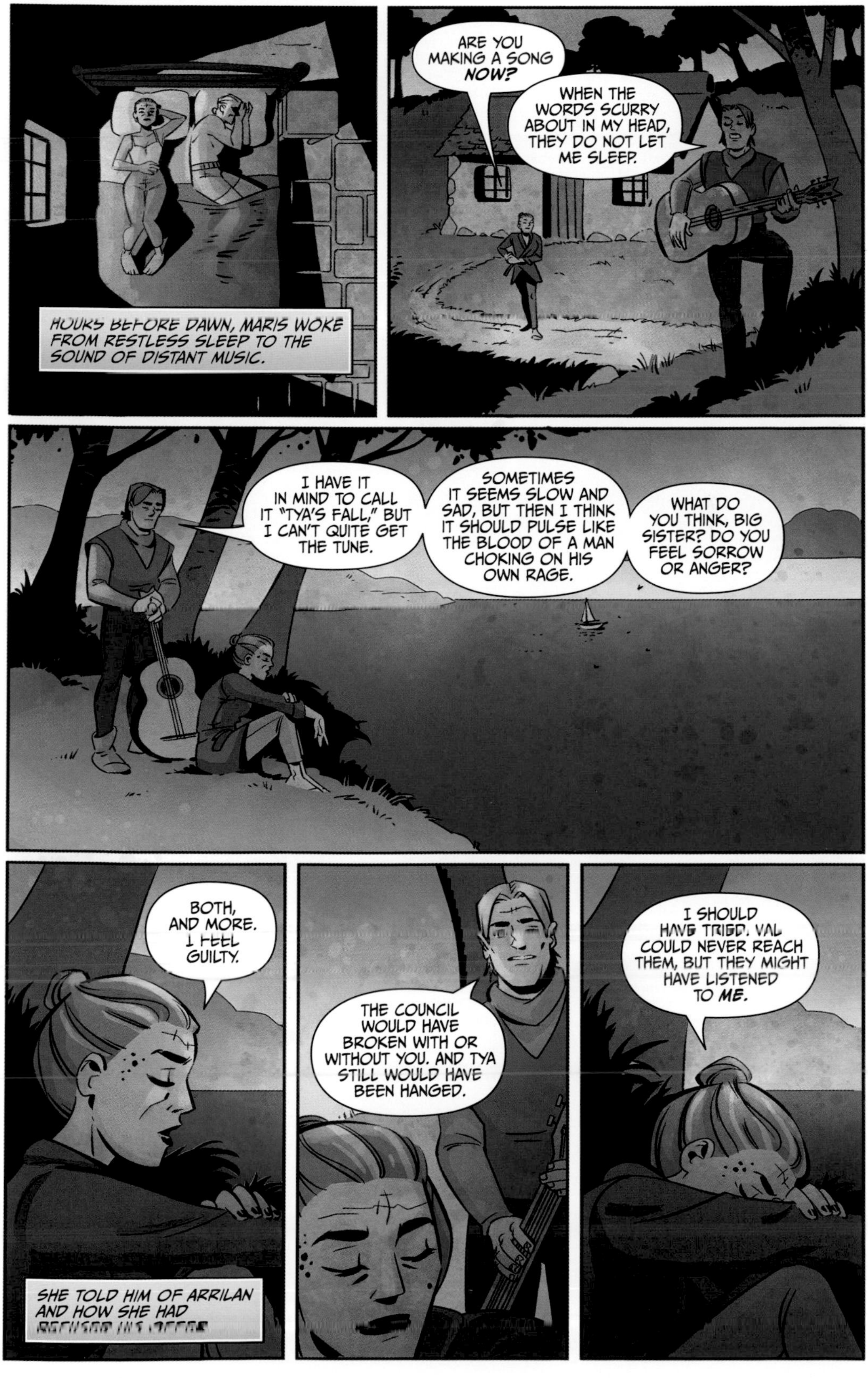
HOURS BEFORE DAWN, MARIS WOKE FROM RESTLESS SLEEP TO THE SOUND OF DISTANT MUSIC.
ARE YOU MAKING A SONG *NOW?*
WHEN THE WORDS SCURRY ABOUT IN MY HEAD, THEY DO NOT LET ME SLEEP.
I HAVE IT IN MIND TO CALL IT "TYA'S FALL," BUT I CAN'T QUITE GET THE TUNE.
SOMETIMES IT SEEMS SLOW AND SAD, BUT THEN I THINK IT SHOULD PULSE LIKE THE BLOOD OF A MAN CHOKING ON HIS OWN RAGE.
WHAT DO YOU THINK, BIG SISTER? DO YOU FEEL SORROW OR ANGER?
BOTH, AND MORE. I FEEL GUILTY.
SHE TOLD HIM OF ARRILAN AND HOW SHE HAD
THE COUNCIL WOULD HAVE BROKEN WITH OR WITHOUT YOU. AND TYA STILL WOULD HAVE BEEN HANGED.
I SHOULD HAVE TRIED. VAL COULD NEVER REACH THEM, BUT THEY MIGHT HAVE LISTENED TO *ME.*

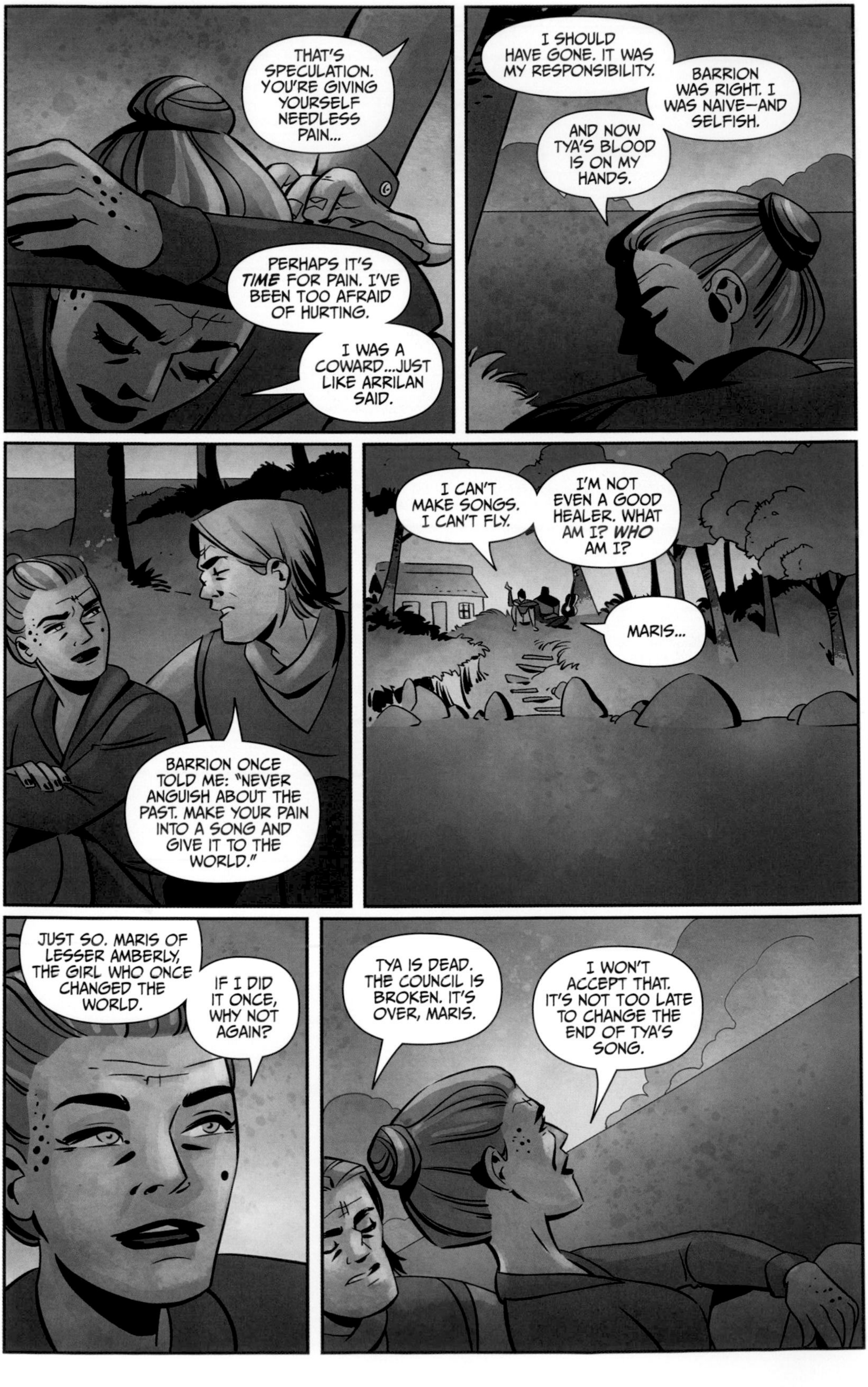
THAT'S SPECULATION. YOU'RE GIVING YOURSELF NEEDLESS PAIN...
PERHAPS IT'S *TIME* FOR PAIN. I'VE BEEN TOO AFRAID OF HURTING.
I WAS A COWARD...JUST LIKE ARRILAN SAID.
I SHOULD HAVE GONE. IT WAS MY RESPONSIBILITY.
AND NOW TYA'S BLOOD IS ON MY HANDS.
BARRION WAS RIGHT. I WAS NAIVE—AND SELFISH.
BARRION ONCE TOLD ME: "NEVER ANGUISH ABOUT THE PAST. MAKE YOUR PAIN INTO A SONG AND GIVE IT TO THE WORLD."
I CAN'T MAKE SONGS. I CAN'T FLY.
I'M NOT EVEN A GOOD HEALER. WHAT AM I? *WHO* AM I?
MARIS...
JUST SO. MARIS OF LESSER AMBERLY, THE GIRL WHO ONCE CHANGED THE WORLD.
IF I DID IT ONCE, WHY NOT AGAIN?
TYA IS DEAD. THE COUNCIL IS BROKEN. IT'S OVER, MARIS.
I WON'T ACCEPT THAT. IT'S NOT TOO LATE TO CHANGE THE END OF TYA'S SONG.

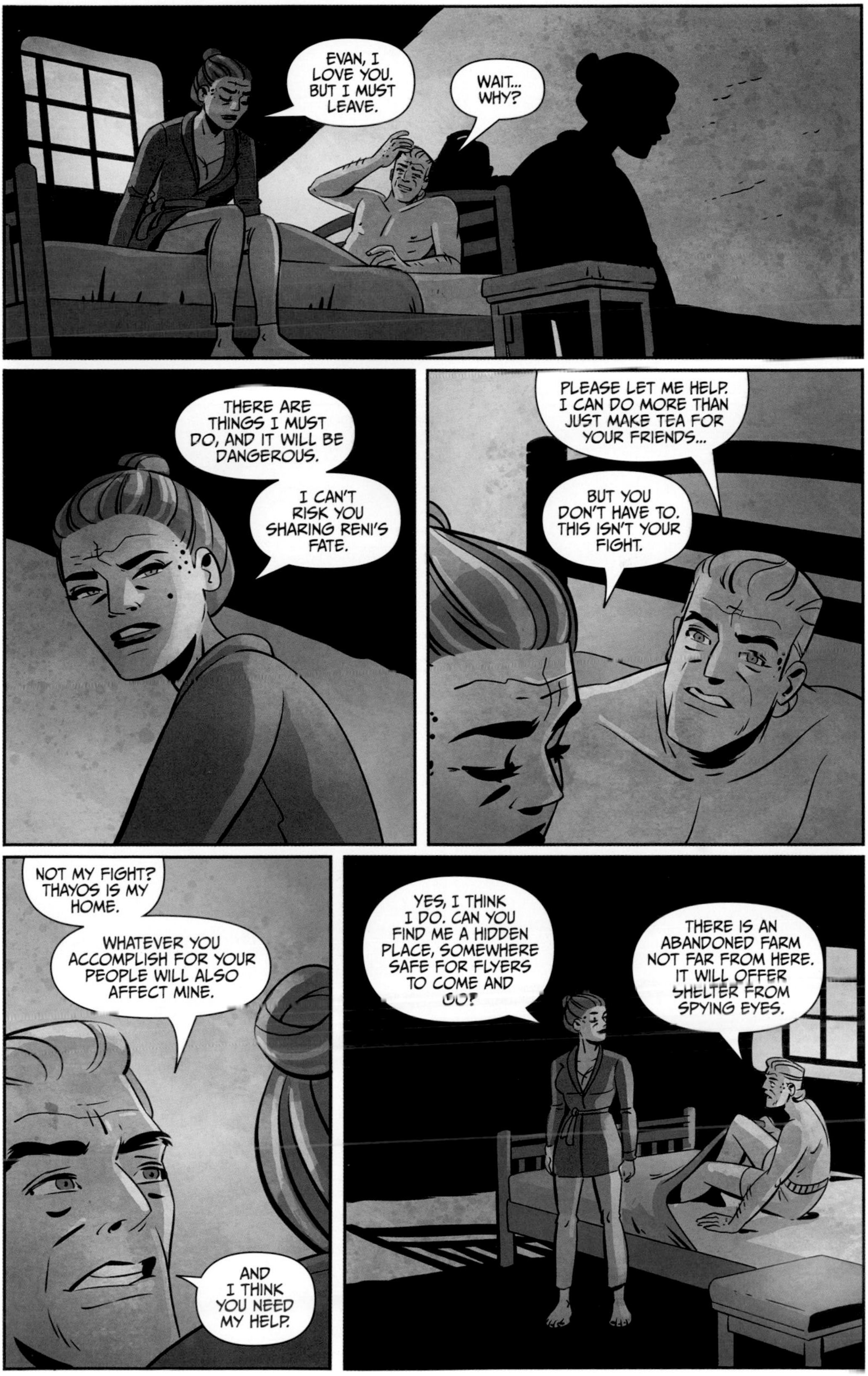
EVAN, I LOVE YOU. BUT I MUST LEAVE.
WAIT... WHY?
THERE ARE THINGS I MUST DO, AND IT WILL BE DANGEROUS.
I CAN'T RISK YOU SHARING RENI'S FATE.
PLEASE LET ME HELP. I CAN DO MORE THAN JUST MAKE TEA FOR YOUR FRIENDS...
BUT YOU DON'T HAVE TO. THIS ISN'T YOUR FIGHT.
NOT MY FIGHT? THAYOS IS MY HOME.
WHATEVER YOU ACCOMPLISH FOR YOUR PEOPLE WILL ALSO AFFECT MINE.
AND I THINK YOU NEED MY HELP.
YES, I THINK I DO. CAN YOU FIND ME A HIDDEN PLACE, SOMEWHERE SAFE FOR FLYERS TO COME AND GO?
THERE IS AN ABANDONED FARM NOT FAR FROM HERE. IT WILL OFFER SHELTER FROM SPYING EYES.

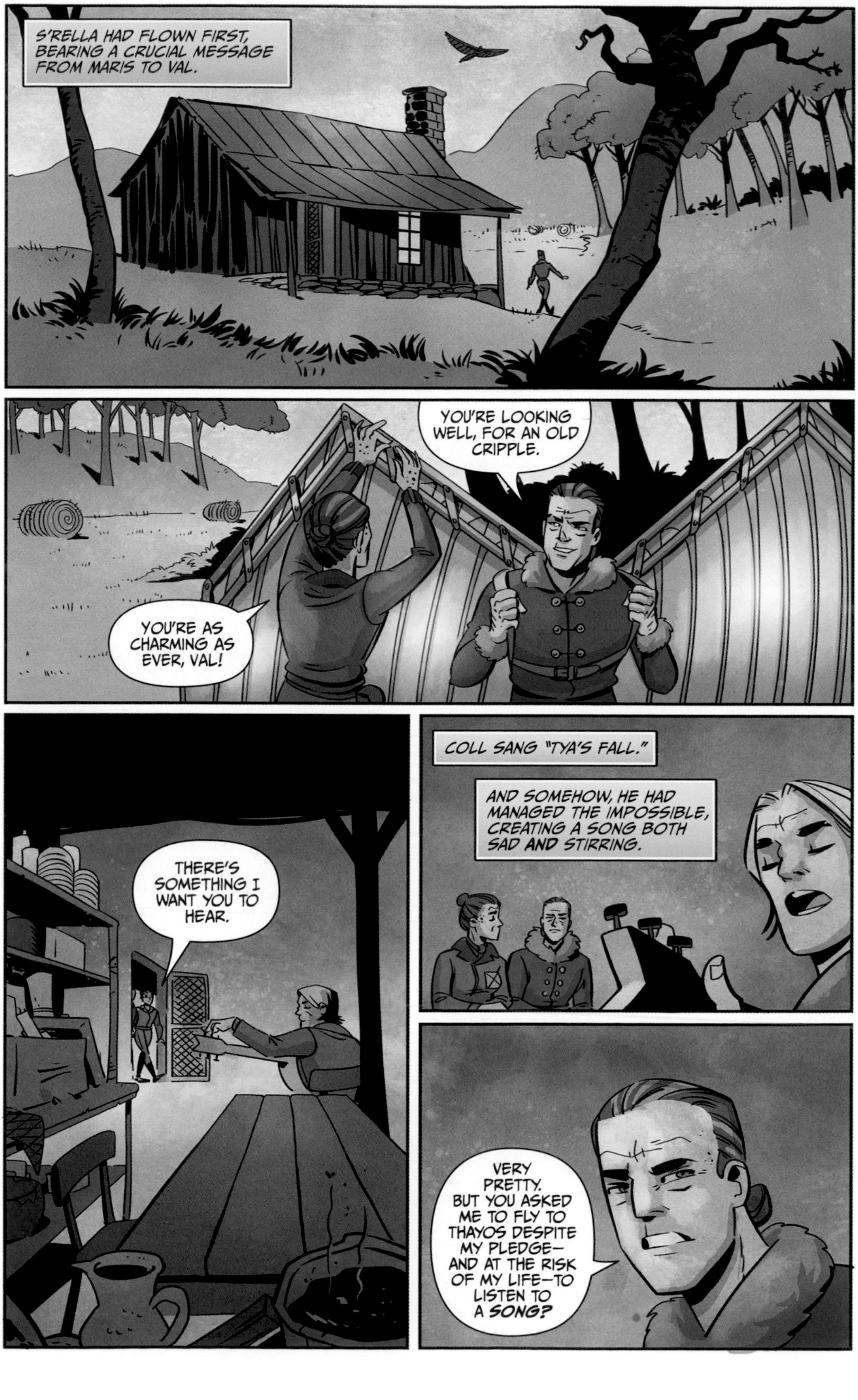
S'RELLA HAD FLOWN FIRST, BEARING A CRUCIAL MESSAGE FROM MARIS TO VAL.
YOU'RE LOOKING WELL, FOR AN OLD CRIPPLE.
YOU'RE AS CHARMING AS EVER, VAL!
THERE'S SOMETHING I WANT YOU TO HEAR.
COLL SANG "TYA'S FALL."
AND SOMEHOW, HE HAD MANAGED THE IMPOSSIBLE, CREATING A SONG BOTH SAD AND STIRRING.
VERY PRETTY. BUT YOU ASKED ME TO FLY TO THAYOS DESPITE MY PLEDGE—AND AT THE RISK OF MY LIFE—TO LISTEN TO A SONG?

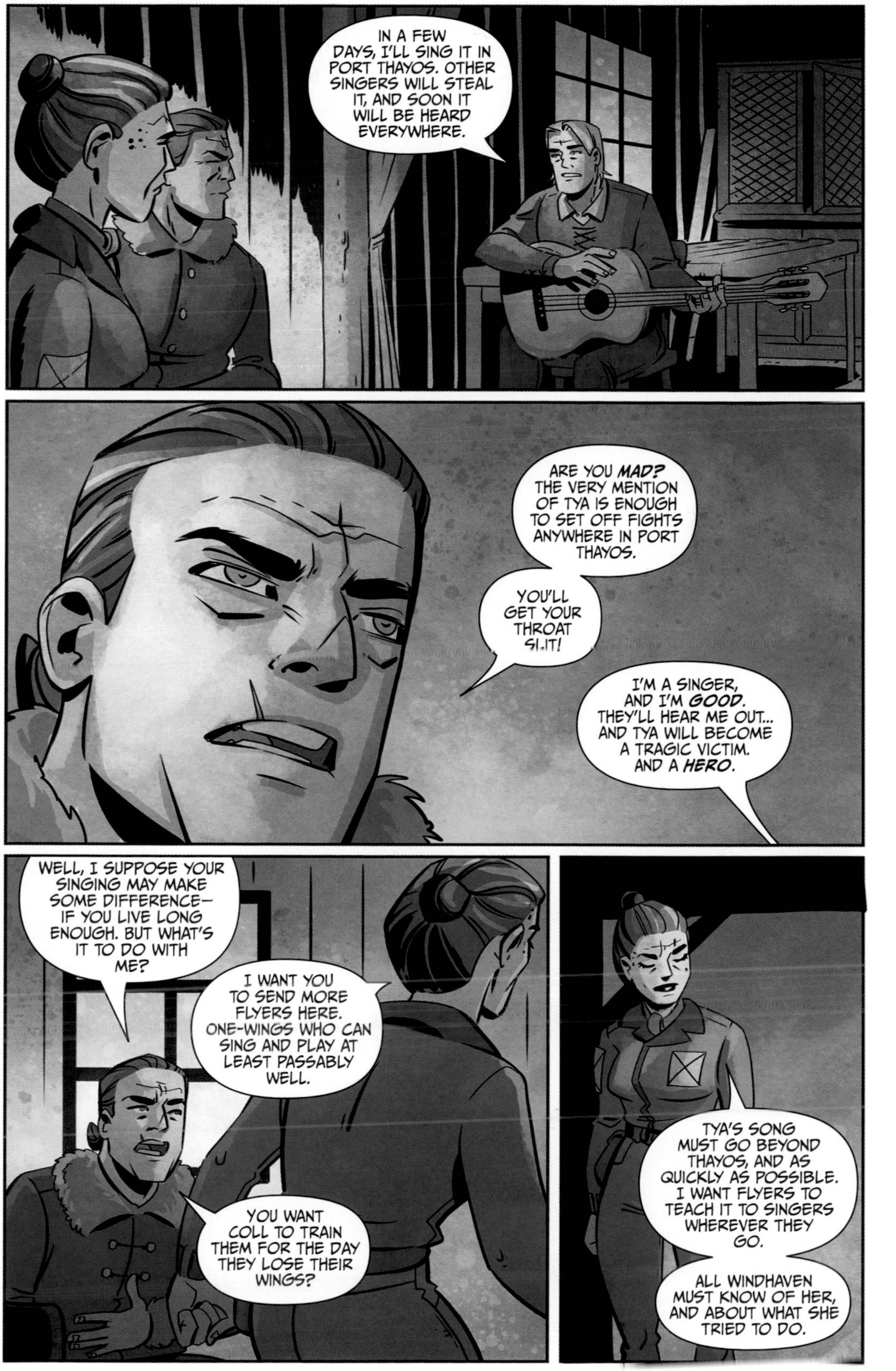
IN A FEW DAYS, I'LL SING IT IN PORT THAYOS. OTHER SINGERS WILL STEAL IT, AND SOON IT WILL BE HEARD EVERYWHERE.
ARE YOU *MAD?* THE VERY MENTION OF TYA IS ENOUGH TO SET OFF FIGHTS ANYWHERE IN PORT THAYOS.
YOU'LL GET YOUR THROAT SLIT!
I'M A SINGER, AND I'M *GOOD*. THEY'LL HEAR ME OUT... AND TYA WILL BECOME A TRAGIC VICTIM. AND A *HERO*.
WELL, I SUPPOSE YOUR SINGING MAY MAKE SOME DIFFERENCE— IF YOU LIVE LONG ENOUGH. BUT WHAT'S IT TO DO WITH ME?
I WANT YOU TO SEND MORE FLYERS HERE. ONE-WINGS WHO CAN SING AND PLAY AT LEAST PASSABLY WELL.
YOU WANT COLL TO TRAIN THEM FOR THE DAY THEY LOSE THEIR WINGS?
TYA'S SONG MUST GO BEYOND THAYOS, AND AS QUICKLY AS POSSIBLE. I WANT FLYERS TO TEACH IT TO SINGERS WHEREVER THEY GO.
ALL WINDHAVEN MUST KNOW OF HER, AND ABOUT WHAT SHE TRIED TO DO.

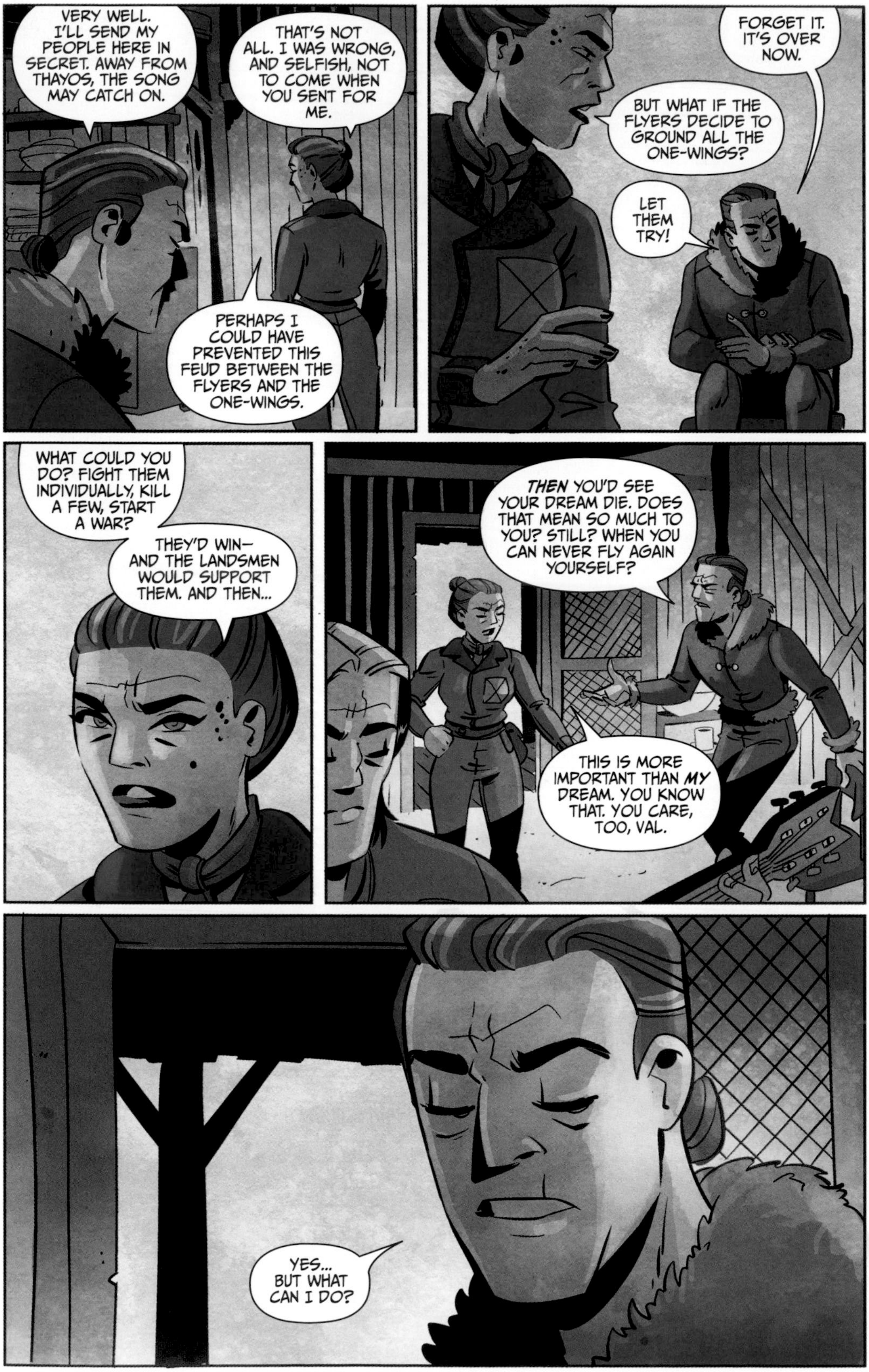
VERY WELL. I'LL SEND MY PEOPLE HERE IN SECRET. AWAY FROM THAYOS, THE SONG MAY CATCH ON.
THAT'S NOT ALL. I WAS WRONG, AND SELFISH, NOT TO COME WHEN YOU SENT FOR ME.
PERHAPS I COULD HAVE PREVENTED THIS FEUD BETWEEN THE FLYERS AND THE ONE-WINGS.
FORGET IT. IT'S OVER NOW.
BUT WHAT IF THE FLYERS DECIDE TO GROUND ALL THE ONE-WINGS?
LET THEM TRY!
WHAT COULD YOU DO? FIGHT THEM INDIVIDUALLY, KILL A FEW, START A WAR?
THEY'D WIN— AND THE LANDSMEN WOULD SUPPORT THEM. AND THEN...
THEN YOU'D SEE YOUR DREAM DIE. DOES THAT MEAN SO MUCH TO YOU? STILL? WHEN YOU CAN NEVER FLY AGAIN YOURSELF?
THIS IS MORE IMPORTANT THAN *MY* DREAM. YOU KNOW THAT. YOU CARE, TOO, VAL.
YES... BUT WHAT CAN I DO?

REVOKE THE ONE-WINGS' SANCTIONS AGAINST THAYOS BEFORE YOUR ENEMIES USE IT AGAINST YOU.
AND WILL THE LANDSMAN REVOKE TYA'S HANGING?
NO, MARIS, THIS IS THE ONLY POWER WE HAVE. THE OTHER FLYERS MUST JOIN US.
THEY WON'T. AND WITHOUT THEM, IT'S A USELESS GESTURE.
ARE YOU REALLY ASKING ME TO FORGET WHAT THE LANDSMAN DID TO TYA?
NO ONE WILL FORGET TYA. MY SONGS WILL ASSURE THAT.
TYA MUST BE AVENGED BY MORE THAN A SONG!
TYA TRIED TO PREVENT WAR, AND PROVE TO THE LANDSMEN THEY WERE NOT ALL-POWERFUL.
BUT THESE SANCTIONS HAVE SPLIT AND WEAKENED THE FLYERS. ONLY BY ACTING TOGETHER DO WE HAVE THE STRENGTH TO DEFY THE LANDSMEN!
TELL THAT TO DORREL.
I INTEND TO. AND I'LL TELL HIM THAT, THOUGH TYA DIED WITH HER WINGS ON, SHE WAS NOT ALLOWED A FLYER'S BURIAL.
WHAT DO YOU REALLY WANT OF ME, MARIS?
I WANT YOU TO MOURN, VAL. THAT'S ALL. I WANT YOU TO MOURN TYA.

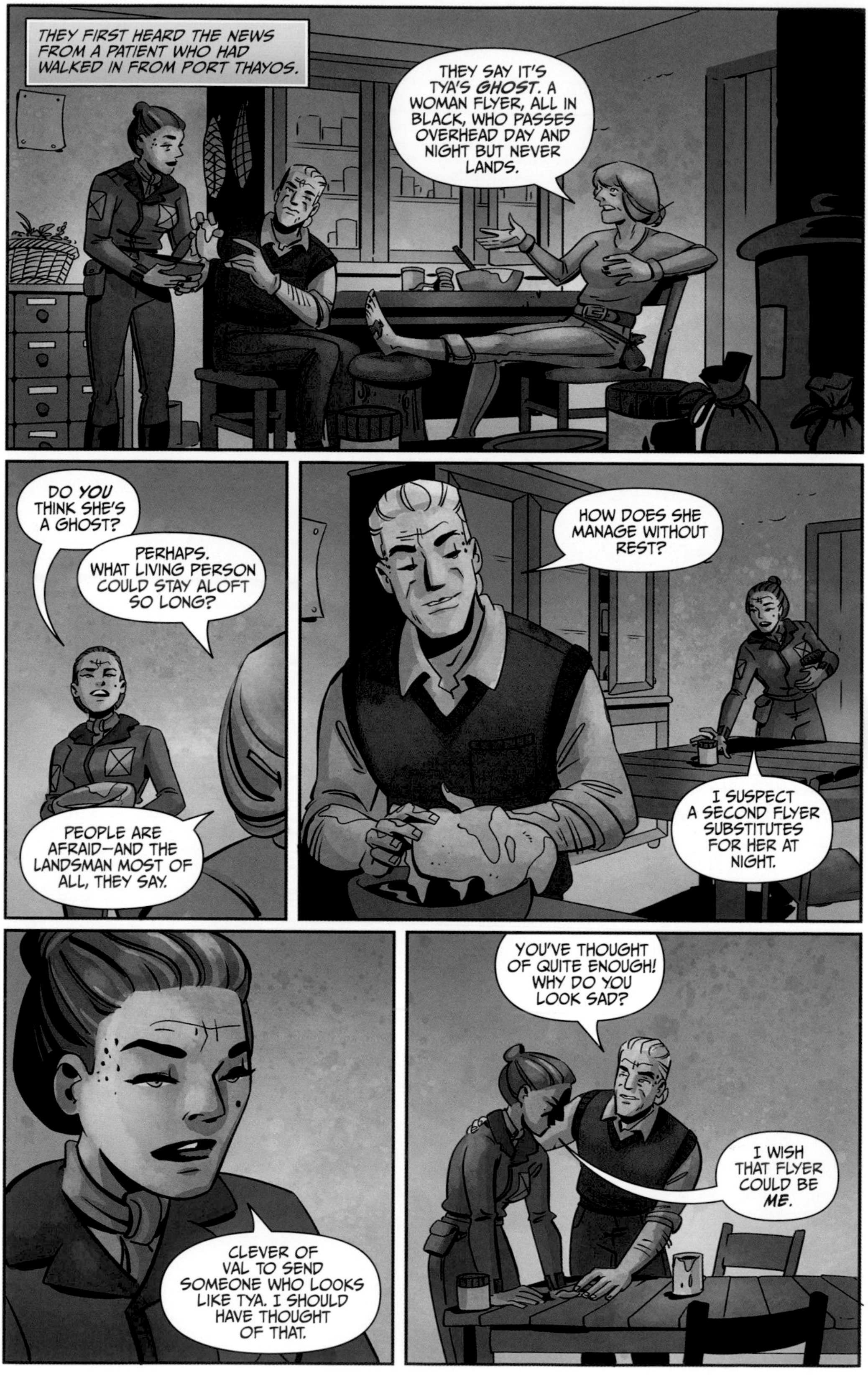

THEY FIRST HEARD THE NEWS FROM A PATIENT WHO HAD WALKED IN FROM PORT THAYOS.
THEY SAY IT'S TYA'S *GHOST*. A WOMAN FLYER, ALL IN BLACK, WHO PASSES OVERHEAD DAY AND NIGHT BUT NEVER LANDS.
DO *YOU* THINK SHE'S A GHOST?
PERHAPS. WHAT LIVING PERSON COULD STAY ALOFT SO LONG?
PEOPLE ARE AFRAID—AND THE LANDSMAN MOST OF ALL, THEY SAY.
HOW DOES SHE MANAGE WITHOUT REST?
I SUSPECT A SECOND FLYER SUBSTITUTES FOR HER AT NIGHT.
CLEVER OF VAL TO SEND SOMEONE WHO LOOKS LIKE TYA. I SHOULD HAVE THOUGHT OF THAT.
YOU'VE THOUGHT OF QUITE ENOUGH! WHY DO YOU LOOK SAD?
I WISH THAT FLYER COULD BE *ME*.

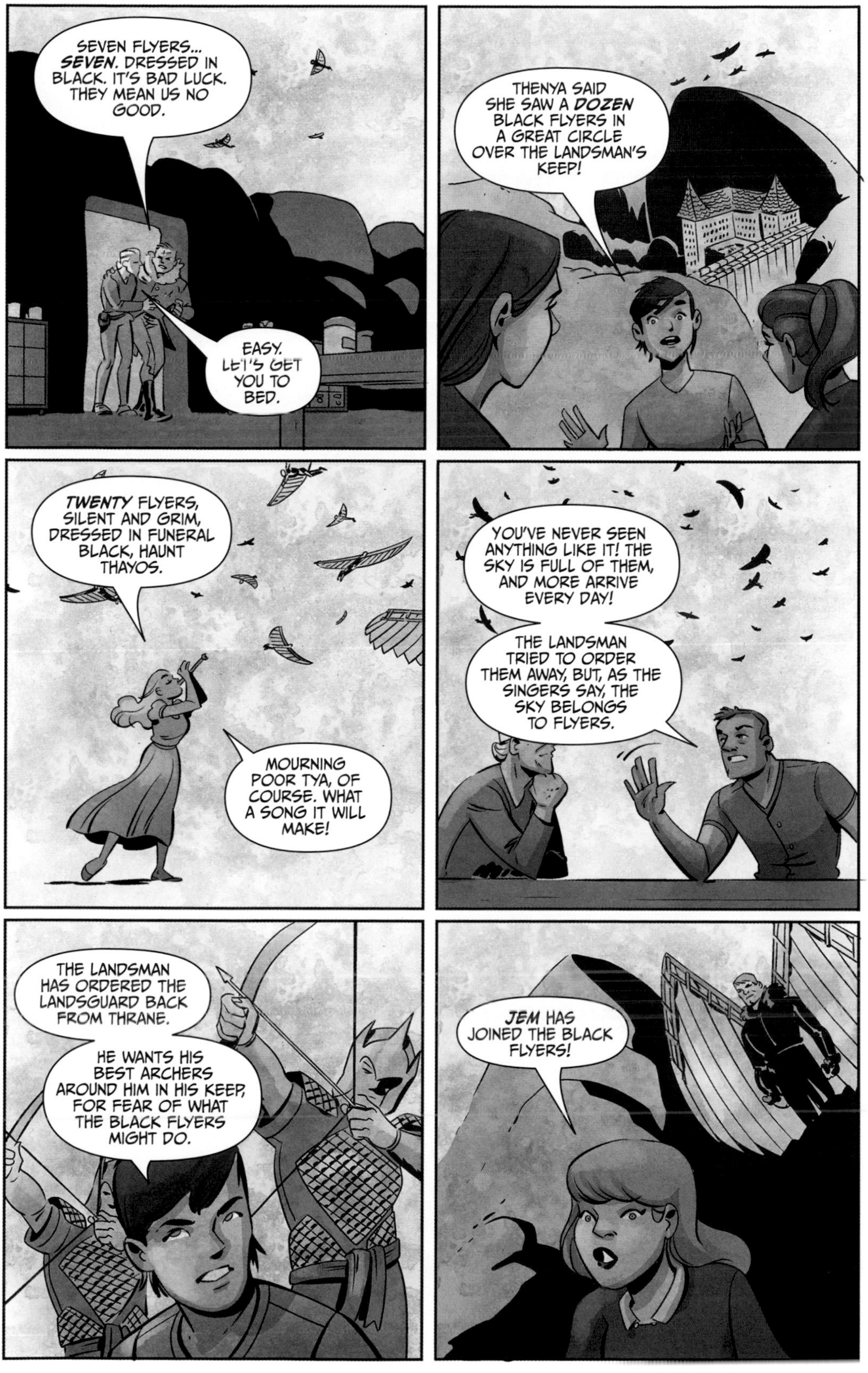
SEVEN FLYERS... *SEVEN*. DRESSED IN BLACK. IT'S BAD LUCK. THEY MEAN US NO GOOD.
EASY. LET'S GET YOU TO BED.
THENYA SAID SHE SAW A *DOZEN* BLACK FLYERS IN A GREAT CIRCLE OVER THE LANDSMAN'S KEEP!
TWENTY FLYERS, SILENT AND GRIM, DRESSED IN FUNERAL BLACK, HAUNT THAYOS.
MOURNING POOR TYA, OF COURSE. WHAT A SONG IT WILL MAKE!
YOU'VE NEVER SEEN ANYTHING LIKE IT! THE SKY IS FULL OF THEM, AND MORE ARRIVE EVERY DAY!
THE LANDSMAN TRIED TO ORDER THEM AWAY, BUT, AS THE SINGERS SAY, THE SKY BELONGS TO FLYERS.
THE LANDSMAN HAS ORDERED THE LANDSGUARD BACK FROM THRANE.
HE WANTS HIS BEST ARCHERS AROUND HIM IN HIS KEEP, FOR FEAR OF WHAT THE BLACK FLYERS MIGHT DO.
JEM HAS JOINED THE BLACK FLYERS!

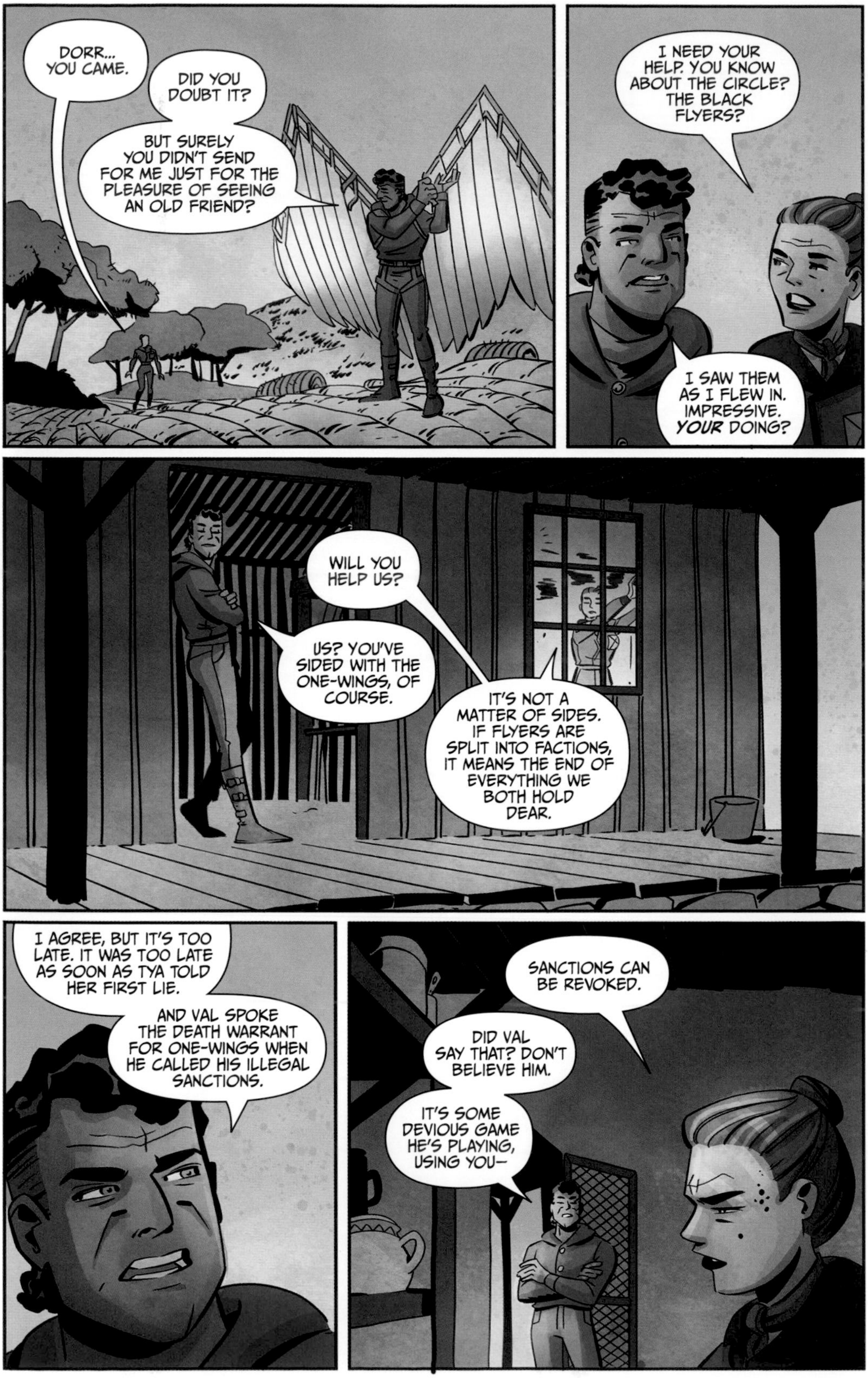
DORR... YOU CAME.
DID YOU DOUBT IT?
BUT SURELY YOU DIDN'T SEND FOR ME JUST FOR THE PLEASURE OF SEEING AN OLD FRIEND?
I NEED YOUR HELP. YOU KNOW ABOUT THE CIRCLE? THE BLACK FLYERS?
I SAW THEM AS I FLEW IN. IMPRESSIVE. *YOUR* DOING?
WILL YOU HELP US?
US? YOU'VE SIDED WITH THE ONE-WINGS, OF COURSE.
IT'S NOT A MATTER OF SIDES. IF FLYERS ARE SPLIT INTO FACTIONS, IT MEANS THE END OF EVERYTHING WE BOTH HOLD DEAR.
I AGREE, BUT IT'S TOO LATE. IT WAS TOO LATE AS SOON AS TYA TOLD HER FIRST LIE.
AND VAL SPOKE THE DEATH WARRANT FOR ONE-WINGS WHEN HE CALLED HIS ILLEGAL SANCTIONS.
SANCTIONS CAN BE REVOKED.
DID VAL SAY THAT? DON'T BELIEVE HIM.
IT'S SOME DEVIOUS GAME HE'S PLAYING, USING YOU—

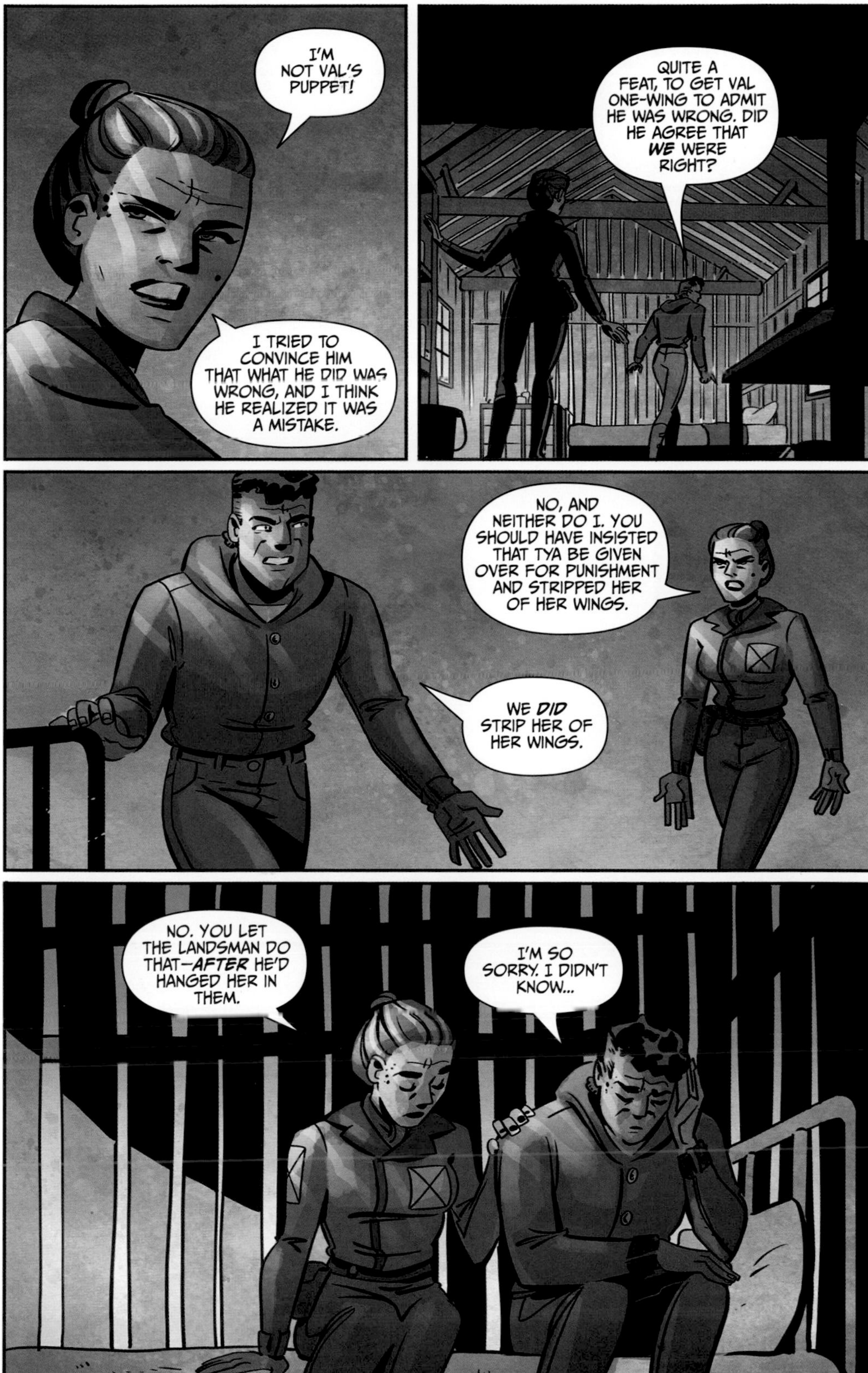
I'M NOT VAL'S PUPPET!
I TRIED TO CONVINCE HIM THAT WHAT HE DID WAS WRONG, AND I THINK HE REALIZED IT WAS A MISTAKE.
QUITE A FEAT, TO GET VAL ONE-WING TO ADMIT HE WAS WRONG. DID HE AGREE THAT *WE* WERE RIGHT?
NO, AND NEITHER DO I. YOU SHOULD HAVE INSISTED THAT TYA BE GIVEN OVER FOR PUNISHMENT AND STRIPPED HER OF HER WINGS.
WE *DID* STRIP HER OF HER WINGS.
NO. YOU LET THE LANDSMAN DO THAT—*AFTER* HE'D HANGED HER IN THEM.
I'M SO SORRY. I DIDN'T KNOW...

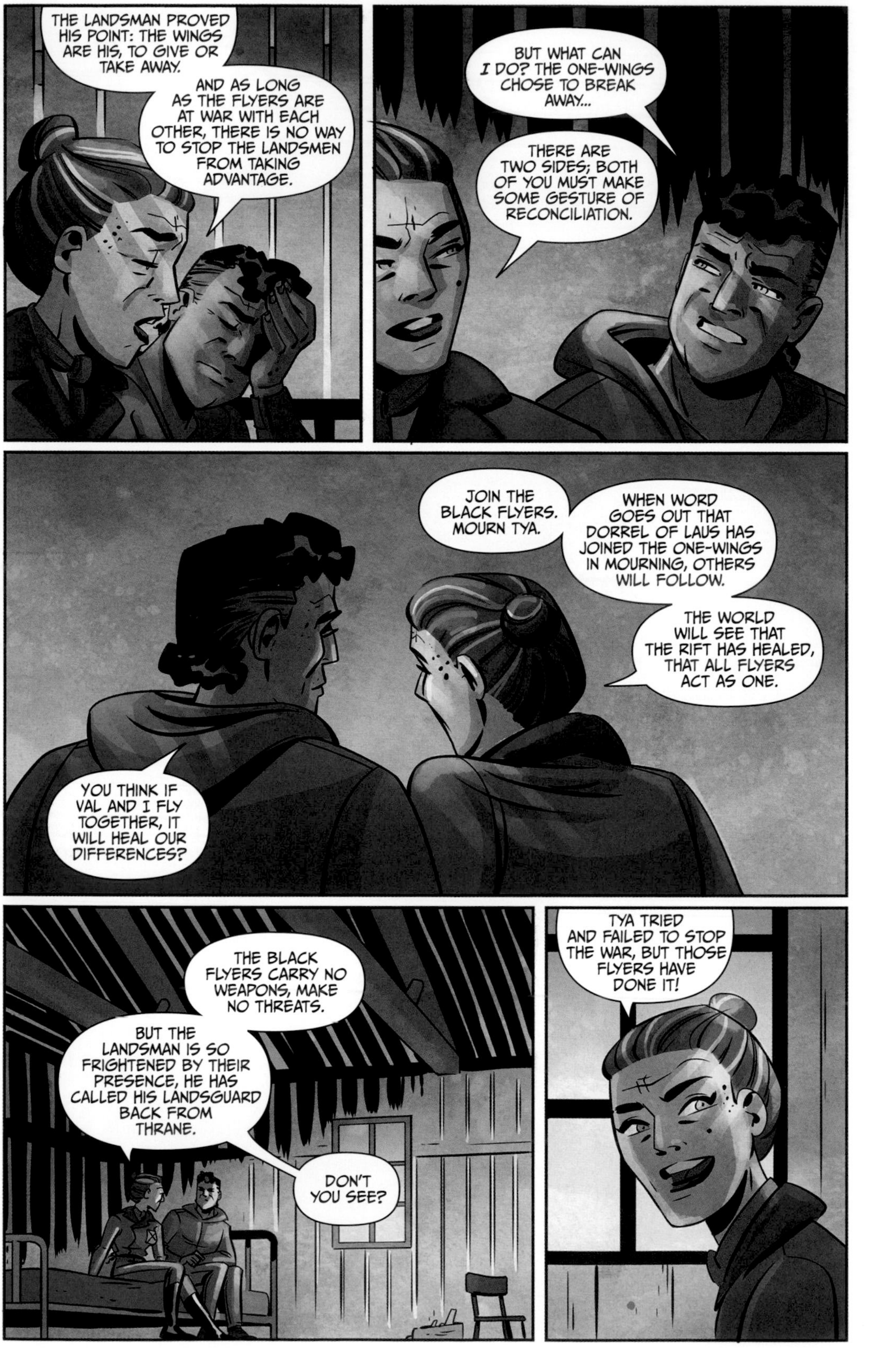
THE LANDSMAN PROVED HIS POINT: THE WINGS ARE HIS, TO GIVE OR TAKE AWAY.
AND AS LONG AS THE FLYERS ARE AT WAR WITH EACH OTHER, THERE IS NO WAY TO STOP THE LANDSMEN FROM TAKING ADVANTAGE.
BUT WHAT CAN I DO? THE ONE-WINGS CHOSE TO BREAK AWAY...
THERE ARE TWO SIDES; BOTH OF YOU MUST MAKE SOME GESTURE OF RECONCILIATION.
JOIN THE BLACK FLYERS. MOURN TYA.
WHEN WORD GOES OUT THAT DORREL OF LAUS HAS JOINED THE ONE-WINGS IN MOURNING, OTHERS WILL FOLLOW.
THE WORLD WILL SEE THAT THE RIFT HAS HEALED, THAT ALL FLYERS ACT AS ONE.
YOU THINK IF VAL AND I FLY TOGETHER, IT WILL HEAL OUR DIFFERENCES?
THE BLACK FLYERS CARRY NO WEAPONS, MAKE NO THREATS.
BUT THE LANDSMAN IS SO FRIGHTENED BY THEIR PRESENCE, HE HAS CALLED HIS LANDSGUARD BACK FROM THRANE.
DON'T YOU SEE?
TYA TRIED AND FAILED TO STOP THE WAR, BUT THOSE FLYERS HAVE DONE IT!

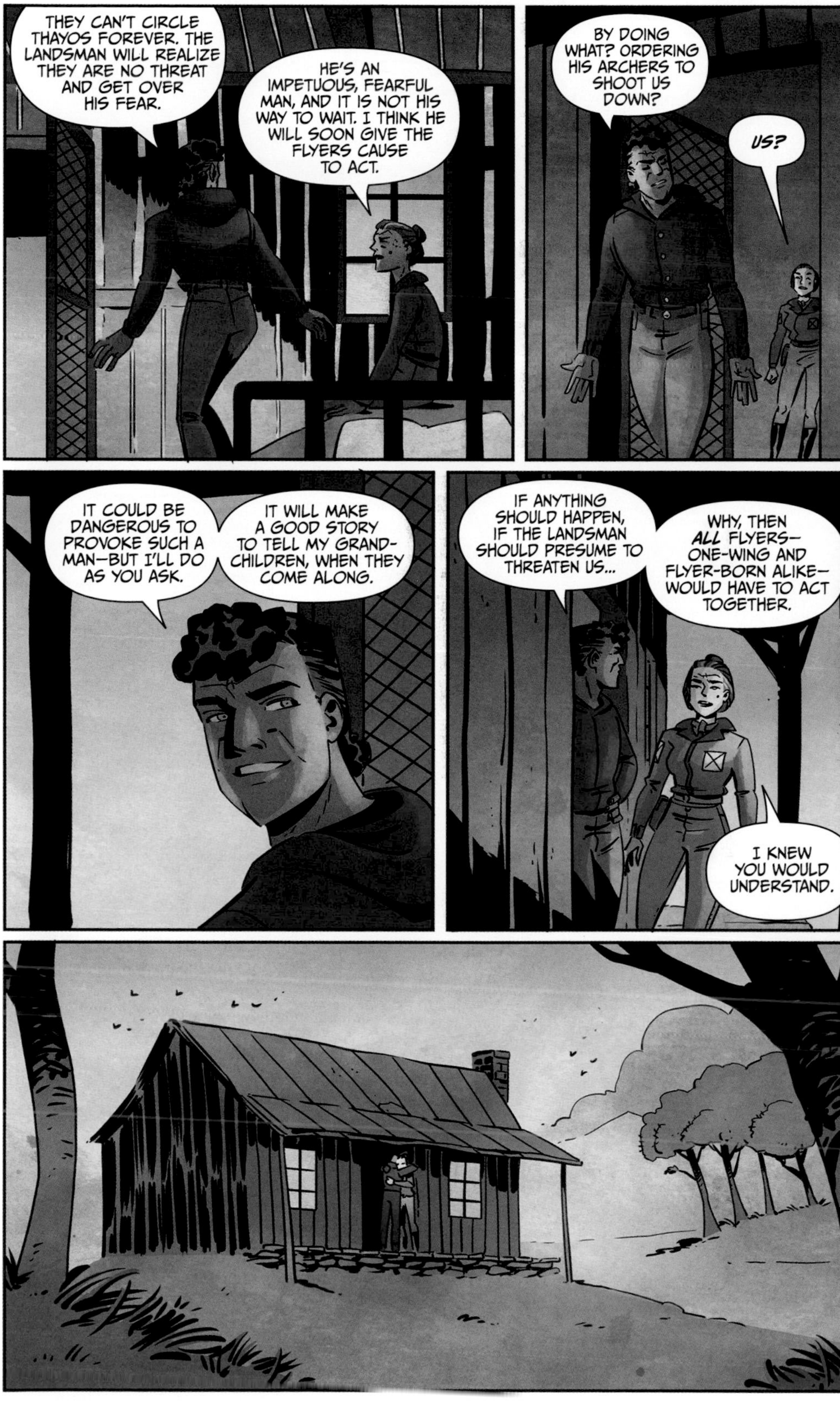
THEY CAN'T CIRCLE THAYOS FOREVER. THE LANDSMAN WILL REALIZE THEY ARE NO THREAT AND GET OVER HIS FEAR.
HE'S AN IMPETUOUS, FEARFUL MAN, AND IT IS NOT HIS WAY TO WAIT. I THINK HE WILL SOON GIVE THE FLYERS CAUSE TO ACT.
BY DOING WHAT? ORDERING HIS ARCHERS TO SHOOT US DOWN?
US?
IT COULD BE DANGEROUS TO PROVOKE SUCH A MAN—BUT I'LL DO AS YOU ASK.
IT WILL MAKE A GOOD STORY TO TELL MY GRAND-CHILDREN, WHEN THEY COME ALONG.
IF ANYTHING SHOULD HAPPEN, IF THE LANDSMAN SHOULD PRESUME TO THREATEN US...
WHY, THEN ALL FLYERS—ONE-WING AND FLYER-BORN ALIKE—WOULD HAVE TO ACT TOGETHER.
I KNEW YOU WOULD UNDERSTAND.

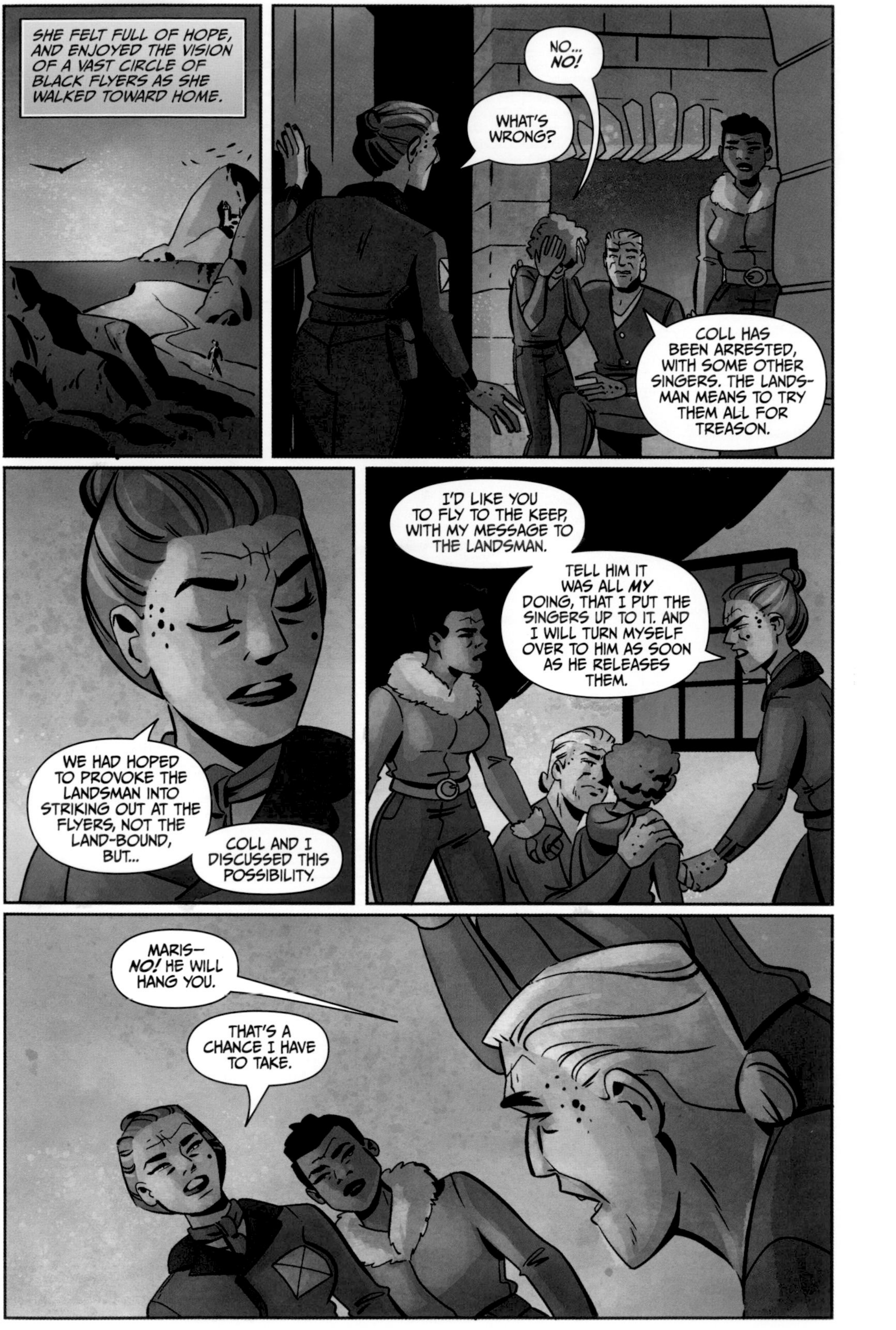
SHE FELT FULL OF HOPE, AND ENJOYED THE VISION OF A VAST CIRCLE OF BLACK FLYERS AS SHE WALKED TOWARD HOME.
NO... NO!
WHAT'S WRONG?
COLL HAS BEEN ARRESTED, WITH SOME OTHER SINGERS. THE LANDSMAN MEANS TO TRY THEM ALL FOR TREASON.
WE HAD HOPED TO PROVOKE THE LANDSMAN INTO STRIKING OUT AT THE FLYERS, NOT THE LAND-BOUND, BUT...
COLL AND I DISCUSSED THIS POSSIBILITY.
I'D LIKE YOU TO FLY TO THE KEEP, WITH MY MESSAGE TO THE LANDSMAN.
TELL HIM IT WAS ALL MY DOING, THAT I PUT THE SINGERS UP TO IT. AND I WILL TURN MYSELF OVER TO HIM AS SOON AS HE RELEASES THEM.
MARIS— NO! HE WILL HANG YOU.
THAT'S A CHANCE I HAVE TO TAKE.

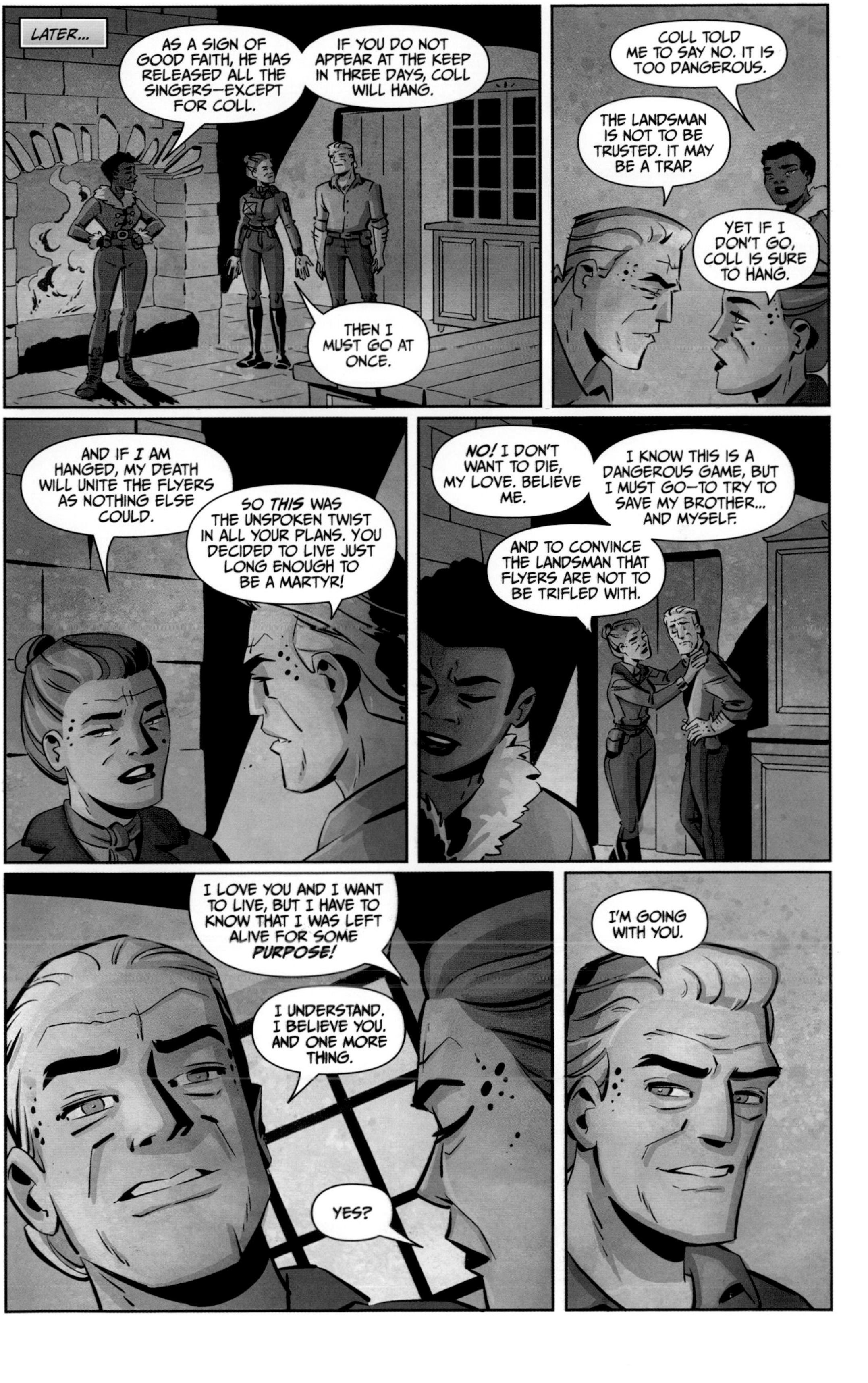
LATER...
AS A SIGN OF GOOD FAITH, HE HAS RELEASED ALL THE SINGERS—EXCEPT FOR COLL.
IF YOU DO NOT APPEAR AT THE KEEP IN THREE DAYS, COLL WILL HANG.
THEN I MUST GO AT ONCE.
COLL TOLD ME TO SAY NO. IT IS TOO DANGEROUS.
THE LANDSMAN IS NOT TO BE TRUSTED. IT MAY BE A TRAP.
YET IF I DON'T GO, COLL IS SURE TO HANG.
AND IF I AM HANGED, MY DEATH WILL UNITE THE FLYERS AS NOTHING ELSE COULD.
SO THIS WAS THE UNSPOKEN TWIST IN ALL YOUR PLANS. YOU DECIDED TO LIVE JUST LONG ENOUGH TO BE A MARTYR!
NO! I DON'T WANT TO DIE, MY LOVE. BELIEVE ME.
I KNOW THIS IS A DANGEROUS GAME, BUT I MUST GO—TO TRY TO SAVE MY BROTHER... AND MYSELF.
AND TO CONVINCE THE LANDSMAN THAT FLYERS ARE NOT TO BE TRIFLED WITH.
I LOVE YOU AND I WANT TO LIVE, BUT I HAVE TO KNOW THAT I WAS LEFT ALIVE FOR SOME PURPOSE!
I UNDERSTAND. I BELIEVE YOU. AND ONE MORE THING.
YES?
I'M GOING WITH YOU.

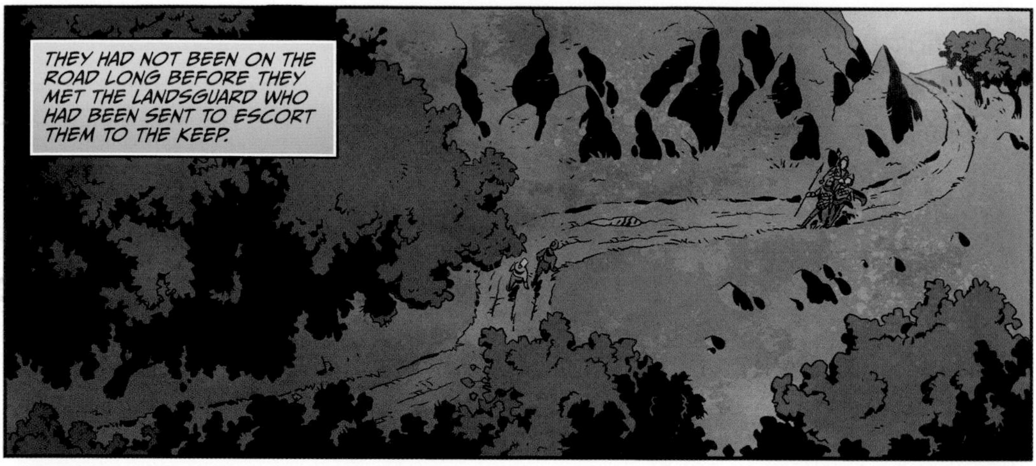
THEY HAD NOT BEEN ON THE ROAD LONG BEFORE THEY MET THE LANDSGUARD WHO HAD BEEN SENT TO ESCORT THEM TO THE KEEP.

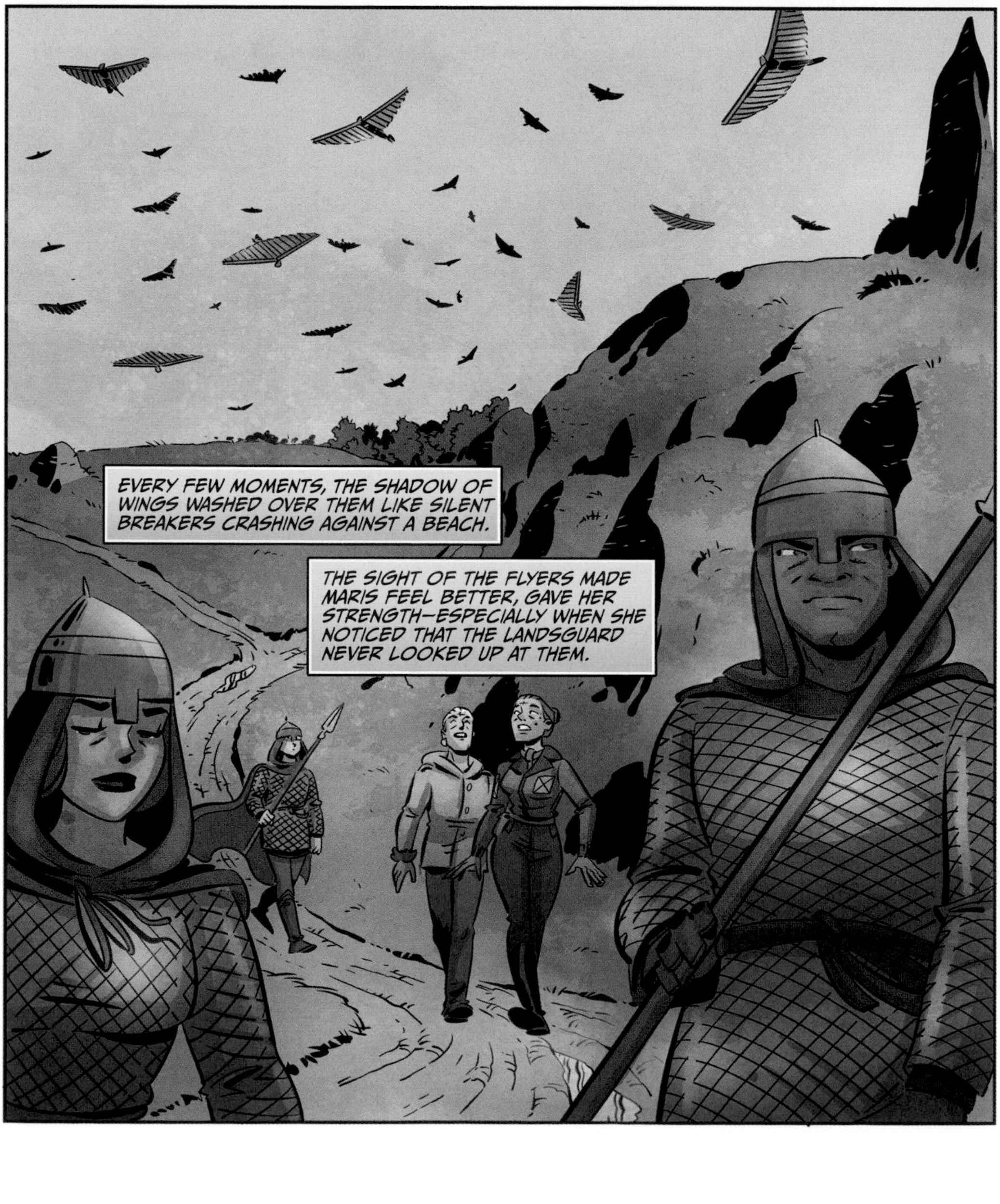
EVERY FEW MOMENTS, THE SHADOW OF WINGS WASHED OVER THEM LIKE SILENT BREAKERS CRASHING AGAINST A BEACH.
THE SIGHT OF THE FLYERS MADE MARIS FEEL BETTER, GAVE HER STRENGTH—ESPECIALLY WHEN SHE NOTICED THAT THE LANDSGUARD NEVER LOOKED UP AT THEM.

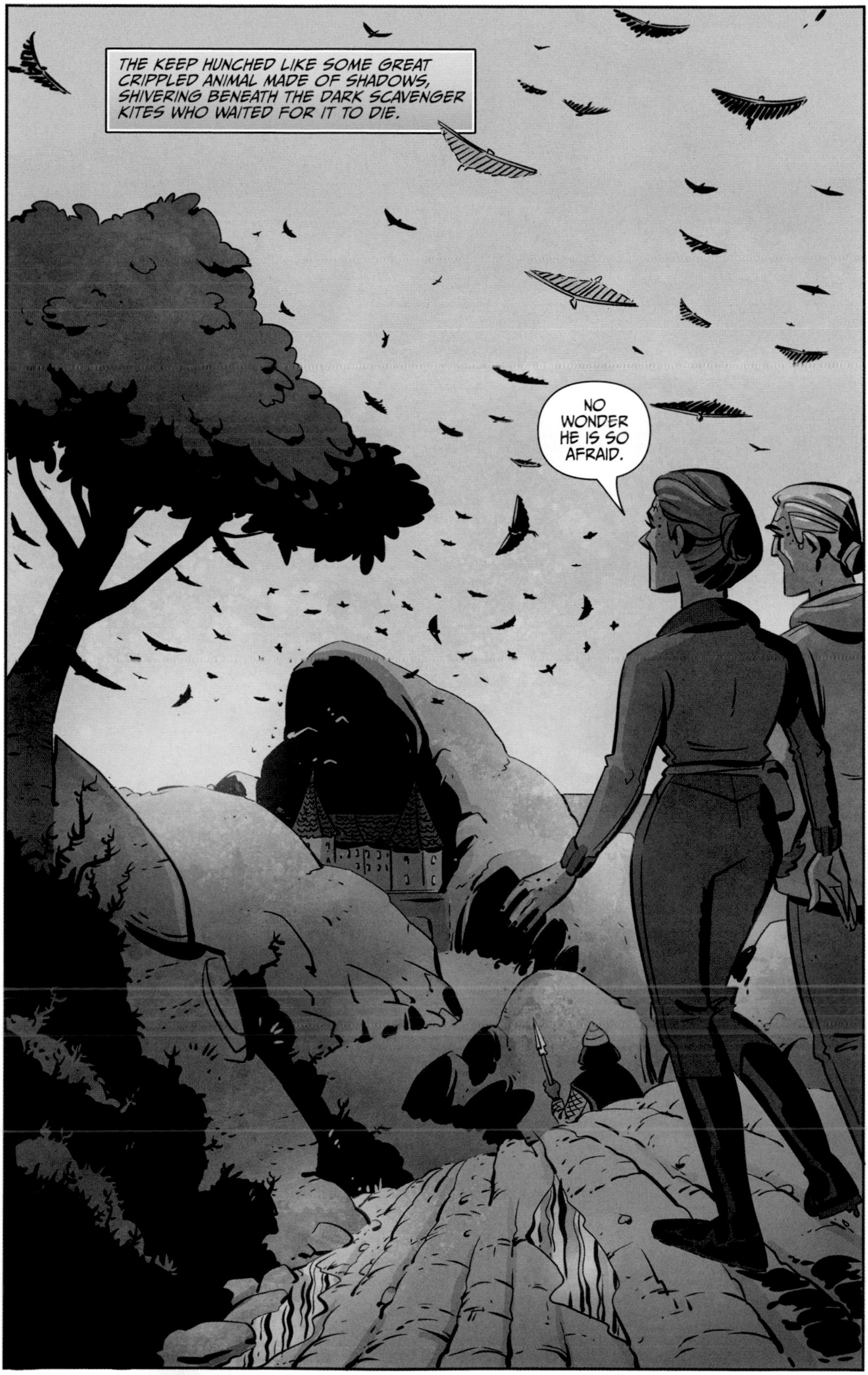
THE KEEP HUNCHED LIKE SOME GREAT CRIPPLED ANIMAL MADE OF SHADOWS, SHIVERING BENEATH THE DARK SCAVENGER KITES WHO WAITED FOR IT TO DIE.
NO WONDER HE IS SO AFRAID.

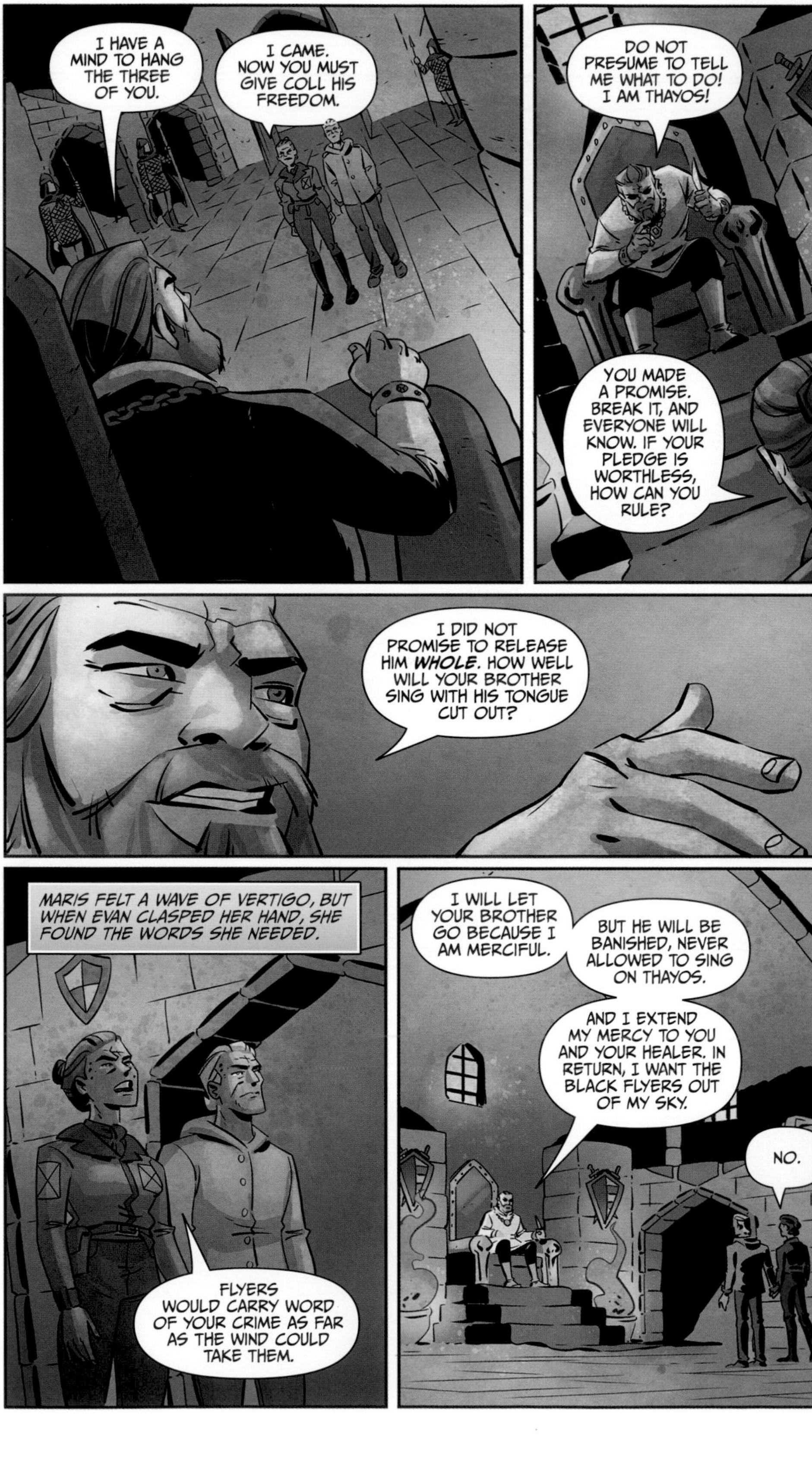
I HAVE A MIND TO HANG THE THREE OF YOU.
I CAME. NOW YOU MUST GIVE COLL HIS FREEDOM.
DO NOT PRESUME TO TELL ME WHAT TO DO! I AM THAYOS!
YOU MADE A PROMISE. BREAK IT, AND EVERYONE WILL KNOW. IF YOUR PLEDGE IS WORTHLESS, HOW CAN YOU RULE?
I DID NOT PROMISE TO RELEASE HIM ***WHOLE***. HOW WELL WILL YOUR BROTHER SING WITH HIS TONGUE CUT OUT?
MARIS FELT A WAVE OF VERTIGO, BUT WHEN EVAN CLASPED HER HAND, SHE FOUND THE WORDS SHE NEEDED.
FLYERS WOULD CARRY WORD OF YOUR CRIME AS FAR AS THE WIND COULD TAKE THEM.
I WILL LET YOUR BROTHER GO BECAUSE I AM MERCIFUL.
BUT HE WILL BE BANISHED, NEVER ALLOWED TO SING ON THAYOS.
AND I EXTEND MY MERCY TO YOU AND YOUR HEALER. IN RETURN, I WANT THE BLACK FLYERS OUT OF MY SKY.
NO.

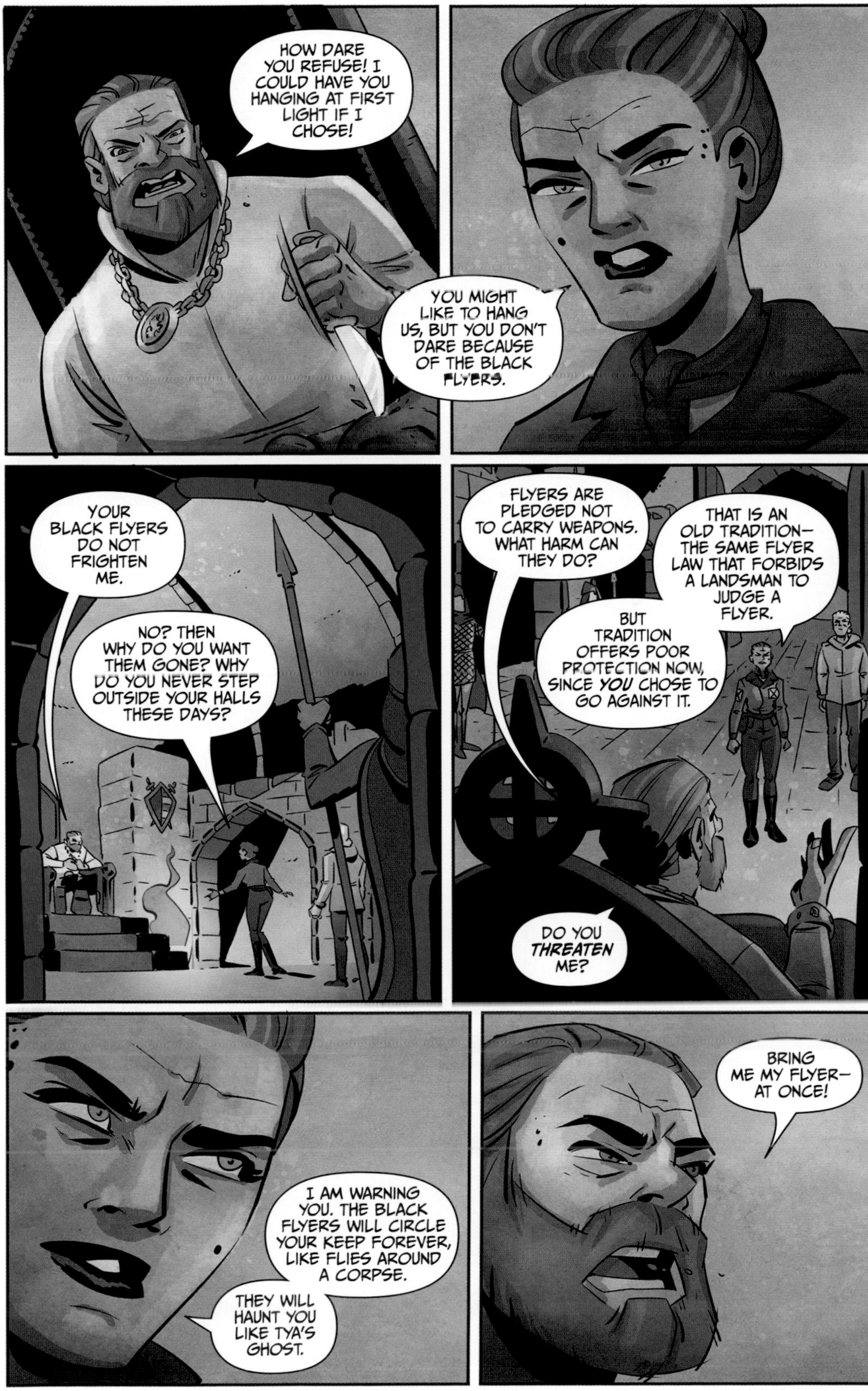
HOW DARE YOU REFUSE! I COULD HAVE YOU HANGING AT FIRST LIGHT IF I CHOSE!
YOU MIGHT LIKE TO HANG US, BUT YOU DON'T DARE BECAUSE OF THE BLACK FLYERS.
YOUR BLACK FLYERS DO NOT FRIGHTEN ME.
NO? THEN WHY DO YOU WANT THEM GONE? WHY DO YOU NEVER STEP OUTSIDE YOUR HALLS THESE DAYS?
FLYERS ARE PLEDGED NOT TO CARRY WEAPONS. WHAT HARM CAN THEY DO?
THAT IS AN OLD TRADITION— THE SAME FLYER LAW THAT FORBIDS A LANDSMAN TO JUDGE A FLYER.
BUT TRADITION OFFERS POOR PROTECTION NOW, SINCE *YOU* CHOSE TO GO AGAINST IT.
DO YOU *THREATEN* ME?
I AM WARNING YOU. THE BLACK FLYERS WILL CIRCLE YOUR KEEP FOREVER, LIKE FLIES AROUND A CORPSE.
THEY WILL HAUNT YOU LIKE TYA'S GHOST.
BRING ME MY FLYER— AT ONCE!

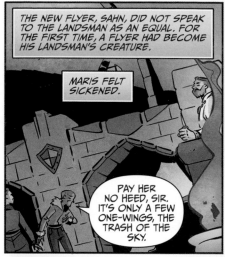

THE NEW FLYER, SAHN, DID NOT SPEAK TO THE LANDSMAN AS AN EQUAL. FOR THE FIRST TIME, A FLYER HAD BECOME HIS LANDSMAN'S CREATURE.

MARIS FELT SICKENED.

PAY HER NO HEED, SIR. IT'S ONLY A FEW ONE-WINGS, THE TRASH OF THE SKY.

AS I THOUGHT. ONE-WINGS ARE ALL LIARS. THE *REAL* FLYERS CARE NOTHING FOR TYA.

SAHN...TELL YOUR LANDSMAN WHO DORREL OF LAUS IS.

DORREL OF LAUS IS A WESTERN FLYER, FROM AN OLD FLYER FAMILY. POPULAR, WELL-RESPECTED... A LEADER.

WHY SHOULD I CARE?

BECAUSE DORREL IS BRINGING A HUNDRED WESTERN FLYERS TO JOIN THE CIRCLE.

IS THIS TRUE?

I...I DON'T KNOW, SIR. DORREL HAS INFLUENCE; IF HE HAS DECIDED... IF HE...

SILENCE, YOU FOOL, OR I'LL FIND SOMEONE ELSE FOR THOSE WINGS OF YOURS!

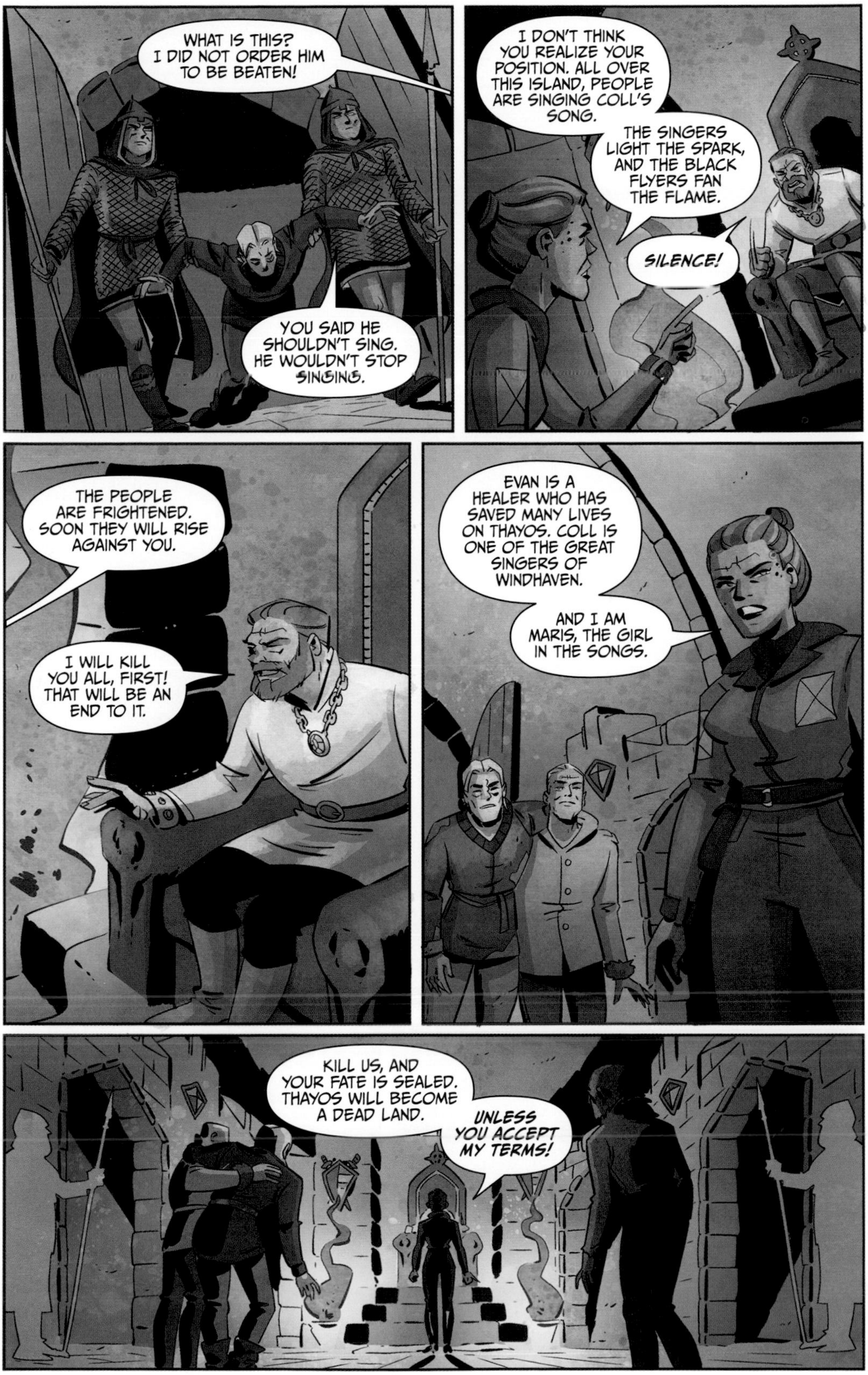
WHAT IS THIS? I DID NOT ORDER HIM TO BE BEATEN!
YOU SAID HE SHOULDN'T SING. HE WOULDN'T STOP SINGING.
I DON'T THINK YOU REALIZE YOUR POSITION. ALL OVER THIS ISLAND, PEOPLE ARE SINGING COLL'S SONG.
THE SINGERS LIGHT THE SPARK, AND THE BLACK FLYERS FAN THE FLAME.
SILENCE!
THE PEOPLE ARE FRIGHTENED. SOON THEY WILL RISE AGAINST YOU.
I WILL KILL YOU ALL, FIRST! THAT WILL BE AN END TO IT.
EVAN IS A HEALER WHO HAS SAVED MANY LIVES ON THAYOS. COLL IS ONE OF THE GREAT SINGERS OF WINDHAVEN.
AND I AM MARIS, THE GIRL IN THE SONGS.
KILL US, AND YOUR FATE IS SEALED. THAYOS WILL BECOME A DEAD LAND.
UNLESS YOU ACCEPT MY TERMS!

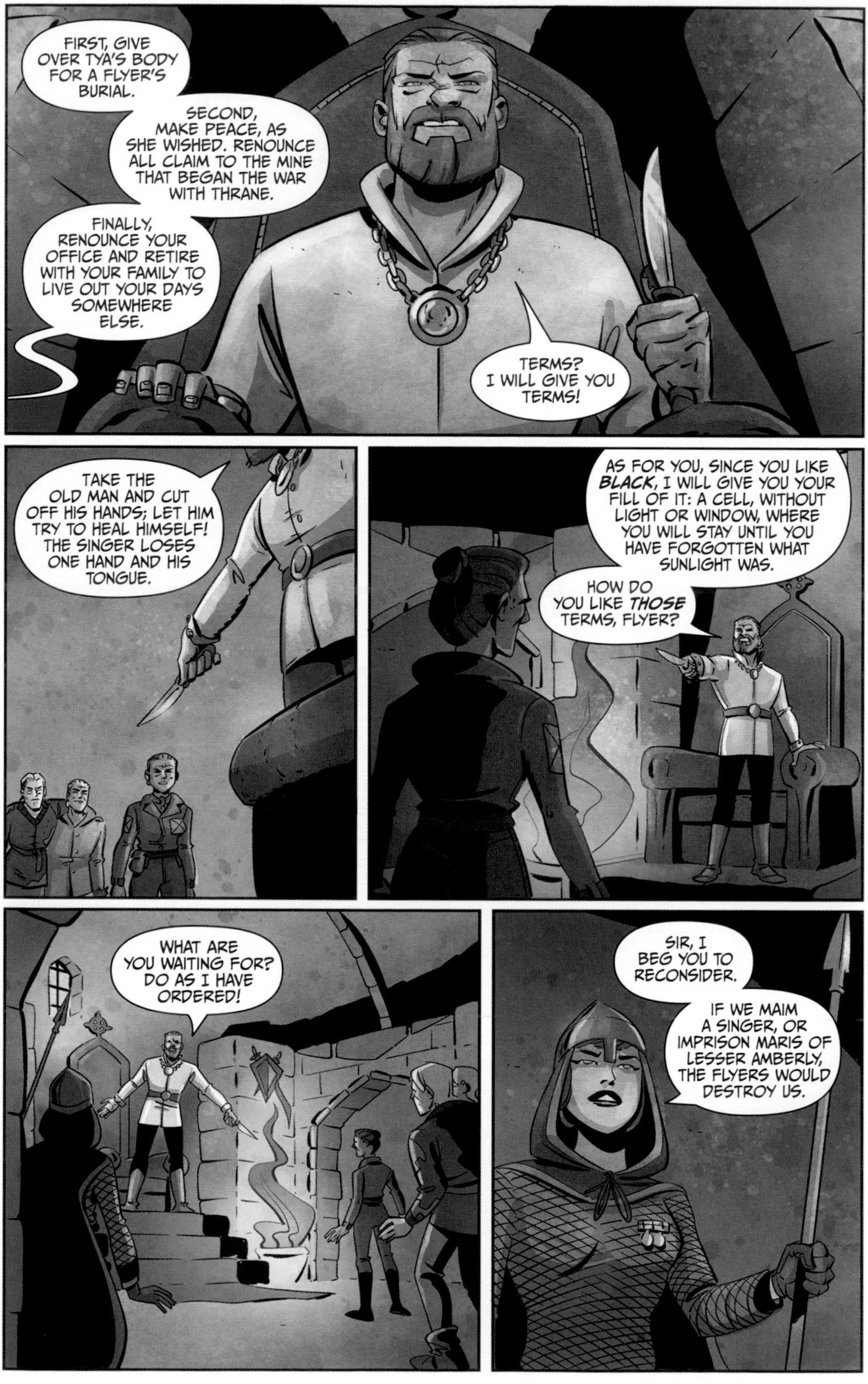
FIRST, GIVE OVER TYA'S BODY FOR A FLYER'S BURIAL.
SECOND, MAKE PEACE, AS SHE WISHED. RENOUNCE ALL CLAIM TO THE MINE THAT BEGAN THE WAR WITH THRANE.
FINALLY, RENOUNCE YOUR OFFICE AND RETIRE WITH YOUR FAMILY TO LIVE OUT YOUR DAYS SOMEWHERE ELSE.
TERMS? I WILL GIVE YOU TERMS!
TAKE THE OLD MAN AND CUT OFF HIS HANDS; LET HIM TRY TO HEAL HIMSELF! THE SINGER LOSES ONE HAND AND HIS TONGUE.
AS FOR YOU, SINCE YOU LIKE *BLACK*, I WILL GIVE YOU YOUR FILL OF IT: A CELL, WITHOUT LIGHT OR WINDOW, WHERE YOU WILL STAY UNTIL YOU HAVE FORGOTTEN WHAT SUNLIGHT WAS.
HOW DO YOU LIKE *THOSE* TERMS, FLYER?
WHAT ARE YOU WAITING FOR? DO AS I HAVE ORDERED!
SIR, I BEG YOU TO RECONSIDER.
IF WE MAIM A SINGER, OR IMPRISON MARIS OF LESSER AMBERLY, THE FLYERS WOULD DESTROY US.

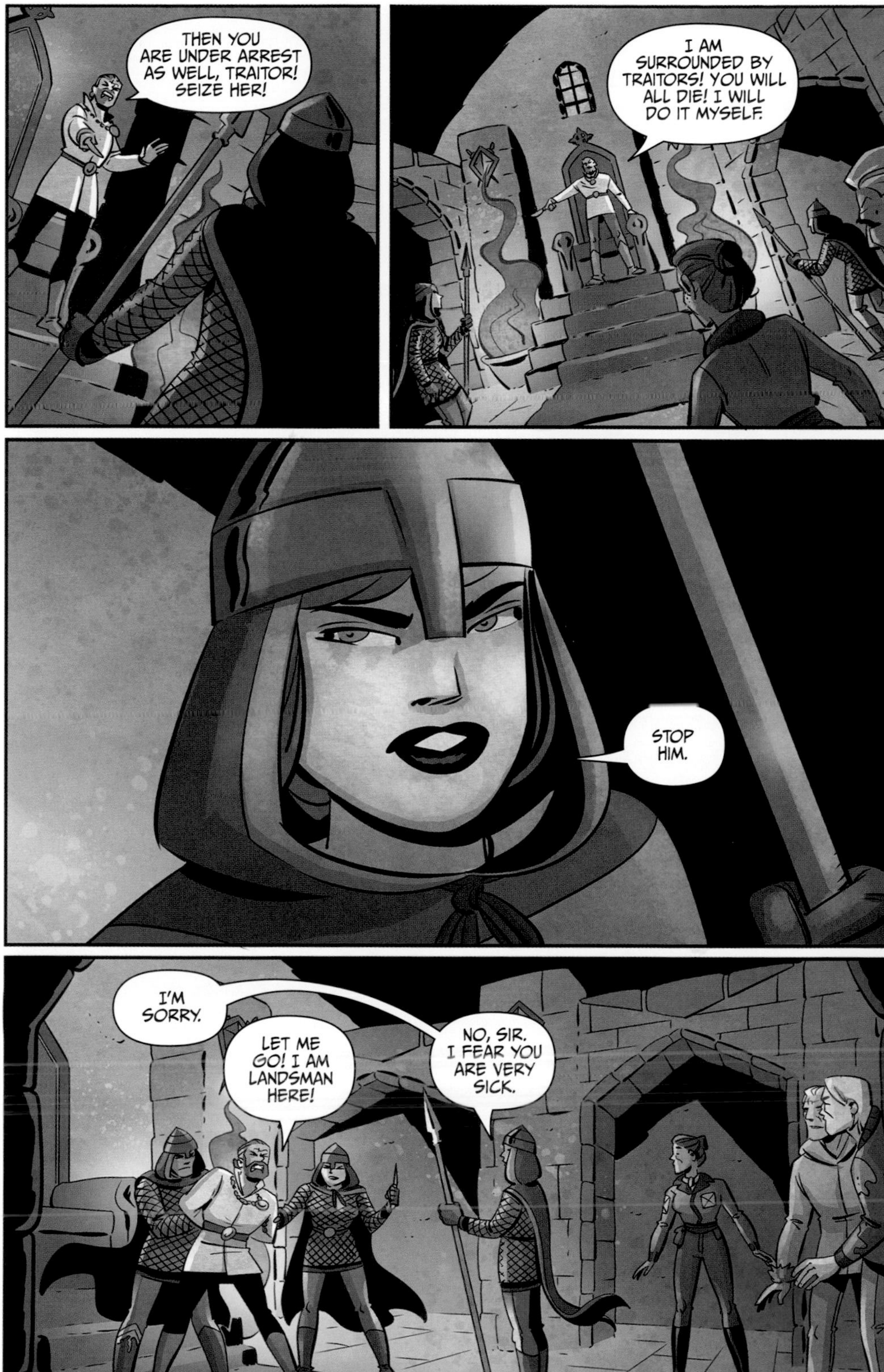
THEN YOU ARE UNDER ARREST AS WELL, TRAITOR! SEIZE HER!
I AM SURROUNDED BY TRAITORS! YOU WILL ALL DIE! I WILL DO IT MYSELF.
STOP HIM.
I'M SORRY.
LET ME GO! I AM LANDSMAN HERE!
NO, SIR. I FEAR YOU ARE VERY SICK.

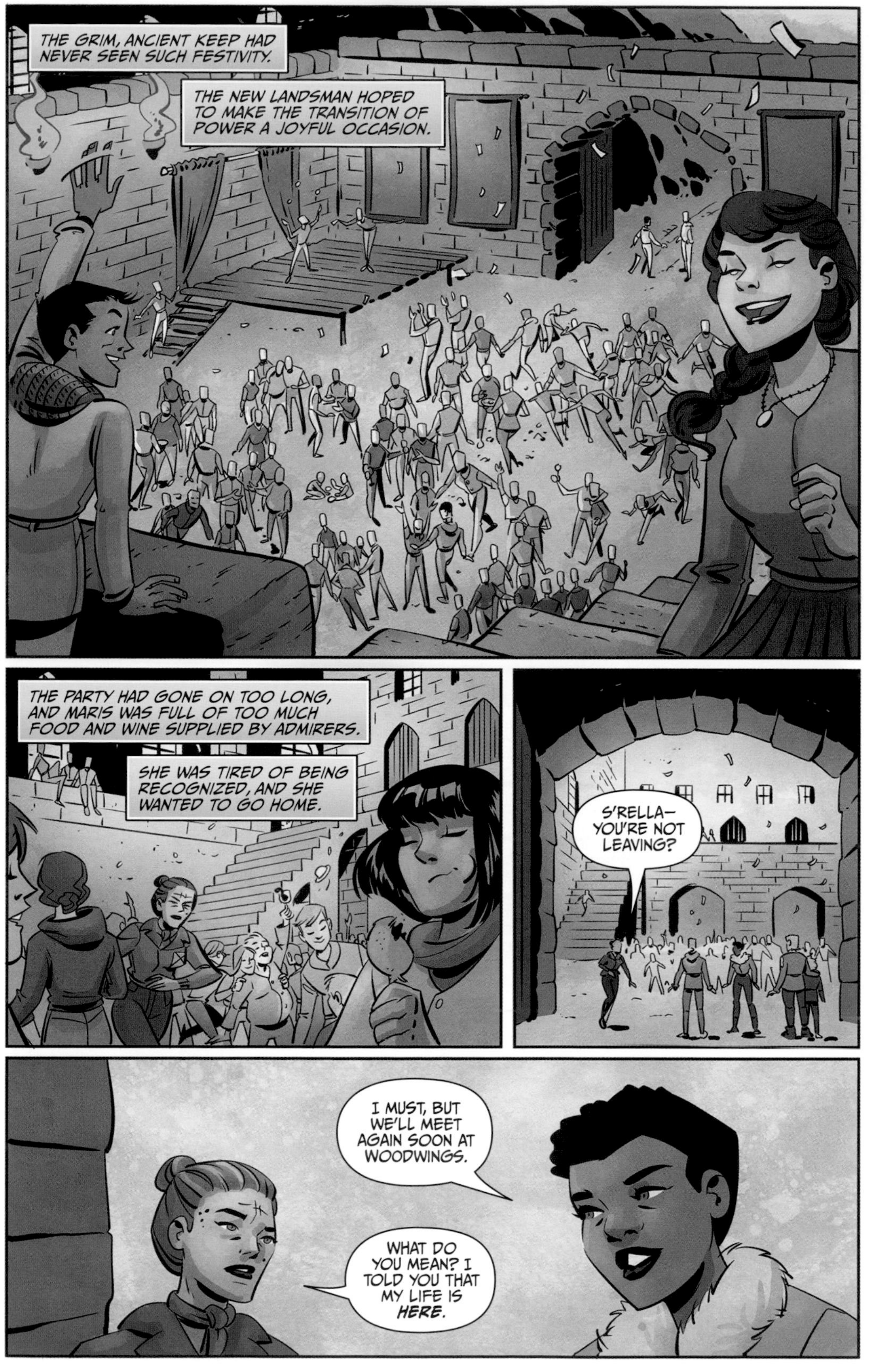
THE GRIM, ANCIENT KEEP HAD NEVER SEEN SUCH FESTIVITY.
THE NEW LANDSMAN HOPED TO MAKE THE TRANSITION OF POWER A JOYFUL OCCASION.
THE PARTY HAD GONE ON TOO LONG, AND MARIS WAS FULL OF TOO MUCH FOOD AND WINE SUPPLIED BY ADMIRERS.
SHE WAS TIRED OF BEING RECOGNIZED, AND SHE WANTED TO GO HOME.
S'RELLA—YOU'RE NOT LEAVING?
I MUST, BUT WE'LL MEET AGAIN SOON AT WOODWINGS.
WHAT DO YOU MEAN? I TOLD YOU THAT MY LIFE IS *HERE*.

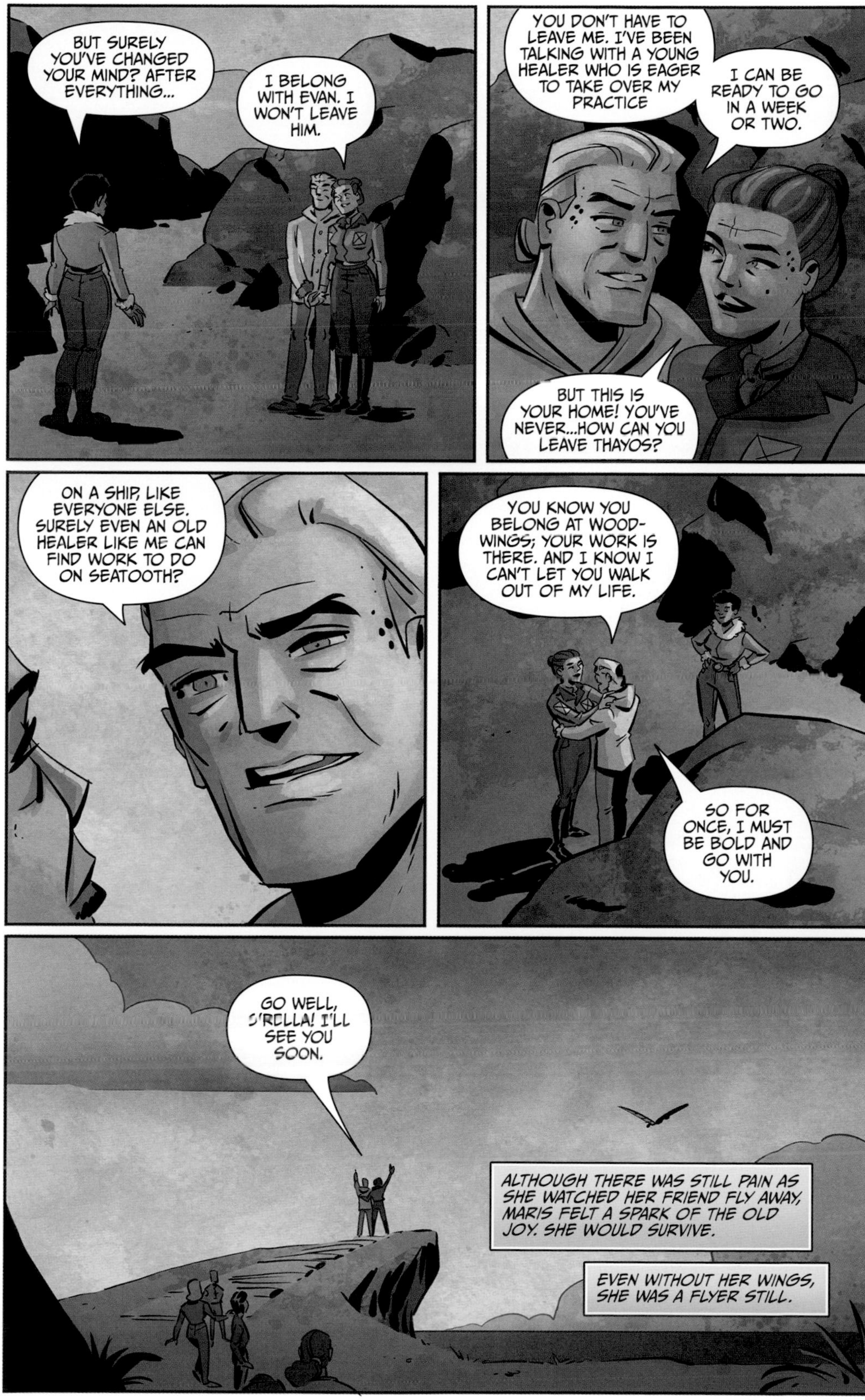
BUT SURELY YOU'VE CHANGED YOUR MIND? AFTER EVERYTHING...
I BELONG WITH EVAN. I WON'T LEAVE HIM.
YOU DON'T HAVE TO LEAVE ME. I'VE BEEN TALKING WITH A YOUNG HEALER WHO IS EAGER TO TAKE OVER MY PRACTICE
I CAN BE READY TO GO IN A WEEK OR TWO.
BUT THIS IS YOUR HOME! YOU'VE NEVER...HOW CAN YOU LEAVE THAYOS?
ON A SHIP, LIKE EVERYONE ELSE. SURELY EVEN AN OLD HEALER LIKE ME CAN FIND WORK TO DO ON SEATOOTH?
YOU KNOW YOU BELONG AT WOOD-WINGS; YOUR WORK IS THERE. AND I KNOW I CAN'T LET YOU WALK OUT OF MY LIFE.
SO FOR ONCE, I MUST BE BOLD AND GO WITH YOU.
GO WELL, S'RELLA! I'LL SEE YOU SOON.
ALTHOUGH THERE WAS STILL PAIN AS SHE WATCHED HER FRIEND FLY AWAY, MARIS FELT A SPARK OF THE OLD JOY. SHE WOULD SURVIVE.
EVEN WITHOUT HER WINGS, SHE WAS A FLYER STILL.

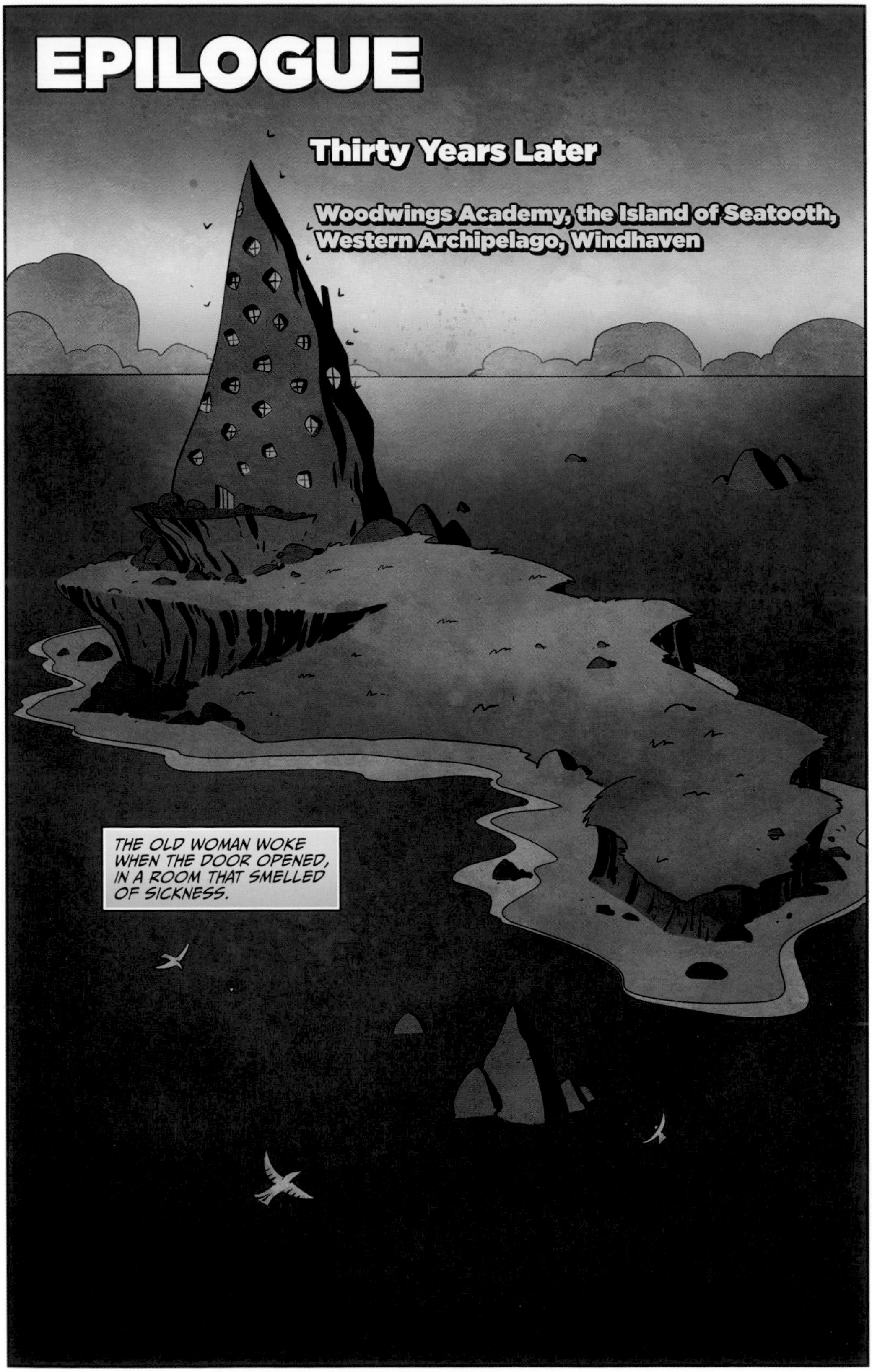
EPILOGUE
Thirty Years Later
Woodwings Academy, the Island of Seatooth, Western Archipelago, Windhaven
THE OLD WOMAN WOKE WHEN THE DOOR OPENED, IN A ROOM THAT SMELLED OF SICKNESS.

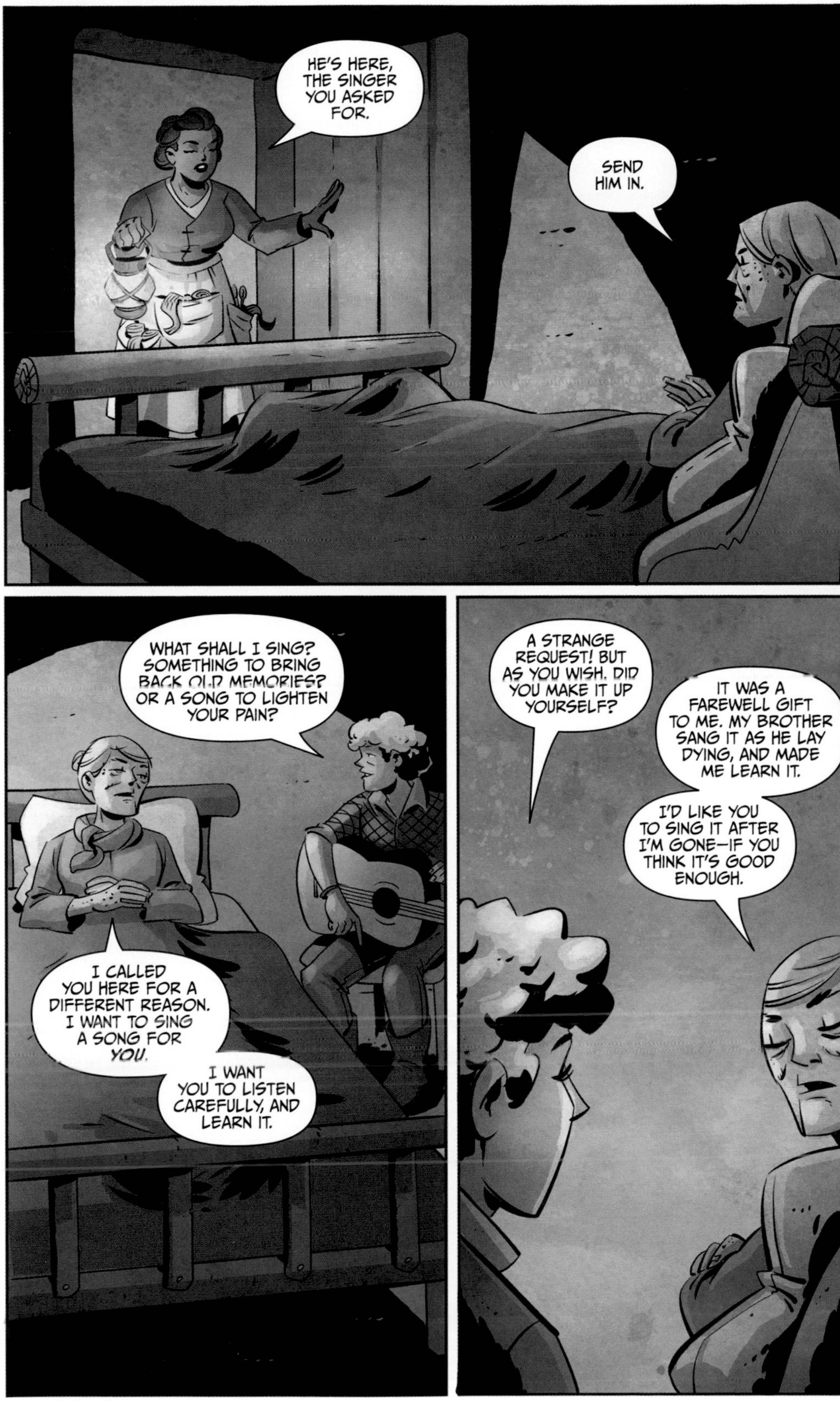
HE'S HERE, THE SINGER YOU ASKED FOR.
SEND HIM IN.
WHAT SHALL I SING? SOMETHING TO BRING BACK OLD MEMORIES? OR A SONG TO LIGHTEN YOUR PAIN?
I CALLED YOU HERE FOR A DIFFERENT REASON. I WANT TO SING A SONG FOR *YOU*.
I WANT YOU TO LISTEN CAREFULLY, AND LEARN IT.
A STRANGE REQUEST! BUT AS YOU WISH. DID YOU MAKE IT UP YOURSELF?
IT WAS A FAREWELL GIFT TO ME. MY BROTHER SANG IT AS HE LAY DYING, AND MADE ME LEARN IT.
I'D LIKE YOU TO SING IT AFTER I'M GONE—IF YOU THINK IT'S GOOD ENOUGH.

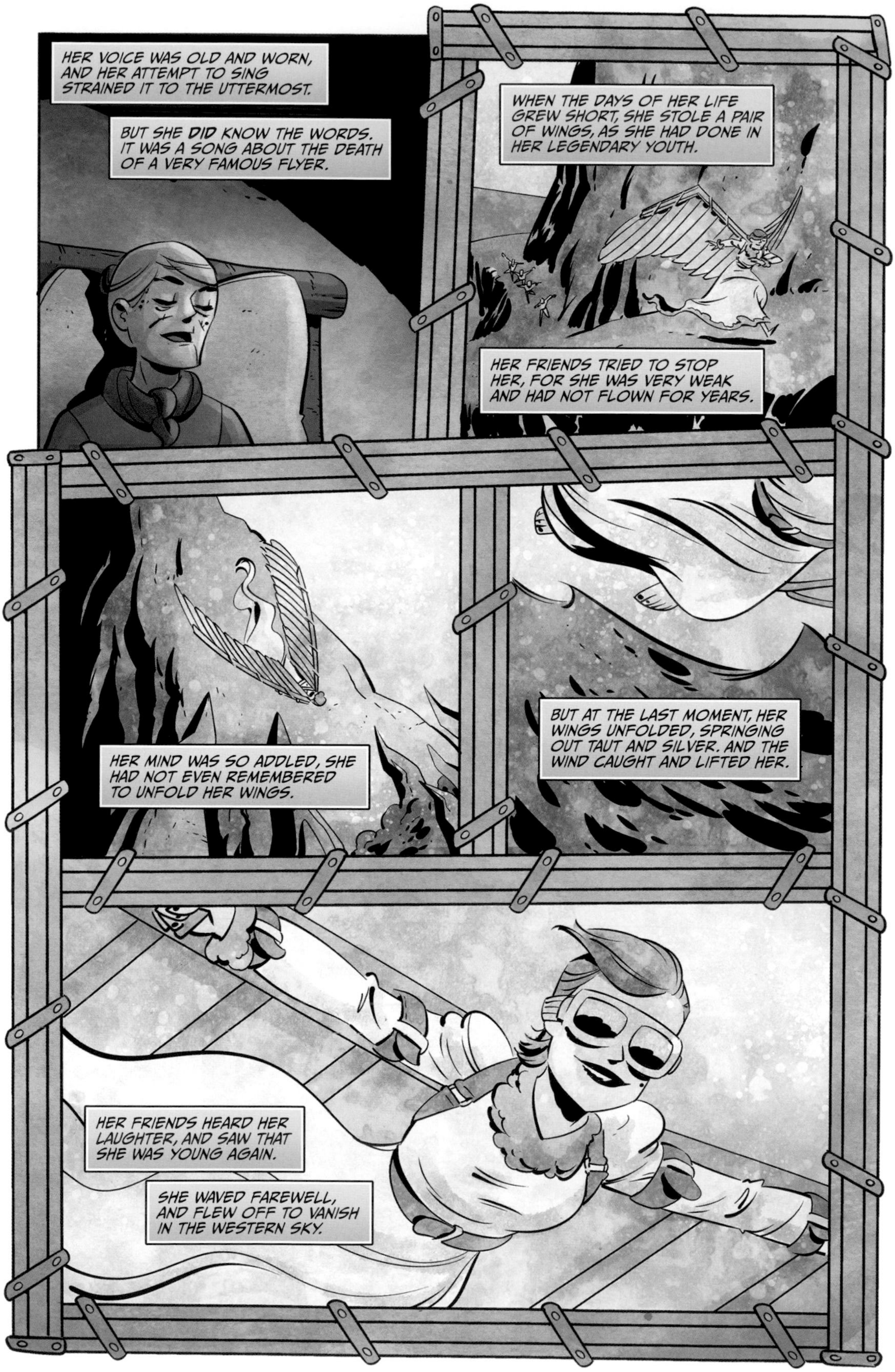
HER VOICE WAS OLD AND WORN, AND HER ATTEMPT TO SING STRAINED IT TO THE UTTERMOST.
BUT SHE DID KNOW THE WORDS. IT WAS A SONG ABOUT THE DEATH OF A VERY FAMOUS FLYER.
WHEN THE DAYS OF HER LIFE GREW SHORT, SHE STOLE A PAIR OF WINGS, AS SHE HAD DONE IN HER LEGENDARY YOUTH.
HER FRIENDS TRIED TO STOP HER, FOR SHE WAS VERY WEAK AND HAD NOT FLOWN FOR YEARS.
HER MIND WAS SO ADDLED, SHE HAD NOT EVEN REMEMBERED TO UNFOLD HER WINGS.
BUT AT THE LAST MOMENT, HER WINGS UNFOLDED, SPRINGING OUT TAUT AND SILVER. AND THE WIND CAUGHT AND LIFTED HER.
HER FRIENDS HEARD HER LAUGHTER, AND SAW THAT SHE WAS YOUNG AGAIN.
SHE WAVED FAREWELL, AND FLEW OFF TO VANISH IN THE WESTERN SKY.

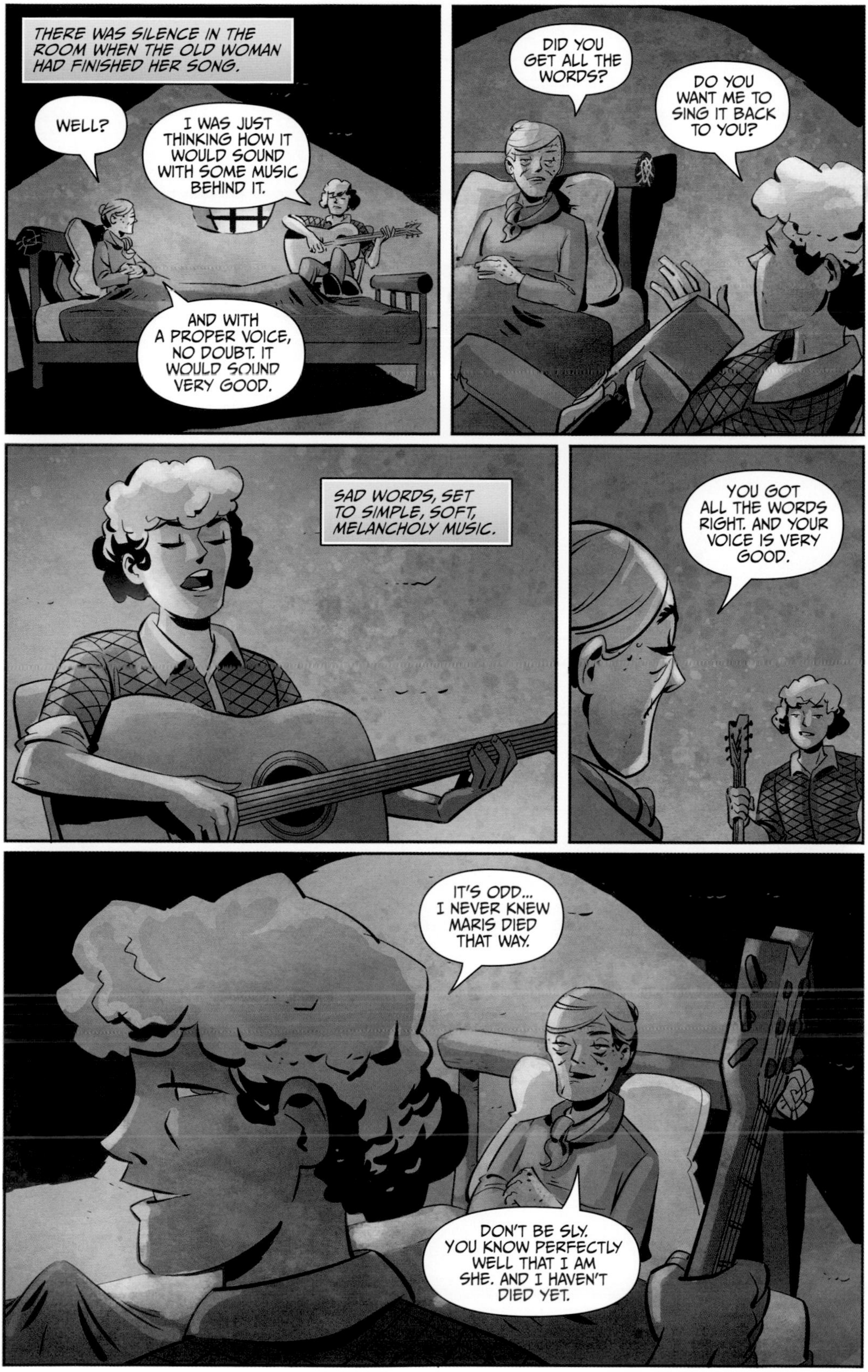
THERE WAS SILENCE IN THE ROOM WHEN THE OLD WOMAN HAD FINISHED HER SONG.
WELL?
I WAS JUST THINKING HOW IT WOULD SOUND WITH SOME MUSIC BEHIND IT.
AND WITH A PROPER VOICE, NO DOUBT. IT WOULD SOUND VERY GOOD.
DID YOU GET ALL THE WORDS?
DO YOU WANT ME TO SING IT BACK TO YOU?
SAD WORDS, SET TO SIMPLE, SOFT, MELANCHOLY MUSIC.
YOU GOT ALL THE WORDS RIGHT. AND YOUR VOICE IS VERY GOOD.
IT'S ODD... I NEVER KNEW MARIS DIED THAT WAY.
DON'T BE SLY. YOU KNOW PERFECTLY WELL THAT I AM SHE. AND I HAVEN'T DIED YET.

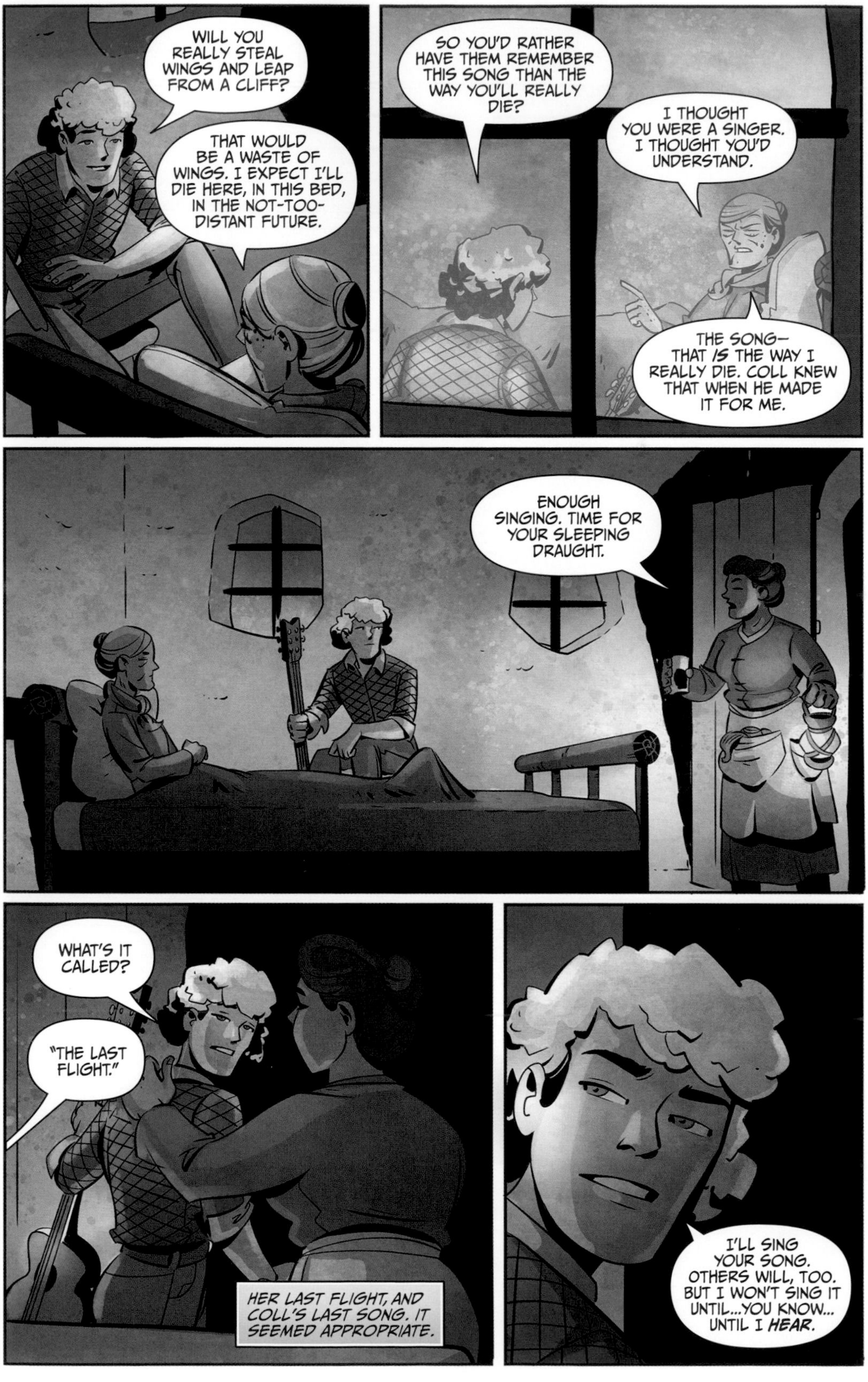
WILL YOU REALLY STEAL WINGS AND LEAP FROM A CLIFF?
THAT WOULD BE A WASTE OF WINGS. I EXPECT I'LL DIE HERE, IN THIS BED, IN THE NOT-TOO-DISTANT FUTURE.
SO YOU'D RATHER HAVE THEM REMEMBER THIS SONG THAN THE WAY YOU'LL REALLY DIE?
I THOUGHT YOU WERE A SINGER. I THOUGHT YOU'D UNDERSTAND.
THE SONG— THAT *IS* THE WAY I REALLY DIE. COLL KNEW THAT WHEN HE MADE IT FOR ME.
ENOUGH SINGING. TIME FOR YOUR SLEEPING DRAUGHT.
WHAT'S IT CALLED?
"THE LAST FLIGHT."
HER LAST FLIGHT, AND COLL'S LAST SONG. IT SEEMED APPROPRIATE.
I'LL SING YOUR SONG. OTHERS WILL, TOO. BUT I WON'T SING IT UNTIL...YOU KNOW... UNTIL I ***HEAR***.

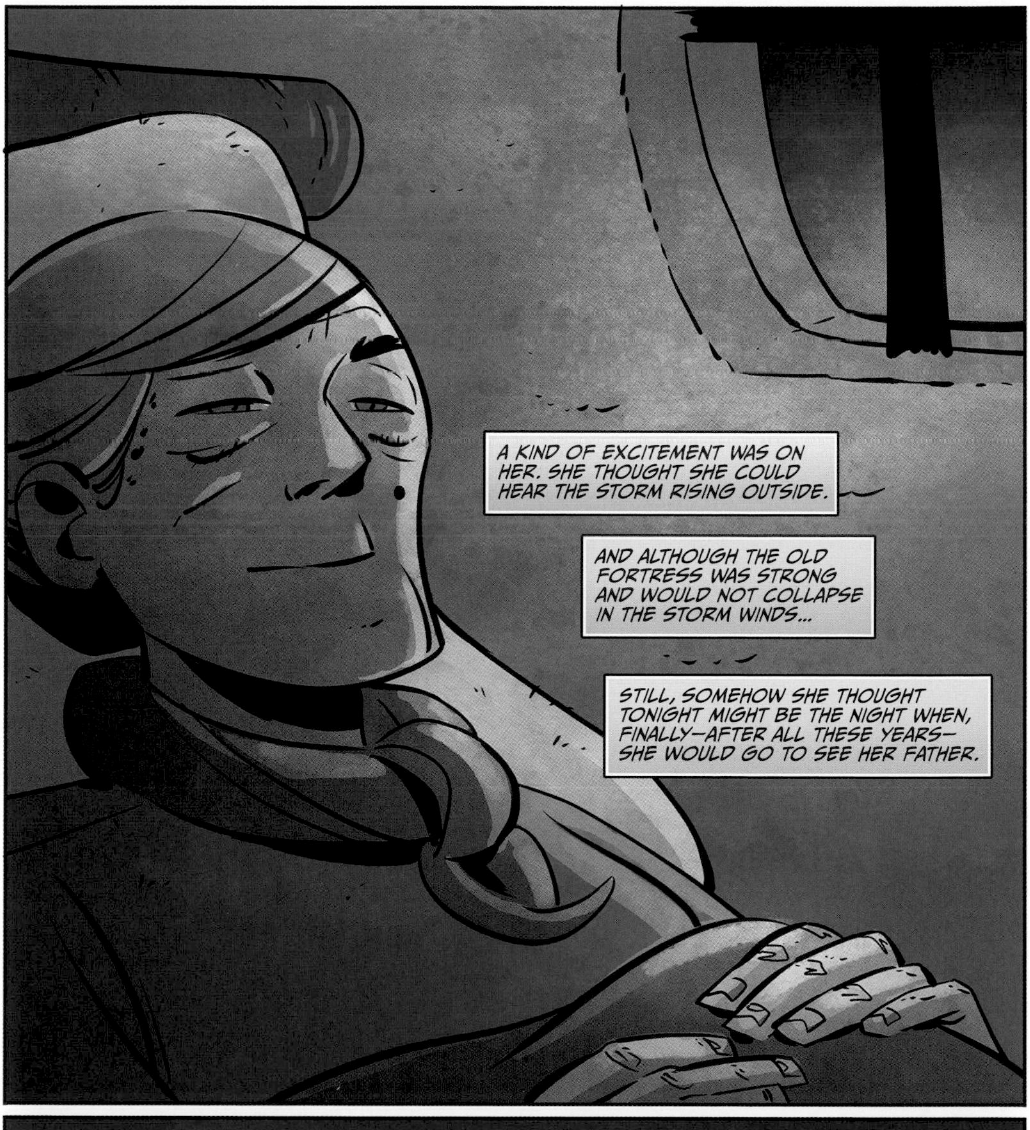
A KIND OF EXCITEMENT WAS ON HER. SHE THOUGHT SHE COULD HEAR THE STORM RISING OUTSIDE.
AND ALTHOUGH THE OLD FORTRESS WAS STRONG AND WOULD NOT COLLAPSE IN THE STORM WINDS...
STILL, SOMEHOW SHE THOUGHT TONIGHT MIGHT BE THE NIGHT WHEN, FINALLY—AFTER ALL THESE YEARS—SHE WOULD GO TO SEE HER FATHER.
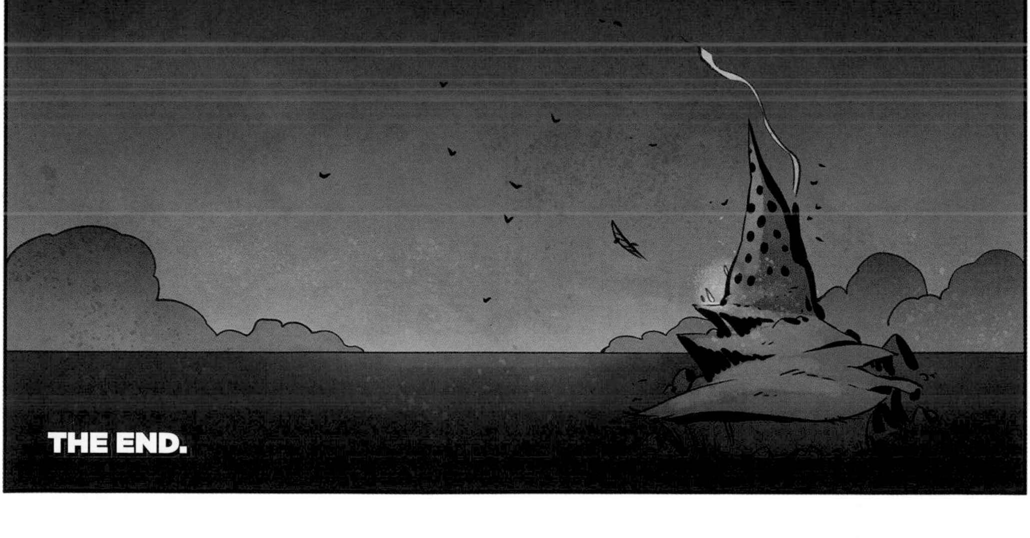
THE END.

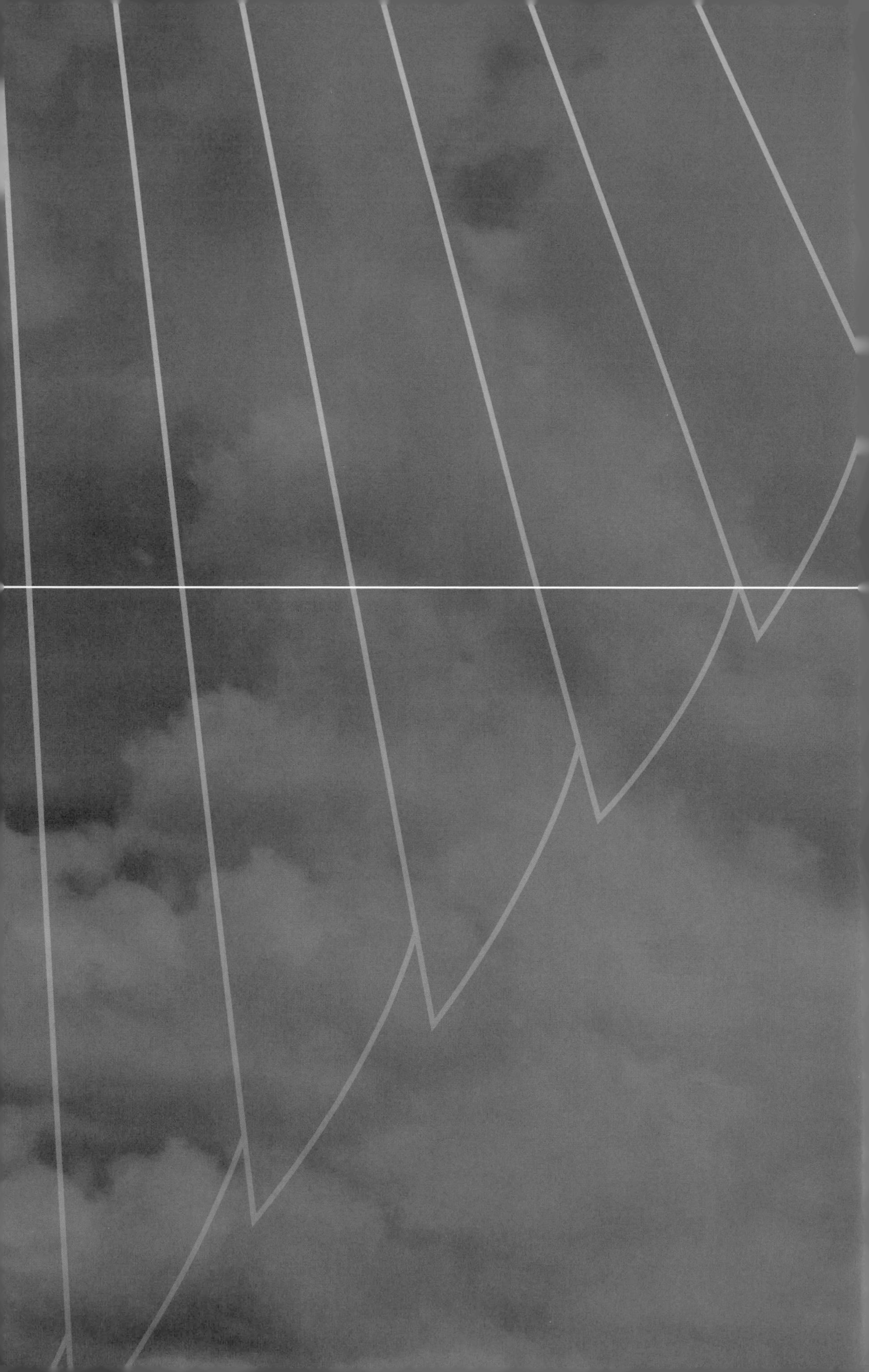

George R. R. Martin

George R. R. Martin is the #1 *New York Times* bestselling author of many novels, including the acclaimed series A Song of Ice and Fire—*A Game of Thrones, A Clash of Kings, A Storm of Swords, A Feast for Crows,* and *A Dance with Dragons*—as well as *Tuf Voyaging, Fevre Dream, The Armageddon Rag, Dying of the Light, Windhaven* (with Lisa Tuttle), and *Dreamsongs Volumes I* and *II.* He is also the creator of *The Lands of Ice and Fire,* a collection of maps from A Song of Ice and Fire featuring original artwork from illustrator and cartographer Jonathan Roberts. As a writer-producer, Martin has worked on *The Twilight Zone, Beauty and the Beast,* and various feature films and pilots that were never made. He lives with the lovely Parris in Santa Fe, New Mexico.

GEORGERRMARTIN.COM

FACEBOOK.COM/GEORGERRMARTINOFFICIAL

TWITTER: @GRRMSPEAKING

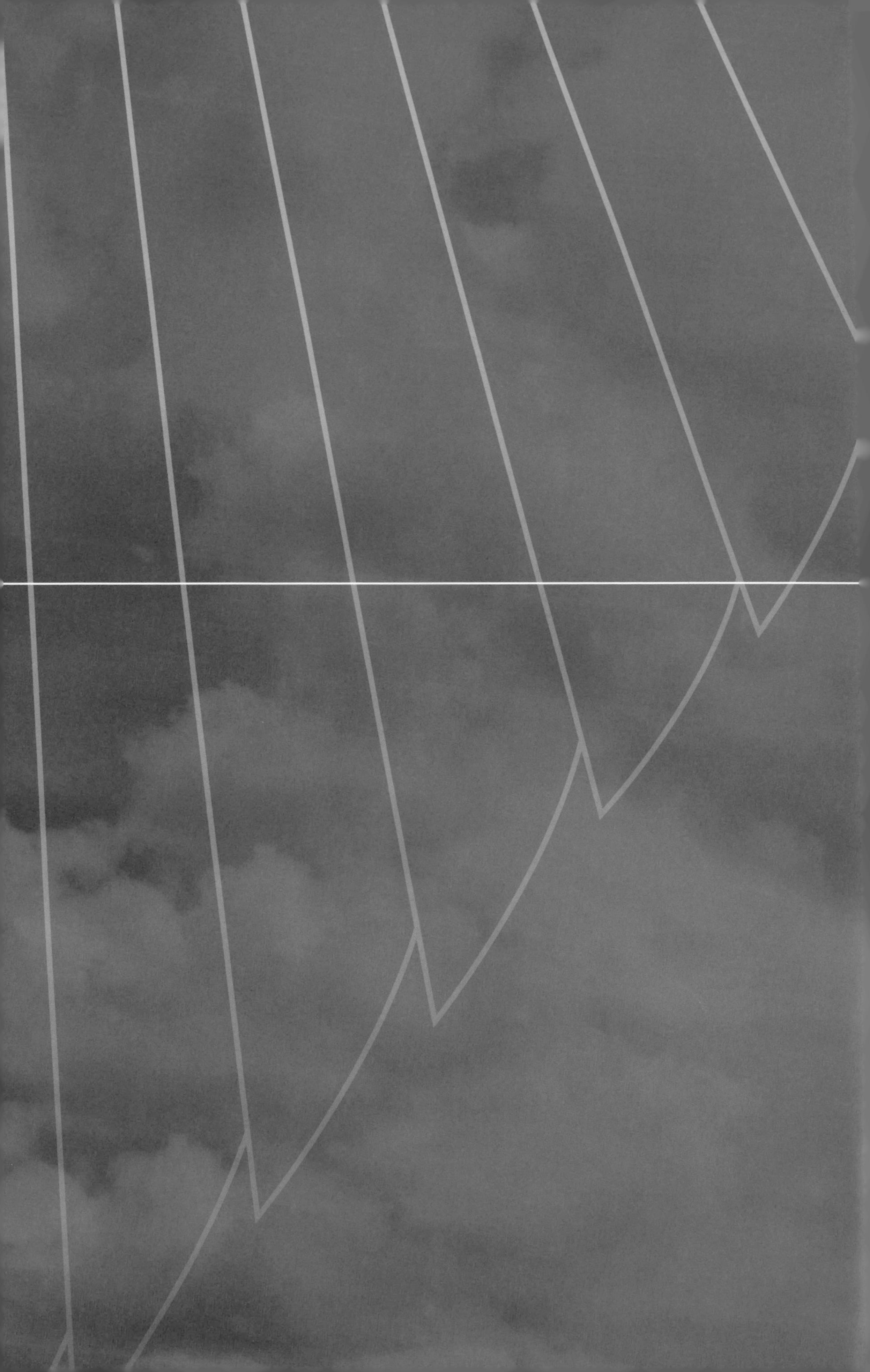

Lisa Tuttle

Lisa Tuttle won the John W. Campbell Award in 1974 at the beginning of her career, and subsequently her short stories have won the British Science Fiction Award and the International Horror Guild Award, as well as being chosen for "Year's Best" anthologies and nominated for Hugo and Nebula Awards. Her novels include *Lost Futures, Gabriel, The Pillow Friend, The Mysteries, The Silver Bough* and, most recently, the first two in a series of supernaturally tinged mysteries set in Victorian England: *The Curious Affair of the Somnambulist and the Psychic Thief* and *The Curious Affair of the Witch at Wayside Cross*. She has also written nonfiction and books for children. American-born, she now lives with her family on the west coast of Scotland, where the weather and scenery are similar to that of Windhaven.

FACEBOOK.COM/LISATUTTLEWRITER

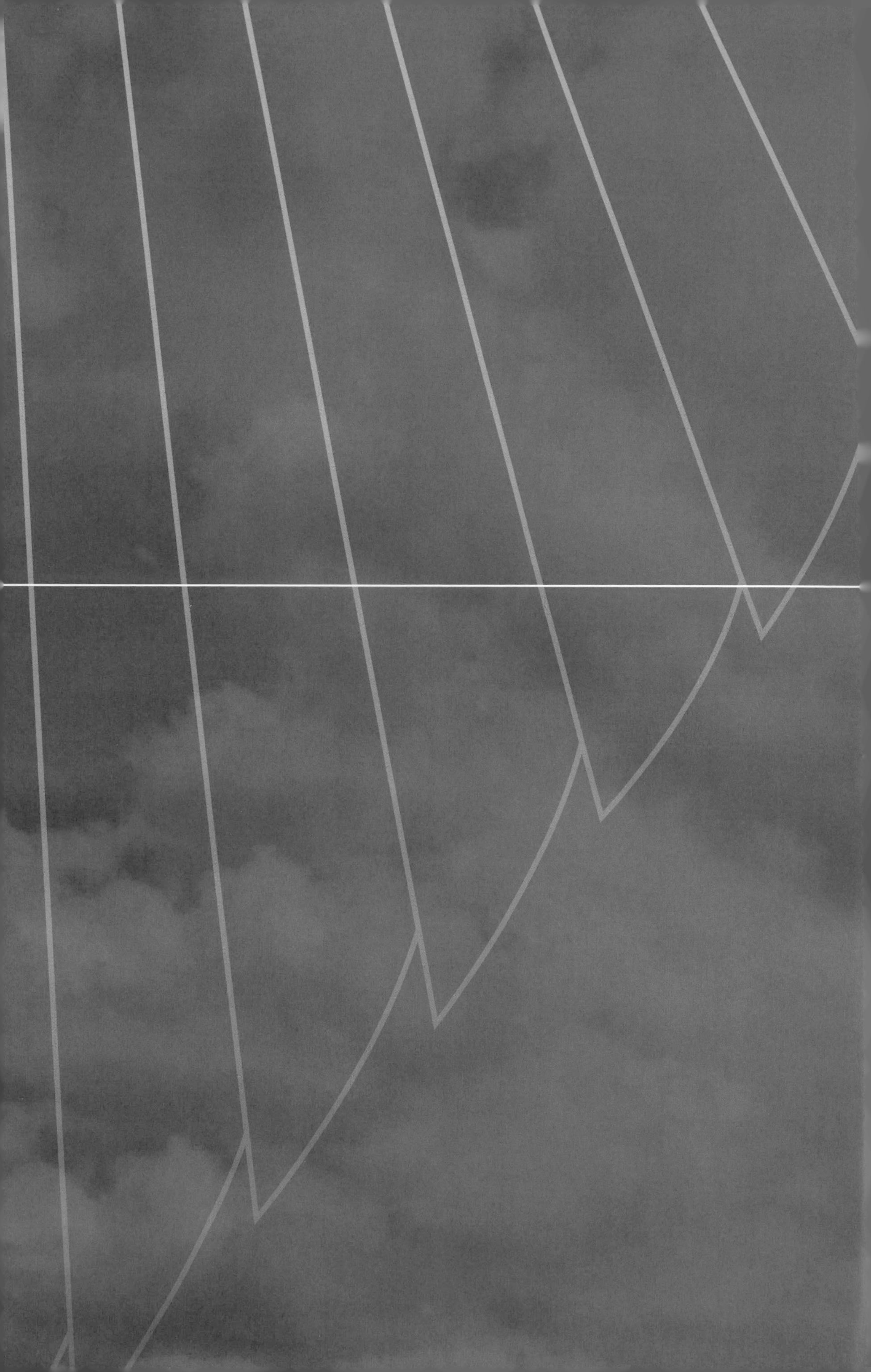

Elsa Charretier

Elsa Charretier is a French illustrator and comic book artist. After debuting on COWL at Image Comics, Charretier co-created *The Infinite Loop* with writer Pierrick Colinet at IDW. She has worked at DC Comics (Starfire, Bombshells, Harley Quinn) and launched *The Unstoppable Wasp* at Marvel. Colinet and Charretier recently co-wrote The Infinite Loop v2 as well as a forthcoming YA miniseries and an issue of *Star Wars Forces of Destiny*.

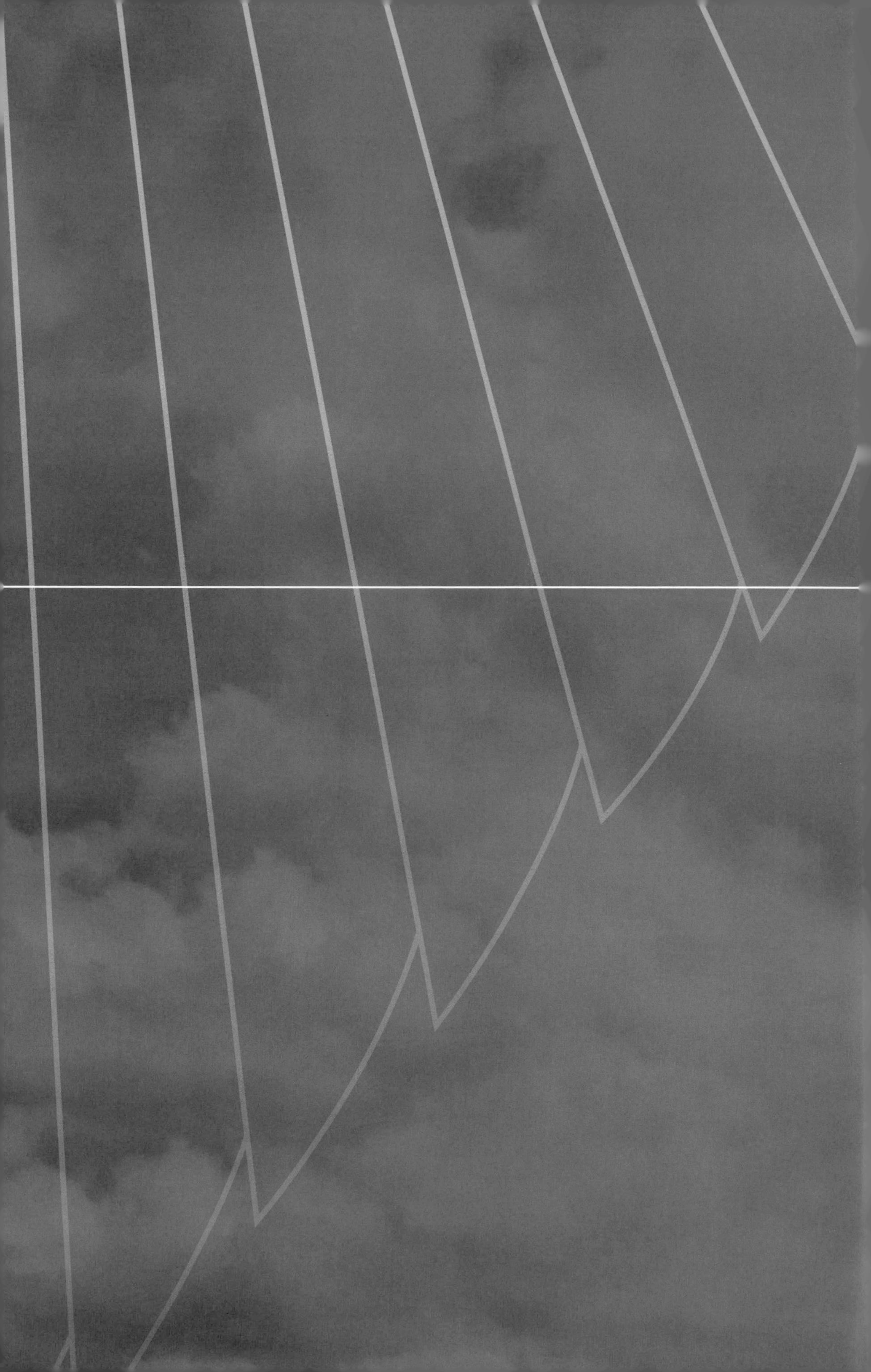

Lauren Affe

Lauren Affe is a freelance artist who has been working professionally in comics since 2010. After making her debut in *Dark Horse Presents*, Affe has worked as a colorist on many creator-owned titles across various publishers, such as Image Comics (Five Ghosts, Buzzkill, The Ghostfleet), Dark Horse Comics (The Paybacks, Rebels2), Aftershock Comics (The Revisionist), and Stela (*Villian*), as well as for Marvel Comics (Spider-Gwen). She currently resides in Albany, New York.

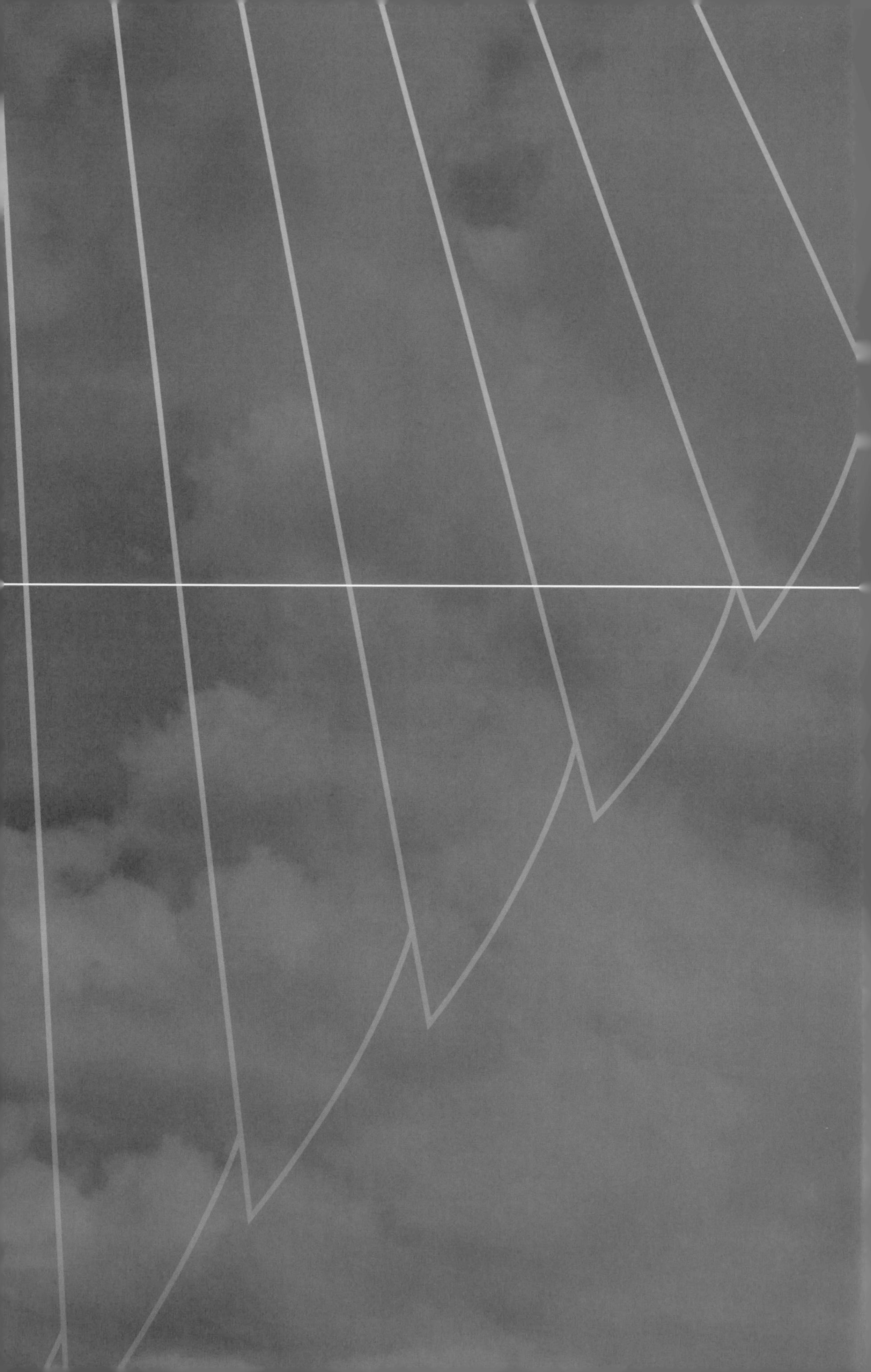

Bill Tortolini

Born and raised in the shadow of Boston, Bill Tortolini graduated from Salem State University. He has been working as a creative director for over two decades. Working on large brands and advertisements for Fortune 500 companies, Tortolini also became involved in the comics industry in 1996. Since then, he has lettered comics for companies including Marvel, Dynamite Entertainment, Random House, Disney, Image Comics, among many others. Notable works include Marvel's Anita Blake comics, the various adaptations of Robert Jordan's Wheel of Time series, Stephen King's *The Talisman*, Jim Butcher's The Dresden Files, and George R. R. Martin's *The Hedge Knight* and *The Mystery Knight*.

Tortolini is an avid Boston sports fan, skier, golfer, and pop-culture aficionado. He lives in Billerica, Massachusetts, with his wife, Kristen, their three children Abigail, Katherine, and Cameron, and his sometimes-loyal dog, Oliver.